THE GRAND GAME
BOOK 3: WORLD NEXUS

THE GRAND GAME
Book 3: World Nexus

Tom Elliot

COPYRIGHT

THE GRAND GAME

Multiplying foes.
A deadly city.
And with no clear path to his goals,
how will Michael survive Nexus?

Michael reaches Nexus but finds advancing more challenging than he'd anticipated. Factions abound, allegiances shift, and separating truth from lies is harder than ever.

The line between friend and foe blurs, and Michael's path grows murkier. Nexus is a place of both opportunity and danger. Sitting at the heart of the world, the city is home to thousands—ordinary people, players, but Powers too. Can Michael remain free of their clutches, or will he become entangled in the Powers' machinations?

Will Nexus be the death of Michael?
Follow Michael on his epic journey and find out!

PRAISE FOR THE GRAND GAME:

"Interesting portal litrpg. Well-paced and the start of a new series. Curious to see where it goes..." —**Tao Wong on goodreads.com.**

"... Great action, great storyline and I honestly binge read it, start to end..." —**Alex Kozlowski on goodreads.com.**

"Smart MC. Great Tension. Full of Action." —**CookieCrumble on RoyalRoad.com.**

"Everything I look for in a LitRPG." —**CosmereCradleChris on RoyalRoad.com.**

"Oh I liked this very much!" —**The Enlightened Beard on amazon.com.**

"One of the best in this category this year." —**kindle customer on amazon.com.**

Author's Note

Dear Readers,

Thank you for reading the Grand Game. This is a self-published book. Even though care has been given to the review and editing of this novel, some mistakes may have slipped through. If you spot any grammatical errors or typos, please get in touch with me via email.

This book also contains game-like elements. They are generally unintrusive and integrated into the story, but beware, they exist. Otherwise, I hope you enjoy Michael's story.

Happy reading!
Tom (**TomLitRPG.com**)
Support me on PATREON[1]

---

[1] https://www.patreon.com/grandgame

CONTENTS

MICHAEL'S EVOLUTION

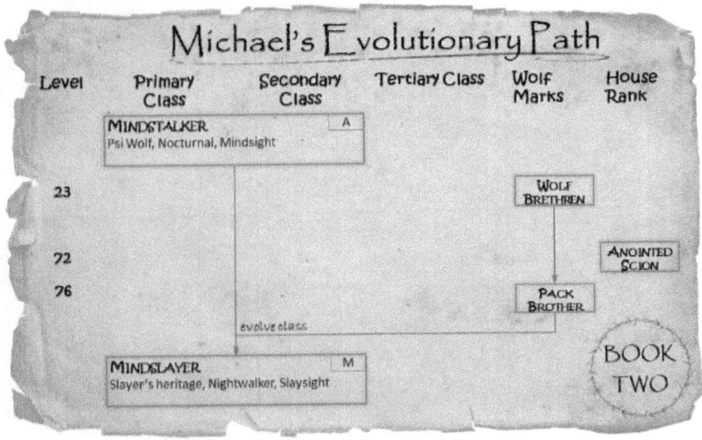

As always, Michael continues to grow during his adventures in the Forever Kingdom. The chart above only illustrates his latest achievements (as accomplished over the course of the last book). If you wish to view Michael's earlier evolutionary charts, please visit my site at the link below.

tomlitrpg.com/michael

THE SYSTEM OF THE GRAND GAME

The universe of the Grand Game continues to expand with every book in the series, and at this point, it no longer makes sense to include all the maps, charts, and diagrams in each new book.

If you wish to learn more about the world of the Forever Kingdom or understand the system of the Grand Game better, please visit my site at one of the links below.

tomlitrpg.com/game-lore
tomlitrpg.com/world-lore
tomlitrpg.com/glossary

MICHAEL AT THE END OF BOOK 2

Player Profile: Michael

Level: 76. Rank: 7. Current Health: 100%.
Stamina: 100%. Mana: 100%. Psi: 100%.
Species: Human. Lives Remaining: 3.
True Marks (hidden): Pack-brother.
False Marks (fabricated): Lesser Shadow, Lesser Light, Lesser Dark.

Attributes

Available: 0 points.
Strength: 2. Constitution: 14. Dexterity: 21 (20)*. Perception: 24. Mind: 41.
Magic: 6 (7)*. Faith: 2 (0)*.
denotes attributes affected by items.

Classes

Available: 3 points.
Primary-Secondary Bi-blend: mindstalker (fabricated), mindslayer (hidden).
Tertiary Class: None.

Traits

Slayer's heritage (hidden): +2 Dexterity, +2 Strength, +4 Mind, +4 Perception.
Beast tongue: can speak to beastkin.
Marked: can see spirit signatures.
Nightwalker (hidden): improved senses in the dark.
Anointed scion (hidden): bound to House Wolf.
Inscrutable mind: +8 Mind.
Secret blood (hidden): conceals your Wolf bloodline.

Skills

Available skill slots: 0.
Light armor (current: 42. max: 140. Constitution, basic).
Dodging (current: 50. max: 200. Dexterity, basic).
Sneaking (current: 61. max: 200. Dexterity, basic).
Shortswords (current: 55. max: 200. Dexterity, basic).
Two-weapon fighting (current: 49. max: 200. Dexterity, advanced).
Thieving (current: 39. max: 200. Dexterity, basic).
Chi (current: 47. max: 410. Mind, advanced).
Meditation (current: 67. max: 410. Mind, basic).
Telekinesis (current: 46. max: 410. Mind, advanced).
Telepathy (current: 46. max: 410. Mind, advanced).
Insight (current: 62. max: 240. Perception, basic).
Deception (current: 57. max: 240. Perception, master).

Abilities

<u>Dexterity ability slots used:</u> 13 / 20.
crippling blow (Dexterity, basic, shortswords).
minor piercing strike (5 Dexterity, advanced, shortswords).
lesser backstab (5 Dexterity, advanced, sneaking).
basic trap disarm (Dexterity, basic, thieving).
simple lockpicking (Dexterity, basic, thieving).

<u>Mind ability slots used:</u> 8 / 41.
simple charm (Mind, basic, telepathy).
stunning slap (Mind, basic, chi).
one-step (Mind, basic, telekinesis).
minor reaction buff (Mind, basic, chi).
simple astral blade (Mind, basic, telepathy).
short shadow blink (Mind, basic, telekinesis).
minor chi heal (Mind, basic, chi).
simple mind shield (Mind, basic, meditation).

<u>Perception ability slots used:</u> 14 / 20.
improved analyze (5 Perception, advanced, insight).
lesser trap detect (Perception, basic, thieving).
conceal small weapon (Perception, basic, deception).
facial disguise (Perception, basic, deception).
ventro (Perception, basic, deception).
lesser imitate (5 Perception, advanced, deception).

<u>Other abilities:</u>
simple slaysight (hidden): (Class, basic, telepathy).

Known Key Points
Sector 14,913 exit portal and safe zone.
Sector 12,560 nether portal and safe zone.

Equipped
spider's bite shortsword (+15% damage, webbed), concealed.
ebonheart (+30% damage), concealed.
common fighter's sash (+3 shortswords).
enchanted leather armor set (+20% damage reduction, −35% Dexterity and Magic).
slotted potion belt (2 minor heal, 3 moderate heal, 1 full heal, 1 full mana potion, 3 invisibility potions).
common thief's cloak (+3 sneaking).
apprentice's ring (+2 Magic).
acolyte's ring (+2 Faith).
troll's talisman bracelet (+6% damage reduction).
gift of the unbound ring (immunity to tier 1 and 2 entanglement spells).
band of stillness ring (immunity to tier 1 and 2 Mind spells).
wayfarer's boots (legendary item, +4 Dexterity).
backpack, small bag of holding, alchemy stone.

medallion of the stygian brotherhood (summon stygian beast).

Backpack Contents

<u>Money</u>: 12 gold, 9 silver, and 0 copper.
20 x field rations.
1 x flask of water.
2 x iron daggers.
1 x bedroll.
1 x goblin writ of safe passage.
1 x bounty letter authorization.
1 x coil of rope.
1 x shortsword,+1 (+15% damage, +10 shortswords).
1 x tavern bill of ownership.
1 x Tartan token.
4 x full mana potions.
8 x major mana potions.

Miscellaneous Loot

13 x enchanted rings, 5 x enchanted robes, 8 x spellcasters wands, 3 x enchanted bracelets, 3 x enchanted boots.

Alchemy Stone Contents

(111 / 150 ingredients stored).
25 x vials of beast blood.
25 x heaps of ordinary bonedust.
9 x sacs of wyvern venom.
1 x set of wyvern fangs.
1 x wyvern heart.
2 sets of wyvern claws.
48 x wyvern scales.

Bank Contents

<u>Money</u>: 3,046 gold, 4 silver, and 9 copper.
2 x full healing potions.
2 x basic steel shortswords.

Open Tasks

Find the Last Wolf Envoy (hidden) (find Ceruvax).
Stay True to Wolf (hidden) (acquire a mana-based Class).

If you wish to view Michael's earlier player profiles, please visit my site at the link below.

<u>tomlitrpg.com/michael</u>

CHAPTER 157: THE HEART OF THE WORLD

Day One in Nexus.

I stepped out of the portal into a world filled with noise.

The transition was sudden and disorientating. Between one step and the next, I moved from the still and quiet darkness of the wyvern's lair to the hubbub and noise of a crowded square.

I tensed, hands reaching for my weapons.

Threats abounded all around me, and my gaze flitted left and right, trying to identify a path to safety. I was standing on a raised dais.

And I wasn't its only occupant.

There were perhaps a dozen or so other players on the stone platform with me. As concerning as this was though, it wasn't *them* that held my attention—it was the sea of people surrounding the dais.

Where the hell did Loken send me?

A Game message dropped into my mind.

You have entered a safe zone.

My apprehension eased and some of the stiffness left my limbs. I wasn't in immediate danger. Moving my hands away from the hilt of my blades, I pivoted in a slow circle and took a second, longer look at my surroundings.

I was in a city.

Behind me, the gate through which I'd entered was receding. It wasn't the only portal on the stage either. Half the other nearby players were travelers too, arriving or departing through their own portals, while the other half were the mages responsible for opening the gates.

The stone platform was a teleportation point, I realized.

More Game alerts flashed for attention, and turning my gaze inward, I scanned through their contents.

The time allotted to your non-aggression Pact with Erebus has expired. Your Pact with the Power is closed!

You have entered sector 1 of the Forever Kingdom.

Congratulations, Michael! You have discovered the city of Nexus, a closed sector under the control of the Triumvirate.

The sector is both the anchor and heart of the Forever Kingdom. More than any other sector, Nexus bridges the gap between the aether and nether, providing multiple, and sometimes ever-shifting, entry points between the twin voids.

A shield generator is in place around the city, preventing portals from opening anywhere except in the designated teleportation zones.

I frowned.

I was unsurprised my pact with Erebus had ended. I had been expecting such a Game alert all day. The second message concerned me more. Once again, I found myself in a closed sector.

And this time, one controlled by a faction.

Who were the Triumvirate? And why did they control Nexus? I'd assumed the sector would be neutral ground, uncontrolled by any faction or Force.

Then there was the other bit of the message. What did it mean that Nexus was referred to as an "anchor" and a "heart"? Based on what I'd learned from Ceruvax, I'd expected the city to contain more than one dungeon entrance, but the phrasing of the Adjudicator's message implied Nexus was more than that.

Stranger and stranger.

"Hey, you!" a voice barked. "Get moving. You're blocking traffic."

Turning my attention outward, I glanced to my left and saw an armored figure striding toward me.

"Are you daft?" the speaker called out angrily when I stared at him, saying nothing. "Did you not hear me? Get a bloody move on!"

The player was dressed in plate armor, complete with metal-tipped boots, solid leggings, embossed breastplate, metal greaves, and an open helm. Coming to a halt in front of me, he crossed his arms and glared down at me. The brute—that's what I labeled him in my mind at least—towered over me.

Making no move to comply with his instructions, I analyzed him.

The target is Trion, a level 159 holy knight and human. He is a player and bears a Mark of Greater Light and a Mark of Herat. Trion is an authorized representative of the sector's ruling faction, the Triumvirate.

My brows lifted in surprise. So, the player before me belonged to the Triumvirate—and his level was twice my own. "What traffic?" I asked innocently.

The knight's eyes narrowed, and a moment later I felt a tingle ripple across me.

You have passed a mental resistance check! An analyze attempt by a neutral entity has failed.

"God dammit," Trion muttered. "A deceiver *and* a noob to boot."

I frowned. Granted, I was half the knight's level, but I was a far cry from being a new player. By my own reckoning anyway.

Trion was still scowling at me. "Last chance, thief," he growled. "Move— or else."

I ignored the insult. "Or else what?" I asked, curious to know what action the knight could take against me.

"Else, I will expel you from the safe zone," Trion snapped.

My eyebrows rose higher. "You can do that?"

"You better believe it. Now get off the damn platform!"

There was nothing to be gained from antagonizing Trion further. "Alright, I'm going." Turning around, I headed toward the stairs leading away from the dais. After two steps, I paused and swung back around. "Can I ask you one more thing first?"

The knight glowered at me. "Make it snappy," he barked.

"What is the Triumvirate?"

Trion stared at me, seemingly unable to believe my ignorance. After a moment, when I said nothing but only waited patiently for his answer, he asked, "You're serious? You don't know?"

I shook my head.

"What rock have you been living under not to have heard of the Triumvirate?" Not waiting for me to answer, he elaborated, "The Triumvirate is only the strongest faction in the Game." He puffed out his chest. "We've controlled Nexus for centuries."

My face crinkled in confusion. Based on Trion's own Marks, I'd assumed the Triumvirate was a Light faction. "But why would Shadow and Dark allow that?"

Trion's smile grew smug. "Because the Triumvirate is as much a part of Shadow and Dark as it is of Light. It is the only faction to have amongst its numbers Powers from all three Forces."

Now I was truly baffled. That went against everything I'd learned about the Forces. "But how can that—"

"Enough!" Trion interjected. "I've answered your damn question. Now get out of here!" Lowering his arms, the knight rested his hand on the big blade sheathed at his side.

Closing my mouth, I swung around and marched off the platform.

✳　✳　✳

I stepped down from the dais but didn't join the crowd just yet. With my back braced against the stone platform, I took in the surroundings.

The square was full of players of all shapes and sorts—tall, wiry, short, round, stumpy, and stout. Nearly every species I knew was represented, and many more that I didn't.

By and large, the players were humanoid. But here and there I spotted an outlier. Sliding across the ground on my left was a serpent-like player—*a naga?* Up ahead, towering over the nearby players, was a centaur. And accompanying him was an arachnoid.

An eight-legged player? I shook my head in disbelief. Could this world get any stranger?

But despite the numerous differences between the species, they all had one thing in common: everyone was in a hurry.

Everyone except me.

No wonder Trion picked me out so easily, I thought wryly. I was the only one standing still for any length of time.

I better get a move on soon then, so I don't attract more unwanted attention. Tearing my gaze away from the players, I resumed my study of the surroundings.

The square was bordered on all sides by imposing and majestic mansions. Each was made of marble, decorated with elaborate stone statues, and had windows shielded by clear-glass panes.

The shortest building was over four stories high, and judging by the windows, the tallest numbered ten floors. The bigger structures were more than mansions. They were palaces really. Flat-topped and edged with crenellations, the buildings were patrolled by smartly attired guards.

I could tell that, whatever else Nexus was, it was rich.

But despite the grandeur of the mansions and palaces surrounding the square, it was the lone structure *in* the square that caught and held my attention.

In what I judged to be the square's exact center, a mammoth crystalline spire rose upward. Formed from multiple bands of white crystals intertwined in the manner of thread, the seemingly never-ending needle-like structure vanished into the depths of the clear blue sky above. Its crystals sparkled in the noonday sun, and beams of light raced through them, making the entire spire appear alive.

What is that, I wonder.

Curiously, I reached out and analyzed the odd structure.

The target is the Adjudicator.

My mouth dropped open in shock.

This was the Adjudicator? I knew the Game had a controlling intelligence, but I hadn't expected it—*him?*—to have a physical form, nor one so unusual.

I need to take a closer look.

Unmooring from the safety of the platform's edge, I sailed into the square.

* * *

Among the sea of players, the first thing I noticed was how little respect they had for personal space.

Within moments of wading into the crowd, I was pushed, shoved, trod upon, and squeezed so tightly I barely had space to move. And despite my determination to remain on guard, it was impossible.

Bloody hell, I cursed.

Forgoing my attempts at caution, I unwrapped my fingers from around the hilt of my blades and used my hands as the other players did—to shove my way through the throng.

It was slow going. At least initially. But once I recognized the crowd's rhythm, I stopped trying to bulldoze my way through and instead moved in tune with it. Cutting through was much easier then.

As I swam through the throng, I noticed other oddities.

Dotted among the heaving mass of players were islands of stillness—stationary wooden stalls. The crowd swarmed thicker around them, almost concealing the wooden structures entirely.

A half-caught glimpse between scurrying players revealed one table to be heaped with merchandise. A second look showed new items appearing on it while old ones vanished.

I frowned. *What?*

Pushing my way past a dwarf and slipping between a giant's legs, I inched closer to the stall. A bored-looking merchant stood behind the table, only engaging with the nearby players when forced to.

Drawing on my will, I analyzed one of the objects on display.

The target is the enchanted helm of Aguiar. This is the global auction block item 324,958. The item's properties have been shielded from direct inspection.

For more information, consult the authorized auctioneer, Seville Ingo. Note, items purchased directly from merchants at the global auction are free of aether handling fees and other surcharges.

My brows rose in surprise. So, this was the auction. And the reason for the square's busyness, I suspected.

Players had mobbed the area, looking for a bargain. Normally, such a place would be a thief's paradise. But with the safe zone's rules and the Game itself protecting the merchants, I imagined they had no fear of losing any of their possessions.

Drifting away from the auctioneer, I resumed my course toward the Adjudicator. While I did, I randomly analyzed passing players.

Most were between level one hundred and two hundred. A few were below rank ten, and even fewer were above rank twenty. I frowned thoughtfully. So, while I was a bit under-leveled for the sector, I wasn't as bad off as I'd feared.

Nearing the spire, I pushed out of the crowd and entered the vicinity of the structure. In comparison to the rest of the square, it was only lightly trafficked. For whatever reason, the crowds seemed to want to avoid the Adjudicator.

Maybe it's because his presence is so keenly felt in the Game that even the Powers are forced to heed his pronouncements.

Not everyone was distancing themselves from the spire though. A few players, musicians by the look of them, were assembled near its base. They played a variety of instruments. Picking one at random, I analyzed him.

The target is Mertil, a saurian bard. He is a player and bears a Mark of Lesser Light.

The saurian had no player level, which meant he was a civilian and no threat. Dismissing him and his fellows from consideration, I approached the Adjudicator.

What is he? I wondered, placing a tentative hand on the sparkling crystal. *Some form of construct?*

A Game message flashed into my mind.

Hail, scion of House Wolf.

Chapter 158: At the Feet of the Adjudicator

The words resonated through my mind, strident and loud. Quickly, I snatched my hand back and looked around.

Had anyone else heard?

But no one was paying me the slightest heed, and my tension eased. Well, no one except the bard standing a few feet away. *He* was looking at me strangely. *Damn.*

"First time in Nexus?" he asked, striding closer.

I studied my questioner carefully. He was dressed as if ready for court and wore a silk shirt, suede pants, and an embroidered waistcoat. *No armor and no weapons,* I noted. *A civilian then.*

But despite the richness of the bard's clothes, he couldn't conceal their poor state. The ends of his sleeves were tattered, and the corners of his coat were fraying. The bard's flute was the only exception to his rundown air. It looked expensive.

My questioner's attire wasn't his most striking aspect though. His features were. While the bard was as heavily muscled as a human, his face had a distinct elven cast. His ears peeked through flowing locks, his eyes slanted upward, and his chin was sharply pointed. *A half-elf?*

"What makes you say that?" I asked finally.

The bard chuckled and rapped his knuckles against the statue behind him. "Your reaction to *him*, for one. Nearly everyone responds that way the first time."

Hmm. There was no glint of suspicion in the bard's eyes. *Perhaps, his sudden interest in me is innocuous after all?*

"He is a bit overwhelming," I admitted, continuing the conversation for no other reason than to allay my concerns. "Is calling it a 'he' even correct?"

The bard laughed. "Who cares? Address him however you like. Everyone else does."

It sounded a bit irreverent, but I only nodded as I glanced up at the looming spire. "Do you know what he is?"

The half-elf shrugged. "I don't. And the way I hear tell, no one does. Like much else about the Game, the Adjudicator remains a mystery."

I nodded thoughtfully and made to swing around. The bard's interest appeared no more than idle curiosity. But before I could leave, he stuck out his hand. "I'm Shael."

So, he does want something.

I hesitated for a moment before reaching out and clasping his hand in turn. I made no attempt to introduce myself though. "If you don't mind me asking, Shael, what are you all—" I gestured behind him, including the other musicians in my question—"doing here?"

My new acquaintance sighed. "I don't know about them, but I'm here because there's nowhere else for me to go."

I stared at him curiously. What did that mean?

"The Triumvirate don't like players to dawdle in the safe zone," he explained. "Normally I would have been expelled already." He chuckled darkly. "But for some reason, they give the Adjudicator a wide berth."

"So why don't you just leave?"

Shael laughed humorlessly. "And go where? The rest of the city is even worse. And leaving the sector isn't an option. I can't afford it."

I stayed silent, not sure what he was getting at.

The half-elf picked up on my confusion. Gesturing to the crowd, he explained. "Haven't you noticed how wealthy everyone here is?"

I nodded. I *had* observed that the players I'd seen were more richly dressed than those I'd encountered in the valley, but I'd assumed that was normal for players of higher ranks.

"Well, I'm not sure how you got here," Shael said, "but Nexus is for the rich—*only* the rich. That doesn't include the faction lackeys, of course. But everything here is expensive, including teleports into and out of the sector." He sighed again. "The short of it is, I can't afford a portal out."

"How expensive?" I asked, deliberately not reacting to his comment about "faction lackeys." Did Shael *know* I wasn't affiliated with any faction?

"The Triumvirate charge five hundred gold for a portal. Though hardly anyone uses them if they can help it," Shael said. "But even the cheapest mage will ask for three hundred gold to open a gate."

I exhaled a carefully concealed breath. Three hundred gold was a lot, but thankfully with the money I had in the bank, it was well within my means.

At least *I* wasn't stuck here.

The half-elf, meanwhile, hadn't stopped speaking. He seemed quite talkative. Maybe he was simply starved for conversation, or maybe he was always this verbose. "... I'm just about at the end of my tether and almost inclined to try escaping through one of the dungeons."

My ears perked up. "What do you mean?"

Shael didn't answer immediately. He studied me from beneath suddenly hooded eyes for a long moment, almost as if he sensed my keen interest. "Look, friend, you look like a likable enough chap, but nothing in Nexus is free, including information." The half-elf lowered his head. "And I'm desperate."

I waved aside the bard's embarrassed explanation, and to be honest, I would rather pay for the information. It was a simple transaction and would mean I owed Shael nothing else in return. "How much for what you know about the dungeons?" I paused. "And the safe zone?"

Shael licked his lips. "I can't tell you much," he said, suddenly more hesitant.

I shrugged. "I'll settle for what you know."

"Five silvers?" the bard suggested tentatively.

I withdrew two gold coins from my coin pouch and placed them in the bard's palm.

Shael's eyes widened, darting from the money to me. "You *are* rich," he breathed appreciatively. Then added offhandedly, "Despite how you're dressed."

I glanced down at my leather armor. It was dusty and scratched but still serviceable. "What's wrong with how I look?" I asked in a puzzled tone.

Shael smiled, his confidence returning as he slipped the coins out of sight. "No offense, friend, but no one wealthy walks around dressed for war in the safe zone." He paused. "Well, except for the knights, but they're just soldiers." The half-elf eyed me critically. "And your gear... I'm no expert, but—" his voice lowered conspiratorially, forcing me to lean in—"it screams noob."

I jerked back and scowled at the bard.

Shael spread his hands. "I meant nothing by it," he reassured me. He gestured to the players in the square. "But that is how everyone will see you."

I bit back a retort. Shael was right. I was underdressed for the sector, but I realized something else too—something I should have caught onto much earlier. Shael couldn't be a civilian, not if he was contemplating entering a dungeon.

Reaching out with my will, I analyzed him.

You have failed a Perception check and are unable to analyze your target. This entity bears a Mark of Moderate Shadow.

My eyes widened in alarm, and my gaze shot back to the bard.

Shael shrugged apologetically. "Sorry. I recognized you as a fellow deception player. That's what drew my interest in the first place."

"You analyzed me?" I asked sharply.

He nodded, confirming my fears. "It's rude, I know, but I didn't think you would sense it. Many players can't."

I blew out a troubled breath. *Damnation.* My deception skill was relatively high and I'd been hoping it would foil most attempts to identify me. But it seemed I'd exposed myself already.

Will he realize there's a bounty on my head?

"Look, Michael," Shael said suddenly—deliberately using my name, I thought. "I can see that me knowing your identity troubles you. You have nothing to worry about though. I don't care who you are or what you've done. I've had my own run-ins with the factions, and I know what it's like to run afoul of them. I won't tell anyone. Promise."

I took a calming breath and let my tension dissipate. Shael knew who I was, and there was nothing I could do about it now—not in the safe zone. "You've seen my Class and level?" I asked with forced indifference.

The bard nodded mutely.

"What level are you?" I asked.

"One hundred and twenty," he replied solemnly, making no effort to avoid the question. "And before you ask, my Class is red minstrel." He made a face. "It's not particularly combat-efficient, but I get by."

He could be lying, but without being able to analyze him, I had no way of knowing. Setting aside the matter, I turned the conversation back to my original point of inquiry. "Tell me about the dungeons."

Shael threw me a lopsided grin. "Nexus has many of them. Which one do you want to know about?"

I shook my head. "We'll get to that. But I'm more interested in what you implied earlier."

The half-elf stared at me blankly.

"Can you leave the sector through a dungeon?"

"Ah," Shael breathed. "I was only being half-serious. Technically it *is* possible though. Some dungeons have multiple exits, and they don't all necessarily lead to the same sector."

I frowned. It sounded simple, yet Shael's phrasing implied otherwise. "But?"

"But," Shael said with a smile, "such dungeons are rare and multi-leveled. Not to mention exceedingly tough to get through."

"I see," I murmured and squirreled away the information. If I ever needed to escape the sector undetected, it was useful to know there was an alternative to using the portals in the safe zone. "Where can I find these dungeons?"

Shael shrugged. "I don't know."

I glanced at him sharply, wondering if he was holding back.

The bard marked my disbelief. "I'm not lying," he protested. "All the bigger and more stable dungeons are under the control of the factions. And knowledge of what lies within them is closely guarded by each faction's players."

My frown deepened. "So, what does that leave?"

"Smaller dungeons," Shael replied promptly. "But their rewards are... let's say, less than valuable." He paused. "Then there are rifts."

I hadn't heard the term before. "What are those?"

Shael sighed. "I'm sure you received a welcome message from the Adjudicator on entering Nexus?"

I nodded.

"Of all the many Kingdom sectors, Nexus lies closest to the Nethersphere, and that makes some of its nether portals volatile. They can randomly change location, appear, or even vanish altogether." Shael shivered. "Worse yet, many of the new portals that open generally lead into the nether itself, creating rifts. When that happens, dark creatures spill out into the city."

My eyes narrowed. "Dark creatures?" I murmured. "You don't mean stygian beasts, do you?"

"Ah, you've heard of them I see," Shael said. "Then you know how hard they are to kill." His gaze flickered over my armor. "Especially for fighters without magic."

I nodded slowly. "And these beasts can appear anywhere in the city?"

Shael bobbed his head. "It's one reason why Nexus is shielded. It stops the stygians from invading other Kingdom sectors." The half-elf grinned suddenly. "But there's no need to look so worried. In three of the city's four quarters, it's almost unheard of for the beasts to appear, and when they do, the faction soldiers make quick work of them. It's only if you venture into the plague quarter that you have to worry."

"The plague quarter?" I asked, not liking the sound of that.

Shael pointed southward. "It lies that way, through the safe zone's south gate. For whatever reason, the plague quarter is the most unstable region of the city. Rifts aren't uncommon there." ·

"Is that why it's called the *plague* quarter?"

Shael smiled. "Yes, but apart from its stygian affliction, the quarter is also prone to actual outbreaks of disease, courtesy of the cursed marsh in its southernmost end."

I nodded vaguely, still deep in thought about the rest of what the half-elf had told me. "What about the other three city quarters?" I asked finally.

Shael pivoted a slow circle. "The Light quarter can be accessed through the west gate, the Dark quarter through the east gate, and the Shadow quarter via the north gate."

So, the factions had divided the city among themselves and in the manner I'd come to expect—by Force affiliation. "What about the safe zone?" I asked, thinking about the palaces I'd spotted earlier. "Who occupies it?"

Shael rolled his eyes. "Who else but the rich and moneyed? The safe zone is the haven of the Game's elite. It holds the most powerful merchant houses, the auction, every major bank, and the mansions of the Powers."

"Then there's nowhere for a traveler to stay in the safe zone?"

"There is *one* hotel: the Wanderer's Delight. It's expensive though." He paused. "But perhaps you can afford its rates," he finished with a hint of question in his voice.

I ignored the half-elf's probing. Rubbing my chin, I let my gaze rove from east to west while I wondered which quarter to explore first. The plague quarter, as intriguing as it was, also sounded dangerous. Venturing there would have to wait until I had a better feel for the city.

"What faction do you belong to?" Shael asked, following the direction of my gaze.

"Why?" I asked distractedly.

"Because you're not getting into any of the Force quarters without being pledged to one."

I broke off from my musings to stare at the half-elf. "What do you mean?" I asked slowly.

"The factions control their city quarters almost as strictly as they do their dungeons. Only members of *approved* factions are allowed inside. And if you don't belong to a faction, forget about getting in at all."

My heart sank. The half-elf could be lying, but I didn't think so. It tied in with the rest of what I knew of the Forces.

"So, which faction is it that holds your allegiance?" the bard asked again. "I can't tell. You bear Marks from all three Forces."

I didn't answer.

Shael opened his mouth to question me again, but before he could, one of his fellows called out from behind, "Shael! Envoy Livitus just sent word. He's looking for a band of musicians to play tonight. You interested?"

The half-elf closed his mouth with a snap and nodded to his companion. "Coming." Turning back to me, he shrugged apologetically. "Sorry, gotta run. Livitus pays well."

I nodded in understanding. "Go. You've earned your two gold already."

The half-elf bowed elaborately and spun about. He took two steps toward his companion, then paused and glanced over his shoulder at me. "If you're ever in need of a friendly bard again, you can find me here." He grinned. "I'll do nearly any job if the price is right."

I nodded.

Shael hesitated. "And if you're looking for a job yourself or for the most up-to-date information on the dungeons, try the bounty hunters' guild or the information brokers in the plague quarter. They're both situated close to the south gate, so you won't have to venture far into the quarter."

"Thanks," I replied.

With a final wave, Shael dashed off.

CHAPTER 159: PONDERING MY RICHES

After the half-elf left, I chewed over his parting words.

I planned on staying far away from the bounty hunters' guild. With a price of one thousand gold on my head, I didn't want to tempt any more hunters onto my trail.

The information brokers and the plague quarter definitely piqued my interest though. If the other three city quarters were closed to me, a visit to the brokers sounded like a good place to start.

But before moving on, I sat down cross-legged at the base of the Adjudicator's feet and reviewed my plans for the sector. My objectives were twofold. One: to find Ceruvax and learn more about House Wolf. All I knew of the envoy's location was that he was imprisoned in one of Nexus' dungeons—which one I'd yet to discover.

Two: I needed to acquire my third Class. A simple enough objective considering that the auction was within easy reach, but if I heeded Ceruvax's words—and at this point, I saw no reason not to—venturing into a dungeon and acquiring my own Class stone would yield better results.

According to the last Wolf envoy, a dungeon was the best place to obtain a new Class. And not just any dungeon. I'd gathered from his words that the more difficult the dungeon, the greater the reward.

Seeing that fulfilling either of my objectives would require me to visit a dungeon, I was reasonably certain that the greater part of my time in Nexus would be spent dungeon diving.

But I still knew little about dungeons in general and even less about those in Nexus. So, task one: *find out everything I can about dungeons.*

The city's dungeons weren't my only concern, however. There was also the matter of Loken's tracking spell. Until I found a way to rid myself of it, I couldn't go anywhere near Ceruvax. Which brought me to task two: *find a mage to remove the tracking spell.*

I expected it was going to be expensive though.

Visiting the auctions and spending my hard-won cash would have to wait. As tempting as it was to hunt down new gear, doing so at the moment was premature.

Rising to my feet, I headed north through the square.

While I was certain of what I had to do, much of it hinged on the information Shael had provided, and before I did anything else, I needed to confirm its veracity.

✳ ✳ ✳

Once I exited the market square, the crowds thinned out.

Nexus' safe zone was enormous, many times larger than both the previous ones I'd been in. Beyond the auction were multiple city blocks. They too were chockful of stone mansions, each as elaborate and richly decorated as those bordering the auction.

Striding down the cobbled road, I admired the neatly trimmed hedges and manicured gardens. Players passed me by in ones and twos. At first I tensed at each look thrown my way, but most barely spared me a glance, and those who did only did so to sneer or wrinkle their noses in disgust.

For the umpteenth time, I glanced down at myself, seeing ripped seams, sullied leathers, and grimy gear. The truth was unassailable. I *did* look like a noob. By contrast, the players who strode past wore well-tailored garments, all in immaculate condition.

Still, despite the poverty of my gear, it seemed the one thing I didn't need to fear was recognition. Among Nexus' thousands I was just one face, and I doubted most of the city's players had even heard of Ishita's bounty.

Eventually, I neared the north gate. The streets around it were busy and I slowed my steps, deciding it prudent to first observe the goings on at the gate before approaching too closely.

A squad of steel-clad players armed in a manner similar to Trion stood on guard inside the gate. *Triumvirate knights,* I thought.

They weren't the only troops on display though.

Another squad of guards accompanied them. They were dressed in gray-leather armor and bore crossbows and smaller blades instead of the giant two-handed weapons the knights carried.

The two sets of soldiers were inspecting the players passing through the gate. Each player was individually processed and examined by a pair of officers before being allowed to enter the quarter beyond.

From this far out I couldn't determine what the guards were doing, but I suspected the players were being thoroughly analyzed. I ducked my head in thought. It seemed like Shael hadn't lied. About this at least.

Discreetly, I let my gaze drift to the fortifications above. Like the safe zone in the wolves' valley, the one in Nexus was ringed by stone walls and topped with ramparts. These, however, were many times higher and patrolled by players—Triumvirate knights, to be exact.

Attempting to bypass the gate wouldn't be easy—but perhaps not impossible. With a thoughtful frown, I swung back around and headed for the south gate.

✳　✳　✳

On my second stroll through the safe zone, I studied the passing mansions more intently.

Some bore signs—either boldly displayed or elegantly understated—that marked them as public places of business. Most, though, did not, and I assumed them to be private residences. A few buildings in particular caught my attention.

One was labeled "First Shadow Bank." Nearly ten stories high, it made for an imposing sight. A constant stream of Shadow-Marked players flowed through its doors. Another, labeled "The Wyne Brothers' Merchant House," was a series of interconnected smaller structures, walled and patrolled by its own guards.

When I reached the northern end of the market square, I decided not to wade through its crowds again and diverted right to stroll through a quieter network of streets.

The mansions on display along its sides were surprisingly uniform. Turning my attention to the nearby players, I saw they were almost exclusively Light-Marked. *Hmm. The palaces here must belong to Light.*

I rubbed my chin in consideration. It appeared that the western end of the safe zone, like the west quarter of the city itself, was the domain of Light, the north belonged to Shadow, while the east was the domain of the Dark. Despite being one city, Nexus appeared to be a sector deeply divided.

Will matters in the plague quarter mirror the rest of the city? I wondered. Would I find that it, *too*, had been divided into little fiefdoms by the factions?

I hope not. Because it seems like it's the only place I can go in this city.

✻　✻　✻

A little later, the gate set in the southern wall of the safe zone came into sight, but I stopped short before reaching it. On my left was a low single-story structure that contrasted sharply with its neighbors. At first glance the building appeared to have been constructed inside a fountain.

Hmm. That's... decidedly odd.

Striding closer, I took a second longer look. Nozzles had been inset into the building's walls and roof. They released a constant stream of water that shrouded the building under a perpetual curtain of rain.

The liquid gathered in the shallow crater dug all around the building, making it accessible only via the thin stone bridge leading to the imposing front doors. Curiously, I studied the plaque affixed to the structure.

It read, "The Albion Bank."

A smile spread across my face. It was just the place I needed to visit.

✻　✻　✻

It was perhaps three yards from the edge of the pool—*moat?*—to the bank's entrance, and I crossed it easily enough. The front doors were unguarded, if wet. Shielding my head from the dripping curtain of water, I ducked within.

You have entered a dampening field. Your mana, psi, and stamina abilities have been inhibited.

The Game alert gave me pause.

I wasn't sure of the need for the dampening field—this was the safe zone, wasn't it?—and the idea of remaining within one made me uncomfortable enough that I almost turned around and left. But I needed to visit the bank;

the bulk of my funds was locked in its vaults. Dismissing my concerns, I took in my surroundings.

I was in a large marble foyer. There were only a handful of players around—the bank didn't seem nearly as popular as the First Shadow Bank. Ignoring the other customers, I scanned the room for a clue as to where to go next.

At the far end of the room behind a white counter, I spied three civilians dressed in uniforms emblazoned with the letters "AB." But the path to the trio was blocked by an array of rune-inscribed rectangular frames.

My brows furrowed. That the frames were magical in nature was obvious. However, I didn't expect them to be harmful—not in a safe zone—and despite my mounting misgivings, I strode through the closest one.

A Game message flashed through my mind.

Watcher activated. Scanning commencing...

...

You have failed a magical resistance check.
You have failed a mental resistance check.
You have failed a physical resistance check.

...

Scans completed.
Anomalous spell(s) detected! Potential threat identified!

Uh-oh.

Hastily, I backpedaled away from the magical device. Checking on my funds could wait, I decided. It was time to beat a retreat.

But it was already too late for that.

The bank doors had already slammed shut, and concealed entrances around the perimeter of the foyer had broken open, spilling out more Albion employees.

I was trapped.

That, though, wasn't the worst of it.

Unlike the trio behind the counter, the new arrivals—guards, I thought— were armored and armed.

And in the strangest of ways.

The newcomers were dressed in bulky suits, giving them a comically rotund appearance. There was nothing funny about their hard expressions, though, nor the oversized mittens they wore on their hands. These, too, were made of some sort of soft, pliable substance.

Understanding flashed through my mind.

The guards' gear had been chosen for subduing interlopers *without* breaking any of the safe zone's rules. I finally realized the purpose of the dampening field too. Without my abilities, I had no hope of escaping.

As the guards converged on me, I raised my hands. There was nowhere to flee, and trying to fight my way out would be counterproductive. Any action I took would likely land me on the wrong side of the Adjudicator's judgment.

"Whoa there," I began. "I'm only here to—"

I got no further.

A guard clamped his foam-covered hand across my mouth, while another wrapped his arms around my torso and a third lifted me off the ground.

Urgh.

In mere seconds, I was effectively disabled.

It was a practiced maneuver, something obviously done on multiple occasions, and even if I wanted to, I could see no way of fighting free.

Held firmly, if gently, the three guards carried me out of the foyer. I tried speaking again, to explain myself, but my captors would have none of it. Sighing, I resigned myself to waiting.

The guards didn't expel me from the premises, as I half expected them to. Instead, they transferred me to a side room behind the now-exposed entrances.

The chamber was sparsely furnished, containing only a metal table and two chairs. Without communicating in any manner I could make out, the guards placed me in one of the chairs and held me down.

In my new position, I was just as firmly restrained as before. But as frustrating as I found the situation, I couldn't help but admire the guard's handiwork. They'd managed to capture and transport me, all without triggering the Adjudicator's ire.

More players entered the room behind me. My head was too firmly clasped to turn around, but listening intently, I was able to identify seven different sets of footsteps. Silently, the newcomers took up positions against the right and left walls, and I saw that they, too, were guards.

The door to the chamber closed with a gentle click. Still, no one said anything.

Now what? I wondered.

I didn't feel particularly threatened. Sure, the bank had bent the safe zone rules enough to subdue and capture me. But I doubted the Game would let them go any further than that.

Eventually, they'll have to release me, I reasoned. *I just need to wait.*

Five minutes passed. Then another ten.

The room we were in looked remarkably like an interrogation chamber, but it didn't seem like the guards intended to question me themselves.

They must be waiting for someone further up the chain to arrive, I decided.

Realizing there was nothing to do but wait, and wondering what exactly the detection ward had revealed about me, I schooled myself to patience.

Chapter 160: A Powerful Casting

Minutes turned into hours, and still no one showed up.

The entire time, none of the ten Albion guards said anything. After the first hour, I was well and truly bored. With little to occupy me, I tried to use my mindsight.

You have failed to trigger your mindsight. The ability has been blocked by a dampening field.

As expected, it didn't work.

After that, I spent long minutes meticulously examining the guards, but other than their species, there was little more I learned about each. Next, I tried to break free of the trio holding me, but no matter how much I struggled, I failed at that too. It was at times like these that I regretted not investing in Strength.

Finally, I sat back and let my thoughts—and worries—run rampant. It hadn't escaped my notice that the Game hadn't defined the rank of the detection ward I'd tripped. My biggest concern was that the Watcher had uncovered my secret blood trait.

I didn't think it likely though.

The blood memory wasn't a spell, after all, and nothing about its description had suggested it vulnerable to detection—of any sort. No, the more obvious explanation was that Loken's spell had been revealed. If so, I had nothing to worry about.

I hoped.

There was no way to know for sure though. But neither was there any benefit to worrying. *Just wait, Michael.*

Closing my eyes, I set about doing just that.

✳ ✳ ✳

Hours later, the door opposite me slid open and two elegantly clad figures walked in. The first player, a step ahead of the other, appeared to be a bodyguard. He was dressed in a cobalt-colored suit. His shirt, his tie, and even his boots were also blue, even if they were different shades.

The guard's scales were nearly as blue as his clothing. Gills flapped open on either side of his cheekbones, and he was clearly a descendant of an aquatic species. At his side, the player carried a longsword with a hilt bedecked with sapphires. Despite the blade's flashy appearance, both its hilt and scabbard were well worn, suggesting they'd seen hard use.

As striking a figure as the bodyguard cut though, it was the woman who followed in his shadow that was more arresting. She was just as blue-skinned as her guard, but despite the unsettling tone of her skin, the rest of the woman was comfortingly human. Except for her eyes. They were a uniform blue.

The woman seated herself in the chair before me without fuss. Planting her elbows on the table, she rested her chin in a cupped palm. It was an artless pose, but I wasn't reassured.

The woman reeked of power.

With a jerk of her eyes, the woman motioned the three guards holding me away, then turned her disturbing eyes on me.

Under her scrutiny, I felt the urge to cower in my chair. Fighting the instinct, I held myself still. There was something about the blue woman's gaze that reminded me of Erebus and Loken. And suddenly, I knew my initial impression was wrong.

She wasn't a player. She was a Power. And an enemy of Wolf.

Fearing the worst now, I stiffened.

Seeing the play of emotions on my face, a small smile tugged at the corner of the Power's lips. "You're an interesting character, Michael." Her voice resonated with the sound of gently flowing water. Like a babbling stream, it was both soothing and pleasant.

Yet, I wasn't set at ease. Despite her easy tone, I knew what she was. Remaining silent, I waited for her to go on.

The Power's smile grew. "Careful too." She tilted her head to the side. "How did one such as you come to be entangled with Loken?"

I didn't let my relief show. *So, it is Loken's spell she uncovered.*

"Still nothing to say?" the Power asked. "Interesting. But I wonder, will you still say nothing if I told you that you've defaulted on your contractual obligations with the bank?"

My alarm grew, but once more I stopped myself from responding. *She's only toying with me.*

"Devlin, please inform the customer of the consequences of his actions," she said when I remained silent.

The guard at her back stiffened to attention and said, "Yes, Lady. By entering the Albion Bank premises with an active enchantment, the player Michael has failed to comply with contract term eighteen fifty, and as a consequence has forfeited his account, all goods, and monies stored with the bank."

This time, I couldn't conceal my outrage. "No! That's bloody—"

The Power spoke over me, her tone hardening, "And how much does that amount to?"

Devlin's eyes flickered inward. "A touch under three thousand gold," he said, sounding surprised.

The Lady, though, showed no reaction to the amount. Her gaze flickered back to me. "So, Michael, are you ready to forfeit all that? Or will you answer my questions?"

I clenched my hands into fists beneath the table, but I knew I was just as helpless to resist her threat as I'd been to escape the three bank guards' grasp. "What do you want to know?" I ground out.

"For one, why did you so willfully break the terms of your contract?" she asked, a hint of exasperation coloring her voice.

"I wasn't aware of the restriction," I replied in a clipped tone.

The Lady's lips thinned. "Ignorance is no excuse. Your obligations would've been clearly spelled out to you when you opened the account."

I grunted. "Be that as it may, this is the first time I've entered the bank. No one told me the terms of use. Hell, I didn't even know there was one."

"Impossible," the Lady snapped.

Before I could reply, Devlin interjected, "Excuse me, Lady. But it seems the customer is correct. According to our records, his account was opened for him by a third party."

The Power sat back in her chair, her face a picture of curiosity. "That isn't something we usually allow," she murmured. "Who opened his account?"

Devlin took his time answering. "Loken."

"Ah," the Lady said, her gaze drifting back to me. "So, you are more tightly entangled in the trickster's clutches than I thought." Her tone grew pitying. "It will not end well for you." She paused. "What does Loken want with you?"

I met her gaze unflinchingly. "I suspect you know that already."

"I do," the Lady said with that amused smile. Her gaze drifted over me. "There aren't many mindstalkers in the Game. I take it your Class evolved early on?"

"It did."

"And Loken is aware of your ability to evolve?"

I nodded mutely.

"Why did he let you go?" she asked, interest peeking through her tone. "From your Marks, it's clear you're not Shadowsworn."

I smiled grimly. "He didn't, not willingly. I refused his offer."

The Lady's eyes widened a touch. "Oh my," she murmured with what sounded suspiciously like delight. "That certainly must not have gone down well. No wonder he placed a tracking spell on you."

Seeing an opportunity to win some sympathy, I said, "Then you understand? I didn't mean to break the bank's rules, nor did I ask Loken to cast his spell on me."

"I believe you," the Lady said.

"Then you won't confiscate my money?"

"I won't," she agreed.

I waited, hardly daring to breathe while I waited for the other shoe to drop. She would obviously demand something in exchange for her magnanimity.

A heartbeat went by, then another, and still the Lady said nothing. "You don't want anything from me?" I asked cautiously.

The Power laughed. "No, Michael, I don't." She paused. "I only request that you continue to bank with us, but that is a request, not a demand." She rose to her feet. "You're free to use the bank facilities as you wish. An exception will be registered in your records until such time as you can free yourself from Loken's spell."

I rose hastily to my feet, relief and gratitude vying with each other. The Power and Devlin turned toward the door, both clearly intent on leaving. "Wait!" I called out.

The Lady turned around.

"Can you remove Loken's spell?" I asked hopefully.

The Lady smiled. "I can," she said. "But it will cost you. The spell of a Power is no small thing to dispel." She paused. "Even for another Power."

Her words confirmed my suspicion. "How much?" I asked.

"One hundred thousand gold," she said.

My eyes bulged.

"That's more than you can afford, I see," she said with a twinkle in her eyes. "Goodbye, Michael."

"Can you tell me who you are, at least?" I called after her.

"I'm Viviane, and the Albion Bank is mine."

CHAPTER 161: BANKING BLUES

I fell back to my chair and sat unmoving for a long while after Viviane and Devlin left.

The Power was only the second I'd met since awakening my Wolf bloodline, and she had been no more aware of my heritage than Loken had.

Only the second?

I snorted at the idea. I was getting too used to rubbing shoulders with the Powers. Still, my confidence in the secret blood trait was now absolute. It had proven its effectiveness, and I could trust it to conceal me.

More concerning, though, was Loken's tracking spell. Viviane had implied removing it wouldn't be easy. I didn't have one hundred thousand gold to spare. Or anything close. And even assuming I could amass the ridiculous sum, I had no wish to spend it on disentangling myself from the Power.

It was a problem for later though.

Raising my head, I studied the guards. They hadn't moved from their posts, nor did they seem inclined to let me leave. "What now?" I asked.

The closest guard turned his head fractionally in my direction. "You wait. Your liaison will be here soon."

I nodded as if I understood what he meant.

This time though I wasn't kept waiting overly long. Less than a minute later, Devlin walked back in. Resting his longsword against the table, the Power's bodyguard seated himself across from me.

"It's time to get down to business," Devlin said.

I eyed the too-blue player. "Business?" Was I going to be interrogated further?

He nodded. "What brings you to the bank today?"

I blinked in confusion for a moment, then took his meaning. "*You're* my liaison?"

"I am," Devlin replied simply.

"Then you aren't just Viviane's protector?"

Devlin's gills trilled outward in what I thought was an expression of amusement. "The Lady's protector? She does not need such." He placed hands covered in delicate scales on the table. "I am the branch manager. The Lady requested me to see to your needs myself."

I stared at him. "Why?"

Devlin's brows crinkled. "Why what?"

"Why would Viviane ask you to deal with me personally? What's her interest?"

Devlin leaned back in his chair. "Ah, you are suspicious. Your question, though, is easy enough to answer. While you *may* have satisfied the Lady's immediate concerns, she is not certain you've been completely honest with her. And it is as much for the protection of the bank's other customers as your own that you don't use the common facilities."

"I see." My eyes dropped to the sword leaning against the table. "Are all Albion bank managers as well armed?"

Devlin's gills quivered again. "I'm not just the branch manager. I'm in charge of security too."

My gaze slid to the silently watching guards. "So, it is *you* that I have to thank for my rough treatment earlier."

"It's standard procedure, I assure you," he replied evenly. "You were treated more gently than you would have been at any other bank."

I sighed. "Then I can expect a similar experience every time I visit a bank?"

Devlin nodded. "Watchers are installed at every one of our branches. As you can imagine, verifying that our customers are truly who they *appear* to be is of utmost importance."

That seemed to be a pointed comment. "What's that supposed to mean?"

"You are a deception player, aren't you?"

I nodded, not bothering to attempt denying it. Devlin's words were more statement than question anyway.

"Then you take my meaning." Devlin pulled out a familiar-looking square from his coat pocket—a keystone—and then four other objects, seemingly from thin air. One by one, he placed them on the table.

I recognized the items. They were the very same ones I'd stored in the bank's vaults.

Devlin pointed to the keystone. "Two thousand, five hundred and forty-six gold." He gestured next to the items. "Two full healing potions and two shortswords. That is the sum of your possessions in our safekeeping." His gaze returned to me. "I must congratulate you, Michael. For a new player, you've managed to accumulate a sizable fortune." He looked at me curiously. "How did you do it?"

I ignored Devlin's question, my attention fixed on something else entirely. "You said two thousand, five hundred," I said abruptly. "That's less than I deposited."

Devlin's eyebrows rose. "You aren't aware of the annual fee?"

"I am, but—"

"Good, then that's settled."

I scowled at him. "No, it's not. The fee is only payable at the end of the year!"

If anything, Devlin's eyebrows rose higher. "A little over a year has passed since the account was opened," he said softly.

"Impossible!" I sputtered. "Loken only opened the account—"

I broke off as I realized I didn't know for a fact *when* the Shadow Power had opened my account. I only had his word for it, and if I had learned anything about Loken, it was that he would lie when it suited his purposes.

My anger deflating, I let the matter be. Devlin wasn't the one who'd swindled me. That was almost certainly Loken.

The bank manager didn't comment on my reaction. "Now, how can the Albion Bank help you today?" he asked again.

Sighing, I leaned across the table and we got down to business.

✳   ✳   ✳

You have stored a stack of 2 full mana potions and a +1 shortsword in the Albion Bank. You have withdrawn 2 x shortswords.

I made only minimal changes to my bank-stored items.

Devlin had assured me that my money would be accessible from anywhere in Nexus, including the plague quarter, and I saw little need for withdrawing any of it.

My primary purpose in coming to the bank had been to ensure that the money I'd received from Tartar, Loken, and Arinna was available, and while the visit hadn't been without hiccups of its own, I'd learned what I'd set out to.

Our business concluded, I rose to my feet. But before leaving, I posed one last question to Devlin. "I have some items to sell. Is there a trader you can recommend?"

The only merchant I knew was Hamish—Loken's alter ego—but after our recent encounter, I was wary of dealing further with the Power.

"Most players sell their goods directly through the global auction," Devlin replied. He made a face. "But, while you will unquestionably receive the best rates that way, it can be tedious and time-consuming. I prefer using a factor as an intermediary."

Pulling out two cards from his pocket, Devlin slid them across the table. "Visit this trading company. As an Albion VIP customer, their services will be available to you at no charge."

I looked at him in surprise. "I'm a VIP?"

"Of course," Devlin replied blandly. "The Lady herself has taken an interest in you. That automatically qualifies you."

I nodded thoughtfully. "Where can I find—" I glanced at the card on top—"the Kesh Emporium Outlet?"

"Two streets over, near the south gate," Devlin said. "Deal directly with Kesh."

"Thank you," I said, pocketing the cards.

You have acquired a token of Viviane. This item cannot be stolen, traded, or lost, even upon death.
You have acquired a Kesh Emporium access card. This item cannot be stolen, traded, or lost, even upon death.

Seeming to deem our business concluded, Devlin rose to his feet and strapped on his sword. On closer inspection, I noticed that the blade's hilt was formed of the same fine-blue scales that covered the bank manager.

"That's an interesting sword," I remarked. "Where did you get it?"

Devlin smiled. "So is that ebonblade you're hiding under your cloak. Tartar does not give those out lightly. How did you manage to get your hands on one?"

I returned his smile with one of my own and just as unashamedly ignored the question.

The corners of Devlin's mouth twitched in barely concealed amusement. "There is one more thing I must tell you. When you triggered the Watcher, a notification was sent to Loken. It's standard bank protocol to inform a Power when one of his agents has been apprehended."

My brows furrowed. "One of his agents?"

Devlin shrugged. "That's what we thought you were initially. Now we know better." He paused. "But it's too late to retract the alert."

"I see," I murmured. "How will Loken react?"

"I don't know," Devlin admitted. "He's always been impossible to predict."

I sighed. That much I'd learned well enough on my own. Bidding a final farewell to Devlin, I turned around and left.

CHAPTER 162: THE PASSAGE OF TIME

You have exited a dampening field. Access has been restored to your pools of mana, psi, and stamina.

I breathed a sigh of relief as I ducked out of the bank. Wanting to put some distance between me and its disturbing dampening field, I hurried across the moat bridge and onto the street without looking up.

"There he is!"

At the thunderous voice, I jerked to a halt. I knew that voice.

Bornholm.

Spinning about, I spied a small group standing to my right: Bornholm, Morin, and Tantor. All three grinned broadly when I spotted them. *What are they doing here?* I wondered.

Racing forward, Bornholm flung his arms about me. "Lad, it's been ages! I never thought I'd see you again. Yet here you are, hale and well!"

Though somewhat confused by the dwarf's greeting—it had only been a week since we'd parted—I nevertheless patted him heartily across the back. "It's good to see you too, my friend," I replied with a smile.

Stepping forward, the high elf greeted me more sedately. "Michael," he said, shaking my hand.

"Tantor," I replied just as formally.

The mage made way for Morin, and I stuck out my hand for her to shake, but she surprised me.

"It's good to see you, Michael," the painted woman said as she pulled me into a hug.

"Likewise, Morin," I replied just as warmly.

Our greetings completed, the four of us stood around in a circle, foolish smiles on our faces. "So, what are you doing here?" I asked finally.

It was good to see the trio again, but the last I'd heard, they'd been heading to a Shadow sector. What were they doing in Nexus?

Morin's smile grew forced. "We—or rather I—was sent to meet you."

My own grin died. "Sent? By whom?" I asked, fearing I knew already.

"Loken," the painted woman answered, confirming my suspicions.

My lips twisted unhappily, but before I could demand an explanation, Tantor interjected, "We shouldn't talk here." His eyes roved meaningfully over the open street. "It's not safe."

Bornholm bobbed his head in agreement. "I know just the place to chat. Come on, it's not far from here!" Not waiting for a response, he spun around and headed south.

Glancing at me, Morin raised an eyebrow in silent question.

Nodding reluctantly, I followed in Bornholm's wake.

I suspected then that whatever the trio had to tell me, I wasn't going to like it.

✳ ✳ ✳

You have left a safe zone.

We passed through the south gate without drawing even a cursory glance from the Triumvirate guards on duty. The players traveling in the reverse direction, on the other hand, were closely inspected.

The establishment Bornholm led us to was built right up against the outside of the safe zone's south wall. It was called "the Southern Outpost" and was quite obviously the local drinking spot.

A place to chat, eh? I thought drily, eyeing the dwarf sideways.

The inside of the bar was packed, and seemingly only by players, as confirmed by the Marks nearly everyone bore. However, there was a distinct difference between the players in the Southern Outpost and the safe zone residents. The bar's patrons were armed to the teeth, boisterous, and drank as if there were no tomorrow.

Fighters and adventurers then?

Standing in the doorway while the others secured a table, I scanned the bar. Everyone was drinking, laughing, or yelling. Too intent on their own conversations, they paid us no heed.

Still, I was wary. One thousand gold, I suspected, would be a fortune for most of the bar's patrons.

"Michael!" Bornholm hollered. "This way."

I turned in the dwarf's direction. He had found a table. Squeezing through the crowd, I joined the others and seated myself.

"Are you sure this is a good place to talk?" I asked dubiously.

The adjacent tables were too close for comfort, and the surrounding noise meant we would have to shout to make ourselves heard.

"Let him do his thing!" Bornholm yelled, gesturing to Tantor.

I glanced at the elven mage. He was mumbling something under his breath. *A spell,* I thought.

You have been enclosed in a ward of silence. This is a sound barrier and will prevent noise from intruding or escaping.

Between one moment and the next, the ambient noise fell away sharply. "That's much better," Bornholm said approvingly. "Now we can talk."

I nodded appreciatively at Tantor. "That can't be a rank one spell. Looks like you've grown more than I have in our week apart."

Strangely enough, my words caused my companions' expressions to turn pained. *Maybe they're just embarrassed by how far behind I've fallen by comparison.*

Deciding to spare them further discomfort, I changed the topic. "Speaking of when we parted ways, there's something I've been wondering."

"Oh, what's that?" Bornholm asked, perking up once more.

"Remember the portal Loken used to teleport you out of Erebus' dungeon?"

Bornholm's smile died again.

Thinking his reaction odd, I went on anyway. "I've since learned a bit more about dungeons. For instance, I now know that *only* ley lines can be used to travel between sectors in the Nethersphere. Power or not, Loken should *not* have been able to teleport you out of the dungeon."

I leaned forward across the table. "So, how did he do it? How did Loken manage to open a portal in a dungeon sector?"

There was a moment of guarded silence before Tantor answered. "He didn't."

"Oh?" I asked dubiously.

"Remember that door with the image of a jester painted on it?" Bornholm asked. "The one that had nothing behind it but solid rock?"

A wry smile touched my lips. "Of course. How could I forget that?"

Morin sighed. "Neither the door nor the rock was real. Both were part of a cunningly crafted illusion to hide a sector exit portal."

I stared at her. "You mean to tell me we had the means to escape the sector right there in front of us... *and Loken concealed it?*"

The painted woman grimaced. "Correct. The 'portal' Loken opened was another fake. It held us in stasis until you left, after which he escorted us through the sector exit portal."

"Remarkable," I said, sitting back in my chair. "Where did the portal take you?" It surely couldn't have been to a Kingdom sector, not given everything else I'd learned in the wolves' valley.

"To another dungeon level," Tantor answered. "From there, a group of Shadow operatives guided us through a series of Dark-controlled sectors before we eventually emerged aboveground in a Kingdom sector."

"I see," I said, shaking my head at the Shadow Power's trickery. It was disconcerting to realize how thoroughly Loken had manipulated events, but it wasn't a matter for contemplation now.

I turned back to the others. "Well, it seems that you three have had quite the adventure." I glanced at Tantor. "That makes what you've accomplished even more impressive. How did you manage to learn that ward spell in only seven short days? Between dodging the Dark and escaping the Nethersphere, you surely didn't have much time to train your skills."

Once more, I was greeted by stark silence. Worse yet, all three of my companions looked away, refusing to meet my gaze.

Something is amiss, I thought. *Something more than them acting as Loken's messengers.* "What's wrong? What did I say?"

Bornholm and Tantor glanced at Morin, fielding the question to her.

"It hasn't been seven days, Michael," she whispered.

I shook my head. "It has. Believe me, I've kept close track of the passing time. I've had to, what with Erebus' dogs straining at the bit to get me. Today is the seventh day since I've left the dungeon, and I'm sure you'll recall—"

"No, lad," Bornholm said, his voice unwontedly serious. "It's not."

I glanced at him, my face creasing in confusion. Morin was avoiding my gaze again. "It's not what?"

"It's not been seven days, lad." The dwarf paused, then added heavily, "it's been a year."

✳   ✳   ✳

"You're joking, you have to be," I said numbly.

He shook his head mutely, as did Tantor when I glanced at him. Slowly, I turned to Morin. My face impassive, I waited.

The druid wilted under my gaze. "Bornholm is right, Michael. A year has passed since we last saw you." She looked at me imploringly. "Believe me, none of us had anything to do with this."

I stared at her wordlessly, my mind turning frantic circles as I tried to make sense of their words.

A year? I've lost a whole year?

How could that be?

Morin lowered her eyes. "I only found out this morning after being instructed to meet you here. That's when I collected Tantor and Bornholm. I thought the news would go down better if you heard it from all three of us."

My eyes flickered over the trio. As much as I wanted to disbelieve them, I could fathom no reason for them to lie.

It's true.

My surprise transformed into anger, and I glared at Morin. "How? How in hells did I lose a year?" I ground out harshly.

Wincing at my tone, Morin pulled out a folded parchment and slid it across the table. "Loken asked me to give you this. He said it would explain everything."

Loken.

I squeezed my eyes shut. *Of course.* The trickster had to be the one behind this. Dreading what I would find, I picked up the letter and began to read.

Dear Michael,

By now Morin has already delivered the news. It's true. You've lost a year. You're probably still in shock and doubtlessly feel angry and betrayed. But know that I did what I did because it was necessary—both for your own sake and mine.

Your sterling work in the valley left Ishita fuming. Her fury knew no bounds, and in her rage she ordered her followers—all her followers—to hunt you down. The spider goddess wanted vengeance badly enough that she willingly abandoned all other ventures to get at you.

But when after months of fruitless searching turned up nothing, Ishita's ire cooled, leading her to abandon her hunt and even retract her bounty. (You heard me right. The bounty on your head is no more).

No doubt, you now realize the part I played in all this.

Thanks to me, you safely weathered the storm of the goddess' fury. (You're welcome, by the way!)

I didn't do all this purely for your benefit, of course. The truth is, I mislike how fortune bends around you, and after you so graciously handed me the keys to the valley, I had my own plans to put into effect.

To be blunt, I couldn't risk your interference.

Pawn though you still are, you have managed to cast a bigger shadow in the Game than you should.

As to how I did all this?

If you think for a moment, you'll figure that out easily enough. The portal you entered was not an ordinary one. Carefully hidden within it was a stasis shell. You

*entered both simultaneously. And for a year, I kept you in limbo in the aether—
safe and unharmed.*

*I can almost see you fuming over there. But don't let your anger consume you.
Be wise and set it aside; we have more immediate matters to deal with. By now,
you know the tracking spell on you is not easily removed. (Yes, Viviane informed
me of your request).*

I will dispel the spell—for a price.

*I have a task for you to perform. Unfortunately, it isn't one I or any of my
agents can be seen to be involved in. Morin will provide you with the details, but
simply put, I need you to steal something for me. The owner is an Awakened Dead
Power. And the location is the Dark quarter.*

*It's no accident that I've chosen you for the job. You are ideal for the task and
will likely succeed where others have failed. And, of course, if you're caught, no
one will question why you would attempt such foolishness—by now, your
vendetta with Erebus is well-documented. It's almost the perfect scheme! (For
me, anyway.)*

*Now, now, Michael. Don't get upset; this is simply the nature of the Game (and
don't lie to me, I know reading this last bit has set your blood boiling!) Do not
forget: stay calm!*

*Remember what's important: do this little task for me, and you won't have to
worry about the tracking spell again.*

Till next we meet!

Loken.

*P.S. I would have preferred delivering this news in person, but for obvious
reasons, we can't be seen together.*

When I was done, I stared at the note, panting heavily.

I didn't know what to do. What to feel. I wanted to be angry. But I also
didn't. Which would give Loken more satisfaction? Me angry, or me being
calm—like a good little boy?

This, I thought. *This... seething uncertainty is what he was after. Loken must
be beside himself right now.*

I gnashed my teeth in frustration. Then I quite deliberately and
methodically ripped the notes to shreds. *Bloody Loken.*

Why did I ever entangle myself with him?

"He's a tricksy bugger, isn't he?"

I looked up to find Bornholm studying me pityingly. Ignoring the dwarf's comment, I planted my elbows on the table and rubbed at my temples as I tried to make sense of the sudden shift in my reality. My time in the Game numbered not days but months.

If a year really has passed—

I broke off. No. There was no point in further denials. A year *had* passed. I had to accept that as fact.

But what did it mean?

My biggest concern was for the dire wolves. With Erebus, Tartar, and Loken up to no good in the valley, were they still safe? The three Powers had had a year—*a whole year!*—to wreak havoc in the sector.

I needed to get back to make sure the wolves were safe. Almost, I rose from my chair and raced back to the teleportation platform.

But then I realized I couldn't.

Not until I removed the tracking spell.

I couldn't afford for Loken to become aware of my association with the wolves. The Shadow Power was too perceptive by far, and he already knew too much about me.

Ironically, I had the Awakened Dead to thank for Loken not knowing more. If not for Ishita's shield generator around the valley, Loken would already know about the dire wolves. But he didn't, and I had to keep it that way—both for their sake and mine.

I sighed. The dire wolves would have to fend for themselves for a while yet. *Duggar and Sulan will keep them safe,* I thought, not certain if I believed it.

And what about Saya? Was the young gnome coping with the tavern? I hoped so.

Ceruvax, I was sure, was alright. He had survived centuries unharmed, and there was no reason to believe he hadn't managed to evade capture for another year. But would he still have faith in me after all this time?

I didn't know, but it changed nothing. I still had to find the Wolf envoy, and I needed to get my third Class.

But after my tasks in this sector were done, I had to return to the valley. Or at least find out how the wolves and Saya were doing. Contacting the pack from Nexus would be impossible, but perhaps there was a chance I could reach the former apprentice alchemist. *Maybe if I—*

"Michael?"

I looked up to find my companions staring at me. *I have to deal with them too.*

Loken wouldn't have chosen Morin as his message bearer simply because of our prior history. *A year is a long time. Are they still who I remember?* Reaching out with my will, I analyzed each of the trio in turn.

The target is Morin, a level 163 shadow druid and painted human. She is a player and bears a Mark of Greater Shadow and a Mark of Loken.

The target is Tantor, a level 157 phantom sorcerer. He is a player and bears a Mark of Major Shadow and a Mark of Loken.

The target is Bornholm, a level 156 gray berserker. He is a player and bears a Mark of Major Shadow and a Mark of Loken.

I sighed.

The others' Marks were no surprise. I'd been expecting something like it, but that they were sworn to Loken left me wondering how far I could trust the trio. And their levels...

Considering the time that had passed, I found their ranks perplexing. Frowning, I tried to make sense of it.

"What's troubling you?" Morin asked.

"Your levels..." I let my voice trail off.

"We know, lad," Bornholm said. "We outrank you, but you must remember it's been a year." He smiled. Of the three, he seemed the least discomforted by the reversal in our roles. "Knowing you, you'll catch up fast."

I shook my head. "It's not that you out-level me," I said, "but as you say, it *has* been a year. Shouldn't you be higher ranked than you are?"

Bornholm blinked.

A moment later, I felt twin ripples pass over me.

An analyze attempt by a neutral entity has failed.
An analyze attempt by a neutral entity has failed.
Your deception has increased to level 58.

Bornholm and Morin frowned. Tantor, though, did not. "He's level seventy-six," the elf said.

Morin's head snapped toward her companion. "Rank seven already? Are you sure?"

Tantor nodded.

Bornholm, meanwhile, was eyeing me in admiration. "How in forges did you manage to gain fifty levels—in what was it?—seven days?"

I shrugged. "By making enemies aplenty and fighting monsters too powerful," I said drily. Before they could think to question me further, I added, "But I'm more curious as to why you three haven't gained more levels than you have. Did you decide to stop leveling?"

The trio looked at each other. "You explain it to him," Morin told Tantor.

The mage studied me thoughtfully for a moment before speaking. "We *haven't*, as you put it, stopped leveling. On the contrary, we've been trying as hard as we can to advance, but since hitting tier four, our experience gains have slowed dramatically."

"Why?" I asked, since he clearly expected me to.

"Because the enemies we've been fighting have *also* been tier four, and experience gain in the Game is inversely proportional to the level gap between foes."

I was familiar with the mechanics Tantor had just described and had felt its effects often enough myself. Still, it didn't account for their low ranks.

"By all accounts, Nexus is rich in dungeons," I said. "Why not find higher-leveled foes? Or are you saying there aren't any?"

Tantor shook his head. "That's not it. The real issue is that the power gap between tiers four and five is extraordinary. Or, to put it more bluntly, it's nearly impossible for tier four players to defeat tier five foes."

I squinted askance at the elf. "Really?" I'd defeated more than a few foes that were higher tier than myself. Granted, it hadn't been easy... but impossible? I wouldn't go that far.

Tantor didn't miss my skepticism. "Believe me, Michael, there's a marked difference between tier four and five, more so than any minor improvements you may have noticed at lower tiers.

"Beyond level two hundred, the Game is wholly different. As a bare minimum, you need a master-ranked blended Class, exceptional gear, and tier five abilities. But even with all that, success isn't guaranteed. Talent and expertise play a big part." He shrugged. "Only true masters of the Game make it to rank twenty."

"Most players die before they can bridge the gap to tier five," Morin added. "Or give up trying."

"We've tried the quick route," Bornholm said, tugging hard at his beard. "Once, anyway." He grunted. "But once was more than enough."

"The quick route?"

"Pitting ourselves against a rank twenty monster," Bornholm replied. "Suffice it to say, we fell short of the mark. Our entire party wiped before we did little more than scratch the beastie."

I winced in sympathy.

"We learned our lesson after that," Tantor said. "Now, we stick to the slow and sure method."

"Meaning entering dungeons with creatures below rank twenty?" I asked.

"Aye," Bornholm said. "It's a grind for sure, but the risk is significantly less. It might take us years to get there, but one day, certainly, we'll see rank twenty."

The others nodded in agreement.

"I see," I murmured. In light of the trio's explanations, I better understood the player levels I'd observed in the safe zone, and the dynamics at play in Nexus were becoming clearer.

I took another long look at the three. I was grateful for their information, but there was still much about my old companions that I was uncomfortable with—not least being their new affiliations.

Focusing on their gear, I studied them anew. Tantor wore shimmering black robes embroidered with arcane insignia. His hands were gloved, but beneath them I noticed the shape of multiple rings.

Morin was clothed in scaled storm-gray armor. It was form-fitting and so tightly enclosed the painted woman that it appeared almost a second skin. Stowed across her back was a wooden staff with glowing white sigils.

Bornholm wore thick plate armor with a greenish-white tinge. I didn't recognize the material, but it wasn't ordinary steel. A large dwarven warhammer of the same material peeked over his shoulder.

Whatever else my former companions had become, they were certainly well-equipped. And they all bore Loken's Mark too.

"You've joined Shadow?" I asked, seeking their confirmation.

Their faces solemn, the trio nodded.

"And you're Loken's agents now?"

"Do not think badly of us for it," Morin said. "It's impossible to make your own way in the Game. It was join Loken's faction or another's."

I didn't respond to the quiet entreaty beneath her words. "What has the Power told you about me and our... interactions?"

Bornholm snorted. "What do you think?" he asked. "Nothing, that's what! All we know is that he stuck you in a stasis field for the better part of a year."

Morin leaned across the table. "What happened to you, Michael? Why did Loken do that?"

I shrugged. "I'd rather not say."

That silenced the trio. "You don't trust us, lad?" Bornholm asked, sounding hurt.

I held the stout dwarf's gaze unflinchingly. "How can I? It's because of Loken that I've lost an entire year, and by your own admission, you three are his sworn servants."

The dwarf bowed his head. "I understand..." he slammed his open palm flat against the table. "But goddamn, I wish things could be different."

I nodded solemnly. "Me too."

Another uncomfortable silence descended upon the table. Not letting it drag on too long, I turned to Morin. "What now?"

The druid appeared resigned. She, at least, seemed to understand how much things between us had changed, and to her credit, she didn't try to convince me to take them into my confidence.

"Did Loken's message mention the task he requires of you?" she asked quietly.

I nodded, my lips tightening at the reminder. Once again, it seemed that I was at the beck of a Power.

Both Bornholm and Tantor turned toward Morin, their interest piqued as well. "What task?" the mage asked.

Morin ignored him, keeping her gaze locked on mine. "The target is Paya. She is a minor Power in the Awakened Dead faction. You're to steal an artifact from her mansion in the Dark quarter."

"What madness is this?" Bornholm roared. "Loken is sending *him* into the Dark quarter? The boy won't survive a day there! What is his high-and-mighty thinking?"

"Deniability," I said softly.

"What's that?" Bornholm asked gruffly.

Tantor was nodding. "Michael has no faction allegiance. If he gets caught, Loken won't be implicated."

"And why would his highness care about that now?" Bornholm demanded. "It's never stopped him before."

"It's the Triumvirate," Morin answered. "Matters in Nexus have been spinning out of control recently. The knights and their patrons are cracking down. Already, two Powers have been expelled for gross violations of the city's laws."

I leaned forward in interest. "I've run across one of these knights, but I admit I'm not certain as to their function."

Morin turned toward me, her face grave. "The Triumvirate are more powerful than most players realize. When it comes to Nexus, their word is absolute, and not even the other Powers will trifle with them in the city. Their leaders, Herat, Mydas, and Rampel, are among the strongest Powers in the Game. Don't toy with them."

I nodded, acknowledging the warning. "How did they come to be?"

"I'm not quite sure," Morin admitted. "Their origins are shrouded in mystery, but it's commonly believed that some long-ago threat forced the Powers to band together. The Triumvirate are the remnants of that alliance."

Some long-ago threat? Was that the ancients? *More than likely.* I didn't voice my suspicions though. "And what is their purpose?"

"To maintain stability in Nexus," Morin said. "The city isn't called the heart of the world for nothing. If Nexus is overrun by chaos, every other sector will be affected. The Triumvirate have been entrusted by the other Powers to keep the city from being torn apart by the factions' perpetual infighting." She shrugged. "As you can imagine, with all three Forces here in strength, tensions always run high in Nexus."

I pursed my lips. "So, the knights are peacekeepers?"

Morin nodded. "In a manner of speaking. They control access into and out of the city and have the authority to expel any faction—or Power."

"But the Triumvirate only concern themselves with stability, not justice," Bornholm warned. "Don't think they'll look out for your own well-being."

I looked at him questioningly.

"What Bornholm means is that the knights don't care about unimportant and unaffiliated players," Tantor said. "If you don't belong to a faction, and if your death isn't likely to spark a faction war, they don't care what happens to you." The elf met my gaze. "Be careful."

"Got it," I said and turned back to Morin. "Now, tell me more about this artifact I need to steal."

Morin described the item and its location at length.

From what I could gather, the object I was to steal was some sort of chalice stored in the vaults of the Power Paya. The Power, it seemed, had only recently risen to the deity ranks—recent being relative, of course—and was still only a junior member of the Awakened Dead ruling council.

When Morin was done, a Game message flashed through my mind.

Loken has allocated you a new task: <u>Heist in the Dark</u>! The trickster has tasked you with stealing an artifact from another Power. In exchange, Loken will remove the tracking spell he has laid on you.

Objective: Recover the mysterious chalice locked away in Paya's vaults. Optional objective: Carry out the theft undetected.

Loken hadn't put a time limit on his mission, which left me plenty of time to prepare. I questioned Morin on the task again, and after I was certain I understood its entirety, I leaned back in my chair. "Well, I guess this is goodbye again."

"Already?" Bornholm asked. "Don't you want to—"

Morin laid a hand on the dwarf, silencing him. She turned back to me. "I'm sorry things have turned out the way they have." She fell silent for a moment. "But if there's anything we can do to assist you, don't hesitate to contact us."

"If you need us, we'll come," Bornholm affirmed. "We owe you that much."

"Thank you," I said gravely to the pair. "Where can I find you?"

"We're billeted in Shadow Keep," Tantor said. "It's in the center of the Shadow quarter. You won't be able to get there yourself, but if you send a messenger, we'll come to find you."

I nodded but didn't say anything else.

After another awkward moment of silence, when it became clear I wasn't going to leave, the three rose to their feet. We shook hands and they departed, taking Tantor's cone of silence with them.

The rowdiness of the tavern rushed back in, and I let my shoulders sag. Only now that I was alone did I let my true feelings show.

I'd done my best to maintain a friendly, if distant, air with the trio, to not let them see how much Loken's betrayal—and by extension, their own—had shaken me.

The sad truth was that I couldn't afford to treat them as friends anymore. They weren't enemies, not precisely, but that could change in an instant. Morin, I thought, had realized that.

Sighing, I bowed my head and contemplated the trio's revelations. But my mind refused to focus, and only one thought kept buzzing to the fore as I tried to figure out what it all meant: *more problems, that's what.*

In a sudden fit of anger, I snapped my head back up. What I needed most right now was *to not think.* Raising my hand, I summoned a waiter.

It was time for a drink.

✳   ✳   ✳

I didn't stop at just one drink.

I kept going, and eventually my rage subsided, helped no doubt by a steady stream of tankards. And then, despite my resolve not to, my thoughts drifted toward Morin's tidings.

Even after escaping the Awakened Dead's clutches, it seemed I hadn't managed to disentangle myself from the Powers and their bloody games. I had intended to maintain a low profile while in Nexus. As large and populous as the sector was, I'd hoped that I could lose myself within the city while I slowly worked toward fulfilling Wolf's tasks.

Loken's machinations put all of that in jeopardy.

If I took on his mission, I would once again be thrown into the limelight. Even if I pulled off the theft flawlessly, I couldn't count on my identity remaining a secret.

For one, Loken would know who had done it, and what little trust I had in the Power had vanished. If it suited his ends, I was sure he would have no compunctions about revealing my identity.

I was well and truly stuffed.

If I could help it, I wouldn't go anywhere near Paya and her chalice. But the alternative didn't bear thinking upon either. I *had* to remove Loken's spell, and I didn't have one hundred thousand gold to do it.

"Goddamn Powers," I muttered and downed another drink.

✳   ✳   ✳

It was early evening when I rose unsteadily from my seat.

I'd had far too much to drink, but I didn't care. Swinging around, I surveyed the bar. If anything, it was more crowded than earlier—*past time to leave.* Slapping down some coins on the table, I stumbled out the door.

The fresh night air whipped against my face, and the hubbub of the bar faded as the door closed behind me. I hadn't had much time to examine the plague quarter earlier, and in my less-than-sober state, I didn't manage to take in much of the surroundings now either.

But one thing was immediately clear: the plague quarter possessed nothing of the safe zone's richness.

Where to now? I wondered hazily. Even with my thoughts muddled, I knew sleeping in the quarter was a bad idea. *Back to the safe zone and the hotel the bard mentioned then.*

Staggering into the street, I turned left. From what I remembered of my outward journey, it was only a few dozen yards to the south gate.

I can manage that.

There was a definite hitch to my step as I headed toward my destination, and I stumbled more than once. *Yikes, I'm a mess.*

And I wasn't the only one who thought so.

Despite my inebriated state, I wasn't totally oblivious of my surroundings, so I didn't fail to catch the loud whispers at my rear.

"... this should be easy."

"What do I keep telling you idiots? Never underestimate a mark!"

"He's drunk!" the first voice scoffed.

"Alone too," another added.

"And below rank ten," a third chipped in.

"Easy pickings," a fourth concluded with unmistakable glee.

"Just don't take any chances," the fifth cautioned, seemingly the sole voice of reason in the group.

The speakers sounded close. Too close. My would-be muggers had gone undetected far longer than they should have.

Through half-lidded eyes, I studied the road ahead. On my left was a dark alley, and up ahead the south gate was in sight. If I made a dash for it, I could probably escape my pursuers.

But escape was the last thing on my mind.

Perhaps it was the drink still sitting heavy in my stomach, but suddenly, I felt in dire need of a good clean fight. Odds be damned.

You picked the wrong mark tonight, boys.

Swaying left, I headed toward the alley.

✳ ✳ ✳

The moment I entered the alley, I let the shadows swallow me.

Five hostile entities have failed to detect you! You are hidden.

"Where'd he go?" a voice whispered, sounding confused.

"Quiet!" another hissed.

I headed deeper into the narrow street. Up ahead, I saw that the alley ended abruptly. *Dead end.*

There were no doors exiting the buildings to my left and right, but nearly ten yards above me was a narrow ledge, and even drunk, I thought I could manage the climb. Setting my hands on the wall, I began scaling it, if less nimbly than I could have.

Halfway up, I made my first mistake and a stone fell loose.

"You hear that?"

"What?"

"I heard something too."

"He's hiding. The noob must have spotted us!"

"There's no escape from here. We've got him boxed in."

"Enough chatter. Draw your weapons and ready your spells."

Cursing my ineptness, I pulled myself up onto the ledge without further mishap. It was barely wide enough to hold me. With my feet and arms spread, I glared down at my prey.

The five had entered the alley two abreast, and the first pair was almost beneath me already. Drawing ebonheart and spider's bite, I dropped like a stone.

But my timing was off.

Instead of landing lightly behind my first target as I intended, I crashed squarely atop one of the players in the second row.

You have crippled Lexion. You are no longer hidden.

In hindsight, I would've been better off using shadow blink, charm, astral blade, or any one of the many abilities available to me, but made overconfident by drink, I'd stupidly believed them unnecessary.

Swearing foully, I rolled free of the moaning body beneath me and struck out blindly with my swords. Fortune must favor fools and drunkards, because both my blades found their marks.

You have injured Rex.
You have critically injured Malik.

"Get him!"

"He's killed Rex!"

"I'm alive, you idiot," Rex swore.

Lightning crackled into existence and sped across the alley. Guided by instinct, I dropped flat on the ground.

You have evaded Gatar's magical projectile.

"Not lightning, fool! You're going to hit us, not him!"

More curses were shouted at the unfortunate spellcaster, and in the chaos, I retreated deeper into the alley.

I was sobering up fast, and the depth of my predicament was finally dawning on me. I was stuck in an alley with five players of unknown levels and capabilities. Never mind that I'd injured three; that had been due more to luck and surprise.

It was too late to back out from the fight now though. And while I'd been stupidly arrogant, my foes had made their own share of mistakes.

"He's running. After him!"

"Hez, tend to Lexion and Malik. Gatar, let's get him," Rex ordered.

Two sets of footsteps rushed toward me, leaving Hez alone with the injured pair. I smiled savagely. *Another mistake.* Drawing psi, I waited for two beats of a heart, then shadow blinked.

You have teleported into Hez's shadow.

Emerging from the aether, I thrust both my blades forward—and found only unyielding chainmail.

Hez's armor has blocked your attack.

Damnation!

My foe swung around, his flail whipping through the air. I ducked under the blow and nearly fell over in the process. But I held my balance and, dropping spider's bite, began summoning an astral blade.

"Rex, he's behind—" Hez began.

My arm flew forward, materializing the psi dagger an instant before my hand made contact with Hez's chest. This time around the player's armor proved no hindrance, and his eyes widened as the nerves in his chest deadened.

Unfortunately, the effect was only temporary.

Hez recovered from the attack a second later, and his weapon jerked back into motion toward me. Swaying out of the way, I slapped him across the face with my empty left hand.

Hez has passed a physical resistance check! You have failed to stun your target.

Well, damn and damn.

From further in the alley, I sensed Rex and Gatar spin around. Lexion appeared out of the fight, but Malik was fumbling with something in his hands.

A potion, I realized, fixing my gaze on the injured player. Hez began backing away, and I let him. I'd wasted enough time trying to kill the fighter already.

Better take care of the injured one first, I thought and took a step toward Malik.

It proved a mistake.

Hez wasn't a fighter. Or at least, he wasn't *only* a fighter.

Hez has cast whip of the divine.

I spun back around in time to see three tentacles of light expanding outward from Hez's flail. Before I could think which way to duck, they wrapped fast around me.

You have failed a magical resistance check.
A whip of the divine has injured you!
A whip of the divine has injured you!
A whip of the divine has injured you!

I convulsed, limbs spasming as waves of charge rolled through me. Worse yet, the whips were drawing tighter.

"Got him!" Hez crowed.

"Good work," Rex said, striding forward to join the cleric. "Now, tend to the others."

"I can't," Hez said. "If I stop channeling, the whips will dissipate."

"Don't worry about him," Rex said confidently. "We've got him."

I was completely sober now.

The agony wracking my body had washed away the last of the alcohol's ill effects, and I realized I'd made a hash of the fight.

I had to turn things around—and fast.

Hez's spell was a vicious one, and second by second my health was plummeting lower. I wasn't stun-locked though. It was the pain and not the casting that was keeping me in place.

I *could* move and cast, and I would.

But first, I needed a target. Through eyes drawn to slits, I studied the four players around me.

Rex, Gatar, and a fully recovered Malik held their weapons ready, waiting for my bindings to drop. For whatever reason, they seemed hesitant to strike while I was still wrapped in the coils of surging current.

The first whip of lightning uncoiled from around me.

My gaze jerked to Hez. He was muttering under his breath. Undoing his spell?

I thought so.

Time to act. Flinging open my mindsight, I targeted the group's leader and cast slaysight.

Strands of psi expanded outward from me to delve into Rex's consciousness. In a heartbeat, I found the nerve centers responsible for his vision and distorted them, erasing my presence from his sight.

Rex has failed a mental resistance check! You have hidden your presence from your target for 10 seconds. Warning: taking hostile action against your target will dispel the spell's effect.

"What happened?" Rex asked, sounding puzzled. "Did he disappear?"

"What do you mean?" Gatar asked. "He's right in front of you."

"I see him too," Malik agreed.

Rex's voice rose an octave. "Well, I can't!"

I smiled in satisfaction. *That's a wonderful ability.*

The second electric coil had unwrapped itself from me. Not waiting for the players to figure out what was going on, I shadow blinked.

You have teleported into Malik's shadow.
You have escaped a whip of the divine.

Of the four players still standing, Malik was the one most lightly armored. Darting forward, I plunged ebonheart through his back.

This time I didn't foul the blow. Death was instantaneous.

You have killed Malik.

"He's escaped!" Hez cried unnecessarily.

Gatar lunged at me while the bespelled Rex spun about, striking blindly at nothing. Jumping backward and out of range of their attacks, I faded into the shadows.

Three hostile entities have failed to detect you. You are hidden.

Safe in the shadows, I ignored the players' confused shouts. Drawing psi, I delayed only long enough to ready myself before shadow blinking behind Hez. The cleric was the biggest danger.

Emerging behind him, I drove ebonheart forward while simultaneously empowering the blow with piercing strike.

This time, Hez's armor failed to stop my blade.

You have backstabbed your target for 2x more damage.

The cleric reeled under the blow. Not letting up, I struck at him again and landed another devastating combination.

You have killed Hez.

Two down, one injured, two left.
A crackling burst of white light caught my attention, and without hesitation I threw myself forward.

You have evaded Gatar's thunderous charge.

A shape wreathed in lightning blurred past. I kept rolling, not stopping until I was in the shadows. Hidden once more, I unfurled my mindsight and identified the figure as Gatar.
He's some sort of spellblade. Drawing psi, I readied a casting.
"Gatar, talk to me!" Rex snapped. "Where is he?"
"I don't know," the spellblade growled. "He's killed—"
A storm of psi descended on Gatar, breaching his defenses and overwhelming his mind.

You have charmed your target for 10 seconds.

"Gatar?" Rex asked.
"Attack," I whispered.
Wordlessly, my bespelled minion pivoted around and strode toward the gang leader.

Your slaysight has dissipated.

The spell's end mattered little. I was out of sight already. Watching Rex intently, I readied myself. Gatar reached Rex and hefted his sword.
Realizing something was amiss, Rex began backing away. "Gatar, what are—?"
He didn't get to finish. The charmed spellblade thrust his weapon forward and ran his disbelieving companion through.

Gatar has injured Rex.

It was the opportunity I'd been waiting for. Blinking forward, I rejoined the fray.
It was time to end this.

Chapter 165: A Good's Night Rest

By the time I reached the battling duo, Rex had retaliated, injuring Gatar in turn, and it was a simple matter to finish off both, as well as the still-gasping Lexion.

I did so without remorse and without pity. Inept as the five had been, I doubted I was their first victim. Perhaps dying would cause them to mend their ways. I doubted it though.

You have killed Rex, Gatar, and Lexion.

My grim work done, I retrieved spider's bite and reconsidered my surroundings.

The rear end of the alley was backed against the safe zone's fortifications, and atop the walls I could see knights patrolling. A constant stream of people passed across the alley mouth too. Despite this, no one had attempted to intervene on my behalf.

I snorted, guessing that muggings were commonplace in the plague quarter.

Reseating myself in the darkest corner of the alley, I spent a few minutes healing and meditating. Once I was done, I attended to the waiting Game messages.

You have reached level 80 and rank 8!

For achieving rank 8, you have been awarded 1 additional attribute point and 1 Class point.

Your dodging has increased to level 52. Your sneaking has increased to level 62. Your shortswords has increased to level 57. Your light armor has increased to level 45.

Your chi has increased to level 48. Your meditation has increased to level 68. Your telekinesis has increased to level 48. Your telepathy has increased to level 47.

Your two-weapon fighting has increased to level 50 and has reached rank 5, allowing you to learn tier 2 abilities.

I whistled appreciatively at my gains.

I must've been under-leveled in comparison to my foes to have advanced four whole levels. *That's netted me a tidy sum of attribute points and a Class point too.*

I needed to see to my player progression but couldn't do so here. *Let's find somewhere safe.*

Turning my attention to the corpses, I quickly looted them. Sadly, none of the five carried anything especially valuable. Even Hez's flail was an ordinary weapon and contained no enchantments.

Still, I took everything the five had and stuffed it into my bag of holding, if for no other reason than to teach the thieves a lesson.

You have acquired 5 x caches of basic items.

You have acquired 6 silver and 3 copper.

Once my scavenging was completed, I slipped out of the alley and back toward the safe zone.

✳   ✳   ✳

As I approached the south gate, I casually, but quite deliberately, ran my gaze over the fortifications. The fight had cleared my mind, and in its wake, I'd come to a decision.

It didn't matter how I felt about Loken, his manipulations, and the fact that I'd been played for a fool, I had to get rid of his surveillance. My eyes drifted over the wall again. Sooner than I'd like, I would have to penetrate them.

The Triumvirate knights ran a tight ship. Three-man-strong patrols paced atop the wall, always keeping at least one other squad in sight. The ramparts themselves were well-lit and had mage globes strung up every twenty yards.

The gatehouse was even more impenetrable. Portcullises were emplaced on either end, and the tunnel which ran between was nine yards long and riddled with murder holes. Thankfully, there was no moat or drawbridge. Nonetheless, the safe zone's defenses were impressive.

I passed unhindered through the gate. Though the Triumvirate guards on duty eyed me carefully, none tried to stop me.

You have entered a safe zone.

Sighing, I closed my mindsight. Here, at least, I didn't need to worry about being ambushed. Advancing to the middle of the street, I surveyed the buildings on either side.

The hotel the bard had told me about was on my right, the Kesh Emporium Outlet on my left, and the Dark quarter farther east. Sleep beckoned, but I hesitated before heading for the hotel.

I'd been foolish tonight and fortunate not to have paid for it with my life. Rex and his fellows had taught me a valuable lesson. I couldn't afford to let emotion cloud my thinking. As much as I hated the thought of doing Loken's bidding, I couldn't dismiss the possibility that it might be the surest way to rid myself of his spell.

Perhaps complying with Loken's wishes will do the trick, or perhaps not.

Either way, I needed to find out more about the task he had set me. I couldn't do that unprepared though.

I had to plan meticulously.

My first order of business would be to scout the target—a venture on its own. To do that, I needed to get over the wall undetected. After seeing the defenses, I knew that wouldn't be easy, but if I prepared carefully, I was certain it could be done.

I'll scout the Dark quarter tonight, I decided. Swinging left, I headed towards the Kesh Emporium Outlet.

First, though, I had some shopping to do.

$$*\quad*\quad*$$

The emporium, as the name implied, was a market. It wasn't for everyone though. The place was run by the merchant Kesh for a select clientele. You couldn't get in without the appropriate references—which, thanks to Albion Bank, I had.

The emporium was enclosed within a walled compound of its own close to the south gate and was unmissable. Golden magelights danced in the starless sky over the compound, bathing the place in a soft, warm glow, and gentle music emanated from within.

I made straight for the wooden gates barring entry into the compound. Two giants clad in a mountain of steel stood before it. Their weapons alone were taller than me.

"Halt," the first rumbled.

"This is private property," the second added. "No riffraff allowed."

My lips twisted in amusement. "Really?" I murmured. "Then it's a good thing I'm not that." Pulling out the card Devlin had given me, I waved it before the pair.

The guards eyed the item. "Let me see that," the first demanded.

I handed over the card without fuss, and while the two bent their heads to scrutinize it, I analyzed both.

The target is Ent, a level 171 giant armsmaster. He is a player and bears a Mark of Lesser Shadow.

The target is Lake, a level 178 giant berserker. He is a player and bears a Mark of Lesser Light.

"That's rude," Lake said, sensing my analyze.

I shrugged. "No ruder than you two," I retorted.

Lake scowled at me. "You little—"

"It's genuine," Ent interrupted.

Lake's expression cleared, and he closed his mouth with a snap. Bowing low, he wrapped his large hands around the handle of one of the doors and pushed it open. "Sorry for the trouble, sir. You may pass."

I flashed him a grin, knowing that apologizing was the last thing the giant wanted to do. "Not a problem," I said and retrieved my card from the silent Ent before strolling into the compound.

$$*\quad*\quad*$$

A hooded figure met me inside. "How may I help you today, sir?"

The player was draped in a formless red robe that completely hid the shape beneath, but from my questioner's voice, I assumed it was a woman.

"Can you direct me to Kesh, please?"

The woman shook her head. "I'm sorry, but Kesh is unavailable."

Pulling out Viviane's token, I tossed it up in the air. The hooded figure locked eyes on the token before turning around. "This way, sir."

My escort led me down an elegant corridor and past rows of closed wooden doors. There was a thick plush carpet underfoot, and gold chandeliers hung down from the ceiling. The occasional player passed us by, each accompanied by another of the faceless figures.

Why the hoods? I wondered.

Finally we passed by an open doorway and, curious, I peered in. The room was configured as a simple, if expensive, office. A customer sat on one side of the desk and a merchant on the other. Unexpectedly, there were no wares in sight.

"Where are all the items?" I asked.

My escort glanced at me. "This is your first time in the emporium I take it, sir? We do not deal directly with merchandise here. As you can imagine, space is at a premium in the safe zone, and it's impossible to keep our entire inventory on the premises."

"Huh," I remarked.

"Our goods are stored in secure vaults outside the sector and only retrieved at need. At the emporium, our customers can peruse our catalogs, which are themselves highly prized. You will not find goods of similar quality or rarity anywhere else in Nexus," she finished with a notable timbre of pride.

All at inflated prices, no doubt, I thought, wondering if I had made a mistake in coming here. The emporium was clearly not a place to shop on a budget.

Before I could question my guide further, she drew to a halt before a double set of doors and knocked.

"Come," a voice called from within.

My escort pushed open the door and waved me through. "This way, sir. Kesh awaits."

*   *   *

The first thing I noticed was that my host was a woman and not a man, as I expected from her name. The second thing that drew my eye was her age.

Kesh was old.

Her face was wrinkled and seamed like aged paper, and her hair was snow white. It was only while studying her that I realized few of the players I'd met had been truly old.

A white shawl was draped over the merchant's head and shoulders, its edges lined with gold embroidery. Folds of a matching garment were wrapped around her body and arms, leaving only her spindly hands and bony fingers exposed.

Kesh wore surprisingly little jewelry for someone as obviously wealthy as she was. Only a single ring adorned her right hand. Her other fingers were bare of ornaments, as were her neck and ears.

The office itself was little different from the one I had glimpsed before. It was decorated with understated elegance. A polished wooden table sat in the center, behind which Kesh waited in a plush leather chair. Curtains draped the windows, a carpet lay on the floor, and bookshelves lined the walls.

My gaze darting back to the merchant, I cast analyze.

The target is Kesh, a human master merchant. She is a player and bears a Mark of Greater Light, Greater Shadow, and Greater Dark.

A dry and wintry chuckle rose from the merchant. "I'm not what you were expecting, I take it?"

I broke off from my stare. "Sorry, it's just that—"

Kesh waved a hand dismissively. "Forget it. Your reaction is little different from thousands of other customers." She gestured to the chair opposite her. "Sit."

I sat. "Do you mind if I ask you a question?"

The elderly merchant smiled. "Anything for a customer," she rasped.

"How old are you?"

Kesh smiled mysteriously. "You won't believe how many times I get asked that," she said while making no attempt to answer the question. Her gaze roved over me, sharp eyes seeming to catalog each piece of my gear. "I'm surprised you managed to attract Viviane's interest," she said bluntly.

I glanced down at myself. "Why? What's wrong with how I look?" I asked only half-jokingly.

"You're poor," Kesh said bluntly. "If there is one thing both Viviane and I have in common, it's that we appreciate refined things."

I didn't miss the warning behind Kesh's words, nor the familiarity with which she spoke the Power's name, and I got the distinct impression she wouldn't hesitate to throw me out if I didn't merit her attention.

I cast her a lopsided grin. "Is this how you treat all your customers?"

Kesh snorted. "Only those I suspect of wasting my time. As you've observed already, I'm an old woman. Others can beat around the bush. Not me." She leaned back in her chair and pinned me with a glare. "Viviane's token was enough to get you through the door, but to stay you have to show me more. Now answer me truly. Can you afford my wares?"

I shrugged easily. "Truthfully? I don't know. I'm newly arrived in Nexus and don't have a feel for the market yet."

Kesh said nothing for a moment, then tapped the fingers of her right hand on the table in a peculiar pattern. In response, a bank keystone emerged in front of me.

"Touch the keystone and let me verify your funds," the merchant demanded.

Mutely, I did as asked.

Kesh's attention flickered inward momentarily before returning to me.

"So. Am I rich enough?"

The old woman's lips widened into a smile. It was answer enough.

"Before we get down to business," Kesh said, "there are a few ground rules."

"Go on," I said.

"One, I will not buy stolen goods. I have neither the inclination nor the patience to fence such items."

I opened my mouth, but before I could interject, the merchant went on, "Looted items are different. I will buy them, but when it comes to high-ranked and unique gear, I will give the original owner the right of first purchase at a *discounted* price. You will only get what I receive, minus my commission of course." She held my gaze, waiting for my acknowledgment.

I nodded slowly, indicating my understanding.

"Two, there will be a ten-percent surcharge on all items I purchase for you through the auction or from third parties and on any that I sell for you. If that's too much, leave now. My commission is non-negotiable."

She waited. I remained seated.

"Good," Kesh said. "Third, and most importantly, I promise you total anonymity in any transaction we engage in. This is at the core of the services I offer and the reason for the premium applied to my goods. The emporium prides itself on maintaining the privacy of its clients. No one, not even the Powers, will learn of the items you buy or sell through me. I have sworn a binding Pact with the Triumvirate, who themselves ensure the secrecy of my customers' trades." She paused. "Now, if you understand all that and still wish to proceed, then we may continue."

"I have three questions," I said.

The merchant's lips twitched. "Only three? Go on, ask away."

"Do you sell information?"

Kesh shook her head. "I do not. If it's gossip and rumors you seek, visit the information brokers in the plague quarter."

I nodded. It was the same advice Shael had given me. "What about bounties?"

Kesh frowned. "I don't deal in them, if that's what you're asking." She paused. "Nor do I care if there are any bounties on your head. A paying customer is a paying customer."

That was good enough for me. "Last question. Your Pact with the Triumvirate, how does that work?"

"Ah," Kesh said. "A very long time ago, the Powers signed an Accord. Every Power and faction in existence at that time—and since—has agreed to the Accord. By its terms, the Triumvirate have been given complete autonomy in Nexus. They alone have the power to decide which factions and Powers can enter the sector. In return, the Triumvirate have relinquished any claim to all other sectors in the Forever Kingdom. Nexus is the extent of their domain." She glanced at me to see if I was following.

"Go on," I said.

"The rest is simple," Kesh said. "I have an agreement with the Triumvirate—a Pact, really. For a not inconsiderable fee, the three Powers have sworn to protect my customers' anonymity. Any Power caught snooping into my records or my customers' identities will be in violation of the Triumvirate's rules and banished from the sector. And no one wants that." She smiled. "Does that answer your concern?"

I returned her smile. "It does. Alright then, let's get started."

✳   ✳   ✳

The merchant Kesh has accepted you as a customer. Henceforth, all your transactions with the emporium are protected under Kesh's Pact of secrecy with the Triumvirate.

By the terms of the Pact, any individual or organization that reveals your dealings with the emporium to a third party, including Kesh herself, will be banished from Nexus.

Kesh reached under the table and pulled out five thin films of metal. Spreading them out before me, she tapped each in turn. "Weapons. Armor. Ingredients. Ability tomes. And miscellaneous gear." As the old woman touched each sheet, words appeared upon them.

Bending my head downward, I read the text. Each metal film contained a catalog, a list of items many hundreds of thousands long that scrolled continuously across the polished surface, appearing at the bottom and disappearing from the top. Curiously, I touched one of the named items.

The scrolling list paused, and a Game message opened in my mind, describing the object in question in detail, along with its price tag. "Remarkable," I murmured.

"The emporium's catalogs are unique. You won't find their like elsewhere in the Game," Kesh said with a proud smile. "They're searchable too."

My head jerked up at that. "Searchable?" That would make the list not just remarkable but priceless.

The merchant's smile widened. "To activate the search function, focus your mind on what you're looking for while touching the catalog. The list will filter itself to show only the relevant items."

"That's... amazing," I managed, momentarily at a loss for words.

"It is," Kesh agreed. "Now, if you can tell me what you're after, I can help speed things along."

I had a fairly good idea of what I needed, but I wasn't sure if such items were available or if Kesh stocked them.

"What I'm looking for is..." I began and rattled off my requirements.

The merchant sat back and studied me with pursed lips. "That's quite the list," she said at last.

"Is it doable?" I asked. I hadn't held back. Trusting in Kesh's Pact, I'd spilled everything I sought to accomplish my immediate goals.

"Let's deal with the items one at a time," the merchant said. She tapped the weapons sheet. "I can get you the swords you're looking for, but I don't advise it. It will cost you the greater part of your funds."

I licked my lips unhappily. "How much?"

"For what you want? One thousand gold." She paused. "Minimum."

I sighed. "Alright, leave the blades out." As a stealth, dexterity-based fighter, my weapons were the most important aspect of my arsenal. Still, the swords I carried were serviceable, and at this stage, better weapons weren't essential.

"The same goes for the armor you requested," Kesh continued.

I sagged further in disappointment. Fulfilling my requirements was going to be more costly than I'd anticipated.

"If I can make a suggestion?" Kesh prompted.

"Go ahead," I said, waving her on.

She eyed my leather armor shrewdly. "Your current gear offers adequate protection for one of your level. To get the enchantment you want, changing your armor isn't necessary. Rather purchase a garment that can be worn over it."

"Oh?" I asked, interest piqued.

The merchant closed her eyes and tapped the armor sheet. A single item appeared in the catalog, and a Game message unfurled in my mind.

Item 7,653 of the emporium's wares is the apprentice rogue's outfit. It is a rank 3 item and consists of a black balaclava, a pair of gloves, a shirt, and pants. The full set increases a player's sneaking by +30 when in dark environments. This item set requires a minimum Dexterity of 12 to use. Cost: 200 gold.

I winced at the price, but the outfit did exactly what I wanted, and despite the cost, I had no hesitation in agreeing to Kesh's suggestion. "That'll do nicely," I said. "I'll take it."

"The young these days..." Kesh said with an indulgent smile. "So impatient. There's another option. It is pricier, I admit, but I think it will suit you better." Without waiting for my assent, she pressed her finger against the sheet again.

Item 47,653 of the emporium's wares is the belt of the chameleon. It is a rank 4 item and has three modes: stealth, simple, and combat.

In simple mode, the belt equips the player with everyday garments that are nondescript but hard-wearing. In combat mode, the clothes are retracted into the belt, leaving the wielder's armor and weapons freely accessible. In stealth mode, the garments transform into a form-fitting mesh designed to absorb incoming light and blend with the surroundings, increasing your sneaking by +20 in all conditions.

Additionally, the belt also includes 10 slots to hold standard crystals. Bonuses provided by this item will not stack with other items. It requires a minimum Dexterity of 8 and a Perception of 8 to use. Cost: 500 gold.

"Whoa," I breathed. "You're right. The belt is *much* better." Despite costing more than double the rogue's outfit, the belt was more versatile.

Kesh smiled in satisfaction. "You'll take it then?"

"I will," I agreed. "One question though. What are crystal slots?"

"Most single-use enchantments these days are infused in small cylindrical crystals like this one," Kesh answered, holding up a translucent sapphire three inches tall.

I nodded in understanding and waved her on. "What's next?"

"Next, the secondary gear you require. I can get all of them," she said, tapping the miscellaneous catalog.

This is a lot consisting of 10 smoke bombs. Cost: 100 gold.

This is a lot consisting of 3 full healing potions. Cost: 300 gold.

Item 81,600 of the emporium's wares is the cat claws. This is a rank 3 item designed to allow a player to climb vertical surfaces and requires a minimum Dexterity of 12 to use. Cost: 100 gold.

Item 127,911 of the emporium's wares is the spectacles of ward seeing. This is a rank 4 item that allows a player to detect wards of tier 4 wards and below. It requires a minimum Perception, Magic, or Faith of 16 to use. Cost: 300 gold.

Item 30,193 of the emporium's wares is a simple potion bracelet. It is worn high on the player's arm and can be activated at will to inject a potion directly into your bloodstream. The bracelet can hold up to three potion solutions. Cost: 200 gold.

Item 104,145 of the emporium's wares is the trapper's wristband. This item not only stores trap components but has been enchanted to simplify their deployment. The wristband can only be used to configure simple traps. Each trap can consist of a maximum of 2 components: one trigger and one trap element.

Currently stored trap-making crystals: 40 / 40.

Available trigger types: pressure plates (for use on floors), sound glasses (omnidirectional), tripwires (between two points), and motion pins (cone).

Available element types: lightning enchantments, poison clouds, fire enchantments, coiled-spring daggers, bear-trap clamps, and small explosives.

Note that the player must still employ the thieving skill to deploy his traps. Furthermore, the components in the trapper's wristband are not pre-configured but are stored as enchanted crystals that can be transformed into the desired component when required. Cost: 100 gold.

I studied the six items avidly. I'd chosen the smoke bombs because they had proven so useful in the valley. They were relatively cheap too, and I'd no compunction about buying them again.

The cat claws would henceforth become my primary climbing tool. A rope was too conspicuous, not to mention more restricted—finding or reaching a point to affix it wasn't always possible — and while the claws would offer less protection against a fall, my other abilities would make up for that lack.

The spectacles of ward seeing was an item I considered essential, especially after repeatedly falling foul of the mages' wards in the valley. While the glasses wouldn't disable any ward I found, they would reveal them. But like all items in the Game, they were limited in their capability.

"Why do the glasses only detect wards up to tier four? Don't you have any better ward detectors?"

Kesh chuckled. "I certainly do. But you can't afford them."

I stared at her uncomprehendingly. The glasses were priced at only three hundred gold. How much more could a higher-tiered detection device cost?

"I see from your expression you don't understand," Kesh said. "Tier five abilities are almost exclusively the domain of elite players — those above level two hundred." She paused and held my gaze. "Few players achieve such rank, and the items necessary to combat their abilities are exceedingly rare. Consequently, there is a significant jump in price from rank four to rank five items."

My brows furrowed in thought. "How much?" I asked.

"For a rank five ward detection device? Three thousand gold."

My eyes widened. "Ten times more?" I gasped.

Kesh nodded solemnly despite the amused glint in her eyes.

"I guess I'll make do with the rank four one then." Bending my head to the slate again, I studied the next item on the list. I'd asked Kesh for an item that automatically dispensed my healing potions, and the bracelet she'd listed fit the brief perfectly. *It'll do*, I thought.

The last item was the most interesting.

In function it was similar to the alchemy stone, except the components it stored were those related to traps, and I was excited at the thought of trying it out.

"I'll take them all," I paused. "How much is that?"

"Sixteen hundred gold," Kesh replied immediately.

I winced at the cost. That was over half my accumulated wealth. Still, the items were necessary, and I didn't quibble. "What about the spellbooks I requested?"

Kesh shook her head. "Unfortunately, with regards to them I can be of much less help."

I stared at the merchant in surprise. I'd asked for tier two tomes for the abilities I'd acquired through the Wolf trials. All four of my mind skills were nearing rank five and I wanted to advance them as soon as I could, yet from Kesh's expression, it seemed like that wouldn't be as easy as I'd thought. "Why not?"

"I'm not sure how you came by such abilities," Kesh said through narrowed eyes, "but they aren't available on the open markets, nor on the private ones I have access to. Two of the abilities you've mentioned I've never even heard of before." She held my gaze. "And let me tell you, there is very little I haven't heard of."

I nodded slowly. "So, are you telling me there's no way for me to upgrade the abilities?"

Kesh's grin returned. "I didn't say that. There is a way, but it's more expensive than purchasing a tier two ability tome."

"Let's hear it then."

"Your abilities are not the only rare ones in the Game and, at higher tiers especially, it is sometimes difficult to find the right ability tome. Thankfully, the Adjudicator has provided a solution: upgrade gems."

I lowered my head into my hands, already knowing what was coming next. "Don't tell me. Their cost is exorbitant."

Kesh nodded. "A single-use ability upgrade gem costs two thousand gold."

"Damn."

"Do you wish to purchase one?"

"Not yet," I said reluctantly. "What about the other tomes I want?"

"They were trivial to acquire," Kesh said, laying a palm on the ability slate.

Turning my gaze inward, I read the Game messages that appeared.

Item 144,951 of the emporium's wares is the simple set trap ability tome. Governing attribute: Dexterity. Tier: basic. Cost: 10 gold. Requirement: rank 0 thieving.

Item 161,411 of the emporium's wares is the lesser lighten load ability tome. Governing attribute: Constitution. Tier: basic. Cost: 10 gold. Requirement: rank 0 armor skill.

Item 113,916 of the emporium's wares is the simple whirlwind ability tome. Governing attribute: Dexterity. Tier: advanced. Cost: 25 gold. Requirement: rank 5 two-weapon fighting.

"Excellent," I said. "I'll take them as well."

CHAPTER 167: ALL DRESSED UP

However Kesh's people stored their wares, it only took a few minutes for my items to arrive, and I wasted no time learning the abilities and equipping my new gear.

You have acquired the basic ability: simple set trap. This ability allows you to deploy simple traps, consumes stamina, and can be upgraded. Its activation time is very slow. You have 6 of 20 Dexterity ability slots remaining.

You have acquired the basic ability: lesser lighten load. This ability reduces the encumbrance from worn armor by 10%, consumes stamina, and can be upgraded. Its activation time is very slow. You have 13 of 14 Constitution ability slots remaining.

You have acquired the advanced ability: simple whirlwind. This ability empowers the caster's limbs with energy, increasing the speed of his attacks by 100% for 3 seconds. You have the necessary skills, rank 5 two-weapon fighting and a rank 5 light weapon skill, to learn this ability.
This ability's activation time is very fast, consumes stamina, and can be upgraded. You have 1 of 20 Dexterity ability slots remaining.

You have equipped a trapper's wristband. Stored trap-making crystals: 40 / 40.
You have equipped a potion bracelet. Potions readied: 3 doses of full healing.
You have equipped the belt of the chameleon. Current mode: combat.

The trapper's wristband was a plain wrap of black leather that fitted snugly around my left forearm. It was unembellished except for the stitching around its ends and a single blue rune in the middle.

The potion bracelet was just as unassuming. It was a sleek band of metal, sized to sit on my arm just above the wrist. Three runes were engraved on its surface, and touching a stone flask to each caused the liquid within to be absorbed and stored as a dose in the enchanted item.

The chameleon belt was the most interesting. Made of fine, soft scales, the item almost seemed to disappear against my black leather armor when I equipped it around my waist. Only the polished black buckle at the center stood out. Toying with it, I saw three studs concealed within the buckle. I supposed they were how I changed the belt's active enchantment.

After I was done, I eyed my bank balance.

You have lost 1,645 gold. Money remaining in your bank account: 901 gold, 4 silver, and 9 copper.

Damn. In one shopping trip, I'd run through more than half my funds. There were still more things I wanted, but I stifled the urge to buy anything else.

There would be plenty of time for that, assuming everything went according to plan later on tonight.

"What do you think?" Kesh asked, watching me test my purchases.

"They're exactly as promised," I said.

"Excellent," the merchant replied. "Now, is there anything else I can do for you?"

"Actually, yes," I said. Upending my backpack, I unloaded the loot I'd marked for selling. Then added a few more items—gear that had become redundant.

You have lost: a common fighter's sash, a common thief's cloak, an acolyte's ring, 71 pieces of miscellaneous loot, and 111 alchemy stone ingredients.

"How much will I get for all this?"

"Hmm..." Kesh murmured as her eyes roved over the loot. "Some of the items are near worthless," the merchant said, holding up the fighter's sash by way of example. "While others are much in demand," she added, holding up the acolyte's ring. "You sure you want to sell this?"

"Well..." I hesitated, debating with myself for a moment. "Could you exchange it for another attribute-type ring?"

Kesh raised an eyebrow. "Any preference for what you want boosted?"

"Strength," I replied. It was my lowest physical attribute, and unlike Faith, I had *some* use for it. And while I wasn't about to invest any of my hard-won attribute points into Strength, a few additional points from a stat-boosting item would be nice.

"Strength I can do," Kesh said. "Such rings are less in demand than Faith buffs—and therefore cheaper." Setting aside the ring, she turned her attention to the remaining items. "The alchemy ingredients are worth a tidy sum. Whoever you got to harvest them did a good job."

I nodded in agreement. The merchant's words also reminded me of something else I needed to attend to, and I made a mental note to follow up on the matter later.

"For all this, I can give you..." Kesh closed her eyes and performed some mental arithmetic, "let's say, on average, ten gold per item and two-hundred and fifty gold for the alchemy ingredients." She opened her eyes to peer at me. "Rounding up, that makes one thousand gold. How does that sound to you?"

It sounded good. *Very* good.

It was a darn sight more than I'd expected, and while I was sure Kesh would make more, I valued the anonymity and ease that came from using the merchant's services over the extra pennies I would receive if I sold the items directly myself.

"Deal," I replied.

"Excellent," Kesh said with a pleased smile. She waved her hand over the items, and just like that they vanished from the table. In their stead, a single ring remained. "That's yours," Kesh said. "Your funds have also been deposited into your account."

Picking up the ring, I inspected and equipped it.

You have acquired a bull's ring, +2 Strength. This is a rank 1 ring and increases your Strength attribute by 2. This item has no requirements to equip.

"Thank you," I said.

Kesh, meanwhile, was studying the rest of my gear. "What about that medallion?" she asked abruptly. "Don't you want to sell it?"

"No," I said.

"And the wayfarer's boots?" Kesh persisted. "For *that,* I can get you a small fortune."

"No," I said even more firmly. "But speaking of the boots, do you have the other items from the set in your stores?"

Kesh snorted. "In my stores? No. The boots and their companion items are part of a legendary set. Such artifacts are rarely—if ever—available on the open market, and when they are, they're quickly snapped up." She paused. "I could see about acquiring the other pieces in the set for you. For that, however, I will charge an *additional* twenty percent. Call it a finder's fee."

"Of course you will," I muttered under my breath. But really, I understood the reason behind Kesh's exorbitant markup. Unlike my other stat-boosting items, the boot's bonuses *stacked* with other items, making each piece truly priceless and highly sought after. Acquiring the full set would require diligence and patience.

Raising my voice, I said, "Go ahead and look."

Kesh nodded. "Don't expect to hear back soon. It could take weeks, months, or even years to put the set together."

"Understood," I said, then hesitated before forging on. "There's just one last thing."

"Yes?"

"As a merchant you have aether magic, don't you?"

Looking puzzled by the question, Kesh nodded. "I do."

I deliberated for a second longer, formulating my thoughts. "There's an... employee of mine in a remote sector that, from time to time, I will need to get into contact with. Do you think that's something you could help with?"

Kesh's eyebrows rose at the strangeness of my request. "You're going to have to give me more details than that."

I sighed, realizing she was right, and then went on to explain about Saya and the tavern.

The merchant leaned back in her chair. "I understand now. You need an agent to act on your behalf, someone to serve as an intermediary between the tavern and yourself as the owner."

I nodded, relieved she seemed to understand the gist of my requirements. "Can you do it?"

Kesh nodded. "Do you have the tavern's bill of ownership?"

"Yes," I said.

"Perfect," Kesh replied. "If you appoint me as your factor, I can do all that you need, including opening an account on behalf of the tavern and acquiring any necessary supplies. Since you're already a valued customer at the Albion Bank, it would be best to establish the tavern's account there. Once that's done, I will establish contact with your tavernkeeper—Saya, was it?—and initiate any transfer of funds required between your accounts. I will do all that and more." She smiled again. "For a nominal price."

"Name it."

"Five-percent commission on all the tavern's profits."

I rubbed my chin in thought. "The services you provide as the tavern's factor, will that be covered under your Pact of secrecy? Will my identity as the owner be protected?"

"Of course," Kesh answered.

Five percent was steep but worth it for the added layer of anonymity it provided. I doubted anyone except Benadean and Saya knew who the tavern's true owner was. Saya certainly wouldn't tell anyone, and the former owner had left too fast to share the news.

I rose to my feet. "Then we have a deal."

✳   ✳   ✳

By rights of your bill of ownership, you have appointed the player, Kesh, as the factor of 'The Sleepy Inn' in the safe zone of sector 12,560.

I left the emporium quickly after that.

It was time to check in at the hotel. The night was still young, and the streets of the safe zone remained busy. For what I planned on doing next, the fewer people around, the better.

Finding a dark alley, I ducked within and changed the setting on the chameleon belt, activating another of its enchantments.

Clothes rippled upward from the artifact to cover my leather armor in a pair of sturdy black pants, a white cotton shirt, and a brown duster jacket.

You have activated the simple mode enchantment of the belt of the chameleon. Your armor and weapons are now hidden.
You have successfully concealed ebonheart.
You have successfully concealed spider's bite.

I ran my gaze over my new apparel. It was as unremarkable as promised and would attract less scrutiny in Nexus. Slipping out of the alley, I made my way to the hotel.

The Wanderer's Delight was a building that stretched nearly ten stories high and was easily visible from a few streets away. The hotel's location was made more obvious by the lurid glowing sign floating above its rooftop.

As I drew closer, I studied the building curiously. Stone crenellations and what looked like gargoyles topped the roof, but I couldn't be certain. It looked like someone had taken a hammer and chisel to the statues, defacing each.

The windows running along the building's length were also odd. They were more arrow slits than anything else. However the Wanderer's Delight had begun life, it had certainly not always been a hotel.

I stepped up to the open wooden doors guarded by two well-dressed servants. "Welcome, sir," the first said.

"How can we help you today?" the second asked.

"I need a room for the night," I said.

"Of course. Come this way."

I followed the doorman inside. The interior of the building was nothing like its bullish exterior and was smartly furnished. Hotel staff and guests were everywhere, bustling around quietly.

The doorman led me to a counter, where I paid for my room—a hefty charge of ten gold per night. I didn't bat an eye at the cost though, and, leaving the servant behind, I made my way directly to my room.

The room was as tastefully decorated as the rest of the hotel. It came complete with running water—heated no less—and many other unexpected amenities. Locking the door behind me, I threw my pack down and lay on the bed. There was just enough time for me to get a few hours of rest.

Closing my eyes, I let sleep claim me.

✳ ✳ ✳

Just after midnight, my eyes snapped open.

For a moment, I stayed unmoving while I focused on my surroundings. The hubbub in the nearby streets and the floors below had died down.

It wasn't completely silent, though, far from it. But I suspected that the conditions were about as good as they were going to get for scouting the Dark quarter.

Rolling off the bed, I began readying myself.

First, I stowed my backpack in a nearby cupboard. I intended to be back before the day was over, and the less weighed down I was for tonight's mission, the better. Next, I sat down cross-legged and turned my focus inward. It was time to attend to my player progression.

I had five attribute points to spend and decided to split their investment in Magic—in preparation for my third Class—and Dexterity—the lowest of my core attributes.

Your Magic has increased to rank 8.

Other modifiers: +2 from your apprentice ring and -1 from your light armor. Magic skills and abilities have been limited to rank 9.

Your Dexterity has increased to rank 22.

Other modifiers: +4 from the wayfarer's boots and -3 from your light armor. Dexterity skills and abilities have been limited to rank 23.

Then, I reflected on my four Class points.

My original intention had been to save them until I achieved a tri-blend, but after observing how well my Class ability, slaysight, had performed against Rex, I was forced to reconsider that plan.

The spell had effectively blinded the gang leader to my presence for ten seconds. Even better, Rex hadn't even seemed to be aware that his sight had been manipulated. If I improved slaysight to tier two—*or maybe even tier five!*—it could make all the difference to tonight's mission, which I hoped to pull off undetected.

It warrants the investment of at least one Class point, I decided. Closing my eyes, I willed my intention to the Adjudicator.

Assessing player's suitability for a Class upgrade...
Class points available: 4.
Player rank: 8.
Upgrade requirements met.
You may advance your Class to rank 2 by improving an existing Class benefit or by selecting new ones. Note, if any of your Class abilities or traits are lost through a future melding, their upgrades will not carry over to your new blended Class.

Do you wish to proceed?

I frowned at the Game's response.

It wasn't unexpected, given what I'd already learned about Class upgrades, but it implied more risk than I anticipated. Still, I was only interested in improving slaysight, and since the ability was more a result of my Wolf bloodline than a Class blend, I didn't foresee losing the ability in the future.

An acceptable risk, I decided and conveyed my response to the Adjudicator.

Commencing Class upgrade...
3 new Class benefits are available, and 2 of 3 existing benefits are upgradeable.
New benefit: mental focus. This trait makes it easier for you to penetrate a foe's mental defenses.
New benefit: hardened mind. This trait makes it harder for a foe to assault your mind.
New benefit: prepared mind. This ability allows you to precast a single ability, releasing it instantly when needed with no additional casting time required.
Existing benefits that may be upgraded: slayer's heritage and nightwalker.
Existing benefits not available for upgrade: slaysight. This ability requires a telepathy skill of rank 5 to advance.
Choose your rank 2 Class benefit now.

I stared at the Adjudicator's words. I couldn't upgrade slaysight yet.

"Bloody hell," I muttered. Disappointed, I willed the Adjudicator to cancel the upgrade.

Warning: You will lose your Class point if you terminate the Class upgrade process at this point. Do you still wish to proceed?

My lips twisted sourly. *Really?*

If I'd known the process couldn't be canceled, I would have waited a bit longer before attempting the Class upgrade. After all, my telepathy was nearly at the required level, but once more, I was caught out by ignorance.

I exhaled noisily. Still, there was nothing to be done. Retracting my request, I scrutinized the available benefits.

Both prepared mind and mental focus seemed useful.

Prepared mind would allow me to retaliate quickly when ambushed, whereas mental focus would act as a buff on my offensive mind abilities. Of the two, mental focus seemed the more versatile and beneficial trait, especially if I could keep improving it.

Decided, I willed my choice to the Adjudicator.

You have gained the trait: mental focus. This trait makes it easier for you to penetrate a foe's mental defenses by increasing the effectiveness of your Mind skills by 10% when applied to enemies.

Upgrade complete. Class points remaining: 3.
Congratulations, Michael, your mindslayer Class has advanced to rank 2!

With a sigh, I rose to my feet. For what it was worth, my Class upgrade was complete, and while the outcome wasn't what I'd desired, it was still favorable.

But now it was time to get to work.

Surveying myself, I conducted one last check. My swords hung loose in their sheaths, and my potions were in place and equipped.

I was ready.

Slipping out the door, I left the hotel.

CHAPTER 168: OVER THE WALL

I reached the safe zone's east gate without incident.

Drawing to a halt thirty yards away, I spent a moment observing the area. Even at this late hour, the gate to the Dark quarter was open and players passed through, if sporadically.

Too busy, I thought.

Slipping away, I turned south and walked along a street running parallel to the wall. When I reached the mouth of a narrow street between two walled estates, I stopped and scanned the surroundings nonchalantly.

The alley was dark and extended all the way to the wall bordering the Dark quarter. No players passed close by, and the east gatehouse was out of sight. It was only magical detection wards and the guards atop the ramparts that I had to worry about.

It was as perfect an entry-point as I could've hoped for.

Drawing the shadows around me, I ducked into the alley and padded to its end. Hidden at the base of the wall, I cast lighten load and reaction buff.

Your Dexterity has increased by +2. Duration: 10 minutes.

Your light armor penalties have decreased by 10%. Duration: 10 minutes.

Then I put on my thieving gear.

You have equipped a set of cat claws.

The cat claws' gloves were made from liquid-black scale hide. They were pliable and soft, except for a hard mass at the end of each finger. Inspecting the fingertips closely, I noticed each had a small hole.

For retractable claws.

The palms of the gloves were covered by tiny suction cups. To improve their grip, I assumed. Both cups and claws would make holding anything cumbersome, and wielding my swords would be nearly impossible.

It's a good thing I don't intend on fighting tonight then, isn't it?

You have equipped the spectacles of ward seeing.

The spectacles were shaded black and more akin to goggles. Their edges were trimmed by dark metal, and their arms wrapped around my head. Craning my neck backward, I gazed up at the wall.

Immediately, my vision lit up.

I pursed my lips in silent appreciation. The fortifications were riddled with wards formed from multi-hued strands of color. Like some strange puzzle, the magical lines traced the wall's brickwork in a crazy pattern.

I wasn't certain if the softly glowing threads were from a single spell, but from the different colors, I guessed multiple wards had been cast. I couldn't tell what the wards' purpose was, only where they had been positioned.

But knowing that should suffice. Scrutinizing the wall intently, I searched for a path through the maze.

After long minutes of study, I mapped out a route. It would require me to scale the wall in a decidedly zigzag fashion, but it could be done.

I flexed my fingers. At the motion, curved metal claws shot out of my gloves. They were as hard as toughened steel and appeared strong enough to grip the wall.

Multiple hostile entities have failed to detect you! You are hidden.

I glanced up. A patrol was passing by atop the wall, but though the Triumvirate knights ran their gazes over the ground below, they failed to spot me.

I smiled grimly. My stealth was holding. I could only hope it would continue to do so while I climbed. Stretching my left arm up, I set a hand on the wall. The glove's claws dug into a seam in the brickwork and held.

Good. Anchoring my left foot on the thin lip atop another brick, I pulled myself upward. Raising my right hand, I repeated the maneuver.

I was on my way.

I didn't hurry. Trusting my stealth to keep me concealed, I inched higher up the wall and made sure not to disturb any of the ward lines crisscrossing its surface.

My biggest concern wasn't the wards I *could* see. It was the ones that remained unseen. My spectacles only revealed tier four wards, after all. But if the knights had thought of placing better wards on the wall, there was nothing I could do about it. And little point worrying about it.

Besides, I was still in the safe zone. That meant any ward—no matter the tier—couldn't be lethal. If I did trigger an alarm, there was a decent chance I could flee before I was captured or identified.

Multiple hostile entities have failed to detect you!

Freezing in place, I glanced up. Another trio of knights marched past. Heart thumping loudly, I waited for them to leave hearing range.

Then I resumed climbing.

✳ ✳ ✳

It took me nearly an hour to scale the wall.

By then, my arms and legs ached from the strain. Yet, when I reached the top I didn't immediately pull myself over. Clinging to the outside of the fortifications like a spider, I extended my senses.

Two patrols were approaching my position. One from the left, the other from the right. They would cross each other almost in front of me.

Remaining motionless, I waited. I was merely one more blot of shadow in the darkness. Pressed flat against the wall with arms outstretched and feet turned sideways, I was indistinguishable and unremarkable.

I hoped.

Three hostile entities have failed to detect you!
Three hostile entities have failed to detect you!

The knights crossed each other, and even though they passed less than a few feet from me, both squads failed to sense my presence. Nearly giddy with relief, I waited for another handful of heartbeats before swinging myself over the stone crenellations.

Neither squad looked back.

Disregarding the retreating knights, I focused on the next—and most difficult—part of my escapade: crossing the ramparts themselves.

I didn't have much time. Another patrol would be by soon, and with the many mage globes brightening the top of the wall, I couldn't expect to remain undetected while on the ramparts. My gaze darting left and right, I surveyed the ground ahead.

The walkway atop the wall was nearly ten yards wide. Stone crenellations bordered both ends, but there was a third set too. It ran along the center of the ramparts, neatly dividing the wall in two.

Strange design, I thought, wondering if the safe zone's fortifications had been extended at some distant point in the past. That would explain the oddly placed crenellations in the middle.

More disturbing though: I spotted no wards.

Why's that? I wondered, thoughts racing.

Maybe the patrols make them impossible. If the wards didn't distinguish friend from foe, then the passing knights would only falsely trigger them. Could that be it?

Movement around the corner of my eye drew my attention. The next patrol was approaching from the right. *Damnit!* I had to make a decision. I bit my lip, weighing the risks. The walkway seemed innocuous, but something about it alarmed me.

The footfalls of tramping feet grew louder.

I was out of time. *I go,* I decided. Reaching into my potion belt, I withdrew a flask and gulped down its contents.

You have turned invisible, completely shielding yourself from sight. Duration: 60 seconds. Note, taking any hostile action will dispel the potion's effect.

The effect wasn't instantaneous.

Holding out my arms in front of me, I watched as they gradually faded. My gaze shot to the approaching patrol and then back to my body, counting down the seconds.

It took a full five seconds for the potion to take effect.

From my visit to the emporium, I'd learned that invisibility potions were expensive and rare. But having decided to cross, I was determined to leave nothing to chance. Now, even if my stealth failed—or unseen wards detected me—the patrol wouldn't be able to stop me before I escaped.

Keeping one eye on the approaching knights, I began crossing the ramparts. I paused between each step, refusing to rush as I examined the stone underfoot with trap detection.

It took longer than I liked, but I forded the first half of the walkway without incident. Reaching the middle, I leaped lightly onto the top of the three-foot-high crenellations emplaced there.

Three hostile entities have failed to detect you!

At the Game message, I glanced behind me. The patrol had closed the distance and was only a few yards away, but I had less to fear from them now. The knights were marching along the inner walkway I had just crossed and wouldn't stumble onto me.

Still, there was no reason to dally. Dismissing the patrol from my mind, I dropped down onto the outer rampart.

You have left the safe zone.

Flinching at the Game message, I tried to reverse course.
But it was too late.

You have failed a magical resistance check! You have triggered an alarm. You have been trapped in a tier 12 paralysis field. Duration: 2 minutes.
Three hostile entities have failed to detect you.

Between one moment and the next, the wall and its environs were transformed. Magelights, brighter than a noonday sun, rocketed into the sky above; rods of energy rippled outward to encase the outer rampart in a cage of crackling white; and finally, as if the light show wasn't warning enough, a deep horn sounded.

In response, voices called out and footfalls sounded loud in my ears.
Worst of all, I couldn't move.
The paralysis field held me trapped, unable to bat an eyelid or even twitch a finger. My only consolation was that I hadn't been found yet. The invisibility potion was still working.
The tread of heavy feet announced the approach of another knight. "Where are the intruders?" he demanded.
"I don't know, sir!" one of the sentries answered.
"Well, don't just stand there. Find them!" the officer snapped.
The commotion behind me escalated as more patrols arrived to assist. Hurrying back and forth on the inner rampart, the knights scoured the area. But none of the players attempted to step onto the outer walkway.
Now, when it was too late, I knew why.
Can I escape?
The first blush of my panic had faded, and my thoughts were churning again. Despite my paralysis, my senses still worked fine, and I heard and saw everything around me as I normally would. Encouraged by this, I focused my psi on a knight at the edge of my vision and cast shadow blink.

You have failed to teleport. This paralysis field precludes the use of all abilities and spells.

Damnation! Until the ward's effects dissipated, I was helpless. Left with nothing else to do, I considered the ward itself. It was a tier twelve spell.
What rank did a player need to be to cast such a spell?
If I assumed that the levels required for each tier were consistent, then it meant the ward's creator had a magical skill of over five hundred and fifty! That could mean only one thing: I had run afoul of a Power's working.
I'd stood no chance from the beginning.

This is what I get for involving myself with Loken.

Letting go of my frustration, I turned my attention inward and focused on the two timers ticking down. The first was for my invisibility potion, and the second was for the ward's paralyzing effect.

There were no prizes for guessing which one would wear off first. But would the knights find me when my invisibility dissipated?

I guess I'll find out soon enough.

CHAPTER 169: THE SOUTHEAST WATCHTOWER

A hostile entity has failed to detect you!
A hostile entity has failed to detect you!
...

The seconds ticked by, and still the knights failed to see me.

"Get a bloody diviner!" the officer roared. "The intruders must be here. Only the alarm in this section triggered."

"Should we summon a Power?" a knight asked quietly.

"Not yet," the officer growled. "There's still time."

Light footfalls approached—too soft to be another knight. "Have you found them yet, Stonebeard?" the newcomer inquired lazily.

"No," the officer replied in a clipped tone.

"Why not?" the newcomer challenged. "This section of the wall has been flooded with light and troops. Your men can't be *that* incompetent."

Who was the newcomer? A second officer?

There was a moment's silence. The insult obviously grated on Stonebeard, but when he responded, his tone was even. "The intruders are hiding, Wilsh."

Wilsh sighed. "If they aren't located, I can assure you, Rampel will be... most displeased." He paused. "With *you*."

"I'm well aware of that, Captain Wilsh," Stonebeard said impassively. "Now, if you'll leave me and my men to do our jobs, we can see this done."

"This inner wall is yours to oversee, of course," Wilsh continued, making no move to leave. "How you conduct your search is your own business, but if you let them escape, it will be on your head. Not mine."

"Enough!" Stonebeard snarled, his temper finally fraying. "Your advice is both unwanted and unwarranted. See to your own responsibilities. The outer wall's wards are still triggered. Have your people—"

Your invisibility potion has worn off.

I cursed softly as my hands began to materialize. The potion had chosen a poor time to dissipate. The two officers and a host of other knights were still close by.

A hostile entity has detected you! You are no longer hidden.

"Sir, I see one! He's stuck in the paralysis field!"

Luck was not with me today. I'd been spotted with almost a full minute remaining on my paralysis.

"Find the others!" Stonebeard ordered. "They can't be far."

"Oh my," Wilsh remarked. "An invisibility potion. This is a well-equipped—if foolish—thief."

Keep talking, I thought. The longer the officers took to act, the better my chances of escaping. I stared at the opposite end of the rampart. It was achingly close. Evading detection was no longer possible, but reaching the Dark quarter... that I might still do.

I'll worry about the consequences later. If I can only—

"You two!" Wilsh barked. "Don't just stand there gaping. Kill him!"

Uh-oh.

"Don't," Stonebeard countermanded. "We should capture him. Then we can—"

"Ha!" Wilsh exclaimed. "There's no 'we' here, Stonebeard. As you pointed out earlier, the outer wall is my responsibility. I, at least, will have something to show when Rampel investigates this mess."

Heavy silence. Then, "As you wish."

The swish of Wilsh's clothes as he spun around was audible even without my acute hearing. "Stop dithering," Wilsh yelled. "I gave you an order! Now, kill him!"

Well, this isn't good, I thought inanely.

A heartbeat later, two arrows screamed through the air.

A hostile entity has critically injured you!
A hostile entity has critically injured you!
Warning! Your health is dangerously low at 5%.

The archers were good.

Both had unerringly found their marks, striking me in the neck. Agony radiated outward from the twin wounds, and if not for the ward holding me up, I would be writhing on the ground.

Any hope I had of escaping had vanished, and I saw no point in attempting to use my new potion bracelet. Even if it worked while I was paralyzed, it would only serve to prolong my suffering.

I was good as dead already. Making peace with my fate, I waited.

I wasn't kept waiting long.

A hostile entity has critically injured you!
You have died.

✳   ✳   ✳

I returned to awareness with shocking suddenness.

I'd died.

I remembered that much but nothing else. My memories would return though. And painfully. Gasping quietly, I steeled myself for what would come next.

Images cascaded through my mind.

Gut-wrenching agony followed.

Convulsing, I curled in a ball, legs tucked in and head bowed as I was forced once more to suffer the sensation of dying. From my one prior experience of death, I knew there was nothing to do but bear through it.

However, that didn't make the experience any less unpleasant. Impatiently, I waited for my mind to accept the truth.

I'm not dead, I told myself. *I'm not.*

Reluctantly, the waves of torment holding me captive receded. Breathing easier, I turned my attention to the waiting Game message.

You have been reborn. Lives remaining: 2. Time lost during resurrection: 8 hours. Rebirth location: sector 1 safe zone. One soulbound item has been restored.

Your task, Heist in the Dark! has been updated. You have failed to enter the Dark quarter. Objective revised: before you can attempt the robbery, find a viable means of entry into the Dark quarter.

I opened my eyes.

I was in a rebirth well—and I wasn't alone. Ignoring the liquid lapping at my face from the shallow pool and the silent figure standing nearby, I sat up and took in my surroundings.

I was in a cell. Stone walls bordered me on three sides, while wrought iron rods barred the way out on the fourth.

The sight took me aback. I was in a safe zone, and while I expected my circumstances to be dire, I hadn't expected to awaken as a prisoner.

Glancing down at myself, I saw I was clothed in a white newbie shirt and shorts. Ebonheart was in the pool too, lying next to me. I retrieved the sword and its sheath—it too appeared soulbound—and affixed them around my waist.

Damn, what now?

I turned my attention to the figure standing opposite me—on the *other* side of the bars. Dressed in unrelieved black, he was studying me inquisitively. "Sirs!" he said, shouting down the corridor. "The prisoner is awake."

I walked up to the bars. Curiously, the guard wasn't dressed like a knight. If it wasn't the Triumvirate holding me prisoner, then who? Reaching out with my will, I cast analyze.

The target is Liam, a level 140 fighter and human. He is a player and bears a Mark of Major Dark and a Mark of Rampel.

My lips twisted sourly. *A Dark player.* Could this get any worse? *Well, I could've landed in the Awakened Dead's hands,* I thought blackly. At that, my lips stretched in a thin smile.

"What are you grinning at?" someone asked.

I recognized that voice. It was the second officer who had been present at my killing. I glanced to my left. Two players were striding down the corridor that ran across the entrance of my cell.

One was Wilsh, and the other a dwarf. I didn't respond to the officer's question and instead studied the newcomers as they drew to a halt before my cell. The dwarf was in full plate mail and clearly a Triumvirate knight. Wilsh, on the other hand, was dressed in a similar fashion to the guard—in reinforced black leather armor.

I analyzed both players.

The target is Stonebeard, a level 169 shadow paladin and dwarf. He is a player and bears a Mark of Greater Shadow and a Mark of Mydas.

The target is Wilsh, a level 165 sorcerer and human. He is a player and bears a Mark of Supreme Dark and a Mark of Rampel.

"Well?" Wilsh demanded again.

I stayed silent.

Wilsh's face tightened, but before he could admonish me, the dwarf spoke. "I'm Captain Stonebeard, commander of the east Triumvirate guard contingent."

I nodded in acknowledgment.

Stonebeard looked at his companion, and reluctantly Wilsh introduced himself. "Wilsh. Blackguard captain," he said curtly. "And who are you?"

Ignoring the question, I glared at the two captains. "What am I doing here?"

"You are being detained," Stonebeard said, stating the obvious.

My eyes narrowed to slits. "Detained? Why?"

"We are not here to answer your questions," Wilsh snapped. "You are here to answer ours. Now, tell me who you are."

I folded my arms and stared at him.

Wilsh's face reddened at my insolence, but he didn't repeat the question. His gaze flickered to the blade at my hip. "You are no legionnaire," he stated with conviction. "Where did you get that sword?"

Ignoring his question once more, I let a slow smile spread across my face.

Wilsh scowled, and a moment later I felt an interrogatory ripple wash over me.

You have passed a mental resistance check! An analyze attempt by Wilsh has failed.

The blackguard captain growled in frustration and spun to face his companion. "I still can't analyze him. You try."

The dwarf cast his fellow captain an opaque look before turning back to me. A second later, I felt the effect of another analyzed attempt.

An analyze attempt by Stonebeard has failed.

"I can't either," the knight said.

I smiled thinly at my two captors. "Will either of you tell me why I am being held?"

"No, we bloody won't!" Wilsh barked out. "Not until—"

"You are being detained because you have committed multiple infractions against the laws governing Nexus," Stonebeard said, speaking heedlessly over his companion.

Infractions? That didn't sound too bad.

Wilsh glared at the dwarf. "Don't answer him!"

"City law is clear," the dwarf replied evenly. "Every criminal has a right to know the offenses of which they have been convicted."

"But you don't have to tell him *right* now!" Wilsh said in exasperation.

Tilting my head slightly, I listened to the pair argue. The two officers were clearly not united in their approach.

"He asked," the dwarf said, unfazed by his companion's anger. Stonebeard held the taller human's gaze. "Now, let me do my duty. I warn you that if you continue to interfere, I will be forced to lodge an objection with—"

"Very well. Go ahead," the blackguard captain said, his face a picture of disgust. Folding his arms, he fumed in silence while Stonebeard turned back to me.

"Where is this?" I asked, testing the limits of what the Triumvirate knight was willing to tell me.

"You are being held in the prison level of the southeast watchtower," Stonebeard replied. He glanced sideways at the other captain. "The tower is under the command of the blackguards."

My lips turn down at that. Given what I had heard so far, I'd rather be in Triumvirate custody than in the hands of the Dark soldiers. "What infractions did I commit?" I asked, although I thought they were pretty obvious.

"You broke city laws four, twenty-nine, twelve, and sixteen. Attempting to illegally enter the Dark quarter. Failure to identify yourself. Trespassing in a restricted zone. And damaging city property."

I frowned. Three of my infractions were self-explanatory. The fourth was less clear. "I didn't damage anything."

"You did," Stonebeard said equably. "You triggered a tier twelve ward. The ward will have to be reset."

I opened my mouth to object. Surely a spell couldn't be considered property?

But before I could speak, the Triumvirate captain went on, "Tier twelve wards are expensive and can only be set by a supreme Power. And they hate being disturbed for such trifles."

I closed my mouth with a snap. *Interesting.* Stonebeard's words were my first solid bit of information about the power differential between players and Powers. *I have a long way to go if I'm going to challenge them.*

"How long will I be held?" I asked.

"For your crimes, three months," Stonebeard answered.

My heart sank. Three months? That seemed like forever. I contemplated trying to escape. Both captains stood in clear line of sight. All it would take was a single shadow blink to leave.

But I restrained myself. I'd already been dealt one harsh lesson about the perils of underestimating the knights. Even if I *did* manage to get out of the cell, there was no telling what other defenses I would have to overcome before escaping the prison entirely.

Meanwhile, the Triumvirate captain continued speaking. "... earlier for a fee."

My ears perked up as I caught the tail end of his words. "What was that?" I asked sharply.

"I was explaining that you may either serve the sentence or pay a fee in lieu of jail time," Stonebeard said patiently.

"How much?"

"Five hundred gold."

I groaned at the cost, but before I could respond another player entered the room. If his uniform was anything to go by, he too was a blackguard.

The newcomer saluted Wilsh. "Sir! The diviner is on her way. She will be here soon."

"Excellent," Wilsh murmured, almost rubbing his hands in glee. At his companion's look of silent reproach, the blackguard captain scowled. "What? The law doesn't stop me from examining our prisoner, now does it?"

Stonebeard shook his head. "It doesn't."

Wilsh smiled in satisfaction and glanced at me. "Despite your poor attempts to conceal your identity, I will soon find out who you are. Rest assured, my diviner will unearth your secrets." His voice trailed off. "There is something familiar about your face..." he muttered. "Something I feel I should remember."

I wasn't sure if I wasn't meant to overhear the captain's last words, but they gave me fresh impetus. I spun back to the Triumvirate captain. "Five hundred gold, you say? If I pay the fine can I leave immediately?"

"Of course," the dwarf replied. "Can you *pay*?"

"Yes," I said shortly. "I only need access to my bank account."

Wordlessly, Stonebeard slid his right hand through the bars, revealing a keystone in his palm.

"Wait!" Wilsh protested. "Don't let him go just yet. Give me a few minutes at least."

A small smile twitched at the corners of the dwarf's mouth. "I can't do that," he rumbled. "The prisoner is prepared to pay his fine, and the law is clear on that score. He must be released immediately."

Ignoring Wilsh's sputtered complaints, I stepped forward and slapped my hand onto the keystone, willing the funds to transfer.

You have lost 500 gold.
You have paid 500 gold in fines to Captain Stonebeard, a representative of the Triumvirate faction. Your infractions have been struck from the city's records.

An instant later, the bars of the cell retracted and I stepped out a free man. I grinned at the Triumvirate knight. "Thank you," I murmured.

He inclined his head in acknowledgment.

"What about my gear?" I asked quickly, knowing I had to get out of the prison fast. "Can I get it back?"

Stonebeard shook his head. "That isn't for me to decide. You were killed on the outer wall, which falls under the jurisdiction of the Dark. To retrieve your items, you must apply to the blackguards."

My gaze flickered to Wilsh. His smile was back. "Of course you may have your gear back." He paused. "For a price."

I didn't have time to negotiate, and if the glint in Wilsh's eyes was anything to go by, revealing my identity would be part of the price I'd have to pay.

Leaving my gear behind hurt, but I had no choice. "No thanks," I replied and dashed out of the room.

CHAPTER 170: A CHANGE IN STRATEGY

The cell where the blackguards had been holding me was on the tower's ground floor, and I raced past the watching mass of dark-clad soldiers without pause.

The building opened directly onto the street, and I made straight for the exit, but as I burst through I almost collided with a colorfully dressed figure coming the other way.

Contorting wildly, I managed to avoid hitting them. Still, I wasn't able to prevent myself from sprawling onto the street.

"Are you alright?" a woman asked.

Glancing up, I saw it was the same figure I'd tried avoiding. She was garishly dressed and had a pair of pink-tinted glasses perched on her nose.

The diviner?

Gods, I hope not.

Rising to my feet, I dusted myself off. "I am," I mumbled, making no attempt to analyze her. If the woman *was* the diviner, the last thing I wanted to do was pique her interest—although I suspected it was too late for that.

"Thank you for your concern," I added, my head still bowed. Before she could respond, I turned about and hurried away, waiting for the telltale buzz of a failed analyze.

None came, but that didn't reassure me. If anything, it only heightened my worry.

Would Wilsh soon know who I was? Was my identity compromised? There was no way to tell. And truly, there was nothing I could do about it if that turned out to be the case.

Ducking around the corner of a building, I slipped out of sight and took a moment to settle my nerves while I studied my surroundings.

Bright sunlight was streaming down from a clear blue sky.

Morning had arrived.

The nearby streets weren't busy though. Hurrying my steps and unhappily aware that I made for a distinctive figure in my newbie clothes, I attempted to lose myself in the sparse crowds.

It didn't work.

Mocking laughter, derisive snorts, and unflattering comments about newbies followed in my wake. *This is useless,* I thought and, creeping into the shadow of a building, concealed myself in darkness.

Multiple neutral entities have failed to detect you! You are hidden.

Better.

Temporarily safe, I considered my options. My backpack and other belongings were still in the hotel, and my first instinct was to head straight there and retrieve them.

But I had no secondary armor to re-equip, and so after a moment's thought, I headed in a different direction.

✳ ✳ ✳

Even slinking through the shadows, it didn't take me long to get to my destination.

Reaching the walled compound, I emerged from the shadows. Surprised by my sudden appearance, the giants guarding the entrance swung my way and drew their weapons.

The guards hadn't changed shifts though. The same two giants I had encountered earlier were on duty, and recognition flickered across their faces.

"Look who's back," Ent said.

"And freshly risen from the dead too," Lake replied.

Both laughed. Ignoring their amusement, I drew to a halt before the pair.

"That's a nice sword," Ent remarked slyly. *For a newbie.* The words went unspoken, but I heard them nevertheless.

"Thanks," I muttered. "I need to see Kesh."

"Again?" Lake grumbled.

"It's urgent," I growled and gestured at my attire. "My circumstances speak for themselves."

Ent chuckled. "That they do." Turning about, he shoved open the door. "Head on in, *sir.*"

Ignoring the mockery in his tone, I inclined my head in thanks and slipped into the confines of the emporium.

✳ ✳ ✳

Kesh, predictably, was not happy to see me again so soon.

The merchant's gaze flickered over my distinctive apparel. "I think... I think I'm going to regret taking you on as a client," she said, her voice stiff with disapproval. "What happened?"

"I died—obviously," I replied.

"I can see that," Kesh retorted. "How?"

"I tried to go over the wall."

The merchant rolled her eyes. "What possessed you to attempt that? Not even the Powers can manage such a feat." She paused. "Or didn't you know that?"

I winced. "I do now," I murmured.

Kesh mumbled something under her breath that I failed to catch. "So, what can I do for you?" she asked in a louder voice.

"You mentioned earlier that you will sell gear I brought to you back to the original owners. Will you do the reverse?"

The merchant frowned. "Meaning?"

"Meaning, I want you to buy back my gear."

Kesh nodded. "I can do that." She paused. "Who has it?"

"A blackguard captain by the name of Wilsh."

"Blackguards," Kesh muttered. "That isn't good. The knights would have been simpler to deal with. The guards can be greedy." She eyed me. "It will cost you," she warned.

"I'll pay," I said firmly. But after a moment's thought I added prudently, "Only what's reasonable."

"Of course," Kesh said. "It may take a while. Where can I contact you?"

"I'll be in the Wanderer's Delight."

She grunted in acknowledgment. "Anything else I can do for you?"

I hesitated then forged ahead, deciding I'd already trusted Kesh with enough of my secrets that one more wouldn't matter. "What do you know about the Powers?"

She snorted. "They're damnably powerful and not to be trifled with."

I couldn't disagree with her on that score. "Any idea how to remove the spell cast by one?"

Kesh sat back in her chair and eyed me shrewdly. "Does this have something to do with why you tried going over the wall?"

I sighed. "It does. A Power has set a tracking spell on me. Suffice it to say, the only easy way of getting rid of it is by entering the Dark quarter."

"Who cast the spell?"

"Loken."

Kesh winced. "Finding someone to get rid of that will be nearly impossible. He's a supreme Power."

"A supreme Power?" I asked. "What does that mean?"

The merchant considered me for a moment but didn't beg off answering. "Just like players, not all Powers are equal. They have their own tiers, differentiating minor, major, and supreme Powers from one another. Loken, of course, is one of the Game's most significant Powers and one of the oldest too." She held my gaze. "And in case you were wondering, that means he's over level five hundred. I'd advise against antagonizing him."

I could see Kesh was curious about how I'd earned Loken's attention, but I didn't enlighten her. I leaned forward in my chair. "But you said nearly impossible, not impossible. Does that mean you can help?"

"Perhaps," Kesh said with her lips pursed. "I can't promise anything. And if I do manage to secure you aid, it'll be expensive."

With a bitter laugh, I rose to my feet. "Isn't it always?"

"That's true enough," the merchant said with a smile.

I turned toward the door, then paused as something else occurred to me. "One more question, if you don't mind."

Kesh groaned. "If I did, would that stop you?"

I ignored her quip. "What can you tell me about the blackguards?"

She sighed. "They perform a similar function to the Triumvirate knights, only their purview is the Dark quarter. If you ever venture into the Light and Shadow quarters, you will find comparable forces policing both. Shadow names them the Gray Watch and Light the Dawn Brigade."

"Fascinating," I murmured. "Who maintains order in the plague quarter?"

Kesh chuckled. "No one. The stygian brotherhood, the Triumvirate knights, and the bounty hunters are all present there, but none have succeeded in bringing the rule of law to the quarter." She cast me another meaningful glance. "If you venture into that hellhole, best you depend on no one but yourself for protection."

I inclined my head in thanks and, with a thoughtful frown, left the compound.

✳   ✳   ✳

Exiting the emporium, I wrapped myself in darkness again. Despite the sun overhead, splotches of shadow cast by the looming buildings were still evident everywhere.

Lost deep in thought, I slunk toward the hotel. The disaster on the wall and what I'd learned since had given me fresh cause to reassess. The unhappy truth was that I was nowhere near ready to pull off a heist on—

An unknown entity has detected you! You are no longer hidden.

I jerked to a halt, head whipping upward.

A figure was blocking my path—and it was the last person I expected to see.

"Loken!" I exclaimed.

"We must talk," the Power said, his face unwontedly serious.

I glared at the trickster. The blame for much of my predicament could be laid at his feet. Though, if I was being honest, I bore my own fair share of responsibility for my circumstances too—mostly because I hadn't cut ties with the Power when I should've. But I wasn't about to compound my errors further.

"Me and you are done," I growled. "I'll have no more dealings with you."

"I never marked you for a fool," Loken snapped. "Stop behaving like one now."

My jaw worked soundlessly for a moment, but sense prevailed and I bit back the retort that fought to get out. "Talk then. I'm listening."

The Power eyed me for a moment and, seeming to realize he would gain no further concessions from me, went on. "Going over the wall was foolish," he said, unconsciously echoing Kesh.

I snorted. I knew that. Now, anyway.

"You aren't ready to take on the task I set for you. Get a few more ranks under your belt, and I'll help you get into the Dark quarter." He paused, waiting to see if I had anything to say. When I only stared back at him in stony silence, he continued, "Morin and the others are on their way back here. They will help you level—"

"No!" I ground out harshly, unable to remain silent any longer.

Loken stared at me with bird-like intensity. "No?"

"I want no more help from you. Either to level or to get into the Dark quarter. I'll get it done myself." *Somehow.*

"You're being childish," the Power chided. "I know you're still annoyed—"

"Annoyed?" I barked in laughter. "I'm a bit more than that at your betrayal."

"Whatever you may think, I did not betray you," Loken said mildly. "If not for me, you'd be dead many times over. Thanks to me, Ishita rescinded her bounty."

My eyes narrowed. "Why should I believe you?"

"You have my word as a Power," he said quietly. "The year I placed you in stasis was as much for your own good as anything else."

"Ha! If you cared that much for my well-being, you wouldn't be setting me on a collision course with the Awakened Dead again."

Loken opened his mouth, but before he could speak, I went on. "No, I suspect the truth is much simpler than you're letting on. You *needed* the bounty removed so I could do this damnable task for you. There's just one thing I don't understand: surely you have enough minions. Why do you need me?"

"So cynical," Loken murmured, shaking his head. He didn't, however, refute any of my accusations. "Let's just say... you are uniquely suited to this task."

"More cryptic statements," I muttered, making no attempt to disguise my disdain.

"Think what you will," the Shadow Power said, his voice hardening. "But without my aid, you will not get my tracking spell removed." He paused. "Despite what Viviane told you, she doesn't possess the ability to dispel my casting."

I glared at the Power. Loken might very well be telling the truth. Or he might not.

"Now, back to business," Loken said. "Will you still fulfill my task?"

I let the silence draw out before answering. "Tell me one thing first. How are matters in the valley?"

"Is that what's been bothering you?" Loken asked, all smiles again. "Matters in sector 12,560 are still unresolved. The valley remains unclaimed, although it has since been flooded with players from all three Forces." Loken paused. "Your alchemist and the tavern are doing well. More than well, if you ask me."

I let no sign of my relief at the news show. I was more concerned about the wolves than Saya though, but of course I couldn't ask Loken about the pack. "I will attempt the task," I said finally. "But my own way, in my own time, *and* without your help."

"Ah, if you must," Loken said. "I'd almost forgotten about that stubborn streak of yours." He shook his head ruefully. "Very well, I will withhold my aid for now, but if you will accept one word of advice?" Not waiting for my response, he went on. "Don't attempt entering the Dark quarter until you've *evolved* further."

I ignored Loken's not-so-subtle emphasis. The Power was up to something, obviously. And I would be damned if I blindly did as he asked.

Until I learned more about what game he was playing, there was no way I was entering the Dark quarter.

Still, it cost me nothing to agree with Loken in the interim, and I nodded curtly.

"Excellent," Loken said, beaming in his usual guileless manner.

I wasn't deceived though. I had seen beneath the Power's mask and knew that a serious—and dangerous—player lurked beneath.

"I guess this is goodbye then," the Power said when I remained silent.

"Bye," I said shortly.

Loken spun away, only to twirl around a moment later. "Oh, and Michael?"

I glanced at him.

"Try not to look so grumpy next time. Pretty please?"

I didn't dignify that with a response, and the Power laughed gaily.

He was still chuckling when he vanished into thin air.

Chapter 171: Doing what Must be Done

How does he do that? I wondered.

My conversations with Loken, as always, left me doubting. Not about how far I could trust him—because I didn't—but about what to believe. The Power had a way of twisting truth and lies, making it impossible to parse one from the other.

Shaking my head, I left the fading echoes of Loken's laughter behind and resumed my crawl through the shadows. Nevertheless, I pondered his words as I made my way to the hotel. As much as I hated to admit it, the Power was right—about some things, at least.

I had overreached.

Nexus was altogether different from the previous two sectors I had been in. Here there were high-level players and Powers aplenty, and I couldn't afford to assume that any challenge was surmountable.

If anything, my experience so far proved the opposite.

I would have to take matters slowly. I didn't like it, but it didn't seem as if I had any other choice. Until I got stronger, I'd have to set aside the pursuit of my primary goals.

Step one would be gaining a few more player ranks. And from every indication, the plague quarter was the only place to do that. Decided on my course, I hurried on my way.

✳   ✳   ✳

I reached the hotel without anything more noteworthy occurring than the occasional strange look from a passerby. Head down, I rushed through the foyer, intent on reaching my room without attracting further attention, but halfway there I stopped as I spotted a familiarly dressed figure.

By the looks of it, the player was one of the emporium's agents, and she was making a beeline toward me. Standing my ground, I waited for her arrival.

"What is it?" I asked as the red-robed figure drew to a halt.

"Mistress Kesh has heard back from the blackguard captain," the agent replied.

My eyebrows lifted. "Already?" How had Kesh managed to elicit a response from Wilsh so soon? I was sure it would take days, if not longer.

The robed figure nodded. "The mistress has negotiated the captain down to five hundred gold."

I nearly sagged in relief. Five hundred gold was a lot, but it was a pittance compared to how much I'd expected Wilsh to try extorting. "What did she do? Threaten him or something?" I asked, only half-joking.

The agent laughed. "Or something. The mistress offered the captain a one-time opportunity to use her service for free. He was quick to accept."

I grinned. The merchant was proving an unexpectedly valuable business partner—or was that ally? "Tell Kesh to proceed with the trade. She can deliver my items here."

"As you wish," the agent said before silently retreating.

Whistling happily, I headed to my room to await my gear.

❋   ❋   ❋

You have lost 550 gold. Money remaining in your bank account: 841 gold, 4 silver, and 9 copper.

Two hours later, I was dressed in my old gear once more.

Kesh had come through spectacularly and had regained all my lost items. She hadn't done it for free, of course, and had charged me a fee for playing the role of intermediary.

I didn't begrudge her her cut though. I didn't imagine I would have been half as successful negotiating with Wilsh.

Feeling whole again, I strode out of the hotel and toward the south gate. I passed through without pause, barely sparing the Triumvirate knights on duty a second glance.

You have left a safe zone.

After I exited the gatehouse, I drew to a halt and took a long, slow look around. This was my first opportunity to really study the plague quarter. I expected I would spend the greater part of my time here in the coming weeks and knew I needed to familiarize myself with its layout.

The first thing I noted was how rundown everything appeared. I'd vaguely noticed the disrepair during my earlier forays into the area, but in the stark light of day the true extent of the quarter's state was laid bare. Dilapidated buildings, broken windows, and filthy streets characterized the surroundings.

But it wasn't just poverty that afflicted the quarter.

Signs of battle damage were everywhere. Doors were clawed through, stone walls were burned, and the roads themselves were pockmarked and scorched.

This is an active combat zone.

The people mirrored the surroundings. Hunched shoulders and downcast eyes were commonplace. Shooting glances and darting gazes too. More surprisingly yet, many of the quarter's residents were *not* players.

There was no shimmer in the air around them, nothing that signified the presence of Marks. Few of the non-players walked alone; most had gathered in groups, seeking protection in numbers.

I frowned as the extent of the quarter's misery seeped in. *Lawless. Poor. Ravaged by stygians. And seemingly abandoned by the Powers.*

Truly, the quarter is plagued.

I was sure the Force quarters were nothing like this. The brief glimpse I'd caught of the Dark quarter while standing atop the safe zone walls had certainly suggested otherwise, and it left me wondering why the Powers allowed this blight in the very heart of their world.

Was it because of the stygian menace in the quarter?

Or was it because most of the residents weren't players—not *true* participants of the Game?

I didn't know, but it left me with a sick feeling in my stomach. I resumed walking, my steps heavier. Given the state of the quarter, it was no wonder I had been mugged last night. Alone and unaccompanied, I would've made for a tempting mark.

But forewarned was forearmed.

Hands hovering close to my blades, I strode down the middle of the street. My first order of business was to visit the information brokers' offices and the bounty hunters' guild.

From the little information I had managed to gather on both, I knew they were near the safe zone. If I followed the safe zone's wall, I was sure I would find the guild and office soon enough.

Reaching a crossroad, I glanced left and right. The roads in both directions ran parallel to the wall. Randomly choosing one fork over the other—the left one—I kept walking.

I hadn't gone far when I smelled something curious in the wind. Tilting my head upward, I sniffed delicately at the air. There was a... saltiness to it.

I stumbled to a halt, long-forgotten memories stirring.

It's the sea.

I was as sure of my conclusion as I was of anything—which was more than passingly strange. I had never encountered the ocean or its like during my time in the Forever Kingdom.

This has to be a memory from my former life... or from one of the fallen scions.

Both possibilities were equally disturbing.

I exhaled slowly. So far, the plague quarter was doing a good job of distracting me. Not even five minutes in the area, I found myself losing track of what I was here to do.

You have a plan, Michael. Stick to it.

I started down the street again. As I did, motion from my rear drew my attention. Someone else had resumed walking in time with me.

I had picked up a tail.

Displaying no sign that I was aware, I listened intently and discerned the tread of another three sets of boots moving in lockstep with the first. A gang of four.

More muggers?

Unfurling my mindsight, I analyzed my stalkers.

The target is Senuka, a level 121 elven thief and player.
The target is Actus, a level 101 human brawler and player.
The target is Rose, a level 105 gnomish scout and player.
The target is Sata, a level 108 human fighter and player.

Hmm... My would-be hunters were lower-leveled than I expected, but that didn't mean they weren't a threat. All four were still players, and even the lowest had more than twenty levels on me.

Keeping my stride even, I scanned the nearby buildings. Some looked abandoned, and within their dark confines I would fare better against my hunters. I wondered, though, if I should pre-empt my foes or wait for them to make the first move.

Abruptly, my pulse spiked.

Danger!

I reacted instantly. Leaping forward, I threw myself into a tumble. Legs and arms tucked in, I rolled over the cobblestones.

You have evaded an unknown hostile's attack.

Beneath the distraction of my own sudden motion and the flashing Game alert, the hiss of an object striking stone went almost unheard.

What was that?

Not an arrow—not small enough. Not a rock either—the impact had been too soft. A dart?

Possibly.

Identifying the projectile was only a secondary concern though. I was too exposed in the center of the street. Rolling onward, I aimed for the shadows of the closest building.

You have evaded an unknown hostile's attack.

A second projectile hit the ground behind me. This time I caught a glint of a polished and sharpened metal tip. I'd been right; it was a dart.

Where's my attacker?

Whoever it was, it was *not* one of the four trailing me. They were still too far back to be firing darts, and the angle of attack was all wrong.

Reaching the building's shadows, I hit the control stud on my belt.

You have activated the combat mode enchantment of the belt of the chameleon. Your armor and weapons are now exposed.

A moment later, I wrapped myself in darkness.

You are hidden.

Rising silently to my feet, I braced my back against the building and scanned the surroundings both with my physical senses and mindsight.

I failed to spot my attacker with either.

Damnit! Either my attacker was shielded or—

Psssh.

At the whisper of sound, I flung myself to the left.

A hostile entity has detected you!
You have evaded an unknown hostile's attack.

My lips twisted in an unhappy smile as the shadows slipped away from me. My foe had to possess high Perception to have uncovered me so easily. More alarming still was that I had failed to detect him in turn.

What was I up against?

Rolling back to my feet, I summoned psi. I may not have spotted my foe, but I had marked where the dart had come from. The moment an astral blade materialized in my hand, I flung it in the same direction.

The glowing dagger of violet hurtled through the air, and a curse erupted from the middle of the seemingly empty street.

You have detected a hostile entity. Gintalush is no longer hidden! Your target has evaded your attack.

Although the astral blade failed to find its mark, it served to flush out my foe. But I had no idea what to make of him.

My attacker was wrapped from head to toe in reams of green cloth, with only a narrow slit left open for his eyes. Two crossed swords were sheathed across his back, and in his right hand he held a blowpipe.

Seeing that he had been uncovered, Gintalush turned about and ran the other way. He was making for the building on the opposite side of the street. To conceal himself again?

Reaching out with my will, I analyzed the green-clad figure.

You have failed a Perception check and are unable to analyze your target.

I hesitated for a fraction of a second, debating whether to let the fleeing figure escape or pursue him in turn. But if I let him go, that would only invite a second ambush—one I might not be as fortunate to evade.

Baring my teeth in anger, I drew ebonheart and spider's bite. Gintalush was too far to reach with shadow blink. So, I did the next best thing.

Kicking off the building, I gave chase.

A dozen steps later, I was back in the middle of the street and under the glare of the bright sunlight streaming down again. Still, I was no closer to running down my target.

Damn, he's fast. This may be a waste—

Psssh.

At the dreaded sound, I dove forward and the dart whistled overhead.

You have evaded an unknown hostile's attack.

Bloody hell! I could still see Gintalush racing ahead of me. *He* hadn't fired the dart. It could mean only one thing.

There was another attacker.

I skidded to a halt and spun around in search of my second foe. Almost as if on cue, Gintalush whipped around and charged back toward me, drawing his swords.

I cursed bitterly, realizing Gintalush's flight had been a decoy.

He'd only fled to draw me out of the shadows. A moment later, the second attacker revealed himself. He, too, was dressed in green and, like his partner, raced toward me with twin blades in hand.

I was trapped in the open and caught between my attackers, with nowhere to hide.

Goddamnit. What now?

CHAPTER 172: STREET-FIGHTING

I spun around to face the attacker closing in from the rear and used a precious second to analyze him.

The target is Wengulax, a level 162 human blade dancer.

My fear ratcheted upward at my foe's rank. I could only assume his partner was the same level—or higher. *I can't win this fight,* I thought, the realization biting deep.

In fact, I was likely as good as dead already.

No, damnit. Think!

There had to be a way out of my predicament. I didn't know what that was yet, but I wasn't going to find it standing in the middle of the street.

Fighting off the almost paralyzing fear, I raced toward my second attacker, closing the distance between us even quicker. While I did, I summoned psi.

Seeing me hurtling toward him, Wengulax raised his blades in anticipation. A few feet short of him, my spell completed, and without hesitation, I cast.

You have teleported behind Wengulax.

I blurred through the aether, one moment trapped between my enemies, the next in the shadow of the one ahead. I didn't turn around or make any attempt to strike at my green-clad foe from behind. Instead, head down, I kept running.

Behind me, I heard the blade dancer's swords clatter on the cobblestones as he spun around. Suspecting what he was about, I jigged left and one-stepped through the air for good measure.

You have evaded Wengulax's attack.

The anticipated projectile whooshed past me, flying well wide of its mark. I smiled grimly. My two assailants might be double my own level, but they weren't infallible.

After another few heart-pounding steps, I reached the building's shadows. Skidding to a halt, I hit the stud on my belt and cloaked myself in darkness anew.

You have activated the stealth mode enchantment of the belt of the chameleon. Your sneaking skill has increased by +2 ranks.

Two hostile entities have failed to detect you! You are hidden.

I shuddered in relief. I'd made it. But I suspected the encounter was far from over.

You have evaded Gintalush's attack.

The dart lodged into the wall, inches from my right shoulder. Ignoring it and the sweat dripping down my face, I braced my back against the same wall. Then, with deliberate care, I sidled along the building, putting some distance between myself and my last known location.

Wengulax and Gintalush had drawn to a halt in the street. Standing unnaturally still, they scanned the shadows.

Two hostile entities have failed to detect you.

Keeping a wary eye on the pair, I slinked away. Since the encounter had begun I'd barely had time to think. Now the questions came boiling out.

Who were my attackers? Where had they come from? And why were they dressed so outlandishly? Then an even more dastardly thought occurred: *are there more of them?*

I sincerely hope not.

The pair, on their own, were proving more than I could handle. My attention slid back to the two masked assailants. Neither was making any attempt to leave.

Well, that's just great.

The fact that the two were hanging around suggested this wasn't some random encounter and I wasn't a chance-met mark. They had to be hunting *me* specifically. What I didn't know was why.

Right now, though, that mattered little. My only priority was escaping.

Gintalush and Wengulax, meanwhile, hadn't broken their statue-like poses. Like hunting cats, the pair held themselves motionless while their eyes swept the shadows. If they caught the least whiff of me, I was sure they would pounce.

Two hostile entities have failed to detect you.

Under my assailants' malevolent gazes, I felt the urge to hurry my steps. Stifling the impulse, I kept my movements slow. My surest protection against the two was my stealth. As long as I stayed hidden, I would be fine.

Or so I hoped.

Two hostile entities have failed to detect you.

The Game messages helped quell my doubts. The increased stealth provided by the chameleon belt was proving enough to defeat my attackers' Perception, and inch by inch, I got farther away.

The two green-clothed fighters still didn't move.

Both stood brazenly in the middle of the road, seemingly unconcerned that anyone would interfere. Wengulax hadn't even bothered picking up his dropped swords. The pair's confidence seemed justified too. To my right, the streets were empty. All the bystanders had long since fled. To my left, the streets were similarly deserted.

No, that wasn't quite true.

The four I had spied trailing me earlier still watched me from around the corner of a building. Were they working with Wengulax and Gintalush?

I didn't think so. The stalkers seemed rather inept by comparison.

At a slip of motion, my gaze darted back to Wengulax and Gintalush. Both were reaching into their shirts. Moving with eerie synchrony, they pulled out a pair of spheres from concealed pockets.

The orbs were made of a lime-tinged metal, and each rested easily on the palms of their bearers. Both my foes stared at the spheres in their hands, and after a moment the devices lifted into the air.

Uneasily, I cast analyze on one of the hovering spheres.

The target is a hunter eye, a rank 3 enchanted item. It is a tracking and scouting device designed to find and follow a subject by a variety of means, including scent, sight, or sound.

This is a single-use item and must be keyed to its designated subject before use.

Urgh, I thought, realizing what the two intended.

Before the hunter eyes could find me, I needed to disrupt my foes' plans. A glimmer of an idea forming, I drew on my stores of energy and wove a spell, releasing it as soon as it was ready.

You have cast ventro.

Projecting my voice back down the street, I growled, "Don't just stand there, you fools! Help me kill them!"

The four stalkers jumped back in alarm. My voice had emanated from an empty spot of air less than two yards from them. Good sense finally overcoming their morbid curiosity, they jerked back out of sight.

But it was too late.

My assailants had spotted them.

More importantly, the hunter eyes had reacted to the timbre of my voice. Buzzing to life, the two orbs zipped down the street to find me.

Wengulax and Gintalush weren't so easily fooled though. Making no move to follow their enchanted devices, the pair stared at each other for a drawn-out moment, and I got the feeling they were communicating.

Finally, Gintalush hurried away to trail after the green orbs while Wengulax returned to scanning the shadows near me.

I ground my teeth in frustration. I'd hoped both would leave, letting me flee as fast as my feet could carry me. Still, my gambit had improved my situation, and now I had only one enemy to contend with. I continued my careful retreat. Only a little further...

Then Wengulax did something unexpected.

His head swiveling left and right, my foe picked a direction, seemingly at random, and jogged along the wall of the building. Worse yet, he picked the right direction—or rather, the *wrong* one, from my perspective. Cursing my luck, I eyed the approaching hunter. Wengulax was moving too fast for me to avoid.

I had no choice but to act again.

My gaze darted back down the street. Gintalush had disappeared from sight. *At least I won't have to worry about him just yet.* Drawing on my will, I readied a casting.

Weaves of psi rippled out from me toward my target, attempting to warp his sight and blind him to my presence.

Wengulax has passed a mental resistance check! You have failed to hide your presence from your target. Your mental intrusion has been detected!

Damnation! My situation had just gone from bad to worse.

My foe jerked to a halt, his head whipping around to stare unerringly at the spot I occupied. Even though I remained cloaked, I knew for certain that my failed casting had just revealed my location.

Wengulax raised his blowpipe to his lips.

I didn't wait for him to complete his attack. Jabbing the stud on my belt, I summoned psi and shadow blinked.

You have activated combat mode. You have teleported behind Wengulax.

I materialized in my foe's shadow and cast whirlwind. In an instant, stamina flooded my arms, invigorating them with extraordinary speed. In the same motion, my swords flashed forward two times quicker than normal.

But my enemy was faster.

Before I was halfway complete with my attacks, Wengulax dropped his blowpipe, spun around, *and* swayed under both my blades.

Impossible! I thought. But I wasn't done yet. Whirlwind buffed me for three seconds, and I still had time to score a hit. My eyes narrowing in determination, I pressed my foe hard, unleashing a flurry of blows.

Wengulax has evaded your attack.
Wengulax has evaded a crippling blow.
Wengulax has evaded a piercing strike.

...

But no matter how well-timed my maneuvers, no matter how flawlessly I executed my attacks, Wengulax avoided everything I threw at him with laughable ease.

I cut left. He slipped right.

I slashed downward. He bobbed beneath.

I lunged forward and he darted backward.

Then whirlwind dissipated and the surge of energy empowering my limbs abandoned me.

In that instant, I was vulnerable.

Wengulax didn't have his swords, but that didn't mean he was unarmed. The moment my frenzied assault died, my foe went on the offensive.

Slipping two punch daggers out of concealed sheaths, Wengulax lunged forward, slashing simultaneously both up and down. I scrambled to defend myself, flinging spider's bite upward to parry the first attack and ebonheart downward to block the second.

I stopped both strikes—barely.

But Wengulax was only just getting started. Flowing forward, he beset me once more. I backstepped, parrying desperately as I tried to open the distance between us again.

It was like trying to fend off a storm.

My foe was relentless. At every opportunity, he nipped at me with his tiny daggers. I held him at bay, somehow. I suspected that all that was keeping me alive was that the daggers weren't Wengulax's weapons of choice. If he had his swords...

Still, even with the advantage in reach, I wasn't winning. In fact, I was most decidedly losing.

Repeatedly, the blade dancer's weapons slipped through my guard, and before long a network of fine slashes and shallow gouges riddled my torso. The entire time I fought defensively, unable to even contemplate counterattacking.

This is useless.

Attempting to engage Wengulax in melee combat had been a mistake. And soon Gintalush would return. Then my fate would be truly sealed.

Taking a desperate gamble, I parried aside Wengulax's latest attack and spun around, leaving my back exposed for a heart-stopping moment. My maneuver caught my foe off guard, and he was too slow to react.

My disengagement successful, I wasted no time fleeing up the street.

Wengulax pursued, of course.

I kept ahead of him—barely—using one-step and my smoke bombs. For all my pursuer's speed and skill with his blades, his senses weren't as finely honed as mine, and he struggled navigating through the smoke.

I didn't make the mistake of attempting to close with him again though. In open combat, Wengulax was clearly my superior.

I'll have to find a more underhanded means of defeating him.

As I made my way further east through the quarter, I kept an eye out for somewhere—or something—to turn the tables on my foe. I passed more than a few buildings, but every door I tried was locked, and with Wengulax hard on my heels, I had no time to attempt picking any of them.

There were plenty of people on the streets too. Most ignored me entirely but bolted at the sight of my hunter. There was something about Wengulax's nature that inspired fear in the quarter's residents.

Finally, though, I spotted three who did *not* flee.

Even without identifying them, I could tell they were players. The trio stood outside the open doorway of a burned and scorched building fifty yards ahead, quietly conversing. At the ruckus that spread like a wave before me and my pursuer, their gazes turned in our direction.

"Mantis!" the elf among them spat.

With admirable speed, his human companion unsheathed the reed-like blade at his hip. "The plague quarter never ceases to surprise," the courtly attired figure said carelessly. "Every time I think I've seen it all, something worse creeps out of the woodwork."

The third—a half-elf—chuckled. Drawing her longbow, she knocked an arrow and held it at the ready. "I told you, Jas. Lowlifes and wretches. That's all you can expect to find here."

Still running hard, I analyzed the players.

The target is Moonshadow, a level 165 elven aeromancer.
The target is Jasiah, a level 152 human duelist.
The target is Simone, a level 155 half-elf sharpshooter.

Perfect, I thought and made straight for the three. They disregarded me entirely, their gazes fixed on my green-clad pursuer. As soon as I closed to within nine yards, I shadow blinked.

You have teleported into Jasiah's shadow.

I emerged from the aether, still moving at a hard clip. Throwing my hands forward, I dropped into a roll to slow my momentum.

"What the—!"

"Who was that?"

Ignoring the consternation of the players, I rose smoothly to my feet and broke left, dashing into the darkened doorway of the abandoned-looking building. Slipping into the shadows, I concealed myself.

A hostile entity has failed to detect you! You are hidden.

Inhaling deeply, I fought to regain my breath while I listened to the ongoing conversation outside.

"Forget him," the human—Jasiah—barked. "Look! The mantis is heading straight for us!"

"Quick, Moon!" the half-elf ordered. "Stop him."

I exhaled, breathing more easily. My ploy seemed to be working. I hated that I had to stoop to using the three players to stave off pursuit, but judging by the trio's levels, they seemed more than capable of standing up to the threat. Peering carefully around the doorway, I observed the encounter.

Jasiah had stepped in front of the mage, his blade thrust out defensively.

"Stop!" Simone, the half-elf, barked from beside the elf.

Wengulax didn't stop—or even slow—and charged headlong toward the three.

The mage finished incanting the casting he'd been preparing, and a moment later the spell snapped outward to trap the blade dancer in a glittering cage of light.

"You were warned, worm!" Moonshadow growled.

For the first time, I heard my hunter speak. "Fools!" he hissed. "You are interfering in mantis business!"

Jasiah threw back his head and laughed merrily. "You don't scare us, you green-skinned devil!"

Simone was less eager for a fight. "We have no quarrel with your order or your master," she said, laying a restraining hand on her companion.

Wengulax glared at the archer. "Then release me!" His gaze slid to the darkened doorway hiding me. "Now!"

"Not until we have your reassurance that you mean us no harm," Simone said smoothly.

I slipped away from the door. I'd heard enough. My ploy had bought me a little time, but it seemed almost certain that the trio wouldn't take care of my problem. They didn't want to entangle with Wengulax any more than I did.

I'll have to deal with him myself.

✳   ✳   ✳

The building was just as desolate and wrecked on the inside as it appeared from the outside. Any furniture it once held had long since been stolen or destroyed. Now only cobwebs, mildew, and dust inhibited its depths.

I climbed up the rickety stair to the second floor, carefully placing each step. There were six rooms. I investigated each and chose the one that was mostly intact.

Ducking into the room, I inspected its surroundings. There were two windows, both boarded up, and a single entrance. *It'll do*, I thought and got to work.

Leaning down beside the door, I tapped at the single blue rune on the trapper's wristband, activating its enchantment while willing the items I desired to appear.

You have passed a thieving skill check! You have removed 4 trap-making crystals from your trapper's wristband. Remaining stored trap-making crystals: 36 of 40.

The crystals materialized, each small enough to fit in the palm of my hand.

The items from the wristband were of premium quality. Unlike those from a basic trap-making kit, the crystals I held were enchanted. Inside each was a spelled trigger or trap element. They weren't purely physical in nature either but also contained a magical component that simplified their deployment. And under my current circumstances, where time was of the essence, I was doubly grateful for that.

Crystals in hand, I cast trap set.

In response, energy thrummed through my fingers and eyes, giving me the ability to manipulate the enchanted components.

In my newly enhanced vision, the spells woven around the crystals burst into sight. Each was riddled with a complex weave of magic that my thieving abilities allowed me to decipher.

Identifying the crystal I wanted first, I set aside the other three on the floor and tapped a complex sequence on it. The item crumbled to dust, leaving behind a slim wire.

You have activated a single-use enchantment and acquired a tripwire trigger.

Working furiously, I placed the trigger.

The wire was no ordinary cord, of course. Tugging on its ends, I stretched the trigger across the doorway and released its enchantment. A moment later, the cord faded from sight and stretched taut, affixing itself to the sides of the door without any physical anchor.

You have concealed a tripwire.

Picking up the second crystal, I extracted its trigger: a plain sheet of metal. Holding the two shorter sides, I tugged hard, causing the spelled object to expand.

When it was large enough to fit the doorway, I placed it beneath the tripwire. A second later, the gray sheet disappeared as it mimicked the appearance of the adjacent dirty timbers.

You have concealed a pressure plate.

Only the trap elements left to place now.

Unlike with the triggers, I didn't need to extract the trap elements from their crystals. All that was necessary was to connect them. The traps would activate automatically once the trigger was disturbed.

Moving carefully, I placed the first crystal on the inside of the camouflaged pressure plate and pulled the magical weave dangling from its end to the trip wire.

You have connected a trap element to a trigger.
A bear clamp trap has been successfully configured!
Your thieving has increased to level 40.

The moment the trap element was in place, it too faded from sight. Hurrying into the room itself, I pressed the second crystal firmly into a blank section of the wall directly opposite the doorway and spell-linked it to the pressure plate.

You have connected a trap element to a trigger.
A lightning trap has been successfully configured!
Your thieving has increased to level 41.

My preparations were nearly done. Crouching down in the darkest corner of the room, I unsheathed my blades and laid them down beside me. Then I pressed the stud on my belt.

You have entered stealth mode, increasing your sneaking by 2 ranks.

There was just one more thing for me to do.
Hiding myself in the shadows, I drew on my small store of magic and slipped mana into the item I held in my hands. It took longer to prepare the casting than it had to set the traps, but eventually the medallion was charged almost to capacity. I held off on adding the last bit though.
The time for that would come later.
I was finally ready.
Now, to see if my hunter appears.
If Wengulax chose to continue his pursuit, I would have more than a few surprises in store for him.

Long minutes passed with no sign of my hunter.

Either he had been unwilling to give the trio the assurances they wanted, or they had deliberately delayed releasing him. Either way, I was grateful to the three players for the unwitting part they'd played in my plan. Although I was sure they were less than happy with the role I had thrust them into.

At the creak of a downstairs floorboard, barely heard above the background noise of the quarter, I jerked upright and returned my attention to my surroundings.

Straining my ears, I listened intently but heard nothing further. I raised my head and sniffed at the air. The faint odor of unwashed cloth and sweat wafted up to me.

Someone had entered the building.

Making certain I remained concealed, I cast my buffs.

You have cast reaction buff, increasing your Dexterity by +2 ranks.

You have cast lighten load, reducing your total armor penalty to 5%. Net effect: +1 Dexterity and +2 Magic.

After that, I set myself to wait again. Soon enough, I would find out if the intruder was Wengulax.

A minute ticked by. Then another.

Still, no one appeared. I didn't dare move though. My hunter was closing in. I was sure of it.

A hostile entity has failed to detect you! You are hidden.

I almost smiled. *There he is.*

A smudge of green inched around the doorway—at floor height. It hung there for a drawn-out moment, almost as if to spur a reaction.

But I wasn't about to be baited. With my target in sight, my impatience fled. My eyes glinting in anticipation, I watched the patch of green with the stillness of a stalking predator. Wengulax didn't know it yet, but our roles had been reversed.

This time, *he* was the prey.

After another heartbeat, the smudge grew larger. More green appeared, and then finally, a pair of eyes narrowed to slits.

Wengulax.

My foe was suspicious. Stretched out flat against the ground and making no attempt to cross into the room, he scrutinized the inside.

A hostile entity has failed to detect you!
A hostile entity has failed to detect you!
A hostile entity has failed to detect you!

The blade dancer's eyes passed over me multiple times but, time and again, failed to spot me. He obviously sensed something was amiss, but it was equally clear he was uncertain as to the cause.

Scarcely daring to breathe, I fed my medallion the final bit of mana it needed. Having come this far, I didn't expect my hunter to retreat.

He's going to enter soon. He has to.

You have fully charged a medallion of the stygian brotherhood. A summoning rift is ready to be opened.

Warning: Your mana is low at 20%.

At the Game alert, my attention shifted downward to the enchanted item clutched in my sweating palm. It was brimming with magical energy that begged to be used. If I didn't release the medallion's spell soon, its mana would dissipate unused.

Wengulax's head drew back.

My shoulders sagged in disappointment. *Is he retreating?* But before my worry could grow, my foe reappeared. Standing tall, Wengulax took a slow, cautious step forward.

It was exactly the wrong thing to do.

A hostile entity has triggered a trap!

Wengulax's head whipped downward, and he jerked his foot back. But even his quick reflexes failed to save him this time.

The blade dancer's foot made contact with the unseen tripwire.

The cord broke.

The bear clamp materialized and snapped closed.

Jagged metal teeth pierced cloth, leather, skin, and bone.

Wengulax has failed a physical resistance check!
Your target has been injured.
Your target is hobbled for 10 seconds.

My assailant shrieked and staggered forward, instinctively bringing his left foot down next to his injured right to relieve it of weight.

Snick!

A hostile entity has triggered a trap!

The sound of the pressure plate activating was almost inaudible beneath Wengulax's surprised yelp.

A heartbeat later, dancing white energy sparked into being and crackled across the room. My foe's head jerked back up, the whites of his eyes showing as the bolt of pure light careened into his midriff.

Wengulax has failed a magical resistance check!
Your target has been injured.
Your target has been stunned for 3 seconds.

Finally, it was time for the last blow.

Releasing the enchantment in the stygian medallion, I directed its spell weaves to appear at a location almost atop the hapless Wengulax.

Energy surged out of the item, and a second later the air was torn open.

You have opened a rank 2 rift into the nether! This rift is large enough for a single stygian beast between levels 50 and 99 to pass through.

Summoning in progress...

...

...

A level 81 stygian nightmare has answered your call!

The rift will remain open for five minutes, after which time the beast will be pulled back into the nether. Warning, you have no affiliations with the Stygian Brotherhood. Your summoned creature will be hostile toward you.

Two hooved feet appeared.

Still dazed, Wengulax didn't react.

The rest of the summoned creature emerged, and a midnight-black horse thundered out. The stygian's outline wavered in the air, indistinct and blurry, partially concealing its form, but I got a strong impression of a powerful torso and muscular hindlegs.

A level 81 stygian nightmare has failed to spot you!

With only a single vulnerable target in sight, the creature wasted no time in flinging itself at my stunned foe. Head lowered, the beast crashed full tilt into the blade dancer.

A stygian nightmare has knocked down Wengulax. The target has been stunned for 3 seconds.

Like a doll with his strings cut, the hunter collapsed. The nightmare was far from done though. Snorting in fury, the creature reared up on its hind legs, its immaterial body passing through the rotten timbers of the building without complaint.

A heartbeat later, the beast brought its forelegs crashing down on the slim green-clad figure at its feet.

A stygian nightmare has trampled Wengulax, dazing him for 10 seconds. Wengulax has been critically injured.

Exhaling noiselessly, I sagged against the wall at my back. Now I could relax. Wengulax's death was a foregone conclusion, and I only needed to wait for the stygian to do its work.

The blade dancer took a long time to die.

Over and over, the stygian smashed its hooves into the delirious player, remorselessly pounding his flesh until nothing remained of him except a bloody mess of bone, blood, and gore.

Wengulax has died.

You have gained experience and reached level 84!

I didn't emerge from concealment. Warily eying the stygian beast, still dancing over the corpse's remains, I decided discretion was the better part of valor and used the time to meditate and replenish my lost psi. The entire time the summoned creature didn't spare its surroundings a second glance, seemingly content to gloat over its kill.

Eventually though, the mana in the medallion ran dry.

A rank 2 rift has been closed. A level 81 stygian nightmare has been unsummoned!

Rising to my feet, I moved to examine my dead foe. After the nightmare's messy work, the body was barely recognizable. Stilling my rebellious stomach, I rifled through the player's belongings.

You have acquired 3 x vials of viper's venom, a rank 4 poison.
You have acquired 2 x full healing potions.
You have acquired a hunter eye.

You have acquired a rank 3 blowpipe. This item has 5 / 10 darts remaining. You do not have the necessary skill, exotic weapons, to use this weapon. None of the Game-gifted benefits and abilities pertaining to this item are available for your use.

You have acquired 2 x rank 3 punch daggers, +3. You do not have the necessary skill, daggers, to use these weapons.

You have acquired an ox ring. This is a rank 2 ring and increases your Strength attribute by 4. This item has no requirements to equip. Note, the attribute bonuses from multiple items do not stack with each other. This excludes legendary and unique items.

You have acquired the band of the cat. This is a rank 2 ring and increases your Dexterity attribute by 4. This item has no requirements to equip.

Despite the gory mess, I recovered multiple items of worth. Curiously though, Wengulax's body was missing his twin katanas and green outfit. The items had definitely been on him when he'd entered the room.

A chill passed through me. The missing gear could mean only one thing.

All three items were soulbound.

"Bloody hell," I muttered. What was the so-called "mantis" that he could afford three such priceless items?

Only now did I truly understand the dread my assailants had inspired in the plague quarter residents. What did it mean for my own future that two such foes had been hunting me?

Nothing good.

Deciding not to waste more time than necessary for fear of Wengulax's partner finding me, I finished my looting and hurried downstairs.

Matters were back to normal on the streets outside.

It was like nothing had happened, and I barely attracted a second glance from the passersby. *Huh, I guess being chased through the plague quarter isn't that unusual.*

I wasn't sure if I could prevent a repeat incident, but it was time I took a few precautionary measures.

Picking a likely subject—a passing elf—I studied his face, gait, and mannerisms intently. The player was a fighter of some sort and about the right size and shape. *Perfect.* After the elf passed out of sight, I wove an illusion around myself.

The lines of my body, clothes, and face blurred as they were overlaid by a casting of light. My voice, though, remained unchanged, having nothing to mimic.

You have cast lesser imitate, assuming the visage of an unknown elven fighter. Duration: 1 hour.

I glanced down at myself.

To my own eyes I looked no different, but hostile eyes would be fooled—hopefully. However the mantises had found me, I suspected they hadn't relied on visual recognition. Still, there was no harm in trying to confound Gintalush. As persistent as my two hunters had proven, Wengulax's partner had likely not given up the chase yet.

Strolling nonchalantly through the doorway, I exited the building and entered the street. No one paid me any heed. I glanced to my left. Back that way lay the south gate—and where I'd last seen Gintalush.

No thanks, I decided and headed farther east.

The road continued to run parallel to the safe zone's south wall and the towering ramparts were a constant presence, but after my encounter with the mantises, I was feeling more kindly toward the Triumvirate knights. I stayed alert for danger, and while some passing groups of players threw me hard, assessing looks, no one tried anything.

Eventually, deciding it was safe enough, I saw to my player progression. I'd gained four levels from the skirmish, and after a moment's thought, I equipped the looted rings from Wengulax—they were the only items of immediate use—and distributed my new attribute points.

Your Magic has increased to rank 10.
Your Dexterity has increased to rank 23. Other modifiers: +5 from items.
Your Perception has increased to rank 25.

With my player progression taken care of, I opened my profile and reviewed the changes to myself.

<u>Player Profile (Partial): Michael</u>
Level: 84. Rank: 8. Lives Remaining: 2.

True Marks (hidden): Pack-brother.

Attributes
Strength: 6 (2)*. Constitution: 14. Dexterity: 28 (23)*. Perception: 25.
Mind: 41. Magic: 11 (10)*. Faith: 0.
denotes attributes affected by items.

New Traits
Mental focus: increases effectiveness of Mind skills by 10%.

Skills
Dodging: 55. Sneaking: 64. Shortswords: 61. Two-weapon fighting: 53.
Light armor: 48. Thieving: 41.
Chi: 49. Meditation: 70. Telekinesis: 50. Telepathy: 47.
Insight: 64. Deception: 59.

New Abilities
Constitution ability slots used: 1 / 14.
lighten load (Constitution, basic, light armor).

Dexterity ability slots used: 19 / 23.
simple set trap (Dexterity, basic, thieving).
whirlwind (5 Dexterity, advanced, two weapon fighting).

New Equipment
simple potion bracelet (3 full heal potions).
trapper's wristband (18 / 20 traps available).
belt of the chameleon.
ox ring (+4 Strength).
band of the cat (+4 Dexterity).

Backpack Contents (Key New Items)
Money: 12 gold, 15 silver, and 3 copper.
1 x Viviane token.
1 x Kesh Emporium access card.
7 x smoke bombs.
1 x cat claws.
1 x spectacles of ward seeing (detect tier 4 wards).
3 x vials of viper's venom (rank 4 poison).
1 x hunter eye (single use).

Miscellaneous Loot
Blowpipe (exotic weapon), **2 x punch daggers** (+3), **bull's ring** (+2 Strength).

Open Tasks
Find the Last Wolf Envoy (hidden) (find Ceruvax).
Stay True to Wolf (hidden) (acquire a mana-based Class).
Heist in the Dark (steal chalice from the Power, Paya).

My skills had advanced nicely in the battle, and another of my Mind disciplines—telekinesis—had advanced to the second tier. I expected the other two would follow shortly, and soon I hoped to be able to upgrade all my Mind abilities.

Assuming I can afford it.

Unfortunately, things in Nexus were more expensive than I anticipated. What had seemed like a small fortune when I'd entered the sector was now mostly gone, and if I didn't want my player growth limited by money—or lack thereof—I needed to find a steady source of income.

Which was partly why I'd changed my mind and decided to seek out the bounty hunters. The other reason being—I needed to confirm the truth of Loken's words.

After the Power's recent deeds, it would be foolish to trust anything he said without verifying it first. And while visiting the guild could prove dangerous if Loken *had* lied, I felt the risk worth taking. Knowing how widely I was being hunted was crucial and would impact my future course.

My thoughts flickered back to my green-clad pursuers. *Although, even if the guild isn't after me, someone else is.*

It was all the more reason to get off the streets quickly. Turning my attention fully outward again, I scanned the passing buildings. Another wall had appeared on the horizon. It ran from northwest to southeast, and judging by its placement, I suspected it formed a divider between the Dark and plague quarters.

Not much further, I thought. *If the information broker or guild is on this side of the south gate, I'll encounter one of them soon enough.*

✳　✳　✳

A short while later, I came across a squat monstrosity of a building with a stark, unpainted signpost. The letters "BHG HQ" had been burned deep in the wood.

BHG HQ? As in bounty hunters' guild headquarters?

I frowned at the sign. There was nothing inviting about it. If anything, it appeared to be little more of an afterthought. *Why use such an ambiguous signboard?* I wondered. It would do nothing to attract prospective clients.

My gaze drifted to the building itself. The structure had quite obviously been designed with defense in mind. The walls were formed from unembellished granite blocks, the windows were arrow slits, and the entrance was protected by a steeply rising staircase and a studded metal door.

There were no guards in sight, neither patrolling the flat-topped roof nor outside the entrance, and the double doors were shut.

I stared at the building for a long moment. It wasn't what I anticipated it would be. Sure, I expected the guild to exude a military air. What I hadn't expected was that its headquarters would be so... unwelcoming.

This has to be the right place.

Before climbing the stairs, I took a long look at my surroundings but failed to spot any green-clad players. Wherever Gintalush was, he hadn't caught up with me yet.

With a shrug, I strode up to the entrance. There was no lock on the door, and left with no other option, I banged a closed fist against its surface. "Hello!" I yelled. "Anyone in there?"

There was no response.

I glanced over my shoulder. My position atop the stair was exposed and left me feeling vulnerable. If Gintalush was anywhere nearby, he was sure to spot me...

I pounded on the door once more. Again, no answer was forthcoming, but I didn't let that dissuade me and kept at it.

"Hello! You have a—"

The door slid open a touch, revealing a pair of angry gray eyes.

I lowered my fist in surprise. Granted, the walls and door of the building might be thick, but I hadn't heard the newcomer approach. My mindsight—which I'd kept active—had also failed to detect the stranger's presence. But, as I well knew, both the ability and physical senses could be defeated.

Whoever this is, they're both shielded and stealthy.

Curiously, I studied the newcomer. Or tried to.

You have failed a Perception check and are unable to analyze your target. This entity bears a Mark of Greater Dark and Lesser Shadow.

My lips turned down. Resorting to more mundane means, I tried to pierce the gloom surrounding the newcomer but failed to make out anything except their eyes.

"What do you want?" the player asked in a gruff—and distinctly male—voice.

I frowned. I couldn't pinpoint where his voice was originating from either. "Who are you?"

"Call me Eyes," he replied laconically.

Appropriate. "Is this the bounty hunters' guild?"

The storm-gray eyes flickered up and down my form. "You don't look like a client," he pronounced.

"I'm not," I said. "I'm looking for work."

"Huh. Check the noticeboard in Market Square then."

I scratched my chin. That was a good point. "I should have," I admitted. "But I'm here now. Can't I see whoever's in charge?"

Eyes was silent for a moment. "Are you a member of the guild?"

I shook my head. "I'm not—"

"Then you're outta luck. This is the guild's headquarters, and only members are allowed inside."

I ground my teeth in frustration. This was taking too long. I scanned the streets again. There were plenty of players about, but none wore the striking green of my hunter.

"What are you looking for?" Eyes asked abruptly.

"Nothing important," I replied before returning to the matter at hand. "Look, let me in, and I'll—"

"That isn't true," Eyes said, interrupting me again. "That's the third time you've scanned the streets."

My eyes narrowed. "How long have you been observing me?"

He ignored my question and shot back one of his own. "Who's hunting you?"

I didn't answer.

"It can't be guild members," Eyes mused absently. "Your bounty was revoked months ago."

My brows flew up. The elf illusion I'd woven around myself was still in place. "You know who I am?"

"Of course," Eyes said, sounding amused. "You were scanned the moment you touched the door. You're Michael. No last name. A level eighty-four mindstalker and former guild mark."

I bit my lip. So Loken had been telling the truth. Ishita really had taken down her bounty.

"Did Ishita hand your death contract over to someone else?" he asked casually.

I sighed. "I don't know. But the ones chasing me are clad in green and named—"

"Mantises," Eyes hissed.

"That's what everyone keeps calling them," I agreed.

"You better go." A hint of pity leaked into Eyes' voice. "I cannot let you in. However you managed to lose your hunters, they will find you again. Mantises are relentless. I don't know who told you to come here, but you won't find sanctuary in the guild."

"I'm not looking for protection," I said patiently. "I told you. I'm looking for work."

"Then check the bloody noticeboard in the square," Eyes said in exasperation. "It contains a listing of all the jobs authorized for non-members." The door began to swing close.

I stuck a foot in the door. "Wait! Does that mean there are *other* jobs, ones reserved for members only?"

"Of course. Now remove your foot."

I kept my leg where it was. "How do I become a member?" I had no particular aspiration to become a bounty hunter, but reserved jobs meant better bounties and—just as importantly—more money.

"*You* don't," Eyes said in annoyance. "Get a few more levels under your belt and maybe you'll be allowed to apply."

He wasn't going to get rid of me that easily. "So, there *is* a level requirement. What is it?"

Eyes sighed. "You're an annoying little noob, aren't you?" he muttered. "No wonder Ishita placed a bounty on you."

I ignored the snide remark. "What's the minimum level required for membership?" I persisted.

"There isn't any," Eyes admitted. "But that doesn't mean there aren't any entrance requirements. To be considered for guild membership, you either need to convince an existing member to apprentice you or complete a few tier four bounties." Before I could ask what those were, he went on, "Those are bounties fit for players of level one hundred and fifty or greater."

I withdrew Gelar's bounty authorization note—still in my possession all this time—and waved it through the narrow slit. "Does this qualify?"

Eyes' gaze dropped lower to scan the parchment's contents. "That's a tier three bounty," he finally pronounced.

"But the wyvern was level one hundred and ninety-eight. That's almost a tier five creature!" I was guessing that bounties followed a similar grading to abilities.

"You don't give up, do you?" Eyes said, answering obliquely.

I grinned, sensing his resistance waning. "I don't."

"Come on in then. Han can decide what to do with you."

The door swung open all the way and I slipped through.

Studying my surroundings, I saw that I was in an enclosed foyer. Contrary to my expectations, the room was well-appointed and looked nothing like the outside led me to expect. A woven rug covered the floor, and gold-frame paintings hung on the walls.

"Wait here," Eyes ordered, floating toward the door at the far end of the foyer.

"Why?" I asked.

"I'm going to fetch Han," he replied.

"Who's that?" I asked absently, studying one of the nearby paintings. It portrayed a troop of soldiers fighting something that looked remarkably like a dragon.

"Someone better off dealing with your incessant questions," Eyes grumbled. He paused outside the door. "Don't think about trying to leave this room," he warned. "The building is warded against intruders, and the traps they trigger are fatal."

"Alright," I said agreeably. "I'll wait here."

Eyes disappeared through the door without opening it. Left to my own devices, I walked a slow circuit around the room, studying each of the paintings in turn. They all depicted players battling monsters, either in groups or individually.

They must all be bounty hunters, I thought, thinking it likely the paintings depicted some of the guild's proudest moments.

I was still inspecting the room when the interior door opened. I turned around and saw a dapper-looking woman standing at the entrance. The newcomer, a young human woman, was elegantly attired in a black suit. Her flowing black hair had a lustrous sheen to it, her fingers were manicured, and her eyebrows were tilted upward, studying me as avidly as I did her.

"Han?" I guessed.

The woman chuckled. "It's Hannah, actually. But Eyes refuses to call me anything other than Han. I'm the guild client liaison officer."

"Ah, I see."

She waved me to a pair of couches sitting against the left wall. "Have a seat, Michael," she said, "and let's talk."

I did as she bid.

"Oh, and you can get rid of that illusion. You won't need it here."

I quirked an eyebrow at her but didn't protest as I let my lesser imitate spell dissipate.

"Thank you," she said with a smile. "Now, from what Eyes has told me, I understand you wish to join the guild?"

I nodded.

"Well, technically this isn't my area of responsibility," Hannah said. "I usually only deal with clients, but none of the other senior guild officers are available at the moment, and Eyes—correctly so—judged himself unqualified to deal with the matter."

I rubbed my chin but said nothing, not missing the implications behind her words. For whatever reason, it seemed for me to become a guild member was no ordinary matter.

"Your file is quite interesting," she continued.

"I have a file?" I murmured.

Hannah nodded. "All our marks do." She paused. "Or, in your case, former mark."

"Alright," I said. "What's so special about my file that it warrants the attention of a senior guild officer?" I asked with a grin.

No answering smile flickered across the client liaison's face. "For one, the bounty taken out on you was for a significant amount," she said solemnly. "For another, the bounty was directly at the behest of a Power. And thirdly, the guild's analysts believe there is a high probability of another bounty being taken out on you in the near future."

I winced, but I couldn't disagree with the guild's assessment. "What does all that mean?"

"It means you're a liability," she stated bluntly. "And the guild will be better served without you as one of its members."

"But?" I asked. "There has to be a but, or we wouldn't be having this conversation, would we?"

Hannah's smile finally returned. "You're right. There are a few counterarguments. You've managed to kill a rank nineteen wyvern, and you appear not to be risk averse."

I snorted. *That* was an understatement.

"Then there's your Class," she continued, her smile growing. "Mindstalkers are rare. Finally, and most importantly, you have attracted the interests of no less than four different Powers." She paused. "All this makes you potentially quite valuable to the guild."

"Enough to let me become a full member?"

She shook her head. "Not quite. But it is enough to let you try becoming one. If you wish, I'll register you as a probationary member."

"Excellent," I replied. "Where do I sign up?"

"Not so fast," she said. "First, tell me what you know of the guild."

"Eh..."

Hannah's lips twitched. "That's what I thought," she murmured. "Before you decide, there are a few things you must know."

"Go on," I said, realizing she was right.

"One, the bounty hunters' guild is not a Game faction," Hannah said. "We have no Power protecting our interests or shielding our members from retaliation by disgruntled parties. You understand?"

I did, and while Hannah might have expected the information to make me less eager to join the guild, on the contrary it made me more willing.

"Two, the guild is nonpartisan. We have no affiliation with any other faction, Force, or Power. The guild respects only one thing: money. We will take any job *except* those that require hunting down a fellow guild member." She smiled. "Which is why we don't grant membership to just anyone."

I grinned happily. Even disregarding the other benefits of membership, that alone was reason enough to join the guild.

Hannah leaned forward, her smile fading. "This is important, so let me be clear. The guild only has *one* rule: don't kill your fellow members. If you're caught, not only will you be expelled, but we will hunt you down with every resource at our disposal." Hannah held my gaze, waiting for my acknowledgment.

"I understand," I said, much more soberly.

She nodded. "Good. Now for the last bit. Every job is voluntary. If we feel you're suitable for a particular job, a guild officer will reach out to you. But the choice of whether to accept the bounty or not is yours alone. The guild also only acts as an intermediary—for which we take our cut—and by itself does not guarantee the success of any job.

"Admittedly, this has made us less than popular with the factions, and over the years it has resulted in them forming their own in-house hunter teams. The mantises are one such group." She paused. "I understand you've already run afoul of them?"

I nodded. "Who are they?"

Hannah's lips thinned. "They are a Dark faction, and their contracts are exclusively from Darksworn. Primarily, they're assassins." She tilted her head to the side. "Do you know who hired them to hunt you down?"

I shook my head. "I don't, but I can guess. It must have been Ishita."

Hannah nodded. "That makes sense in light of her cancellation of your bounty with us. The Power must have been frustrated at the lack of results." She met my gaze. "Do you still want to join up?"

"You haven't mentioned the benefits of joining," I pointed out.

She smiled. "As a member, you will gain access to exclusive jobs and will earn a greater percentage of the profit. Advance high enough in the guild, and you'll also gain access to our exclusive stores and the dungeons we control."

I nodded. It was as I'd thought. "And in return?"

"In return, you complete your prescribed minimum number of jobs annually. Any other questions?"

"Just one. How do I become a full member?"

Hannah grinned. "The standard requirement is three tier four bounties. Given the difficulty of the tier three bounty you managed already, for the purposes of your membership application we'll allow it. That means you'll need to complete two more tier four jobs."

I bowed my head in my hands and groaned. That wasn't going to be easy.

The client liaison chuckled. "Don't look so disheartened. Study the Nexus bounty ledger." She waved a hand and a book appeared on a nearby table. "It lists all the currently open jobs in the sector and those available to you as a probationary member. You'll find most tier four jobs aren't as difficult as the tier three one you attempted."

I raised my head. "They aren't?"

"They aren't," Hannah said, still smiling. "Tier four jobs are generally for multiple subjects or items. Study the ledger," she repeated, "and you'll see."

I nodded. "I'll do that."

Reaching into her coat pocket, the guild officer pulled out a small brown card. The letters "BHG" were engraved in silver across the middle of the card's lacquered surface. Below it, in smaller text, was my name, followed by the words, "probationary member."

Flipping the card over, Hannah handed it to me. "That's your guild identification." Game messages unfurled in my mind as I took the offered item.

You have acquired a BHG ID. This is a writ of authorization, marking you as a probationary member of the bounty hunters' guild. As a probationary member, you may be in active pursuit of five bounties at any one time.

This item cannot be stolen, traded, or lost, even upon death. Note, if your membership is revoked by the guild, this writ will be destroyed.

The Adjudicator has allocated you a new task: <u>Probie!</u> The bounty hunters' guild has accepted you as a provisional member. Fulfill the guild's requirements to become a full member. Objective: Complete two tier 4 bounties.

"Congratulations, Michael," Hannah said warmly. "You are now a guild member, if only a temporary one. You may explore the rest of the rooms in the building if you wish, but you'll find that as a probationary member, you'll be barred from entry into most." She rose to her feet, signaling an end to our meeting.

I rose with her. "Thank you," I said, watching her walk off.

✳　✳　✳

After Hannah left, I strode over to the bounty ledger to inspect its contents. There were dozens of bounties listed within. In fascination, I perused the list.

The jobs were categorized by tier. The first thing I noticed was that all bounties of tier five or greater were reserved for full guild members. Comparatively, there weren't many such jobs, but invariably they were unique and paid handsomely.

More interesting, though, was that most of the high-tiered jobs listed marks in other quarters of the city. That gave me pause, and I frowned thoughtfully at the book.

Does that mean those jobs are only open to guild members who are Force sworn, or do guild members have special dispensation to enter the other city quarters?

I'd have to remember to ask Hannah the next time I saw her, but for now, I set aside the question of high-tiered bounties and turned my attention to the jobs at the low end of the scale. Most of these were open to anyone— probationary members and non-members.

Almost immediately, I dismissed the idea of attempting any of the tier one and -two bounties. Their tasks were unappealing and repetitive and consisted mostly of collecting ingredients, delivering messages and goods, or finding specific individuals. Their pay was nothing remarkable either.

The tier three jobs were more interesting and seemed to focus on escort duty, stealing, spying, information gathering, and even serving as a henchman. Curiously, I read the description of one such job.

Job number: 921. Job name: fighter henchman wanted. Tier: 3. Bounty: 50 gold. Payment is guaranteed by the guild, and the job is available to both guild members and non-members.

Job description: A melee-based fighter player between levels 50 and 100 is required to serve as a henchman to the player Sykes for a single dungeon run through the tier two dungeon: infested gutters. The henchman will be fitted with a guild-approved control device that will force him to obey Sykes for the duration of the dungeon run. A penalty of 200 gold will be levied against Sykes if the player deviates from the job parameters or the henchman dies in service.

There were other details too, like where Sykes could be found, the job start date, and so on, but I didn't bother reading any of it.

My lips twisted in disgust at the thought of leashing my will to another. It went without saying that the job didn't appeal to me.

Flipping over the page, I studied the next set of jobs.

The tier four jobs were primarily kill orders.

As Hannah had said, most were for multiple targets. A disproportionate number, though, were for stygian beasts. But that stood to reason, given what Shael had told me about the city's problem with nether rifts.

Carefully, I read the description of the first such job.

Job number: 674. Job name: cleanse the quarter (weekly). Tier: 4. Bounty: 100 gold. Payment is guaranteed by the guild, and the job is available to both guild members and non-members. Job description: assist the Triumvirate knights to maintain order in the plague quarter by slaying 20 stygian beasts in 7 days. For permission to pursue this bounty and claim your reward, visit knight-captain Orlon in the Triumvirate citadel.

This is a bounty I can complete, I thought. Tracing my fingers over the page's text, I wondered how to accept the job. A Game message opened.

You have been granted authorization for bounty 674.
Your BHG ID has been updated. Active bounties: 1 of 5.
Note, as a guild member, you are automatically authorized when you accept a job and are not required to visit the bounty holder to obtain permission to pursue the bounty.

"Huh," I murmured. "That's nice." Pulling out my recently acquired BHG ID, I studied its contents. Sure enough, etched in small letters on the rear of the card was the mentioned authorization.

Stowing away the ID, I continued to peruse the jobs and stopped as I came across one that wasn't a kill order.

Job number: 1,240. Job name: capture a stygian beast. Tier: 4. Bounty: 150 gold. Payment is guaranteed by the guild, and the job is available to both guild members and non-members. Job description: disable or imprison a rank ten or above stygian beast in the plague quarter and inform huntmistress Kartara at the stygian brotherhood chapterhouse when the deed is done.

Hmm... I rubbed my chin. It was an interesting bounty and not one I was certain I could fulfill. Nevertheless, I accepted the job.

You have been granted authorization for bounty 1,240.
Your BHG ID has been updated. Active bounties: 2 of 5.

I continued scrolling through the list. Many were for specific dungeon creatures, and others were for players. I was hesitant about accepting either just yet. Mostly because I wasn't certain which dungeons I intended to explore, and finding the players, I suspected, would be more work than they were worth.

I began flipping over the page faster, my eyes skimming the text each time I saw phrases such as *'can only be found in a dungeon...'* or *'the mark is a player...'*

I was mostly finished with the tier four job list when, almost unnoticed, my gaze passed over a most intriguing word: *werewolf.*

My eyes jerked to a stop, and I exhaled sharply.

Werewolf?

Bending my head over the page in question, I read the bounty notice.

Job number: 428. Job name: hunt for a criminal. Tier: 4. Bounty: 150 gold. Payment is guaranteed by the guild, and the job is available to both guild members and non-members. Job description: knight-captain Orlon requires assistance in apprehending a convicted thief named Anriq. The thief escaped custody and is thought to be in the saltmarsh district. The mark is a player and a known werewolf. Knight-captain Orlon can be found in the Triumvirate citadel.

The bounty notice contained disappointingly little information, yet I knew it wasn't one I could ignore. *I have to find this Anriq, if only to learn more about werewolves.*

Did they carry the bloodline of Wolf?

Possibly, if not probably. Running my hand over the page, I accepted the job.

You have been granted authorization for bounty 428.
Your BHG ID has been updated. Active bounties: 3 of 5.

After that, I closed the bounty ledger. The three bounties I'd selected would give me enough of a start, and if necessary, I could always come back to pick up other jobs.

Setting aside the book, I glanced at the inner door of the foyer. Further exploration of the guild could also wait for later, I decided. After the mention of werewolves, I was eager to venture deeper into the quarter.

Restoring my disguise with lesser imitate, I swung around and exited the building.

✳   ✳   ✳

Before descending the stairs, I took a moment to scan the streets. Everything looked normal. Satisfied, I ducked my head and hurried down the steps.

At the base of the staircase, I stopped again, wondering which way to go. I still needed to find the information brokers' offices before I headed further south. To my left, the eastern boundary wall of the quarter loomed large.

East, I decided, seeing as there wasn't much more for me to explore in that direction. Stepping onto the street, I swung left.

You have failed a mental resistance check! An unknown hostile has pierced your disguise.

The Game message was unexpected, but my reactions were well-honed and I didn't hesitate. Picking a direction at random, I flung myself away.

You have evaded an unknown hostile's attack.

A heartbeat later, a metal dart pinged against the cobblestone. My lips tightened.

Gintalush. It had to be.

Somehow, the mantis had tracked me down. Bouncing back onto my feet, I whipped around. A blur of green sped toward me. With almost no time to react, I did the only thing I could think of—I shadow blinked.

You have teleported behind Gintalush.

The assassin skidded to a halt and swung around, both blades flashing in the sunlight as they rushed toward me. But I was already moving.

Slapping my left hand to the concealed stud on my chameleon belt, I activated its combat mode and retreated out of reach of the mantis' swords.

You have evaded Gintalush's twin attacks.

My foe danced forward, seeking to close the distance between us again. I didn't let him. Backstepping, I summoned and threw an astral blade in a single motion.

Gintalush dodged the psi dagger easily, but the evasive maneuver cost him, knocking him off his stride and delaying his advance.

I unsheathed my own blades.

The mantis rushed in, simultaneously attacking from the left and right. I swept the first blow aside with spider's bite, dodged the second, and then riposted with ebonheart.

Gintalush didn't even bother parrying.

Sliding past my counterattack, he launched a new offensive. Desperately, I fended him off. From the opening exchange, I realized Gintalush was as skilled as Wengulax *and* armed with swords, not knives.

I couldn't let myself become entangled in another sword fight, but I struggled to disengage. The assassin was pressing me too hard. Dancing across the cobblestone road, we traded blows.

Inevitably, the blade dancer pierced my guard.

Gintalush has struck you a grazing blow.
Gintalush has struck you a grazing blow.

"Damnation," I growled as I felt the bite of my foe's swords twice over. I'd managed to turn aside the blades enough that the wounds barely tickled, but if either attack had penetrated a little deeper...

I took a step back. Then another, weaving a desperate defense.

You have blocked Gintalush's attack.
You have evaded Gintalush's attack.
You have...

It was too much. Soon my foe would penetrate my guard again, and I would be dead. Searching for inspiration, I retreated again.

The back of my left foot hit stone. I'd reached the base of the staircase leading up to the guild, I realized. *If I can get to the door, maybe—*

My foe vanished.

Huh?

My head swung right, tracking the assassin. Gintalush had thrown himself to the side and *away* from me. *What did he do that for?* I wondered, lowering my uselessly hanging blades.

I had no idea, but this was too good an opportunity to waste.

My gaze never leaving my foe—it could be some elaborate trick, though it wasn't like he needed one—I retreated further up the staircase.

Gintalush sidestepped again, then ducked and rolled.

I frowned, perplexed by my foe's mad dance. In other circumstances, it would've made for an amusing sight. But Gintalush's deadly menace was all too real, as was the intense focus of his maneuvers.

It was almost as if the green-clad assassin was fighting an unseen foe...

Two gray orbs appeared, floating at eye level with Gintalush.

Bloody hell.

It was Eyes. The mantis was battling the guild's doorkeeper.

A moment later, Eyes' body materialized, and involuntarily I backed up another step. The guild's doorkeeper was the strangest species I'd yet seen in the Game. There was nothing remotely humanoid about him.

Eyes had no legs, no hands, or even a body that I could discern. He consisted entirely of thick, writhing tentacles—and of course, the two gray orbs that served as his eyes, each attached on the end of their own appendage.

Wielding no weapons, Eyes struck at Gintalush with sucker-like tentacles. The assassin did his best to evade their grasp and even managed to slash off two—to no noticeable effect.

Eyes' remaining limbs bore relentlessly down on the green-clad figure.

Finally, one of the thick tentacles landed on Gintalush's right arm and stuck fast, sucking on the assassin like a leech. It slowed him only a touch.

But enough that a second tentacle landed.

A third followed.

Then a dozen more, until eventually both Gintalush's limbs were covered in the writhing appendages and held fast. The assassin had been disabled. Eyes was far from done though. Bringing more of his tentacles to bear, the doorkeeper enfolded Gintalush entirely, freezing him immobile.

My mouth dropped open in awe. The seemingly unstoppable assassin had been stopped.

Then the strange sight turned even stranger.

Before my stunned gaze, Gintalush began to shrink. *No, not shrink,* I realized. *Shrivel.*

I gulped. Eyes was leeching the life out of the mantis through his tentacles.

Gods. That's no way to go.

The mantis fought at first, but then little by little he began to sag in the guild doorkeeper's grasp until matters reached their inevitable conclusion.

Gintalush has died.

A second later, Eyes turned invisible again, or the most disturbing aspects of him did. His gray eyes remained, floating serenely in the air.

"Urgh," Eyes spat. "That was foul."

My gaze drifted from my benefactor to the pile of discarded possessions that was all that remained of the former assassin. "Uhm, you mean the mantis?"

Eyes snorted. "Of course I mean the mantis. What else would I be talking about? I don't know when last I ate something that horrible."

"Ate...?" I asked, edging backward again.

The two gray orbs bobbed cheerfully in the air. "Ate," he agreed. "Humans taste much better."

I had no response to that.

A moment later, Eyes bellowed in laughter. "I'm only joking, of course." He paused. "You humans taste nearly as bad."

I glared at the doorkeeper, coming to the belated realization that he was teasing—or so I hoped. Unbending from the crouch I'd unconsciously fallen into, I strode back down the stairs with affected nonchalance and inclined my head to Eyes.

"Thank you," I said gravely. Whatever the doorkeeper was, I wouldn't begrudge him a little fun at my expense.

He'd saved me, after all.

"My pleasure," Eyes remarked. "Anything to take down those green bastards a notch. Can I ask you a favor?"

I nodded. "Of course."

"Will you carry my loot back into the foyer? It will be much easier than me trying to drag them."

"You got it," I said and did as he bade.

✳   ✳   ✳

A minute later, I was done mopping up and stood at ease with the doorkeeper in front of the guild.

"You have eight hours now," Eyes remarked, his tone markedly more serious than earlier.

I glanced at him. "What?"

"Eight hours," he repeated. "Mantises don't give up. *Ever.*" He bobbed his eyes toward the spot where Gintalush had died. "That one will be back on your trail as soon as he resurrects. You have at least eight hours to prepare before that happens. Use the time wisely."

I nodded. Eyes was right. I would have to make sure I was ready for a repeat encounter—with both assassins. "I'll do that," I said, then paused as something else occurred to me. "If I send Gintalush to his final death, what then?"

Eyes chuckled. "I like your confidence. You sure you can manage that?"

"I will," I stated grimly. "What happens to the mantis contract on me then?"

Eyes was silent for a moment. "I'm not sure," he admitted at last. "I've never heard of anyone surviving a mantis hunt. The assassins will keep hunting you until your final death. And even if you somehow manage to permanently put an end to one, I suspect more will be sent after you. The faction prides itself on *always* completing a contract." He paused. "I'm afraid, human, that your chances aren't great. Your best hope would be to find the one who placed the contract and convince them to retract it."

I nodded slowly in understanding.

On behalf of Wolf, the Adjudicator has allocated you a new task: <u>Preying Mantises</u>! An unknown entity has placed a kill order with the mantis faction, marking you for death.

This goes against the tenets of Wolf. Wolf does not flee; Wolf is never prey. Wolf is the hunter—always. Rectify matters and appease Wolf by teaching the assassins a lesson.

Objective: stop the mantises from hunting you. Optional Objective: discover the identity of the one who has marked you for death.

My lips tightened in a grim line at the Adjudicator's message. *As if I don't have enough to deal with already.*

Dismissing the Game alert, I glanced down the street before turning back to Eyes. "Mind pointing me in the direction of the information brokers?"

"Follow the street west. You'll find the brokers only a little way beyond the south gate to the safe zone. Their offices are usually busy, even at night, and you should see a crowd gathered outside it."

I nodded. "Thanks again," I said in farewell before leaving the guild and its strange doorkeeper behind.

CHAPTER 178: THE COST OF A LITTLE KNOWLEDGE

Disguise back in place, I strode down the street.

While I did, I checked the gains I'd earned from the last encounter. My player level hadn't advanced—but then it was Eyes who had done all the work killing Gintalush.

Still, many of my skills had progressed.

Your dodging has increased to level 57. Your shortswords has increased to level 62. Your two-weapon fighting has increased to level 55. Your telekinesis has increased to level 51. Your deception has increased to level 61.

Your light armor has increased to level 50 and has reached rank 5, decreasing your light armor penalties by 25% and allowing you to learn tier 2 abilities. The net effect of your armor is now -1 Magic and -3 Dexterity.

My lips twitched upward.

While I was still no match for the mantises—or most other players, for that matter—if I kept advancing at the rate I was going, soon I'd be able to hold my own against all but the very best.

I found the progress of my light armor skill to be especially pleasing. The skill had advanced appreciably since I'd entered the Game, and the attribute penalties I now suffered were significantly reduced. In fact, taking into account the effect of the enchantments on my gear, the final debuff incurred by my Magic and Dexterity was only ten percent.

Negligible really.

With a contented sigh, I turned my attention back to my surroundings. Reaching the safe zone's south entrance, I kept walking and soon enough found the building Eyes had told me about.

The structure was constructed from slatted white timbers and had a large white sign gilded in gold affixed to it. Clumps of players milled around the entrance in greater numbers than I'd yet seen in the plague quarter.

Striding up to the sign, I scanned its contents.

The first line read: *"Welcome to the offices of Nexus' information brokers. We are professional rumormongers and the best source of gossip in town."* Below that, in smaller text, was a second line: *"Strictly no guarantees will be provided as to the veracity of any disclosed information."*

I scratched my head, not sure what to make of the sign.

The second sentence sounded like a joke, but after reading the third one, I wasn't so certain. Right now, though, I was too desperate for information— even unconfirmed rumors—to turn my nose up at the brokers.

Slipping through the crowd, I entered the building. It was even busier inside. Players were pressed up at the counter that stretched the room's length, waiting to gain the attention of one of the uniformed gnomes sitting on high stools on the other side. A screen of bars separated the gnomes from the players.

From the layout of the room and the behavior of the other players, I guessed the gnomes to be the brokers. *Curious*, I thought and studied them more closely.

The gnomes were dressed in white suits with gold embroidery that matched the building's decor. Reaching out with my will, I analyzed the closest one.

The target is Meson, a level 28 gnome.

Surprisingly, the information broker wasn't a player. I analyzed the other gnomes and saw that none of them were. *Interesting*, I thought and joined the line of queueing players.

I kept a wary eye on my surroundings as the line inched forward, but nothing untoward happened before I reached the counter.

"Buying or selling?" the broker asked in a bored tone, not looking up from the book in which he was scribbling furiously.

"Excuse me?"

The gnome looked up, his eyes assessing me. "Ah, a new customer. And a newcomer to the sector as well, I take it?"

I nodded.

"Then you're here to buy," he said with confidence. He flipped open his book to a blank page, pen poised in readiness. "I'm Arden. And you are?"

I told him.

"Class? Level? Home sector?" Arden asked.

Those particulars I was less inclined to share. "Why do you need to know all that?"

The gnome grinned. "I don't. But the more you tell me about yourself, the bigger your discount."

I eyed the broker suspiciously, not trusting the glint in his gaze. I suspected any information I shared with him would be sold to whoever requested it. "I'll forego the discount," I said blandly.

The broker shrugged. "Suit yourself," he said and closed his book. "Before we begin, there's one thing you should know. For every question I answer, no matter how mundane, you will be charged a fee." He paused, waiting for my nod of acknowledgment. "Now, what can I do for you?"

I had already thought the matter over on my way here and knew what information I desired. "For starters, I want a book on the Game's mechanics."

Arden sighed. "Not another one."

I stared at him blankly. "What?"

"Do you know how many players come in here asking for a Game manual?"

I didn't, but judging from his expression, it was a lot.

The gnome didn't wait for my answer but forged on. "We don't have any, nor would the Triumvirate allow us to sell them if we did. And do you know why?"

I shook my head.

"Because knowledge like that is too powerful and reserved for the factions' elite. If you want a Game manual, join a faction and rise among the ranks of its sworn."

Biting back a sigh, I let the matter go. "In that case, I want a map. Do you think you could help with *that*?"

Arden brightened. "Of the plague quarter?"

I nodded. "And of the rest of the sector too."

Arden bent under the counter and rifled through some papers. "How recent a map do you want?" he asked from below.

I opened my mouth to respond, but before I could he fired off more questions.

"How accurate should it be?"

"Do you need it with or without street names?"

"What details do you need to see?"

"Do you need any specific locations shown?"

He finally ran down and I managed to get in a word. "Erm... I don't know."

"That figures," Arden muttered and bobbed back up, his arms ladened with rolled-up parchments.

Withdrawing one from the stack, he placed it before me. "This map is only twenty hours old. It has the updated location of every dungeon portal and rift in the sector. It includes street names and the last known position of the Powers currently in the city. It *also* includes a basic analysis of every major faction in the sector."

"Wow, that sounds useful," I said, reaching for the map.

Arden snatched it back. "One thousand gold first, please."

I gaped at him. "That's ridiculous!"

"Information is power in the Game," the gnome replied without the least trace of a smile. "It doesn't come cheaply."

Clearly it didn't. But one thousand gold was beyond my means. My gaze drifted to the other maps in Arden's hands. "Do you have anything... cheaper?"

The broker sighed. "What's your budget?"

"Ten gold?"

The gnome winced. Executing an intricate gesture with his fingers, he caused all the maps but one to disappear. "For ten gold, I can offer you this." He unrolled the parchment on the counter. "It shows the basic layout of all four city quarters and the plague quarter in a bit more detail."

I let my gaze rove over the map. It didn't include any street names and contained disappointingly little information on the other quarters, but it showed key structures in the plague quarter. A few dungeons were also marked on it. I already knew, though, that nether portals in Nexus weren't always stable. "How outdated is this information?"

"It was last updated ten years ago," Aden replied.

My lips turned down, and I pointed out the dungeons on the map. "Do these even exist anymore?"

Arden nodded. "They do. This map only shows the most stable dungeons in the plague quarter. Those three have existed in the city for eternity, and their entrances are still at the locations marked on the map."

The map had value then. "I'll take it."

"Excellent," Arden said, some of his smile returning. "Now, what else can I help you with?"

I scrutinized the map again, noting the ocean that surrounded the city. It explained the whiff of sea breeze I'd caught earlier. Nexus, it seemed, was an actual island. I focused on the plague quarter, and my brows furrowed as I noticed one area of particular interest to the southeast. "Tell me about the saltmarsh."

"The marsh is a low-lying district that is periodically flooded by the ocean's tidal currents," the broker answered. "It is also responsible for much of the quarter's woes, and few players venture within its depths."

My frown deepened. "What does that mean?"

"The plague quarter isn't called such for nothing," Arden said with a smile. "Disease and sickness oftentimes run rife in the quarter—most of which are born in the saltmarsh. Unsurprisingly, the worst illnesses and plagues can be contracted in the marsh itself. Here, close to the safe zone boundary, we're rarely affected, but if you venture farther into the quarter, I'd advise you to purchase ointments to treat disease." He paused. "You will not survive long in the quarter otherwise."

Arden's information tallied with Shael's, and his warning was timely. "I see," I murmured. "Where can I find such ointments?"

"You'll find the biggest selection and best prices for cure disease potions in the Triumvirate citadel at the center of the quarter," Arden said. "Of course, you could also buy them through the global auction."

I glanced at the citadel in question. Assuming the map was drawn to scale, the Triumvirate castle didn't appear far away. "Do the knights patrol the plague quarter?"

"If you're asking if they serve the same function in the quarter that they do in the safe zone, then the answer is no. However, you will find squads of knights roaming the region. Their mission, though, isn't establishing order but hunting down any nether beasts running loose and closing open rifts."

I pointed to the stygian brotherhood chapterhouse. "And what do they do?"

"The brotherhood also hunts the nether beasts that enter the city. But unlike the knights, who seek only to kill the creatures, the brotherhood are more interested in capturing and taming the stygians for their own use. At times this puts them at odds with the knights, but the two groups have had centuries to work out an accord between themselves, and these days quarrels between them are rare."

I nodded thoughtfully. The glint in the broker's eyes hadn't escaped my notice, and I was certain he would bill me for every explanation I asked for, but the background knowledge he was providing was invaluable, and I didn't stop my questions.

"Where is a safe place to rest in the quarter?"

Arden chuckled. "Safe? Nowhere in the plague quarter is truly safe, not like the safe zone. And arguably that isn't all that safe either. But if you intend on spending a night here, you can sleep in the taverns along the south wall with minimal risk. And, of course, the lodging provided by the knights in the citadel is also quite secure."

"Thank you. Now, tell me about the three dungeons on the map," I said, returning to my primary reason for entering the quarter.

"They are all public dungeons. In the scorching dunes, you will usually find rank twelve players and desert creatures. Your biggest challenge there will be combating poison and fire.

"The haunted catacombs, as you can guess, are infested with undead. The catacomb's depths provide a healthy challenge for most players between the ranks of twelve and fifteen.

"The guardian tower is inhabited by the hooded savants, and in there you can expect to face all manner of elemental magic. I wouldn't advise entering without a strong and well-knit team, all of whom exceed level one hundred and fifty. Even though it's a public dungeon, few venture within the tower."

The gnome paused to glance at me. "That's the basic rundown, but I can expand further on any particular dungeon if you so wish."

I digested the information but didn't ask him to elaborate. "Why do you call them public dungeons?"

"Because they're just that—dungeons unclaimed and uncontrolled by any faction. Unlike the more prestigious dungeons, the rewards from the three are of relatively little value and not worth the resources of any faction to protect and control. The Game itself seeds the three dungeons, and any player is free to enter."

"Huh," I muttered, wondering what that meant for my chances of discovering a rare master Class stone. But regardless of whether I found Class stones in the public dungeons, they would still be useful for leveling.

I'd learned all I wanted to know about the quarter, though, and rolled up the map. As I did, I asked offhandedly, "You brokers aren't players. Why is that?"

Arden's eyes twinkled. "Before I answer your question, I'm obliged to inform you that your tab has reached one hundred gold for the information already provided."

I scowled at the gnome. "One hundred gold? That's steep."

"I must insist that you settle the outstanding amount," the broker said, ignoring my comment.

I sighed but didn't protest further. "Do you have a keystone?"

"Of course," the gnome said and laid one on the table. I placed my hand on the device, authorizing the transaction.

You have lost 100 gold.

"Thank you," Arden said, beaming happily. "Now, do you still wish me to answer your last question?"

I waved off his request. "Forget it." Something else had occurred to me. "If I wanted to find out the identity of an individual who placed a bounty on me, could you help me with that?"

The gnome's smile faded. "Ah, that's a more serious request and one not likely to be fulfilled immediately. We can, of course, attempt to uncover the information you require but can make no guarantee as to the success of our queries. And, of course, the price will vary depending on the parties involved." He paused. "Who holds the bounty?"

"The mantises," I replied simply.

Arden sucked in a breath. "That will be expensive indeed."

"But not impossible?" I asked.

The broker's smile returned. "But not impossible," he agreed. "I'm afraid, though, because of the nature of your request and the risk of er... non-recovery, we will have to demand payment upfront."

"Naturally," I murmured.

"The transaction will also have to be handled by a senior broker. Do you wish me to call my supervisor?"

I shook my head. The cost was probably going to be exorbitant and not one I could afford now. Still, it bore consideration for the future.

"No, thank you," I said. "I have all the information I need. But you mentioned something about buying information too. What do you think about this..."

I attempted to sell what I knew about sector 12,560 and the Awakened Dead's machinations in the wolves' valley to Arden. However, because of the age of the information and the fact I had no evidence, the gnome refused the transaction.

It seemed that despite their disclaimer on the sign outside, the brokers wouldn't purchase unverified information. Still, I left the office happy with the outcome of my dealings.

Breaking away from the crowds, I found a quiet spot to consider my next move. It was time to head deeper into the quarter. But where exactly?

I need to gain more levels—and fast. I also needed money almost as badly. Dungeons would do for the one, and bounties for the other. But both would require me to spend significant time in the quarter.

Best to heed Arden's advice then and purchase some cure disease potions.

Orienting myself with the map, I strode southeast in the direction of the Triumvirate citadel.

* * *

As I moved deeper into the quarter, the streets became quieter. Fewer players were about, and those who were moved in groups.

My lone form attracted more than one curious glance, but I paid them no heed. I had no option but to travel alone, having as much to fear from other players as I did whatever horrors the quarter might hold.

One particular street, though, was busier than the others.

It ran directly from north to south, and multiple Triumvirate knights traveled along its length. The road was wide, and its cobblestones were clean and less pockmarked than other streets. Considering its placement, I suspected it was the main artery between the south gate and the citadel.

Given what Arden had told me, I suspected the knights' outpost in the quarter would serve well as my base of operations. It was centrally positioned, and if the broker was to be believed, offered safe lodgings and merchants to trade with.

Halfway to my destination, I stopped short as a tortured howl cut through the air.

My head whipped around. The cry had come from the right. The sound was full of pain and anguish and was one I recognized intimately.

Someone was dying.

No one else nearby had reacted though. The scream had come from too far off for most to hear. A moment later, a second howl split the air. This one was closer. It was followed by footsteps. *Lots* of footsteps.

A crowd was fleeing my way.

I debated my options. The smarter choice would be to hurry on and ignore the fleeing people, but that didn't sit well with me. I wanted—*no, needed*—

to know what was going on, especially if the plague quarter was going to be my home for the near future.

I surveyed the area and spotted an alley on the opposite side of the street. It offered both a shadowy refuge and safe observation point. Crossing the road, I slipped into its darkness, then turned around and fixed my gaze on where the crowd would emerge from.

The seconds ticked by, and eventually the other travelers on the road sensed the onrushing disturbance. Heads turned. Whispers followed. And many, wisely, hurried away.

The crowd's forerunner—a human player—emerged from the side street, the whites of his eyes showing. Dropping his hands to his knees, he gulped in deep breaths.

A knight hurried toward him. "What's going on?" he demanded.

The exhausted man took a moment to answer. Straightening, he gasped, "Stygians! A rift has opened!"

The knight's hand tightened around his blade. "How many?"

"I don't know—an entire army! The city's been invaded!"

The knight's brows drew down. "Where? What levels?" he barked.

The player didn't hang around to answer though. Taking off running again, he headed north for the safety of the safe zone.

"Come back here!" the knight roared.

The frightened man kept running. The knight swung back to face the side street. More people were emerging, and the Triumvirate soldier fired off another volley of questions.

None stopped to enlighten him.

Throwing up his hands, the knight hurried back to his companions. After a short conversation, the entire group hurried south and back to the citadel. To get reinforcements, I presumed.

The streets had become disturbingly empty. But I stayed where I was, curiosity growing. Finally, it seemed I had stumbled on an opportunity to come face to face with the stygian menace plaguing the quarter.

The trickle of fleeing people became a flood, a sea of incoherence—howling men and women and babbling children. Disturbingly, there were nearly as many players as there were non-players. What could terrorize so many so?

I could do nothing for the crowd though. Panic had dug its claws deep into them, and it would be awhile before any were fit to talk. Loosening my blades in their sheaths, I readied my blades.

Flee or fight, I would do as the circumstances demanded.

✳   ✳   ✳

Just as quickly as the crowds had appeared, they vanished.

The wave of noise receded, and in nearly pin-drop silence, I waited. The seconds ticked by. A minute passed. Then another.

Yet no horde of stygian beasts arrived.

Perplexed, I uncoiled. *False alarm?* I wondered.

Has to be.

My gaze swung up and down the road. It was starkly empty in both directions. Word had spread, and others were keeping away. I hesitated, then entered the side street the crowds had emerged from.

Hugging the sides of a tall building, I crept further down the road, retracing the path of the fleeing crowd. My senses were extended, and I was alert for danger. But it was a good few minutes before I heard anything that warranted concern.

From up ahead, around the corner and out of sight, I heard the faint rasp of a blade. It was followed by clipped orders and the sizzle of something...

A spell hitting its target?

Whatever the furor was all about, it was just a few streets ahead. But it certainly didn't sound like an invasion. The ground didn't shake, the building didn't tremble, and a horde of stygian beasts most emphatically did not appear. The fleeing human had exaggerated, I thought, or so it seemed.

Still, caution was necessary.

Glancing upward, I scanned the nearby structures. They were all multi-storied buildings. *Better to approach from up high.*

Equipping my cat claws, I slunk to the side of the building I had marked as an easy climb and began scaling its heights.

Less than a minute later, I was atop the building's tiled roof. Through my mindsight, I could sense the minds huddling inside. The building's interior was occupied, as were many of the nearby structures.

The residents who had chosen to remain, cowering behind their locked doors, appeared exclusively non-players, and I knew I would get no help from them.

Darting across the roof, I reached its edge and threw myself across the stretch of open air to the next building. The distance was too large to ford in a single leap, but with one-step I managed the feat easily.

I rolled to a stop on the next building. Then, with nimble steps, I crossed its length and hopped over the next street and onto the adjacent building.

After another series of jumps, I reached the source of the noise. Stretched out flat, I pulled myself forward with my elbows and peered over the roof's edge.

A battle was in progress below.

And much to my surprise, the fleeing player had been somewhat correct in his report. Most of the combatants were stygian creatures. They were far from a horde though.

Taking a quick tally, I estimated there were seventeen slithering stygians—serpents by the look of them—and one larger six-headed horror—a hydra.

Facing off against the nether creatures were four players, three of whom I recognized. It was the same trio I'd used to escape Wengulax. Accompanying them was a centaur covered from hooved feet to shoulders in armor formed of overlapping plates.

Corpses—the majority dead stygian beasts—littered the streets. The four seemed to have killed a fair number of the "invaders" already.

Running my gaze over the centaur and two of the stygians, I analyzed them in turn.

The target is Barac, a level 160 centaur crusader.
The target is a level 110 stygian serpent.
The target is a level 180 stygian hydra.

The players had drawn up against the side of the building on the opposite side of the street, and the serpents had formed a half-circle around them.

Despite the numbers arrayed against them, the party seemed to be holding its own. Barac swung his heavy two-handed axe with wild abandon, keeping the snakes at bay, while from within his shadow the duelist, Jasiah, nipped at the creatures with his slim blade. The archer, Simone, and the mage, Moonshadow, threw spells and arrows to protect the party's flanks.

An experienced party, I thought, watching them fight.

Though, as well as the party seemed to be doing, I thought matters would change quickly once the hydra reached them. And from the glances the four kept shooting at the approaching monster, they seemed to know it too.

From the neck down, the hydra was built like any other four-footed creature, if only one more immense than most, outmatching even the centaur in height. Its six heads, snapping jaws, and snaking necks made it truly monstrous though. What the hydra lacked in speed, it made up in might. The beast was thirty yards away from the party, but every moment it crept closer.

I should help them.

Given the hydra's slowness, the party had some time before they were overwhelmed, but that they would be seemed assured. Although the group were strangers to me, three of them had aided me against the mantis—unwittingly or not—and I owed them.

How do I help though?

I studied the ground. The four were too far away from me to use shadow blink. Besides, I wasn't sure another blade—especially from an under-leveled player—would make much difference. Somehow, I needed to change the balance of the fight.

Most of my tricks weren't suitable for group combat. If I smoked the area, I would only blind the players. Nor would summoning a stygian beast help in this instance. Charm should work, but I suspected it would take multiple attempts—and time the party didn't have—to bespell one of the serpents.

There was only one other thing I could think to attempt.

My gaze flickered to the opposite building, measuring its height. *It could work.* The street the battle raged in was wider than the others I'd crossed so far, and fording the distance wouldn't be easy.

Still, it was worth a try.

Decided, I rose to my feet and backed away a few yards. Then I hurled myself forward, accelerating to full speed by the time I reached the edge of the roof.

Springing off my right leg, I leaped through empty air, legs windmilling. When I passed the top of my arc, I cast one-step and flung myself forward again, hands outstretched. My reaching fingers curled around the edge of the opposite rooftop.

I'd made it.

Pulling myself up, I looked back down. Neither the players nor their foes had noticed me yet. Removing the coiled rope from my backpack, I tied it around the nearby chimney and, standing at the roof's edge, let its length unravel to the ground.

The rope end smacked the archer on the cheek, attracting her attention. Breaking off from her attacks, the half-elf's gaze whipped upward.

I smiled and, cupping my hands around my mouth, shouted, "Get up here!"

Simone didn't reply. Bending her head back down, she whispered something to the elven mage. Moonshadow glanced upward and, after a curt reply to his companion, began climbing.

Good. I'd almost feared the party would refuse my aid. However, my actions had only increased their danger in the short term. Until the mage reached the rooftop, the remaining three would have a much harder time holding off the stygian creatures.

I turned my attention back to the fight. Seeming to realize they needed to buy their companions time to reposition, the centaur and the duelist intensified their attacks.

Forgoing defense, they laid into the serpents with abandon, causing the creatures to hiss and recoil in pain. The pair's blades fared better than my own had in my single encounter with a stygian, which meant theirs had to be enchanted to inflict magical damage.

Let's see if I can help them even the odds.

Drawing on my psi, I targeted the nearest serpent and cast simple charm. Strands of my will reached into the creature's mind but were adamantly rebuffed.

You have failed to charm a level 101 stygian serpent.

I grimaced at the failure but didn't give up. Drawing on my psi again, I sent more strands searching outward. *This time, I'll—*

Your spellcasting has been interrupted!
You have been teleported. Simone has swapped positions with you.

What the—!

For a moment, I stood frozen in disbelief before understanding dawned. My gaze flew upward to meet the self-satisfied smirk of the half-elf. She spared a moment to wave cheerfully at me before returning her attention to the serpent and taking aim with her bow.

God dammit, I cursed. *That bloody ungrateful—*

I broke off as the irony of the situation hit.

Simone had only done to me what I had done to her with Wengulax. *Turnabout is fair play, and besides—*

"Stop standing there and gaping like a fool!" Barac roared. "Draw your blade and join the bloody battle!"

My gaze flickered to the centaur. He was right. The party's two ranged combatants were now safely atop the roof, where they could rain down their projectiles to devastating effect.

It was time I did my part.

Stepping forward, I shadow blinked into battle.

CHAPTER 180: STYGIAN HORRORS

I stepped out of the aether and into the shadow of a stygian. Both my blades were still sheathed. They would be of no help in this battle.

But that didn't mean I was helpless.

My empty right hand flew forward. Midway to my target, an astral blade coalesced in my palm, and I buried it hilt-deep in the smoky outline of the serpent's neck.

You have backstabbed a level 108 stygian serpent for 2x more psi damage!

The nether creature jerked upright, hissing in surprise. I readied a second astral blade, but before I could strike I spotted a second form rushing downward upon me. Aborting my attack, I blinked away and flung the psi dagger at a different target instead.

You have backstabbed a level 110 stygian serpent for 2x more psi damage!

I'd done better choosing my second prey. The beast in question was already engaged with the centaur and considerably injured. Not letting the opportunity pass by, I struck again.

You have injured your target, inflicting psi damage.

The snake shuddered, and I sensed it was almost done for. A shadow grew behind me. It was from another foe drawing closer.

Ignoring the new attacker, I stayed focused on the injured serpent. Kept busy by the crusader, it hadn't turned around to face me. Whipping my right hand forward again, I flicked a third astral blade at my target.

You have killed a level 110 stygian serpent.

There was no time to celebrate the kill. The serpent behind was diving. But I knew already that it was too late to avoid the onrushing blow. I whirled around, determined to not let the creature escape unscathed.

Neither I nor the serpent got to complete our attacks.

A streak of light—a glowing projectile—flashed past me to bury itself deep in the open mouth of my striking foe.

Simone has killed a level 109 stygian beast with a fatal blow.

My head jerked up in surprise, and I threw the archer on the rooftop a grateful nod. Reassured that I could count on the party's assistance—for this encounter at least—I threw myself back into the fray.

Shadow blinking, I teleported forward to emerge on the opposite flank of a serpent Jasiah battled. I was already poised to strike and activated whirlwind the moment I emerged from the aether.

You have cast whirlwind, increasing your attack speed by 100% for 3 seconds.

The spell energized me, and, my form a blur, I lunged forward to strike with the astral blade in my right hand.

You have backstabbed a level 102 stygian serpent for 2x more psi damage!

Even before I completed the first blow, my left hand was flashing forward. Alas, it was absent an astral blade. Despite my new speed, I couldn't summon the psi daggers fast enough to keep up, and rather than delay my attacks, I struck out in another manner.

Drawing psi from my mind, I sent it coursing through my muscles, out my open palm, and directly into my foe.

There was no resistance at the moment of impact, of course.

My blow passed unheeded through the creature's wavering form. Still, as my hand waded through the cloying ichor and gelatinous lumps that passed for the serpent's body in the physical realm, invasive energy flooded the serpent.

A stygian serpent has passed a physical resistance check! You have failed to stun your target.

I was undaunted by the Game message. If anything, it pleased me. I'd been unsure if stunning slap would work, what with the spell being at least partially physical in nature, but the message's phrasing implied it could succeed.

I struck out again, this time with the open palm of my right hand.

A stygian serpent has failed a physical resistance check! You have stunned your target for 1 second.

I grinned at the spell's success. Astral blade was ready again, and with my foe still stunned, I plunged the psi dagger in my left hand into its neck.

You have backstabbed your target for 2x more psi damage! You have killed a stygian serpent.

"Nice work," Jasiah said as the serpent collapsed between us.

I nodded perfunctorily. "Let's get the next," I said, already moving.

"No," the duelist barked abruptly. "Moon has gotten his act together. We need to clear the field." Raising his voice, he yelled, "Barac, heads up! Incoming!"

The centaur glanced upward and his eyes widened. Following his gaze, I spotted three roiling balls of light and energy floating downward from the rooftop.

While we'd been trading blows with the stygians, the party's mage hadn't been idle. Making use of the protection afforded by his elevated position, Moonshadow had cast a spell more complex than the simple lightning bolts he'd been using earlier. And judging from the reaction of his companions, it was a powerful one.

"Back!" Barac roared.

Trusting the fighters to know what they were doing, I obediently swung around and headed after Jasiah, who had braced himself against the side of the building.

Two steps into my retreat, I glanced over my shoulder and saw that Barac wasn't following. Worse yet, bereft of other targets, the serpents were converging on the lone crusader.

The centaur was surrounded.

I stumbled to a halt and my eyes darted upward. The slowly descending crackling orbs were only seconds away from impact. The hydra, too, drew closer, and while it was still not an immediate threat, it would be soon. On his own would the crusader be able to survive orbs, stygians, *and* the hydra?

I doubted it. *I should assist him.*

Barac, though, didn't need help.

Before I could move in his direction, the crusader rose up on his back legs and brought his forelegs crashing down.

Barac has cast hoof stomp.

The ground bucked and shockwaves rippled outward from the impact, overtaking the serpents, the hydra, and my own position.

I flung out my arms, trying to maintain my balance on the suddenly heaving ground. It was no use. Like the stygians, I was flung off my feet.

You have failed a physical resistance check! You have been knocked down. You have been stunned for 3 seconds.

Urgh. Flat on my back and helpless to move, I stared up at the sky and what I was sure was my onrushing doom—the three glowing orbs of Moonshadow's spell.

A furious face appeared above me. "Idiot!" Barac yelled. "Didn't I tell you to retreat?"

He had, and I was sorry now that I hadn't listened. But still reeling from the stun, I couldn't seem to get my mouth to work and voice an apology.

"Why do I bother?" Barac growled. With another angry mutter, the centaur reached down and dragged me away.

✳ ✳ ✳

Despite the ignominious manner of his conveyance, Barac got me to safety in time. Moments after we took shelter against the side of the building, the mage's spell hit.

The charged orbs, sailing gracefully downward, splashed into the ground in slow motion to create three expanding pools of lightning.

The serpents, most of whom were still recovering from Barac's spell, were trapped in the charged fields and writhed helplessly as the destructive coils of energy crackled through their wavering forms.

A level 105 stygian serpent has died.
A level 109 stygian serpent has died.
A level 103 stygian serpent has died.

...

With my mouth hanging open, I watched in awe as, one by one, the serpents collapsed into motionless heaps.

"Thanks for the assist earlier," Jasiah remarked from above me.

I dusted the debris still clinging to me and rose to my feet. "You're welcome," I replied absently, not tearing my gaze away from the dying beasts.

For the next twenty seconds, Moonshadow's spell continued to wreak havoc. Of the original pack of seventeen serpents, only five remained alive, and they too looked nearly dead. Barac had charged forth again to engage them and seemed to have matters well in hand.

This time, I left him to it.

My gaze drifted past the centaur to the hydra. It was the only stygian to have escaped the destruction of Moonshadow's spell.

The creature had come to a halt a safe distance from Barac and, with frightful intensity, watched the demise of its fellows through six pairs of eyes. I glanced at Jasiah. He was studying the hydra too.

I jerked my chin at the creature. "How do we deal with that?"

"Not easily," he replied with a sour laugh. "Hydras may be slow, but they're tough. And they're a damn sight smarter than the average stygian."

"You guys have a plan though?"

There was no response.

"Don't you?" I asked, turning around to stare at him.

Jasiah still didn't reply, but before I could badger him further the final serpent perished and I returned my attention to the battlefield.

Barac was looming over his last kill, eying the hydra. Staring at him in turn, the beast remained where it was. *Why isn't it attacking?* I wondered. *Or fleeing?*

At a whistling sound from behind, I glanced back to see Moonshadow and Simone slipping deftly down the rope.

The elven mage scowled at me, recognition sparking in his eyes. "I *thought* you looked familiar. Why have you come to trouble us again?" He craned his head to peer behind me. "You don't have another mantis on your tail, do you?"

"You know him?" Barac asked, returning to rejoin us.

The hydra, I noted, still hadn't moved.

"He's the one I told you about," Moonshadow said. "The noob who slipped the mantis on us."

"Hmm," the centaur remarked, hefting his large axe in a manner that wasn't very comforting. "Maybe we should—"

"Enough," Simone said, cutting through the chatter. "We'll sort out that mess later." She jerked her chin toward the hydra. "For now, we've got to see to that." Her gaze flitted to me. "You've proven useful so far, and we could use the help. Are you still with us?"

I nodded. I'd come this far and saw no reason to back out of the fight now. "What's it waiting for?"

"The beast is smart enough to realize it's too slow to flee *or* to catch us," Simone answered grimly. "So, it's doing the only thing it can: waiting for reinforcements. The rift is just beyond that corner," she added, gesturing down the street. "And it's still open." The archer eyed her companions. "If we're going to tackle this monster, it's now or never. We doing this?"

The other three nodded.

From the group's interactions, I guessed the archer was the party leader, and I watched her intently, curious to see what plan she came up with for tackling the hydra.

Simone glanced at the elf. "Moonshadow, you ready?"

"Just about," the mage replied. Pulling out a flask, he gulped down its contents.

It was a mana restoration potion, I realized. Both Jasiah and Barac were drinking potions too, although I didn't recognize the contents of their own vials. *This party is well-equipped.*

"I am now," Moonshadow said a heartbeat later.

"Alright," Simone said, speaking rapidly now. "For those who don't know—" her gaze fixed meaningfully on me—"hydras can soak up loads of damage. On top of that, they can regenerate too. So, if we're going to slay the beast, we're going to have to hit it hard and fast, overwhelming it. Understood?"

I nodded.

"Another thing," Simone went on. "The hydra itself may be slow on its feet, but those heads of it are anything but. Six converging simultaneously on you is no joke. Beware of them." She eyed me from head to foot. "I can see you're not equipped to go toe to toe with the beast. It's best if you hang back. Do you have a ranged weapon?"

I shook my head. "Don't worry about me. I'll be fine up close."

The archer opened her mouth, then closed it with a snap. "It's your funeral," she said with a shrug.

"Do you even have a blade that can hurt it?" Jasiah asked.

I hesitated, then replied in the negative. "I don't, but I have a spell that can serve as a substitute."

The duelist snorted. Digging into a pouch at his waist, he extracted a shortsword seemingly from thin air. The pouch had to be a bag of holding, I realized. The fighter held the blade out to me, hilt first. "Here, use this."

I took the offered weapon.

You have acquired a rank 3 stygian shortsword, +3. This item has been enchanted to increase the wielder's shortsword skill by +3 ranks.

Stygian weapons are forged from materials harvested from the corpses of nether creatures. Imbued with the essence of a stygian, this weapon will inflict necrotic damage instead of physical damage. This item requires a minimum Dexterity of 12 to wield.

With an effort, I kept my eyes from widening. "Thank you," I managed.

"It's a loan only," he said.

I inclined my head, grateful nonetheless.

"One more thing," Simone said, drawing my attention to her. "The hydra is different from most other stygians you may have fought—" her gaze darted meaningfully toward the dead serpents — "including those. The beast is more fully present in this world than most of its brethren manage."

I frowned at her. "What does that mean?"

It was Moonshadow who answered. "What Simone is getting at is that hydra will have *real* weight and presence. You won't be able to pass through its form as you may have done with other stygian beasts. Got it?"

I nodded slowly in understanding. "Got it."

"Alright then," Simone said. "Let's get down to strategy. Ideas, anyone?"

CHAPTER 181: A MAGE, A THIEF, AND AN ARCHER

While the others readied themselves for the battle, I saw to my own preparations. Turning my attention inward, I acknowledged the waiting Game messages.

Status of bounty 674 updated. You have slain 2 / 20 stygian beasts. Time remaining to complete the bounty: 7 days.

You have reached level 86!

Your dodging has increased to level 58. Your sneaking has increased to level 66. Your telekinesis has increased to level 52. Your telepathy has increased to level 48.

Your chi has increased to level 50 and has reached rank 5, allowing you to learn tier 2 abilities.

I'd gained more levels, and while I couldn't derive any benefit from my increased chi rank yet, I had gained two attribute points.

How to spend them? My Magic had reached a comfortable level and didn't need to be increased further—not until I obtained my third Class. Dexterity was the next best choice, seeing as how I had only a few ability slots remaining in it. Decided, I invested in the attribute.

Your Dexterity has increased to rank 25. Other modifiers: +5 from items.

Opening my eyes, I returned my attention to the surroundings. The party had begun its advance on the hydra, and it was time to join them. Drawing the sword Jasiah had loaned me, I admired its length.

Clouds of gray billowed across the surface of the blade, giving it an indistinct appearance not unlike the stygian creatures it had been forged from. It was a beautiful weapon. Deadly too, and I wished I possessed its like.

Yet it's only Jasiah's spare blade. Which begged the question, how much more powerful were the duelist's primary swords?

I shook my head in wry realization. I had a long way to go in the Game. *Time to get going,* I thought and strode forward to join the others.

✳ ✳ ✳

Barac, Jasiah, and I spread out to surround the hydra. Weapons held at the ready, we approached from three different directions while Simone and Moonshadow hung back.

From what I understood, the archer and mage would be the party's main damage dealers. It was up to Barac, Jasiah, and me to keep the beast distracted so the other two could do their work unimpeded.

According to Simone, Moonshadow's most lethal spells were multi-target ones that hurt everything in the field of effect, but to protect his companions in the upcoming battle he would restrict himself to seeking spells only.

I hadn't even known such spells existed, but it seemed some higher-tiered spells were advanced enough to differentiate friend from foe. But despite the limitations, the party was sure the mage and archer combined could deal enough damage to whittle down the hydra's health fast enough.

"Remember, we take out the head on the right first," Simone whispered.

The plan wasn't complicated.

We would cut off the hydra's heads one by one. That would slow the beast's regeneration and deprive it of its most potent offensive weapons — its six deadly jaws. Without its heads, finishing off the creature would be simple, or so the others believed.

I held back slightly, waiting for my companions to engage first. While I did, I summoned psi and reached out to the hydra's mind. I didn't expect my spell to work, but it was worth a try.

Weaves of energy spun out from me and toward the beast, attempting to blind it to my presence.

A level 180 stygian hydra has passed a mental resistance check! You have failed to hide your presence from your target. Your mental intrusion has been detected!

One of the hydra's heads turned my way, and the beast hissed angrily — or was that mockingly? — in my direction.

My lips thinned. As expected, even with my high Mind, slaysight had failed. The beast was more than double my own level, after all.

I guess there is going to be no easy way to do this. Hefting the blade in my hand, I advanced on the creature. Meanwhile, the others were concluding their own opening attacks.

With an ear-splitting war cry, Barac charged the monster from the left. Using his bulk to good effect, the centaur pushed the hydra off-balance, causing it to stumble momentarily.

Barac has staggered a hydra. Target dazed for 10 seconds.

Exploiting the distraction created by his companion, Jasiah dashed in from the right and slashed open a jagged cut down one of the hydra's necks.

Jasiah has struck a hydra with a glancing blow.

The beast attempted to retaliate, but before its striking heads could descend on the duelist, Moonshadow lowered his staff and cast.

A widening beam of white light expanded outward from the mage, passing harmlessly through Jasiah to envelope all twelve of the hydra's eyes.

Moonshadow has cast moonbeam. A hydra has failed a magical resistance check. Target blinded for 10 seconds.

Hissing in fury, the beast reared back. An eldritch arrow blurred past me, striking the targeted head that, just for a split-second, had been perfectly framed for the shot.

Simone has crippled a hydra. One of twelve eyes permanently blinded.

"Wow," I murmured, impressed anew by the party's level of coordination and skill. *Time to play my own part.*

Sprinting forward, I wove psi and my left hand flashed forward, releasing the astral blade that materialized in it.

The hydra, though, was no longer an easy target. Realizing its vulnerability—the beast was still blinded and dazed—the creature flung its necks into motion, swaying them back and forth.

Despite this, the hydra didn't see the incoming projectile, and the ethereal blade found its mark, if not quite where I intended.

You have struck a hydra a glancing blow, dealing psi damage.

I wasn't disheartened. With the creature still blinded, there was ample opportunity for me to do further damage, and I kept running.

Peripherally, I was aware of the others continuing their own attacks, but I had eyes only for my target. My feet pounding against the road, I kept my gaze fixed on the hydra's swinging heads.

A heartbeat passed, then another, and I judged myself in range.

Springing off my left leg, I went airborne. A second later, I pushed off again with one-step, correcting my trajectory midair to follow the motion of the swaying head I'd picked out.

I'd timed the leap perfectly. My outstretched left arm wrapped around the creature's oily neck and my legs quickly followed, anchoring me firmly in place.

Sensing my sudden weight, the hydra reared back its neck, but I clung on tenaciously and it failed to dislodge me. Before the creature could react further, I attacked with the stygian blade in my right hand.

You have cast crippling blow. A hydra has passed a physical resistance check! You have failed to cripple your target.

While my first blow had failed to cripple my target as I'd hoped, I kept striking, activating my other abilities. Energy gushed into my arm, empowering each hit.

You have cast whirlwind, increasing your attack speed by 100% for 3 seconds.

You have cast piercing strike, doubling the damage dealt on the next attack.

Once. Twice. Thrice. In rapid-fire fashion, I plunged my shortsword through the hydra's neck.

You have injured a hydra.
You have injured a hydra.
You have injured a hydra.

I didn't stop there. With whirlwind my attacks were a blur, and I kept going, stabbing into my foe with berserker frenzy. Each strike caused blood to spurt and the beast's head to sag further.

You have injured a hydra.
You have injured a hydra.
You have...

Hissing in pain from the damage, the hydra withdrew two of its heads from its battle with the others and sent them racing toward my own position.

But I'd anticipated the ploy.

Loosening my grip momentarily, I flipped around to hang off the underside of the creature's neck. The hydra hadn't regained its sight yet, forcing it to strike blindly, and not unsurprisingly, its seeking heads failed to find me.

Once the danger passed, I flipped back over and kept stabbing.

You have injured a hydra.
You have injured a hydra.
...
1 of 6 of your target's heads has been permanently damaged.
You have crippled a hydra!

The flurry of blows proved too much, and eventually the neck I clung to sagged as the head I'd assaulted died. The hydra roared in fury and pain and, abandoning all its other attacks, sent its five remaining jaws hurtling toward me.

It was too little too late, of course.

Focusing on Simone, I shadow blinked to safety.

You have evaded a hydra's attacks. You have teleported 8 yards.

I emerged from the aether at the party leader's side and found Moonshadow staring at me aghast.

"You're crazy," the mage pronounced, his gaze roving over my gore-spattered form.

I admit I did look a sight, but it was only blood, and none of it was mine. I opened my mouth to retort, but before I could Simone intervened. "That was insane, agreed." She pinned me with her gaze. "But can you do it again?"

I grinned wolfishly. "Of course."

CHAPTER 182: UNWRITTEN RULES

Rinse and repeat.

That was what the next few minutes amounted to. We replayed the same successful battle sequence five times over, with Barac staggering the hydra, Moonshadow casting moonbeam, and me severing the creature's heads while the others kept it distracted.

Of course, it wasn't all easy going.

After the loss of its first head, the hydra focused exclusively on me whenever I fell within range of its jaws. And while that made me less effective, it gave the others free rein with their own attacks, and soon enough we had the creature on its knees.

The others allowed me to strike the final blow. It didn't increase the experience I'd earned from the battle, but it helped with my bounty task.

You have killed a level 180 stygian hydra.
You have slain 3 / 20 stygian beasts required for bounty 674.
You have reached level 88!

Rising free from the corpse beneath me, I cleaned Jasiah's stygian blade of blood and grime and looked up to see the party approaching.

"Thanks," I said, offering the blade back to the duelist.

Ignoring the outstretched sword, Jasiah glanced at Simone. "The rift?"

The archer nodded, eyes darting from the dead hydra to the street beyond. "Go keep watch on it. It won't be long now before more of the creatures emerge."

Jasiah ran off, leaving me still holding his bare blade.

Feeling self-conscious and aware of the others' watchful gazes, I sheathed the sword and held it awkwardly in my hand. "What now?"

For a drawn-out moment, no one said anything.

I kept my gaze on Simone, waiting for her response. But to my surprise, it was Barac who broke the silence. "You did well, noob," he said grudgingly. "If not for your fast work there, I doubt we would have killed the beast before more of its fellows joined the fray."

"I still think he's crazy," Moonshadow muttered.

My gaze flitted between the two in confusion. The party leader still hadn't said anything, but I got the sense that I'd joined the conversation midway. It almost sounded as if they were trying to decide something...

"What now?" I asked, looking at Simone again.

The archer folded her arms and stared at me with hard eyes. "Why did you help us?"

Ah, I thought, realizing that this w be an interrogation. I shrugged. "I felt bad about what I did earlier."

"About the mantis, you mean?" she asked.

I nodded. "I shouldn't have used you three as a decoy."

Moonshadow snorted but didn't interrupt his party leader further.

"Why was the mantis chasing you?" the archer asked.

"I don't know," I replied honestly.

Simone frowned as she contemplated my answer. "And where is he now?"

"Dead," I replied simply.

"Dead?" she repeated. "Did you kill him?"

"I did."

Another hush descended upon the trio, and once more it was broken by the centaur. "Well, I'll be damned." He guffawed. "Looks like our boy here has some skills."

Simone didn't say anything, and I couldn't tell if she believed me. A moment later, her gaze drifted to the mage.

"He's only rank eight," the mage protested obliquely.

The half-elf stared at him.

Moonshadow sighed. "Alright, but I still think it's a mistake."

Simone nodded and glanced at the centaur.

"You know what I think already," the crusader responded. "We're short on firepower, and this won't work any other way."

"Agreed," Simone replied. She turned back to me. "We're about to enter the rift and do our damnedest to close it. Barac is right. We could do with an extra blade." She held my gaze. "You're in?"

Now I know why Jasiah didn't take his sword back. *His vote must've been yes too.* "I don't know much about the rifts," I admitted, glancing at the corpses strewn about the street. "Will what we face there be as tough as these?"

Barac threw back his head and laughed uproariously.

I suppose that's answer enough.

"Tougher," Simone replied, an amused smile on her face. "So, what will it be?"

I thought about it for a moment, then grinned back. "Count me in."

❋   ❋   ❋

My decision wasn't as reckless as it seemed at first glance.

I knew I was under-leveled for the rift. Hell, I seemed to be under-leveled for everything in the sector.

But at the back of my mind was the thought that if I was going to do something as dangerous as entering the nether—the very lair of the stygians—it was best I did it with a team of players as skilled as the four seemed to be.

And, of course, I expected I would gain a wealth of experience in the process.

Simone turned to Barac and Moonshadow. "Loot the corpses. Quickly."

The two hurried off, pulling out small objects that looked like alchemy stones.

The half-elf glanced at me. "This your first time in the quarter?"

I nodded.

Simone pursed her lips. "I thought so. There are no laws in the plague quarter; you must know that already. But that doesn't mean anything goes. The players who frequent this part of the city have a few unwritten rules, and they take it upon themselves to punish any who break them. You understand?"

"I do. What are they?"

"One, stay the hell away from battles between other players, and most definitely don't attempt to score easy kills from any who are wounded in the conflict. If it doesn't involve you, it's not your fight." She paused, waiting for my acknowledgment.

"Understood."

"Secondly, don't loot any kills that aren't your own." She gestured to the player corpses lying nearby. "Especially those of fellow players. Doing that is a surefire way of earning a reputation as a scav. And believe me, you don't want that."

"Got it."

"Good," Simone pronounced. "Now, do you have a means of gathering alchemy ingredients?"

I nodded.

"Perfect. You can loot the two serpents you killed earlier but nothing else." Simone grimaced. "I'm sorry we can't share the spoils further, but we need the reagents too badly ourselves."

I tilted my head to the side. "Why's that, if you don't mind me asking?"

The archer shrugged. "It's no secret. We're on a mission for a Light Power."

"Oh? And you've been given a task to collect the reagents? They must be important then."

"They are," Simone said, not elaborating further. "And we're drawing near the end of our time limit." She hesitated, then added reluctantly, "That's the only reason we're risking the rift."

My eyebrows furrowed in concern. Suddenly, my decision to enter the nether with them didn't seem that wise anymore. "You're worried about our chances there?"

Simone shrugged. "The biggest risk, as always, is getting overwhelmed. So long as we maintain our lines of retreat, we'll be fine."

I nodded, unsure whether her answer relieved me or not.

"Anyway," she continued, "since you'll officially be a member of our party during our time in the nether, the loot distribution will be fairer there. You'll get one-fifth of everything we collect."

"Sounds good," I said.

Seeming to consider the discussion closed, Simone moved off to begin her own looting and I did the same.

Stopping in front of the first stygian serpent I killed, I placed the alchemy stone on it, or rather *inside* it—even dead, the creature didn't seem to possess a true body.

The stone activated, pulsing emerald. With each pulse the serpent shrunk, shriveling before my eyes, and in less than a minute the corpse vanished entirely.

The light from the alchemy stone faded, its work done. Leaning down, I picked up the object.

You have retrieved an alchemy stone. New ingredients acquired: 2 x lumps of necrotic plasma and 1 x vial of nether residue.

Hmm. I rubbed my chin thoughtfully at the Game message as I strode to the next corpse and began collecting its loot too. Given the party's task, I assumed stygians' reagents were valuable.
But how valuable? I wondered.
If the reagents were expensive enough, they could prove a viable source of income. The serpents, at least, I was sure I could kill by myself. But first I would need to get a stygian blade of my own.

New ingredients acquired: 3 x lumps of necrotic plasma and 1 x vial of nether residue.

Done with my looting, I glanced about and saw that the others were still busy. I had a few minutes at least before they were done. After munching quickly through a ration bar, I sat down cross-legged, closed my eyes, and meditated to regain my lost psi.

✳   ✳   ✳

"Hey, noob! You just gonna sit there staring off into space? Or are you gonna join us?"
I opened my eyes to see the centaur shifting impatiently before me. "Coming," I murmured and rose to my feet.
Not waiting for me, Barac spun about on his hooves and headed down the street at a steady clip. Following more slowly, I checked the waiting Game messages and saw to my progression.

Your psi is now at 100%.
Your dodging has increased to level 60. Your shortswords has increased to level 65. Your chi has increased to level 52. Your telekinesis has increased to level 54. Your meditation has increased to level 72.
Your Dexterity has increased to rank 27. Other modifiers: +5 from items.

Satisfied that I was ready as I could be for the rift, I surveyed the surroundings. The streets were still empty of life, and I spotted signs of fresh damage on the nearby buildings.
The residents had fled, and there was no telling when they would be back. If every influx of the stygians was this disruptive, it was no wonder the plague quarter was in the state it was.
As we turned down the corner, the rift came into view, and I stumbled to a halt. Less than a dozen yards ahead was a hole in reality.
Where open air and sunlight should have existed was... nothing.
It was a blackness so complete that it seemed solid, and not even my night vision could penetrate its depths. But for all that, the void of nothingness was remarkably similar to the opening Worca—and come to think of it, I,

too—had created when performing a stygian summoning, if only many times larger. This one was wide enough that it occupied the entire width of the street and tall enough that it rose above the nearby buildings.

So that's a rift.

At a more wary pace, I resumed walking. The rest of the party was gathered before the floating void. I noticed that it didn't quite touch the ground, and I wondered idly what would happen if the rift cut across the road or, for that matter, through the adjacent buildings.

Would they have vanished into nothingness?

I shuddered at the thought. Living in the plague quarter was more dangerous than I realized. As I neared the party, Simone turned to face me, seemingly unfazed by the nothingness behind her.

"This is for you," she said, handing me a small cylindrical-shaped object.

I took the proffered item. It was a three-inch-tall crystal similar to the trap-making ones I'd used against Wengulax. "What enchantment does it hold?"

"A ward of protection," Moonshadow said.

My eyebrows rose.

"The rift opens directly into the nether," Simone said, answering my unspoken question. "The air there is thick with a dark miasma, and it goes without saying that breathing it will do you more harm than good. The ward will shield you from the nether's negative effects."

I nodded. "How do I use it?"

"Break the crystal while holding it," Moonshadow instructed.

I did as he bade, the slim crystal cracking easily as I applied pressure to its ends.

You have activated a single-use enchantment, casting a ward of nether protection around yourself. For the next hour, you will be shielded from the ill effects of the nether at tier 4 and lower concentrations.

"Done," I said.

"Let's go then," Simone said. Without further ado, she swung back around and dashed toward the rift.

CHAPTER 183: INTO THE NETHER

In a flash, Simone disappeared, teleported presumably to the nether.

The others followed quickly on her heels, and I scrambled after, surprised at the alacrity with which matters were moving. I'd been expecting Simone to outline the plan at least.

"Why the rush?" I called out to the others before they could vanish.

Barac and Moonshadow didn't bother responding, and a second later they also disappeared through the rift. Jasiah, though, paused and waited for me to catch up.

"Because we're on a time limit," he said when I reached his side. "We only have one hour to find the stygian seed, destroy any nether creatures guarding it, and head back."

"Stygian seed?" I asked in confusion.

"The thing that's created the ley line to this sector. We have to remove it to seal the rift."

I nodded in understanding. "And we don't have any more of the protection crystals?"

"We do," Jasiah said. "But they're too expensive to spend frivolously."

I bit my lip, frustrated anew by my ignorance of so many aspects of the Game. "What can I expect on the other side of the rift?"

"You'll find out soon enough," he said and, without further explanation, dove into the black void.

I stared at the spot where the duelist had vanished and then, with a shrug of my shoulders, followed on his heels.

✳ ✳ ✳

You have entered sector 6,910 of the Nethersphere. This area is outside the boundaries of the Endless Dungeon and has been claimed for the Nethersphere by a mature void tree. Warning: the ley line connecting this sector to the Kingdom is unstable and may close at any time.

You have entered the nether. The dark miasma infecting the region is unconducive to life and will cause your health, psi, stamina, and mana to degenerate by 10% per minute. Nether toxicity: tier 1. Current status: Protected. Remaining duration: 59 minutes.

I stepped out into a world of gray.

The journey through the rift had been no different from traversing a portal. The transfer had been instantaneous and smooth, but the sector I found myself in was wholly different.

The air was hazy and thick, enveloped by heavy banks of smog. Visibility was poor. I could see, but not more than a few yards ahead of me. After that, everything transformed into a wall of gray that even my nightwalker senses couldn't pierce.

I looked back. The rift behind me was also obscured. Even the void of nothingness was seemingly not proof against whatever hung in the air. Glancing down, I saw the ground was rocky and hard, reassuringly solid. At the scuff of a stone I peered up, the stygian blade held at the ready. Four shapes had emerged from the mists.

It was the party.

As the others drew closer, I noticed Moonshadow's eyes were closed and his mouth was moving rapidly. Casting a spell?

I had my answer a moment later.

Moonshadow has cast purifying dome. Duration: 10 minutes.

An electric ring rippled outward from the mage, passing harmlessly over his companions but causing the thick tendrils of mists to dissipate. The circle kept expanding until it passed over both me and the rift to my rear.

You have entered a purifying field. All environmental ill-effects have been nullified.

I turned around in a slow circle. The dome was about ten yards in diameter, and inside it the air had been entirely cleared of smog.

Moonshadow opened his eyes to rest them upon me. "So you came through after all," he said, sounding disappointed.

"Huh, didn't think you would," Barac added. He attempted to speak in a low voice but wasn't at all successful.

Ignoring the pair's comments, I turned to Simone. "Are we safe here?"

Barac snorted. "Of course not," he replied before the archer could, his words another dull rumble. "This place is infested."

"Shh, you big oaf," Jasiah hissed, nudging the crusader in the ribs. "Or you'll bring them down upon us."

The centaur muttered something under his breath, too low even for me to catch.

"Relax, Jasiah," Moonshadow said. "I've cast my net. There are no stygians within fifty yards," he said confidently.

Simone glanced at him. "Have you found the seed yet?"

"Still looking," the elf replied, his eyes half-lidded. He was scrying with his mage senses, I thought.

"Well, hurry up then," Simone said. Ignoring the glare the mage threw at her, she turned to me. "Until Moonshadow finds it, there's nothing for us to do but wait."

I frowned and gestured to the dome above us. "Is that a good idea though?" The spelled circle of purified air had to be a beacon to the stygian creatures in the region, and I felt vulnerable beneath it.

Simone smiled, if a bit grimly. "The dome exposes us, I know, but it's actually our best option in this scenario. It lets us keep an eye on the rift to detect if it's closing." She paused. "And it keeps our lines of sight clear in case we're attacked."

I nodded slowly. I understood her reasoning, even if the tactics they'd chosen weren't the ones I would have employed myself. I would've preferred to have skulked in the mists, poor visibility or no.

"Besides," Jasiah added, "stumbling through the mist is more dangerous."

I glanced at him. "But it isn't mist, is it? This stuff feels heavier and moves strangely. What is it?"

"What else? It's the dark miasma of the nether itself. You don't want to feel its touch while unprotected," he warned.

"Right," I muttered. My gaze flickered back to the party leader. "When Moonshadow finds the seed, what then?"

She eyed me for a moment in silent contemplation. "We don't have the numbers for a straight-up fight, and normally we'd wait for the knights' assistance before attempting this."

"I see," I said, my concern mounting that perhaps this venture wasn't as well thought out as I'd originally assumed. "What's the plan then?"

"You're a good sneak, aren't you?" Simone replied obliquely.

I folded my arms and stared at her, not sure I liked where this was going.

"You hid successfully from the mantis, no mean feat," the archer continued, ignoring my unhappiness. "If you managed that, you should be able to pull this off."

"The plan, Simone," I growled. "Tell me."

She shrugged. "You sneak into the stygian's lair, grab the seed, and hurry back."

I scowled at her in disbelief. "What about the rest of you?"

"We hold this point and create a distraction."

"So, you want me to venture into that—" I gestured to the swirling mists—"alone while the rest of you stay here safe?" I asked in a half-strangled voice.

"In essence, yes," Simone replied unapologetically.

My gaze drifted from her to the rest of the party. Jasiah wouldn't meet my eyes. Lost in the midst of his scrying, Moonshadow paid me no attention, while Barac only smirked in response.

From what I'd seen of the party, none of them were stealthy. Without me, their scheme—such as it was—wouldn't work. My suspicions hardened. "This was the plan all along, wasn't it? This is the only reason you invited me along?"

"Yes," was the unflinching response.

I bowed my head in disappointment. The party didn't consider me an equal member. I'd only been brought here to attempt a gamble—and a risky one by the sounds of it.

"Extra blade, eh?" I remarked bitterly. I wasn't that—far from it. I was a sacrificial lamb. A noob of no consequence.

Simone sighed. "Look, I admit what I'm asking you to do is dangerous. But I wouldn't have wasted our time and, more importantly, our resources if I didn't think you had a chance of pulling it off."

I said nothing.

"The truth is," Simone continued, "the five of us can't take on an entire stygian nest on our own. But the four of us may be able to hold off one long enough for you to retrieve the seed and return here. Believe me, in drawing the nest's attention, we'd be risking as much as you."

Not quite. The four would still have an easy line of retreat if things went sour. Me—not so much.

Still, the archer's arguments did assuage some of my doubts. *Maybe this can be done.*

"What if I die?" I asked eventually.

Barac laughed—quietly. "Don't," he said in a clipped tone. "This sector has no safe zone to resurrect you."

It took me a moment to digest that, and I finally understood their reluctance to leave the safety of the rift. Better to retreat through the portal and die on the other side than risk permanent death on this side.

That one little fact raised the stakes significantly though.

"Will you do it?" Jasiah asked softly.

I didn't answer immediately. My failed attempt at crossing over the safe zone wall and even my encounters with the mantises had driven home how under-leveled I was for the sector. Given my player rank, doing what the party requested would be a gamble. I'd be risking permanent death too.

But on the other hand, if I took no risks, I wouldn't go far in the Game. *No,* I thought, *the real question isn't that of risk but of confidence.*

Did I believe I could sneak into a lair of monsters and steal the prize they guarded?

I did.

Moonshadow opened his eyes. "Found it!" he pronounced in satisfaction. A moment later, his face crinkled in confusion as he sensed the tension around us. "What's going on?"

"Simone told him the plan," Barac replied laconically.

"Oh." The mage turned my way, a surprisingly sympathetic look in his gaze. "Not too keen on the idea, are you?"

Before I could respond, Simone tugged on the elf's arm. "Where is it?" she demanded.

Moonshadow pointed to his left. "Three hundred yards in that direction. There's a nest surrounding it." He paused. "A large one."

The party leader turned back to me. "Well, are you in?" She gestured to the rift at our rear. "If you're not, there's the exit. Time to decide."

"Fifty," I said.

"What?" Simone asked with a frown.

"I want fifty percent of the loot," I clarified.

Barac barked in laughter. "Nice try, noob, but no way."

I didn't glance at the centaur and kept my gaze fixed on Simone. "I'm the one who will be shouldering all the risk."

The party leader stared at me impassively. "Thirty percent."

Barac jerked in surprise. "Simone, you can't—"

The half-elf held up a hand, silencing him.

"Forty percent," I countered.

"No," Simone said flatly. "Thirty percent and not one iota more." I opened my mouth, but before I could speak she went on. "We need that much of the seed to meet our quota, or else all of this is for nothing."

I held her gaze for a moment, then conceded the point. "Alright, but I have a few other demands."

"Name them."

I raised the stygian blade still in my hand. "I get to keep this."

Simone glanced at Jasiah, and the duelist nodded. "Done," she said. "Go on."

"The seed stays with me until I get my share of the loot," I said. I was still uncertain what the seed was or its value in monetary terms, but I was betting there would be less chance of the party double-crossing me if I had the prize they seemed to want so keenly.

A frown flickered across Simone's face. She clearly didn't like the idea, but she didn't demur. "Acceptable."

"Lastly—" I began.

"Finally," Barac muttered.

Ignoring the interruption, I went on, "Lastly, I want two more of the nether protection crystals."

Simone's brows drew down in consternation. "Why?"

"If I'm going to hazard permanent death, I'm not going to risk rushing. I'll do this *carefully*. And if it takes longer than an hour, so be it."

Simone nodded slowly. "Alright. Is that all?"

"It is," I said, ignoring the sharpness of her tone.

"Then let's get started."

✳ ✳ ✳

Now that our course had been set, the party moved quickly.

Barac and Jasiah re-entered the rift, and when they returned I saw that they had piles of miscellaneous junk in tow. With Simone's help, the two began erecting makeshift defenses.

Moonshadow, meanwhile, pulled me aside and, in excruciating detail, described the lay of the land as revealed by his scrying efforts. After he was done, I was confident I would find my target. The mage went on to map out the layout of the stygian nest and the location of the seed.

"But what is it?" I asked, interrupting him when it appeared he wasn't going to address this crucial aspect.

Moonshadow frowned at me. "What is what?"

"The seed," I said. "I still don't even know how to recognize what I'm looking for!"

The elf grinned. "Oh, you'll recognize it when you see it. The seed looks much like the rift. It's a void of nothingness, only one condensed to the size of an egg. It's hard to miss."

I nodded.

"As for what the seeds are," Moonshadow went on, "that's less easy to answer. I doubt any except the stygian brotherhood knows the truth; they study the subject fanatically. As for the rest of us, many believe the seeds are birthed by the nether itself. Others that there is a great stygian monster swimming in the void, dropping seeds in its wake. Suffice it to say, the seeds are the means by which the nether spreads."

"Spread?" I asked, startled.

The mage nodded. "The seed has only begun to sprout, but once it's fully germinated, a void tree will be born, anchoring the ley line and creating a more stable conduit to the aether. And that's bad."

I was almost afraid to ask. "Why bad?"

"You saw how large the rift in Nexus was? That's nothing. Once the ley line is anchored, the rift's borders will begin to expand and swallow up the adjacent buildings. If left unattended, the rift will eventually consume the entire sector and claim it for the nether."

Seeing my horrified look, Moonshadow smiled. "Thankfully, the process isn't all that quick and can take weeks to months. Years, perhaps, for a sector as large as Nexus." His expression grew somber. "But it does make the rifts dangerous, especially for ordinary people."

"Why? What's different about them?"

Moonshadow shrugged. "No one is entirely sure, but for some reason players have a natural resistance to the nether, enough so that its effect on us are only fleeting. Once we leave it, we will suffer no ill effects from any nether toxins we may have inhaled."

He paused. "Not so for non-players. A single whiff is enough to afflict even the strongest of them with a debilitating illness that only the most powerful healers can cure. In the more remote regions of the Forever Kingdom, it isn't unusual for the rifts to wipe out entire sectors before help can arrive."

I shuddered.

"And that's why the Adjudicator rewards players well for closing them," Moonshadow finished heavily.

Before I could ask him what he meant by that, Simone walked up to join us. "Is he ready?"

Moonshadow nodded. "Almost. There's just one more thing." He turned to me. "Don't be alarmed, but the farther away you move from the rift, the denser the surrounding miasma will become. The nether toxicity will increase, but it shouldn't go beyond what your ward can handle."

I looked at him skeptically. "Shouldn't? What if it does?"

Moonshadow's expression turned bleak. "Then I suggest you don't dally out there." He turned back to Simone without giving me a chance to respond. "Now, he's ready."

"Good," Simone said and tossed a small object my way, which I instinctively caught.

This is a farspeaker bracelet. This item is 1 of 2 in a matched set of devices and will allow you to communicate through the aether with the other bearer while you both occupy the same sector. It has no minimum requirements to use.

"Put that on," Simone instructed.

I turned the object over in my hands, making no move to comply. "Who has the other one?"

Simone pulled down her left sleeve. "I do. The bracelet will let us coordinate from afar. Once you reach the nest, you give me the signal and we'll create a distraction. It should draw most of the nest out, leaving you free to nab the seed."

"Only most?" I asked.

Simone nodded grimly. "I'm afraid so. While your typical stygian possesses only the crudest intelligence, the beasts will never leave the seed entirely unguarded; their protective instincts regarding the damn thing are too deeply ingrained. You'll have to find a way of dealing with those that stay behind."

"Understood," I said. Slipping on the bracelet, I swung around to face the boundary of the purifying dome. The mists on the other side were thick, but with mindsight I was sure I could navigate their murky depths.

"Last thing before you leave," Moonshadow said.

I glanced over my shoulder at him. The mage was muttering the words of another spell under his breath.

"Mind, Strength, or Dexterity," the elf said. "I can buff one. Choose."

I pursed my lips in thought. "Mind," I decided. It was my most versatile attribute and the one I had the most abilities for. A moment later, I felt the weaves of a spell settle on me.

Moonshadow has cast mage's aid on you, increasing the effectiveness of all your Mind skills and abilities by 25% for the next hour.

"Thank you," I said gravely. The boost provided by the elf's spell was substantial and would come in handy. With a final wave at the party, I tiptoed into the mists.

✳   ✳   ✳

The moment I crossed the boundary of Moonshadow's spell, the smog enveloped me and visibility shrunk. Still, I could see well enough to navigate the route the mage had provided, and my other senses were unimpeded.

The terrain itself was mundane, a dried-out riverbed, and its very ordinariness made me wonder about the sector we were in. Had it at some stage been a Kingdom sector that had the misfortune of being swallowed by the nether?

Just as troubling was what it said about the Forever Kingdom. More and more I got the sense that this was a world in conflict, whether between new Powers and old, the aether and nether, or the Forces of Light, Dark, and Shadow themselves. Life in the Forever Kingdom seemed harsh, a constant struggle, and I could only imagine what my future held.

I banished my morose musings. I had a mission to complete, and this was no time to get philosophical. Giving my surroundings my full attention, I activated the stealth mode on my belt and faded from sight.

You are hidden.

Concealed in the mists, I continued my careful approach. According to the mage, the ravine I was following led directly to the stygian nest and the seed. When I judged I'd traversed nearly three hundred yards, I slowed my advance to a crawl.

If Moonshadow's information is correct, I should be coming up on the nest just about now.

Sure enough, a minute later my mindsight pinged. Ten yards away, at the very limit of the ability's range, two brightly burning consciousnesses had appeared.

I dropped into a crouch and, reaching out through mindsight, analyzed both targets.

The target is a level 115 stygian serpent.
The target is a level 113 two-headed stygian snake.
Stygian serpents are one of the most primal and ancient of nether creatures. Over eons, their evolutionary paths have diverged. But despite the many variants in existence—two-headed snakes, winged serpents, and hydras—all stygian serpents are renowned for the fearsome speed of their striking jaws and strong necrotic attacks.

I pursed my lips at the Game's response. Moonshadow hadn't been able to tell me anything about the nest's inhabitants—something about living creatures being harder to scry than terrain—but we'd anticipated the presence of serpents. The real question, though, was whether anything more dangerous lay deeper in the lair.

I would have to investigate further. But first I needed to report back. Focusing my thoughts on the bracelet around my wrist, I projected my words to Simone. *"I've reached the nest."*

Her response came back sharp and swift. *"What do you see?"*

"Not much. Just two rank eleven serpents."

"More snakes," Simone muttered, a tinge of revulsion in her voice. She paused. *"You're ready to begin?"*

"Not yet."

"Call me when you are then," she said and dropped off the communication link.

I turned back to the foes ahead. The mists were too thick for me to see them yet, and I was forced to observe them with only my mindsight.

While the pair didn't appear to be guarding the nest's entrance, they were most definitely blocking my path through the ravine. I'd have to find another way.

I glanced to my left. The slope there was steep but still scalable. The biggest challenge would be remaining undetected. Retreating a few yards, I began climbing.

✳ ✳ ✳

A few minutes later, I stood atop the bank bordering the ravine. The climb had been uneventful, if more difficult than I anticipated.

I took a moment to study the ground underfoot. It was just as barren as the riverbed itself, and traversing it would be no great hardship. Resuming my advance, I slipped soundlessly forward.

Two hostile entities have failed to detect you! You are hidden.

I paused at the Game message. The hostiles in question were the serpents in the ravine that lay just a few yards to my right. Staying frozen in place, I waited to see if the stygians would detect me. If my stealth wasn't up to the task of sneaking past the creatures, it was better I knew that before I penetrated the lair too deeply.

A minute went by and the snakes failed to sense me. Judging it safe to proceed, I crept forward. Only a few yards later, I stopped again. The fringes of my mindsight were crawling with more targets.

I had found the nest.

✳ ✳ ✳

It took only a moment to confirm the identity of the creatures ahead. All were stygian serpents between rank ten and twelve, and from the unhurried nature of their movements, they didn't appear particularly alert.

I crept forward.

Simone had instructed me to kick things off when I'd reached the nest, but before I gave the party the go-ahead I wanted to set eyes on the seed. Once things were in motion, time would be in short supply, and the success of the mission would depend heavily on how long it took me to complete my own part. I wanted that to be as quick as possible.

If that meant taking more risks upfront, so be it.

Multiple hostile entities have failed to detect you!
Multiple hostile entities have failed to detect you!

Multiple hostile entities have failed to detect you!

I paused again.

I'd reached the edge of a steep bank. Based on Moonshadow's information, I guessed I stood on the edges of the dead freshwater lake that the ravine fed into. According to the mage, the nest was in the lake itself.

At the bottom of the bank, a serpent slept fitfully. At least, I thought it was sleeping. Less than three yards separated me from the creature, and it was fully visible. The creature was no different from those we had fought on the streets of Nexus and seemed blissfully unaware of me.

I scanned the area with my mindsight. The next closest hostile was six yards to my right. *That's far enough to go unseen,* I thought and shadow blinked into the lake.

CHAPTER 185: DANGER FROM ABOVE

You have teleported into the shadow of a level 114 stygian serpent. A hostile entity has failed to detect you! You remain hidden.
Warning: the nether toxicity has increased to tier 3!

The sleeping snake didn't stir as I emerged beside it. Leaving it undisturbed, I crept away and deeper into the nest. The increase in the miasma concentration perturbed me, but there was little I could do about it, and it was still within manageable levels.

Hostiles surrounded me on all sides. Without an unobstructed view of the entire lair I couldn't accurately gauge their numbers, but if I had to guess, I would place them at more than one hundred.

Simone hadn't been lying. There was no way our small party could've taken on the entire nest.

The lair itself was characterized by oddly glistening ebony boulders and broken-off shards of the same material. According to Moonshadow, the boulders could be found in every known stygian nest and were assumed by many to be what gave birth to the nether creatures.

Up ahead, a trio of serpents slithered across my path. Drawing to a halt, I waited for them to pass.

Thankfully, the nest was large enough that its denizens were spread out, and as long as they continued to move languidly, mindsight gave me enough forewarning to weave a zigzag path through.

The snakes ahead disappeared into the mist, and I slunk onward, making for the center of the nest. It was there that I would find the seed.

"What's the hold-up? Why aren't you in position?"

Simone's voice, loud with impatience, broke my concentration and almost caused me to stumble. *"Shh,"* I murmured back. *"I can't talk right now."*

There was a moment of heavy silence. *"Where are you?"*

"In the nest," I replied curtly.

"What are you doing in there, you idiot!" Simone hissed angrily. *"Have you forgotten the plan? You're supposed to—"*

"I'll call when I'm ready," I replied and cut the link.

Simone could, of course, always reestablish communication, but I was betting she wouldn't once she thought matters through. Disturbing me would benefit no one, least of all her party.

Refocusing on my surroundings, I resumed my careful skulking.

✳ ✳ ✳

It took me another ten minutes to reach the center of the lair and catch my first glimpse of the seed. Moonshadow had been right; it *was* unmissable.

The seed was thirty yards ahead but burned with a darkness so dense that not even the mists could obscure it.

Unfortunately, the same couldn't be said of the creatures about it. From this far out, I could make out nothing of their numbers or levels. But I was sure the region was thick with stygians.

Focusing on the bracelet, I said, *"I've found it."*

"The seed?" Simone shot back.

Glancing around, I searched for somewhere to hide. *"Yes,"* I answered absently. Three yards to my right was a large boulder nearly twice my height. It wasn't much of a hiding place, but if I crouched down at its base...

"Well done. Are you ready to begin?"

"Give me a minute." Padding forward, I slipped into the boulder's shadow and braced my back against it. Then I uncorked the flask I held ready and gulped down its contents.

You have turned invisible, completely shielding yourself from sight. Duration: 60 seconds.

"Do it now," I instructed.

The response was instantaneous.

A guttural roar shattered the bleak quietness of the nether. Deafening, resounding, and savage. It was Barac, his already loud voice amplified tenfold by Moonshadow's magic.

The nest's denizens reacted exactly as predicted.

All around me, serpents stretched up tall and hissed angrily, only to drop down a moment later and slither toward the rift.

The call to arms had been sounded, and the challenge had been accepted.

Pressed up against the boulder, I ducked my head into my hands and curled into a ball. All I needed to do now was wait. With the boulder at my back, it was unlikely any of the beasts would stumble upon me.

A serpent slipped up the rear of the boulder.

Not daring to move, I didn't look up. A moment later, it dropped to the ground, landing three feet away.

A hostile entity has failed to detect you!

The invisibility potion did the trick, and I went undiscovered as the beast shot forward toward the ravine. *"The nest is on the move,"* I reported.

On my right a large group surged past, then three more on my left. They, too, fail to sense me.

Shortly, the trickle became a horde. A young hydra thundered across the ground to my left, more snakes slithered past on the right, and wings fluttered above me.

At the last, I looked up, sneaking a peek through my hands.

Serpents, half as huge as a full-grown wyvern, were propelling themselves ponderously through the air. I bit my lip in worry. Airborne foes weren't something we'd planned for. Reaching out with my will, I analyzed one of the creatures before it could disappear.

The target is a level 136 flying serpent.

"Simone, we have a problem..."

✳   ✳   ✳

"We'll handle it," the party leader said when I was done explaining.

I took a moment to digest her response. There was no doubt in her tone. *"You sure?"*

"I am." She paused. *"Against the numbers you've described, we can hold for... ten minutes, no more. Can you finish things on your end before that?"*

It was more time than I expected to have. *"I will,"* I replied just as firmly.

"Good. Simone out."

Closing down the communication link, I turned my attention outward again. The exodus was fully underway. With nothing else to do, I watched the beasts streaming past. Based on the direction they were heading, it seemed the crawling serpents were reacting as expected and using the ravine to reach the rift. Which was all to the good.

The plan called for the party to keep the nest's denizens bottled in the ravine. That would work well enough for the landbound horde, but not so much for the airborne ones.

Yet Simone had taken the news of the flying snakes better than I anticipated, and I wondered if I was still underestimating the party's abilities.

How the party expected to hold back the flying snakes I wasn't sure, but I couldn't afford to worry about that now. I had my own problems to deal with. The exodus had come to an end.

Not all the stygians had abandoned the lair though.

Even thirty yards from the seed, I could hear the angry hiss of the beasts that remained. From the sounds of it, they didn't intend to leave.

Bent in a half-crouch, I slunk closer. Ten yards out, my mindsight lit up. I kept advancing, wanting to get a firm handle on my foes' numbers. Six yards away, I stopped again and took count.

There were a dozen serpents guarding the seed.

Damnation. That was far more than I'd anticipated. Worse yet, Barac's roar had alerted the creatures, and I could feel them probing the mists attentively.

If I snuck closer, I was sure to be detected.

Remaining in position, I analyzed the beasts. The highest serpent was only rank twelve. However, *that* one had wrapped itself around the seed. I wasn't going to be able to blink in, grab it, and flee.

My lips turned down sourly. I had no choice but to deal with the seed's guards first. I didn't have much time either. The clock was ticking.

I scanned the terrain, but visibility was still poor and I saw nothing I could exploit. *I'll have to create my own advantage.* Coming to a decision, I retreated a few yards and searched around until I found a sizable boulder.

Then I got to work.

Tapping the blue rune on my trapper's wristband, I extracted the items I needed.

You have passed a thieving skill check! You have removed 8 trap-making crystals from your trapper's wristband. Remaining stored trap-making crystals: 20 of 40.

As the enchanted crystals fell into my waiting hands, I cast set trap. A moment later, my eyes and fingers thrummed with energy and I began preparing the killing ground.

Releasing the enchantment on the first crystal, I extracted a pressure plate trigger and extended it to its maximum length—some three yards. Carefully, I positioned it next to the boulder.

You have concealed a pressure plate.

Releasing the enchantments on the other trap-making crystals, I placed them too.

You have concealed 3 motion cones.

I'd positioned all three cones atop the boulder and angled them downward so that their fields of detection overlapped with that of the pressure plate.

My hope was that the traps would trigger simultaneously, transforming the area around the boulder into a maelstrom of destruction. Four traps were probably overkill, but I couldn't afford to be careless and chose to err on the side of caution.

Next, I seeded the area around the boulder with the trap elements—fire enchantments. Unfortunately, I had no way of predicting precisely what path the serpents would take once I initiated my ambush. All of this forced me to allow for a wide margin of error with the placement of the trap elements.

Lastly, I connected triggers and elements.

You have connected 4 trap elements to 3 motion cones and 1 pressure plate.

4 x Firebomb traps have been successfully configured!

Sitting back, I studied my handiwork. Everything was ready and good to go.

There was only one more thing to do: lure the serpents.

Chapter 186: Painting the Mists Red

I returned to my original observation point.

Crouched down on my haunches, I took a moment to watch the serpents. Their positions remained unchanged. *Right, let's get started.*

Readying my voice, I cast ventro.

"Yoohoo!" I yelled at the top of my voice, projecting the words to appear as if originating from the trapped boulder. "I'm over here!"

Twelve heads reared up. Staring at the ground to my left, the snakes hissed angrily but none moved.

"Come on, come and get me!" I roared.

The serpents stayed put.

Bleh. Looks like they need a bit more motivation. Using mindsight to locate a target, I cast simple charm and sent strands of psi reaching out to it.

A level 115 two-headed stygian snake has failed a mental resistance check! You have charmed your target for 10 seconds.

I smiled at the ease with which I overcame the creature's defenses. Unlike my previous charm attempts on the streets of Nexus, I'd succeeded on the first try this time. And it was Moonshadow's buff that had made all the difference.

Tugging on the mental leash I'd wrapped around my minion's mind, I commanded it toward the ambush spot. Obedient to my will, the charmed snake slid in the direction I indicated.

But none of the other serpents followed.

My hands tightened painfully around my weapons. *Damn, these snakes are stubborn.*

My improvised plan looked to be failing—spectacularly. There was only one more thing to do: play the bait myself. *So be it,* I thought and began to rise.

One of the seed guards uncoiled itself. Then another.

I sank back down to the ground in relief. *Finally!* Seeing their fellow race toward my supposed location, the other serpents were following in its wake.

I yelled further encouragement using ventro. "That's it! Come and get me!"

Predatory instincts stirred, overwhelming the creatures' more protective urges, and the trickle toward the trapped boulder became a stream.

The remaining time on my charm spell was passing quickly. Still, I ordered my minion to slow down a touch. It wouldn't do for the bespelled creature to trigger the ambush early.

Caught up in the frenzy of the hunt, the other serpents barely noticed and narrowed the gap in an impressively short amount of time.

Excellent, I thought, eyeing the mass of writhing snakes hurrying to their doom. My gaze slid back to the seed.

Not all the stygians had abandoned their post though.

Four remained, including the largest—still wrapped about the seed. *Four I can manage.* Drawing my blade, I rose into a half-crouch and waited.

A moment later, the ambush was sprung.

A stygian serpent has triggered a trap!
A stygian serpent has triggered a trap!
A stygian serpent has triggered a trap!
A stygian serpent has triggered a trap!

The ground shook, and the air burned as four explosions rocked the dried-out lakebed. Dense orange flames mushroomed outward, swallowing the eight blindly swarming serpents.

A stygian serpent has been killed.
A stygian serpent has been killed.
Your charmed minion has been killed.
A stygian serpent has been injured.
A stygian...

Game notices scrolled heedlessly through my vision, a testament to my ambush's success. While the serpents hadn't been as tightly grouped as I'd hoped, they'd all been caught in the killing ground, and none escaped unscathed.

I smiled grimly. The odds had swung in my favor. Turning back to the four stygians protecting the seed, I fixed my gaze on the largest serpent and cast again.

Waves of psi swamped the beast's mind, overwhelming its mental defenses, and in short order the creature was mine.

You have charmed a level 121 stygian serpent for 10 seconds.

"Attack," I breathed across the mental conduit linking us. Obediently, my minion uncoiled itself from the seed and lunged at its nearest companion.

The assaulted snake hissed in shock as the bespelled serpent's jaws clamped down on it. Flinging itself erect, the victim tried to escape, but my minion's teeth were sunk deep into its skin and it failed to free itself.

The remaining two serpents shrank back, their forked tongues hissing out in unmistakable warning to their battling fellows. It was the perfect opportunity for me to execute my next attack.

Blade in hand, I blinked into the shadow of one of the bystanders.

You have teleported 8 yards. You are still hidden. Warning: the nether toxicity has increased to tier 4!

With its malevolent gaze fixed on the battling duo, my target hadn't noticed my arrival at its rear. I didn't waste the opportunity and activated whirlwind, piercing strike, and crippling blow one after the other.

Then I struck.

Flowing forward, I plunged my stygian shortsword deep into the oblivious beast.

You have backstabbed a two-headed snake for 4x more damage. You have crippled your target's torso!

Sadly, the blow didn't prove fatal.

Still, the attack was devastating and the stygian shuddered, its head sagging lower. Moving faster than thought, I struck again.

You have critically injured your target. You have killed a two-headed snake!

The kill didn't go unnoticed.

Observing its fellow's death, the other unengaged serpent flew at me, jaws unhinged and ready to clamp down. But with whirlwind still empowering my limbs, my own limbs were faster.

Disdaining to dodge, I flung up my left hand and slapped the striking snake away.

You have stunned your target for 1 second.

Dazed senseless, the snake flew harmlessly past. But it didn't get far. The stygian blade in my right hand was already in motion, and before the creature could fly out of reach, I hacked off its head.

You have killed a level 110 stygian serpent with a fatal blow.

Backing away from the corpses, I chanced a quick glance around.

My minion and its foe remained locked in combat and coiled around each other. The ambush survivors, meanwhile, were slithering back, dragging themselves across the ground despite their wounds.

Knowing I was nearly out of time, I dashed to the seed. The object was a little larger than my hand. Bending down, I tugged it free.

Or tried to.

The seed was fused to the rock beneath it.

Damn it, I growled. It would take me more than the few seconds I had remaining to free the thing. Abandoning the seed, I swung around. I would have to deal with the remaining serpents before I could attend to it.

My gaze sweeping over the remaining hostiles, I formulated a hasty plan.

My bespelled minion was still the biggest threat on the battlefield, and the spell I'd woven around its mind was about to expire. Slipping further tendrils of will into its mind, I cast slaysight.

You have hidden your presence from your target for 10 seconds.

The second spell overcame the creature as easily as the first had, penetrating its already compromised defenses and blinding it to my presence.

A second later, my charm spell dissipated.

You have lost control over a level 121 stygian serpent.

Returned to its senses, my former minion tried to disentangle itself from its foe. The other snake, however, was having none of it and only coiled itself tighter about it.

The larger serpent thrashed violently—in a frenzy to get free. It couldn't see me, but the beast clearly realized something was wrong.

I smiled tightly. The slaysight spell hadn't been necessary, after all. Dismissing the dueling pair from consideration, my gaze slid to the returning snakes.

There were three of them, all bearing one injury or another. Focusing on the one I judged to be the greatest threat, I blinked into its shadow and buried my sword in the back of its head.

You have killed a stygian serpent.

The beast on my left snapped at me. Rolling under the blow, I bounced back to slash at its torso.

You have injured a stygian serpent.

Creeping up from behind me, the third snake lunged forward. Forewarned by my mindsight, I sidestepped the attack and pivoted on my heel to slap the surprised serpent across the side of the head.

You have stunned your target for 1 second.

For just a moment, the creature froze. Leaping onto it, I took my stygian blade into a two-handed grip and plunged it down to seal the beast's jaws forever.

You have killed a stygian serpent.

I swung back to face the last of the trio. Grievously injured, it was attempting to crawl away. Striding over to the beast, I stabbed it through the left eye without the least flicker of remorse.

You have killed a stygian serpent.

There were only two more serpents remaining.

Still embroiled in their own struggle, neither was paying me any heed. My former minion was losing and sagged listlessly in the second serpent's jaws. Soon it would be dead, leaving me to contend with the other.

Hanging back, I slammed my will into the smaller of the battling duo. The creature was no more able to resist me than its fellows had been and fell under my control.

Ordering my new minion to disengage, I blinked into the other's shadow and waited. Obediently, the bespelled serpent released its prey and slid back. The larger serpent swayed uncertainly, confused by its foe's abrupt withdrawal.

Raising the stygian shortsword high overhead, I brought it flashing down and through the injured serpent's neck.

You have killed a stygian serpent with a fatal blow.

One to go.

Dashing forward, I plunged my blade into the last snake, delivering it to the same fate as the others.

You have killed a stygian serpent with a fatal blow.

With a tired sigh, I sheathed my blade and surveyed the lakebed. The battle was over, and I had won.

My gaze dropped to the stygian seed. *Time to get what I came for.*

CHAPTER 187: A RUNNING BATTLE

In the end, retrieving the stygian seed didn't take as much effort as I feared. After a few solid blows from ebonheart, it broke free and fell into my waiting hands.

You have acquired a stygian seed. This is an artifact of unknown rank. You are unable to discern its properties.

"I have the seed," I reported through the farspeaker bracelet.

"Excellent! Now get it back here!" Simone replied, the words spilling out of her in a rush. She paused, then continued a touch more calmly, *"I may have been a bit optimistic about those ten minutes. Hurry, Michael."*

"Understood," I responded, sensing the urgency behind her words. *"I'm on my way."*

Securing the seed in my bag of holding, I dashed toward the same bank I'd first descended to get to the lake bed. I had no intention of traveling through the ravine and risking an encounter with more stygian creatures.

I scaled the bank easily and, dropping my head, ran flat-out across the rocky ground toward the rift. But I only managed half the distance when Simone contacted me again. *"Michael, you've got trouble incoming. The flying snakes have withdrawn. They must be heading your way."*

"Got it," I said grimly. The creatures must have sensed the seed's removal somehow. Skidding to a halt, I surveyed the surrounding terrain.

There were no handy boulders to hide behind, and besides, I couldn't afford to remain stationary. The only safe harbor was beyond the rift. Pulling the mists around me, I cloaked myself and kept moving, albeit at a more cautious pace.

Slipping softly across the hard-packed ground, I kept one hand on the still-sheathed stygian blade across my back and my head turned upward, listening intently.

It wasn't long before I heard what I searched for.

The flutter of approaching wings—three sets of them.

Multiple hostile entities have failed to detect you! You are hidden.

That was quick, I thought bleakly. How had they reached me so fast? It didn't matter though. I had to keep going.

I maintained my careful advance. My foes hadn't spotted me yet. *And with a little luck, maybe they won't find me at all.*

Three hostile entities have failed to detect you!
Three hostile entities have failed to detect you!

...

Moments later, the Game alert was still scrolling through my mind. But it only told me what my senses had already picked up on.

The stygians flying overhead hadn't passed me by.

Instead, they circled above my position, keeping pace with me. Somehow, despite failing to pierce my stealth, the flying snakes were still able to home in on my location.

My brows drew down. *How are they doing that?*

The three hovering creatures dropped lower. I realized they had to *know* where I was, if not precisely, then generally. I drew my blade. A fight seemed inevitable.

My ears pricked at a whistling rush of air and I froze, listening harder. Only two sets of wings were flapping now.

The third snake was diving.

I unfurled my mindsight and waited. A moment later, a bright consciousness crossed over the edge of my awareness, hurtling downward.

Remaining still, I tracked the descending creature. A heartbeat later, it struck the ground with a resounding thud—five yards in front of me.

A hostile entity has failed to detect you!

The beast had dived blindly, I realized.

The ground shook, but I kept my feet easily and watched the blurry figure through the mists. The snake was tasting the air, its forked tongue slipping out intermittently while it rotated its head clockwise.

When it faced my direction, the creature stilled abruptly.

A hostile entity has failed to detect you!

The knuckles of my hand whitened around the hilt of my blade, not at all comforted by the Game message. The creature had sniffed me out.

The snake slithered tentatively forward.

I grimaced. My stealth was affording me less protection than I'd anticipated. *I can't stay here,* I thought and began moving. Keeping my actions slow and smooth, I crept sideways.

A hostile entity has failed to detect you!

The grounded beast's forked tongue flickered out again, and its head shifted minutely to fix on me once more. The beast was tracking me. Not accurately or easily, but well enough to eventually locate me.

I kept moving, cutting a wide arc around the snake.

The air whistled again, and my head jerked up. I'd almost forgotten about my other two foes. Both were diving.

A heavy body thudded down and then another, the second snake landing on my right flank and the third on my left.

Damn it! The creatures had me neatly trapped. *That can't be by chance.*

Three hostile entities have failed to detect you!

I ignored the Game message. It meant little. All three snakes were slithering toward me now. In their soft hissing, I imagined I could sense predatory anticipation.

Slow and steady isn't working. Time to speed this up.

Picking up my pace, I charged the snake on my left. Almost instantly, my stealth broke.

Three hostile entities have detected you! You are no longer hidden.

The snakes darted forward the moment I was revealed—just as I expected. I let them come. An instant before the closest could strike, I shadow blinked.

You have teleported 4 yards.

I emerged behind the first serpent, out of the trio's trap and with the way to the rift clear. The snake I'd used to teleport whirled around, jaws snapping. But I was already gone, sprinting for the rift.

The stygians chased after, the closest two slithering across the ground in pursuit while the third creature winged aloft. I kept my attention fixed on that one—an attack from above would be harder to fend off.

After a few feet, the beast spread its wings to glide in my direction and begin an attack run. I clenched my jaw in frustration. Despite my head start, the snake had caught up swiftly.

The beast swooped and I zigzagged, barely evading its snapping jaws. The snake glided away, still airborne. It would only be a matter of time before it returned for a second attack, I realized.

The other two stygian snakes took to the air—no doubt to mirror their fellow's tactics.

Urgh. This wasn't going well.

"Michael, where are you?" Simone's voice barked out from the farspeaker bracelet.

"About a hundred yards from the rift. I have three flying snakes on my tail," I replied in a clipped tone. *"Can you help?"*

"No," she said heavily. *"We have our hands full here."* A drawn-out moment of silence. *"I'm sorry, Michael, but if you don't get here soon, we'll have to—"*

I cut the link, not bothering to listen to the rest of what she had to say. It was obvious, anyway. I was on my own.

The other two serpents, meanwhile, had begun their dives. I darted left, sidestepping the first, then rolled forward, dodging the second. But almost before I regained my feet, the third started its next attack.

I growled in frustration. Attempting to evade the swooping dives of the three snakes was another losing proposition. I'd barely made any headway toward the rift, and time was not on my side.

There was only one thing to do.

I skidded to a halt. The unexpected maneuver foiled the diving stygian's attack, and it overshot my position. Winging aloft, the creature began circling back once more. The other two were doing the same too.

Working fast, I unhooked my backpack. At best, I had a few seconds before the next attack. Digging into the pack, I found what I needed: my bag of holding. Opening it, I withdrew the stygian seed and tossed it to my left.

Then I dashed away in the opposite direction.

After I had covered ten yards, I skidded to a stop and spun around. Panting slightly and with blade in hand, I waited.

As I'd suspected, the attacks halted.

Paying me no heed, the three flying serpents landed near the seed and formed a defensive huddle about it. They hissed triumphantly, seeming to think they'd chased me off.

But I was far from done. Melting into the mists again, I cast my buffs and padded silently toward the trio.

Three hostile entities have failed to detect you!

It was time to do what I should have attempted from the start. Drawing on my psi, I sent searching tendrils of will into the mind of the closest snake.

A level 136 flying serpent has passed a mental resistance check! You have failed to charm your target. Your mental intrusion has gone undetected!

Shrugging off the failure, I tried again and sent more psi rippling toward the snake.

A flying serpent has failed a mental resistance check! You have charmed your target for 10 seconds.

Much better.

The charmed snake stopped hissing. Its fellows didn't notice. *"Attack!"* I bellowed through my mind link to my minion.

Contorting itself, the bespelled snake dug its fangs into one of its companions. The victim hissed in surprise but wasted no time in counterattacking in the same manner, and a heartbeat later both serpents were writhing across the ground, their bodies coiled tight about each other.

The third serpent remained by the seed. Ignoring its fellows' antics, the creature flared its wings in warning and hovered protectively over its charge. Fixing my attention on the beast, I cast again.

You have teleported into the shadow of a level 138 flying serpent. You are still hidden.

I'd chosen my re-entry point well and emerged unseen beneath the shadow of the snake's left wing. Taking my shortsword in a two-handed grip, I cast whirlwind and piercing strike.

Your attack speed has increased by 100% for 3 seconds.
You will deal double damage on your next attack.

Spelled energy rushed into my arms, redoubling their speed and power. Finally ready, I lunged upward.

You have backstabbed a stygian serpent for 4x more damage! You have critically injured your target.

At the bite of the blade, the stygian hissed in pain. Flaring its wings higher, it whipped its tail around.

Ignoring the incoming attack—completing my objective was more important—I one-stepped upward and kept slashing at the wing, striking thrice more in quick succession.

You have injured a flying serpent.

You have injured a flying serpent.
You have injured a flying serpent.
A flying serpent's left wing has been permanently damaged. You have crippled your target!

I smiled tightly as the Game message I'd been waiting for finally arrived. I'd done it. I'd crippled the snake. Stopping my attacks, I fell back to the ground—and straight into the onrushing tail.

A level 138 flying serpent has critically injured you!
You are bleeding internally. Ongoing damage sustained. Your health is at 40% and dropping.

I'd known the blow was coming but had accepted it as the price I had to pay to cripple my foe. Yet what I hadn't anticipated was the strength of the attack.

The serpent's tail crashed into my torso, compressing my ribcage and expelling the air out of me in a rush. But the damage didn't stop there.

Bones splintered under the force of the blow, puncturing organs. Blood rushed out of my arteries, rendering me weak and lightheaded. I wasn't allowed to regain my feet and recollect myself either. The striking tail flung me upward, propelling me through the air at a dizzying velocity.

Confused, disorientated, and with the edges of my vision blackening, I struggled to think. One thought shone clear through my battered thoughts though. The damage from the attack was mounting, and I needed to halt it. As if in confirmation, a Game message unfurled in my mind.

Warning! Your health is dangerously low at 15%.

Marshaling the tattered shreds of my will, I concentrated on the bracelet on my arm. In a heartbeat, soothing waves of energy rushed through my body, mending flesh and bone.

You have restored yourself with a full healing potion. Your health is now at 100%.

The fog around my mind cleared, and my thoughts snapped back into focus. Taking stock of my situation, I saw I was still tumbling through the air.

My charmed minion and the other snake remained locked in combat. Better yet, the crippled serpent stayed near the dropped seed, seemingly disinclined to pursue me.

A smile flickered across my face. It was time to regain my prize.

My gaze turned to the onrushing ground, and before I could crash I cast one-step, halting my rapid descent to land gracefully. Immediately, I took off running—toward my injured foe and the seed it protected.

The creature saw me coming but, cradling its injured wing, stayed where it was. As I drew nearer, its head darted forward. I ducked under the attack and thrust my sword upward into its lower jaw.

You have injured a flying serpent.

Feeling the touch of my blade, the beast hissed in anger and brought around its tail in a blistering arc, attempting to repeat its earlier attack.

I wasn't about to make the same mistake again though. Giving the attack my full attention, I leaped over the blow.

You have evaded a flying serpent's attack.

My eyes glinted in anticipation. I had the creature now. *Time to finish this.*

Rolling back onto my feet, I cast whirlwind and threw myself at the serpent again. Its head darted forward, but I sidestepped the blow as easily as I had the first and launched my own attack. Matching the snake for speed, I slashed out with my stygian sword and tore open the skin of its neck as it passed me by.

My foe shrieked and brought around its uninjured wing to batter me. But in the next instant I was gone, shadow blinking to its opposite flank, where I scored another line of red along its torso.

Bleeding profusely, the creature was slow in reacting to my rapid repositioning, leaving me free to follow up with another piercing attack.

You have critically injured your target. You have killed a flying serpent!

The dead beast sagged to the ground, and I leaped over it to retrieve the seed sitting unprotected at its rear. I spared a glance at the other two serpents. They were still engrossed in their own conflict.

Leaving them to it, I took off running toward the rift.

CHAPTER 188: FRUITS OF A DARK LABOR

Alas, the other two serpents didn't keep fighting.

Moments after I grabbed the seed and fled, the flying snakes disentangled themselves from each other and, taking to the air, gave chase. It seemed the threat of losing the seed was enough to spur them to set aside their own conflict.

Once aloft, both serpents' jaws yawned open to emit piercing whistles. At first I didn't understand the sounds' purpose, but when I heard a responding cry from the left—the direction in which the ravine lay—I realized they were calling to the rest of the nest.

Reinforcements were inbound.

I'm not going to make it, I realized. Not without some help, at least.

"Simone, you guys still here?" I panted.

"We are," she replied. *"The stygians aren't pressing us as hard anymore. I think they're retreating."*

If only.

I chuckled grimly. *"They're not. They're heading my way. The two flying serpents on my tail are drawing the others to my location."*

A pregnant pause. *"What happened to the third one?"*

"It's dead. Can I expect any aid?"

"We'll think of something," the archer replied. *"Just keep on your current heading."*

"Will do," I acknowledged. Saving my breath, I put my head down and ran flat out.

Unfortunately, it did me little good. The flying snakes were too fast to escape. I had covered less than twenty yards before the two caught up. From up high, the duo swooped down together.

Smart, I thought grudgingly.

Dodging both attacks would be near impossible. Tracking their approach by sound alone, I kept running. At the same time, I spun psi in preparation. The two plummeted fast. Holding my spell at the ready, I waited.

The first crossed the edges of my mindsight, no more than a fast-moving blur passing through my awareness.

I reacted instantly, shadow blinking.

You have teleported onto the back of a flying serpent.

The startled snake hissed and jerked around its head to nip at me. I was faster though. Before the creature could halfway complete its attack, I plunged my blade hilt-deep through its neck.

The snake shrieked and flipped over, trying to fling me off.

Obligingly, I let go.

In free fall, I kept my gaze locked on my foe. The creature's maneuver had left it stranded upside down and with no time to pull out of its dive. Even its incredible agility wouldn't save it now.

In a flurry of wings, the snake hurtled into the ground. I grinned as I heard the snap of fragile bones. The serpent had inflicted more damage on itself than I'd managed.

Momentum kept the crashed snake going, and it only narrowly escaped colliding with its fellow, which was forced to swerve left at the last minute.

A yard from the ground, I cast one-step and broke my own fall. I landed in a sprawl but was a little worse for wear. Not bothering to get up, I shadow blinked immediately.

You have teleported onto the back of a flying serpent.

I emerged in nearly the same position where I'd first landed on the snake. Activating one ability after another, I yanked out the still-embedded stygian blade and struck the dazed beast in a series of rapid-fire attacks.

You have cast whirlwind, increasing your attack speed by 100% for 3 seconds.
You have crippled your target's neck for 3 seconds.
You have struck your target for 2x more damage with a piercing strike.
You have critically injured your target.
You have killed a flying serpent.

I had little time to celebrate. Sensing a fast-approaching form from my rear, I rolled off the corpse and took shelter beneath its large wings.

The second flying snake rushed overhead, its jaws clamping on nothing but empty air. Thwarted, the beast winged aloft.

I plucked my bloodied sword free and took off running again. At the sounds of enraged hissing from my left, my gaze darted in that direction.

The stygian reinforcements had arrived.

A tightly grouped clump of a dozen serpents was slithering rapidly across the ground. Given their bearing and speed, they would intercept me well before I reached the rift.

"Damnit, Simone! Where are you people?"

There was no answer.

Clenching my jaw in frustration, I kept fleeing. Sooner or later my luck would run out, but I was out of options. There was no point in stopping to fight either; each delay only worsened my predicament.

The approaching stygians drew closer, and I readied my psi, picking out a likely target at the group's rear for shadow blink. The flying snake was rushing in for its next attack too.

It was going to be close.

The last serpent in the landbound group drew into range and I blinked, teleporting into its shadow.

The way to the rift was clear. Not looking back, I fled.

Behind me, I sensed the serpents slither to a halt and turn. I had no attention to spare them though. The flying snake was diving.

But I was out of tricks.

Shadow blink wasn't ready for recasting, and there was no time for anything else. Throwing myself forward in a halfhearted dodge, I squeezed my eyes shut, imagining the serpent's fangs digging deep into my exposed back.

Almost unnoticed, something whizzed past.

Simone has killed a flying snake with a fatal blow.

I could hardly believe the Game message. But it didn't stop me from acting. Rolling out of my dive, I bounced back to my feet and resumed sprinting.

Standing a few dozen yards in front of me—and miraculously unobscured by the nether's smog—were Simone and Moonshadow.

The archer was raising her bow again, and the mage... the mage was chanting.

Suspecting what was about to come, a bloodthirsty grin spread across my face.

Moonshadow has cast heaven's fury.

Three charged orbs of roiling energy emerged from the elf's hand to arc gracefully over me. *That'll do it,* I thought, laughing in anticipation.

Glancing over my shoulder, I watched the balls splash into the ground to create three expanding pools of lightning that neatly trapped my pursuers.

All the serpents were caught and writhed helplessly as destructive coils of energy crackled through them. A moment later, Game messages flooded my mind.

A level 115 stygian serpent has died.
A level 108 stygian serpent has died.
A level 113 stygian serpent has died.
...

The chase had come to an end.
About bloody time, I muttered and resumed my jog toward the rift.

✶   ✶   ✶

Simone and Moonshadow didn't wait for me.

Spinning around, they fled toward the rift. With their motion, whatever had been holding the smog at bay dissipated and the mists rolled back in to obscure them from sight.

Despite this, unhampered by pursuit, I quickly covered the remaining distance to the waiting party.

When I broke through Moonshadow's purifying circle—still in place around the rift—I skidded to a halt as I beheld the devastation the party had wreaked in my absence.

The entrance to the ravine was piled high with stygian corpses, but plenty more were still alive. A wall of roaring flames patrolled by Barac and Jasiah held those back though. Some serpents, more foolish than others, braved the fire but were summarily dispatched by the waiting Barac and Jasiah.

At my appearance, the pair retreated from the ravine mouth. "You have it?" Jasiah yelled.

I nodded. "In my backpack," I replied.

"Then let's go," Simone said. Spinning on her heels, the archer raced toward the rift.

The rest of us followed, and as one the party plunged through the curtain of shimmering nothingness.

✻   ✻   ✻

The moment I stepped out of the portal, an avalanche of Game messages scrolled through my vision. Ignoring them, I spun around to see how many serpents would follow us through. But I need not have bothered.

The rift was gone.

Dumbfounded, I stared at the space where it had hung.

From beside me, Jasiah chuckled wearily. "Check the Adjudicator's messages and you'll understand."

I did as he bid.

You have slain 16 / 20 stygian beasts required for bounty 674.

You have removed a stygian seed from the nether, disrupting the ley line it was forming to this sector.

A stygian seed has died.

A rift has been closed.

You have accomplished the feat: Rift Defender! Requirement: close your first rift. You have been awarded an additional life! Total lives: 3.

You have reached level 95!

Congratulations, Michael! You are now a rank 9 player.

Your dodging has increased to level 63. Your sneaking has increased to level 70. Your shortswords has increased to level 68. Your thieving has increased to level 45. Your light armor has increased to level 53.

Your chi has increased to level 54. Your telekinesis has increased to level 57.

Your insight has increased to level 66. Your deception has increased to level 62.

Your telepathy has increased to level 51 and has reached rank 5, allowing you to learn tier 2 abilities.

"Woah," I exclaimed softly, not sure if I was more amazed by the life I'd gained or the seven whole levels. *Damn, that was a profitable venture.*

"Your first rift I take it?" Moonshadow asked, coming up from the other side of me.

I nodded, still scanning the Game messages.

"I can still remember my first," the elf said musingly.

"You can?" Barac snorted. "That must have been at least a hundred years ago!"

The rest of the party chuckled, and the mage glared at the centaur in mock anger.

"So, does closing a rift always grant you a life?" I asked.

"If only that were true," Jasiah said glumly. "But the Game isn't that easy. The requirements for rift-related feats increase exponentially each time. You'll have to close nine more rifts before you can earn another life."

"Still," Moonshadow said. "Rift diving is always profitable."

"But dangerous," Jasiah added.

"That it is," Barac agreed with another laugh.

Laying a hand on my shoulder, Simone stopped me. The others, still laughing, kept walking. The maneuver felt pre-arranged, and I sensed the party leader wanted to chat with me alone.

What now? I wondered.

"You did well back there, Michael," the archer said. "Better than we could've asked, in fact." She sighed. "I fear I gambled too much on this venture, and I placed not just you, but the entire party, at risk. If not for your quick thinking..." She shook her head. "Anyway, for a moment there it was all touch and go."

I smiled, if a trifle bitterly. "Not bad for a noob, heh?"

Simone met my gaze unflinchingly, not looking away. "Don't judge me too harshly, Michael," she murmured. "Someday, you too may have to use others to achieve your goals."

I winced at her words; they struck deeper than she realized. I'd manipulated others in the past for my own ends—just as she'd used me. Exhaling heavily, I let go of my animosity. "What now?"

Simone glanced at me. "I don't suppose you'd trust us to sell the seed and deposit your share of the proceeds into your bank account?"

I smiled with no trace of humor.

Simone grinned. "Just as I thought. Then I guess we're heading to the citadel."

The citadel Simone spoke of was the Triumvirate castle in the center of the quarter. According to Jasiah, it was close by.

Once we set out, I turned my focus inward and saw to my player progression. I'd gained seven attribute points in the battle. Before spending them, I pondered over my performance in the rift.

I had done well in melee combat, and my thieving skills hadn't let me down either, but it was my Mind skills that had made all the difference. If not for charm, shadow blink, and slaysight, I wouldn't have been able to overcome foes so much higher-leveled than me.

What made them so effective? I wondered.

Part of it, I realized, was Moonshadow's buff and my Class trait, mental focus. Then, too, thanks to my Wolf scion trait my Mind attribute was higher than what I guessed to be normal. All three, working together, had let me achieve more than most players at my level could.

I pursed my lips. It was certainly food for thought and highlighted the benefits of specialization.

My gaze darted toward my companions. I would need to enter a dungeon soon, and it was unlikely I would find a strong party to accompany me. There would be no Moonshadow to buff me again or a dead-eyed archers to cover my back.

Perhaps, I reflected, *it's time to specialize*. Both my telepathy and chi had also reached rank two, making the idea of doubling down on my Mind skills more attractive, and I did just that.

Your Mind has increased to rank 48.

Refocusing on my surroundings, I noticed a commotion ahead. A large squad of players was approaching from farther up the street.

"Bloody knights," Barac snorted. "Always too late."

I studied the nearing figures more closely and, sure enough, realized that at least half were Triumvirate knights. Catching sight of our party, the two figures at the front of the group made a beeline for us.

"Who's holding the rift?" asked the first, an armored human knight with a jagged scar running down his cheek.

Before anyone could answer, the second—a mage, I thought—spoke up. "And what can you tell us about the emerging stygians?"

Jasiah smiled and spread his arms. "Gentlemen, the rift is closed."

The two players stared at him blankly.

"Impossible," Scarface spat. "The knight-captain dispatched only a single troop to deal with the menace. Us," he added, in case any of us mistook his meaning.

Jasiah's grin broadened. "*We* closed the rift."

I glanced at the duelist askance. Jasiah was toying with the pair, and I wasn't sure how wise that was, considering how large and well-equipped their group was. Still, Simone and the others seemed content to let Jasiah do the talking, and I didn't interfere.

"Then where is the seed?" Scarface growled.

"Safe," Jasiah said, his own face hardening. "And its location is no concern of yours."

The faces of the mage and knight tightened at Jasiah's curtness, but before they could say anything Simone intervened. "Relax, friends. You don't have to take our word for it." She pointed over her shoulder. "As I'm sure you know already, the rift opened somewhere back there. Go and have a look for yourself if you don't believe us."

The Triumvirate knight's look turned sour. "We will," he said and motioned his company forward.

✳   ✳   ✳

We waited for the column of players to pass us before continuing onward. The streets grew busier, but no one else accosted us, and eventually we reached our destination: the Triumvirate citadel.

Barac paused at the edge of a large square, and the rest of us drew up alongside him. The entrance to the citadel was on the opposite side, and a near-continuous stream of players flowed in and out of its open gates.

It seemed the castle itself was the hive at the center of the activity.

While the others stood idle, I studied the Triumvirate citadel. It was a veritable fortress consisting of a separate outer wall and an inner central keep.

Wall and keep were replete with ramparts and looming towers, and both boasted a heavy presence of patrolling knights. But despite the display of martial strength, the citadel's gates stood open.

It's been built to intimidate and protect, I thought. But protect against what? Stygian incursions?

"Everyone ready?" Simone asked.

I frowned, glancing at her. What was there to be ready for?

The archer pursed her lips as her gaze crossed mine, and she correctly interpreted my confusion. "You *do* have a ward of disease protection, don't you?"

I didn't.

I'd planned on purchasing some from the citadel itself, but before I could say so, Barac snorted in disdain. "Of course he doesn't. He is a bloody noob. I bet he doesn't even know why he needs to activate his disease protection *before* entering that bloody pile of stones."

He was right—*not* about me being a noob, but about not knowing why I needed one right now. Still, I ignored the centaur's caustic remarks and addressed Simone directly. "I don't."

The archer sighed and gestured to Moonshadow. Tugging a crystal off his belt, the elf tossed it my way.

You have acquired a crystal of rank 4 disease protection.

"That will protect you against the more common infections running rampant in the quarter," Jasiah said from beside me.

"Why do I need it?" I asked, voicing the question most on my mind. "I thought it was only in the saltmarsh that I had to worry about disease."

Barac crowed in vindication. "Told you! He's as ignorant as a day-one noob!"

I rolled my eyes but didn't retort.

Jasiah's eyes twinkled, but he too ignored the centaur as he explained, "You're right. The saltmarsh is the primary source of disease in the quarter. Unfortunately, it's not the only place you may contract an illness. Us players are the biggest carriers of plague in the quarter." He gestured to the fortress. "Outside of the safe zone, you won't find a larger concentration of players than in there. If you enter unprotected, you'll likely be diseased within the hour. And you don't want that, not if you can help it."

"Alright, lecture time is over," Simone said impatiently. She glanced at me. "Activate the enchantment already."

I did as she bade and broke the crystal in my hand.

You have activated a single-use enchantment, casting a ward of disease protection around yourself. For the next 4 hours, you will be shielded from tier 4 and lower infections.

"Right, let's go," Barac said. Without waiting for a response, he entered the square and made for the citadel's gates.

The rest of us followed on his heels. "Why are the knights in the plague quarter?" I asked no one in particular.

Simone glanced at me. "What do you mean?"

"I mean, they're tasked with protecting the safe zone, right? Why would the Triumvirate construct a fortress here?" I gestured to the castle ahead. "It seems a bit much to go to all that trouble just for the benefit of having a force ready to close the occasional rift."

Simone nodded. "True," she said. "But it's not only to fight off stygian incursions that the knights are here. They have other reasons for occupying the quarter."

Before I could inquire further as to what she meant, we neared the gate and joined the streams of people entering and leaving and, of necessity, the conversation lapsed.

Swiveling my head left and right, I studied the crowd. Most, I noticed, were players, and they almost all appeared to be in a hurry. Although many of the players were near the party's own level, few appeared nearly as well-equipped.

We passed through the gate without fuss and entered a large bailey full of merchant stalls and carts. While the courtyard wasn't as congested as the market square housing the global auction, it was certainly busy. Barac forged a path through the square, and most players got out of his way readily enough.

"So, which merchant should we approach to sell the seed?" I asked, yelling to be heard over the crowds.

"We won't be dealing with any of *these*," Jasiah said, gesturing disparagingly at the packed bailey. He pointed to the central keep. "The more prosperous traders are inside. Our contact is there too."

"Your contact?" I asked, realizing only then that the party was looking for someone in particular.

"There aren't many who can afford to deal in stygian reagents," the duelist replied offhandedly. "If we don't want to be ripped off, we have to approach the right trader."

"I still don't know what's so valuable about the reagents," I pointed out.

Jasiah shrugged. "Necrotic plasma, nether residue, and even the stygian seeds themselves are all used to make one thing: stygian powder."

"And what's that?" I asked.

Jasiah pointed to the blade on my back. "The powder is what's used to craft stygian artifacts like the shortsword you're wielding." He grinned. "In fact, most enchanted items require a pinch of stygian powder to make." He shrugged again. "But if you want to understand more of the process, ask Moonshadow."

The mage snorted. "How many times do I have to tell you, Jas? I'm no alchemist. I'm a damn mage."

The two began bickering, and I left them to it as I scanned the surroundings. By this point, we'd traversed the length of the square and had reached the doors to the central keep. A squad of knights was standing guard outside it and were turning away all the players who approached them.

This didn't faze Simone though. Strolling forward, the archer exchanged a few words with the sergeant-in-charge, and a moment later he drew back the doors to let us in.

I seem to have fallen in with a well-to-do bunch, I thought in bemusement as I followed the party inside.

Chapter 190: The Price of a Seed

We passed through the citadel's main doors and entered a foyer. An elegantly attired, if overweight, human stepped forward to greet us. By his garb, I marked him as a civilian.

Simone strolled across the checkered tiles of the foyer. "Constable Richter, it's good to see you again."

"Simone," Richter replied, opening his arms in welcome. "As always, it's a pleasure to have you and your party visiting with us. What can I do for you today?"

"Is Trexton in his room?" Simone asked.

The constable rolled his eyes. "When is he not?" His gaze drifted from the party leader to the rest of us. "Will you be staying long this time?"

Simone shook her head. "We're only here to see Trexton. Then we must hurry back to the Light quarter. We've business to attend to over there."

"As always, all work and no play," Richter said with a smile. "I won't keep you then." He paused, his gaze resting on me. "But who's this? Not one of your party, if recollection serves."

"He's not," Simone agreed. She hesitated for only a fraction of a second, then went on. "But he is a friend. I trust he will be welcome in the citadel?"

"If you vouch for him, then of course," the constable replied smoothly. His lively gaze roved over me as if fixing me in memory. "A mindstalker," he murmured. "How nice."

Before I could respond to that, Richter swung away in what was a clear dismissal.

The foyer had three doors leading further into the keep. Leaving the constable behind, Simone strolled purposefully through the middle one and into a carpeted passage.

"Thanks for vouching for me," I said grudgingly as I stepped up beside her.

She threw me a wry grin. "Don't make me regret it."

I nodded, but the archer had already turned away. We'd come to a fork in the passage, and without hesitation Simone turned down the left one. She seemed to know her way around well enough to navigate through the warren of corridors inside the keep.

I turned to the others. "So, I guess the knights don't let just anyone wander in here?" I asked, thinking of the exchange with the constable.

Jasiah shook his head. "Of course not," he replied. "Even we are restricted to the public sections of the keep."

I nodded and studied the rooms we passed through their open doors. Most appeared to be shops, offices, or workshops. On the left, I spied a smithy; on the right, a carpenter's store; and in the next corridor, a merchant's shop. All looked open for business, and players freely entered and exited.

I even spotted a familiar-looking, red-cloaked figure. Stopping short, I read the sign above the door's lintel: *"Kesh Emporium Outlet."* Marking the location of the shop in my mind, I hurried on after the others.

Eventually, Simone found the room she was looking for and strolled through its open door. I entered with the party, glancing at the sign at the entrance as I did. It read: *"Trexton. Herbalist Extraordinaire."*

There were no customers inside the shop and only a single dark-skinned elf behind one of the counters. That had to be Trexton.

"Simone!" the elf exclaimed as he stepped out from behind the counter. "Why am I not surprised to see you here?"

"What does that mean?" Simone asked as she pulled him into a hug. From the enthusiastic manner of the pair's greeting, I took them for old friends.

Trexton laughed. "Oh, I meant nothing by it. Only that the rumors of a new rift appearing aren't even an hour old, and here you are already. Are you and your friends planning on joining the rift dive?"

"Not exactly," Simone said, grinning broadly. "This time, we beat the knights to it. We've cleared the rift already."

"Ooow," the herbalist said, his eyes gleaming. "Then you're here to sell. Tell me what you have."

Pulling Trexton aside, Simone began a low-voiced conversation clearly not intended for the rest of us. I left them to it. From the sounds of it, the two were haggling amicably. While I waited for them to finish, I perused the store.

Trexton had a wealth of potions, ointments, and ingredients on display, including full health and mana potions that I assumed he'd made himself. *He certainly appears to be living up to his self-styled title of 'herbalist extraordinaire,'* I thought.

Eventually, Simone beckoned me over. "Michael, give him the seed."

Obligingly, I passed him the item. The dark elf turned it over in his hands, his excitement palpable. "Ah, this will do nicely," he crooned.

"Then it'll suffice?" Simone asked, more stiffly than I expected.

I looked at her curiously. I'd stopped paying attention to the pair's conversation, and it seemed I'd missed something of import.

"It will," Trexton replied, and Simone visibly relaxed.

"Excellent," the archer said. "Now, for the matter of payment."

"Two thousand gold, just as I promised," the herbalist said, holding out his keystone for Simone.

I whistled in appreciation. The stygian seeds were more valuable than I'd thought.

"Deposit one thousand, four hundred only," Simone said. She gestured to me. "The rest goes to him."

The pair completed their transaction, and Simone gestured to me. "Your turn."

Wordlessly, I placed my hand on Trexton's keystone, and a moment later the Game confirmed the transfer of funds into my account.

You have acquired 600 gold. Money remaining in your bank account: 1,341 gold, 4 silver, and 9 copper.

"Thank you," I murmured.

"You can sell your other stygian reagents to Trexton too," Simone said. "He won't cheat you," she added with a meaningful glance at the herbalist.

The dark elf chuckled and held out his palm. "May I?"

After a moment of silent deliberation, I handed over my alchemy stone and the herbalist extracted the ingredients. "Hmm, for this, I can give you... one hundred gold. Does that sound fair?"

I shrugged, having no idea of their actual value. "I'll trust you."

✳   ✳   ✳

You have lost 5 x lumps of necrotic plasma and 2 x vials of nether residue. You have acquired 100 gold.

After I and the others concluded our transactions with Trexton, we ducked out of his shop to gather in the corridor, where Simone wasted no time in addressing me. "This is where we part ways, Michael." She held out her hand. "Bracelet, please."

I nodded, having expected this moment, and handed over the item in question. "It's been... educational."

You have lost a farspeaker bracelet.

"Good luck in your travels," Simone said, smiling as she shook my hand. "If you ever find yourself in the Light quarter, look us up."

"Perhaps I will," I replied.

Jasiah stepped forward and clamped a hand down on my shoulder in farewell. "You can rest here for the night," he advised.

"I'll do that," I said. I hesitated, my gaze drifting across the group, wondering if I should ask the question on my mind. When it came to dungeons, I knew players didn't like to share what they knew, but some of the party—notably Moonshadow and Jasiah—had been more forthcoming with their knowledge than I expected, and I thought there was an even chance they'd answer me. "Before you all go, will you answer one question?"

"Go ahead," Simone said, waving permission.

"What do you know about the dungeons in this quarter?"

Barac snorted in laughter. "Goddamn, Michael. Your ambition is going to be the death of you!"

I waited, not saying anything—*his* response I'd expected. And at least the centaur was addressing me by my name now and not "noob."

The others looked amused too, but there was no mockery in Simone's gaze when she turned to me. "Do you have a party to tackle them with?"

I shook my head.

"Then I'd advise you to stay away until you do," she replied. "Dungeons are serious business. One misstep can mean *final* death for you—no matter how many lives you have remaining. Without players who you trust guarding your back, things can quickly go wrong."

I rubbed my chin. I knew better than to ignore her advice, but I needed to know how far it held true. "Does the same go for the public dungeons?"

"Those are cesspools," Moonshadow scoffed. "You're better off avoiding them."

All the others nodded in vigorous agreement, even Jasiah.

I frowned. "Why?"

"Because dungeons are all about risk versus reward," Moonshadow answered obliquely. "And the rewards in the public dungeons just don't justify the risk."

I wasn't sure I agreed. Even if I didn't gain any monetary rewards in the public dungeons, I still thought I could use them as a training ground to advance my player level and skills.

But I didn't bother arguing and returned to my original query. "So, are there no *other* dungeons in the plague quarter?" I persisted.

The party exchanged glances, seeming hesitant to answer, and when they did, it was Simone who fielded a response. "Dungeon locations are not freely shared, Michael," she said softly. "And normally I'd ignore the question." She held my gaze. "But you've done us a favor that has more than made up for your earlier mishap."

Barac snorted.

Ignoring him, Simone went on, "So I will tell you this. Excluding the public dungeons, there are three others in the quarter—that we know of, of course."

"Three, I breathed. "Where?"

"The first is here, right below your feet," Simone said.

My eyes widened. "Here?"

"Don't get too excited about that," Jasiah warned. "The entrance portal is in the keep's basement and heavily guarded. The Triumvirate *own* the dungeon, and its depths are reserved solely for their knights."

Simone nodded. "The dungeon is the real reason why the Triumvirate chose to build their citadel here, and it's one of the knights' most prized possessions. You will not gain access to it," she concluded with disheartening certainty.

I nodded slowly in understanding but probed for further information nonetheless. "How high-leveled is the dungeon?"

Simone shrugged. "From the little we know, the dungeon sectors within are suitable for a wide range of players. Knights of all ranks train here."

I stroked my chin. "I see. And the next dungeon?"

"That you will find at the stygian brotherhood chapterhouse," she said. "Like the knights, they've chosen to locate their group's main base at the dungeon's entrance. It, too, is heavily guarded and reserved for the exclusive use of brotherhood members."

I didn't let my disappointment show. Finding a suitable dungeon to enter seemed like it was going to be more of a challenge than I expected.

"And the last one?" I asked finally.

For a long moment, Simone didn't say anything. "That one I know little about. And truth be told, I'm not certain it even exists."

My curiosity was piqued. "Why's that?"

"We've never seen it," Simone admitted. "Nor has anyone who I trust visited it either. But the rumors of its existence are too persistent to shrug off as mere gossip."

"Where can I find it?" I asked eagerly.

"In the saltmarsh, on the very outskirts of the quarter," Moonshadow answered.

I frowned at him. "The marsh?"

The elf nodded. "If I were you, I would stay well away from there. The saltmarsh is disease-ridden and not with the run-of-the-mill variants you see in the rest of the quarter. If you venture into the marsh's depths, you'll be infected with high-tiered blights and plagues. Don't do it."

My frown deepened, but I said nothing.

"Moonshadow is right," Jasiah added. "No one is foolish enough to venture into the marshes." He paused, then added almost offhandedly, "Well, no one except for the werewolves that is."

A thrill of excitement shot through me at his words, and I struggled not to show my sudden interest. "There are werewolves in the marsh?" I asked as nonchalantly as I could.

At my question, Jasiah's eyes narrowed a touch. Clearly, I hadn't been as successful as I'd hoped in disguising my interest. "Yes, there are," he replied. "Only they have a strong enough Constitution to resist the diseases infecting the region."

"Damn shapeshifters," Barac muttered. "They can regenerate even faster than a bloody hydra."

Interesting, I thought.

"Well," Simone said. "We've told you all we know." She stuck out her hand again and I shook it.

"Goodbye, Michael," she said. Pivoting on her heel, she strolled away without further ado. The rest of the party exchanged their own farewells with me before following in her wake.

I watched them go, a faraway look in my eyes. As unexpected as the encounter with the party had been, I had learned much from them.

And they'd given me much to think about.

CHAPTER 191: RANKING UP

After the others disappeared from view, I followed in their footsteps, retracing my steps back to the room with Kesh's agent.

My wolf senses led me true, and after only a few missteps and wrong turns, I found the Kesh Emporium Outlet. The day was growing late, but the shop remained open. Peering inside, I saw there were no other customers.

"Hello," I greeted, approaching the red-cloaked figure sitting idle behind the desk in the room's center.

"Good afternoon," the figure replied automatically before looking up. She fell silent then as she took in my appearance. "I'm sorry, but this shop is reserved for—"

I flashed my emporium access card.

"—customers like you," she continued without skipping a beat. "How may I be of help today, sir?"

I smiled. "You're one of Kesh's agents?"

The cloaked woman nodded.

"How should I address you?" I asked, pulling out an empty chair to seat myself.

"Agent is adequate," she replied. She cocked her head to the side. "You're Michael, aren't you?"

In the act of sitting, I paused. "You've heard of me?"

The woman nodded. "Kesh sent word to expect you," she added with unmistakable curiosity.

I sat down. "I take it that's unusual?"

"Very," the agent said drily. "Kesh rarely troubles herself to deal directly with clients these days."

I rubbed my chin thoughtfully but didn't respond to her subtle prompt to fill in the details. I wasn't sure myself that I could explain Kesh's interest.

When it became apparent I wasn't going to reply, the agent asked, "What can I do for you?"

I withdrew the items I had marked for sale from my backpack. "For starters, I want to sell these."

Then I unequipped my trapper's wristband and potion bracelet. "And I need these recharged as well."

The agent studied the objects I'd spread out on the table. "I can give you four hundred gold for the blowpipe, punch daggers, and bull's ring. Will that do?"

I simply nodded in return, not inclined to either haggle or verify if the agent's price was a fair one.

"As for these," the agent said, picking up the wristband and bracelet, "recharging them is simple enough, but I'm afraid it can't be done here. The items will have to be sent back to the emporium for that. I can have them ready for you to collect tomorrow morning," she finished, looking at me questioningly.

"That should be fine," I said, having already decided to spend the night in the citadel.

"It will cost you one hundred and fifty gold," she warned.

I didn't even blink at the amount, growing used to spending large amounts of gold.

"Very well," the agent said, taking my silence for assent. "Is there anything else you need?"

"Yes," I replied. "I'm looking for these ability tomes," I said and rattled off a list.

The agent was silent for a minute before replying. "The emporium has the five books you mentioned in stock. Their total cost is one hundred and twenty-five gold."

I nodded, unsurprised at the tomes' relative cheapness. "I'll take all of them."

"Excellent," the agent replied, sounding pleased. "Which tier two charm spell variant do you wish me to supply?"

I frowned. "What do you mean, 'which?' Is there more than one option?"

"Of course. There are two variants of the tier two charm spell in stock: mass charm and advanced charm. The first allows you to apply the ability to multiple targets, while the second significantly increases the spell's duration on a single target."

"Hmm..." I mused uncertainly.

"You can buy and learn both," the agent said helpfully.

I was tempted. I really was, but while the monetary cost was negligible, the cost in ability slots was exorbitant. "No," I said regretfully. "I'll take only the mass charm tome."

She nodded. "Then, if you can place your hand on the keystone, I'll finalize the transaction."

I did as she asked, and a moment later the books I requested materialized on the table.

You have lost a blowpipe (exotic weapon), 2 x punch daggers (+3), and a bull's ring (+2 Strength).

You have acquired 400 gold.

You have acquired a minor lighten load ability tome. Governing attribute: Constitution. Tier: advanced. Cost: 25 gold. Requirement: rank 5 armor skill.

You have acquired a simple mass charm ability tome. Governing attribute: Mind. Tier: advanced. Cost: 25 gold. Requirement: rank 5 telepathy.

You have acquired a two-step ability tome. Governing attribute: Mind. Tier: advanced. Cost: 25 gold. Requirement: rank 5 telekinesis.

You have acquired simple reaction buff ability tome. Governing attribute: Mind. Tier: advanced. Cost: 25 gold. Requirement: rank 5 chi.

You have acquired a superior ventro ability tome. Governing attribute: Perception. Tier: advanced. Cost: 25 gold. Requirement: rank 5 deception.

"Thank you," I said. Storing the books in my bag of holding, I rose to my feet.

"It's been a pleasure doing business with you, Michael," the agent said and shook my hand.

"Likewise," I replied. I began to swing away, then paused. "One more thing. Do you know how I can get a room in the citadel?"

∗ ∗ ∗

It turned out it was Constable Richter himself who assigned rooms to guests. After I returned to the keep's entrance foyer and handed over the requisite four gold, I was led by a page to the room I'd been allocated.

Entering the simple stone chamber, I locked the door behind me. The room was on one of the upper levels, but the window was shuttered, letting little light in.

Turning a slow circle, I scanned the room. *It'll do*, I decided. The room was about as secure a location as I was going to find to sleep in—outside the safe zone itself, of course.

Setting my pack down on the only table, I extracted the ability tomes I had purchased and sat down to read them.

You have upgraded your lighten load ability to minor lighten load. This ability reduces the encumbrance from worn armor by 20%. It is an advanced ability and requires 4 more ability slots than its basic variant. You have 9 of 14 Constitution ability slots remaining.

You have upgraded your charm ability to simple mass charm. This spell temporarily overrides the consciousness of 5 targets, forcing them to serve the caster for 10 seconds.

You have upgraded your one-step ability to two-step. This ability allows you to take two steps in the air as if it were solid ground. You have 32 of 48 Mind ability slots remaining.

You have upgraded your reaction buff ability to simple reaction buff. This is a self-use ability that increases your Dexterity by +4 ranks for 20 minutes. You have 28 of 48 Mind ability slots remaining.

You have upgraded your ventro ability to superior ventro. This ability conceals the source of your voice, projecting it to anywhere within a 20-yard radius of yourself. You have 7 of 25 Perception ability slots remaining.

A little later, I leaned back in my chair, my head swimming with new knowledge. I was pleased with the result of my choices. Wary of the rising attribute cost of advanced abilities, I'd picked the ones to upgrade carefully, and already I felt better about facing the plague quarter's challenges.

Unfortunately, neither crippling blow nor stunning slap was an upgradeable ability. There were no higher-tiered variants of them. They were useful as they were nonetheless. But there was still one more ability I had to upgrade. Closing my eyes, I willed my intention to the Game.

You may advance your Class to rank 3 at this time.
Class points available: 3.

Do you wish to proceed?

I signaled my intent to proceed to the Adjudicator and selected slaysight for upgrading.

Commencing Class upgrade…

…

Upgrade complete. Class points remaining: 2.

Congratulations, Michael, your mindslayer Class has advanced to rank 3!

You have upgraded your slaysight ability to improved slaysight. The second tier of slaysight ability adds another mental manipulation to a mindslayer's arsenal: terrify. Additionally, the range and number of targets the spell can affect has also doubled.

With improved slaysight, you may terrify or cloak your presence from any 2 targets within a 20-yard radius for 10 seconds. This is a Class ability and does not occupy any ability slots.

"Ah," I breathed in quiet satisfaction. The spell had increased in range, effects, *and* the number of targets affected. *Handy*, I thought, rising from the chair to lie down on the bed.

The time had come to decide my next move.

Folding my arms behind my head, I closed my eyes and considered the past two days.

Since coming to Nexus, little had gone as I'd envisioned. I had made no headway, either with finding Ceruvax or gaining my third Class. Still, I *had* progressed in other ways.

My knowledge of the Game, and Nexus in particular, had improved vastly. I was far better equipped too. And even though the knowledge and gear had cost me the greater part of my accumulated wealth, I didn't regret their loss.

The money had been well spent—mostly.

Unfortunately, I'd made mistakes too.

My trust in Loken had been misplaced, *and* I'd underestimated the difficulties I'd face in the sector. Worse yet, I'd let my enemies find out I was in the city. It was unclear whether those who'd sent the mantises were old enemies or new. But either way, it didn't matter.

I was being hunted—and vigorously.

Yet, despite my many missteps, it was time I got back on track and focused on what was important. Getting rid of Loken's tracking spell was still beyond my reach, but with my two other goals—finding Ceruvax and obtaining my third Class—I thought I was better placed to make *some* progress.

And while I'm about it, I best see that I make enough money to keep at it too.

Obtaining a third Class seemed the most straightforward task. If I followed Ceruvax's advice—and at this point, I was determined to do so— the best place to acquire a master Class was in a dungeon. According to the Wolf envoy, the harder the dungeon, the better.

Fetching the map I'd bought from the information broker, I unrolled it on the bed.

Letting my eyes rove over the map, I picked out the three public dungeons: the scorching dunes, the haunted catacombs, and the guardian tower. Jasiah and the others had advised against entering them, but I couldn't afford to be as picky as their well-outfitted party.

If I ignored the public dungeons, my only choices were the Triumvirate dungeon beneath me, the brotherhood one at their chapterhouse, or the wild card—the mysterious dungeon in the saltmarsh.

But I wasn't about to underestimate the Nexus factions *again*.

I suspected that the dungeons belonging to knights and the brotherhood would be too well-guarded for me to gain access. The saltmarsh dungeon was also a non-starter. If even Simone's party was hesitant to enter the marsh, I was loath to try.

A public dungeon it is then.

Which to attempt though?

I frowned, puzzling over the question while I weighed the potential risks. Sadly, I didn't know enough about the three dungeons to answer the question in any meaningful way.

Why not enter all three then?

My brows drew down further as I considered this possibility. What was stopping me from doing so?

Nothing.

Well, nothing except the mantises. But given the capabilities of the assassins' hunter eyes, I had an idea of how to stay off their radar. And if I could hide from the mantises, then... there was no reason to hurry.

No reason at all... except to return to the valley and check on the wolves.

I sighed. Revisiting the valley, though, was dependent on getting rid of Loken's spell, and until I figured out how to do *that*, I could take my time exploring the dungeons one careful step at a time.

It was a startling thought and, given the frenetic pace of my days in the city thus far, one I had a difficult time accepting.

I'll do it, I decided. *I'll visit all three public dungeons.*

Even if none of them proved profitable, the experience would better prepare me for future dungeon dives. And admittedly, I was curious to see what the dungeons looked like. With my path decided, I lay back down on the bed and closed my eyes.

Tomorrow was a new day, and one I was looking forward to.

Chapter 192: A Note-worthy Occurrence

Eight hours later, I woke up rested and restored.

From the light filtering in between the gaps in the shuttered windows, I could see that the sky was just beginning to turn gray.

Dawn had arrived.

Rolling off the bed, I gathered my possessions, readied myself, and hurried out of the room. My first destination was Kesh's agent.

Even at this early hour, the keep's corridors were busy, and not unexpectedly, the doors to the emporium's offices were open. I ducked inside and found the red-cloaked figure seated at her table and reading a letter while she sipped from a steaming mug.

"Good morning, Michael," she said, setting down the parchment and rising to her feet. "Your items are ready and waiting."

Two objects materialized on the table.

I smiled, appreciating the efficiency of Kesh and her agents. Striding forward, I examined the items. Just as promised, my wristband and bracelet had fully charged, and I equipped both.

Your potion bracelet has been refilled with a full healing dose. Cost: 100 gold. Your trapper's wristband has been replenished with 10 traps. Cost: 50 gold.

The agent moved her hand back toward the letter, then paused as she caught my thoughtful expression. "Is there something else you need?"

I nodded. "Do you stock wards of disease protection?"

"Yes, of course. How many do you want?"

"Hmm... for now, I only require enough for one day."

"I have these," the agent said, laying down a familiar-looking object on the table.

This is a rank 4 disease protection crystal. Cost: 20 gold. Each crystal contains a single-use enchantment that grants you protection from tier 1 to tier 4 infections for 4 hours.

My brows rose slightly. The cost of the enchantment crystals was a bit steeper than I anticipated. Still, I couldn't do without them. "I'll take five."

"Easily done," she said.

"Out of curiosity," I asked idly. "How expensive are higher-ranked disease protection crystals?"

"A rank five one will cost you two hundred gold, and a rank six five hundred gold," she replied. "The cost escalates quickly after that."

I winced. It was just as expensive as I expected.

"If you think you may contract a disease of a higher level than rank four, you're better off using a cure disease potion instead of a ward. They're cheaper."

"Oh," I said, perking up in interest. "Do you have any?"

The agent shook her head. "Try the herbalist, Trexton. Do you know his shop?"

"I do."

"In that case, is there anything else I can help you with?"

"Yes," I said, then took a minute to gather my thoughts as I wondered how to describe what I needed to hide from the mantises.

I knew already that the hunter eyes tracked their targets by sight, sound, and scent. With my deception abilities, I could disguise both my appearance and voice. Scent, though, was trickier...

"I'm looking for some way to hide my smell," I said finally.

"Your... uh, smell?" the agent asked hesitantly and in a tone that made me sure her face was screwed up in confusion beneath her concealing hood. "Like a, uhm... perfume?"

A smile twitched at the corners of my mouth. "I don't think I've done a good job of explaining. But yes, perfume *should* work, if it's overpowering enough. I'm looking for anything that will make me smell different, really." I paused. "And that will last a whole day."

The agent pondered my request for a moment. "A perfume will be... inefficient," she said at last. She placed an object—another crystal—on the table. "This will work better, I think."

I frowned. I was unsure what use an enchantment crystal would be, but I inspected the item nonetheless.

This is a scent concealment crystal. Cost: 20 gold. Each crystal contains a single-use enchantment that completely masks your scent for four hours.

An involuntary bark of laughter escaped me. "Really?" I asked, lifting my gaze back to the agent. "Is there anything an enchantment crystal *won't* ward against?"

The agent laughed lightly, sharing in my amusement. "Very little." She paused. "So, will these suffice?"

I nodded. "They will. I'll take five of them as well," I said and touched her keystone to conclude the transaction.

You have acquired 5 x rank 4 disease protection crystals.
You have acquired 5 x scent concealment crystals.
Money remaining in your bank account: 1,366 gold, 4 silver, and 9 copper.

"Thank you," I said and turned to go.

"One second, please, Michael," the agent called out.

I swung back around to find her holding two pieces of paper. "Yes?"

"I spoke to Kesh yesterday. She asked me to give you this," the agent said, handing me the pages. They were from the letter I'd seen her reading earlier.

I frowned. The letter was for me? Reaching out, I took the pages and began to read. The first was a note from Kesh—short and to the point.

Michael,
*I've established contact with Saya, the tavernkeeper of the Sleepy Inn. She is
not very trusting. Read her letter and you'll understand what I mean.*
Kesh.

My interest quickened. Kesh had heard back from Saya! Hurriedly, I set
down the first page and scanned the second.

Dear Michael,
*I am glad to finally receive word from you—if this is really you, of course.
When weeks went by, and then months, and you still didn't return, I feared you
never would.*
Now I have hope again.
*It's been an eventful year, and much has happened that I must tell you about.
But given the... questionable manner in which you've reestablished contact, I
think you would be the first to advise caution. You're in Nexus and rich enough to
afford a factor?—I don't believe it!*
*You will understand—I hope—that before I can give your agent access to the
tavern's books, I need you to verify your identity. To that end, please answer the
following questions.*
Question one: why did Gelar kick me out?
Question two: what was the wyvern's mother's name?
Question three: where did you find me?

Yours truly,
Saya.

A broad grin split my face. Saya was proving to be an even better choice
for the tavern than I'd expected. Not only did I think her caution necessary,
I heartily approved of it!

Chuckling, I turned over the page and scribbled out my answers with the
pen the agent handed me. "Send this back to Kesh with my compliments," I
said when I was done.

The agent inclined her head. "I'll deliver it myself."

"Thank you."

Still smiling, I left the shop.

✳　✳　✳

I didn't exit the citadel immediately after that. Taking the agent's advice
to heart, I made my way to Trexton's shop. I didn't think I would run across
any potent diseases during the day's outing, but if I ventured into the
swamp, I might need one... In any case, it paid to be prepared.

I found the herbalist pottering around with his alchemy equipment. He
swung around when he noticed me. "Ah, an early morning customer.
Michael, wasn't it?"

I nodded.

"Was there something you forgot yesterday?" Trexton asked.

I shook my head. "No, but seeing as you are a herbalist, I was wondering if I could commission a few potions."

"Of course," Trexton replied. He studied me curiously. "What are you looking for?"

"Cure disease potions," I replied.

The herbalist smiled. "Those are easy. Given where we are, I always keep some in stock."

"I'm looking for something stronger than usual... a rank eight potion, maybe?"

He looked at me strangely. "You're not intending on visiting the saltmarsh, are you?"

I shrugged. "I may need to," I admitted. "I have a bounty to chase down there."

"A bounty in the saltmarsh? How curious," the herbalist mused. "But you won't need a rank eight potion. A rank six should suffice." He looked down his nose at me. "Can you pay?"

I nodded.

The herbalist withdrew something from his robe's inner pocket. "These should do."

I studied one of the items in his hands.

This is a rank 6 cure disease potion. It will treat any affliction, plague, or blight of tier 6 or lower.

"That looks like what I need," I said. "How much?"

"Two hundred and fifty gold. Each."

I didn't quibble. At half the price of an equivalent enchantment ward, the potions were the better buy. Mutely, I set my hand to Trexton's keystone, and he concluded the transaction with a smile.

You have lost 500 gold. You have acquired 2 x rank 6 cure disease potions.

"A pleasure doing business with you, Michael," Trexton murmured in farewell.

✳   ✳   ✳

After I left the herbalist's shop, I headed for the keep's exit. While I hurried through the corridors, I saw to my preparations for the day.

You have activated a disease protection crystal.
You have activated a scent concealment crystal.
You have cast facial disguise, assuming the visage of Jasiah. Duration: 1 hour.
You have activated the simple mode enchantment of the belt of the chameleon. Your armor and weapons are now hidden.

I'd chosen to conceal my identity with facial disguise instead of lesser imitate because the lesser imitate spell was susceptible to damage and would unravel if I was hit.

Facial disguise was a less complete illusion—it wouldn't change my body shape or alter my voice—but it *would* stay in place even if I was struck, and considering I planned on entering a dungeon, I couldn't afford my face to be revealed mid-fight.

Looking markedly different and hopefully unrecognizable by the mantises, or anyone else for that matter, I stepped into the keep's entrance foyer. Constable Richter was absent, and no one stopped me as I slipped out the main doors.

Despite the early hour, the citadel's bailey swarmed with players. My lips twisted. I'd been hoping to avoid the crowds. With a sigh of disappointment, I stepped into the courtyard.

Immediately, I was accosted.

Seeing me emerge from the keep and perhaps mistaking me for a richer player, vendors tried to flog their wares on me. Ducking my head, I shoved my way through the crowd.

It didn't deter the merchants though, some sticking with me all the way to the citadel's outer wall. But eventually I passed through the gates and my "escort" faded away.

Exhaling in relief, I headed northwest through the quarter—toward the scorching dunes dungeon. Of the three public dungeons, it was the easiest and, logically, my first destination.

The rest of the plague quarter was blissfully quiet, most of its residents still asleep. Enjoying the silence, I strolled through the streets.

My journey was uneventful, and with the gnomes' map I found the dungeon easily. Emerging out of the narrow streets, I stepped into a paved city square. The entrance to the scorching dune dungeon sat in its center, marked by two towering statues standing sentinel on either side of a portal of shimmering white.

To my disgust, though, the square was nearly as packed as the citadel's bailey had been. *So, this is where all the players in the quarter are,* I thought.

The portal itself was at the center of the chaos and was mobbed on all sides by a surging crowd—just as many entering the shimmering curtain as exiting it. My lips thinned in disappointment. If these many players were outside, the inside of the dungeon was likely overrun.

Still, I didn't turn away.

I'd come to see the dungeon, and even if it proved a wasted trip, I was going to do that.

Making sure all my belongings were firmly secured to my person—who knew how many pickpockets were running around—I joined the crowds.

The mob was rowdy.

Players shouted and hollered at one another. Some even plied goods and loot. No one attempted to maintain order or guide the press of bodies into and out of the dungeon. To get to the portal, I had to push and shove my way as I saw others around me doing.

It took some time, but eventually I reached the dungeon's entrance. While I waited for those ahead of me to enter, I glanced up, studying the giant marble statues that stood on either side of the portal and seemingly guarding it.

Whoever had carved the statues had managed to etch an astonishing level of detail in the stone. The human one had a falcon perched on his shoulder, and the elven one's hand rested on the head of a hunting cat.

I found the incorporation of the animals in the statues strange—it didn't seem something popular among the Powers—but before I could dwell much on it, the bodies before me disappeared.

It was my turn to enter the portal.

Before anyone could think to shove me aside, I darted forward and into the shimmering portal of white.

This nether portal is uncontrolled by any faction and may be used by any player.

Transfer through portal commencing...

...

...

Passage completed!

Leaving sector 1. Entering the Endless Dungeon.

Chapter 193: The First Cesspool

You have entered sector 101 of the Endless Dungeon.

This sector is part of a closed region named the Scorching Dunes. It consists of 1 unclaimable sector and 1 two-way portal.

There is no restriction on the number of players that may be in the Scorching Dunes at any one time. The dungeon is repopulated on a continuous basis and has a fast respawn rate.

Recommended player levels: 100 to 120.

Recommended party size: 1 to 4.

You have entered a safe zone.

Facial disguise dispelled. This spell cannot be maintained while within the bounds of a safe zone.

I emerged under a sky of startling orange.

The light was so harsh I had to narrow my eyes to slits to shield them from the glare. *Ouch, that's bright.* Ducking my head, I waited for my eyes to clear off the dancing afterimages that felt like they'd been burned onto my retinas.

Almost immediately, I was shoved from the rear.

"Damnit, man!" a voice growled from behind me. "What are you doing standing around at the portal?"

"Get out of the way, idiot!" another added. "Don't you know more players are incoming?"

"I'd listen to them," a third quipped, "or the Adjudicator may interpret your actions as hostile. This *is* a safe zone, you know."

The third speaker had a point, and I moved.

Keeping my head bowed—I hadn't missed the Game message about my spell dispelling—I forged a path through the press of bodies. The inside of the dungeon was as crowded as the outside, and a constant stream of players moved both toward and away from the gate.

It was chaos, but amicable chaos, given the safe zone restrictions.

As I weaved through the crowd, I risked the occasional look to orientate myself. Spotting a rise of land in the distance, I made my way toward it.

The ground underfoot was soft and grew softer with each step. Glancing downward, I saw the sand was loosely packed, dry, and lifeless.

I'm in a desert, I thought, finally recognizing the source of the dungeon's name.

I reached the base of the dune I'd been aiming for and climbed it, feet sinking deep into the soft sand with each step. I persevered, though, and finally I topped the rise.

You have left a safe zone.

The Game's message was a relief, and I wasted no time in recasting facial disguise. After my false visage was in place, I looked up.

The dungeon wasn't what I expected.

Instead of narrow corridors and countless rooms filled with enemies, the dungeon was one large open space. Standing atop the hill, I could see its entirety.

Behind me, in a dip formed by the encircling sand dunes, was the safe zone. The nether portal was at its center, nearly obscured by the players buzzing around it. But the crowd thinned rapidly the farther out one traveled in the safe zone, leaving me with plenty of breathing room at its edge.

Ahead of me and to my left and right were hills upon hills of rolling sand dunes.

There were monsters aplenty too.

Nearly every dune sported one, and more kept surfacing from the sand. Troubled by the possibility of a predator lurking underfoot, I unfurled my mindsight.

Strands of my will darted out, encompassing me in a bubble of awareness twenty yards in radius. Eight shining consciousnesses were within range. All were aboveground though and accounted for by nearby players. I relaxed minutely and turned back to the distant monsters.

They were all under attack.

As soon as a new dungeon denizen emerged from the sands, players mobbed it. My lips twisted unhappily, finally understanding why Moonshadow had labeled this place "a cesspool."

Despite the abundance of hostile life in the dungeon, there was almost nothing to fight. And given the hordes of players charging back and forth or throwing spells with abandon, the chances of me suffering "accidental" damage were high.

Worse yet, not every battle I witnessed was between players and monsters. I counted at least three different skirmishes between large groups of players—fighting over kills or loot chests.

It was a free-for-all.

Clearly, the plague quarter's "unwritten rules" *didn't* apply to its dungeons. I sighed, not at all eager to join in the madness.

But I've come all this way already. The least I can do is explore the dungeon more fully.

Readying myself, I cast my buffs.

You have cast reaction buff, increasing your Dexterity by +4 ranks for 20 minutes.

You have cast lighten load, reducing your total armor penalties to 0% for 20 minutes. Net effect: +3 Dexterity and +1 Magic.

The corners of my lips twitched upward. Despite my lack of enthusiasm for the dungeon, I couldn't help but be pleased by the performance of my upgraded buffs. Their effects were perceptible now.

Right, let's have at it, I thought.

Jumping down the ridge, I headed deeper into the dungeon.

✳   ✳   ✳

The sand shifted under my feet as I slid down the dune, but I was agile enough to maintain my balance. Other players, I noted, weren't faring so well in the terrain.

All around me, I saw mages slipping, archers stumbling, and fighters falling over—sometimes even while in the midst of battle. But none of their mishaps proved costly. Almost always, they were saved by their companions. What my fellow dungeoneers lacked in skill, they made up for with numbers.

Nearly every party had more than ten players—more than twice the Game-recommended size. Idly, I analyzed some of them.

The target is Wayne, a level 101 human sharpshooter.
The target is Lagar, a level 112 giant shieldbreaker.
The target is Nek, a level 103 saurian wizard.
The target is ...

The scorching dunes was clearly not the haunt of high-ranked players.

Nor the most skilled, I thought disparagingly, watching the antics of one particular party. Despite the overwhelming odds in their favor, the two dozen players were making a hash of battle against their solitary target. Skirting around the chaotic skirmish, I turned my attention to the dungeon denizens themselves.

They were uniformly large, menacing, and more interesting than my fellow players.

Most were giant scorpions—rust-colored and armored in chitin. Some were mammoth worms, with pale, translucent skin and teeth larger than my arms. There were even a few flying monstrosities—flying raptors, sleek and agile. Picking out targets at random, I analyzed the dungeon creatures.

The target is a level 140 giant rock scorpion.
The target is a level 130 sand worm.
The target is a level 145 desert raptor.

My interest quickened. The dungeon denizens would make for worthy adversaries and were sure to reward me with enough experience to make the trip here worthwhile.

I only needed to find one to fight.

Perhaps things will be quieter away from the safe zone, I thought and scanned the horizon.

At the very limit of my vision, I noticed a dark tinge. It was still too far away to make out clearly, but I suspected that whatever it was, it marked the limits of the dungeon. Fixing my gaze on the distant speck, I headed toward it.

A little later, my suspicions were confirmed, and the far-off smudge revealed itself to be a towering obsidian wall. It extended hundreds of feet into the sky—at one time both too tall and too smooth to scale.

Right, that has to be the edge of the dungeon.

It took me another ten minutes to reach the wall, and when I did, I couldn't resist running my hand along its polished black surface.

Immediately, a Game message blared in my mind.

This is the boundary of sector 101. The barrier protects the sector and its occupants from the dark miasma of the nether that lies on the other side. Warning: once the barrier is crossed, there is no way back. Re-entry into the dungeon from the nether is not permitted.

I dropped my hand hastily.

I'd had my fill of the nether already and didn't want to risk returning to it so soon. In fact, knowing the nether lay so close, I felt a strong desire to retreat. Stopping myself, I glanced around.

It appeared I wasn't the only one who was reluctant to remain near the wall. There were fewer players in the area than anywhere else in the dungeon.

Perfect.

Stalking clockwise along the barrier, I began hunting for my first kill.

✳   ✳   ✳

Five minutes later, I was still looking.

The hordes of players present elsewhere in the dungeon were absent around its rim, but so too, it seemed, were the dungeon's denizens. I kept searching, though, intent on completing a full circuit of the dungeon before I gave up.

The entire time, the sun beat down remorselessly, and its heat, I realized, was a real danger—the dungeon was truly scorching.

Pausing to rest, I took a sip of water from my flask. Then another.

Not too much, I warned myself. I hadn't thought to replenish my stores of water before entering the dungeon and would have to remember to do so next time—assuming I ever came back, of course. But for now, I needed to ration my intake. Reluctantly, I returned the water flask to my backpack.

That's when I saw the sand ahead of me swirl.

I paused. The air inside the dungeon was still, with not even an errant breeze to relieve the stifling heat. Was something hiding under the sand? Extending my mindsight, I probed the area.

Nothing.

The sands shifted again, sinking slightly.

Frowning, I strode closer to the disturbance. I was in a shallow dip formed by the dune to my right and the sector barrier to my left. Consequently, I was partially hidden from the rest of the dungeon's occupants.

If I'm lucky, maybe there is *a monster lurking under the sand—one I'll have all to myself.* I chuckled wryly. I was sure most people would find the thought passing strange.

But I was a player. And this was the Game.

Kneeling down, I removed my gloves and rested bare palms against the ground.

The sands vibrated minutely.

Something's definitely down there.

Whatever it was, it was likely far enough away to be beyond the range of my mindsight. Rising back to my feet, I re-equipped my gloves and drew my stygian blade.

I took one last look around. No one was nearby, but I doubted it would remain that way if a monster showed up. I shrugged. There was nothing I could do to stop other players from interfering except to kill the emerging creature quickly. *Time to do this,* I thought and stamped down with my foot.

The sands' movements grew more agitated.

I waited, hand tightening around the hilt of my blade, but nothing surfaced. *Let's try that again.* Jumping up, I stomped down again, harder and with both feet this time.

The ground trembled.

I smiled. *That did it.*

Chapter 194: A Stolen Kill

Stepping back, I dropped into a crouch.

The stygian sword was in my right hand, my buffs were cast, and my face was concealed by an illusion. I was as ready as I could be. For a moment I contemplated drawing ebonheart, but the blade was too distinctive and, in the crowded dungeon, would attract the wrong kind of attention.

A presence swam across the boundary of my mindsight.

My foe.

Reaching out with my will, I analyzed it.

The target is a level 128 giant rock scorpion.

My lips turned down. I would have preferred battling one of the giant worms. From what I'd seen of the other fights, it would've made for an easier foe.

Still, this was no time to get picky.

Blade at the ready, I began casting slaysight. Tendrils of my psi reached toward the scorpion rushing up through the earth, slipped past its mental defenses, and erased me from its mind.

A rock scorpion has failed a mental resistance check! You have hidden your presence from your target for 10 seconds.

A moment later, the creature burst free of the sand.

Remaining unmoving, I inspected the monster from less than a few feet away. It dwarfed me, a true behemoth. I didn't let that faze me though. I'd fought bigger.

The scorpion's face was flat, and its heavy pincers dragged along the ground. They were sure to pack a punch. Both the creature's mandibles and its clawed tail dripped with a thick viscous liquid. *Venom*, I thought with a shudder. Remembering the wyvern, I knew I couldn't afford to let myself be poisoned.

The counter on slaysight was running out. Still, I didn't move. Maintaining my predatory stillness, I waited for the perfect opportunity to strike.

The scorpion's head swung to the side—searching for whatever had disturbed its rest, no doubt.

Now, I thought.

Eyes fixed on the segment between the creature's head and thorax, I dashed forward. Two quick steps and I was in position. Raising my sword aloft, I gripped its hilt with both hands before whipping it downward in a deadly arc.

You have cast piercing strike. You have backstabbed a rock scorpion for 4x more damage!
You have critically injured your target.
Slaysight has dissipated.

With barely a hitch, the stygian blade pierced the scorpion's chitin armor to cut through nerves, tissue, and muscle.

Yellow ichor spurted free, hissing and steaming as it hit the ground.

Almost certain the spraying liquid was venomous, I leaped backward.

I dodged the scorpion's spilled blood easily, but before I could move into position to strike again, the beast responded with an attack of its own. With an eerie shriek that gave voice to its outrage, the scorpion brought its tail hurtling around.

I didn't stay to meet it.

You have teleported 9 feet.

I emerged from the aether atop the scorpion's head and attacked immediately, casting crippling blow as I plunged my sword downward.

A rock scorpion has passed a physical resistance check! You have failed to cripple your target.

My second attack was only half as successful as my first, but my blade still sank hilt-deep, tearing a second hole in the beast's armor.

My foe screamed again and both its pincers reached upward. Yanking my blade free, I somersaulted forward and down the creature's face.

You have evaded a rock scorpion's attacks.

Halfway down the scorpion's face, I surged upright, but almost as soon as I regained my feet I knew it was a mistake. Despite my agility, my boots struggled to find purchase on the slick surface of the creature's chitin plate armor.

Seeming to sense my sudden vulnerability, the scorpion wrenched back its head, leaving me stranded midair.

A moment later, the creature's head whipped back around, mandibles clicking as it tried to pluck me out of the air. Glimpsing the movement, I cast two-step.

The air solidified beneath my feet and I dashed forward, no longer falling.

You have evaded a rock scorpion's attack.

My abrupt change in vector caught my foe by surprise, and its jaws snapped close on nothing but air. I smiled grimly. I could almost taste the beast's frustration.

Landing lightly on the sand, I spun about to face my opponent. Sadly, despite bleeding profusely from the two holes punctured through its chitin, the creature still appeared to have plenty of fight left in it.

In an abrupt turn of motion, the scorpion spun around, its tail cutting through the air in a whistling arc. I threw myself down, barely avoiding the deadly tip.

Time I did something about that.

Casting shadow blink, I teleported onto the exposed back of the scorpion, near its tail, and slashed at the still-raised stinger.

You have cast whirlwind. You have injured a rock scorpion.

The scorpion was still spinning around, and the rapid motion threatened to fling me off. Dropping onto one knee, I slapped my empty left hand onto the beast's torso and cast stunning slap.

You have immobilized your target for 1 second.

My foe stilled with startling abruptness, but expecting it, I rode the sudden stop without falling off. *Now, I have it where I want it.* Keeping my left palm fixed in place, I hacked at the scorpion's tail with the blade in my right hand.

You have immobilized your target for 1 second.
You have injured a rock scorpion.
You have injured a rock scorpion.
You have immobilized your target for 1 second.
You have...

...

...

It took about as long as I anticipated and drained my psi to its dregs, but eventually I disabled the beast's stinger.

You have crippled a rock scorpion's tail!

Now to finish it.
Sliding down the scorpion, I circled around the crippled beast toward its head. The creature was still battling to regain its senses, and it was stumbling unsteadily. *This will be easy,* I thought, readying myself to attack.
The sky turned incandescent.
My head whipped to my left.
Standing atop the dune, in a long line spread across the ridgeline, were a group of players. It was they who were responsible for the light show. Their staffs, wands, and bows raised, the uninvited party was releasing a storm of magic on my foe.
Well, damn.

✻   ✻   ✻

Tightlipped, I watched the hail of descending projectiles.
The storm of magic was too dense for me to weather, and I was forced back. Grim-faced, I watched the projectiles splash into my half-dead foe.

A rock scorpion has been injured.
A rock scorpion has been injured.

...

The barrage failed to finish the scorpion. Still, by the end of it, the beast was visibly worse for wear. Gravely injured, the creature wavered unsteadily. I took a step forward, intending to slay the creature myself.
At a second burst of light on the horizon, I stopped.

The damnable players had unleashed another volley. I shot them an angry look. None so much as bothered to glance my way. In fact...

Not waiting for their second wave of attacks to land, the party was preparing a third assault!

I ground my teeth in frustration. *This is useless.* Sheathing my blade and turning my back on the scorpion, I stomped up the dune.

A giant rock scorpion has died.

Ignoring the Game message, I kept advancing. I shouldn't have bothered though. At the Adjudicator's words, the players broke ranks and descended the bank in a wave of their own, slipping and falling in their haste to get to the corpse—and the loot chest that had no doubt appeared.

My mouth opened, an outraged demand for the scavengers to stop on the tip of my tongue. Whooping and hollering, the players rushed past me, unheedingly. My hand flew to the hilt of my sheathed blade.

Almost, I drew it. Almost.

But prudence held me back. If I started a bloodbath here, it wouldn't end with this party. Others would come, drawn by the killings, and then—

Another Game message opened in my mind.

You have passed a mental resistance check! Multiple neutral entities have failed to pierce your disguise. Your deception has increased to level 63.

Eyeing the Game alert, I snorted in disdain. The encounter hadn't been a complete waste after all. If nothing else, it had confirmed my disguise would hold up to casual scrutiny.

Releasing my sword hilt, I resumed my climb up the dune. I didn't bother returning to the scorpion. The only way I was going to get my fair share of the loot was if I fought for it, and I wasn't about to risk that. Not for what was likely to be only a paltry sum.

Turning my focus inward, I scanned the other Game alerts awaiting my attention.

You have reached level 96!
Your dodging has increased to level 65. Your shortswords has increased to level 69. Your chi has increased to level 59. Your telekinesis has increased to level 58. Your telepathy has increased to level 52. Your insight has increased to level 67.

I sighed. I'd gained only a single level from the battle. No doubt that was thanks to the other players. The Adjudicator must have granted them a portion of the experience as well.

Coming here was a mistake. Time to leave.

CHAPTER 195: A SECOND UNWELCOME SURPRISE

"Hey you, hold up!"

In no mood to chatter with the fools who'd stolen my kill, I almost didn't look up. But the cry had come from up ahead, not behind me.

Glancing up, I saw that not all the players from the uninvited party had rushed to the scorpion's corpse. A smaller company remained atop the hill. A gnome there was hailing me, his arms swinging wildly as he tried to gain my attention.

My lips thinned. *Now, what does he want?* But I wasn't interested enough to find out. Lowering my head, I altered my course to avoid the players.

Unfortunately, my attempted evasion didn't work. After a whispered conversation among themselves, the entire group hurried down the dune on an intercept course.

"Stop, please!" the gnome called out as he drew closer. I didn't stop, but I *did* analyze him.

The target is Genmark, a level 125 gnomish ward architect.

My brows crinkled at the unusual-sounding Class. It still wasn't enough to make me want to talk to him though, and I angled away again.

The gnome didn't take the hint.

Drawing up alongside me, Genmark shot me curious glances. For a second I worried his intentions might be nefarious, but no, the rest of his group was hanging back. If they were going to attack, the players wouldn't send one of their own into easy range of my blade.

They might not mean me harm, but they're still scavs. But before I could decide how to get rid of the gnome, another Game message dropped into my mind.

You have passed a mental resistance check! Genmark has failed to analyze you.

My lips twitched in amusement at the gnome's failure. He had to realize I possessed deception—a skill most other players seemed to despise. *Maybe it'll be enough to scare him off.*

Sadly not.

"We caught the tail-end of your fight," Genmark said brightly. He paused, waiting for a response.

I looked resolutely ahead.

"You were quite impressive," Genmark said, forging on bravely. "I've never seen anyone take on a giant rock scorpion alone before. Weren't you scared?"

Ignoring the question, I sped up, leaving the smaller player behind.

But only for a moment.

Breaking out in a run, Genmark caught up with me again. *Whatever he wants, he's persistent, I'll give him that.*

"Look, I understand you're angry," the gnome panted. He gestured to the players gathered around the scorpion. "I tried to tell them not to steal your kill. But they wouldn't listen." He shrugged. "You know how players are sometimes."

"I do," I said, finally speaking. "So you would do well to leave me alone."

Even the thinly veiled threat didn't deter Genmark. "I have a proposition for you. Or at least my party does."

"Not interested," I said tersely.

"We're all ranged casters, you see," the gnome said, going on as if I hadn't spoken. "We can't take on any of the dungeon creatures ourselves, not without a melee fighter of our own. That's why we joined the group down there." He looked at me. "But if you join us... we wouldn't need them. We can tackle the monsters on our own."

"I'm no tank," I growled. "And like I said—not interested."

"Why not?" Genmark asked sincerely. "I can't tell your level, but if you're here you must need the experience, and I promise you you'll get a fair share of the loot. Even better, we can make it difficult for others to disrupt our hunts."

Although I found the last bit intriguing, I wasn't tempted. The quicker I got out of the dungeon, the better, and there was no way I was going to trust a random group of players. Reaching the top of the hill, I turned right, walking along the ridgeline.

Genmark kept following. "What can I do to convince you?"

He's not going to give up, I thought. *Not unless I make him.*

Jerking to a halt, I spun around to face the gnome. "Listen carefully, Genmark," I hissed. "I *will* not—"

I broke off, noticing a distant speck on the horizon.

I almost ignored it, thinking it was another desert raptor. But then my mind caught up with what my instincts were telling me: the far-off figure was too small to be one of the dungeon's flying monsters. Narrowing my gaze, I scrutinized the shape more closely.

It was small, round, and green.

A hunter eye.

The color drained from my face. Taking my sudden silence as a positive sign, Genmark began pleading his case again. Ignoring him, I slowly ran my gaze from left to right, scanning the dungeon. There was no way the hunter eye's appearance could be a coincidence.

Somewhere in the dungeon, there was a mantis.

Or two.

It didn't take me long enough to spot the pair of green-clad figures. Making no attempt to disguise their presence, the assassins stood sentry atop the dunes ringing the safe zone.

It was Wengulax and Gintalush.

I beat back the urge to retreat down the dune. *No need to panic—yet. They can't see me.* From where I stood, I could barely make out the two figures. And after our previous encounters, I was sure the mantises' senses weren't as sharp as mine.

My gaze flew back to the hunter eye. It was midway between me and the safe zone and seemed to be flying in a search pattern. Now that I looked more closely, I saw that it wasn't alone. There were other hunter eyes around, but unlike the first one I'd spotted, the rest remained in the safe zone, circling high overhead.

The assassins' strategy was becoming clear. The pair were using the screen of hunter eyes to supplement their own senses and guard the dungeon's exit portal.

Which meant they had to know for sure I was here.

But how?

Facial disguise hid my features, and the scent concealment crystal did the same for my smell. So if it wasn't by sight or smell, how had mantises tracked me from the knights' citadel?

I had no idea.

God dammit, I ground out. *Are they using some sort of spell to find me? Am I never going to escape these two? How do I—*

My internal monologue ran aground as I saw the hunter eye break off from its slow, careful drift through the dungeon and accelerate on a straight-line path... directly toward me.

I paled further. *Now, why has it done that?*

My eyes darted left and right, searching for somewhere to hide, but the dungeon's harsh light meant there were few shadows around.

Hiding would be all but impossible.

My gaze swung back to the hunter eye. It had slowed down and was moving more tentatively now, but it hadn't veered off course and, moment by moment, drew closer.

I gripped the hilt of my sword. *If I can't hide, then I'll fight,* I thought grimly.

The hunter eye sped up.

My eyes narrowed. It was almost as if... as if it had heard my mindvoice.

I stilled, a new and more startling thought occurring. Could the hunter eyes track my consciousness, seeing me the way I saw others with my mindsight?

It was certainly possible. Wasting no further time, I cast mind shield, wrapping my consciousness in steel-like protective bands of psi.

Your psi pool has been transformed into a mind shield. While the shield remains active, all your psi abilities are unavailable.

The moment my spell was completed, the hunter eye lurched to a halt.

It stayed like that, hanging motionless in the air for what felt like an eternity before eventually wandering off to resume its search pattern. I exhaled a slow, relieved breath. That had been too close.

"Are you even listening to me?" Genmark yelled suddenly. He'd been babbling at me all along, I noted absently.

"No," I replied, not even looking at him as I tracked the retreating hunter eye with my gaze.

Now that the immediate danger had passed, it occurred to me to wonder why this hunter eye was the *only* one searching the dungeon. Wouldn't the mantises have been better served by sending out all the hunter eyes to sweep the dungeon?

I scanned the dungeon's skies again but failed to spot any more of the mechanical devices outside the safe zone. I frowned, not sure what to make of it.

Just then, a raptor dived out of the clear blue sky to snap up the green orb I'd been watching, eating it in a single gulp.

I grinned. I had my answer.

In fact, as my gaze swept the crowded dungeon, I realized that despite the lack of shadows, the mantises wouldn't have an easy time finding me. In the dunes I was one among thousands, and as long as I *stayed* in the dunes, the odds of Wengulax and Gintalush finding me were low. The pair dare not leave the safe zone themselves. If they did that, I'd be able to sneak past.

Still, the mantises' tactics were effective. While they and their hunter eyes stood guard over the safe zone, I was trapped in the dungeon.

I swung back abruptly to Genmark. "I'll do it," I said.

He blinked in confusion. "Do what?"

"I'll join your party," I replied.

I might not be able to escape the dungeon undetected by the assassins, but I *could* wait them out.

✳   ✳   ✳

While Genmark and his group—ten players in all—readied themselves, I descended to the base of the dune again.

The scavs were long gone, having cleaned out the scorpion's corpse and loot chest already. Out of sight of the safe zone, I saw to my own preparations: renewing my disguise, meditating, and investing my new attribute point.

Your meditation has increased to level 73.
Your Mind has increased to rank 49.

When I was done, I joined my new party. "How do you want to do this?" I asked Genmark, ignoring the glances the rest of the group were throwing me.

"Let's find a monster spawn closer to the center of the—" he began.

"No," I said, cutting him off.

He looked at me curiously.

"It's better to stay here, around the edges where the crowds are sparser," I explained.

It wasn't the crowds I worried about, of course. It was the mantises. Gintalush had seen through my lesser imitate spell once and would probably be able to pierce my facial disguise illusion just as easily.

Then, there was also the analyze ability to worry about too.

If, by some misfortune, the mantises chose me out of the thousands of players in the dungeon to analyze, they would either uncover my identity or realize I was a deception player.

Neither outcome was desirable.

"Hmm, alright," Genmark replied. "There are spawns aplenty near the barrier too."

I inclined my head, grateful he'd not chosen to argue the point.

"Move out," the gnome called out to the group as he began to trace a slow circuit along the dungeon's outskirts. I kept pace beside him while the others followed in our wake.

"What should we call you?" Genmark asked suddenly.

I shot him a questioning look.

"None of us have been able to analyze you," Genmark explained. "And I don't want to shout 'hey, human!' every time I need you," he added with a grin. "So, what should we call you?"

"Uhm," I said, rubbing my chin in thought. "Mika will do."

"Mika it is," Genmark said, eyes twinkling.

The gnome obviously knew the name I'd given him was an alias. He didn't belabor the point though, and I turned back to the dunes ahead. They appeared empty, but I didn't trust to that.

The slain scorpion had appeared at the edges of my mindsight as if from nowhere, and if one monster could do that, then so could others. It got me wondering how the creatures spawned. "When will they run out?" I asked absently.

Genmark's face grew puzzled. "Run out?"

"The dungeon creatures, I mean. How many will we have to kill before the dungeon is cleared?"

"Ah," Genmark said, understanding dawning on his face. "This is your first time here, I take it?" He didn't wait for my response but went on, "The scorching dunes is different from other dungeons. It has no sector boss, *and* it produces an endless spawn of monsters."

Wondering if he was joking, I turned to stare at him. But there was no hint of a smile on the gnome's face. "Endless?" I asked disbelievingly.

Genmark nodded. "The Game notice when you entered the dungeon should have told you as much."

Now that Genmark mentioned it, I recalled mention of the dungeon spawn rate being defined as "continuous," but distracted by the heat and crowds, I hadn't given much thought to what it meant.

"It's what draws the crowds you know," the gnome added.

"Oh?"

"Truly. For lower-leveled players like ourselves—" Genmark waved his arms to take in his entire party— "the scorching dunes offers a sure means of advancing. Of course, it has its downsides too. For one, the loot is horrendous; for another, the dungeon's open design and continuous spawning nature make the risk of a party being overrun high. In fact, if not for the ever-present army of players that keep the monster population at a manageable level, this dungeon would be impossible." He chuckled. "So you see, we should all be grateful for the crowds."

I wasn't sure I agreed, but I took his point. "I guess. Still, if it weren't for—"

I broke off. Up ahead, something was wriggling free of the sand. "I think we've found our first prey," I said, gesturing to the disturbance.

Genmark squinted in the direction I pointed. "Well spotted! You have good eyes, Mika." Rubbing his hands together in glee, the gnome swung back to the party. "Alright, people, let's go bag a monster!"

Chapter 196: Eyes in the Sky

The sandworm went down easily.

Given the manner in which we'd met, I didn't expect Genmark's party to be any good. But they surprised me, and under the gnome's leadership, they seamlessly coordinated their attacks and spells with my own.

I ran circles around our prey, keeping it focused on me while the party assaulted it from afar. Throughout the fight, I kept one eye on my foe and the other on my allies, wary not so much of betrayal but of friendly fire.

The party surpassed my expectations though. Not once was I forced to dodge any of their own missiles, and in short order we killed the sandworm.

The rest of the morning passed quickly thereafter. Following Genmark's lead, our group traced a path of destruction around the dungeon's rim.

Finding monsters to fight was the easy part; securing the kills was more difficult. Genmark and two others in the group were crowd control specialists, and together they managed to fend off most of the encroaching players using spells of illusion, wards of keep-away, or magical obstacles. It didn't always work, but the trio turned back enough players to make dealing with the stragglers easier.

Genmark had been right about the rewards too.

Although each kill manifested a loot chest, the contents were disappointingly meager. Thankfully, the gnome's group was disciplined, and no one stole—not that I saw, anyway.

Genmark alone looted the chests and claimed all the alchemy reagents. The agreement among the group was that all the loot would be sold and the proceeds evenly divided. When the gnome had told me, I had merely shrugged in acceptance.

After all, it wasn't for the loot that I had joined them.

During our dungeon crawl I kept a close watch on the mantises, regularly surveilling them from afar. Every time, I found the assassins at their posts.

The pair sat atop the dunes bordering the safe zone with unnerving stillness and gave every impression of being content to remain that way— forever, if necessary. I did my best to not let myself be affected by their resolve, but despite myself, I was impressed.

The assassins possessed the patience of true predators.

Other players were likewise affected, and despite the thick crowds in the safe zone, a circle of emptiness surrounded each of the green-clad hunters.

Morning turned to afternoon, and I lost count of the number of creatures we killed. Sandworms, raptors, rock scorpions, and even a chimera—we slew them all.

I took frequent rests between fights. Genmark thought it was to restore my stamina, and I didn't dissuade him of the notion. In reality, it was to regain my lost psi and refresh my facial disguise.

I didn't, of course, use any psi in battle, but maintaining the shield around my mind drained my psi more quickly than any stamina I lost from combat. In fact, in nearly every skirmish I barely worked up a sweat.

Genmark's people did most of the damage, and I was rarely called upon to do more than land the occasional blow. I didn't even have to heal myself either. Each time I was injured, the party's two clerics restored me almost before I suffered any pain.

As a result, my player progression was glacial.

You have reached level 99!
Your Mind has increased to rank 52.

Despite the many battles, I gained only three levels over the course of the day. I suspected a large part of that was due to the number of players involved in every conflict. But there was another aspect to consider too.

Today wasn't the first time I'd fought in a group. However, it *was* the first time that my own contribution was minimal. In previous conflicts where I'd fought in a party, I'd done so almost *apart* from the party, picking my own targets and inflicting huge swaths of damage on them.

Not so this time.

But, while the experience I earned was negligible, the same couldn't be said for my skills. They improved steadily—the ones I chose to use anyway.

For the entire day, I fought one-handed and without spells, deliberately refraining from doing anything that would lead an observer to believe I was anything but a simple human fighter. As a result, my shortswords, dodging, and light armor skills all increased.

They weren't the only skills to improve though. Three others—meditation, insight, and deception—also advanced. Being in close proximity to others, with a concealed weapon *and* facial disguise cast about me, meant my deception was almost always in use. It didn't fail me, not even once. And, of course, I took every opportunity to analyze passing players.

All in all, it was proving to be an unexpectedly fruitful day.

✳ ✳ ✳

When the sun set—it turned out the dungeon's sky mirrored that of the city outside—it brought more good news.

The mantises had finally withdrawn.

Peeking over the crest of a dune, I breathed a sigh of relief. The two assassins no longer stood sentry over the safe zone, and their screen of hunter eyes was gone too.

About damn time, I thought.

I'd begun to fear the assassins would never leave. But even though I was eager to escape the dungeon, I made no move toward the safe zone.

Best to wait a while longer in case this is some sort of elaborate trap.

"Mika?" Genmark called. "Hey, Mika, you still with us?"

Belatedly I realized he was addressing me and turned around. "What?" I yelled back. The group was gathered at the bottom of the dune.

"Rest's over," he replied. "Time to find the next beastie."

"Coming," I said and rejoined them. Despite the darkening sky, Genmark's people showed no sign of wanting to quit the dungeon yet. *I'll stay as long as they do,* I decided. It would serve me better to leave the dungeon as part of a group instead of on my own.

And besides, while my skills are advancing, there's no reason to stop.

✻   ✻   ✻

It was close to midnight when Genmark finally called it quits. "Alright, everyone, let's round it up. Time to leave."

I nodded and dropped in line at the back of the group. Everyone was weary but satisfied. The day had gone better than anyone expected, and as we made our way to the exit portal, I tallied my gains from the dungeon.

Your dodging has increased to level 71. Your shortswords has increased to level 76. Your light armor has increased to level 61.

Your meditation has increased to level 79. Your insight has increased to level 78. Your deception has increased to level 73.

A smile stole onto my face. Despite my initial misgivings and the forced nature of my time in the dungeon, I'd emerged from it vastly improved.

Now, to get out of here safely.

When we reached the dunes bordering the safe zone, I dropped farther back from the group. No one noticed. Other than Genmark, the rest of the party remained tight-lipped, and over the course of the day, I'd barely exchanged more than a handful of words with anyone besides the gnome.

Almost there, I thought, lowering my head as we neared the invisible line separating the safe zone from the rest of the dungeon.

You have entered a safe zone. Facial disguise dispelled.

My face was hidden, and no one marked the sudden change in my features. Descending the dune, I was swallowed by the crowds. Despite the lateness of the hour, the area around the exit was still packed—which suited me just fine. Tracking Genmark's group with mindsight, I followed them to the nether portal.

We reached the exit, and the others passed through without looking back. I hesitated a touch and snuck a quick look around. No one was paying me the slightest heed. If an ambush awaited me, it was on the other side. *That, or my watchers are too good to give themselves away.*

Still, I couldn't delay any longer. Shoving through the press of bodies, I followed on the party's heels.

Transfer through portal commencing...

...

...

Passage completed!
Leaving sector 101. Entering the Forever Kingdom.

✻   ✻   ✻

You have left a safe zone.
You have entered sector 1 of the Forever Kingdom.

I emerged with my head still lowered and spinning psi, only looking up to scan the area after my facial disguise was in place.

The city square surrounding the dungeon was as full as when I'd entered the portal earlier in the day. I spotted no blur of green—either in the sky or within the crowds. Some of the tension in my shoulders eased. I was safe, for the moment anyway.

Escaping the mass of players gathered around the gate, I made my way to the east side of the square where Genmark's group had gathered, all the while darting furtive looks at the overlooking buildings.

But I saw nothing that warranted a second look or caused my senses to prickle, and the last of my worries faded.

"Mika," Genmark called, waving me forward as he spotted my false visage, "we were just discussing the loot distribution. Today turned out to be more profitable than I'd anticipated, and I'm afraid it's going to take more than a few hours to sell everything. Will a deposit into your bank account tomorrow suit you?"

It did not. Giving the gnome my bank details would reveal my identity.

"What's my share?" I asked, evading the question.

Genmark smiled, sensing my hesitancy. "If I had to guess? Fifty gold." He shrugged. "But that's a conservative estimate only. Until I sell the reagents and items we recovered, I can't say for sure what the final amount will be."

I rubbed my chin thoughtfully. That meant the party had made at least five hundred gold today. Not a small sum by any means. But if I had been alone, I doubted I could've slain so many of the dungeon denizens or as quickly. "I'll take my cut now if you have it," I said at last.

The gnome nodded. "I thought that would be your preference," he said, handing me a coin pouch.

You have acquired 50 gold.

"Thank you," I murmured with a smile. Genmark and his fellows were proving to be a better sort than I'd initially assumed. "Well, I guess this is—"

"Hold on one second," Genmark said, interrupting me. "The others and I have discussed the matter, and we'd like you to join us tomorrow."

My brows rose. "Tomorrow?"

Genmark nodded. "We intend on returning to the dungeon. You in?"

I pursed my lips, thinking it over. Revisiting the scorching dunes hadn't factored into my plans, but... but the day *had* been profitable, in skill gains alone if nothing else, and I *had* resolved to take matters slower.

I'd been intending on entering the haunted catacombs tomorrow, but would things be any different there? And in the scorching dunes I would at least be in the company of a group I'd already grown familiar with.

"Alright," I said finally. "I'm in."

Genmark grinned. "Excellent! In that case, we'll see you here at first light." He paused. "Unless you wish to lodge with us tonight...?"

I was tempted by the offer, but I couldn't keep facial disguise active while I slept, and letting them see my true face would invite too many unwelcome questions. "Sorry, can't. I have some of my own business to attend to tonight," I said, which was true enough.

"Suit yourself," Genmark said with a shrug. Shepherding his party away, he headed east, in the direction of the gate leading to the Dark quarter, I noted.

After scanning the surroundings one more time and finding myself reassuringly unwatched, I turned north toward the Nexus safe zone.

CHAPTER 197: GUEST RIGHTS

I slipped into the shadows at the first opportunity.

Nestled in darkness, I crept toward the safe zone's south gate. As I traveled, I reflected on the assassins and their ongoing hunt.

As disconcerting as I found the mantises' persistence, the day's events had given me a better grasp of their abilities. My precautions had defeated their hunter eyes. And while that reassured me, there was still the question of how the pair had known to look for me in the dungeon in the first place.

I hadn't told anyone where I was heading today, nor was it likely that the assassins had followed me from the citadel—otherwise, I was sure they would've ambushed me earlier.

Wengulax and Gintalush had obviously been tracking my consciousness. The hunter eyes had certainly been capable of sensing my unshielded mind, and it was no stretch to believe that the mantises could do the same over a much larger distance.

But if that was the case, why hadn't the assassins been able to pinpoint my precise location?

Could whatever spell the pair had been using not be accurate enough? Had it only given them my general position? Was that why they'd resorted to using the hunter eyes to locate me in the dungeon?

Makes sense, I mused.

Of course, there was another, simpler possibility: Loken had told them where I was.

The Shadow Power was the only one that I knew for certain was tracking me. But according to the bounty hunters' guild, the mantises only worked for the Dark, and despite what I'd recently learned of Loken's machinations, I couldn't see the Power attempting to kill me.

If he'd wanted me dead, Loken had ample opportunity to make certain of that in Erebus' dungeon. And besides, killing me seemed... entirely too mundane for him. Nothing with the trickster was ever that simple.

Me dead benefited the Shadow Power little.

But me *alive...* that was someone Loken could exploit to his own ends.

No, I concluded. *Loken and the mantises aren't working together.*

Still, I had to assume that wherever I went, my hunters would be able to locate me. And that meant... My steps slowed, and I came to a halt.

I can't go to the safe zone, I realized.

There was only one way in and out from there for me—the south gate. All the mantises would have to do was lie in wait at the gate's exit and follow me when I entered the plague quarter.

I grimaced. *Which is likely how they found me during my second day in the city.*

Swinging back around, I headed southeast. Until I dealt with the mantises, the safe zone was no longer a viable refuge.

I would have to find somewhere else to spend the night.

*   *   *

The best alternative to staying in the safe zone was spending the night in the Triumvirate citadel. Slinking through the darkened quarter, I reached the square bordering the keep without mishap.

Before leaving the shadows, I cast lesser imitate, wrapping myself in the illusion of an ordinary and forgettable human warrior.

I passed through the outer gates—still open at this late hour—and into the courtyard, but when I reached the steps leading up to the keep, I let the illusion drop.

The constable knew me as Michael, and I feared that if I approached as someone else I would be barred from entry. Sure enough, the moment I climbed the stairs, the gaze of the duty sergeant fixed on me. "Identify yourself!" he barked.

I paused. "Michael," I said.

My response did nothing to thaw the knight's frosty glare.

"I was here yesterday with Simone's party," I added helpfully. "Constable Richter will recognize me." At least, I hoped he would.

My words had the desired effect, and the knight-sergeant turned back to mumble something to someone on the other side of the door.

After the return message, I was let in.

"Ah, the mindstalker," the constable said as I stepped into the entrance foyer. "Welcome. Looking for a room again?"

I nodded.

"How many nights will you be staying with us this time?"

I hesitated.

Sensing my uncertainty, Richter added, "If your stay extends beyond a single night, you can keep the room key. It alone will suffice to gain you entrance into the castle—" he looked me over—"no matter the manner of your appearance."

I eyed him carefully, not missing his meaning. The constable, I was sure suddenly, already knew I could disguise my form. Was it a guess based on my Class? Or had Richter somehow observed me wearing an illusion earlier?

However he'd figured it out, the constable's words served to convince me. "Alright, I'll take a room for three nights."

Wordlessly, Richter held out a key. I took the item and paid the required fee.

You have lost 12 gold.

You have acquired a Triumvirate citadel room key. This item cannot be stolen, traded, or lost, even upon death. After three days have passed, this item will automatically be returned to the issuing authority.

My eyebrows rose at the Adjudicator's message. This wasn't the same key I'd been given during my previous one-night stay and seemed to be far more than a simple room key.

Seeing my expression, Richter smiled. "The Triumvirate takes its obligation to its guests seriously." He jerked his chin toward the key. "That marks you as a temporary resident of the citadel. You can sleep easy knowing

that for the duration of your stay, you will be officially under the knights'
protection."

"Well, that's... uhm, nice," I said, not knowing what else to say.

The constable waved his hand, accepting my thanks as no more than his
due. "Of course. Now, I believe you know your way to the room?"

I nodded and, without further conversation, strode away.

✳   ✳   ✳

Before turning in for the night, I had one stop to make.

Hurrying through the citadel, I made my way to the Kesh Emporium
Outlet. I needed to stock up on my wards. During my time in the scorching
dunes, I'd employed four scent and four disease protection crystals, and I
expected to do much the same tomorrow.

Considering the price of the crystals, I realized that I'd ended the day at a
loss. I'd spent eight wards—valued at one hundred and sixty gold—and in
return gained only fifty gold. From a purely monetary perspective, the day
hadn't served me well, but that was alright. The skills I'd improved on more
than made up for that lack, and I was confident that after a few more days, I
could turn around the equation and start earning real money.

Once again, I found the emporium offices empty but for Kesh's agent. The
red-cloaked woman was in nearly the exact same position I'd left her in the
morning. *Does she never sleep?* I wondered.

"Welcome back, Michael," the agent said, greeting me warmly.

I inclined my head in response.

"Have you come to inquire about your correspondence?" she asked. "I
handed over your letter to Kesh this morning, and she promised she would
see it delivered to your tavernkeeper soon."

"Ah, that's good. Thanks," I replied. "But no. I actually came here for
another reason. I need to stock up on disease protection and scent
concealment crystals again," I said, getting right to it.

"Of course," the agent replied. "You wish to purchase another lot of
five?"

I nodded, and we concluded the exchange without fuss.

You have acquired 5 x rank 4 disease protection crystals.
You have acquired 5 x scent concealment crystals.
Money remaining in your bank account: 666 gold, 4 silver, and 9 copper.

"Is there anything else?" the agent asked.

I began to shake my head, then stopped. "You know... I still don't know
your name," I said.

It was more than idle curiosity that sparked my statement. This was the
third time I'd dealt with the agent—despite not having seen her face, I was
sure it was the same woman I'd spoken to on all three occasions—and I felt
I was beginning to get to know her.

But I realized I wasn't. Not really.

I didn't know the agent's name or what she looked like. Even her scent was masked. Her voice and mannerisms were the only means I had of identifying her.

Caught by surprise, the agent hadn't responded to my question yet. "I've none to give," she said finally. "While I wear the garb of the emporium and act as Kesh's factor, I must remain nameless."

I nodded, having suspected as much already. "That's to keep your identity secret, I presume." I paused. "But why go to such lengths?"

"I'm sure you know by now that Kesh has sworn to protect the anonymity of her customers under the auspices of a Pact?"

I nodded.

"Then you know the why of it already," she replied, the smile evident in her voice. "We conceal our identity to prevent anyone from forcibly attempting to extract information from us when not on duty."

I frowned. "But what about when you *are* on duty? What's stopping me from attacking you now?"

The agent laughed gently. "I'd caution you against trying. The consequences will be quite... severe." She gestured downward. "My robe protects me."

I blinked. "Your robe?"

"It is a high-tiered artifact crafted by one of the Triumvirate Powers. The robe both conceals my identity and protects me from attack." She paused. "*Any* attack."

It took me a moment to catch her meaning. "What, you mean it's proof against Powers too?" I asked half-incredulously.

"It is," she confirmed.

"Well, isn't that something," I murmured. Kesh had gone to greater lengths than I'd realized to keep her secrets. I glanced at the agent again. "Can I analyze you?"

"You can try," she said, amusement coursing through her voice again.

Gathering my will, I reached out and, for the first time, attempted to analyze the agent.

You cannot analyze your target! This entity is immune to this ability!

The Adjudicator's message added further weight to the agent's words, and I found myself believing the rest of what she'd said. I thought for a second further, then asked, "What about Kesh?"

"Kesh?"

"She doesn't wear a robe," I said. "Why not?"

"Ah," the agent said. "Kesh never leaves the Nexus safe zone. Ever. It's part of the price she's been made to pay for her bargain with the Triumvirate."

I nodded thoughtfully. "Thank you," I said and spun about to leave. Midway, I paused and swung back around.

"Cara," I said abruptly.

I could sense the agent's sudden confusion.

"That's what I'd like to call you. If it's not too presumptuous, of course. 'Agent' is just so... formal." I stared into her hood. "Can I call you that?"

The agent was silent for so long that I thought she wouldn't answer. "Cara will do," she said at last.

I smiled and, waving farewell, headed to my room for a well-deserved night of rest.

Day Four

Six hours later, I was up again.

Rising quickly, I exited my room, sealing the door behind me. The first rays of sunlight had appeared on the horizon, and I had to hurry if I wanted to join Genmark and his fellows before they entered the dungeon.

I dashed through the citadel's corridors, my mind full of plans for the day. Yesterday's skill gains had been particularly pleasing, yet they had transpired less by design and more by happenstance, and I was sure I could find ways to advance my skills even further today. I was still toying with the notions of how to go about it when a dull rumble echoed through the corridors.

What's that?

Pausing in my steps, I cocked my head to the side and listened intently. It sounded like the tramp of heavy feet and was coming from a passage I'd just passed. Keen to find out what was going on, I backpedaled and peered down the corridor in question.

A troop of Triumvirate knights marched by.

They were armed and armored for war. Wearing heavy plate mail, with their visors closed and clenching bared weapons, the twenty-odd knights looked ready to do battle. One player's helm creaked in my direction, but the procession didn't stop as they jogged down the corridor.

My brows furrowed. The troop were the first knights I'd seen within the citadel itself. *Where are they going in such a hurry?* I wondered, resuming my journey with much slower steps.

*　　＊　　＊　　＊*

A short while later, I had my answer as I entered the citadel foyer.

The troop I'd spotted was standing guard at the main doors. They crowded the small chamber, leaving barely any elbow room. The constable noticed me and shoved his way through the press of soldiers to my side. He too was armed—if only with what looked like a dress sword.

Something is definitely up, I thought.

"Good morning," Richter said. "Sleep well?"

"I did, thank you," I replied. My gaze drifted toward the knights. "What's going on?"

"Nothing we can't handle," the constable said. "The knights are here merely as a precaution."

I frowned. "Precaution against what?" I asked, not liking his evasive response.

The constable didn't meet my gaze. "Oh, don't worry. As a guest, you have nothing to fear. This matter will be cleared up soon, and you will be free to leave."

I stared at him for a moment. "I can't leave?" I asked, my voice rising. "For how long? Am I a prisoner then?"

Richter opened his mouth to reply, but before he could, a Triumvirate knight walked over. "Something the matter here, sir?" he asked, addressing the constable.

Richter shook his head. "No, sergeant. Everything is fine. You can go back to your men."

My jaw tightened. Whatever was going on, the constable clearly didn't want it known, but I wasn't about to be kept in the dark. Something unusual had happened, and unusual meant trouble. I turned to the knight. "What's going on?" I asked bluntly.

The sergeant looked to the constable for direction, and Richter sighed. "Tell him."

"Assassins have been spotted outside the citadel's outer walls," the sergeant said, answering me just as forthrightly. "Knight-captain Orlon decided a show of force is necessary to prevent them from doing anything... rash."

"Assassins?" I asked with a sharp intake of breath. "Not mantises?"

Both the knight and the constable's gazes shot in my direction. "How did you know that?" the constable asked softly.

Silently, I cursed myself for my lack of restraint. However, it was too late to take back the words. "I've had a few run-ins with them already. Nothing I couldn't handle," I replied blandly.

The constable's lips twitched as I parroted his earlier words back at him. The sergeant, though, wasn't as amused. Scowling at me, he took a step forward—no doubt to demand further information—but before he could speak, the constable laid a restraining hand on his arm and whispered something that caused the knight to rejoin his troop.

I turned back to Richter to find him scrutinizing me. "I've observed a few mantis hunts in my days, you know," he said casually. "But I've never known them to impinge on Triumvirate territory before." He peered at me from beneath lidded eyes. "Just how badly do they want you?"

I said nothing.

The constable sighed. "In that case, is there anything I need to know?"

"Only that the sooner I leave, the sooner you'll be rid of your mantis problem," I said shortly.

Richter nodded and stroked his chin. "You should know that the mantises are no friends of the knights." He paused. "But neither are we enemies. As long as they're discreet, we turn a blind eye to their activities." He fixed me with a piercing gaze. "Do you understand what I'm saying?"

I nodded, catching his drift. The knights wouldn't aid my hunters, but nor could I expect any help from them.

"Excellent," the constable said. "Now, you're a guest, and like all our guests, while you remain within our territory you will be protected. But once you pass through our gates..." He opened his hands and shrugged.

"Understood. Now, can I go?" I asked, eager to be gone.

"There's just one more thing," the constable said.

I stared at him, waiting for him to go on.

"It's fortunate you've purchased a room for three nights," he mused.

"Why's that?" I asked, suspecting what was about to come next.

"Like I said last night, we take our obligation to our guests seriously. Having said that, the mantises are a powerful faction, and the Triumvirate will not needlessly antagonize them." Richter held my gaze. "I won't throw you out of your room, but if I were you, I wouldn't expect to be allowed inside the castle once your access key expires."

I nodded in grim understanding. "Then I better make the most of my time," I said and exited the foyer.

✳ ✳ ✳

The moment I left the inner citadel, my gaze flew upward to scan the sky.

There were no hunter eyes around—yet.

Lowering my gaze, I scanned the crowded courtyard. No green-clad assassins lurked there either, but then, if the constable was to be trusted, the mantises knew better than to let their hunt spill into Triumvirate territory.

I was safe until I passed beyond the outer walls.

Striding casually into the courtyard, I lost myself in the crowds, and then, when I was sure as I could be that no one was watching, I made my way toward the nearest wall and cloaked myself in its shadow.

Multiple neutral entities have failed to detect you! You are hidden.

With my back braced against solid stone, I stared unseeing into the crowd, my thoughts far away. It was time to figure out my next move, but before I could decide what that would be, I had to puzzle out the answer to the question at the forefront of my mind.

How did the mantises find me?

The entire way back to the citadel yesterday, I'd kept my mind shielded, my features disguised, and my scent masked. In fact, the only time my protections had been absent was when I'd fallen asleep.

That must be it.

The mantises must've tracked my unshielded consciousness last night.

Unfortunately, keeping my mind shielded while asleep wasn't an option. I'd tried but failed. It seemed that the spell needed active direction to maintain.

So, now what?

Knowing that the mantises prowled outside the walls, I could possibly—*probably?*—slip past unnoticed. But what then? Returning to the scorching dunes dungeon seemed... unwise.

Wengulax and Gintalush had to have realized that I'd somehow escaped their grasp yesterday, and if I ventured into the dungeon again today, I could expect them to be better prepared. The chances of me escaping a second time weren't good.

221

I grimaced, realizing I needed to cancel my plans for the day. Genmark and his fellows would have to be left wondering as to my whereabouts.

But what did I do instead?

Wherever I went, I was sure that mantises would dog my heels. And to be honest, I was tired of being their prey.

It is time I showed them some teeth.

But was I ready to face my hunters? Pensively, I opened my profile and studied it.

Player Profile (Partial): Michael

Level: 99. Rank: 9. Species: Human. Lives Remaining: 3.
True Marks (hidden): Pack-brother.

Attributes

Strength: 6 (2)*. Constitution: 14. Dexterity: 33 (27)*. Perception: 25. Mind: 52. Magic: 11 (10)*. Faith: 0.
denotes attributes affected by items.

Class (2 points available)

Primary-Secondary Bi-blend: mindslayer III (hidden).

Skills

Dodging: 71. Sneaking: 70. Shortswords: 76. Two-weapon fighting: 55. Light armor: 61. Thieving: 45.
Chi: 59. Meditation: 79. Telekinesis: 58. Telepathy: 52.
Insight: 78. Deception: 73.

New Abilities

Constitution ability slots used: 5 / 14.
minor lighten load (5 Constitution, advanced, light armor).

Mind ability slots used: 20 / 52.
simple mass charm (5 Mind, advanced, telepathy).
two-step (5 Mind, advanced, telekinesis).
simple reaction buff (5 Mind, advanced, chi).

Perception ability slots used: 18 / 25.
superior ventro (5 Perception, advanced, deception).

Other abilities:
improved slaysight (hidden) (Class, advanced, telepathy).

New Equipment

1 x stygian shortsword, +3, concealed.
1 x simple potion bracelet (3 full heal potions).
1 x trapper's wristband (20 / 20 traps available).
1 x belt of the chameleon (2 x rank 4 nether protection crystals, 5 x rank 4 disease protection crystals, 5 scent concealment crystals).

<u>**Backpack Contents (Key New Items)**</u>
<u>**Money**</u>**: 50 gold, 15 silver, and 3 copper.**
2 x rank 6 cure disease potions.
1 x Triumvirate citadel room key (2 nights).

<u>**Open Tasks**</u>
Find the Last Wolf Envoy (hidden) (find Ceruvax).
Stay True to Wolf (hidden) (acquire a mana-based Class).
Heist in the Dark (steal chalice from the Power, Paya).
Probie (complete two tier 4 bounties).
Preying Mantises (stop the assassins hunting you).

I frowned as the Game data confirmed what I already knew. I wasn't ready—nowhere near as much as I'd like.

The mantises still outclassed me, but I was no pushover either. I understood the assassins' limitations better than I'd had a few days ago. And as my previous encounter with Wengulax had shown, if I chose my battleground wisely, there was a chance I could emerge victorious.

Sure, given the level disparity, the outcome of any clash between the mantises and me would always be in doubt—no matter how carefully I planned.

But for the chance to rid myself of my hunters... it was a risk I was prepared to take.

It's high time I flipped the tables on them, I decided. For the hunted to become the hunter.

And I knew just the place to do it.

CHAPTER 199: FINDING THE RIGHT SPOT

Before leaving the safety of the shadows, I activated a scent ward, wrapped my mind in a shield, and cast lesser imitate, transforming myself into the likeness of a Triumvirate knight.

A moment later, I strode boldly into the bailey.

The crowds parted for me, instinctively making way for one of the citadel's custodians, and I reached the citadel's southern wall without incident. As I drew closer to the gate positioned there, my steps slowed.

The crowds were thin at this end of the bailey. Few players appeared inclined to visit the plague quarter's more southerly districts, and this was the first time I'd come this way myself. On my previous visits to the citadel I'd always used the north gate, and the keep itself was about as far south as I'd ventured into the quarter.

Will the mantises think to watch the south gate? I wondered. *Or just the north one?* I was ready for them in any case. With my senses extended and my mindsight opened, I passed under the open portcullis and into the square beyond.

No attack followed.

But something else caught my attention.

Intermingled with the saltiness of the sea was the stench of something rancid. I wrinkled my nose. The salt marsh and the ocean had to be close by, I realized.

No wonder this area is so lightly trafficked.

Despite my sudden worry about virulent diseases, I didn't pause in my stride as I marched through the square. There weren't many others around, and I was sure to be spotted by an astute observer. Trusting my disguise, I kept going, my gaze fixed on the buildings at the far end.

I'd almost reached them when my intuition prickled.

You have passed a mental resistance check! A hostile entity has failed to pierce your disguise. Your deception has increased to level 74.

I was being watched. *Mantis*, I thought. *Where is he?*

It took an effort of will not to flinch or hurry my steps. Expecting an analyze attempt at any second, I held my nerve and kept my stride even. The shadows were *so* close.

A moment later, I passed out of the square and sagged against the side of a building. Would whichever mantis had seen me follow after? Or would he think nothing of the lone knight passing through?

The streets weren't an ideal battleground for squaring off with the mantises, but if it came to it, I would make the best of it. Concealing myself in the shadows, I drew my blades and waited.

Five long minutes passed.

And still, no attack came.

I did it. I'd escaped undetected. Letting the lesser imitate spell around me lapse, I replaced it with facial disguise before slipping west through the quarter and in the direction of the haunted catacombs.

My chosen battleground.

✳   ✳   ✳

To fight the mantises, I realized I would need an environment suited to my talents. While the assassins were stealth fighters, they seemed to rely more on their blade work and toxins.

My own ability to hide surpassed theirs, and I suspected a dungeon like the haunted catacombs—which, if its name was anything to go by, was dark, enclosed, and deep underground—would suit me better than it did my foes. Certainly, it would be better than fighting under the harsh light of the scorching dunes.

Navigating by my map, I reached the haunted catacombs without mishap. Its entrance was situated in an open square on the western side of the quarter, and to my surprise, I found the players waiting to enter assembled in a long snaking line.

Well, things here are certainly more orderly than at the scorching dunes.

A portal was in the square's center, and on either side of it towered two giant statues—one depicting a dwarf and the other an orc. Like the other marble figures I'd seen in the city, these two were also accompanied by animal companions. The dwarf cradled a mole in his arms while the orc had a snake draped across his neck.

Once again, something about the statues struck me as odd, but I couldn't quite place my finger on what bothered me about them. Shrugging away the mystery, I entered the square to join the queue.

But as I padded closer, another oddity caught my attention: the snaking line of players was static.

No one is entering the dungeon.

My expression twisted into a frown. *What now?* I wondered. I couldn't afford to stand around like the others though. Sooner or later, the mantises would start searching the plague quarter, and I didn't want to be caught out in the open.

I was nearly certain the assassins wouldn't be able to track me—not with all my defenses active, but *nearly* certain and certain weren't the same thing, and too many of my assumptions in Nexus had been proven wrong for me to put much faith in them anymore.

Coming to a decision, I cut through the line of patiently waiting players.

You have passed a mental resistance check! Multiple unknown entities have failed to pierce your disguise or analyze you.

Glares and muttered oaths were thrown my way; curses and the occasional limb too. No one drew a blade though. Smiling tightly, I ignored the attention directed my way as I slipped deftly through the crowd to draw up short at the dungeon's entrance.

The nether portal's shimmering curtain of energy was dull, nowhere near as bright as the one to the scorching dune had been. *Is it inactive?* I wondered worriedly. Was that why no one was entering?

"Hey, you! What do you think you're doing?" someone shouted.

I glanced at the player who'd addressed me. It was an ogre standing near the front of the line. He was more than twice my own height and armored in a mountain of steel. Ignoring his question, I asked my own instead. "Why is no one going in?"

The elf standing beside the ogre sniggered. "Oh, Powers, not another noob!"

The ogre proved more gracious. "Because the team inside has nearly cleared the dungeon," he explained patiently. He spread his arms to encompass the twenty players gathered around him. "There is no point in our party entering until they're finished."

I shrugged, not making much sense of his response except to pick out one important bit: entering the dungeon was possible, even if the players chose not to do so. "You don't mind me entering then?"

The ogre's bushy brows drew down. "Why would you want to?"

"I'm kind of in a hurry," I said.

"You're not a scav, are you?" the elf asked suspiciously.

An unknown entity has failed to pierce your disguise or analyze you.

I ignored the elf—and his failed analyze attempt—and kept my gaze fixed on the ogre. One way or the other, I intended on entering the portal. It was just a few steps away, and even if they wanted to, I couldn't see the nearby players stopping me before I ducked inside.

But if they pursued... it might prove problematic.

The ogre shrugged. "Be my guest."

"What? No, Toff!" the elf exclaimed. "Why would you—"

"We're not knights," the ogre rumbled. "Policing the dungeon isn't our job. If the noob wants to go in, he can. And if he *is* a scav, well, the guys inside will deal with him quickly enough."

"Thank you," I said. Ignoring the ongoing sputtered protests of the elf, I slipped into the shimmering curtain.

Transfer through portal commencing...
...
...
Passage completed!
Leaving sector 1. Entering the Endless Dungeon.

✳   ✳   ✳

I emerged in a small room.

The chamber was unlit—and just as dark and dank as I hoped it would be. It appeared empty, except for the zombie corpse at the far end and the portal at my back. Slipping into the shadows, I crouched down in the corner of the stone chamber and unfurled my mindsight. It confirmed what my physical senses told me.

I was alone.

Satisfied I remained safe for the time being, I studied the Game alert buzzing for my attention.

You have entered sector 102 of the Endless Dungeon. This sector is part of a closed region named the Haunted Catacombs. It consists of 3 unclaimable sectors and 3 two-way portals.

A maximum of 24 players may be in the Haunted Catacombs at any one time. The dungeon is only repopulated once all the sector bosses have been killed.

Recommended player levels: 120 to 140.

Recommended party size: 4 to 6.

Players currently inside the dungeon: 21.

Sector bosses remaining: 1 of 3.

In light of the Adjudicator's message, the ogre's remarks began to make sense. This dungeon imposed a limit on the number of players that could enter, and it did *not* respawn continuously.

No wonder the players outside are content to wait. It wouldn't be much of a dungeon dive for any party entering the dungeon now, but that didn't matter to me.

I was here to slay the mantises, not hunt monsters.

Dismissing the Game notice, I studied the nether portal again. It glimmered a dull white, marking the portal as active. That was good.

It meant I could leave anytime.

But it meant too that the mantises could appear without warning.

I had to be ready before that happened. I planned on ambushing the assassins, and the Game message gave me an inkling of how to go about that.

According to the information it provided the dungeon consisted of three sectors, and two of its sector bosses were dead already. That meant the first two levels of the dungeon were likely free of denizens, or mostly so, and hence safe to explore.

Step one, then: get a better handle on the terrain.

Rising into a half crouch, I padded across the room and through the open doorway at the far end. A long corridor lay beyond. I scrutinized it for a moment. The corridor disappeared into the distance, beyond my line of sight, and was peppered with doors on either side, but like the entry chamber, it seemed empty of threats.

I crept into the corridor, pausing every so often to scan the surroundings with mindsight. The adjacent rooms were barren too. A few dozen yards on, I came across another corpse. This one was that of a bleached skeleton. Bending down, I examined the remains.

The target is a slain level 120 skeletal warrior. Reanimated skeletons are among the most common type of undead and can be raised from the dead to perform a variety of functions.

Your insight has increased to level 79.

The undead had been stripped bare of equipment, and the nearby area was littered with debris—mostly shards of shattered bone.

There wasn't enough to identify, much less analyze. But given the intact skeleton, I thought the other remains were also that of slain skeletal warriors and had likely been obliterated by a spell. Rising to my feet, I shook my head in wry admiration. Whichever party had passed this way, they had been quite thorough in their destruction.

That should make things easier.

Leaving the slain undead behind, I delved deeper into the dungeon.

Chapter 200: Preparing the Ground

It took me nearly two hours to explore the first sector and memorize its layout. My scouting took me through a dizzying array of barren corridors and rooms, all empty of loot or living creatures.

The level had been thoroughly cleansed.

There were plenty of dead monsters though. I inspected each one, and slowly the dungeon's design became clear. The first sector of the haunted catacombs was infested by rank twelve undead—zombies, ghouls, wights, skeletons, and the like.

But at what I'd judged to be the far end of the level, I found the sector's safe zone and a dungeon denizen that didn't fit the pattern of the rest of the level. It was the corpse of a level one hundred and fifty death knight. *It's three whole ranks higher than the rest of the creatures on the level,* I mused.

It was the sector boss. Had to be.

Pivoting about, I scanned the chamber the dead boss occupied. It was larger than other rooms on the level, and its door was an oversized grille metal gate in place of the plain wooden doors found elsewhere on the level.

This is definitely the sector's final chamber, I thought. Unfortunately, the room was devoid of cover or anywhere to hide.

Exiting the room, I entered the adjacent one. It held the safe zone. Unlike the previous safe zones I'd visited, this one was small, barely a few yards across. It contained only two objects of note: a rebirth well and a shimmering curtain of energy.

The nether portal to the next level.

Only staring at the portal did it occur to me to wonder what would happen once the dungeon was cleared. Would all the denizens respawn immediately? Or would all the players inside—including me—be given time to get to an exit portal?

No point worrying, I thought. *It's out of my control. Still, best I finish my scouting while I can and plan for the worst.*

Hurrying my steps, I strode through the portal.

✳   ✳   ✳

You have entered sector 103 of the Endless Dungeon. This sector is level 2 of 3 of the Haunted Catacombs.

A moment later, I was in a room that was a replica of the first level's entry chamber. Wrapping myself in shadow, I began exploring.

The second dungeon level was laid out in the same manner as the first. And, like the first sector, it was very much empty.

The dead I encountered were different though. The second level's denizens were all rank thirteen and more varied, including vampires and wraiths among their number. It was an unsurprising discovery. Clearly, the dungeon was designed to increase in difficulty at every succeeding level.

Once more, I found the entrance to the next level at the southern end of the sector. It, too, was protected by a safe zone, and in the chamber next to it was a dead sector boss.

Not wasting further time scouting the level, I slipped into the portal.

You have entered sector 104 of the Endless Dungeon. This sector is level 3 of 3 of the Haunted Catacombs.

Emerging in the third level, I slowed my steps. I expected that the dungeon team was still busy in the level, and it wouldn't do to run afoul of them.

I exited the entry chamber and found myself in another darkened—and empty—passage. *This looks familiar,* I thought and ventured deeper into the level.

It took me only a few turns to confirm what I suspected: the floorplan of the third level was identical to the first two.

With growing confidence, I crept through the empty passages, heading in the direction of the sector's safe zone and final chamber. Eventually, I came to a stretch of corridor different from the others.

Like elsewhere in the dungeon, corpses littered the floor, but here not all the dead had been stripped clean of their gear. Leaving the loot untouched, I kneeled beside one of the corpses and inspected it.

The target is a slain level 141 ghost hound. Ghost hounds are loyal beasts that follow their masters into undeath, serving them even beyond the grave. 'Ghost' is a misnomer though. The creatures are not ethereal and are entirely from the physical plane.

I rose thoughtfully. The hound in question was nearly as large as me and, from its level alone, would be a tough foe to battle. Turning to the humanoid corpse lying close by, I analyzed it too.

The target is a level 149 undead hound keeper.

Both hound and undead master had been freshly killed, and the trails of blood spattering the wall had still not congealed.

The dungeon party must be close.

Slipping back into the shadows, I advanced cautiously down the tunnel. I passed more rooms but didn't bother venturing into any; I expected I would find nothing in them but dead dungeon denizens. Less than a minute later, I heard voices from further down the passage.

Players.

They still weren't in sight though. In the quiet corridors, sound carried a long way. I kept going; my every sense extended for the least sign of danger.

I had no intention of interfering with the dungeon party or alerting them to my presence, but I needed to learn as much of the dungeon as I could before it reset.

I found the group of twenty players in the large vault-like room that served as the level's final chamber. The grille gate was locked—magically by all appearance—trapping the party inside with the boss.

Boss and players were locked in combat and too preoccupied with each other to notice me. Peeking through the gate, I studied the combatants. The sector boss was a humanoid undead magic user encased in a shield of pulsing black energy. Gaunt and with skin that was pale and wrinkled, he loomed over all the players—even the giants among them.

A rank seventeen lich. No easy foe, I realized after analyzing the undead and the magic he threw with abandon.

But despite their foe's level and the monstrous amount of magic he wielded, the players weren't only coping—but winning.

Arrayed in two loose lines—fighters out front, mages and archers in the rear—the dungeon team whittled down their foe's defenses. From the looks of it, the players had been at it a while and would soon have the lich's shield down.

Knowing I didn't have much time remaining, I retreated from the gate and entered the adjacent chamber. Like the previous levels, it held a safe zone, but this time there was no nether portal.

I frowned. That meant the only way to exit the dungeon was back the same way I'd entered. Leaving the chamber, I explored the nearby rooms, taking special note of the creatures they contained. I had a plan in mind already, but that didn't mean I couldn't refine it further.

Halfway through my investigations, a Game message dropped into my mind.

The final sector boss has been slain! The Haunted Catacombs dungeon will reset shortly. Warning to all players inside: collect any unclaimed loot and exit the dungeon.

I smiled after reading the Game message. *That simplifies matters.*

Turning my attention inward, I dropped the shield around my consciousness. *There.* If the mantises were tracking me by my mind, they would have my location now.

I hurried back to the second level. It was time to prepare for my hunters.

✳   ✳   ✳

I'd only just entered the second sector when another Game alert arrived.

The dungeon will reset in 10 minutes.

I eyed the message askance. I'd expected to have a bit more time than that, but it didn't matter; I would make do. Racing through the corridors, I made my way to the chamber I'd chosen and ducked inside.

It was time to get ready. First, I saw to my stealth.

You have activated the stealth mode enchantment of the belt of the chameleon. Your sneaking skill has increased by +2 ranks.

Next, I opened my backpack and retrieved the hunter eye I'd looted from Wengulax. I wasn't completely sure how the device worked, but if there was ever a time to use it, it was now. Cupping the small green orb in my hands, I brought it to life.

You have activated a hunter eye.
To enable all tracking features, provide the spirit signature of the target.

Unfortunately, I didn't know how to do that and replied in the negative to the Game message.

No target has been provided.
Automated tracking mode has been deactivated. Entering scout mode, manual piloting required. For the next 4 hours, this item will share its sensors with you.

I grinned. The functionality available on the hunter eye was less than I'd hoped for but would still suffice to serve my purposes.

Closing my eyes, I connected to the device through the mental link forged between us by the artifact's enchantment. Piloting the orb, I navigated it out of the room, through the empty level and the next, and finally out through the portal and back into Nexus.

"Hey, will you look at that!" I heard someone exclaim.

I started in surprise and my head swiveled back and forth, searching the room. I'd been sure I was alone.

"What do you think that is?"

"Looks like a scouting pet."

Belatedly, I realized the sound was coming from the hunter eye and admonished myself for not catching onto the fact sooner. Reconnecting my sight to the object, I peered through it.

The hunter eye was hovering over the ogre, Toff, and his group. I saw his elven companion point upward. "Shoot it," he suggested.

Worried that someone would do just that, I ordered the eye to climb higher until it was little more than a speck in the sky. Looking down from it, I could still see the portal and the surrounding area, but the players staring upward were too far away for me to hear anymore.

I heaved a sigh of relief. The eye was in position, and so was I. There were only a few more things to prepare.

And after that, all that was left was to see if the mantises would come as expected.

CHAPTER 201: STALKING PREY

The Haunted Catacombs dungeon will respawn in 5 seconds. All keys, doors, and traps will be reset, and the dungeon's denizens will be repopulated.

I opened my eyes at the Game message. I'd fallen into a light trance while I waited and hadn't noticed the passage of time. Dropping down into a crouch, I gripped the hilts of my swords.

Four...
Three...
Two...
The dungeon reset has been completed.

A resounding boom echoed through the level.

It was the sound of dozens of doors slamming and traps resetting, I realized a moment later. The door of the chamber I was in banged shut too. I eyed it worriedly.

Was I locked in?

If so, it could ruin all my plans. But I had little time to dwell on the issue as a tear rent the air and an emaciated figure with the unmistakable pallor of death stepped out. I held my breath for a moment, but no second figure followed, and I exhaled slowly.

It was exactly as I'd hoped.

I'd chosen my refuge based on the single corpse I'd found inside the chamber during my scouting. While that was no surety of the number of inhabitants *after* the dungeon reset, I'd been banking on the fact that I would be facing only a single occupant.

The undead shuffled in my direction.

I stiffened, but the creature's eyes were wide and vacant. It hadn't spotted me. The undead reached the wall I sheltered against but failed to see me hiding just a few feet away and swiveled around, dragging itself toward the chamber's opposite end. Mindlessly pacing.

But not for long.

With bated breath, I watched as the undead's steps carried it to the room's center—and straight into the ambush I'd prepared earlier.

A hostile entity has triggered a trap!
A hostile entity has triggered a trap!
A hostile entity has triggered a trap!

The three snares activated simultaneously, unleashing a torrent of damage on my hapless target.

A level 138 undead warlock has been backstabbed by a trap dagger!
Your target has taken fire damage!
Your target has been hobbled for 10 seconds.

Somehow, the warlock survived the hurricane of damage. But I wasn't done yet. Casting shadow blink, I stepped through the aether and followed up with a second devastating volley.

You have cast whirlwind, piercing strike, and crippling blow.
You have backstabbed a warlock for 4x more damage!
You have critically injured your target.
You have critically injured your target.
You have killed an undead warlock!

It was enough.

Caught by surprise and unprepared, the undead succumbed without mustering a response of its own, and with a bitten-off shriek, it slumped to the ground.

Ignoring the corpse, I swung to face the still-closed door. My earlier foray through the dungeon had led me to believe that the corridors were patrolled.

But no noise penetrated from without. Nor did I sense any presence in the corridor beyond. I relaxed; the warlock's scream had gone unnoticed.

The chamber I occupied was more remote than most, and that had served me well. Content that I was safe—at least temporarily—I turned my attention to the hunter eye.

The orb remained on station above the portal, and looking down through it, I saw the tail end of a column of players entering the dungeon. *Toff's team,* I thought.

But they weren't the only ones to enter the dungeon.

Materializing from somewhere unseen, a four-man party rushed toward the gate. They hadn't been waiting in line, and the other players shouted abuse at them. Ignoring the crowd's outraged screams, the small party dived into the dungeon.

But when their last man attempted to enter, the portal's shimmering curtain hardened and the player bounced off the suddenly opaque surface.

His expression a mask of anger, the player tried again. It was no use though. I knew what had happened. The dungeon had reached its limit of twenty-four entrants—one of which was me. I'd stolen the unfortunate player's place.

Oops.

I felt little sympathy for the player; he was probably up to no good. *Like me.* His fellows didn't re-emerge from the dungeon, and stranded alone to face the crowd's anger, the player turned and fled.

I kept watch for a while longer, but the mantises didn't appear. Realizing I had a potentially long vigil ahead of me, I split my focus and saw to the waiting Game messages.

You have reached level 100!
Congratulations, Michael! You are now a tier 3 player. Your experience gains have decreased further. For achieving rank 10, you have been awarded 1 additional attribute point and 1 Class point.

The level-up notice was accompanied by a heap of skill-gain messages, but I paid them little heed as I considered my new attribute points. Stealth would be my greatest asset in the coming battle with the mantises, and I wanted to increase its effectiveness. That made the choice of how to invest the points simple.

Your Dexterity has increased to rank 29. Other modifiers: +6 from items.

I searched the room next. No loot chest had appeared; given what I'd seen of the dungeon layout earlier I hadn't expected one, but that didn't prevent me from being disappointed.

The undead warlock's gear also proved lackluster. He carried only three items of value, all of little use to me.

You have acquired 2 x minor mana potions.
You have acquired 1 x Death magic wand.

My looting done, I tiptoed to the door. As I feared, it seemed locked. But was it trapped too?

Equipping the spectacles of seeing, I inspected the door for magical wards. There were none. This time around, I was certain I could trust the spectacle's findings. The dungeon was designed for tier two players and surely didn't contain wards higher than tier four.

Which left only one other possibility.

Activating trap detect, I ran my hands lightly along the door's wooden surface, searching for anomalies.

You have failed to spot any traps.

I took my time, double-checking and triple-checking the area before I was finally satisfied that there were no traps to find. Only then did I turn my attention to the lock itself.

Crouching down on my haunches, I set my head against the door and activated simple lockpick. With my hearing enhanced—to discern even the smallest of clicks—and the dexterity of my fingers increased—for finer control—I inserted a slim dagger into the lock and manipulated it carefully.

You have failed to pick a lock.

The lock's mechanism defeated my efforts. Grimacing, I tried again.

You have failed to pick a lock.

The second failure no more daunted me than the first, and staying hunched by the door, I kept trying. Until...

You have successfully picked a lock.
Your thieving has increased to level 50 and reached rank 5, allowing you to learn tier 2 abilities.

I grinned. *Finally!* Sitting back, I rolled my shoulders, easing the stiffness from my joints as I memorized the precise sequence of rotations and clicks required to unlock the door.

Then I locked it again.

I had no plans of exiting the room just yet. Until the mantises appeared—or the dungeon party did—there was no reason for me to abandon my refuge.

Returning to the corner, I closed my eyes and gave the hunter eye my full attention once more. The assassins had not yet made an appearance, but it was too early to know conclusively if they would or not.

And until such time, there was nothing to do but wait.

✳   ✳   ✳

An hour later, I was still waiting.

My hunt was turning out to be less exciting than I'd expected, becoming more an excruciating exercise in patience than anything else. *If this is how the mantises spend their days stalking their prey, I want none of it,* I thought drily.

I didn't even know if the assassins would show up. *Perhaps, I'm wrong about how they're tracking me, or maybe they'll decide against entering the dungeon, or—*

I broke off from my musings—they weren't helping—and turned my thoughts to the dungeon party instead. Their progress was surprisingly slow. I had no means of tracking them, of course, but I'd received no notification of a sector boss dying and knew they still had to be on the first level. Their glacial pace didn't concern me though.

My plan catered for multiple contingencies, including if the dungeon party descended to my location before the mantises arrived or if they cleared the dungeon altogether before that happened. I was prepared to wait however long I had to—even through multiple dungeon resets if necessary.

Closing my eyes, I returned to my vigil.

Around noon, I was rewarded for my efforts as I spotted two shapes of bright-green entering the square.

The mantises had arrived.

Rousing myself to full alertness, I watched through the hunter eye as the familiar figures of Wengulax and Gintalush cut through the crowd. No one got in their way, much less objected, as the assassins pushed their way to the front of the line and placed gloved hands onto the rim of the portal.

They didn't enter though.

I assumed that was because the dungeon was still at maximum capacity. Remaining where I was, I continued to watch the assassins. Until the pair entered, there was nothing for me to do. Nevertheless, the mantises' arrival heartened me; it meant that my preparations weren't in vain.

Another hour went by.

During that time, my targets remained oblivious of my observation. Neither assassin looked up, nor did any of the other players inform them of the hunter eye. Eventually, just as the enchantment on the little green orb began to run dry, another Game alert dropped into my mind.

The first sector boss has been slain! Sector bosses remaining: 2 of 3.

My eyebrows rose at the message. It had taken the ogre's party nearly four hours to clear the first level. If they kept going at that rate, they wouldn't finish the dungeon today. *It looks like I might have to spend the night in the catacombs. I better start preparing for—*

I broke off.

Wengulax and Gintalush had vanished.

They've entered the dungeon. I stilled and rose warily to my feet. At least two players must have died during the confrontation with the sector boss. That was the only explanation for the assassins' sudden disappearance.

I took a deep breath. My hunters were in the dungeon, and Toff's party would soon descend to the second floor.

The time to act had come.

✳ ✳ ✳

Unlocking the door to my refuge, I slipped out into the corridor beyond. Pressing my back up against the wall, I scanned the passageway in both directions.

No one—neither undead nor player—was nearby.

I crept down the corridor, stealthily making my way to the portal at the start of the level. Reaching the first crossroads along my route, I paused as a wall of noise rolled over me.

Startled, I dropped into a crouch. *What in hell is that?* Through my palms, I could feel the very floor vibrating.

The noise reached a crescendo, then faded, its echoes reverberating through the corridors. Tilting my head to the side, I tried to identify the noise. It sounded like a roar, a clarion call full of bestial rage.

A shape flashed through my mindsight. It was a vampire, and it was charging down a side passage in the direction the sound had originated from, the direction in which I myself was heading—the sector's entrance portal. It confirmed my suspicions.

The roar was a player's taunt, one meant to draw *all* the sector's creature patrols to the waiting dungeon party.

A bold strategy. Or a foolish one.

I chewed on my lip, pondering my next move. At this very second, Toff's party was likely battling the level's roving undead at the entrance portal, but where were the mantises?

I checked on the hunter eye. Less than five minutes remained on its enchantment. *More than enough time for one last scouting mission,* I thought.

Focusing on the green orb, I ordered it back toward the nether portal. There was a chance—possibly even a high one—that the assassins would spot the eye once it was in the dungeon, but that didn't bother me. I *wanted* Wengulax and Gintalush alert and suspicious.

Ignoring the exclamations of the players outside the portal, I navigated the hunter eye into the dungeon. The orb descended into the first level, and I sent it on a direct course for the portal to the second level.

Halfway there, it found the mantises—or they found it.

A flash of green was the only warning I had before twin daggers hurtled into the orb.

A hunter eye has been destroyed.

My vision went blank, and my consciousness dropped back into my body. My lip curled upward. Now Wengulax and Gintalush knew I was in the dungeon and aware of their presence—just as they were of mine.
The game was on.

Before moving onward, I cast my buffs and renewed my protections.

You have cast reaction buff, increasing your Dexterity by +4 ranks for 20 minutes.
You have cast lighten load, reducing your total armor penalties to 0% for 20 minutes. Net effect: +2 Dexterity and +1 Magic.
You have cast mind shield.
You have activated a disease protection crystal.
You have activated a scent concealment crystal.

I wasn't going to make it easy for the mantises to locate me. In fact, I was hoping to find them first. Hands gripping my blades, ready to draw them at a moment's notice, I crept toward the sector's entrance.

All the corridors I passed were pitch black and eerily quiet.

No undead patrolled the passages, and the doors leading into the side rooms were securely fastened. Idly, I wondered how the dungeon party was faring. Given the tactics they'd chosen, the players had to be confident of the size of the sector's roving denizens and their own ability to defeat them.

Sure enough, when I reached the entrance portal, I was greeted by the sight of Toff's party holding firm against a tide of undead. The ogre's party was still twenty-strong; they hadn't lost anyone yet. But there was no sign of the other three-man team. They'd either perished in the battle with the sector boss or from conflict with the larger party. Their fate mattered little though.

Crouched in the darkness outside the range of the magelights hovering over the ogre's party, I studied the battle. The players were mopping up. Over two-thirds of the undead had fallen, and those that remained—ghouls and zombies—seemed no match for the party.

There was no sign of the mantises though.

They couldn't have beaten me here, and I could only assume the encounter with the hunter eye had slowed them down. *They must still be searching for me on the first level.*

By necessity, my plans for the mantises were fluid. There were too many unknown variables for me to control them all, and rather than stay married to any one strategy for dealing with my foes, I had a few in mind.

The present circumstances—encountering the dungeon party first—allowed for the execution of one of the more promising ones.

Closing my eyes, I cast lesser imitate. Holding the image of my target in my mind, I spun an illusion of light around myself, blurring the lines of my body, clothes, and face.

Once my new guise settled into place, I rose to my feet and stepped out of the shadows. None of the players noticed me at first, too caught up with battling the ghouls between them and me. But the distinctive green-clad garments I wore were nearly impossible to miss, and eventually one of the players in the party's back lines—a mage—spotted me.

You have passed a mental resistance check! An unknown entity has failed to pierce your disguise.

The player's eyes grew round, and his head snapped back around for a second look. "Mantis!" he mouthed.

Even over the distance that separated us, I could read the fear on the mage's face, and I smiled in satisfaction. *It's working.*

Drawing to a halt, I mimed reaching for a dagger on my belt.

Panic suffused the mage's face, and he dashed forward to attract the attention of his leader. Standing on the party's front lines and battling a ghoul, Toff ignored the feeble pounding on his back.

"There's a mantis here!" the mage tried again.

"Shut up and fight!" Toff roared.

"Just look!"

Involuntarily, the ogre's gaze jerked in my direction, and consternation flickered across his face.

Toff has failed to pierce your disguise.

Perfect. Dropping my mind shield, I whipped back my arm and flung a psi dagger at the ogre.

Toff sidestepped the astral blade easily—I hadn't taken any particular care aiming it—and, bashing in the head of his foe, turned to face me. "You green whoreson! What is one of your stinking kind doing here?" the ogre roared. He fairly trembled with anger, displaying not an ounce of fear.

Not bothering to attempt a rejoinder, I melted back into the shadows.

Multiple hostile entities have failed to detect you! You are hidden.

Bewildered cries and shouts of dismay followed in the wake of my disappearance.

"Where did he go?"

"What's a mantis doing here?"

"How did that Dark bastard get ahead of us!"

"Is he hunting you?"

"Don't worry, Toff. We'll protect you! Those cowards will never get their hands on you."

"What nonsense! Listen to me, Toff. You're better off fleeing. If the mantises are after you—"

"I won't run!" the ogre roared. "Now, enough of this useless prattle. Fight, and let's be done with these wretched undead."

Despite Toff's command, the party continued to whisper and speculate among themselves, if in much softer tones. Sitting in the shadows and observing them, a small smile played on my lips.

The ogre's party was twenty-strong, and they had nothing to fear from Wengulax and Gintalush. If anything, it was the mantises who were in for a surprise, especially now that the other players had been primed for their appearance. With my mind shield down, the assassins had to be already homing in on my location.

Wengulax and Gintalush would certainly suspect a trap, but perhaps not the one that awaited them. Eyes glinting in anticipation, I kept my gaze fixed on the entrance portal.

It won't be long now.

✳   ✳   ✳

Five minutes later, Toff's party slew the last undead.

Their chatter hadn't stopped, however. Looting the corpses, they continued to discuss the mystifying appearance of the mantis in the dungeon and why it had attacked the ogre.

It was then that the assassins chose to appear.

This time around, the party was quicker on the uptake. "More mantises!" an elf yelled.

Without further prompting, weapons were drawn and pointed at the two green-clad figures that had emerged from the portal, and a heartbeat later the air began to buzz with magical and physical projectiles.

Wengulax and Gintalush didn't retreat though.

Despite the swiftness of the party's response, the pair weren't caught flatfooted, and an instant before the first attack descended upon them, the assassins multiplied.

Suddenly, there weren't two mantises, but ten.

Cries of consternation erupted from the other players. Crouched in the darkness a few dozen yards away, I was as perplexed as Toff's team.

What had just happened? Had more assassins arrived through the portal?

Just as the first of the party's projectiles struck, the ten mantises dispersed, running in different directions. More attacks followed, but now the players had ten targets, not two. Renewing my mind shield, I watched the battle play out while I tried to make sense of what I was seeing.

An ice shard struck one of the green-clad figures, and it flickered. An arrow passed harmlessly through another. A whirling blade cut through three with no effect.

Illusions, they're illusions.

Toff's party came to the same realization. "It's a mirror image spell!" an archer shouted.

"Mages, launch area attacks. Now!" the ogre ordered.

Three of the images had disappeared already, but at Toff's words the other seven turned on their heels and descended on the ogre's party, bare blades at the ready. My mouth went dry at the sight.

My ploy had gone horribly wrong.

Had I overestimated the party's abilities? Were they about to be slaughtered?

But a moment later, I realized the seven attacking "mantises" were doing no damage. Despite them striking at the players with abandon, their blades passed harmlessly through body and armor alike.

They're *all* illusions. They had to be.

If Gintalush and Wengulax aren't among the images... where are they?

Hiding. Stalking me.

Realizing my own danger, I shifted position abruptly and scanned the surrounding darkness.

You have failed a Perception check and are unable to find your targets.

I grimaced but kept at it, sure now that the two mantises were likewise searching for me in the shadows.

You have failed a Perception check!
You have failed...
...

But both I and the assassins had forgotten the dungeon party. They hadn't been standing idly by.

"Get ready," one of the mages shouted.

I broke off from my search to stare in her direction. Ready for what?

"Dispelling now!" she yelled obligingly.

A heartbeat later, an angry-orange pulse rippled outward from the player's upraised staff. It passed harmlessly over Toff's party members. But when it touched the images they vanished in a puff of smoke, and soon all seven disappeared.

The pulse didn't stop though.

It kept going, expanding faster until...

...three yards beyond the party, it revealed a green-clad form, caught bent in half and creeping in my direction. Gintalush.

"There's one!"

...and eight yards farther, it uncovered another figure, this one with drawn blades. Wengulax.

"And there's the other!"

I gripped my blades, waiting for the inevitable. Only a dozen yards separated Wengulax from me.

But it made all the difference.

Halfway to me, the pulse stopped short and vanished. I sagged in relief. *I* wasn't about to be exposed. My gaze flickered upward to the two revealed mantises, wondering what they'd do next.

But before the pair could react, the party took the decision out of their hands.

"Kill them!" Toff roared.

Bows were aimed and staffs were lowered.

Wengulax and Gintalush shared a look, then as one they took off running—down opposite side passages.

"After them!" an elf screamed.

My eyes narrowed as I saw my prey fleeing. Which one to pursue? *Gintalush*, I decided and slipped down another side passage on an intercept course.

Chapter 203: A Fight Amongst the Dead

Wrapped in shadow, I sat in vigil at the intersection of four of the dungeon corridors. It had taken me five minutes of breathless and silent running to get here.

Behind me, I heard nothing.

Either Toff's party had chosen to pursue Wengulax instead, or they'd abandoned the chase altogether. I didn't care much which. Going at the hunt alone suited me just fine—this way less would be left to chance.

I was under no misapprehension though. Gintalush wouldn't be an easy quarry. Nor would he remain in flight forever. Soon, I expected, the mantis would begin hunting me in turn.

If he wasn't already.

But I had a few things in my favor, not least of which was that I'd memorized the sector's floor plan. It thus came as no surprise to me when less than a minute after I'd positioned myself, a Game message unfurled in my mind.

You have detected a hostile entity. Gintalush is no longer hidden!

The green-clad mantis materialized less than nine feet from me, entering the intersection from the north. It was exactly where I'd anticipated intercepting him. I, myself, had raced through the western fork to get here.

The assassin spun around as the shadows fell away from him. He must've received a notice from the Adjudicator informing him that he had been revealed.

Standing stock-still, the mantis scanned the darkness behind him. His thoughts were easy to decipher. Gintalush suspected someone of following him down the northern corridor.

I didn't move.

I was sitting just inside the western passage and was confident of my own ability to remain hidden from the mantis. I'd done it before, and this time my stealth was higher. But even with Gintalush standing in easy reach, I knew better than to attempt fighting him in hand-to-hand combat again.

Before I engaged the assassin, I would do my utmost to ensure it was *not* a fair fight.

Extending my mindsight, I probed the adjacent chambers. A trio of skeletons was to my right, behind a locked door just a little way down the southern passage. To my left was a room filled with ghouls, while a solitary vampire occupied one of the chambers across the intersection.

My gaze flicked back to Gintalush. He still hadn't moved. Then, in what I took to be a sure indication the assassin intended to confront his pursuer, the mantis reached into his pocket and withdrew a handful of hunter eyes.

I stayed where I was.

I didn't fear the scouting orbs anymore. Hidden, shielded, and protected by a scent ward as I was, the hunter eyes would be blind to my presence. Just like Gintalush was.

Still, it would suit me if the assassin was less wary.

My eyes drifted back to the locked rooms. The skeletons seemed the most suitable for what I had in mind, and I analyzed all three.

The target is a level 133 skeleton warrior.
The target is a level 138 skeleton knight.
The target is a level 136 skeletal mage.

They'll do, I decided. Gintalush, meanwhile, had flung the hunter eyes in the air, sending them racing back up the passage from which he'd come.

I waited until the orbs had disappeared, then dropped my mind shield and sent psi reaching into the southern chamber. Working quickly, in case the orbs returned, I divided my casting into three separate weaves and simultaneously flooded the minds of the skeletons in the room.

You have cast mass charm.
A skeletal mage has passed a mental resistance check!
A skeleton knight has passed a mental resistance check!
A skeleton warrior has failed a mental resistance check!
You have charmed 1 of 3 targets for 10 seconds.

My spell was less successful than I hoped, but the one minion I'd managed to acquire would still suffice for what I had in mind. Reaching out to the skeletal warrior, I gave it its orders before renewing my mind shield.

A resounding bang echoed through the corridor, and Gintalush dropped into a half crouch as he whipped around.

The heavy thud came again.

There was a moment of stark silence.

Another thud.

Realizing the source of the sound, the assassin rose to his feet and padded up to the door in question. More thuds broke the silence. It was the sound of the skeleton warrior hacking at the door with his axe.

Gintalush listened intently at the door. A moment later, he relaxed and scanned the corridor in both directions. Then with an shrug, he headed south.

I smiled grimly. My ploy had worked, and the assassin had been tricked into believing it was a hostile inside the room that had detected him earlier.

For a handful of seconds, I watched the mantis as he slipped away. Gintalush didn't bother recloaking himself in shadow, nor did he recall the hunter eyes he'd sent north.

He's feeling safe again.

After the distance between us had drawn out sufficiently, I followed in my quarry's wake.

*　　*　　*

I followed Gintalush for ten long minutes as his wandering took him eastward and toward a remote quarter of the dungeon. During that time, the assassin periodically released more hunter eyes—to search the tunnels, I presumed—but not once did he look back or hide again.

It was almost as if Gintalush was inviting an attack.

I was tempted to do just that, but I schooled myself to patience and waited for the right moment. Just *what* that moment was, I wasn't sure—not until I saw Gintalush slip into a passage that I knew was a dead end.

This is it.

I waited for the assassin to disappear from sight. He would be back once he reached the cul-de-sac, but that would take at least five minutes, giving me enough time to prepare for his return.

Opening my mindsight, I scanned the rooms on either side of the corridor. All were overflowing with undead. I smiled tightly. It seemed like I was spoiled for choice.

Picking the most appropriate rooms and monsters, I got to work.

✳   ✳   ✳

A little later, my ambush was set.

Crouching in the shadows ten yards from the spot I'd chosen, I watched Gintalush saunter up the passage. He looked no more wary than when he'd left. *Perfect.*

My traps had been laid, my blades were drawn, and I'd renewed my buffs and precast ventro. I was as ready as I could be.

Eyes narrowed, I waited for the right moment to launch my ambush. This time, I'd taken the added precaution of laying my trap triggers in out-of-the-way corners. There was no chance of Gintalush stumbling upon them beforehand.

Blissfully unaware of the fate awaiting him, the mantis entered the trapped area. I rose silently to my feet. Gintalush took two more steps.

Now.

"Boo!" I whispered, using ventro to project my voice to the hidden triggers behind the mantis.

Gintalush spun around, searching for the half-caught sound.

In the same heartbeat, the sound glasses shattered.

You have triggered 4 x traps!

The assassin's response was immediate. Reacting like a scalded cat, he backed up against the wall to his left, his gaze flitting over the floor suspiciously. Gintalush's reaction was understandable—if mistaken.

It wasn't the ground I'd trapped.

In the next instant, the doors of four rooms—two on either side of the assassin—yawned open as the explosives I placed on their locks detonated.

The undead spilled out in a rush.

There were over a dozen of the creatures—ghouls, skeletons, and zombies—and Gintalush was stuck between them. Reflexively, the assassins' blades flew up.

But this time, not even the assassin's exceptional blade work would save him. In a mad dash, the undead converged on their target.

A zombie slashed at the mantis with blistering speed. The assassin dodged the blow easily enough and the next too, from a skeletal knight, but not so the third—an open fist from a diseased ghoul. Gintalush flinched at the impact but kept fighting.

More blows rained down on the beleaguered assassin. The mantis did his best, but he was outmatched. As many attacks as he parried away, he was struck by twice as many.

Safe in the shadows, I observed the fight impassively. Gintalush was doomed. Seeming to realize the same, the assassin attempted to escape. Stilling momentarily, the mantis split into five—no, six—copies.

As one, all the illusions—one hiding the real Gintalush—turned to escape in my direction.

But fleeing the undead proved harder than the mantis' previous getaway. For one, the monsters were *much* closer, and almost as soon as they appeared two of the images were cut down. The other four replicas escaped destruction but suffered heavy damage.

My hands tightening around my blades, I studied the four onrushing figures. There was nearly as much red as green on the mantis' clothing, and I knew I had to finish Gintalush before he escaped and recovered. My gaze skipping over the replicas, I analyzed each in turn.

You have passed a Perception check!
The target is an illusion.
The target is an illusion.
The target is an illusion.
The target is Gintalush, a level 171 insectoid blade dancer.

Got you, I thought. Readying my blades, I placed myself in the fleeing mantis' path.

A hostile entity has detected you! You are no longer hidden.

A second before he ran into me, Gintalush sensed my presence. His eyes grew round, and he frantically tried to bring up his lowered blades. But the mantis' wounds were too severe, and he moved only at half-speed.

Far too slow to stop me.

My stygian blade and ebonheart plunged forward, one to rip out the mantis' throat, the other to pierce his heart.

You have killed Gintalush.
You have slain a disciple of Menaq, earning his ire!
You have gained in experience and reached level 103!

One down, one to go, I thought.

Turning around, I fled down the passage.

The other three images of Gintalush had vanished with his death, and with no other target to hold their attention, the undead charged straight for me. But unhampered by injuries, I was able to easily outrun them, and after a few random turns, I concealed myself in the shadows.

Panting for breath, I reflected on the battle. It came as no surprise that Gintalush was a sworn servant of a Dark Power. *Menaq*, I repeated, tasting the name on my tongue. He had to be the head of the mantis faction.

A new foe. My third. First Ishita, then Erebus, and now Menaq. All Powers too.

How many more enemies would I collect? My foes were multiplying at a frightening rate, yet those I could count on as allies were few and far between.

If I keep going like this, I won't survive this Game much longer.

It was a depressing realization, but I adamantly shoved it aside to dwell on happier things—like the three whole levels I'd gained from killing Gintalush. *Where should I invest the new attribute points?*

After a moment's consideration, I decided to improve my Dexterity again. I still had Wengulax to kill, after all.

Your Dexterity has increased to rank 32. Other modifiers: +6 from items.

What now? I wondered. There was still Gintalush's corpse to loot. With the undead chasing me, I hadn't had time to do so earlier. But the creatures must have dispersed by now, and with the shadows assisting me I was sure I could pick them off one by one and get to the body.

It would take time though.

Time I couldn't afford just yet. *I'll take care of Wengulax first, then come back*, I decided.

Heading northwest, I went in search of the other assassin.

✳   ✳   ✳

Two hours later, I still hadn't found Wengulax.

I'd been up and down dozens of different corridors, come across multiple dead hunter eyes—Gintalush's, I presumed, deactivated when he died—and even spied Toff's team again—from a safe distance, of course—but of Wengulax, I saw no sign.

Finally admitting defeat, I traced my steps south and toward the ogre's party. I knew where to find them, and in the absence of any better plan, I had it in my head to ask the players about Wengulax.

Who knows, maybe they've killed the mantis already. I judged that unlikely to be the case though.

From my earlier observations of Toff's team, I knew they'd resumed their dungeon dive. The party had given up on the slow, careful approach they'd likely used on the first level and instead were seemingly intent on carving a direct path to the second sector's boss.

I suspected the players' encounter with the mantises had spooked them, and now they wanted nothing more than to be done with the dungeon.

As I drew closer to the southern end of the dungeon, I heard the now-familiar voice of Toff shouting out orders amidst what sounded like a large battle.

Looks like they've almost made it to the boss, I thought, hurrying my steps. Once the party entered the final chamber, they would be beyond reach until the boss was dead.

I was about to turn the last corner and enter the passage leading to the final chamber when a sixth sense warned me of danger.

Heeding the instinct, I dived forward and rolled across the cold, hard stone floor. A blade slashed down. It cut through the empty spot of air I'd only just occupied and bounced off the nearby wall in a shower of sparks.

You have evaded an unknown hostile's attack.

Leaping back to my feet, I spun around in time to meet the charge of my green-clad attacker.

Wengulax had found me.

Or perhaps he had been hovering around the edges of Toff's party all along, waiting for me to appear.

Whatever the case, the assassin didn't look best pleased, and he threw himself at me with almost palpable ferocity. The attacks came thick and fast, seemingly from all angles and all at once. I'd only faced such a savage assault on two prior occasions, and both times I'd barely survived.

But I was no longer the same fighter I'd been just two short days ago.

In the interim, I'd gained two whole player ranks, improved my sword skills, and, most crucially, significantly advanced my Dexterity. So, despite the blistering pace of Wengulax's strokes, I managed to hold him back. I wasn't quite a match for him in skill or speed, but I *was* good enough to foil his attacks.

In the first handful of seconds, we traded over a dozen blows—without Wengulax managing to score a single hit.

I saw the assassin's eyes narrow as he came to the same realization I had: I wasn't the same easy mark. At that moment, just for a second, the ceaseless flow of the mantis' attacks relented as he reassessed his strategy.

It was the opportunity I'd been waiting for.

Not to counterattack, but to disengage. Tugging free a stone bottle from my belt, I flung it on the floor.

You have ignited a smoke bomb, creating a smoke cloud.

Dark gray clouds ballooned out from my feet, blinding Wengulax and hiding me from sight. Choosing a direction at random, I threw myself sideways. Hearing soft footfalls, I knew my foe had likewise repositioned.

I had no interest in finding him though. Not yet. Darting forward, I turned the corner and, feet pounding against stone, raced down the corridor.

A moment later, I heard the sound of pursuit.

Wengulax was following. *Good.*

I kept running, my ears straining to hear the telltale snicker of a blowpipe as I opened the distance between my hunter and me. Gintalush hadn't carried a ranged weapon—or if he had, he hadn't used it—but there was no telling if Wengulax was. Just in case, I jinked erratically to confuse my foe's aim.

I wasn't fleeing blindly, of course. There was method to my flight. Toff's party and the final chamber were maybe fifty yards ahead. Both had just come into sight—mine, at least. I didn't know if any of their players could see as well as I could in the dark and couldn't be certain I'd been spotted in turn. But I couldn't wait for confirmation.

Wengulax was gaining, and I had to act while I still could.

Unclipping another bomb, I threw it hard against the floor and, without pause, flew through the thick plumes of smoke that appeared. Emerging out the other end, I dove into the shadows and wrapped myself in darkness.

You are hidden.

Struggling not to pant, I shifted silently sideways and summoned psi in preparation.

Seconds later, Wengulax flew through the selfsame cloud and ground to a halt as he failed to see me. Knowing I had to be close, the mantis scanned the corridor ahead of him.

Wengulax has failed to detect you! You are hidden.
Wengulax has failed to detect you!
Wengulax has...

Bare blades at the ready, the assassin padded forward. From farther up the corridor, I heard renewed shouting. Had Toff's party spotted the smoke cloud? Or Wengulax?

I couldn't tell, but I dared not tear my gaze away from the searching mantis to check. Besides, if my spell worked, it wouldn't matter one way or the other.

The last weaves of my casting fell into place, and I released it, flinging a torrent of psi at my target.

You have cast simple slaysight.

I had tried once before—and failed—to use my mental abilities on the mantises, but like my blade skills, my telepathy had come a long way since then. *This time will be different,* I told myself, half-hope, half-promise.

The strands of psi I sent seeking outward seeped into Wengulax and, finding his mind's fear centers, incited them to a fever pitch.

Wengulax has failed a mental resistance check!
You have terrified your target for 10 seconds. Warning: taking hostile action against your target will dispel the spell's effect.

Between one heartbeat and the next, the assassin went from assured predator to frightened prey. Freezing in place, the assassin stood stock-still, eyes bulging and chest heaving.

I didn't hesitate with my follow-up. Shadow blinking, I stepped through the aether to emerge behind the bespelled mantis.

But I was too late.

Panic had dug its claws deep in Wengulax, and before I could strike he took off running—down the corridor and toward the assembled dungeon party, who I saw now had indeed *spotted* us.

With a pleased smile, I followed more slowly on the heels of the fleeing mantis.

Up ahead, the party didn't stand idle, nor did they question their good fortune. Staffs were lowered, bows were raised, and in a frighteningly short time, a lethal flight of missiles was racing toward Wengulax.

This time, the bewitched assassin made no attempt to dodge, and the storm descended upon him unopposed.

An unknown player has injured Wengulax.
An unknown player has critically injured Wengulax.
...
Wengulax has died.
You have gained in experience and reached level 104!

Your task, <u>Preying Mantises</u>! has been updated. You have twice-over orchestrated the death of the assassins sent to kill you, even sending one of them to his final death. Wolf is pleased. But only time will tell if your actions have sufficed to convince Menaq to call off the hunt. Your objective remains unchanged.

A broad grin broke out across my face.

Despite the somewhat ambiguous nature of the task update, I was ecstatic with my day's efforts. I'd faced both of my nemeses and triumphed without even suffering a scratch in return.

That'll teach the mantises, I thought in savage satisfaction. *Let Menaq send more of his minions to hunt me. I'll give him nothing in return except more dead followers.*

My gaze slid to the puddle of green and red that was all that remained of Wengulax. This time, I'd gained only a single level from the assassin's death. I was certain that was because I'd done no damage in the encounter myself. The bulk of the experience must have gone to Toff's party.

Speaking of which...

My eyes drifted farther up the corridor to see a crowd of players bearing down on me. They didn't look very pleased, but I was sure I could talk my way out of any unpleasantness.

I wonder if they'll let me loot the corpse, I mused idly. Folding my arms nonchalantly, I waited to greet the angry party.

The players were still muttering among themselves as they drew to a halt in a ragged line before me. Fingers were pointed, and the epithet "scav" was thrown around more than once.

Saying nothing, I waited for someone to address me first.

Toff and the same elf who'd accompanied him outside the dungeon stomped forward. "Who the blazes are you?" the ogre growled.

I hadn't had the opportunity to again assume the facial disguise I'd worn when I first met the pair, and they didn't recognize me. Right now, I wasn't sure if that was a good or bad thing.

"My name is—" I began.

"Are you responsible for that?" the elf demanded, his hand snapping out to point in the direction of the dead mantis.

I shifted minutely to face him. "If by responsible you mean did I terrify him...?" I drawled, "Then yes, I am."

My answer seemed to confound the elf but not the rest of the party, and a moment later an avalanche of analyze attempts—*failed* attempts—washed over me.

The corner of my lips twitched upward in satisfaction.

Toff took another step forward, placing his broad chest inches from my nose. The threat was unmistakable. "Are you the one the mantises are hunting?"

"Were hunting," I corrected. "The other one is dead too. And as to your question: yes, I *was* their quarry."

The ogre peered down at me, his face an inscrutable mask as he considered my response. "Then why did they attack me earlier?"

"They did?" I asked, feigning ignorance. "I don't know anything about that."

"You're sure?" the elf asked suspiciously. "What are you doing in the dungeon then?"

"Hiding from the mantises," I said, giving him a hard stare of my own. "Obviously."

The elf scowled, not liking my response, but before he could respond, Toff intervened. "Well, they're dead now, so you can get yourself gone." His piece said, the ogre turned about and walked away.

I glanced beyond Toff's retreating figure to the still-sealed gates of the final chamber. "Need any help with the boss?" I called after him.

"No, the elf snapped before the ogre could correspond. He laid a threatening hand on his sword, and the players behind him followed suit. "And now, like Toff said, you better get going."

I raised my hands and backed away. "Alright, no need for us to fight. I was only asking."

The elf gestured six players forward. "Escort him out," he ordered, glaring at me. "I don't trust him."

"Now, there's no need for that," I said hastily, thinking about all the other undead still waiting to be slain on the level. "I'll see myself out."

The elf snorted. "No, you won't." The six players surrounded me. "We'll see you out ourselves."

✳   ✳   ✳

My escort accompanied me all the way to the dungeon exit on the first level, not letting me out of their sight the entire way.

Of course, had I truly wanted to I could have escaped them at any point, but I decided against it. I was drearily tired of making enemies. I didn't need more players hunting me, and besides, I'd already accomplished what I'd set out to do in the dungeon.

"Out you go," one of my escorts snapped.

I bowed mockingly to him. "Safe hunting," I said in farewell and stepped through the portal.

You have entered sector 1 of the Forever Kingdom.

A second later, I found myself blinking under the sun's harsh light. Nearly the entire day had passed while I was in the dungeon, and it was late afternoon in Nexus. Turning about, I surveyed the square.

"Hey, you," a dwarf called. "How is the dungeon run going? Will they be done soon?"

"Not long now," I assured him. "They're about to tackle the second boss."

"About time," the dwarf grumbled.

I strode away, leaving the crowd behind. No one appeared to be watching me, and why should they? I was just some random noob fleeing the dungeon. Exiting the square, I slipped into an adjacent street.

It was time to decide my next move.

✳   ✳   ✳

Information, I decided. *That's what I need first.*

For the time being, matters with the mantises were about as resolved as I could expect them to be. At the very least, I'd bought myself a few hours.

But with any luck, it would take Menaq much longer to find a replacement for whichever mantis I'd sent to his final death. I was hoping for a few days at least and planned on using the time wisely. Namely, on obtaining my third Class.

Turning my steps north, I made my way to the information brokers' offices. I didn't have much gold remaining, but I couldn't afford further delays, and if I needed to spend all of it in pursuit of my third Class, so be it.

While I walked, I renewed my protections—the enchantments had run dry—and saw to my player advancement, investing my latest attribute point.

Your Dexterity has increased to rank 33. Other modifiers: +6 from items.

It didn't take me long to reach my destination. Cutting through the waiting crowd outside the brokers' offices, I slipped into line inside. Eventually, my turn came, and I stepped up to the counter.

"How can I help you today?" the uniformed gnome on duty asked.

I'd given the matter serious thought on the way over and was ready with my questions. "I'm looking for information on the dungeons in the plague quarter."

"Certainly, sir," the gnome replied. "The plague dungeon is a large area and holds a multitude of dungeons. First, there are the three public—"

"You mistake me," I said, interrupting him. "I don't want generic information. I'm looking for *detailed* data—floorplans and the like—on four specific dungeons."

The gnome's interest sharpened. "That will be costly. What's your budget?"

I hesitated for only a fraction of a second. "Five hundred gold." That would leave me with a little over two hundred gold to purchase whatever equipment and consumables I needed.

"That's not enough," the broker said slowly, "not for the floorplans of four different dungeons." He looked me over carefully. "Do you want to restrict your query to one or perhaps two dungeons?"

I sighed. I couldn't do that. As yet, I didn't know which dungeon would best suit my purpose, which was *why* I needed the information in the first place.

"That won't work," I replied. "Leave out the floorplans then. I'll take the information only. As complete and accurate as you can provide for the price."

The gnome nodded. "Very well. Which dungeons are the subject of your query?"

I ticked off points on my fingers. "The guardian tower. The Triumvirate dungeon. And the one beneath the brotherhood chapterhouse." I eyed the broker. "You think you can help with all that?"

"The guardian tower is a public dungeon, and information on it is easy enough to obtain," the gnome said. He coughed delicately. "On the other hand, knowledge of the dungeons controlled by the knights and brotherhood is a bit more difficult to come by. However, for that price... we can certainly help."

I nodded curtly. I'd half-feared the broker would claim the information on the private dungeons was restricted.

The gnome scribbled down my request on a piece of paper. "What about the fourth dungeon?" he asked, not looking up.

I hesitated again. "I don't know much about it," I admitted. "Only that it is located somewhere in the saltmarsh."

The broker looked up quickly. "The saltmarsh, you say?"

"From your expression, I take it you've heard of it," I said, leaning eagerly over the counter. "What can you tell me about it?"

For a split second, the broker's mask of unassuming affability cracked. "I–I'm not... sure," he stuttered.

Before I could query this surprising response, the gnome jumped off his stool and hurried away. "Stay right there," he called over his shoulder.

I stared at the broker's disappearing form in disbelief. What was it I'd seen on his face? Worry? Fear? Neither response made much sense.

Why would talk of the saltmarsh dungeon perturb the broker when he'd not so much as batted an eye at the thought of revealing information on the powerful Triumvirate dungeon?

And where's he run off to?

Fuming in impatience at the enforced delay, I drummed my fingers against the counter.

The broker kept me waiting ten long minutes, and when he returned, it was only to point me out to his companion before disappearing again.

I focused my attention on the second gnome. He, too, was dressed in a broker's uniform, but he looked nothing like the other gnomes in the office. For one, he was old, with a beard that stretched down to his waist, and for another, his coat was decorated with symbols and medals whose meaning escaped me.

The old gnome sat on the stool before me. "Good day, young fellow," he said in a spritely voice that belied his obvious age. "I'm master broker Cyren." He leaned forward, his voice dropping to a conspiratorial whisper. "My colleague tells me you're looking for information on the dungeon in the marsh. Is this true?"

Not sure what to make of the new broker, I nodded mutely.

"Excellent!" Cyren exclaimed, his bushy brows quivering with lively interest. "Tell me, what is the reason for your inquiry?"

My own eyebrows flicked upward. "Why is that any of your business? I thought this was a simple monetary transaction: information in exchange for money."

"It is, it is," Cyren said, nodding agreeably. "But you must understand, young man, some information is more sensitive than others—" he shot me an all-too-shrewd look—"and some matters we dare not entangle ourselves in, not for all the money in the Game." He paused. "Now, I'm afraid, until I know more about the nature of your request, I will not be able to help."

I hesitated, torn between my need for secrecy and my desire for information. It was obvious the old codger knew something worth hearing, but how did I convince him to tell me what that was?

"I'm looking for a dungeon to enter," I said finally. "Somewhere off the beaten track to level up."

"Ah, you're an adventurer then," Cyren said, a strange look passing too quickly over his face to decipher. Was that disappointment I'd seen?

"In that case," he continued, "I regret to inform you—"

"Wait!" I interjected, sensing a refusal coming. "That's not the entire reason."

I leaned forward across the counter. I wasn't sure why the gnome was being so cagey, but I realized if I wanted to find out more, I would have to risk sharing some truth. "I have other reasons, reasons that are my own. I

will tell you, but to be clear, it's not information that's for sale. To *anyone*."
I eyed Cyren meaningfully.

The old gnome gazed back at me solemnly. "We are brokers of information," he said. "But we do not trade secrets that our clients are unwilling to share. You can trust me."

I wasn't sure about that, but I didn't see that I had much choice.

I could always blindly search the swamp, but given the diseases that were said to run rampant there, I doubted I would find the dungeon before I was infected. Still, I hesitated.

"Does it have something to do with your Class?" Cyren prompted suddenly.

I glanced at him sharply. "What do you know about my Class?"

Cyren ignored the bite in my voice. "Mindstalkers are rare these days. I can't recall the last time one was spotted in the city." A knowing smile tugged at the corners of his mouth. "And I've been around for a *very* long time."

I stared at the gnome. How had he figured out my Class? More importantly, what else did he know? If his expression was anything to go by—too much.

Is this even a gnome in front of me?

Reaching out with my will, I analyzed Cyren.

The target is Cyren, a level 128 loremaster and gnome.

Cyren's level was surprisingly high, but if the Game's response could be trusted, he was an ordinary gnome—and not a player.

But could the Game's response be trusted?

Is Cyren Loken in disguise? Or some other player? Amgira, for instance? And how would I even know if he was?

I rubbed at my temples, feeling the onset of a pounding headache. The truth was, there was no way to know. And suspecting everyone I met of being someone else was a sure path to madness.

Curbing my paranoia, I answered Cyren as vaguely as I could manage. "You're right. My Class is a large part of why I'm seeking a rare and dangerous dungeon like the one in the saltmarsh. Someone told me it's in such a dungeon that I would find the third Class I needed."

The gnome's eyes narrowed almost imperceptibly. "Someone? A... blood relative, perhaps?"

I forced myself not to react. Cyren's rejoinder sounded innocent enough, but I was sure I hadn't imagined the slight stress he'd placed on the word "blood."

Careful, Michael, you're swimming in dangerous waters now.

"You could say that," I answered just as obliquely. "It's something of a dying wish of one of my elders." I paused, then added casually, "He's quite ancient these days."

"Ah," Cyren replied. The gnome's expression remained just as impassive as mine, but he was unable to hide the sudden flare of interest in his eyes at my use of the word "ancient."

He fell into meditative silence, and I let him, waiting with thinly disguised impatience for him to go on.

"Perhaps if your family elder is as old as I am, he will remember the past as fondly as I do," the gnome mused. "In my more sentimental moments, I find myself wishing for a return to those times."

I nodded mutely.

Despite the strangely coded manner of our discussion, I understood Cyren: he, like Sulan, yearned for a return of the ancients.

As tumultuous as the last few days had been, I hadn't failed to see what the plague quarter had made self-evident: the common people of Nexus were not well-treated. Players, if not the Game itself, seemed to have a callous disregard for them. And from that perspective, I could understand why it was non-players, more than players, who took a keener interest in the ancients and their bloodlines.

I truly did sympathize with Cyren and Sulan's hopes. Scions—or players—should do better, should *be* better. The strong protected the weak. It was a motto of the Pack, and one I wholeheartedly agreed with.

But.

But I didn't know Cyren well enough to speak more openly on the topic. I had already gone out on a limb, revealing as much as I had to secure his help. Now, it was up to the gnome to decide if he would aid me or not.

"On second consideration," Cyren said, disrupting my musings, "I think I may be able to help."

Before I could respond, Cyren disappeared into the back office, only to reemerge a few minutes later with a sheaf of papers. He laid the documents on the counter. "This is what five hundred gold buys you on the three dungeons."

I made no move to pick up the papers. "And the fourth dungeon?"

Cyren laid another parchment atop the others. "This is *everything* our archives hold on that one." His eyes glinted. "It's worth considerably more than five hundred gold. Consider it my gift."

I bowed gravely and, picking up the papers, laid my hand on the master broker's keystone to complete the transaction.

"Thank you," he murmured. "Now, is there anything else I can help you with?"

I rubbed my chin. "Actually, there is." I was convinced I had rid myself of the mantises—for the time being, anyway—but there was no point in taking chances. "Do you know how I can shield my mind while asleep?"

"You don't know already?" Cyren asked, his bushy brows wagging. "It's no great secret." He smiled. "I won't even bother charging you for the answer."

I threw him a dry look but said nothing as I waited for his response.

The gnome chuckled. "There are any number of solutions, but the simplest is a mental concealment crystal. Most merchants stock them."

I smacked my head. "I should've thought of that."

Cyren bobbed his head. "What else do you need?"

"Nothing, thank you. You've been a big help already." I turned to go. "Goodbye, Cyren."

"Goodbye," he replied, watching me go, then added so softly I nearly didn't hear him, "and luck upon your house, stranger."

✻   ✻   ✻

Leaving the information brokers' offices, I hurried east toward the Southern Outpost. I needed somewhere to read the documents Cyren had provided, and the tavern was close by.

As I walked, I mused over the gnome's parting words. Like his previous utterances, they were ambiguous enough to be dismissed as nothing out of the ordinary, but it wasn't by happenstance that Cyren had used the word "house."

The gnome was a secret supporter of the ancients and perhaps a potential ally too. How much I could rely on him, though, was yet to be seen.

Before entering the Southern Outpost, I cloaked myself in illusion, and no one spared me a second glance. The tavern was packed, but there were still a few empty tables. Shoving my way through the patrons, I sat down in the room's darkest corner.

After ordering a drink and waiting for it to arrive, I pulled out the notes Cyren had given me and spread them across the table. The stack of papers consisted of four separate documents, one pertaining to each dungeon.

The first was titled *"The Guardian Tower,"* and just as Cyren had promised, contained detailed information on its denizens. Picking up the notes, I began to read.

The guardian tower is one of the few dungeons in Nexus open to players unaffiliated with a faction. It consists of five sectors and is filled with denizens between ranks ten and twenty. But despite being freely accessible, the guardian tower is considered to be one of the hardest dungeons in Nexus. And not for the usual reasons.

For starters, the dungeon's nether portals are all one-way. Once you enter a sector, the only way out is through. Turning back is NOT an option.

This design choice is made worse by the fact that each sector has only one exit—this being the entrance to the next level. Thus, when players enter the guardian tower, they are committing themselves to completing all five of its levels.

Beware, if you enter the guardian tower, you either finish the dungeon in its entirety—or die trying.

But that's not all. What makes the dungeon immeasurably more difficult is that only six players may be in the dungeon at any one time. This is a far greater restriction than encountered in most other dungeons and raises the stakes significantly.

There is nothing remarkable about the dungeon's denizens themselves. The guardian tower is inhabited by savants—physically weak magic and mind users—and their horde of minions: monsters and beasts enslaved to do their masters' bidding. While overcoming the savants and their slaves can be difficult at times, the challenge this presents is nothing unexpected from a tier four dungeon.

The same, unfortunately, cannot be said of the guardian tower's loot. In another extraordinary deviation from standard dungeon design, the first four sectors contain no loot chests, while the fifth has only the single one. Worse yet, the chest—and coincidentally, the exit portal too—can only be accessed by using the amulets taken off the sector bosses in the previous four levels.

Beware, if you enter the guardian tower, you will not be able to bypass any of its sector bosses. You must kill them all to receive your "reward" and exit the dungeon.

Note, too, that if you are expecting great loot, you are destined to be disappointed. Players have consistently reported finding little or nothing of value in the dungeon except for the guardian amulet itself. And while the item in question is worth a tidy sum, it does not warrant the extraordinary risks necessary to acquire it.

Understandably, given everything spelled out above, the guardian tower is unpopular, and all players are advised to stay away.

I sat back in my chair, a frown on my face. The dungeon notes were certainly helpful but seemed a tad... light on details.

This is what five hundred gold had bought me? Where was the detailed breakdown of creature numbers, locations, and weaknesses?

I shook my head. *It doesn't matter. This is what you got; work with it.* Setting aside my regret at the loss of coin, I considered the information itself.

The guardian tower intrigued me. In particular, the reference to "beasts" attracted my interest, but my overall assessment was that the dungeon was too dangerous to venture within. *A dungeon without retreat? No, thank you.*

Setting aside the first document, I turned my attention to the next. It was titled, *"The Minotaur Maze."*

The minotaur maze is a plague quarter dungeon that has been under the control of the Triumvirate knights for centuries. It is a single-level dungeon and, to date, is the single largest dungeon sector ever discovered.

As the name implies, the dungeon is home to minotaurs of all types and levels, ranging from rank five to nineteen. Minotaurs usually favor heavy weaponry and multiple layers of armor. They are social creatures and frequently gather in large groups.

Most are primitive, barbaric, and brutish fighters. Some, though, are cunning, and given the creatures' love for puzzles, they can make the dungeon... unexpectedly challenging. It is no secret that minotaurs love to build—and break—things. As a result, the dungeon is often changing, with new corridors and junctions appearing with every iteration.

The maze's ever-shifting layout is a key feature of the dungeon. It contains multiple secret rooms, traps, pitfalls, and hidden loot chests. In fact, the maze is so large and its frequent changes are so extensive that large sections of it are said to lie forgotten and unvisited for decades.

Truly, the maze is a dungeon with no one true path to success.

However, no matter which road one takes, they all eventually lead to the center of the maze and its dungeon boss: the minotaur king.

The minotaur king is a behemoth said to dwarf even the tallest of Nexus's buildings. He is reputedly so fearsome a foe that even parties of well-prepared and trained knights have a low success rate against him, killing him in only one out of two attempts.

Slaying the king is, of course, not necessary to escape the dungeon, but it is required to obtain the best rewards. In conclusion, it is advised players only enter the maze in large groups and with a hefty surplus of lives.

"Minotaurs," I muttered when I was done. The thought of facing such creatures wasn't appealing.

Admittedly, the rest of the dungeon was intriguing. Hidden chests, secret rooms, and traps... were all challenges I was uniquely suited to face.

But.

But the minotaurs themselves would be a problem. Not to mention all the trouble I would have to go through in the first place to penetrate the knights' defense and enter the maze.

And while several smaller treasure chests sounded great in theory, their very number meant their rewards would be diluted. I wasn't looking for heaps of loot, but one item *only*—the best of its type that I could find.

I turned to the next parchment. It was titled *"The Coral Palace."* Hopefully, it would make for better reading.

The coral palace is a dungeon along the southern rim of the plague quarter and has been under the control of the stygian brotherhood ever since it was first discovered. Given the dungeon's proximity to the sea, it is perhaps not surprising that its many sectors are populated by denizens of the ocean.

The coral palace is a ten-sector dungeon—one of the deepest of its kind. Levels are highly stratified, with the first level containing foes of rank twelve and the last enemies of rank twenty-one. Exit portals are present in every sector, allowing players to withdraw if necessary.

The dungeon itself consists of a myriad of winding tunnels. They are frequently dark, water-logged, and cramped, making the dungeon unsuitable for claustrophobic players. Many of the palace's halls and chambers are also either partially or fully submerged in water, this being the preferred habitat of the occupants.

Water-breathing and darkvision spells or enchantments are a must.

The coral palace's denizens are among the most varied of any dungeon and run the gamut of all aquatic life—including the merfolk. Players can expect to face enslaved fighters, sorcerers, witches, and clerics.

Many of the encounters will take place underwater, and despite whatever water-breathing apparatuses you may have, the advantage in speed and maneuverability will almost always lie with the dungeon denizens.

The coral place does not restrict the number of players that can enter. However, due to the confined nature of most areas in the dungeon, party numbers will count for little, and you can expect most battles to be resolved by no more than a handful of participants.

In short, the coral palace is a dungeon for players who are most at home in aquatic environments or, conversely, those who wield fire, especially in forms that can resist the dousing touch of water.

I sighed noisily. The coral palace was as problematic as the other two dungeons.

While I was certainly not opposed to fighting in the dark, neither cramped tunnels nor submerged ones sounded like much fun. In both, I wouldn't be able to use one of my greatest assets: my speed. If anything, it sounded like the merfolk would have the upper hand on me in that regard. And then, of course, I would have the same difficulty accessing the coral palace as I would the minotaur maze.

It's not for me, I decided.

That left only one option. The most dangerous sounding and most mysterious: the saltmarsh dungeon.

CHAPTER 207: THE OLD GNOME'S GIFT

The first thing I noticed was that the notes on the saltmarsh dungeon were untitled. It appeared that the dungeon had no name, at least none known to the gnomes.

I didn't let that daunt me though and began reading.

Little is known about the dungeon in the saltmarsh. Even its name has been lost over time. But despite this, rumors of the dungeon persist to this day. Some of these tales have no doubt sprung from ancient texts on the subject. Many older historical accounts make reference to the saltmarsh dungeon, all without actually naming it.

And while some scholars may point out that old tales and gossip hardly constitute proof, they lend weight to the theory that the saltmarsh dungeon truly exists—or did exist.

According to the oldest texts on the subject, each saltmarsh dungeon sector is larger than the minotaur maze, and there are many more such sectors than even in the coral palace. The authors who penned those descriptions undoubtedly stretched the truth. But even accounting for their exaggeration, it seems clear the dungeon must be huge.

As for the inhabitants? Information on them is even more scarce. One word, though, is used repeatedly in reference to the dungeon: 'pestilence.' From this, it can be postulated the dungeon favors diseased creatures, contains multiple contagions, and is replete with infections.

Of course, given its location, some treatises have drawn parallels with the dungeon and the plague quarter. A few have even gone so far as to suggest it is the dungeon itself that is the source of the saltmarsh's contamination. This, of course, is an impossibility. The wards on a dungeon's entrance portals are strong enough to hold back the nether, and there is no way any mere disease could spill through.

Lastly, we broach the question that most preoccupies adventurers: where to find the dungeon. Sadly, the ancient texts are of little help. They are all emphatic that the dungeon lies somewhere in the saltmarsh but are vague as to its precise coordinates.

In fact, the only clue to the dungeon portal's location is a cryptic excerpt from an ancient treatise on a feud between two warring houses. It had this to say: 'to find pestilence, search beneath pestilence.'

As you can imagine, this obscure piece of advice has led many adventurers to plumb the depths of the saltmarsh in hopes of finding the lost dungeon. But despite numerous expeditions over the centuries, all such ventures have turned up empty, and these days most scholars dismiss the text as no more than a fanciful turn of phrase.

In conclusion, the only advice we may offer you is the obvious: if you intend on seeking the lost saltmarsh dungeon, make certain to stock up on disease protection enchantments and be prepared for a long and potentially fruitless search.

"That's it?" Unbidden, a growl of disgust escaped me. *Beware of disease and failure? That was all the gnomes could offer me?*

The information on the saltmarsh dungeon was sketchy—at best. The first three parchments had contained hard details, but to even label the saltmarsh dungeon notes as speculation was being generous!

With a sigh, I let the document fall from my fingers. Bracing my elbows against the table, I leaned over and rubbed my temples. If I was being honest, I was less unhappy about the information than how unready I appeared to be. I had hoped to enter one of the four dungeons soon. But if nothing else, the gnome's notes made clear that would be foolish.

The guardian tower left no room for retreat.

The minotaur maze seemed to favor brute strength—*not* my forte.

The coral palace would nullify my advantages in speed.

As for the saltmarsh dungeon... it seemed highly improbable I would even be able to find the bloody thing!

Of course, I could still plunge ahead and attempt one of the dungeons, but the odds of me actually succeeding were low. *So what do I do now?* I wondered. I wasn't sure.

Perhaps it's time to leave Nexus.

Picking up the documents, I sifted through them while I toyed with the notion. I could always return later—when things settled down. And truthfully, I could acquire a third Class anywhere.

But it wouldn't be a *great* Class.

And while taking on any old Class seemed the safer option right now, it would leave me vulnerable in the long run. My Classes might never meld. Or worse, I could find myself lacking the skills and abilities necessary to keep leveling and end up with my player growth capped.

That *would* spell disaster.

Sooner or later, my bloodline would be exposed, and when that happened, I couldn't be weak. Or seen to be weak.

And would matters be any better elsewhere? The mantises would surely follow me wherever I went. *No, leaving isn't a good option.*

A tiny slip of paper fell out of the stack of documents.

I studied it curiously. It had been stuck to the back of the saltmarsh dungeon notes and was a scribbled message penned by Cyren himself. Picking it up, I began to read.

P.S. There is one other rumor about the saltmarsh dungeon that bears consideration. Most scholars dismiss it as mere fancy, but I thought it might pique your interest.

Sometimes, when the saltmarsh dungeon is brought up in recent histories—those chronicling the rise of the new Powers—mention is also made of an 'ancient adversary.'

The relationship between adversary and dungeon is unclear though. Some texts imply the dungeon is the adversary's prison, others their refuge. Who or what the adversary is, is also never described. Details on he/she/it are scantier than on the dungeon itself.

Perhaps this will help you on your quest. —Cyren.

"An ancient adversary?" I murmured. It wasn't much to go on. Ancient could just mean old. Though I doubted that. Cyren obviously thought it significant enough to be worth mentioning.

Most likely, it was a reference to an old Power.

Or one of their envoys.

I stared at the scribbled words, my thoughts far away. Was this the clue I'd been searching for? Was Ceruvax hiding in the saltmarsh dungeon?

Who else can it be? I wondered. *It must be him.*

Your task, <u>Find the last Wolf Envoy,</u> has been updated. You have received unverified information that Ceruvax is the one trapped in the saltmarsh dungeon. Your objective remains unchanged: find the envoy to learn more about the way of the Wolf.

Setting down the note, I sat back in my chair and sipped at my drink. *So, now I have the Wolf envoy's location.*

But it didn't change anything.

I still had no idea where the dungeon entrance was, and I didn't have the time, not to mention the equipment, to search the saltmarsh for days on end.

The question remained: what now?

✳   ✳   ✳

By the time I finished my drink, I had the makings of a plan.

My initial assessment hadn't changed. I wasn't ready for any of the four dungeons, but that didn't leave me without plenty to do.

I still had my room in the knight's castle for two more nights. Even if my nemeses or their replacements resumed hunting me sooner than expected, with a secure base and enough enchantments to protect me, I wasn't unduly worried about being able to stay out of the mantises' clutches—for the next couple of days at least.

I had to use that time to prepare for my dungeon crawl. I needed money and training. Lots of both.

Packing away the parchments, I rose to my feet. If I was going to enter one of the four dungeons in two days, I couldn't afford to waste even an hour. I had to begin now.

Exiting the tavern, I glanced up. There were still a few hours left in the day. *Train today, finish my bounties tomorrow,* I decided. With my course set, I headed south—back to the scorching dunes dungeon.

✳   ✳   ✳

The scorching dunes dungeon was welcomingly familiar. It was just as I'd left it, with hordes of players outside and inside.

Surprisingly, Genmark's party was still in the dungeon, and more surprisingly, they welcomed me back with open arms despite my tardiness.

I was just as glad to see them, and without hesitation I threw myself into the role of party tank.

The next few hours passed by quickly. Forgetting the future and whatever it held, I focused solely on the rather simple task of slaying the desert denizens. Like it had the first day, my skills ticked upward nicely, even if I gained little in the way of experience.

Your dodging has increased to level 77. Your shortswords has increased to level 83. Your light armor has increased to level 68.

Your meditation has increased to level 86. Your insight has increased to level 88. Your deception has increased to level 83.

It was again close to midnight when Genmark finally led the party out of the dungeon. Whatever else they might be, the gnome's team was committed to their own progression, and I found myself admiring their tenacity.

"So, can I count on you to show up tomorrow?" Genmark asked, glaring at me in mock anger as the group gathered outside the dungeon to divide the day's spoils.

I frowned while I considered the day ahead. I had lots to do, but I also knew I couldn't ignore my skills training. *I'll have to squeeze it in,* I decided. "Maybe," I allowed. "But I can't promise anything. It depends on whether—"

Genmark chuckled and held up his hand. "Don't worry, I'm only teasing. But if you *do* decide to join us, we'll be here." Not saying anything further, the gnome dropped a small pouch in my hand.

You have acquired 40 gold.

I looked at him in surprise. "What's this?"

"Your cut from today," Genmark said, "*and* the rest of what I owed you from yesterday. The reagents sold for more than I expected."

"Thank you," I murmured with a smile. Given how late I'd joined the party today, I hadn't been expecting a share of the loot, and it spoke well of the gnome's integrity that he saw I was compensated anyway.

Attempting one of the four dungeons will be easier with a few companions by my side, I thought suddenly. I scrutinized Genmark more closely. Could I trust the gnome that far?

Perhaps. Let's see how tomorrow goes first.

With a final farewell to the group, I turned around and headed toward the citadel and a night of well-deserved rest.

I entered the Triumvirate castle without fuss. Constable Richter was absent but showing the guards my citadel room key sufficed to gain me entry, and no questions were asked as I slipped into the keep.

Before heading to my room and the sleep that beckoned, I stopped by Kesh's offices.

"Hello, Cara," I said, stifling a yawn as I entered the shop.

"Michael," Cara greeted, looking up. She studied me for a moment. "You've been out late again, I see."

"And you're still here," I rejoined. "Don't you ever sleep?"

She chuckled. "I do, actually. These robes are good for more than concealing my face, you know. They do a good job of hiding when I'm napping too."

I laughed. "Ah, so that's your secret." I glanced around the room. As always, it was empty. "And what's the story behind this shop? I've never seen anyone in here. How does Kesh manage to keep the place open?"

I sensed more than saw Cara's grin.

"My primary purpose in the citadel is more buying than selling," she replied. "Walk-ins such as yourself are a bonus."

I frowned. What could Cara be buying, and in such volume, as to warrant Kesh establishing an office here?

Then realization dawned. *The dungeon.*

The knights had to be selling their loot from the minotaur maze through Kesh. "So, the Triumvirate are also emporium customers?"

Cara shrugged eloquently. "I couldn't say."

As an agent of the emporium, Cara was, of course, constrained from discussing its customers, but her response cemented my certainty that I'd guessed right.

"I heard you created quite the stir this morning," Cara said in an abrupt change of topic.

I raised one eyebrow. "Oh?"

"The knight-captain roused the entire keep. Every Triumvirate knight was put on alert." She paused. "Is it true the mantises were hunting you?"

I nodded.

Cara tilted her head to the side and studied me curiously. "Yet here you are. Alive and well."

I grinned. "I'm not so easy to kill."

Cara didn't laugh as I expected. "Don't underestimate the mantises, Michael." The agent's tone was grave, and she almost sounded... worried. "They will not stop."

My own amusement faded. "Speaking of the assassins, they're why I'm here, actually."

"Oh?" Cara asked, mimicking my earlier response.

"I used up nearly my entire stock of crystals today. Do you have more disease and scent enchantments?"

"How many do you need?"

"Five each. And five mental concealment crystals too, if you have them."

"I can supply all of that," Cara confirmed. "But the mental concealment crystals are more expensive." I opened my mouth to protest, but before I did, she went on, "Each one lasts twice as long as the others."

"Oh, alright. Two should suffice then." I paused. "How much will all that cost?"

"Three hundred gold."

I winced. That was more money than I had left. I was bleeding gold and knew I had to curb my spending soon. But I couldn't afford to stop altogether. Time was in far shorter supply.

"Is there anything else?" Cara asked, mistaking the reason for my silence.

I hesitated, pondering my choices. There were a whole host of things I wanted. Many of my Mind abilities were still not upgraded, my thieving skill had reached tier two, adding to the list of abilities requiring attention, and my trapper's bracelet needed refilling, but with money problematic, I had to confine my purchases to only what was critical.

"Michael?" Cara prompted again.

"Sorry, just thinking." I exhaled slowly and made my choices. "I also need tier two ability tomes for trap disarm, detect trap, and lock picking."

I'd decided to go with advancing some of my thieving abilities. The cost to upgrade the mind abilities I'd earned in the Wolf trials was exorbitant, and until I had enough money to afford better traps, it didn't make sense to improve the set trap ability or refill my trapper's wristband. "Can you get all that?"

Instead of answering, Cara placed the three items in question on the table.

This is an improved trap detect ability tome. Governing attribute: Perception. Tier: advanced. Cost: 25 gold. Requirement: rank 5 thieving.

This is a superior lockpicking ability tome. Governing attribute: Dexterity. Tier: advanced. Cost: 25 gold. Requirement: rank 5 thieving.

This is an improved trap disarm ability tome. Governing attribute: Dexterity. Tier: advanced. Cost: 25 gold. Requirement: rank 5 thieving.

I glanced at Cara in surprise.

"The ability tomes are commonplace," she replied, seeing my look. "There are stacks of them in the warehouse. It was simple enough to bring through what you needed."

Meaning she'd used the merchant's ability to teleport items through the aether to fetch the books. Pulling another twelve objects from thin air again—the enchantment crystals I asked for this time—Cara laid them atop the books.

When I still made no move to take the items, Cara added delicately, "That will be three hundred and seventy-five gold."

"I don't have the money," I admitted heavily. I laid my coin pouch on the table. "That, plus what I have in the bank, comes to about two hundred gold."

Cara sat back and considered me silently for a moment. "What can you offer in trade?"

I set down the death magic wand I'd retrieved from the haunted catacombs dungeon. "Will this suffice?"

You have lost a death magic wand.

"Kesh allows me some leeway in the trades I make," she said softly. "But even at the best prices I can offer you, the wand is insufficient. I'm sorry, Michael."

I sighed, but I had suspected that would be the case. "I understand," I said and retrieved spider's bite from my backpack.

I'd had the shortsword nearly since the beginning of my time in the Game and was sad to part with it. The weapon had served me well, but I had little use for it now. Laying the sword beside the wand, I looked at Cara in silent question.

She shook her head mutely.

A grimace crossed my face, but I didn't argue. If Cara said it wasn't enough, it wasn't. Taking off the medallion around my neck, I laid it on the table as well. It was the least useful of my gear.

You have lost a medallion of the stygian brotherhood.

Leaning forward, Cara inspected the artifact closely. "Almost there," she said encouragingly.

Drawing out one of my mana potions from my backpack, I laid it on the table and, when she still didn't say anything, added another.

You have lost 2 x major mana potions.

"It's enough," Cara confirmed.

I sighed in relief. The trade was costlier than I expected, but crucially, I'd gotten what I needed. Sweeping up the items, I placed my hand on Cara's keystone and concluded the exchange.

You have acquired 5 x rank 4 disease protection crystals, 5 x scent concealment crystals, and 3 x tier 2 ability tomes.

You have acquired 2 x mental concealment crystals. Cost: 100 gold. Each crystal contains a single-use enchantment that hides your consciousness for 8 hours.

You have lost 196 gold, 4 silver, and 9 copper. Money remaining in your bank account: 0.

"Well," I said with a lopsided grin. "That officially makes me a penniless player."

"But a well-equipped one," Cara quipped.

I laughed. "That too." Bidding her farewell, I headed up to my room.

✳   ✳   ✳

I reached the tiny chamber I'd been allotted without encountering anyone. Closing the door behind me, I sat down at the wooden desk and began to read.

You have upgraded your trap disarm ability to improved trap disarm, allowing you to deactivate tier 2 traps. You have upgraded your lockpicking ability to superior lockpicking, allowing you to open tier 2 locks. You have 5 of 32 Dexterity ability slots remaining.

You have upgraded your trap detect ability to improved trap detect, increasing your chances of spotting higher-tiered traps. You have 3 of 25 Perception ability slots remaining.

The last tome vanished and, closing my eyes, I let the new knowledge seep into my mind. My experience in the haunted catacombs had once again demonstrated the benefits of the thieving skill, especially in dungeons with narrow corridors or locked chambers.

I hadn't decided yet which of the four dungeons to tackle once I adjudged myself ready, but in at least two of them—the minotaur maze and the coral palace—I could see myself making extensive use of my thieving abilities.

Laying down on the bed and folding my arms behind my head, I considered the upcoming day. I hoped to complete at least two of my allotted bounties, then take on as many others as I could reasonably conclude. Doing that would leave me with enough gold to advance my set trap ability and replenish my traps. Then I would take time to train my skills further and perhaps gain a few more levels.

But first, I need a good night's rest.

Tugging free the mental concealment crystal from my belt, I considered it for a moment. Hopefully, it performed as advertised. *Here goes,* I thought and closed my fist around the slim shape.

The delicate crystal cracked, releasing the stored enchantment.

You have activated a single-use enchantment, casting a ward of mental concealment around yourself. For the next 8 hours, your consciousness will be hidden. Casters without direct line of sight of you will be unable to target you with mind spells.

Perfect, I thought in satisfaction.

Safe in the knowledge that, tonight at least, the mantises wouldn't find me, I closed my eyes and let sleep take me.

CHAPTER 209: WHY WON'T THEY STOP?

Day Five

I awoke to a loud bang.

Sitting up but making no move to leave the warmth of the bed, I rubbed my eyes. What time was it? Checking the state of my mental concealment ward, I saw that little over six hours had passed.

It's too damn early, that's what, I thought grouchily.

A fist hammered on the door again.

Who's disturbing me at this hour?

"Open up!" a voice barked. "If you don't unlock this door right this instant, I'll bloody well kick it in!"

From the sounds of it, I had a knight at the door, and he seemed to be in a fine mood too. Slipping off the bed, I yanked open the door just as the player was about to pound on it again.

My early-morning visitor stumbled forward and nearly fell but caught himself in time. "Who are you?" I asked before he could get a word in.

"Teg," the knight replied. Straightening, he glared at me. "What took you so long?"

I folded my arms. "I was sleeping. Now, explain yourself. Why are you disturbing me at this ungodly hour?"

"The knight-captain wants to see you," he responded curtly.

I stayed where I was. Whatever this was, it couldn't be good, not if the citadel's commander wanted to see me. "Why?"

"Come with me and find out for yourself!" Teg growled.

My lips tightened, and I contemplated refusing.

The knight jerked his thumb behind him. "If you resist, we'll be only too pleased to drag you to him," he said, eyes gleaming at the idea.

My gaze skipped over Teg to the squad of soldiers at his back. "Alright," I conceded. "I'll come."

✳ ✳ ✳

The soldiers led me upward and not down to the foyer as I expected.

Eventually, my escort came to a halt outside a steel door on what had to be the highest floor of the castle. At our appearance, the knight on guard slipped into the room beyond.

Five long minutes dragged by, and still the guard didn't reemerge.

Despite the urgency of my summons, it seemed I was to be kept waiting. I turned to Teg. "Where are we?"

He appeared disinclined to answer but humored me nonetheless. "Captain's office," he said in a clipped tone.

I nodded thoughtfully as I tried to puzzle out the reason for the odd summons. I didn't know the knight-captain, and as far as I knew, he knew nothing of me either. Why would he want to see me?

The door was yanked back, and the guard waved me inside. "Knight-captain Orlon will see you now."

I strode forward. Teg stepped forward too, but his fellow's hard stare stopped him. "Not you." His gaze back darted to me. "Him only. Alone."

Slipping past both knights, I entered the room, eager to discover what was going on. The door closed shut behind me, leaving me alone with the room's two occupants.

One I knew. It was Constable Richter. The other was a large, bearded man—Knight-captain Orlon, I presumed. Even at this early hour, he was fully armored. His gleaming breastplate was proudly adorned with the Triumvirate's insignia, and below it were other markings that denoted his rank and office.

"So. You're the one," Orlon said, fixing his gaze on me with hawklike intensity.

Ignoring the cryptic comment, I nodded in greeting to the constable before turning back to the knight-captain. "I'm Michael." I held out my hand. "I don't believe we've met."

The bearded knight snorted. "This is no time for pleasantries, boy," he said, ignoring my outstretched arm. "We've mantises on our door baying for blood."

Alarm flickered through me, but I let no sign of it show on my face as I lowered my hand. At least the reason behind my summons was apparent now. What was unclear, though, was how the assassins had found me. I'd carried no scent trail into the citadel, and I had been shielded the entire time I'd been here, even while asleep.

"What, nothing to say for yourself?" Orlon demanded.

I met his gaze, my own expression bland. "Don't tell me you woke me this early for a pair of mantises? Surely the mighty Triumvirate knights aren't scared of—"

The knight-captain barked out in laughter. "Stow the attitude," he growled a moment later. "I don't have the time for it."

"And it's not a pair of mantises," Richter said, speaking softly for the first time.

I turned the constable's way. "Oh?" Did just the one assassin come hunting me this time? But if that were the case, why did Orlon look so troubled? Because despite the knight-captain's prickly air, I could smell the worry lurking beneath.

"There are five dozen mantises outside the citadel," the constable said, the tremble in his words betraying that he, too, was unnerved.

My eyes grew round. *"Five dozen?"*

"And those are only the ones we can see," Richter added. "There must be many more hidden in the shadows."

I said nothing, still struck mute by the magnitude of the disaster I was facing. Not in my most pessimistic moments had I imagined the mantises would escalate matters so quickly. And all for what, killing Wengulax and Gintalush?

I shook my head in disbelief.

Orlon chuckled suddenly, and I looked at him in surprise. In the face of my own concern, the knight-captain's worries had evaporated.

"Not so blasé about it now, are you?" he quipped.

I didn't dignify that with a response. "When did they arrive?" I asked Richter.

"An hour ago," the constable answered.

I began pacing. "And you're certain it's me they're after?"

Richter's brows creased in confusion. "Who else could they be looking for?"

That was true enough. I drew up short. "Maybe they don't know," I muttered. "Maybe they're just guessing I'm here."

The constable shook his head. "They know, Michael." Then seeming to choose his words with care, he added, "They've demanded you be handed over."

I wasn't able to stop myself from tensing or letting my hands stray closer to my sheathed blades.

Orlon noticed. "Don't worry, boy," he snorted. "We aren't about to let them have you." He paused. "Yet."

Drawing back my hands, I folded my arms. "Then why am I here?"

Again, it was the constable who answered. "To decide how we proceed."

I glanced at him. "What is there to decide?" I wondered aloud. "Wasn't it you who told me that the citadel is sacrosanct? That the knights *protect* their guests?"

A pained expression flitted across Richter's face. "It's not that simple anymore."

"Why not?" I challenged.

"Because Menaq has gotten involved," Orlon interjected. He held my gaze, making sure I understood the significance of what he said next, "The leader of the mantis faction has appealed *directly* to the Triumvirate. He has requested—most graciously, I may add—that we release you into his followers' custody."

My anger deflated abruptly. If the Powers had bestirred themselves, then Orlon was right; there was nothing the knights could do to gainsay them.

"What did you do?" the constable asked in the sudden silence. He looked at me with morbid curiosity. "What could you have possibly done to make Menaq want you this badly?"

I saw no reason not to tell them. "I killed his sworn. Three times by my own hand and once with help. He must not have liked that," I said matter-of-factly.

That surprised a laugh from the knight-captain. "Well, I'll be damned," he said, still chuckling. "That's another point in your favor."

My brows rose. "*Another* point?" I asked. "What was the first?"

Orlon waved aside my question. "Doesn't matter." He tugged restlessly at his beard. "What we have to figure out now is what to do with you."

"You want to turn me over," I guessed.

Orlon shook his head. "*I* don't. But I don't see that I will be left with any other choice."

"Then the knights' much-vaunted honor and adherence to the laws count for naught," I whispered bitterly.

I knew that my words were harsh. Orlon and Richter were both helpless in the face of any decision taken by their liege lords, the Triumvirate Powers. But my insides were curdling with dread, and I couldn't stop myself from voicing the sentiment. Whatever happened, I wouldn't let myself be handed over to the mantises.

Even if it means dying at the knights' hands instead.

Orlon swung around to face me; his hands clenched into fists. "Don't you dare mock us. The law is *everything*. It is what defines us. Believe me, if there was another way, I would take it!"

I opened my mouth with a ready retort, but the constable spoke over me. "I warned you about this, didn't I? When the Powers get involved, the law counts for little. *If* the Triumvirate decides it best serves their interest to hand you over to Menaq then, law be damned, that's what will happen." He sighed with what appeared to be genuine regret. "I'm sorry, Michael, but once the order comes through, we'll have no choice except to comply."

I fell silent for a moment. Richter's words had given me an idea. "But the Triumvirate haven't decided my fate yet, have they?"

Orlon shook his head. "It's only a matter of time before—"

"Yes, yes," I said, cutting him off. "I'm sure you're right. But until their orders come through, you're free to act. Aren't you?"

He eyed me carefully. "I am."

I withdrew the citadel room key from my pocket. "Then I have a trade to propose." I gesture to the key. "I'll hand this over, freeing both you and the Triumvirate of all obligations to protect me. In exchange, I require only one small favor."

Orlon's eyes widened. "What favor?" he asked, leaning forward unconsciously.

I told him.

CHAPTER 210: FOCUSING THE MIND

"Get me out of the citadel."

I'd thought about asking for access to the minotaur maze, but that would've still left me in the knights' sphere of control, and when the Triumvirate order to hand me over *did* come through—I no more doubted it would than Orlon—it would leave me vulnerable and exposed.

And besides, I didn't think the knight-captain would let me in the dungeon anyway. No, the best approach was to get as far away as I could from the Triumvirate's followers and take the decision out of their hands.

I turned back to the knight-captain to find him frowning at me, his eagerness fled. "How would we do that?" Orlon asked. "The mantises are gathered in strength at both exits."

I shrugged. "Subterfuge. A secret tunnel. I don't care. Just get me out."

Richter and Orlon exchanged glances. "There may be a way," the constable said slowly.

Orlon shot him a look. "Go on."

"A knight detachment is scheduled to set out in an hour to close the new rift that opened last night. The mantises must know about it. They will have no reason to stop or question the detachment." He glanced at me. "We could disguise him in their midst."

Orlon eyed me dubiously. "He doesn't look like a knight."

"Put me in armor," I said, enthused by Richter's idea. "No one will be able to tell the difference. One knight looks much the same as another."

The knight-captain scowled but didn't dismiss my suggestion out of hand.

"It could work," the constable said quietly.

Orlon bowed his head, considering the matter. A moment later, he looked up and nodded decisively. "Let's do it." He glanced at me. "The detachment has already begun gathering at the citadel entrance. I'll ask one of the sergeants to prepare you. Head there now and report to—"

"I have an errand to run first," I said, interrupting him.

Orlon glared at me.

"I'll be quick, promise."

The knight-captain shook his head in disbelief but didn't gainsay me. "You have twenty minutes. Not a minute more. Understood?"

I nodded curtly and spun toward the door.

"Don't be late," the constable yelled after me.

"Send my armor to my room," I called back. "I'll equip it there."

✳ ✳ ✳

I raced back to my room.

I didn't have much time, and I had much to do. Thoughts, plans, and speculations whirled around my head. Mostly, they concerned the mantises.

Against all reason, the assassins had found me again. I'd been so sure I had figured out how they were tracking me.

I'd clearly been wrong.

It couldn't just be a guess on the mantises' part that I was in the citadel. They *knew* I was here. Given the lengths they'd gone to, they had to. Demanding the knights hand me over *and* contacting the Triumvirate directly—neither of those things spoke of uncertainty.

The mantises were sure of my location.

And how could they be?

It was unlikely my protections had failed. I'd tested them on multiple occasions. So, either someone in the citadel had betrayed me, or... someone else had.

I'd had no way of testing the first possibility—there were too many potential suspects—but the second... I knew just how to go about doing that.

More importantly, though, if what I now suspected was true, then I was out of time. I couldn't remain in Nexus much longer. But I still needed my Class.

Which was why I was about to take an unimaginable risk. It was the only way I could see to escape the fate in store for me.

Reaching my room, I dashed within and began undressing. I stripped down to my newbie clothes and stored nearly everything else in my bag of holding. The only items I kept were my sword belts, a pair of crystals, and ebonheart. The black blade was soulbound and couldn't be lost. If the worst befell me, I didn't want to lose my hard-earned gear.

And the chances were good that, by day's end, I would most likely be dead.

At a soft knock, I turned around and yanked open the door. Two boys, too young to be players, stood waiting outside, their hands full of pieces of armor.

"For you, sir," the lead boy said. "From the constable."

I took the offered items.

You have acquired a rank 2 longsword. This item requires a minimum Strength of 8 to equip.

You have acquired a rank 2 set of Triumvirate squire's armor. This item requires a minimum Constitution of 8 to equip. It is of similar design, but of lesser quality, than a full knight's armor. The squire's armor is provided to probationary members of the knighthood and can be worn by non-faction members.

The plate armor was cumbersome and heavy, but I could use it. Not only that, it would also hide my features better than any illusion.

Thanking the boys, I closed the door and began dressing in the new gear.

✳   ✳   ✳

You have equipped a set of squire's armor. This item set reduces the physical damage you sustain by 40% and penalizes your Magic and Dexterity by 70%.

Warning: you do not have the necessary skill, heavy armor, to use this item. Armor benefits not received. Penalties are in effect. Current modifiers: -23 Dexterity and -7 Magic.

It took me longer than I thought to equip myself in the plate armor. I'd been right about the armor's clunkiness though. It was noisy, screeching with the sound of metal on metal each time I moved. I winced. There'd be no sneaking around in it.

I took one last look around the room. I was almost ready to go, but before I got going, there was something else I needed to do.

Sitting down on the bed, I considered my Class points.

What I set out to do today would be difficult, if not impossible. Still, I wouldn't be attempting it if I didn't think there was a chance of success, and employing my Class points might tilt the odds further in my favor.

Casting my mind back to the rift dive with Simone's party, I considered the buff Moonshadow had cast upon me. It had proved hugely beneficial. With it, I'd managed to charm creatures of significantly higher levels than my own.

And if I was going to succeed today, I would need to be able to do that again.

You know the rainy day you were saving your Class points for, Michael? Today is it.

Turning my focus inward, I queried the Game.

You may advance your Class to rank 4 at this time.

Class points available: 3.

You may advance your Class to rank 4 by improving an existing Class benefit or by selecting new ones. Note, if any of your Class abilities or traits are lost through a future melding, their upgrades will not carry over to your new blended Class.

Do you wish to proceed?

I ignored the Adjudicator's warning *and* the options. I was committed to my path and didn't want to become distracted by new choices. What I needed now wasn't a plethora of additional Class traits or abilities but to specialize in *one* particular trait, improving it until it forged my Mind into a finely honed weapon.

Closing my eyes, I willed my intent to the Adjudicator.

Commencing Class upgrade...

...

Upgrade complete. Class points remaining: 2.

Congratulations, Michael, your mindslayer Class has advanced to rank 4!

You have upgraded your mental focus trait to mental focus II. The second tier of this trait increases the effectiveness of your Mind skills by 20%.

Through patient observation during my time in the Game, I knew that both skill level and attribute rank affected the success rate of any ability.

Indeed, it was likely only my high Mind attribute that had allowed me, time and again, to charm or otherwise mentally impair those of higher level than me.

And with the additional boost provided by mental focus, I expected to reap even more benefits from my Mind abilities.

With that in mind, I advanced mental focus again.

And again.

You have upgraded your mental focus trait to mental focus IV. The fourth tier of this trait increases the effectiveness of your Mind skills by 40%.

Congratulations, Michael, your mindslayer Class has advanced to rank 6! Class points remaining: 0.

I stared at the Game message. *A forty-percent boost,* I mused.

It was an even higher buff—and a permanent one too—than Moonshadow had cast over me. As far as I knew, there was no exact science in determining whether an ability would fail or succeed, but based on past evidence, I reckoned the upgraded trait gave me a better-than-even chance of charming foes at rank fifteen.

It'll do, I thought in satisfaction. Picking up the two enchantment crystals, I crushed both.

You have activated a disease protection crystal.
You have activated a scent concealment crystal.

Rising to my feet, I cast mind shield.

I'd done all that I could to prepare and was ready. Picking up my bag of holding, I exited the room, not bothering to lock the door behind me.

* * *

I had just one more stop to make before meeting the knight detachment in the entrance foyer. Moving with painful slowness—the armor felt like it weighed a ton—I entered the emporium outlet.

"Good day, sir knight," Cara began. "How may I—"

She broke off to study me quizzically. "Michael?"

Lifting the visor of my helm, I grinned at her. "How did you know it was me?"

Cara laughed. "I can't tell you all my secrets now, can I?" She paused. "Why are you dressed like that?"

"I need to leave the citadel incognito. My enemies are at the door. Literally."

"The mantises, you mean," she said.

I nodded, unsurprised at how well-informed she was. "Anyway, I must leave quickly and unseen." I held out the bag of holding. "And I need a favor."

Cara took the bag unquestioningly. "How can I help?"

"Can you use your aether magic to deliver the bag to Kesh?"

"It doesn't quite work like that," she murmured. "But I'll see that it gets to her."

"Safely?" I asked.

"Safely," Cara agreed. She hefted the bag of holding. "This feels like it has all your gear."

"Not all," I said, raising my arm to show her ebonheart.

"One sword?" Cara snorted. "Are you on a suicide run then?"

My lips turned up in a wry grin. She was too perceptive by far. "You could say that. My chances of surviving the day are... slim."

Cara was silent for a moment. "And there's no better way?"

"None that do me any good in the long run."

"I see," she said softly.

"One more thing," I said, changing the topic. "Can you retrieve an item for me from my bank account?"

"Of course," she said. "What do you need?"

I touched her keystone. "The shortsword I have stored there." A moment later, the item in question appeared on the table, and I sheathed it in the second sword belt I'd kept for that purpose.

You have acquired a shortsword, +1.

The shortsword was part of my backup gear and not an item I minded losing. Unfortunately, I hadn't thought to store a second set of armor, nor did I have the money to buy one. I would just have to manage without.

"Thank you," I said. "And in case we don't see each other again..." I shifted uncomfortably, uncertain of what to say. "Best of luck, and thanks for everything," I finished awkwardly. Turning on my heel, I prepared to leave.

"Michael," Cara said, stopping me. I glanced back to see her holding something in her hand. "This came for you this morning," she said.

"What is it?" I asked curiously.

"A letter."

Taking the parchment, I began to read. It was from Saya.

Dear Michael,

It's really you! Suspecting a scam, I didn't want to get my hopes up before, but your reply really put a smile on my face (even now, I can't stop grinning). To say that I'm ecstatic you're alive is, well... an understatement!

But down to business. You will be happy to learn the tavern is prospering. With the dungeon's wealth now an open secret, the sector has become a hub of activity, and I've taken the liberty to renovate the Sleepy Inn, adding additional levels and rooms. As the only tavern in the safe zone, we're in high demand.

Unfortunately, success has brought its own share of problems. Nothing insurmountable, I hasten to add, so don't worry!

As per your request, I've given your factor access to the tavern's books. I'm sure you will be pleased with what you find therein.

I look forward to your return—or at the very least, a visit!

Yours truly,

Saya.
P.S. We can't keep calling the tavern the Sleepy Inn. It's hardly that anymore!

A small smile stole onto my face as I folded up the letter and handed it back to Cara. It was good that Saya was doing well, but I still worried about the wolves. Once I was done here, I would have to go back and check on them.

"Kesh wants to see you too," Cara said, disrupting my musings. "She has much to discuss with you."

"Tell her I'll see her as soon as I can." My smile grew lopsided. "Things are a tad busy at the moment."

Cara nodded. "She'll understand."

I turned again to leave. "Good luck, Michael," Cara called softly as I walked out.

"Thanks," I replied. "I think I'm going to need it."

When I reached the foyer, I found Richter, Orlon, and three other knights waiting.

At my appearance, one of the knights—Teg, I noted—swung around to face the knight-captain. "Him? Really? We have to pretend *he* is a knight."

The second knight snorted. "He'll be spotted as a fake from a mile away."

"This is a bad idea," the third added.

"Enough," Orlon snapped. "It's been decided. The Triumvirate themselves have given their approval."

I looked at him curiously, surprised by this latest development. When had the knight-captain spoken to the Powers? The other knights had more to say though and continued protesting, leaving me with no chance to question Orlon further.

Stepping forward, the constable pulled me aside. "You seem to be struggling," he said.

I bared my teeth in an unfriendly smile. "This thing is bloody heavy." While I technically met the requirements to equip the armor, its weight was another thing. With every step I took, the armor dragged me down, and I was unsurprised to find I was losing stamina just by wearing it.

Richter chuckled. "I thought you might have some difficulty. That's why I brought this along," he said and handed me a slim object.

You have acquired a rank 4 Strength enhancement crystal. It contains a single-use enchantment that increases your Strength by +8 for 1 hour.

Realizing the purpose of what I held, I wasted no time crushing the crystal and activating its enchantment.

Your Strength has increased to rank 10. Current modifiers: +8 from enchantment.

Immediately my shoulders straightened and I breathed easier. "Wow," I exclaimed. "That's much better."

"The extra Strength makes it easier, doesn't it?" Richter said, looking me up and down. "Now you look like a proper knight," he pronounced in satisfaction.

"Thanks," I said, nodding at him in renewed respect. "I must admit to being a bit surprised though. The knights are going further than I expected to pull off this deception."

The constable shrugged. "You heard the knight-captain. The Powers have approved the scheme."

"Did they really?" I asked in a low voice, studying his face closely. "I thought perhaps..."

"Orlon was stretching the truth a bit?" Richter finished for me.

I nodded.

"The knight-captain spoke truly," the constable confirmed. "The Triumvirate liked the idea. The law is upheld, the knights' honor remains intact, and, at the same time, they rid themselves of an unwanted headache."

I grunted. "How convenient," I muttered.

Richter beamed. "It is, isn't it?" He glanced over his shoulder. The raised voices had died down. "Come on, it looks like they're done."

"All set?" Orlon asked as we rejoined the knights.

Richter nodded.

I glanced at Teg and his fellows. Anger still clouded their faces, but after the stern lecture they had no doubt received from their commander, they stayed tight-lipped.

The knight-captain studied me for a moment and gave a curt nod of approval. "These three," he said, gesturing to the other knights, "will be leading the detachment. Obey them at all times, and they'll get you out safely."

"Understood," I replied.

"Sergeant Teg," Orlon barked.

Teg stepped forward and held out his hand. "Give those to me," he said, gesturing to the two belts and swords I carried.

I looked at him blankly.

"Those are not knightly weapons," he explained. "I will stow them in my bag." He eyed ebonheart's black hilt with grudging respect. "Have no fear; they will be returned to you."

Reluctantly, I handed over the items. Save for the longsword buckled across my hip, I was weaponless now. Still, I had to admit, I looked the part of a proper knight.

"One last thing," the knight-captain said. Laying a hand on my shoulder, he chanted the words of a spell.

Orlon has cast Mydas' sheltering hand on you. For the next hour, you are immune to all player abilities of tier 4 and lower. Warning: taking hostile action will break the effect of this spell.

My brows rose as I read the spell's description. It was a powerful, if somewhat strange, buff.

"All the other knights are similarly warded," Orlon explained. "The mantises will not be able to analyze you. To them, every knight in the detachment will be faceless and unknowable."

I smiled in understanding. "Thanks."

He nodded curtly. "Now, close your helms and get going. It's time."

✳   ✳   ✳

Exiting the citadel, I found a contingent of a hundred knights waiting in the bailey. Teg pulled me into the middle of the formation while the sergeant's two companions—officers, by the look of them—moved to the head of the column.

"Move out," one of the officers roared a moment later.

Almost as if they were a single entity, the knights marched forward in lockstep with one another. "Follow my lead," Teg growled from beside me as I stumbled.

Doing my best, I mimicked his stride and soon got the hang of it, well enough to withstand momentary scrutiny anyway.

As the detachment's pace increased, merchants and other players in the courtyard scampered out of the way. The two officers led us unerringly toward the citadel's north gate, and in the formation's center, I relaxed. I was just one knight among many and safe from prying eyes.

The contingent marched through the gate without pause, and despite being tempted to search the shadows on either side, I kept my gaze fixed straight ahead, just like the other knights around me.

Still, even without looking, I couldn't help but notice the line of silently watching green-clad figures. Richter hadn't exaggerated their numbers. By my count, there were nearly two dozen near the gate.

Feeling the assassins' probing gazes, sweat broke out across my brow and dripped unseen down my face. Neither Orlon nor Richter had mentioned what the knights would do if the mantises spotted me. Would Teg and his fellows aid me?

I doubted it.

I wasn't blind to the risks I was taking. If I was discovered, there would be no hiding or fleeing. Paradoxically, the mountain of armor encasing me had made me more vulnerable—not less.

I'd placed my faith in Orlon and Richter, and if they chose to betray me... I was dead. Quite simply, I was betting my fate on how well I'd judged the two men. Nothing about either had smelled of betrayal, and the knight-captain, in particular, seemed like a poor liar.

Really, I'd been out of options. Going along with Richter's scheme was a risk. But so, too, was everything else I would do today. My only consolation was that if I died, my losses would be minimal.

Despite my worry, the mantises let us pass unhindered.

With the tramp of heavy feet underscoring our steps, the column of triumvirate knights marched northward. Little by little, my tension dissipated as the distance between me and the assassins widened.

I wouldn't feel truly safe again, not until I took off the ridiculous armor, but the further we marched, the less I feared betrayal or discovery.

Reaching a crossroads, the column of knights turned right. My helmed head creaked left, wondering if now was the time to part ways with them.

"Wait until we get to the rift!" Teg hissed, catching the drift of my gaze.

I hesitated, then nodded imperceptibly. I'd trusted the knights this far; a little longer wouldn't hurt.

The detachment kept marching. It attracted plentiful whispered comments and stares and forced more than a few passersby off the streets but was itself unhindered.

A few minutes later, the officers called a halt. Floating in the air before the column was a void of nothingness. The rift.

"Fall out, people!" the officer yelled. "Battle positions, everyone."

The formation disintegrated as the knights separated themselves into squads and began positioning themselves around the rift. I stayed where I was, having no intention of venturing into the nether.

More players were also flooding into the street, I noted. Sensing that a rift dive was about to commence, they gathered around the knights, supplementing their numbers.

Before my own inaction could be noticed, Teg clamped a hand on my shoulder. "Follow me," he whispered. Swinging about, he strode toward an abandoned-looking house, and I followed on his heels.

Before entering the hastily vacated building—the door was lying open, and food still lay on the table—I unfurled my mindsight. I might have placed my faith in the knights, but I hadn't altogether thrown caution to the wind.

I detected no one but the sergeant inside, and I ducked within. Teg closed the door behind me. "This is as far as you go," he said in a clipped tone. "Now, remove the armor."

Relieved that I could finally rid myself of the armor, I ignored his rudeness and undressed.

Teg watched mutely, making no move to help. When I was done, he gathered up the gear and returned my swords. Then, without saying another word, he strode out of the building, leaving me alone.

I didn't bother waving goodbye.

Setting the knight out of my mind, I pulled my sword belts over my shoulder to lie in their usual place across my back and looked down at myself.

Except for my swords, I was in newbie gear.

An involuntary chuckle escaped me at my strange appearance. If I went out like this, I was sure to be noticed. *A problem easily rectified,* I thought, casting lesser imitate.

A moment later, appearing to all the world like an elven ranger, I opened the door and stepped outside. No one paid me the slightest heed.

Now, I thought, *let's find out how wide a net the mantises have cast.* Turning north, I headed toward the safe zone's south gate.

I remained on high alert but was still more relaxed than I'd been as a knight in disguise. My fate was in my hands alone now.

Reaching the walled boundary of the safe zone, I drew to a halt. Just as I'd suspected, the south gate was blockaded. A squad of mantises was barring the way, inspecting everyone closely before letting them through. There would be no getting past them.

I was trapped.

CHAPTER 212: NO WAY BACK

I didn't bother checking the eastern and western exits of the plague quarter.

If the mantises had gone to the trouble of blocking one gate out of the quarter, I was certain they'd done the same to the other two. And besides, it wasn't like I would be allowed into the Light or Dark quarters either.

There was no getting around it. Until I dealt with the mantises, I was stuck.

Of course, I could just attack the assassins, earning myself a sure death and a quick passage into the safe zone in the process. Eventually, I might end up doing just that, but while the mantises had me trapped in the quarter, my escape from the citadel had left me free to maneuver.

And I had a plan.

Resuming my stroll, I veered east without attracting the notice of the mantises at the gate. I had a destination in mind already. My suspicions of how the assassins were tracking me had hardened, and I thought I knew how they were doing it. But I had thought so too before and had been proven wrong.

This time, I intended on making doubly sure.

The first test was to see if my hunters found me at my next destination. If they did, it would be the confirmation I desired. And if they didn't, well... at least the time would've been well spent.

One way or another, I intended on uncovering the truth by day's end. Even if it meant I had to die a few times in the process.

At ease with my decision, I made my way to the guardian tower.

✳   ✳   ✳

Of all the places to search for my third Class, I chose the guardian tower, not because it was the easiest to reach, but because it was the most restrictive.

If the mantises found me, at most, only five of them could follow me inside, and facing five was far better than battling a few dozen at a time. Of course, if—*no, when*—I exited the dungeon, I'd likely find the rest of the mantises waiting for me.

But I didn't care about that.

By then, I would have gotten what I needed.

There was no getting around it though. I was taking a grave risk entering the guardian tower. But despite the dungeon's daunting reputation, I was *reasonably* certain I could finish it.

A large part of my confidence stemmed from the gnomes' dungeon notes and their description of the savant inhabitants as "physically weak." I chuckled darkly. Physically weak foes were my favorite kind. Even without most of my gear, I fancied my chances against most spellcasters.

The guardian tower was located at the northeastern end of the quarter, and when I got there I found the area almost deserted. The streets adjoining the square were quiet, and the windows of the nearby buildings were dark and shuttered. The dungeon entrance was in the center of the square, in plain sight.

There were no players near it. None.

Remaining in the shadows, I studied the entrance. After a moment, I realized there wasn't one nether portal in the square but two. Standing side by side, they were so close together that, at first, I'd mistaken them for a single portal.

I frowned. *Why two entrances?*

Then realization dawned. According to the gnomes' notes, the guardian tower portals were all one-way. There would be no leaving the dungeon through the portal I entered. That meant the second portal was likely an *exit*, one from the final sector.

Letting my gaze drift away from the nether portals, I studied the statues standing sentry over them. This time around, there were four. All were cloaked, hooded, and towered two dozen feet high. Interestingly enough, one of the marble statues had a hound kneeling beside it, another a jaguar, the third rode a bear, and the fourth flew astride a wyvern.

Once more, I wondered as to the statues' purpose. *I have to ask the gnomes about them next time,* I thought.

If there is a next time.

Slinking out of the shadows, I entered the square and approached the dungeon's portals.

One shone nearly as bright as the sun, while the other was as dim as the moon. Guessing which was which, I touched the border of the dulled portal.

A Game message dropped into my mind.

Passage denied! This is a one-way portal. You may only enter this portal from the other side.

I smiled in satisfaction. It confirmed my earlier deduction. *I guess that means the other one is the entrance.* Inching closer to it, I scanned the surroundings. No one was watching.

Here goes. Stepping forward, I ducked into the shimmering portal of white.

Passage granted!
Transfer through portal commencing...
...

...
Passage completed!
Leaving sector 1. Entering the Endless Dungeon.

✳ ✳ ✳

You have entered sector 105 of the Endless Dungeon. This sector is part of a closed region named the Guardian Tower. It consists of 5 unclaimable sectors and 6 one-way portals.

A maximum of 6 players may be in the Guardian Tower at any one time. The dungeon is repopulated daily.

Recommended player levels: 140 to 160.

Recommended party size: 4 to 6.

Current number of players in the dungeon: 0.

Sector bosses remaining: 5 of 5.

I dropped into a crouch as I emerged from the portal.

Once again, I found myself in an entry chamber. It seemed commonplace in most dungeons. Remaining where I was, I inspected the room carefully.

The walls were formed from gray rock, and there was only a single light source—a magelight inset in the roof. The light wasn't bright enough to banish all the shadows though, and the edges of the room were dim enough for me to hide in.

If the rest of the dungeon was similarly laid out, it boded well for my dungeon dive. Glancing over my shoulder, I saw there was no curtain of shimmering white.

That settled it. There was no way back.

The only way out now was through. I had five levels to conquer, three lives to spend, and nothing except my swords and abilities to aid me.

Despite my dire straits, I laughed.

The sound was shockingly loud and untroubled, joyous almost. Unexpectedly, I found myself more relaxed than I'd been in a long time.

For days now, since even before I entered Nexus, my life had been growing more complicated as my responsibilities, my foes, and those who depended on me multiplied. I had been forced by circumstances and my hunters—Erebus, Ishita, Menaq—to execute complicated stratagems just to stay one step ahead. The weight of it all had been crushing almost.

Now I was a lone wolf again.

And for a time at least, the wider Game mattered little. It was just me, the dungeon, and the mantises. Kill or be killed.

Refreshingly simple.

My objects were clear, and my path was straightforward. Succeed or fail, I would move boldly forward. *And now that you've gotten all that out of the way, let's get this dungeon dive moving, shall we?* Still smiling, I refocused on the task at hand and tiptoed toward the room's sole exit.

The exit was blocked by a door made from solid sheets of metal and looked strong enough to stop a goliath. There was no bar or lock on it though, just a simple metal handle.

Before opening the door, I scanned it with trap detect. Finding nothing, I probed the area beyond with mindsight. It, too, came up empty. Judging it to be safe enough, I turned the handle and let the door swing open.

Nothing jumped out at me.

But I barely registered that fact as the "room" beyond the open door was revealed. Although calling it that was hardly correct.

The entry chamber was perched atop a cliff. Only a few feet separated the door from the steep, near-vertical slope leading down. Glancing left and right, I saw the cliff curved inward in both directions.

It's a basin, I realized. *I'm crouched at the edge of an underground basin.* One that was filled with a glowing liquid.

Lava.

I stifled a groan. What lay before me was nothing like what I thought the inside of a tower *should* be. My gaze drifted upward and found only rough, unadorned rock, inset with the occasional magelight.

Would the sector's strange design make things harder or easier? I wasn't sure.

I glanced behind me at the still-vacant entry chamber. If my suspicions were correct, it wouldn't take the mantises long to learn that I'd fled the citadel. And when that happened, I expected they would be hard on my heels. But I wasn't going to hang around waiting for them. *Let them find me among the monsters.*

Inching forward, I crossed over the threshold of the doorway. Despite the glowing lava in the basin below and the few magelights above, the cavern was dimly lit, and I had little trouble staying concealed. Reaching the edge of the cliff, I studied the area anew.

It was a sharp drop of perhaps thirty yards to the basin floor. The cliff's edge continued in an unbroken circle around the entirety of the basin, but there were no other doors along its rim. The only way forward was down.

Glancing downward, I turned my attention to the basin itself. It was about two hundred yards in diameter and was filled almost entirely with gently bubbling lava. The only exceptions to this were the outcroppings of black magma rocks that every so often grew large enough to breach the molten lake.

The outcroppings in the middle of the basin were more substantial and concentrated, and they'd grown enough interconnections to each other to form what could loosely be termed an island.

Sitting atop the center of the island was a portal.

The luminescent orb of brilliant white light captured my interest immediately. It had to be the gateway to the next level, and thus my primary objective in the sector.

I hadn't expected to find the next portal so soon upon entering the sector. But despite its closeness, getting to the gateway was going to be no simple matter.

Its defenses were formidable.

For starters, the portal was enclosed within a dome of hazy red. *A magical shield of some kind*, I thought.

Outside the dome and seated upon a throne-like chair carved from black rock was a cloaked figure so still and unassuming that I'd almost missed him—as I had the two large creatures looming behind him, but for entirely different reasons.

The pair were made from the selfsame lava and magma rocks that formed the basin, and on first glance I'd taken them for yet more outcroppings, if ones scarred more deeply than usual by veins of lava. But the creatures' eyes—pulsing orbs of red—gave them away.

Reaching out with my will, I analyzed all three hostiles.

The target is a level 155 savant acolyte.
The target is a level 150 magma elemental.
The target is a level 151 magma elemental.

My lips twisted sourly. *Right, that's the second barrier to reaching the portal.*

Unfortunately, the trio and dome weren't the sum total of the defenses I had to overcome. There was the molten lake too. While crossing the lava itself didn't trouble me overmuch, the creatures in it did.

Letting my gaze drift away from the central island, I studied the creatures idly gliding atop the lava bed. Picking one at random, I analyzed it.

The target is a level 125 fire slug.
Fire slugs are creatures born of fire. Fire is the slugs' lifeblood, both nurturing and nourishing them. The creatures spend their entire lives in it and can be found in some of the hottest regions in the world. The hotter it is, the more the creatures thrive.

I sighed. The fire slugs' comparatively low levels were a relief, but there were so many of them that it didn't lessen their threat much. After a swift count, I estimated there were at least thirty-five slugs in the basin. Too many for comfort.

The fire slugs weren't the only creatures in the lava fields either. I spotted two more cloaked figures standing sentry atop small rock outcroppings. I analyzed both.

The target is a level 135 savant mage.
The target is a level 137 savant scholar.
Savants are humanoid creatures with unusually high mental and magical abilities. Despite this, they lack the intelligence of truly sentient beings. They generally possess a wealth of magic and psionic abilities at their fingertips but little ability to communicate.

Alrighty. So that's the third ring of defenses.

Worse yet, given the open design of the level, there was no way I could tackle my foes individually. I suspected the moment I attacked one, I would invite a storm of attacks from the others.

Well, I thought glumly. *This isn't going to be easy.*

CHAPTER 213: THE BASIN OF FIRE

A few minutes later, I had a plan.

My primary goal was to get to the exit portal, and to do that I needed to defeat the savant acolyte and the magma elementals. Given their positioning, it was clear they guarded the exit.

Still, it would be foolish for me to descend into the basin just yet. *Better to whittle down my foes' numbers from above first,* I thought.

My gaze fixed on one of the savants. He would be my first target. Given the fire slugs' low levels, I foresaw no problems charming them. The savants, though, were an unknown quantity. Given the Game's description of them as talented mind users, I suspected I wouldn't be able to charm or otherwise mentally assault the savants.

But I needed to be certain.

Slinking along the rim, I crept away from the door to a spot where the shadows were thickest and readied myself.

You have cast reaction buff, increasing your Dexterity by +4 ranks for 20 minutes.

My target stood idle atop one of the closer magma outcroppings and was clearly visible. Summoning psi, I began casting slaysight.

Of all my mental abilities, slaysight was the one that succeeded most often, and if any of my mind spells were going to work against the savants, it would be it.

Searching tendrils of my will expanded toward my target and, entering his mind, attempted to erase me from the creature's awareness.

A savant scholar has passed a mental resistance check! You have failed to hide your presence from your target. Your mental intrusion has been detected!

I sighed. The spell's critical failure confirmed my fears—to slay the savants, I would have to get up close. My gaze drifted back to my target. The savant was turning around in frantic circles, searching for his attacker.

A hostile entity has failed to detect you!

Failing to pinpoint his foe, the savant threw back his head and emitted an unearthly shriek. *Well, that's not good,* I thought, suspecting what was about to happen next.

The basin came alive.

The fire slugs cut through the lava fields, the magma elements dashed around their tiny islands, and the other savants executed their own pirouettes.

Multiple hostile entities have failed to detect you!

But despite the dungeon denizens' sudden flurry of activity, their search was undirected. They had no idea where to find me. Safe in the shadows, I stayed put, watching keenly to see if any of the creatures would leave the basin.

None did.

Better, I thought. As long as my foes couldn't find me or leave the basin, my plan was workable.

My relief was short-lived though.

Perhaps grasping the futility of their search, the savant acolyte changed tactics. Raising his hands, the creature sounded out the words of a spell in a sibilant, unintelligible hiss. A moment later, a ball of blinding white light sailed over the basin to splash onto the wall above the doorway.

The orb exploded on contact.

And for a stark instant, the area was set ablaze with light.

A savant acolyte has cast revealing light. You have failed a magical resistance check! Multiple hostile entities have detected you! You are no longer hidden.

Uh-oh. Time to go.

My eyes still dancing with afterimages from the dazzling light, I rose to my feet. In the same motion, the heads of the three savants swung my way, and in what was an almost choreographed move, they raised their arms together.

A heartbeat later, three new orbs of light arced over the basin. But this time, they churned with shades of angry orange and red.

Fireballs.

Head down, I raced along the basin's rim, making for the safety of the entry chamber. Out of the corner of my eye, I noticed the fireballs shift trajectories.

Damnit! They were tracking me.

Realizing I wouldn't reach safety in time, I readied myself to meet the flaming projectiles.

The first fireball rushed nearer. A second before it could make contact, I dove forward. The fireball hurtled past to splash onto the cavern wall.

You have evaded a savant scholar's magical projectile.

The raging torrent of fire had missed me by less than a foot, and the back of my head and shoulders felt as if they had been burned raw by the heat alone.

I had no time to see to my injuries though. The next projectile was closing in rapidly. Grimacing against the pain, I sprung back to my feet and cast two-step.

The second fireball accelerated across the final stretch. Dashing forward on steps of solidified air, I climbed up and over the magic missile as it exploded against bare rock.

You have evaded a savant acolyte's magical projectile.

The heat was no less scorching from above than it had been from below. But despite a sudden outbreak of sweat, I was unaffected. Somersaulting off my airy perch, I resumed my flight.

The last fireball screamed through the air, homing in on me. At the last second, I skidded to a stop and let the inferno screech past.

You have evaded a savant mage's magical projectile.

The wall and ground ahead turned sullen red as angry flames hissed and spat across them. But there was no time to delay. The savants had already launched another volley.

Gritting my teeth against the pain, I pounded across the heated surface. Out of the corner of my eye, I tracked the second wave of projectiles.

They wouldn't reach me in time.

Flinging myself into the entry chamber, I slammed the metal door closed and retreated to the far end of the room.

A moment later, the chamber shook under the impact of three resounding thuds.

But despite turning an angry red, the door held.

Exhaling in relief, I panted for breath. I was safe—for now. Wondering what the savants would do next, I drew my blades and waited.

✳   ✳   ✳

The dungeon denizens didn't abandon the basin to pursue me. Maybe they couldn't. Or maybe they saw no need.

Whatever the case, five long minutes went by as the door rebuffed fireball after fireball. During that time, I remained hidden in the corner, watching both the door and where the portal opened.

But neither the mantises nor any other foes entered the chamber.

Eventually, the magical assault on the door subsided. I waited five more minutes before rising to my feet and tiptoeing to the door. Despite causing me to flee, my opening foray had been... educational.

I knew my mind tricks wouldn't work on the savants, but I'd also learned hiding from them was possible. It gave me the opening I needed. I realized, too, that there was going to be no quick resolution to the upcoming confrontation. It would take time and patient work to whittle down the sector's denizens.

Time I might not have, I thought, my gaze darting to the entrance portal. *Better get started then.* With my bare fingers, I tested the door handle. It was cool to the touch.

Cranking the handle down, I slid the door ajar. Only a little.

Poised for flight or fight, I waited.

But despite the revealing slit of magelight emanating from the doorway, no attack followed. Tensing in anticipation, I pushed the door open farther, just enough to slip through.

Still nothing.

Judging it safe enough, I dashed through the opening and immediately sidled left, putting some distance between me and the door.

I covered a dozen yards without incident, then another, but I kept going. I'd realized that the entrance chamber, despite serving as a refuge, was also a magnet for the savant's attacks. Being the spot from which their enemies always emerged, it was the first place the creatures would look for me, and I was determined not to be found again. When I put sufficient distance between me and the door, I let my gaze drift back to the basin.

The occupants' attention had waned.

The fire slugs had resumed their glacial glides through the lava, and the elementals had stilled. Only the savants showed any sign of agitation. Occasionally one of the trio would raise his head to restlessly scan the basin's rim. Despite this, I went undetected.

Let's keep it that way. Drawing on my will, I began my second assault.

This time around, I targeted a group of fire slugs wandering aimlessly near the center of the basin and, coincidentally close by the savant mage. The tendrils of psi I sent the creatures' way slipped past their defenses and wrenched control of their minds without resistance.

You have cast mass charm. 5 fire slugs have failed a mental resistance check! You have charmed 5 of 5 targets for 10 seconds.

Well, that was easy, I thought with a delighted grin. *Now, to see what they can do.*

Tugging on the mental leashes wrapped around my minions' minds, I ordered them to attack the nearby savant. As one, the fire slugs swung around to face their designated target and unleashed a torrent of flame.

Five jets of fire spewed from the slugs' mouths to bathe the savant mage in flames, and in a heartbeat the hapless creature was the center of a roaring inferno.

I rocked back on my heels, amazed by the unexpected violence and suddenness of the attack. My minions' victim was similarly surprised.

But he wasn't shrieking in agony.

Instead, the savant was turning—slowly—to face his attackers, seeming only slightly inconvenienced by the torrent of fire pouring into him.

I grimaced as I realized why.

A savant mage has passed a magical resistance check, reducing the damage he has sustained from your minions' attacks.

My attack had stirred up the basin's other inhabitants too. Flinging up his hands, the acolyte cast revealing light. Not bothering to move, I watched the white orb sail over the basin.

A moment later, the entrance chamber and its immediate surroundings were lit up brighter than a street under a noonday sun, causing all three savants to swing that way. They were almost quivering in their eagerness to get at their foe.

But, of course, I was nowhere near the blaze of light, and their search turned up empty.

I couldn't see their savants' faces, but their body language was easy enough to read. The creatures were perplexed. Angry. Bewildered. I almost laughed, my good humor restored by my foes' confusion.

The acolyte flung a second ball of light at the same spot again—as if that would make a difference—while the scholar began throwing fireballs in random directions.

The mage, meanwhile, had turned back to face the fire slugs. He was still bathed in fire from their attacks but appeared only a little worse for wear. Raising his right arm, the savant waved his hand negligently in the direction of one of my minions.

A savant mage has cast mental domination. You have lost control over a level 125 fire slug.

My eyebrows shot up. The mage hadn't just broken my hold on the slug; he had taken control of it himself. He didn't stop with the one either. Pointing at each slug in turn, the savant dominated them in quick succession.

Holding back from taking further action, I waited to see what the savant would do next. But after capturing the slugs' minds and stopping them from drenching him in fire, the mage seemed to lose interest in his new pets. Turning around to scan the basin's rim, he joined his fellows in throwing fireballs at the unoffending cavern walls.

The basin was too large and attacks too scattered to pose any real danger to me though, and I barely paid the fireballs any heed. Instead, I continued to observe the dominated slugs.

It was a full thirty seconds before the creatures broke free from the frozen poses they'd fallen into after being dominated and resumed their slow, aimless path through the lava fields.

My ploy, it seemed, was in shambles.

The mage hadn't died in fiery agony as I'd planned. In fact, he'd barely sustained any damage. Worse yet, I'd quickly lost control of my minions.

So how was I going to kill the savants? *If I can't use the fire slugs to—*

I paused. Did it mean that?

My gaze slid back to the savant mage. He was hunched over ever-so-slightly. My eyes narrowed. Was he still hurt? Reaching out with my will, I reinspected the creature, this time querying his health status.

The target is a savant mage. He is barely injured.

He hadn't healed.

Was that because he couldn't? Or because the damage was too minor to bother with? *Let's hope it's the former,* I thought, my eyes gleaming with new hope. It would be a slow grind to kill the savants with the fire slugs, but if they were unable to heal themselves, then, with some effort, I could see it done.

Drawing on my will, I got to work again.

CHAPTER 214: A SPELL OF HEAT

My suspicion proved correct. The savants couldn't heal themselves.

It was a dire weakness, and one I was ruthless in exploiting. Time and again, I charmed the fire slugs and sent them against the savant mage, and despite my foe repeatedly wresting back control of the creatures, I was able to inflict an infinitesimal amount of damage each time.

Inevitably, he fell.

Your minions have killed a savant mage.
You have reached level 105!

The mage's death sent the acolyte and scholar into a frenzy, and for a time fireballs and revealing light spells filled the cavern. In response, I broke off my own attacks and gave the glittering orbs sailing overhead my full attention. Anytime one appeared too close, I repositioned.

Not unexpectedly, the two savants failed to find me.

When the pair finally gave up, I resumed my assault. Notably exhausted, the savant scholar barely put up a fight, and it wasn't long before he, too, went the way of the mage.

Your minions have killed a savant scholar.
You have reached level 106!

Elated by my successes, I turned my attention to the last savant. Charming the five slugs closest to the tiny island, I sent them surging across the molten lake to the acolyte. But before the creatures could draw close enough to use their fire-breathing spells, the magma elementals stirred to life and waded into the lava, rock fists clenched and held at the ready.

Sensing an opportunity, I redirected the slugs to attack the elementals. Obediently, the bespelled creatures bathed the two in fiery flames.

It didn't stop the elementals.

Ignoring the flames wreathing them, the acolyte's guards wadded deeper into the molten lake and hammered large, stone fists into my minions' squishy bodies.

The fire slugs stood no chance.

Your minion has died.
Your minion has died.

…

My assault was over almost before it began.

Rocking back on my heels, I considered the elementals and the quick work they'd made of the slugs. The pair were returning to the tiny island, their job done. They moved slowly but surely, seemingly unfazed by being knee-deep in lava.

How much health did that little maneuver cost them? I wondered. Narrowing my gaze, I inspected both creatures.

The target is a level 150 magma elemental. It is uninjured.
The target is a level 151 magma elemental. It is uninjured.

"Well, that's just peachy," I muttered, realizing the magma elementals were immune to fire damage.

It left me in a bit of a quandary. I could send more charmed fire slugs to attack the savant, but I expected the result would be no different the second time around. While the acolyte's rock guardians were around, there would be no using the slugs against him.

I had to get rid of the magma elementals first.

My gaze slid back to the two creatures. They were back in their original positions and loomed like frozen statues behind the savant. *Perhaps, charming them will work...*

Summoning psi, I extended tendrils of my will toward the closer of the pair. But no sooner had I entered the creature's mind than I was met by an opaque wall and firmly rebuffed.

You have failed a Mind check! You are unable to wrest control of your target from its master.

My mouth dropped open in shock at the Game message. It was far different from any I'd received on previous failed charm attempts, and it implied that the magma elemental's mind was already dominated.

My gaze flickered to the savant acolyte seated negligently on his black throne. He was obviously the elemental's "master." He hadn't reacted to my mental assault though. Had my spell gone undetected? *Possible.*

Shrugging, I tried again.

And again.

And again.

Ten times, I attempted charming one of the elementals, and ten times I failed.

Finally, my shoulders sagging, I admitted defeat. My telepathy skill, even boosted by mental focus, was insufficient to overcome the acolyte's hold on the elemental.

Drumming my fingers on my leg, I considered my next move. I still had over thirty foes in the sector, and the three most powerful were impervious to my mental attacks. To kill the acolyte and elementals, I would have to choose a different tack entirely—and that meant getting close.

First, though, I'd have to deal with the fire slugs. *That's easy enough.*

I couldn't use the slugs to kill the elementals or the acolyte, but I *could* use the elementals to kill the slugs.

Charming the next group of fire slugs, I sent them racing toward the island.

✳ ✳ ✳

Your minion has died.
You have reached level 107!

A few minutes later, every fire slug in the basin was dead. The elementals had considerately slain them, and best of all, the Adjudicator seemed to have granted me full credit for their deaths.

Now I had only three more foes to deal with.

My gaze fixed on the tiny island and the nether portal's three guardians. It hadn't escaped my notice that I was ill-suited to face off against the magma elementals.

The pair's rocky exterior would be difficult—if not impossible—to penetrate. And while at close range I *might* find some chinks in their hides, I had to wonder if there was going to be anything beneath soft enough for my blades to cut into. I shook my head. Sparring with the elementals was going to be a losing proposition and to be avoided if possible.

The acolyte, on the other hand, wouldn't do well in a physical confrontation. After observing the fire slugs' assault, I knew the savants had high magic resistance, but I doubted they would be able to shrug off physical attacks as easily.

The only problem would be getting to the acolyte. The elementals made for formidable guards.

But are they willing *guards?* I wondered.

What would the mind-controlled elementals do if their charge was dead? Celebrate their master's death or attack his slayer? There was no way to tell. I bit my lip, considering my options.

I didn't fancy being stuck on the tiny island with two angry elementals. I would have little room to maneuver, and until I figured out how to deactivate the dome protecting the exit portal, I wouldn't be able to leave the sector either.

But I didn't see that I had much choice. I had to take the attack to the trio.

My gaze drifted to the entry chamber. Time was slipping by too. Sooner or later, the mantises would appear. *Best to get this done before they arrive.*

Decided, I turned my attention to the magma outcroppings sprinkled around the basin. They were my only means of crossing the lava. It would be an arduous journey but manageable nonetheless.

Slipping closer to the edge of the basin, I prepared myself to enter its molten depths.

✳   ✳   ✳

For my entry point into the basin, I chose a spot opposite the direction the acolyte and two elementals were facing. The red dome was between me and my targets, and through its hazy glow I could just make out the back of the acolyte's black throne.

The lava lit the basin floor too brightly for me to stay hidden while crossing it, and the only way for me to escape the acolyte's wrath was to go unseen and unheard.

Slipping over the lip of the basin, I touched down lightly on the steep slope leading to the molten lake. Despite the sharp gradient and loose rocks, it appeared navigable. Moving with care, I began descending.

Unfortunately, the slope wasn't all that stable, and not even five steps into my descent, a boulder broke free.

I froze and my head whipped upward to study my distant targets.

They hadn't moved.

Still, I kept my gaze fixed on them, alert for the slightest hint of danger as the rock continued to tumble down the slope, the sounds of it scraping preternaturally loud to my own ears.

Gathering momentum, the boulder continued accelerating until it bounced free and splashed into the lava. I winced at the noise, but once again, there was no reaction from the acolyte or elementals.

Finally daring to breathe, I let myself relax.

In hindsight, I realized my foes were too distant to hear anything. The lava's incessant bubbling was loud enough that even my own sharp hearing would've had trouble picking out the sound of the boulder's fall.

All the same, better I avoid doing that again, I told myself drily. Redoubling my caution, I resumed my descent.

✳   ✳   ✳

A few minutes later, I reached the bottom of the basin.

Warning: the ambient heat is approaching dangerous levels. If you remain in the vicinity, your body will suffer damage.

I dismissed the Game message wryly. I didn't need it to tell me what I could already sense.

This close up, the heat exuded by the lava was palpable. It assailed me in waves and would only get worse once I stood atop the lake. Already, my thin cotton clothes were drenched in sweat.

About ninety yards separated me from the central island. There were multiple outcroppings between though, and with two-step I foresaw no problem getting to the island—except managing the raging heat, of course.

Let's do this fast and quick.

Dashing forward, I kicked off a large boulder and went airborne. I flashed over the red-hot lava and, a moment later, crouched on the flat top of an outcropping.

You have failed a physical resistance check! Due to the harsh environmental conditions, you have been afflicted by heatstroke. Your health is degenerating by 0.5% per second.

The scorching heat hit me like a physical blow. The skin on my hand, my knee, and the soles of my feet—everywhere I was in contact with the rock—boiled and blistered. The only surprise was that my newbie clothes remained intact; it was weathering the heat better than I was.

Steadfastly, I blocked out the pain—before I reached the island, it would only get much worse—and turned my attention to my targets. Their positions remained unchanged.

Again.

Rising to my feet, I repeated my jump, this time using two-step. Eschewing the smaller, jagged outcroppings in between, I landed on another smooth surface six yards away.

Your health is at 98% and dropping.

Once more, my leap went unnoticed. The damage to my body was mounting though, and I'd barely begun my crossing. *I have to hurry this up,* I thought, eyeing the Game message in concern. Wiping away the sweat dripping down my nose, I kicked off again.

Your health is at 96% and dropping.
Your health is at 94% and dropping.
Your health is at 92% and dropping.
...

Damage messages scrolled steadily through my vision as I leapfrogged from one outcropping to another, but I didn't dare stop to tend to my injuries.

My steps had begun to falter, and once or twice I had almost fouled my landing. Worse yet, dizziness was setting in, and I was struggling to concentrate. It was taking everything I had just to make my jumps.

Pausing to heal didn't bear thinking about.

Your health is at 74% and dropping.
...

...
Your health is at 30% and dropping.

Eventually, after what seemed like an eternity, I touched down on the tiny island.

My insides felt as if they had been scorched dry, and simply breathing hurt. I ached to suck in a deep lungful of the blessedly cooler air, but I was painfully aware too that my foes were less than twenty yards away.

My body's needs, as urgent as they were, would have to wait.

Lowering myself gently to the ground, I scanned the surroundings through eyes gone red and swollen. The crossing had left me half-blind, but I could still see well enough to pick out features in the terrain. My gaze fixed on a boulder larger than its companions.

There. The rock in question was about nine feet away. *I can make that,* I thought with grim determination. Planting my elbows in front me, I dragged myself across the ground toward it.

The magma rock beneath me was warm—hot even—but its temperature was nothing compared to the lava's, and ever so slowly, the raging heat inside me dissipated. By the time I reached my destination, the ambient temperature had dropped further, warranting another—more welcoming—Game message.

You are no longer afflicted by heatstroke. Your health is at 20%.
You are hidden.

A quiet sigh escaped me. I'd made it. And now, finally, I could heal myself. Squeezing my eyes shut, I began spinning psi.

CHAPTER 215: THE PERILS OF DOMINATION

A few minutes later, my body was fully restored, the last of its injuries washed away by soothing waves of chi heal.

Opening my eyes, I found myself looking out on the molten lake and repressed a shudder. The journey across had been harrowing and wasn't an experience I cared to repeat. *Don't die,* I told myself grimly, *and you won't have to.*

Reminded of the task before me, I rose into a crouch and peeked around the boulder. The edge of the red dome hung a few inches away, close enough to touch. The gateway itself was just a few yards beyond. Achingly close. Moving with deliberate care, I reached out and touched the dome.

This is a protective barrier formed of fire. Until it is removed, you cannot pass through, nor can the nether portal be accessed.

As I thought. I suspected the means of lowering the barrier was somewhere among the acolyte's possessions. He was the strongest creature in the level and almost certainly the sector boss. Until I killed him, I wasn't progressing.

Withdrawing my hand, I studied my three foes on the opposite end of the island.

They hadn't moved.

The dome covered the bulk of the island, and to reach the trio I would have to sneak either clockwise or anticlockwise around its rim.

Can I reach them undetected though?

Between the light given off from the molten lake, the portal, and the dome itself, the shadows on the island weren't as thick as I liked, and I realized I would have to rely heavily on the terrain for cover. Thankfully though, the tiny island was far from flat, and there were ample dips, rises, and tall rocks to hide me.

And really, I only needed to get within nine yards of my target.

Pursing my lips, I considered the two paths before me. *The right one,* I decided after a moment. Slipping out from behind the boulder, I began my final approach.

*　　*　　*

Staying low and moving with torturous slowness, I circled the red dome. Every few feet, I paused and ran a leery gaze over my foes. But the elementals and the acolyte didn't glance my way, not even once, leaving me to wonder if my abundance of caution was unnecessary.

In any case, I reached the outcropping I'd been aiming for without mishap. With my back braced against the rock, I peered around the edge. The black throne was eight yards away, and within it I could just make out the acolyte.

The savant was still and unmoving. With his head bowed and his arms folded in his lap, he seemed the perfect target. Oblivious and vulnerable.

Smiling grimly, I drew my swords.

Three hostile entities have failed to detect you! You are hidden.

Both blades came free of their sheaths with barely a whisper of sound. Closing my eyes, I took a moment to prepare myself, casting reaction buff, piercing strike, and whirlwind.

Your Dexterity has increased by +4 ranks for 20 minutes.
You will deal double damage on your next attack.
Your attack speed has increased by 100% for 3 seconds.

I wasn't sure if the acolyte was truly as defenseless as he appeared. But it didn't matter. Whether or not he was riddled with unseen protections, it didn't change what I needed to do.

Strike hard. And strike fast.

If my attack failed, I was prepared as I could be for any eventuality, and if it succeeded, well then, the battle was half won already.

Time to act. Exhaling softly, I raised my blades and shadow blinked forward.

You have teleported 8 yards. You are still hidden.

I flickered back into existence beside the black throne, a barely seen shadow. I was already poised to act too. My gaze fixed on my unsuspecting target, I brought my swords rushing down, plunging first one, then the other into one side of the acolyte's throat and out the other.

You have backstabbed your target for 4x more damage!
You have backstabbed your target for 2x more damage!
You have killed a level 155 savant acolyte.

I didn't pause to celebrate.

Despite the success of my sneak attack, I still had a second foe looming at my back and another nearly as close. Not waiting to observe the elementals' reaction, I wrenched my blades free and dropped into a roll.

A few feet away, almost at the edge of the molten lake, I sprang back to my feet and whipped around, swords held at the ready.

The magma elementals hadn't shifted out of position.

Indeed, they seemed to have been frozen into inaction. Only their heads had swung my way, the pulsing of their red eyes increasing in tempo as they studied me from impassive faces.

Summoning psi, I wove a charm spell in my mind and dropped into a wary crouch. But I didn't release the casting. The elementals weren't attacking.

Yet.

The tableau held for a drawn-out moment. The two creatures studying me, and I scrutinizing them in turn, both parties waiting to see what the other would do.

I shifted uneasily. *What are they thinking?*

I didn't relish the prospect of fighting the elementals. Even if I succeeded in charming them—which wasn't guaranteed by any means—I suspected it would be a long and protracted battle.

Much better if they flee.

The elementals tilted their heads to the side... almost as if they'd heard me. But before I could figure out what that meant, the pair dissolved, their magma forms liquifying into lava to seep into the ground.

Mouth dropping open, I gaped at the two already cooling puddles that were all that remained of the elementals. "Well, I'll be..." I murmured.

Unbending from my crouch, I cleaned and sheathed my blades. Only then did the enormity of my accomplishment penetrate. I'd done it—I'd cleared the level.

Raising my head, I glanced at the portal. The fire barrier protecting it had vanished the moment the acolyte had died. The way to the next level was open.

But before I could move on, there were a few things that needed doing.

Striding up to the throne, I yanked back the acolyte's hood. The savant was a strange-looking being. His face, while humanoid, was distinctly inhuman. He had neither teeth nor nose. His lips were gummy, and his eyes were round and bulging.

In death, the savant made for an altogether pitiful sight. But the creatures have proved themselves my foes, and I could afford them no mercy.

Splitting open the acolyte's robe, I inspected it carefully. The fabric was bulky and torn, and I judged it would offer little protection. *My newbie gear is better,* I thought, flinging away the garment to riffle through the rest of the corpse's belongings.

Unfortunately, that didn't amount to much.

Beneath its robe the savant was naked, wearing not so much as a pair of boots. Other than the robe, the acolyte bore only two other items: a necklace around its neck and a bracelet on its right arm. Ripping both free, I inspected each in turn.

The target is a bracelet formed from shards of polished glass.

The target is the amulet of fire, the first piece of the guardian amulet of elements. In its present form, the amulet grants the bearer +10% resistance to fire magic.

I dropped the bracelet—it was worthless. The amulet, though, was worthy of more attention. It consisted of a medallion attached to a thin metal chain. Four quadrants had been etched in the round metal disc. Three were empty, while the last was filled by a ruby crystal.

Pulling the amulet over my head, I tucked it beneath my cotton shirt. I recalled mention of the amulet in the gnomes' notes and knew I would need it on the final level.

If I make it that far.

Ignoring the errant thought, I turned around to stare at the molten lake. I'd seen the savant mage's corpse slip into the lava earlier, and like the bodies of the fire slugs, it was lost to me.

The scholar's corpse remained on his lonely perch. But after what I'd found on the sector boss, I wasn't about to brave the lake again to search it.

With a shrug of disappointment at the lackluster loot—I'd been warned though, so I hardly had cause to complain—I strode up to the portal and concealed myself in a shallow crevice. I hadn't forgotten about the mantises, hence the precautions. They hadn't shown up yet, but I didn't doubt they would.

Safely shrouded in shadow, I finally turned my attention to the waiting Game messages, including the ones I'd suppressed from the earlier encounters.

The first sector boss has been slain! Sector bosses remaining: 4 of 5.
You have reached level 109!
Your sneaking has increased to level 79. Your shortswords has increased to level 84. Your two-weapon fighting has increased to level 58. Your meditation has increased to level 90. Your telepathy has increased to level 61. Your insight has increased to level 89. Your deception has increased to level 85.

I'd gained a total of five levels in the sector, which was low considering the number of higher-ranked foes I'd slain. But I still had five attribute points to spend, leaving me with a difficult choice.

Dexterity or Mind? I wondered.

I'd come into the dungeon realizing I would have to depend heavily on my Mind skills. My faith in my mental abilities had been borne out in the first sector, and I expected things in the second sector to be no different.

The question though was, did I keep pushing my Mind *higher*?

As my player level and telepathy increased, eventually I would reach the point where I could overcome the savants' mental resistance—and perhaps even their hold on their minions.

But would I get to that point while still in the dungeon? And dare I delay reaching that point by *not* investing in Mind?

No. That would be too risky, and I'm already playing for keeps. Decided, I spent my new attribute points.

Your Mind has increased to rank 57.

My player progression seen to, I rose to my feet. Almost involuntarily, my gaze slid to the distant entrance chamber, and for a brief moment I contemplated staying on longer in the level to await the mantises.

But after further consideration, I decided against it.

This sector's design was too open, and once I revealed myself, I doubted I would be able to easily hide again. Ideally, I wanted to strike at the assassins from the shadows and just as quickly fade back unseen.

Maybe the next level will suit me better. Resolved, I slipped through the gateway.

Transfer through portal commencing...
...
...
Passage completed!

Leaving sector 105 of the Endless Dungeon.

CHAPTER 216: DELVING THROUGH THE EARTH

I spilled out of the portal into darkness.

Dropping into a crouch, I extended my senses. The ground beneath was hard, cold, and rough-hewn, while above I could feel a weight of rock pressing down. And the air... it tasted of rock, soil, and dirt.

I'm deep underground, I realized.

Pivoting around in a slow circle, I scanned the surroundings. Lightless though the area was, its every detail was laid bare in my night vision. Naked rock, glistening with water, surrounded me on most sides. Only up ahead did the rock give way to empty air.

I'm at the end of a tunnel. Or rather, considering how I got here, the start of one.

The passageway was about three yards across and nine feet high, leaving me plenty of space to maneuver if the need arose. Feeling more relaxed than I had in hours, I straightened from my crouch.

The darkness was... soothing.

Within it, I had less to fear than I ever had in the lava basin or even Nexus. I bared my teeth in a wolfish grin. *This level may turn out to be easier than the first.* Padding forward, I advanced down the tunnel.

The passageway corkscrewed madly, twisting left, right, up, and down with little rhyme or reason. Sometimes, it even felt like I was doubling back. But no matter how wildly the tunnel contorted, the darkness embracing it remained constant, and I stayed relaxed.

An hour went by, then another, and still I kept walking. I didn't encounter any forks or side passages, or, strangely enough, any whiff of hostiles.

That is, until the third hour.

* * *

There was an unfamiliar smell in the air.

Something was up ahead.

Something I hadn't encountered before.

Shaking myself alert, I broke free from the trancelike state I'd been lulled into. The gyrating tunnels were almost hypnotizing in their effect, and if not for the taint on the wind, I might not have recognized the danger until too late. Drawing to a halt, I tasted the air again.

And immediately wrinkled my nose.

Whatever was up ahead, it smelled unclean... filthy.

The tunnels' twisting nature meant I couldn't see whatever awaited me. *But there's more than one way to see.* Opening my mindsight, I probed the surroundings.

Nothing.

I frowned. I didn't hear anything out of the ordinary either. Perhaps whatever I'd smelled was still too far away. Shrugging, I strode on.

The stench grew stronger, and a new sound entered the tunnels too. Under the slow drip of water, I heard... squeaking? Growing more puzzled, I continued advancing.

Then the darkness brightened.

That gave me pause, and I stopped again. Somewhere up ahead, there was a source of light. Light meant life—*hostile life, no doubt.* Dropping into a crouch, I padded forward softly.

Nine feet later, the tunnel went through another of its abrupt changes. Turning a sharp corner, I found myself in an arrow-straight corridor that stayed unbending as far as I could see. The walls were smoother too, and even the roughness of the ceiling and floor had been chiseled away.

Had I finally reached an inhabited section of the tunnels?

I thought so.

Eighty yards in front of me, under the light of two torches, were a pair of furry creatures. *The source of both the light—and stench.*

Neither creature gave any sign that they'd seen me, but if they required torches, they had to have poor night vision. Staying where I was, I studied the pair intently.

Both were humanoid and about five and a half feet tall. Their feet and hands were uncovered, revealing clawed fingers and toes. They had long elongated snouts and large square teeth. Their eyes were round and large, as were their ears. The pair were clad in rags and armed, if with only primitive-looking weapons. One wielded a crude spear and the other a studded club.

Reaching out with my will, I analyzed both creatures.

The target is a level 110 ratman warrior.
The target is a level 116 ratman warrior.
Ratmen are a savage and almost feral species of were-men. Like with many other blends of sentients and beasts, their animalistic nature is the more dominant of the two. But despite their somewhat lowly origins, ratmen possess the crude cunning of their forebearers and should not be underestimated. They prefer living in dark underground spaces and are fiercely territorial and protective of their nests.

Rat... men?

I'd never heard of the like but could definitely see the resemblance. What was confusing though was the pair's levels. I was almost a match for both, and in a tier four dungeon I didn't expect that.

Staying unmoving, I continued to observe my targets.

Neither moved from their position, and after a while, I became convinced they wouldn't. *They're guards*, I concluded. But how much threat are they?

Low levels didn't necessarily equate to low threat. I knew that better than most. If the Game's description and the ratmen's gear were anything to go by, the creatures possessed a rudimentary intelligence. *Enough to call for help?* I wondered.

Likely.

The passage beyond the two guards was dark and unlit, but I was sure that somewhere beyond more ratmen awaited. *I'll have to dispatch the pair quickly and quietly.*

The best way to do that would be up close. Drawing my blades, I crept up the tunnel, placing each foot with care. My footfalls were so soft I doubted even a wolf wouldn't have heard me coming.

Two hostile entities have failed to detect you! You are hidden.

Little by little, I closed the distance, eyes fixed on my targets and blades held at the ready. As I drew nearer the tunnel grew brighter, but the flickering torches weren't large enough to banish all the shadows, and I stayed unseen.

Two hostile entities have failed to detect you!

I was thirty yards away and nearing striking distance. Suddenly, the ratmen on the left swung toward his companion and emitted a strange sequence of squeaks and grunts.

Squeaks and grunts that I understood.

"You smell dat?"

Startled, I froze. The ratmen could talk? *And what does he mean 'smell'?*

A second later, I had my answer as the second guard raised his snout and sniffed. "Human!" he growled.

A hostile entity has detected you! You are no longer hidden.

Goddamnit! I cursed as the guards' heads swung around to fix unerringly on my position. The pair couldn't see me, but that hadn't stopped them from locating me.

Letting the shadows unravel, I dashed forward. I couldn't let them sound the alarm.

The ratmen's eyes widened, and reflexively they hefted their weapons. In an eyeblink, I covered half a dozen yards. *Almost there,* I thought grimly.

Then the ground fell away.

You have triggered a trap!

I had only a split second of warning.

Danger! my intuition screamed, the same intuition that had saved me multiple times. Despite the warning, I was moving too fast to halt, so I did the only thing I could think of.

I began casting two-step.

The air rushed by, and I dropped like a stone. But even as my legs windmilled for purchase, I wove psi frantically. Half-caught glimpse of the surroundings flashed by. Dirt covered walls. A gleam of steel.

Two grinning faces?

A spiked trap has injured you!

I didn't finish my spell in time. My right leg crunched down the pit floor, bringing my fall to an abrupt end and driving one of the thin metal stakes that had been planted there up and through the arch of my foot.

Searing white agony jolted through me and my leg quivered, almost giving way beneath me. But somehow, I managed to hold onto both the threads of my spell and my footing.

Fighting against the nauseating agony, I completed my casting. A heartbeat later, my left leg came down on solid air, inches above another metal spike.

Yes!

Wrenching my right foot free, I leaped forward onto a step of air and flung up my head.

The guards were peering over the edge of the pit, staring down at me. I was no expert in ratmen expressions, but even I could tell neither was grinning anymore. Indeed, both seemed suitably horrified to see me still alive.

I started falling again, but thanks to the guards' inquisitiveness, I had a way out. Smiling in savage satisfaction, I cast shadow blink and pulled myself free of the pit.

You have teleported 6 yards.

I emerged from the aether behind the spear wielder, and without hesitation I plunged ebonheart through his back and out his chest.

You have killed a ratman with a fatal blow.

The second guard spun around to face me, his club rising. Turning aside his descending blow with the sword in my left hand, I wrenched ebonheart free of the corpse, then darted forward and skewered my foe through the throat.

You have killed a ratman with a fatal blow.

I sank to the floor with the body, my breath coming in short gasps. The encounter had come to a brutal and abrupt ending, and adrenaline still choked my system.

Ignoring my bloodied right foot for a moment, I glanced farther up the tunnel. The alarm hadn't been given, and it remained dark and silent. The last of my tension fading, I closed my eyes and summoned psi.

A moment later, soothing ripples of energy spread into my leg, mending some of the damage done by the damnable trap. It was as bad as it felt and would take multiple attempts to heal fully.

The Adjudicator was right, I reflected. *The ratmen are not to be underestimated.*

CHAPTER 217: A REAL RAT'S NEST

A few minutes later, I was back on my feet.

My right foot was as good as new. The same couldn't be said of my newbie shoes. It had endured the heat of the previous sector better than it had being skewered.

Fingering the large hole in my abused shoe, my gaze drifted to the ratmen. Neither had any footwear to speak of. Sighing, I slipped the shoe back on and investigated the corpses.

The two guards carried nothing of use besides their weapons, but I was ill-suited to wielding either. Leaving the spear and club where they lay, I considered the ratmen's clothing. They were stained, torn, and disgustingly filthy. Hardening myself, I brought one of the rags up to my nose and took a deep whiff.

Urgh.

My stomach heaved rebelliously. The ratmen's clothing smelled as awful as I'd feared.

But I needed them.

I hadn't forgotten how the pair had located me, and if I didn't want to be found out again, I would have to disguise my scent. Working quickly, I stripped both corpses of their garments and took my sword to the rags, fashioning one into a crude skirt and the other into a misshapen vest.

Then for good measure, I pulled out tufts of fur from one of the ratmen and brushed my arms, legs, and face with it. Straightening, I took another deep breath.

All I could smell was rat.

Good enough, I decided. On the off chance that it would fool any other ratmen that happened along into believing the guards' deaths the work of the trap and not an intruder, I flung the two corpses and the club into the pit.

Then I inspected the trap itself.

It was simple in concept—a false floor set above a deep hole—but the execution had been brilliant. Not even my sharp senses had spotted anything amiss until too late.

Where there's one trap, there are likely more.

It was this thought that spurred me to retain the spear. It just might come handy after all. There was just one more thing to see to. Turning my attention inward, I considered the waiting Game messages. There were disappointingly few.

Only two of my skills, chi and mediation, had increased during the encounter, and I hadn't even gained a single level. *Oh well.* It wasn't unexpected, given my foes' low levels. But I was sure whatever else awaited me in this sector, it included plenty more ratmen.

My work done, I doused the torches and ventured deeper into the tunnel.

* * *

Inky darkness suffused the corridor the moment the torches were snuffed. I didn't let this lull me though. Activating trap detect and moving no faster than at a crawl, I meticulously probed the ground ahead before taking each step.

My precautions were tedious and perhaps unnecessary, but a few dozen yards later, I was thankful for my care as the glowing dust particles flitting at the edges of my enhanced sight coalesced into a red line, revealing the tripwire stretched across the tunnel.

You have spotted a trap! Your thieving has increased to level 53.

Drawing to a halt, I scrutinized the trap carefully. The tripwire was held taut by two stakes driven into the ground. A second cord ran from the trigger and up the tunnel wall before disappearing into a hole in the ceiling. There were four other holes in the roof too, spread evenly in a line above the tripwire.

What did they conceal?

Knives? Darts?

Whatever it was, I was sure it couldn't be anything pleasant. Stepping gingerly over the tripwire, I resumed my journey.

✳ ✳ ✳

I encountered six more traps.

Five of them I spotted early enough to avoid triggering. The sixth foiled my best efforts and only the outstretched spear and my reflexes saved me.

Jumping back from the pressure plate the spear had uncovered, I shook my head ruefully at the axe that swung like a pendulum over it. *Too close,* I thought. Ducking beneath the axe, I continued onward.

Since encountering the two ratmen warriors, the tunnel hadn't diverged from its arrow-straight course. I judged I must have walked at least a half mile down its length, and inevitably I began to wonder if it was ever going to lead me anywhere.

My musings were cut short though, as a little past the sixth trap the passage began to brighten again. Noise, whose source I couldn't quite place, was also filtering down the tunnel. I sniffed delicately. There was a familiar stench in the air too.

There are ratmen up ahead, I concluded. Keeping a wary watch on the gradually brightening surroundings, I continued my cautious advance down the passage.

Eventually, I reached a bend in the tunnel.

This one was just as sharp as the one that heralded the start of this particular stretch of passage. Drawing up short, I braced my back against the wall and peered around the corner.

Multiple hostile entities have failed to detect you!

Twelve yards up ahead, the tunnel came to an abrupt end.

A large underground chamber lay beyond. Tall poles with torches affixed on their ends had been staked in the ground, illuminating the cavern's entirety. However, it wasn't the brightly burning torches that drew my attention but the ratmen.

The cavern teemed with the creatures—the source of both the noise and smell. Most of the ratmen held a pickaxe or other sharp implement and were industriously chipping away at the walls and large boulders strewn around the cavern.

They're mining? I thought in amazement. *What are they mining for?*

It seemed a wholly strange occupation for a dungeon's denizens, and I was curious to find out what the ratmen were unearthing. Unfortunately, I couldn't advance closer just yet.

While the cavern entrance wasn't barricaded, it was guarded by six ratmen.

Despite my proximity, I went undetected. I glanced down at myself. *I guess that means this ridiculous getup is working then,* I thought wryly.

Satisfied I was safe for the time being, I began counting the ratmen in the cavern but had to stop when I reached a hundred. Whatever their actual number, there were too damn many of them. Pursing my lips, I considered my next move.

Retreating wasn't an option. I had to locate the sector boss and exit portal, and wherever they were, they weren't behind me. I'd encountered no forks or branches in the tunnel, after all. In fact, the only thing waiting for me to my rear were probably my hunters. No. I had to go forward.

How though?

Fighting my way through the horde of ratmen in the cavern was certainly not an option. And sneaking past seemed equally unlikely. That left only... deception. My gaze slid back to the chamber's entrance.

The six guards bore an assortment of weapons and looked entirely too alert for my tastes. I didn't fancy my chances of strolling past them unchallenged. They would have questions. Questions I was in no position to answer.

The guards will have to die, I decided. *And in a manner that doesn't alert the cavern's inhabitants.*

A tall order. Reaching out with my will, I analyzed one of the sentries, then, for good measure, some of the workers beyond.

The target is a level 118 ratman warrior.
The target is a level 103 ratman miner.
The target is a level 105 ratman miner.

I nodded thoughtfully, my suppositions confirmed. It was the ratmen's numbers, not their levels, that was the true threat. Satisfied I understood what I was facing, I withdrew deeper into the shadows to formulate a plan.

*　　*　　*

A little later, I was ready to act.

Peeking around the corner, I checked the position of the guards. They remained where I'd last seen them. Keeping my movements slow and deliberate, I crept out from behind the wall and to the opposite wall.

Six ratmen warriors have failed to detect you!

Crouching down, I measured the distance between me and the guards. Twelve yards separated us. *Just a little closer.* Eyes fixed on the ratmen, I shuffled closer.
One foot. Two feet. Three... Six.
Perfect.

Six ratmen warriors have failed to detect you!

I was now close enough to react instantly in case my plan went awry. *Time for the next step.* Opening my mindsight, I sent tendrils of psi racing toward the clump of guards.

You have cast mass charm. 4 ratmen warriors have failed a mental resistance check! You have charmed 4 of 5 targets for 10 seconds.

I realized there was no way I could quietly slay all six guards, not while they remained in open view of the miners. So, I planned on doing the next best thing: drawing them away.
"*Come,*" I ordered, reaching out to my minions across our newly forged mental link.
The four bespelled ratmen abandoned their post and, in lockstep with each other, marched toward the corner. One of the guards had resisted my spell. But there was no helping it, and anyway, I'd know beforehand that I wouldn't be able to draw all six away in one go.
There was a chance, of course, that the remaining guards would sound the alarm, but I was banking on the fact that as long as my minions took no hostile action, the pair wouldn't realize anything was amiss.
"Hey, Gurk!" one of the unaffected guards called. "Where you go?"
Gurk obviously didn't answer.
Narrowing my eyes to slits, I watched the two guards still at their post. If they became suspicious, I'd have to accept the risk of being spotted and shadow blink forward and kill them.
But the two didn't raise the alarm.
When no response from Gurk was forthcoming, the pair exchanged uneasy glances and hurried after their fellows. I relaxed. Things were proceeding even better than anticipated.
In obedience to my commands, my four minions had hurried past me and turned down the unlit corridor. They were still running through the tunnel and would keep doing so for as long as the charm spell remained active—which I saw was only another five seconds.
The other two guards, meanwhile, failed to spot me as they hurried past my crouched form. Their gazes fixed on the backs of their disappearing companions, they didn't spare a glance in my direction.
I waited until they also rounded the bend.
Then I acted.

Rushing through the aether, I emerged behind the pair. Neither ratman sensed me at their back, and my sneak attack caught them wholly unprepared.

You have killed a ratman with a fatal blow.
You have killed a ratman with a fatal blow.

Wrenching my blades free, I raced down the tunnel. My charm spell had expired, and the cries of the freed ratmen carried to me clearly. None of them could see me, of course. Without torches, they were completely muddled. Barely able to see each other, they milled around in confusion.

Drawing within striking distance, I struck.

You have teleported 9 nine yards.
You have backstabbed a ratman warrior for 2x damage!
You have killed a ratman.

My blade dripping blood, I whirled away from the corpse and plunged ebonheart into the next closest target.

You have killed a ratman with a fatal blow.

By now, the three remaining guards had realized something was amiss. Not hanging around, they fled. One directly into a side wall, another farther away from the cavern, and last, more by luck than anything else, toward safety.

I chased him down first.

Diving through the aether, I appeared beside the fleeing ratman, keeping pace easily. Some sixth sense must have warned him of the danger. The whites of his eyes showing, the guard swerved away abruptly.

Not fast enough, as it happened.

Before he could take more than a step away, my blades flashed, snuffing out the light from his eyes.

You have killed a ratman with a fatal blow.

Drawing to a halt, I turned around. *Time to finish this.*

Chapter 218: Being Gurk

You have killed a ratman.
You have killed a ratman.

After slaying the last ratman I searched the bodies, but the guards had carried as little of value as the first two I'd killed, and I came away with nothing. The Adjudicator hadn't awarded me with levels from the fight either, only a few skill gains. Shaking my head at the poor recompense, I made my way back up the tunnel.

It seemed impossible that my skirmish with the guards had gone unnoticed, but when I peered in the cavern, I saw the miners' demeanor remained unchanged—they still chipped industriously at their rocks, unconcerned by the unguarded entrance.

Good. Sheathing my blades, I wove an illusion around my form.

You have cast lesser imitate, assuming the visage of the ratman warrior, Gurk. Duration: 1 hour.

Judging by the eight foes I'd slain so far, I was a bit tall for a ratman, but I was hoping that in the bustle of the cavern, my unusual size would go unnoticed. If I was found out... well, then things would go badly for me. Hunching my shoulders, I ambled into the cavern.

No alarm was sounded. And no one demanded I identify myself.

In fact, my arrival went entirely unmarked.

None of the miners so much as bothered to look up from their digging, not even those closest to the entrance. I exhaled softly, relieved by their disinterest.

But it was time I got moving. A lone warrior by the entrance, I was too conspicuous. Ducking my head, I waded deeper into the cavern. As I weaved between the clumps of ratmen, I stole quick glances at what they were mining. It was a reddish-colored ore, but the type defeated my analyze attempts.

Shortly, I reached the cavern's center. Setting aside the puzzle of the unknown ore, I lifted my head and took a good long look around the chamber.

The cavern was as large as I thought, but to my dismay, it had not one or two exits but a dozen. *Damnation. Which one do I explore first?*

I doubted I had time to venture down all twelve passages. Eventually the absent guards would be missed, and when that happened I wasn't sure that my disguise would stand up to close scrutiny. Resuming my quiet walk through the cavern, I searched for inspiration.

I had nearly completed three full circuits when I found it.

Or rather, it found me.

Out of the corner of my eye, I spotted a cloaked figure enter the cavern. Escorting him were two hulking forms. I turned their way immediately, but before I could get a clear view of the trio, they disappeared down another corridor.

Still, I didn't doubt the cloaked figure was a savant.

With no other leads to go on, I trailed after the trio.

✻   ✻   ✻

The tunnel the three had entered was dimly lit by torches. My targets had already disappeared from view though. I glanced around. No other ratmen were in sight either. Intent on catching up to the trio, I sped up, my footfalls silent despite my increased pace.

As I dashed through the corridor, my gaze darted left and right, searching for side passages. I saw none, which was a relief. Fifty yards later, I came across the first door. It was shut. Slowing down, I opened my mindsight and probed the room beyond.

No glowing minds appeared.

Empty, I concluded and hurried onward.

I passed over a dozen more doors, all closed. Each time, I dragged my steps and interrogated the rooms beyond with my mindsight. Most were empty, but a few were occupied by dozing ratmen. The enforced delays were frustrating but necessary. I couldn't afford to miss the savant.

The corridor I was in seemed to hold the ratmen's sleeping quarters, which opened up all sorts of interesting possibilities. Did the savants sleep? And could I catch one napping? *It would make things measurably easier if—*

I broke off.

The two hulking figures I'd glimpsed earlier were up ahead. Both were standing stock-still outside a closed door—*standing guard?*—and, thankfully, hadn't caught sight of me yet. Slowing my steps, I resumed my pretense of being an idle ratmen warrior.

As I drew closer, I realized the pair were ratmen. Overly large and muscular ratmen, but ratmen nonetheless. Finally spotting me, the savant's bodyguards swung around to fix me with inscrutable gazes. Affecting a nonchalance I didn't quite feel, I kept advancing.

You have passed a mental resistance check! Two hostile entities have failed to pierce your disguise.

That ratmen said nothing, but they didn't look away either. Keeping their eyes on me, they watched me saunter closer. *The savant must be inside the room they're guarding.*

Reaching out with my will, I analyzed the ratmen.

The target is a level 120 ratman brute.
The target is a level 121 ratman brute.

Brutes, eh? Well, that explained their size. Drawing even with the two bodyguards, I lowered my gaze in pretended subservience. The ratmen's hard stares followed me, but they let me pass unchallenged.

When my back was to the pair, I opened my mindsight and scanned the room.

But no bright bubble of awareness popped into sight.

I frowned. The savant had to be in the room. Where else could he be? Either he was shielded from my mindsight, or the room beyond was bigger than I thought and he was out of reach.

Whichever it was, I was determined to get to him.

✳   ✳   ✳

I waited until after I'd passed out of the brutes' sight to duck into the shadows. Despite the torches inset at regular intervals in the corridor, there were more than a few pools of darkness around.

Wrapped in shadow, I crept back up the tunnel to observe the brutes. I had to get into the room, obviously. The surest way to do that would be to slay the bodyguards first.

Killing the two wouldn't be difficult... doing it silently though, that could prove troublesome. And if I could help it, I didn't want the savant alerted to my presence until it was too late.

Another option would be to charm the pair. But that brought its own complications. Once I bespelled the two, I'd have ten seconds to get in the room, kill the savant, *and* stop the brutes from raising the alarm.

All possible to accomplish. But it would be risky and left no margin for error. Besides which, there was no certainty I *could* charm the brutes. If the pair were dominated by the savant, there was no chance of that.

How else can I get in? I wondered. Deception? Somehow, though, I doubted the brutes would let a random ratman wander into the savant's rooms unchallenged.

But what if... I imitated a savant? *Hmm, that might work.*

Bowing my head, I began working out the details of my plan. Once I set it in motion, there would be no time for hesitation or second-guessing.

"He late," one of the brutes barked abruptly.

Raising my head, I studied the bodyguard curiously. Who's late?

"Boss won't be happy," the second agreed. He rubbed his tummy. "Me hungry too."

Brute one turned down the corridor to stare in my direction. I stilled. Could he see me?

"Should I go fetch Wick?" brute one asked.

I relaxed. The bodyguard's words made apparent the reason for his glance: he was searching for the missing Wick.

Brute two shook his head. "No. Boss will be angry. Better he angry at him than you."

The first guard nodded vigorously and they both subsided.

I bit my lip. *Food,* I mused. Was that why the savant was in his room? Was he waiting for his meal to be served?

I glanced behind me. My sight was better than the brutes, but even I couldn't see any ratman making his way up the tunnel. Nor did I actually know what lay farther down the passageway. I hadn't explored it fully yet.

Let's find out. Turning around, I headed deeper into the tunnel.

✳   ✳   ✳

Five minutes later, I happened upon a slim ratman rushing up the tunnel. Two trays overloaded with food were precariously balanced in his arms.

This has to be the missing Wick. In his haste to reach his destination, the servant was barely paying attention to his surroundings.

It was too good an opportunity to ignore.

Flinging open my mindsight, I scanned the rooms on either side of me. They were empty. *Good.* Drawing on my psi, I cast charm.

A level 97 ratman has failed a mental resistance check! You have charmed your target for 10 seconds.

Wick wrenched to a halt, upsetting some of the dishes on his trays, but thankfully he didn't drop anything.

Striding boldly out of the shadows, I wordlessly relieved the ratman of his burdens. Setting them aside on the floor, I studied Wick for a moment and got the distinct impression he was young. *Too bad,* I thought.

I couldn't afford to let Wick go free, and I didn't have time for anything fancy. *Sorry, friend.* Slipping forward, I buried ebonheart hilt deep into the ratmen's chest.

You have killed a ratman with a fatal blow.

Catching the body as it fell, I dragged it inside one of the empty rooms and patted it down quickly. The ratman had only one item of value on him, a slim dagger.

Taking the weapon, I stuffed it in my belt, then shoved the corpse beneath a wooden bed. Hopefully, it would be awhile before Wick was found.

Returning to the corridor, I wove a new illusion about myself.

You have cast lesser imitate, assuming the visage of the young ratman, Wick. Duration: 1 hour.

Picking up the two trays, I hurried back up the corridor. I was late for an appointment with a savant.

✳   ✳   ✳

The moment they saw me, the two brutes fixed hungry gazes on the food I carried. Seeing their expressions, any concern I had about my illusion passing scrutiny vanished.

Before I could even draw to a halt, brute one snatched a tray from my hands and, ripping off one of the bowl covers, stuffed his mouth full of food. Brute two quickly followed suit.

A moment later, brute one came up for air and, seeing me still standing in front of them, snarled, "You late."

I nodded, not trusting my speech patterns not to give me away.

"Well? What you wait for?" Brute two demanded querulously. "Go in before boss kill you!"

Brute one hooted. "He might anyway."

Hastily complying, I pushed open the door and slipped inside. Shutting the door firmly behind me, I scanned the room.

The savant was awake.

Sitting at a table on the left side of the room, he was bent over in fascinated study of, of all things, a rock. At my entrance, he looked up and cocked his head to the side, a faint frown marring his face.

A hostile entity has failed to pierce your disguise.

The Game messages didn't reassure me. The savant was still studying me the way one would a particularly puzzling conundrum, and I was sure he would figure out the truth soon enough.

Displaying none of my anxiety, I laid down my tray on the nearby dining table. I felt the savant's gaze on me the entire time. Straightening, I summoned psi and met the creature's lifeless gaze.

You have failed a mental resistance check! A level 135 savant scholar has pierced your disguise.

The scholar's gummy lips parted and his eyes widened. I let a cold smile touch my lips, then I was moving.

Crossing the intervening space between us in an eye blink, I emerged out of the aether behind the savant just as he rose from his chair. The creature raised his hands, preparing a casting.

But I was quicker.

Wrapping my left hand around his throat, I yanked him off his feet, casting stunning slap for good measure.

You have stunned your target for 1 second.

Before the spell's effect could dissipate, I drew ebonheart and ran the savant through.

You have killed a savant scholar with a fatal blow.

The savant died with a quiet sigh in my arms. Hugging the body tighter, I held it upright while I listened intently.

The only sound penetrating through the thick door was the noise of the two brutes' jaws working.

The pair were still eating.

The bodyguards hadn't sensed the killing, which meant they hadn't been mentally enslaved by the savant either. Lowering the corpse to the floor, I chuckled softly. Matters were proceeding even better than I could've hoped.

I dragged the corpse to the bed and shoved it beneath before returning to the center of the room. There, I let the illusion of Wick dissipate and replaced it with another.

You have cast lesser imitate, assuming the visage of a savant scholar. Duration: 1 hour.

Concealing myself behind the door, I drew my second blade. It was time to deal with the brutes.

I didn't exit the chamber.

It was far better to make the brutes come to me. Drawing on my psi, I sent probing tendrils of energy into the pairs' minds and overcame their defenses with laughable ease.

You have charmed 2 of 2 targets for 10 seconds.

With a grim smile for what I knew needed to happen next, I ordered the guards into the room. Obediently, brute one opened the door and stepped inside; brute two followed, shutting the door behind him. Neither spied me hidden in the shadows.

"*Sit,*" I commanded the first guard. He sat, back to me, leaving the second guard where he was.

Moving swiftly—my charm spell would lapse soon—I stuck both my blades into brute two.

You have killed a ratman with a fatal blow.

He died instantly, his corpse hitting the ground with a resounding thud.

Ignoring the body on the floor, I sheathed my bloodied blades. As I'd anticipated, they faded from sight, hidden by the illusion of a robed savant woven around me. There was nothing left to do now but wait. Folding my arms across my chest, I glared at the back of brute one's head.

It didn't take long.

You have lost control over a ratman brute.

The moment brute one slipped my mental leash, he swiveled around in his chair. Spying his dead companion on the ground and me standing over the body, his eyes grew wide as saucers.

"Face forward!" I snapped. The words came out harsh and guttural, nothing like my own voice.

Brute one whipped back around, hiding his face but not the tremble in his limbs. The ratman was scared. *Excellent*, I thought, letting him stew in his fear a while longer.

In my interactions with the two bodyguards—brief though they'd been— brute one had seemed the more voluble of the two, which was why it was him I'd chosen to interrogate. If I wasn't going to waste hours searching every tunnel in the sector for the boss and exit portal, I was going to have to locate them by other means.

Let's hope this works.

Pacing around the table in slow, ominous steps, I came to a halt directly opposite the quivering bodyguard. "Boss control me?" he asked, pointing a stumpy digit at his temple. "In here?"

I said nothing.

Brute one licked his lips, then with more courage than I'd suspected he had, he burst out, "Boss kill Ngor?"

That had to have been brute two.

I let my gaze drift meaningfully to the slowly growing puddle from beneath the bed. "And Wick too," I growled.

Following my gaze, the bodyguard bit off a yelp. "But why, boss?" he asked, voice reedy with fear. "Wick harmless! He no—"

"Wick was not Wick," I drawled. "Wick was an assassin." I paused. "And you two let him in."

Panic flitted across the ratman's face. He'd recognized the threat. "No! We-we didn't. *I* didn't!"

I resumed pacing, cutting another circuit around the table. "I don't believe you," I said from behind the brute. "You, too, must be an assassin."

The bodyguard's head whipped back and forth, trying to keep me in his line of sight. "I'm not. Promise. I no assassin."

"Prove it," I snapped.

Confusion and hope warred on the ratman's face. "How, boss?"

"Tell me things no imposter would know."

The brute frowned, trying to work out what I meant. Before he could, I barked out, "Where are the other bosses now?"

The ratman's face fell, and his lip began to tremble. I held back a sigh. Clearly, this was a question the brute didn't know the answer to. Before he could respond, I held up a hand, stopping him. "Wait. Tell me the location of their rooms."

At this the brute's eyes lit up, and he began to babble out a response.

I cut through his chatter. "Stop. Start again, and this time leave nothing out. I want to know exactly how you would get there. Every turn and tunnel. Understood?"

The bodyguard nodded vigorously and started again.

A faint smile on my lips, I closed my eyes and listened intently.

✳   ✳   ✳

Ten minutes later, brute one was done.

I'd made him go over the details multiple times until I was sure I had it all memorized. When he was done, I had what I needed: the location of the other savant's rooms *and* that of the nether portal.

I was halfway to escaping the sector already.

"Boss... can I ask something?" brute one asked cautiously when, after a drawn-out moment, I said nothing.

I nodded absently, still pondering on how best to use what I'd learned.

"You speak our language?"

I shook off my musings and threw the ratman a sharp look. "Why do you ask?"

I wasn't really speaking the ratmen's language, of course. I suspected the only reason I could understand the ratmen—and them me—was because of my beast tongue trait.

"No reason," brute one blurted, sensing my displeasure. "It's just..." he scratched his nose. "Boss never speak before."

I stared at the bodyguard expressionlessly. The ratman was certainly no Klaxis. The goblin shaman from the wolves' valley had been quick enough to uncover my deception. But even now, despite my behavior being uncharacteristic of a savant, brute one didn't seem to suspect anything amiss.

And I can't keep calling him that. Yet, it wasn't like I could've asked him his name earlier, was it? I could now though.

"What is your name, brute one?" I asked, pacing around the table again.

That ratman looked at me strangely. "What?"

"Your name?" I asked softly from behind him.

"Rugar," he said. "But why—"

"Thank you, Rugar," I said gravely. "You've done me a great service."

The ratman puffed up proudly.

My blades flashed.

You have killed a ratman with a fatal blow.

✳   ✳   ✳

Resting Rugar's head gently on the table, I searched the room and the three corpses strewn around it.

There were some odd-looking artifacts in the room, including the strange rock the savant scholar had been studying, but they were all bulky and not worth the effort of lugging around. Even the food was... unappealing. A single bite was enough to convince me to leave the rest untouched.

In the end, I decided to take nothing. I was managing well enough in just my newbie clothes and two swords, and I decided to continue as I was.

Returning to the center of the room, I turned my focus inward to the waiting Game messages; I hadn't checked my skill gains since the previous sector.

You have reached level 111!
Your sneaking has increased to level 81. Your thieving has increased to level 56. Your telepathy has increased to level 62. Your insight has increased to level 91. Your deception has increased to level 88.

Much better, I thought, smiling in quiet satisfaction. So far I'd gained two levels from my kills in the sector, and without needing to ponder the matter, I invested the new attribute points I'd earned.

Your Mind has increased to rank 60.

There was just one more thing I needed to do before leaving. Concentrating, I wrapped myself in a new illusion.

You have cast lesser imitate, assuming the visage of the ratman brute, Rugar. Duration: 1 hour.

Ready to face the sector again, I slipped out the door. The tunnel was just as empty as before. Marching up it, I headed back to the main cavern with the miners. It was the central hub of the ratmen's nest, and to get to any of my target destinations, I would have to navigate through it again.

According to Rugar, there were three more savants on the level, the sector boss and his two lieutenants. I decided to forgo slaying the lieutenants—I'd left a trail of bodies in my wake, and I wouldn't go undiscovered much longer—but I had to kill the sector boss. His amulet was required to unlock the final chamber on the last level.

The sector boss was likely in one of two locations: his rooms or at the nether portal. Given how well my encounter with the savant scholar had gone, I decided to head to the boss' chambers first. If I could catch him unawares there, killing him would be a trivial matter—hopefully.

✳　✳　✳

The moment I stepped into the main cavern, the gazes of the nearby miners flickered my way before returning to their labors.

Multiple hostile entities have failed to pierce your disguise.

I frowned. Perhaps choosing Rugar's form to imitate hadn't been the wisest choice. I certainly stood out more among the sea of smaller ratmen in the cavern, but it was too late to change my mind now.

Ignoring the sidelong looks I was attracting, I searched for the exit I needed. According to the instructions I memorized, it was the third tunnel over. Spotting it, I stomped toward it.

Halfway there, I paused.

There was a commotion on the opposite side of the cavern. A large group of ratmen—a mix of warriors and brutes—were shoving their way through the miners. In their midst was a savant. Not wanting to attract attention, I resumed walking, but out of the corner of my eye I continued to observe the creature.

Physically, the savants were indistinguishable from one another, so there was a chance the creature I was looking at was the sector boss. But I doubted it. Still, I reached out with my will and analyzed him.

The target is a level 138 savant sorcerer.

One of the lieutenants then.
After a moment, I realized the savant and his escort were heading for the nest's main entrance—the same tunnel where I'd slain the six guards.

Well, that blows it, I thought. *They know they have an intruder on the loose now. Time to hurry this up.*

Increasing my pace, I ducked into the tunnel mouth leading to the sector boss' chamber. Unlike the other passageway I'd just traversed, this one had no rooms or branches along its length, and I encountered no one despite the stir of activity in the rest of the nest.

This tunnel leads to one place only: the sector boss's chambers.

The passageway was long too, seeming to go on forever before terminating in a large cul-de-sac. The room in question was situated at the far end, and as its closed doors came into sight, I drew up short.

Six brutes were standing guard outside the chamber.

I felt a rush of excitement. Did that brutes' presence mean the sector boss was inside? Spotting me, one of the guards called out. "What you want?"

Despite the brute's belligerent tone, there was no undertone of suspicion in his voice, and I responded in kind. "I look for boss. He inside?"

The ratman shook his head. "He at portal readying troops."

"Bosses found dead guards," one of his companions added. "They think players around."

Another hefted his weapon. "You be careful."

Nodding wordlessly, I turned around and left. *Well, this certainly complicates things.*

I hurried through the main cavern for the third time. The ruckus around the nest entrance had increased with many more squads of ratmen assembling. I didn't dare linger. Counting off passages quickly, I located and entered the one leading to the sector's exit portal.

It, too, was flooded with ratmen.

Most were hurrying in the same direction as me—toward the portal chamber. *This isn't good,* I thought. More and more, it was looking like I'd underestimated the ratmen's numbers. *There must be thousands of them in the nest, not hundreds.*

How many would I find near the portal?

Seeing me striding alone, a brute at the head of a squad of marching warriors beckoned me to him. Not wanting to give him cause for alarm, I obliged.

"Where be your squad be?" the brute demanded.

I shrugged. "Not sure."

"Get in line," he ordered.

I didn't demur—they were heading in the right direction, after all—and dropped into place beside him.

So far, my lesser imitate spell was holding up well. None of the ratmen seemed able to pierce my guise, and while they knew they had an intruder, they seemed to have no idea I looked just like them.

I glanced at my fellow brute. "Bosses find intruders?"

"No," was the clipped response.

I scrunched up my face in pretended consternation. "Why we go to portal then?"

The squad leader shot me an irritated look. "Intruders always look for portal."

Huh. That sounded true enough. "What intruders look like?"

"I donno know!" he growled. "Elf, dwarf, or maybe human. Wherever they be, bosses find them," he finished with a note of finality.

Nodding sagely, I fell silent for the rest of the trip.

* * *

A little while later, we reached our destination.

The cavern housing the nether portal was huge. And majestic too. Its ceiling soared high overhead and was rife with stalactites that gleamed in the magelights dancing among them. Thin stalks of stalagmites taller than trees lined the cavern's edges, while the center had been smoothed into a single expanse of space.

One that was filled to bursting with hostiles.

My heart beat faster as I took it in. There had to be at least a thousand ratmen present.

"Move," the brute next to me snapped.

Realizing that I'd drawn to a halt in the tunnel mouth and was holding up the rest of our squad, I trailed after the brute while I studied the cavern and its inhabitants.

The ratmen were formed up in small squads that neatly encircled the cavern's only structure—the raised nether portal in its center. There was only a single entrance leading into the cavern too, I noted. The very same tunnel by which we'd entered.

The gateway itself looked like the one on the previous level, except this one was surrounded by a dome of vibrant green. The horde of ratmen weren't the nether portal's only guards though. A hooded figure—wrapped in his own jade bubble—and two brooding forms also stood in front of the dome.

The sector boss and his bodyguards.

The boss' presence came as no surprise. His guards, though, were not what I expected. For one, they were most emphatically *not* ratmen—brutes or otherwise—and for another, they were covered in armor that shone like burnished silver.

Holding back my trepidation, I analyzed the boss, dome, and bodyguards.

The target is a protective barrier formed from earth. Until it is removed, you cannot pass through, nor can the nether portal be accessed.

The target is a level 161 savant disciple.

The target is a level 154 iron golem.

The target is a level 155 iron golem.

Iron golems! I stifled a heartfelt groan. From the time I'd spent as one in the Wolf trials, I knew just how tough the constructs were. My blades would do little more than scratch their bodies. Worse yet, the golems had no consciousness.

That's both of my strongest abilities made useless.

By this point, our small squad was halfway to the portal, and I realized from our line of march that the brute-in-charge meant to go all the way and, maybe, even report to the sector boss himself.

For just a split second, I was tempted to stay.

An impromptu assassination could solve all my problems. But there were too many variables to control. The boss might sense my deception before I reached striking range, or the golems could block my escape through the portal, or worse yet, I might fail to find the amulet. Not to mention I had no idea how difficult it would be to penetrate the disciple's jade shield.

Better to await another opportunity.

I'd seen what I needed to, and it was time to leave. Whipping my head to the right, I pretended something there had caught my interest. "I see me squad," I said to the squad leader. "I go!" Not waiting for his reply, I dashed off.

No cry or shout followed in my wake.

Weaving out of the crowds of ratmen, I made for the rim of the cavern. While the center was brightly lit by the hovering magelights, there were shadows aplenty among the stalagmites lining the edges. Hidden in their midst, I could safely observe my quarry.

Head bent and feigning having lost something, I broke out of the ranks of ratmen and slipped between stalagmites. I glanced about casually. No one was looking my way. Stepping behind one of the tall ivory stalks, I faded from sight.

You are hidden.

Turning around, I peered around the edges of the stalagmite. From my observation point, I had a clear view of both the sector boss and the tunnel mouth.

I settled down, preparing for a long wait.

I didn't know how I was going to kill my quarry yet; I only knew it couldn't be done in this cavern. When he left, I would follow.

And then I would strike.

✳   ✳   ✳

Hours went by, and my enemies' disposition didn't change.

Overseen by the sector boss—who stayed shielded the entire time—and his bodyguards, the ratmen kept a vigilant watch on the gateway. Any hope I had of escaping the second sector quickly had long since faded, and I'd resigned myself to remaining in the sector for however long it took.

Idly, I wondered what had happened to the mantises. The assassins should have found me by now. Either they had failed to enter the dungeon as I expected, or... they had some other strategy in mind.

I wasn't sure which perturbed me more. But whatever the mantises did wasn't in my control, and I set aside further thoughts on them.

Movement in the cavern drew my eye.

The ratmen in the rear were turning around. I exhaled a relieved breath. The sector boss was finally standing down his forces.

Intently, I watched as the ratmen squads began to disperse, first in ones and twos, then in a rush. Not all of them were preparing to leave though. Nearly a hundred of my foes made no move to depart—including, unfortunately, the savant disciple and his two golem bodyguards.

A hundred ratmen, one savant, and two golems were still too many for me to take on at once.

Hell, even the boss on his own will be a challenge.

The reorganization of the enemy forces around the portal wasn't quite done though. While I was pondering my options, the two savant lieutenants and their escorts entered the cavern. My focus intensified. *Now, this is interesting. Why have they come?*

The three savants gathered near the portal, silently communing with each other, and a moment later the golems jerked to life.

My intuition sparked. *This is a change of the guard,* I realized.

The boss is going to leave.

I was certain of it. My mind raced, forming and discarding plan after plan. I could follow on the savant disciple's heels and strike at him from the shadows. Or I could go ahead and lay an ambush in the tunnels.

But neither of those options appealed to me, especially not with the golems accompanying my mark and the lieutenants close by.

There's a surer way to do this. Resuming the guise of Rugar the brute, I stepped out of the shadows and slipped in behind one of the squads.

Among the stream of ratmen exiting the cavern, I went unnoticed. Skipping quickly through the nest's central hub, I ducked into the tunnel leading to the boss' chambers.

It was as deathly quiet as before.

This time, knowing what awaited me at the end, I stayed hidden, creeping through the pools of shadow between the torches. As I neared the cul-de-sac, I slowed to a halt.

Six hostile entities have failed to detect you!

The brutes I'd spied earlier still stood guard outside the boss' chamber. I was nestled deeply enough in darkness though to escape their notice. Dispatching the six wouldn't be difficult, but I doubted the savant would enter his room if his guards were dead or missing.

I had a better plan in mind.

Letting my gaze drift around the surroundings, I studied the cul-de-sac in more detail. It was more brightly lit than the rest of the tunnel and had torches inset in the wall every three feet, leaving me no shadows deep enough to hide in.

The walls were smooth and unclimbable, and the roof was out of reach, even with two-step. I turned my gaze to the room's doors. They looked ordinary enough, but I hadn't forgotten the ratmen's fondness for traps.

Casting trap detect, I enhanced my sight.

Glowing, dust-like particles appeared in my vision, swirling around whatever my sight touched. When my gaze rested on the door, they coalesced into sharp red lines, signifying danger.

You have spotted a trap!

Well, well. The door and the ground underfoot were outlined in a crimson haze. Guards *and* traps. The savant disciple was a careful one.

However, for my intended purposes, it wasn't enough to simply know there was a trap; I needed to identify it too. Letting my gaze linger on the door, I traced each individual line of magic woven between the trigger and trap elements.

It was harder to do from a distance than if I was right beside the door. Still, slowly but surely, I learned the intricacies of the trap's design.

You have successfully identified a trap. This is a rank 1 explosive trap formed of two trap elements: an explosive fire enchantment and a motion pin.

My lips curved upward in a smile. The savant disciple had certainly not skimped on his defenses. But that would only make his surprise all the more complete when I penetrated them.

It was time to put my plan in motion.

Retreating from the cul-de-sac, I backed far enough away that the brutes wouldn't see what I was doing.

Then, one by one, I began dousing the torches.

It took me less than a minute to get ready.

Working quickly, I put out the torches in a stretch of tunnel between the miners' cavern and the cul-de-sac, transforming the space into an ideal hunting ground.

I'd chosen the spot with care, ensuring it wasn't visible from either the start or end of the tunnel. When I was finished, I hid in the darkness and waited.

It wasn't long before I heard the tramp of marching feet.

Many feet.

I frowned. It didn't sound like it was just the boss and the golems approaching. Listening intently, I counted footsteps.

There were... fifteen, no... twenty incoming hostiles.

If it was indeed the sector boss up ahead, he'd brought along an entire retinue for company. But my frown cleared as I realized it had to be ratmen making up the numbers. The additional bodies wouldn't aid the boss. In fact, I could already see how to turn their presence to my advantage.

Summoning psi, I readied myself.

A tense few seconds later, the enemy column appeared in sight. It *was* the savant disciple—still shielded. Accompanying him were his bodyguards and two squads of brutes. I waited, not releasing my spell. The moment wasn't quite right yet.

The enemy party drew closer.

Nearly simultaneously, the brutes at the head of the formation stumbled to a stop, their faces falling into comically identical expressions of suspicion. It had taken them long enough, but finally the pair had spotted the snuffed-out torches. The ratmen yelped in alarm, and the entire column ground to a halt.

Now.

Between one breath and the next, I released the weaves of psi I'd been holding, targeting not those at the fore but the ones in the rear.

You have cast mass charm. 4 ratmen brutes have failed a mental resistance check! You have charmed 4 of 5 targets for 10 seconds.

My spell completed, I refocused on the enemy column. They hadn't moved and appeared uncertain about how to proceed. The boss wasn't issuing commands either. His focus turned inward, the savant was muttering—the words to a spell, I thought.

The golems were creaking forward while the brutes craned their heads left and right, searching for an enemy they couldn't see. No one was looking to the rear, where my four minions stood still, waiting on my command.

"*Attack,*" I whispered.

The four bespelled brutes drew their weapons and, without compunction, hacked into their former companions.

Your minion has critically injured a ratman.
Your minion has injured a ratman.
Your minion has injured a ratman.
Your minion has killed a ratman with a fatal blow.

In an instant, pandemonium broke out, all semblance of order in the enemies' formation vanishing.

The golems swiveled around, gazes fixed on my minions.

The unaffected brutes, not realizing what was going on, growled and snapped at one another.

The disciple, finally sensing the chaos in his company, broke off his casting. Spinning around, he raised his arms. Realizing what the savant was about to do, I began a second casting.

Our spells were completed near simultaneously.

A savant disciple has cast mental domination. You have lost control over 4 ratmen brutes.

You have cast mass charm. 5 ratmen brutes have failed a mental resistance check! You have charmed 5 of 5 targets for 10 seconds.

I almost laughed aloud.

I hadn't targeted the same brutes again, of course. I was fairly certain if I'd done that I would've failed, the savant's mind magic being superior to my own. Besides, it didn't matter to me which of the ratmen I charmed. My only objective with the ambush had been to delay the boss' party.

Ordering my new minions to attack, I turned around and withdrew deeper into the tunnel.

✳ ✳ ✳

The moment I was safely out of sight range from the boss' company, I ducked out of the shadows and raced flat-out toward the cul-de-sac. I was still in my "Rugar" persona and had no fear of being seen.

In fact, I was counting on it.

My feet pounding against the ground, I hurtled through the tunnel. The clock was ticking. The darkened stretch of tunnel and the chaos I'd sown among the savant's escorts would only hold them for so long, and I still had a lot to do.

Panting for breath, I skidded to a halt in the cul-de-sac. Immediately, the six brutes accosted me. "What go on?" one demanded. "We hear fighting."

I exhaled noisily. "Intruders!" I blurted. "Quick, go help. Boss in trouble!"

The guards didn't need to be told twice. Without a backward glance, they raced up the corridor. Pretending to follow, I jogged after them for a few seconds, and when it seemed certain they weren't going to look back, I stopped altogether and rushed to the door.

It was time to break into the savant's rooms.

Taking a deep breath to settle myself—the run really had left me breathless—I cast trap disarm. A moment later, the spell took effect and energy flooded my eyes and fingers.

I had learned the configuration of the door's trap earlier and already knew how to go about deactivating it. Focusing intently, I disconnected the spell weaves connecting the trigger on the door latch with the explosive bomb hidden beneath my feet, making certain to leave as much as possible of the trap undisturbed.

You have successfully disarmed a rank 1 explosive trap.

Halfway there.

Next, I cast simple lockpicking. While the ability activated, I risked a glance up the tunnel. No ratmen had appeared yet, nor could I hear anyone approaching.

My ambush earlier had been nothing more than a diversion, a way to keep the disciple and his guards occupied while I broke into his chamber. My intent, however, wasn't just to get into the savant's rooms but to do so in a manner that left him unaware of my intrusion. Hence my ruse and diversion.

I was betting that once the dust settled, the one unaccounted-for brute— Rugar—would go unnoticed, and as wary as the boss was, with his rooms' defenses uncompromised, he would feel safe inside.

That's when I would strike.

Don't get ahead of yourself, I cautioned myself wryly. *You still have to get in first.*

I turned back to the door as the lockpicking ability took effect and my hearing was enhanced to discern every click and turn of the lock. Inserting Wick's dagger into the keyhole, I jiggled the lock until it sprang open.

You have successfully picked a lock.

Nearly there.

Turning down the handle, I darted into the room and, using my lockpicking ability again, locked the door behind me. Then I cast set trap. With most of the trap's spell weaves still in place, resetting it was almost trivial.

You have connected a trap element to a trigger.
An explosive trap has been successfully configured!

Only then did I breathe easier.

I'd done it. I'd made it into my foe's lair undetected. *Now to hide.* Staying by the door and wary of more traps, I scanned the surroundings twice over.

The results were enough to convince me there were no further traps. But about magical wards... I was less certain. The savants had displayed no talent in that direction so far though, and I could only hope that continued to hold true.

Turning my attention to the chamber itself, I studied its layout. In the room's center was a large double bed. Cupboards and shelves covered the left wall, and a table was placed near the right one. The room was also thick with shadows, but I didn't think it would remain that way once the boss arrived.

That doesn't leave many options.

My gaze dropped to the bed. It offered the only viable hiding spot. But it was also the most *obvious* spot. If the disciple was the least bit suspicious and had his minions search beneath the bed, I would be easily found.

I shrugged. There was no helping it. My planning had brought me this far, but the room's layout hadn't been something I could've accounted for.

Time to trust my abilities.

If I was discovered, I'd just have to improvise. Stretching flat out on the ground, I shuffled into position beneath the bed and wrapped a mind shield around my consciousness. I was as concealed as I could be.

Now all that was left was to wait and see if my preparations had been in vain.

✳   ✳   ✳

The savant disciple kept me waiting.

Ten minutes after I'd slipped into the boss' chamber, there was a ruckus outside the door. I tensed in anticipation, but after a few seconds I realized it was only the sound of the brute squad returning. I strained my ears to hear what they were saying, but their words were too muffled for me to pick out through the thick door.

Another hour went by, and I began to wonder if my earlier ambush had scared off the boss. But before I could worry in earnest, I felt the floor vibrate.

It was being caused by the tread of heavy feet.

The golems were approaching—which meant the boss was finally here. Forcing myself to relax, I kept my eyes glued to the entrance.

The door swung open.

Bright light spilled into the room—from a magelight, I suspected—and three sets of feet appeared, two of burnished steel and one robed. The boss halted in the doorway, and I could almost imagine his gaze sweeping the room.

Would he sense anything amiss?

Not daring to move, I studied the three pairs of legs that were all I could see of my foes. The golems were inhumanly still while the disciple remained cloaked in a shield of shimmering green.

So, he's not entirely at ease.

Tightening my grip around the hilt of my drawn blade, I prepared for the worst.

I was thus pleasantly surprised when, without further ado, the disciple crossed over the threshold. Striding across the room, the sector boss sat down abruptly on the bed. He wasn't the only one to enter though.

The golems and magelight followed on his heels. The bright orb sailed inward to hover over the bed while the constructs took up guard positions inside the door.

Uh-oh.

I'd been hoping the golems would remain outside. From outside the chamber a brute pulled the door closed, and silence descended. Barely breathing, I waited.

After a drawn-out moment, the shield surrounding the disciple vanished and the bed creaked as he lay down on the bed. A second later, the magelight disappeared too, plunging the room into darkness.

I exhaled softly. Not much longer now.

* * *

Ten minutes later, the boss was snoring.

I guess he's had a long hard day, I thought with a grin. My gaze drifted to the golems. They hadn't shifted an inch since they'd planted themselves on either side of the door. I wasn't sure if they remained a threat or if they too were asleep—in the constructs' version of sleep anyway—but I couldn't afford to treat them like anything but.

Minutely, I flexed my hands and legs to ease the stiffness that had set in. Then, I lowered my mind shield and unfurled my mindsight.

My awareness expanded outward, revealing six bubbles of consciousness—the brutes outside—but *only* six. Neither the disciple nor the golems appeared in my mindsight.

I sighed. Another wrinkle.

I'd been planning on shadow blinking into position and slaying the boss in one swift, sure blow, but that wasn't possible now. *Looks like I'll have to do this the old-fashioned way.* Ever so slowly, I slid out from under the bed.

Two iron golems have failed to detect you! You are hidden.

Well, that answers the question of whether they're alert or not. Doubly grateful for the lack of lighting, I rose silently into a crouch, no more than a blotch of darkness in the greater darkness of the room.

Two iron golems have failed to detect you!

Keeping my eyes fixed on the constructs, I unbent, an inch at a time, until I stood erect. A loud snore escaped the savant. Wrenching my gaze away from the golems, I pivoted toward my target, my every movement slow and measured.

Two iron golems have failed to detect you!

I was nearly in position. Placing my feet with care, I stepped up to my target's side and raised ebonheart in a two-handed grip. I held the pose for a moment, imagining the strike in my mind. I couldn't afford to err now. *Go.* In a sudden explosion of motion, I plunged the sword downward.

There was no resistance.

Cloth, skin, muscle, and bone: ebonheart pierced all.

You have killed a savant disciple with a fatal blow!
The second sector boss has been slain! Sector bosses remaining: 3 of 5.

You have reached level 113!

Metal creaked.
Retracting my blade, I whipped around, ready to fend off the golems. But the pair weren't advancing. The sound I'd heard was that of their helms sagging.
My forehead crinkled in confusion. *What?*

You have freed two spirits from captivity!
An iron golem has been disabled.
An iron golem has been disabled.

Realizing what had happened, I lowered my blade. But there was little time to relax. If this sector's configuration was the same as the first one's—and I didn't have any reason to believe otherwise—the boss' death would have triggered the collapse of the dome around the nether portal, alerting the hostile forces standing guard around it.
Which meant that, very soon, I was about to have company.

Returning to the boss, I tugged free the artifact from around his neck.

You have acquired an amulet of earth, the second piece of the guardian amulet of elements. In its present form, the amulet grants the bearer +10% resistance to earth magic.

The artifact was nearly identical to the other one I'd collected, except its crystal was emerald, not ruby. Drawing the necklace over my neck, I conducted a cursory search of the rest of the room.

I turned up nothing, but I didn't have time for a more thorough examination or to attend to the waiting Game messages. It was time to go.

Returning to the door, I listened intently.

The brutes outside hadn't been alerted yet, and no sound emerged from without. That didn't mean much though. I was sure more enemies were already hurrying this way, and once they entered the tunnel it would be all too easy for them to bottle me in.

I didn't intend to let that happen, but first I had to deal with the guards.

I do this quick and dirty.

Opening my mindsight, I fixed my attention on the brutes outside and cast mass charm.

You have charmed 5 of 5 targets for 10 seconds.

Perfect. Shadow blinking through the aether, I materialized before the one brute who had escaped bespelling.

"Wha—?" the startled guard began.

My blades were already in motion. Snaking forward, they ripped into my foe's torso and disemboweled him in a single strike.

You have killed a ratman with a fatal blow.

Even before the corpse sank to the floor, I spun to face the charmed brutes. They remained locked motionless, faces drawn in rigid lines. Hefting my blades, I padded toward the closest. There could be no witnesses to direct the search.

Ebonheart flashed out.

You have taken hostile action against your minion! Control of target lost.

You have killed a ratman with a fatal blow.

Six seconds to go. Four guards left.

Stepping over the body, I buried my swords hilt-deep in the next pair of guards. I didn't pause for breath. Withdrawing the bloodied blades, I slew the last two with neat surgical strikes.

Marionettes with their strings cut, the corpses thudded to the ground.

My bloody work done, I spun to a halt and cocked my head to the side, finally able to focus on what my senses had been screaming about for the last few seconds.

The sound of dozens of marching feet.

I was too late. More enemies had already entered the tunnel.

Damnation. I had half a minute—at best—before they got here. My gaze skipped from the dead brutes to the closed door and then from the brightly lit cul-de-sac to the darkened stretch of corridor ahead.

Where and how to meet them?

✹　✹　✹

If I could've been certain the two savant lieutenants weren't accompanying the enemy reinforcements bearing down on me, I would've had no compunctions about trying to sneak or bluff my way past.

But I had no such certainty.

So, I did the only thing I could think of: I doused out all the torches in the cul-de-sac and hid in the shadows. The larger volume of darkness gave me more options.

Just seconds later, the white glow of a magelight spilled into the cul-de-sac. A column of ratmen brutes, with a savant sheltered in their midst, followed hard on its heels.

Multiple hostile entities have failed to detect you! You are hidden. Your sneaking has increased to level 83.

Despite the new brightness in the cul-de-sac, the shadows around its edges were still deep enough to hide in. Besides, no one was bothering to look in my direction. All eyes were fixed on the six dead brutes and the closed door they had guarded.

The enemy's distraction was the perfect opportunity.

Bracing my back against cold stone, I edged closer to the tunnel mouth, inching my way out of the cul-de-sac. The enemy column, meanwhile, had spread in a half circle around the entrance to the boss' chamber. They numbered at least five full squads of brutes. Too many for me to tackle.

The savant strode up to the door.

He means to enter the chamber. I paused. *Doesn't he realize the trap is still active?*

Reaching out, the lieutenant yanked down on the latch.

Apparently not.

A hostile entity has triggered a trap!

The fire enchantment beneath the door detonated, and an explosive mix of flames and air mushroomed out. The ground shook, the walls cracked, and I lost my footing, as did all the ratmen.

The savant wasn't so lucky.

Caught in the center of the concussive blast, the lieutenant was flung aloft and struck the hard rock ceiling with bone-shattering force.

A savant sorcerer has died.
Six ratmen have been injured.

"Bloody hell," I muttered. *That was some trap.*

Rising back to my feet, I dusted myself off. The shadows concealing me had been torn away during the height of the blast. But all eyes had been turned the other way, and no one had noticed. Wrapping myself in darkness again, I glanced over my shoulder.

Pandemonium reigned.

Brute officers shouted useless orders, ratmen huddled over the lieutenant trying to revive him, while yet others poked cautious heads through the destroyed remains of the door.

I didn't stay to observe further. I'd gotten what I came for, and staying would only tempt fate. Hurrying into the tunnel, I left the enemy behind me in disarray.

* * *

Halfway down the tunnel, the shouts of the ratmen behind me faded to murmurs. I kept going, only stopping when I neared the central hub. From the sounds of it, things were no less chaotic there.

Weaving illusion, I assumed the guise of Rugar once more. Three of the savants on the level had been dealt with, but that still left one more to contend with—not to mention the hordes of remaining ratmen—and I had no desire to fight the entire way to the exit.

Better to bluff my way through.

Feigning panic, I hurried into the main cavern. I needn't have bothered though. As just another ratmen, my entry went unremarked. Swiveling my head from side to side, I took stock of the situation. The place was in an uproar.

Under the watchful eyes of the brutish officers, miners were dropping their picks and arming themselves with the weapons being brought in by teams of warriors. *They look ready for all-out war,* I mused.

Weaving deftly around the smaller miners, I made a beeline for the tunnel leading to the nether portal. A ratman officer spared me a glance but didn't inquire as to my business.

I reached the exit portal chamber without incident.

Other ratmen were streaming into the cavern too, and minute by minute the already formidable cordon around the gateway grew larger.

I didn't hesitate. Striding boldly into the cavern, I pushed my way through the ratmen squads on a straight-line course for the portal. The time for caution had passed. Now I had to be bold and hope the enemy didn't realize what I was until too late.

As expected, the earth barrier encasing the exit had disappeared. But ratmen weren't the gateway's only protection. Standing beside the shimmering curtain was the last savant. Casually, I shifted my hands closer to the hilt of my blades and readied a spell.

A brute waved me down as I drew closer. "Halt, soldier! Where you go?"

I didn't stop. "Message for boss," I said, gesturing to the savant.

A hostile entity has failed to pierce your disguise. Your deception has increased to level 91.

The brute frowned but let me pass.
The savant was turned the other way, listening to the report of another ratman. I had less than a dozen yards to go. *Nearly there.*
Suddenly, the lieutenant stilled and his head jerked around to stare piercingly at me.

You have failed a mental resistance check! An unknown hostile has pierced your disguise.

Reacting instantly, I released the spell I'd been holding.

You have teleported behind a ratman. Your telekinesis has increased to level 60.

In a split second, I covered the remaining distance to the portal, appearing behind the brute standing closest to it. The savant's hands were raised, preparing a casting. He was too late though.
Turning around, I dove through the gateway.

Transfer through portal commencing...
...

...
Passage completed!
Leaving sector 106 of the Endless Dungeon.

CHAPTER 223: THE WHITE-WASHED PLANE

You have entered sector 107 of the Endless Dungeon. This sector is level 3 of 5 of the Guardian Tower.

I rolled to my feet in a world of white.

It was cold. Blisteringly cold.

Wind tugged at me, and I staggered. Icy fragments whipped into my eyes, and my feet were buried in snow. I turned around in a slow circle but beheld the same thing in every direction.

A wall of white.

The ground—hard-packed snow—was white. The sky—overcast and heavy with clouds—was white. Even the air—full of falling snow—was white.

Goddamnit. Where am I?

Already, I could feel the cold seeping in. Neither my thin newbie clothes nor the smelly ratmen rags I'd draped around myself earlier offered any protection. Shivering, I hugged myself tight and searched again for a landmark. *Anything.*

Nothing caught my eye.

I opened my mindsight, but it was likewise empty. Worry nagged at me. Without a landmark, I had no way of navigating. And it was palpably obvious I couldn't stay where I was.

How in hells do I—

I broke off.

A consciousness had tumbled into the range of my mindsight—less than three feet behind me. *Impossible.* How had it gotten so close? I spun around.

It was a ratman.

My eyes widened. He'd come through the portal.

Realizing the danger, I tugged free my weapons and rushed forward, slashing simultaneously at the creature from the left and right. My foe appeared as befuddled by the weather as I'd been and didn't notice my attack until too late.

You have killed a ratman.

Another ratman emerged from the gateway—a brute this time. Lunging forward, I speared him through the throat.

You have killed a ratman with a fatal blow.

More ratmen spilled through the portal. Swirling among them, I dealt death. I plunged ebonheart through the gut of one, slashed the throat of another, staked a third through the heart, and chopped off the head of a fourth.

You have killed 4 ratmen. Your two-weapon fighting has increased to level 61.
You have reached level 114!

I stepped back, chest heaving and bloodied blades at the ready. If the savant himself emerged, I was going to be in trouble, but I wasn't yet ready to flee aimlessly into the sector's snowy depths.

A squad of ratmen poured through in a single group.

I was on them before they realized the danger. Bobbing and weaving, I cut and slashed. The ratmen were disorientated and disorganized and, despite their greater numbers, put up little resistance as I slew them indiscriminately.

You have killed 10 ratmen.

In a shockingly short span of time, I was done, and more ratmen lay dead at my feet. Covered in blood and gore, I fixed my gaze on where I knew the portal to be and waited.

A slow minute went by, but no more foes appeared.

My teeth chattered. In the heat of the skirmish I'd forgotten the cold, but now I could feel its icy claws digging deep.

I need to get warm, or the ratmen will be the least of my problems.

I couldn't afford to wait any longer. Relaxing from my tense pose, I sheathed my blades and surveyed the butchery I'd wreaked. Already the weather was whitewashing the bodies, but the ratmen's rags were still salvageable.

My lips curling in disgust at the need, I began stripping the bodies of their clothing. On its own each "garment" was insufficient, but tied together... they would provide more protection against the cold than I had right now.

✳   ✳   ✳

A little later, I rose to my feet draped in a cloak of rags. But by then it felt as if the cold had already settled in my bones. I shivered uncontrollably, leading me to wonder if the time I'd spent clothing myself had been worth it.

More alarming was that I didn't feel notably warmer in the cloak. Either the rags were doing little to shield me or... or my physical condition was worse than I thought.

Almost as if on cue, a Game message dropped in my mind.

You have failed a physical resistance check! Due to the harsh environmental conditions, you have been afflicted by frostbite. Your health is degenerating by 0.5% per second.

Well, that's just dandy.

Another grimmer thought followed on its heels. *If I don't find shelter, I'm going to die out here.*

Pivoting in a slow circle, I wondered which way to head.

There was still nothing to distinguish one direction from another. Realizing I had no other choice, I picked a heading at random and began wading through the snow. At the same time, I cast chi heal. I couldn't warm myself, but I could at least slow down the damage I suffered from the cold.

For as long as I had psi, anyway.

✳   ✳   ✳

I trudged through the snow for what felt like days—but in reality was probably less than an hour—searching for some relief from the expanse of ice.

I failed to find it.

The landscape remained unrelentingly white.

This has to be a tundra of sorts, I thought. It got me wondering about the level's design. The link between the elements and each dungeon sector was obvious.

In the first sector, I'd encountered fire creatures; in the second, denizens of the earth; but so far on this level, I'd encountered... nothing.

Where were all the water creatures? Had I chosen the right direction to explore? What if, instead of heading along any point of the compass, the right course had been... down?

Was there an ocean beneath the snow? Was *that* where I was supposed to go?

Gods, I hope not.

But surely, if this was a water-type level, the gnome's notes would have said *something*. It was a key piece of information, after all.

But truthfully, it didn't matter. Even if the right way was down, I couldn't go that way. I wasn't equipped for a prolonged dunk in water, much less water as icy as this sector's was likely to be. Setting aside the unsettling possibility, I scanned the horizon—again.

It hadn't changed.

The snowstorm hadn't let up either, and my frostbite was steadily worsening. So far I'd managed to keep it at bay, but a new concern had arisen.

I was starving.

I hadn't eaten anything since entering the dungeon, and I found myself regretting not eating the ratmen's food when I had a chance. Right now, it would've made for a veritable feast.

If wishes were horses, pigs would fly.

Sighing, I put my head down and kept moving.

✳   ✳   ✳

Your meditation has increased to level 93. Your chi has increased to level 63.

The hours passed slowly. And with it, all my concerns—be they of mantises, ratmen, or even hunger—diminished to nothing. My world had shrunk to my feet, and only two imperatives drove me: placing one foot in front of the other and casting chi heal.

I no longer looked up to scan the horizon. Hell, for all I knew I was walking in circles. It didn't matter. Nothing did except the need to keep moving. I wasn't sure why I bothered, but it wasn't in me to give up.

Twenty steps. Heal. Another twenty steps. Heal again.

It became my mantra, and sticking to it kept me upright long past the point when I should have been.

Game messages scrolled endlessly through my mind, warning me of the damage I was sustaining. And I knew I had attributes points to spend too. But I couldn't seem to muster the energy to bother with either.

Still, despite my single-minded focus on walking, I wasn't completely oblivious of my surroundings, and gradually the prickling at the back of my neck percolated through my mental fugue.

Danger.

Blinking half-frozen eyelids, I jerked my head upright and glanced over my shoulder.

I wasn't alone.

A sleek shape shadowed me. How long it had been there, I had no idea, but I suspected the creature had been trailing me for some time.

Analyze it.

Obeying the mental urge, I did.

The target is a level 118 snow leopard. Your insight has increased to level 93.

Despite me looking straight at it, the beast didn't attack. It met my gaze fearlessly but hung back. It was waiting, I suspected. For the weather to do me in.

A careful hunter then.

I shook myself into a semblance of alertness. Here, if not shelter, was sustenance. *I have to kill the beast*, I determined, nearly salivating at the thought.

I measured the distance between me and the leopard. Maybe eighty yards separated us. I could charm the beast. But would I be able to cover the intervening distance in ten seconds? Not in my present state.

Make it come to you.

That sounded reasonable. I stopped moving, and almost of their own accord, my legs collapsed beneath me.

There. Surely now *I must make for irresistible prey.* Lying flat on my back, I gripped ebonheart in one hand and waited.

A minute passed, but still the leopard didn't approach. Snowflakes piled atop my body, though I barely felt their touch. Opening my mindsight, I searched for the beast.

It was nowhere to be seen.

My eyelids closed. I snapped them back open. I tried to tell myself it had only been a slow blink, but I knew better. Unconsciousness beckoned. I was falling asleep.

Maybe this wasn't such a smart plan after all.

At any other time the thought would have warranted a chuckle, at least. Now, though, even smiling felt like too much effort.

A shadow fell over me. The patient predator had arrived.

Displaying no little patience of my own, I did *not* look the beast's way. Padding softly over the snow, the leopard lowered its head over my feet and snuffled.

I didn't react.

Emboldened by my inaction, the beast stepped closer. Tightening my grip on ebonheart, I waited. Its breath coming out in frosty white clouds, the leopard's head moved up my legs, over my stomach, past my chest, and toward my—

I struck.

It was the moment I'd been waiting for. The beast's position left it exposed and almost perfectly framed for stabbing. Wrenching ebonheart upward, I plunged the black blade through my target's neck.

You have injured a snow leopard.

Sadly, the blow was far from flawless, and I failed to kill the beast or even impale it properly. Thankfully, the creature didn't flee. Seeming determined as I to finish the kill, the leopard thrust its head downward, searching for my throat.

Expecting the move, or something like it, I thrust my left arm into the beast's open jaw, foiling its attack. Then, using every ounce of my remaining strength, I flung myself sideways, toppling the beast and shoving ebonheart deeper into the creature.

The black blade sliced through muscle and bone to emerge out the other end.

You have critically injured a snow leopard!

The beast meowed pitifully. Realizing its fight was nearly done, the creature tried to get its legs under it and flee.

I didn't let it. Hanging on grimly, I worked ebonheart back and forth, widening the already gaping hole in its neck.

It was enough.

You have killed a snow leopard.

Your dodging has increased to level 78. Your shortswords has increased to level 86.

CHAPTER 224: THE FROZEN WASTES

Getting back to my feet took nearly as much effort as slaying the leopard. The kill had given me new hope though, and I forced my tortured body into motion.

But I didn't sate my hunger immediately.

Instead, I began stacking snow.

The fight had cleared my mind, and I realized I couldn't keep searching for shelter. After hours of finding none, it would be foolish to expect to find any soon. The solution was obvious.

I had to build my own.

Packing and stacking blocks of snow together, I painstakingly constructed an igloo. The work went slowly, but I wasn't about to give up, not with a reprieve from the weather almost within my grasp.

An eternity later, I was done.

Returning to the leopard, I dragged it through the small hole I'd left open, then sealed it off with more snow. Finally, I turned back to the corpse.

It was time to eat.

Unsheathing the slim dagger I'd taken from Wick, I began cutting. The beast's body was already half-frozen, but I didn't let that stop me. Sawing off a fistful of raw meat, I shoved it into my mouth.

It was tasteless, mushy, and nearly inedible.

But it was sustenance. Ignoring my rebellious stomach, I chewed and chewed. Then chewed some more before finally swallowing.

Right, next bite.

Returning to the corpse, I cut another slice.

✳   ✳   ✳

A little later, I was sated.

Despite being forced to ingest the meat uncooked, I had no complaints about how nourishing my meal had been. My ice hut was also doing its job, and the numbness was disappearing from my extremities. I was far from warm, but I was no longer a poor excuse for an icicle and could think again. Sitting down cross-legged in the center of my small abode, I took stock of the situation.

There was no getting around it: I was lost.

I was adrift on a frozen tundra that, while not entirely barren of life, was at best sparsely populated. *Where to from here?* I wondered. I had to find the sector boss and nether portal, obviously. But how?

I had no idea.

Figuring out how to navigate the icy wasteland was beyond me. And if what I'd seen of the sector thus far was any indication, it was both larger and harsher than the previous two.

So, for now at least, I had to accept that my main objectives were out of reach. Where did that leave me? My gaze drifted back to the leopard corpse.

Control what you can.

The things I *could* control were few, but thanks to the snow leopard, they included two things vital to my survival. Staying warm. And staying fed.

I drew my knife. *Right, let's get to work.*

* * *

A few hours later, I'd skinned the leopard, cut and packed the edible bits, set aside anything remotely useful, and cleaned the bones.

Sitting back, I surveyed what I had to work with.

ebonheart, soulbound shortsword.
shortsword,+1
amulets of earth and fire.
a slim dagger.
a rag cloak.
10 x portions of raw meat.
an untreated piece of animal skin.
animal fat.
animal sinew.
bone slivers.
miscellaneous large bones.

My possessions were undoubtedly meager, but they were a damn sight more than I'd had a few hours ago, and if I put them to good use they might just see me through the next few days.

Digging a small hole in the snow, I buried the meat to freeze it all the way through. It would make for passable rations. I had nothing to carry the frozen food in though, and after a moment's thought I cut off a small piece of leopard's skin and fashioned it into a crude bag. The animal skin, even bloodied and untreated, was cleaner than the ratmen rags and a better choice for storing the meat.

Holding up the rest of the snow leopard's skin, I ran my fingers through the fur. It was surprisingly warm and would make a good addition to my cloak.

I unwrapped the ratmen rags from around my body. Calling it a cloak was a bit of a misnomer. I'd thrown the "garment" together in haste, and the workmanship was definitely shoddy.

Time to do something about that.

I had tools now—bone splinters for needles and sinew for thread. Better yet, I had one single large skin to act as a frame and animal fat for added insulation.

Head bent, I began crafting.

* * *

I had no crafting skills, of course.

But despite my lack of Game-gifted knowledge on the subject, that didn't stop me from muddling through.

Fashioning a bone needle was hard and entailed a lot of cursing. Sewing with the sinew fibers was even harder and left my fingers bloody. But I persevered, and when I was finally done I had a half-decent item to show for my efforts.

You have created a leopard cloak. This garment is crudely made from uncured animal skins and will rot in hot climes. Due to its poor construction, the cloak offers only the most basic protection from the cold. Additionally, due to the item's weight you will suffer a -20% movement penalty while it is equipped.

I snorted in derision at the Adjudicator's description.

The cloak was definitely nothing much to look at, but it was certainly warmer than anything else I had. Wrapped inside it, I could already feel my body temperature rising. With my immediate needs met, I turned my attention inward and checked my player status.

You have reached level 114 and have 3 attribute points available.

I pursed my lips as I considered my attribute points. Given my current predicament, I didn't think it wise to invest in Mind again. Constitution would likely serve me better in the debilitating weather.

But for all I knew, I might find a way out of the tundra tomorrow. In that case, increasing my Constitution would be the *wrong* choice.

Better to bank the points for now, I decided. *Until I have a better picture of what I'm facing.*

With nothing else to do, I lay down on a bed of snow. It was time to grab what sleep I could.

✳ ✳ ✳

I awoke blissfully warm and to a welcome Game message.

You are no longer afflicted by frostbite.

Smiling, I sat upright and flexed my hands. They felt normal again. I didn't know how long I'd been asleep, but I felt much better for the rest.

Things were looking up.

Rising to my feet, I picked up one of the discarded leopard bones and broke through a hole in the igloo.

It was still snowing. I stared upward. Thick clouds blanketed the sky, hiding the sun. My good mood evaporated. Nothing about the landscape had changed. Retrieving my rations, I waded out into the snow and looked for the leopard's tracks or my own.

I found neither.

Damnit! Kicking the snow in frustration, I turned around in an angry circle. Somewhere in this godforsaken tundra, there had to be shelter. The snow leopard had to have come from somewhere after all. But from where?

The answer eluded me.

Sighing in defeat, I picked a direction at random and began walking.

✳ ✳ ✳

Three days passed.

Three long, horrible days during which the weather didn't let up. Not once.

The only change I observed during all that time was the periodic darkening of the sky brought on by nightfall. I didn't encounter any other beasts either. I had no plan. No strategy. Except to keep walking—in the hope I would get somewhere eventually.

On the second day, I received a Game alert.

The allotted time for bounty 674 has expired. You have failed the job. Your BHG ID has been updated. Active bounties remaining: 2 of 5.

The Adjudicator's message was a not-so-gentle reminder that time was not standing still in the outside world, even if it felt like that inside the dungeon. It made me wonder about the mantises again.

What had happened to them?

It was long past the point when Menaq's disciples should've located me. *Perhaps my theory about how they're finding me is wrong,* I reflected.

Or perhaps, they *knew* where I was but couldn't get to me. Or maybe the assassins' reasons were more insidious. Maybe they believed I was irreparably lost and were content to let the dungeon do what they couldn't.

I shuddered. It wasn't a pleasant thought.

But, right now, strange as it sounded, the mantises were only a secondary concern. Turning my attention outward again, I scanned the horizon in the vain hope something had changed. But once more, the featureless landscape defeated me.

Sighing, I forged onward.

More time passed and I covered untold miles, traveling only in the day and sleeping during the night. There was no reason to do otherwise.

By the end of the fourth day, my stores of food were half-depleted. I'd been rationing them carefully, eating only when I absolutely had to. Still, I knew I would have to find more food soon or risk starvation. The fifth day came and went with no change to my solitary existence.

But on the sixth day, the monotony was finally broken.

✳ ✳ ✳

My morning began like any other. Waking early, I packed my meager belongings and started walking.

Over the last few days, I'd taken to following the wind. I suspected it was a far from a reliable compass, but for lack of anything better, it would do.

Very quickly, I fell into the rhythm I'd become accustomed to. Walking across the tundra in newbie shoes wasn't easy. With each step, my legs sank inches deep into the snow, and I was forced to alter my stride to compensate for the need to wrench my feet free each time.

In hindsight, I realized that in addition to the cloak, I should've fashioned a pair of snowshoes as well, but I'd been so happy to be warm that I hadn't spared a thought for other concerns. Given my odd gait, I'd gotten in the habit of dropping my head and watching my feet.

Which was why I almost missed the shape approaching from the left.

Something—a scent on the wind or perhaps a half-caught glimpse—made me look up and scan the surroundings. A four-footed beast was churning through the snow toward me.

Dropping my food pack, I threw off my cloak. The onrushing creature was some way off, yet it still loomed large in my vision.

It's big then.

Narrowing my gaze, I took in the rest of the creature's appearance. The beast's coat was ice white, making its form difficult to pick out from the terrain. But judging from the amount of snow the creature was kicking up, it was not only large but fast too.

Reaching out with my will, I analyzed the beast.

The target is a level 130 cave bear.

This shouldn't be too difficult. Weaving psi together, I cast charm.

You have failed to charm a cave bear. The target is in the grips of a berserker fury and, while in this state, is immune to mental manipulation.

Well. Not so simple after all. But despite the danger of facing down an angry bear without armor and in its own territory, I was eager for the fight.

I hope it tastes better than leopard, I mused idly while drawing my blades.

The beast drew closer, and more of its features became apparent: a bared muzzle, black lips, razor-sharp claws, and cold blue eyes, both of which were fixed unerringly on me.

"Come on, big boy," I whispered, dropping into a crouch. "I'm waiting."

Whether or not the bear grasped my words, it certainly seemed to understand my tone. The rage in its gaze grew, and it sped up a notch. I smiled. An angry foe was a careless foe.

The bear closed to within four yards, casting me in shadow and causing the saner parts of me to gibber in terror. Its true size was now glaringly obvious: the bloody thing was more than twice my own height.

You can't kill that! my rational mind screamed. *Run!*

I ignored it.

Two more yards and the bear reached striking range. A meaty paw—bigger than me—swiped downward.

I didn't wait to meet it.

You have teleported 5 yards. You have evaded a cave bear's attack.

I emerged out of the aether on the beast's back. Dropping to one knee, I plunged both my blades into my foe.

You have struck your target with a grazing blow.

Wow. My mouth rounded in shock. Both my swords were buried hilt-deep into the bear, yet they barely seemed to have penetrated through its protective layer of fat.
The bear twisted around, jaws snapping.
Jerking into motion, I yanked my blades free and somersaulted backward.

You have evaded a cave bear's attack.

Midair I cast two-step, breaking my fall as I landed lightly on the snow again. The bear swung around, fury rimming its eyes. Then before my startled gaze, it grew even larger.

A cave bear has cast primal wrath, temporarily doubling its size.

I gulped. *Alrighty. Maybe angering it wasn't such a good idea.*

Chapter 225: Frigid Encounters

The bear charged again.

I dove out of the way and it rumbled past. Staying down, I tried to conceal myself in the snow.

You have failed to hide.

So much for that, I thought, rising to my feet. Stealth wasn't going to work. I needed another plan.

The bear skidded to a halt and swiveled around. Then, predictably, it charged again. An instant before impact, I cast shadow blink.

You have teleported 9 yards. You have evaded a cave bear's attack.

Emerging from the aether, I dropped onto the beast. This time I barely reached its back. *It better not grow any bigger,* I groused. Before the creature could react, I slapped my left hand down.

A cave bear has passed a physical resistance check! You have failed to stun your target.

Well, that isn't good. I tried again, this time using the blade in my right hand.

A cave bear has passed a physical resistance check! You have failed to cripple your target.

Urgh. Double fail. The bear's head swung around, and with no other choice, I fled its snapping jaws using two-step. Landing in the snow, I backed farther away while I considered my options.

Hiding was out. Mental assaults too. And the bear's physical resistance seemed too high for either stunning or crippling to succeed.

What did that leave? Short of slicing away at the beast until I penetrated its skin, there was nothing else to try. Such a strategy was fraught with peril too. A single hit from the bear would be fatal. Did I dare take the—

—*wait.*

What about astral blade? The spelled dagger dealt psionic damage *and* should bypass the bear's physical defenses. *It's worth a try,* I thought, weaving psi.

The bear turned around and began another charge, setting the ground rumbling in time to its stride. Simultaneously, my left hand flicked forward, releasing the newly materialized psi dagger.

The violet blade streaked through the air, striking the bear squarely in the chest.

You have injured a cave bear, inflicting psi damage. Nerves at the point of contact have been weakened. Inflict further psi damage to deaden them entirely.

For just a second, the behemoth's stride faltered, and I could almost read the confusion in its eyes as the tiny pinprick of violet hurt it.

I smiled even as I dodged out of the lumbering beast's way.

Now, I had a plan.

* * *

The cave bear was fast, but with two-step and shadow blink, I was faster.

Using both abilities to good effect, I kited the beast. Circling the creature, I kept the distance open between us while I hammered it with a constant stream of psi daggers.

I focused my assault on the bear's left foreleg—I would've preferred trying to blind the beast, but its eyes were too difficult to hit with any regularity.

It took dozens of successful attacks, but eventually the Game message I'd been waiting for arrived.

You have inflicted irreparable nerve damage on a cave bear. A cave bear's left foreleg is permanently paralyzed.

The beast lurched.

Suddenly deprived of one of its legs, my foe crashed into the snow. It got back up, of course. Eyes blazing with fury, the beast limped after me. *It's determined; I'll give it that.* But with one of its legs paralyzed, the bear was no longer a threat.

Forming another astral blade in my hand, I flung it at the bear's broad chest.

It was time to end this.

* * *

You have killed a cave bear.
Your telepathy has increased to level 64. Your meditation has increased to level 95. Your telekinesis has increased to level 61.

Minutes later, the bear thudded to the ground, never to get up again.

Elated but exhausted and cold, I slipped my leopard coat back on and approached the corpse. The bear was notably smaller. The spell that had enlarged the creature had dissipated, and it had shrunk back to its normal size.

That still left a few tons of bear sitting in front of me though.

The beast would feed me for weeks to come, if not longer. But the bear was good for more than just meat. Its fur, fat, sinew, and even bones were just as valuable.

I glanced up at the sky. The day was still young, but I didn't think I was going anywhere today. Harvesting the corpse would take the whole day.

Hefting my blades, I began cutting.

✳ ✳ ✳

Dissecting the bear was laborious and tedious work.

But I didn't rush. On the icy tundra, time was the one commodity I had no shortage of, and I took pains to preserve as much of the bear's fur and insides as possible.

Cutting away the meat in long strips, I buried them in the snow. The bones I cleaned and polished. The furs I scraped clean, stretched out, and staked down on the ground.

I was only three-quarters done by the time the sun set though. The darkness didn't bother me, but I'd learned the hard way that the temperature plummeted even further during the night.

I didn't want to be out and about when that happened.

Abandoning my work, I set about constructing my igloo. I'd gotten better at it with practice, and now I fancied my icy abodes were almost homely. But only almost.

Sealing off my igloo, I lay down on a bed of furs and closed my eyes. I was well satisfied with my labors today. Tomorrow was when the real work began though: transforming the material I'd harvested into usable gear.

✳ ✳ ✳

I awoke to the sounds of a whimpering whine.

My eyes snapped open, and I rolled free from the heap of bear furs I had buried myself under.

What's that noise?

My gaze roved over the igloo's interior. It was free of threat. But on my right, bits of snow were falling away from the wall.

Something was trying to get in.

Drawing my swords, I waddled silently to the spot in question. A paw appeared. Small, doglike. The paw withdrew, and a moment later a brown snout shoved through the hole.

Excited yelping followed.

I frowned. Was the creature friend or foe? Blades held at the ready, I reached out and analyzed my nighttime visitor.

The target is a level 105 young arctic hyena.

My lips turn down. A scavenger. *Foe then.*

The snout disappeared, only to be replaced by two frantically digging paws. It was no great mystery what had attracted the hyena. Although, even if I had thought to do so beforehand, there was no way I could've secured the bear's remains.

But the question now was: how many scavengers did I have to contend with? Unfurling my mindsight further, I scanned the surroundings.

The hyena wasn't alone.

A pack, at least a dozen strong, had gathered around the bear's remains. Briefly, I contemplated my response. It was just after midnight, I thought, and achingly cold outside. I couldn't afford a prolonged fight. Whatever I did, it would have to be quick. And vicious too. Drawing on my psi, I buffed myself.

You have cast reaction buff, increasing your Dexterity by +4 ranks for 20 minutes.

The hyena trying to get in stopped digging.
Its entrance now large enough, the beast stuck its entire head through. I didn't hesitate. Ramming ebonheart downward, I pinned the beast's skull to the ground.

You have killed a young hyena with a fatal blow.

Shoving the corpse back out, I sealed the gaping hole—no sense letting the igloo's remaining heat escape. Then I blinked out.

You have teleported into the shadow of a level 115 arctic hyena. You are hidden.

I emerged out of the aether in the heart of a raging storm. The wind howled and snow flew sideways, each a tiny ice shard of biting cold.
This is a *true* storm, I realized. One that made the constant snowfall I'd witnessed since entering the level seem like a spring rain by comparison.
The wind tugged at me, doing its best to push me off-balance, but I retained my footing. Snowflakes swathed my face, deadening my face and distorting my sight. I didn't let that dissuade me though. Shutting my eyes, I turned instead to my mindsight for guidance.
Twelve bubbles of awareness snapped into view.
Like all its fellows, the hyena in front of me remained unmoving—the storm had to be confounding its senses as much as mine—and though I couldn't see it, I suspected the beast's head was buried nose-deep in the bear's corpse.
Estimating where the hyena's vital organs lay, I struck.

You have cast whirlwind, piercing strike, and crippling blow.
You have backstabbed a hyena for 4x more damage!
You have killed a hyena!

Before the rest of the pack could react, I blinked away and into the shadow of another target.
Then struck again.

You have backstabbed a hyena for 4x more damage!
You have critically injured your target.
You have killed a hyena!

It took a few more blows the second time around, but my third victim died nearly as quickly as the one before.
The pack finally realized they had a killer in the midst. Abandoning their feast, they converged on me. Standing tall and guided by my mindsight

alone, I swept ebonheart in a wide arc at the closest beast—a lunging shape on my right.

The blade connected with something. It kept going, cutting through with barely any resistance.

You have critically injured a hyena.

The creature collapsed, alive but gravely injured. Kneeling on the beast, I pinned it in place and stabbed blindly downward with the sword in my left hand.

You have killed a hyena.

By luck, more than anything else, I hit something vital, and the creature died without protest.

Another beast was hurtling toward my exposed back. The hyenas could obviously see better in the storm than I could. Not waiting to meet the attack, I blinked away.

You have teleported 8 yards.

I emerged on the flank of another of the scavengers—a beast running full tilt toward where I *had* been. Yelping in surprise at my sudden appearance, the hyena wrenched to a halt and turned to attack.

I was quicker.

Swinging and stabbing wildly, I beat at the creature. My assault lacked any of my usual precision but was effective nonetheless.

You have injured your target.
You have injured your target.
You have critically injured your target.
You have killed a hyena.

The kill had taken too long to execute though, and another beast was already airborne, leaping at me from the right. I turned to face the creature, but before I could raise my blades to ward off the attack, the beast bowled into me.

A hyena has struck you a glancing blow.

I landed flat on my back and half-buried in snow. The beast was on me in a flash, its salivating jaws searching for my neck. Dropping the blade in my left hand, I slapped an open palm onto my foe.

You have stunned your target for 1 second.

I didn't waste the opportunity. Thrusting ebonheart upward, I impaled the beast straddling me.

You have critically injured a hyena.

The blow didn't kill my foe, but I wasn't about to stay to finish it. Stretched out on the ground, I was too vulnerable. Picking another hyena at random, I teleported toward it.

I dove out of the aether, poised to strike.

But the pack had had enough.

Yapping and howling at each other, the surviving scavengers fled into the storm.

Standing stock-still, I observed their retreat through my mindsight. Then shivered.

Now that I'd stopped moving, the cold penetrated. Even through my leopard cloak, its effects were biting. Sheathing ebonheart, I raced toward my igloo and shelter.

Come morning, there would be enough time to clean up.

CHAPTER 226: FITTED FOR BEAR

I woke again a few hours later, yawning and red-eyed.

The events of last night seemed almost surreal, and for a moment I wondered if I hadn't dreamt it all. But a quick check on the waiting Game messages was enough to convince me otherwise.

You have reached level 115!
Your dodging has increased to level 80. Your shortswords has increased to level 87. Your two-weapon fighting has increased to level 64. Your telekinesis has increased to level 62.

Right, so all that did happen. Now, let's see if the storm has let up. Breaking open my icy shelter, I ducked outside.

The weather had returned to its default setting: moderately miserable. *As opposed to what? Insanely miserable?* Chuckling at my poor humor, I surveyed the area.

The landscape was a picture of white. Pristine and seemingly untouched.

Snow had buried all the bodies—just how deep wasn't something I wanted to contemplate—and no trace remained of last night's skirmish. Even the bear's remains had disappeared, leaving only a largish size mound to mark its location.

I sighed, realizing what this meant. I was going to spend the better part of the day digging up the corpses, not to mention the other supplies I'd stored in the snow.

Well, best I get to it then.

* * *

It took me as long as I feared to dig out the bodies, but in the end I uncovered my supplies, the bear, my dropped sword, *and* all six hyena corpses—it turned out the one I'd injured had died too.

By then, the day was already waning. Not wanting a repeat of last night's fiasco, I built an oversized igloo and stored everything inside—except for the bear's bones, of course, which were simply too large. There was no way I was going to risk the hyenas stealing any of my hard-earned spoils again.

Although, truly, the scavengers' arrival last night had raised my spirits.

Encountering the bear and the hyenas so quickly after one another gave me hope that I'd found a more inhabited region of the tundra. I was wary of falling prey to false hope though, and so, despite my optimism, I planned for the worst.

Sitting down inside my new igloo, I got to crafting.

The first thing I did was create better needles. The first one I'd made had been done in haste, and this time around I fancied myself wiser and more experienced.

Using ebonheart, I carefully shaved thin long bone splinters from some of the hyenas' softer bones. Despite the soulbound weapon being larger and more unwieldy than my dagger, its hard, unyielding edge was more aptly suited to the task.

Next, I rubbed the bottom ends of the splinters against rougher bones until they were needlepoint sharp. And then, finally, I drilled tiny holes through the upper ends using the pointed tip of ebonheart.

You have created a set of primitive needles. Crafted from soft bones, the needles have poor durability and will be prone to breaking.

I smiled, satisfied with my creations despite the Adjudicator's somewhat disparaging description of them. Setting aside the needles, I tackled my next job: creating string.

This was tedious, if less taxing. Picking up the pieces of bear sinew I'd cut yesterday, I pried free the fibers and began twinning them into string over and over until, hours later, I judged I had enough to work with.

You have created a large ball of string made from animal sinew.

Lastly, I turned to the furs. I had far more than I actually needed. Selecting the best pieces, I cut them into the shapes I desired.

Then, picking up needle and thread, I got sewing.

✳ ✳ ✳

You have created a winter fur suit consisting of an overcoat, cap, face mask, jacket, pants, and snowshoes. Each item is distinct and separate and has been individually crafted from the hide of a cave bear. The garments have poor durability but are well insulated and provide adequate protection against the cold.

The suit is cumbersome and will inhibit your movement speed by -20%. Additionally, due to its native coloring, the suit will improve your sneaking by +5 when in snowy environments.

A weary smile lit my face at the Game message. The so-called winter fur suit had turned out better than I could have hoped for. It was bulky, yes, but that hardly mattered in the face of the cold protection it offered.

The only items my new outfit lacked were gloves. Sadly, they were beyond my meager sewing talents, and while I probably could have created *something* to cover my hands, I wasn't willing to compromise my blade skills with poorly made hand wrappings.

Removing my leopard cloak, I put on my new gear.

You have equipped a winter fur suit. Effects: +5 sneaking, protection from cold, -20% movement speed.

"Better," I grinned.

The night was well-advanced, but before I could retire for the day, there was one more bit of crafting I needed to perform. Cutting the hyena furs into long thin strips, I twined them around one another and bound them tightly together.

You have created simple but strong rope.

"Excellent," I murmured, stifling a yawn. Tomorrow, I'd fit the ropes and see if what I had in mind would work.

With a satisfied smile, I went to sleep.

✳   ✳   ✳

Day eight of my time in the tundra saw me rising early. The hyenas had not returned last night, and my sleep had been undisturbed.

Dragging the fur ropes and a stack of unused skins behind me, I ducked out of my shelter and inspected the bear's remains. The weather had finished what the hyenas and I had started, and now the bones were picked clean. Smooth and dry, they were perfect for what I had in mind.

Raising ebonheart—I really was misusing the poor weapon—I hacked apart the bear's skeleton until I had multiple long bone pieces ready for use. Then, using short pieces of rope, I tied them together to create a flatbed. Beneath this, I affixed two leg pieces running lengthwise.

Next, I stretched out the animal skins over the top of the flatbed and tied them down. And finally, I fitted one end of the flatbed with long running ropes and attached them to a harness designed to go around my torso.

I had, of course, built a sled.

There was no way I was going to be able to carry everything I'd harvested from the bear—and hyenas—on my back, but I wasn't about to leave any of it behind, hence the need for the sled.

Stepping back, I inspected my handiwork.

You have created a bare-bones sled. Crafted primarily from the remains of a cave bear, this device is a simple contraption designed to haul goods across snowfields.

Bare-bones sled? "Cute," I laughed.

Returning to the igloo, I hauled out my supplies and stacked them onto the sled. The meat alone made for a sizable pile. And when I added the furs and the other odds and ends, well...

That's not going to be easy to pull, I thought, eyeing the sled and its contents. But I was loath to leave anything useful behind. Fitting on the harness, I readied myself.

Here goes, I thought with some trepidation. Leaning forward, I heaved.

The sled moved. Barely.

Sighing, I dropped the ropes. I knew what I needed to do, but I'd been hoping it wouldn't be necessary. Turning my attention inward, I checked my player status and specifically my attribute ranks.

You have reached level 115 and have 4 attribute points available.
Strength: 2.
Constitution: 14.

Dexterity: 33.
Perception: 25.
Mind: 60.
Magic: 10.
Faith: 0.

I could triple my Strength in one go. That would make hauling the sled significantly easier. But...

I glanced up at the gray sky. *How long am I going to be stuck here?* I wondered.

I'd spent eight days on the tundra already yet was no closer to finding a way out of the sector. How long would it take? Another week? Two? A month?

I didn't know.

Thanks to the bear and the hyenas, I had the means to survive that long, if not longer. I was cautiously optimistic, too, about my chances of finding more game to hunt.

I knew from the Adjudicator's message when I entered the guardian tower that it was repopulated daily. In most dungeon sectors, this would have determined the time a party had to finish the level. But in *this* sector? With its open terrain and miles and miles of empty space, the dungeon's respawn rate counted for little.

Except.

Except that it also ensures my food source is replenished daily. Hence my belief that I would find more beasts to hunt.

But I also couldn't forget that I had gone six long days without encountering anything. Six days that could easily have become ten or even thirty, and I did *not* want to risk dying of starvation.

It hadn't escaped my notice that I hadn't found the safe zones of the first and second sectors. I didn't doubt they had one, just as this sector must. But I had to wonder how useful resurrecting in some random location—without any cold protection gear—would be in this sector. My first death, I was certain, would quickly be followed by my second and third.

Don't die then. I laughed grimly. *Easier said than done.*

So, where does all this leave me?

It left me without the luxury of being able to take any risks, that's what.

I didn't know which direction to head in. Hell, I didn't even know how to plot a heading. And if I didn't want to die, whether of exposure or starvation, I would need everything on the sled.

With that in mind, I invested the points I'd been saving.

Your Strength has increased to rank 6.

Time to get moving. Rubbing my hands together for warmth, I hauled on the sled again. This time it slid smoothly into motion.

The day passed slowly.

I fell into an easy rhythm, placing one foot in front of the other while trying to maintain a steady heading. All the while, my gaze roved over the horizon, searching for a landmark, a shift in the terrain, anything.

As I'd come to expect, the falling snow remained a constant presence. It no longer bothered me as it once had though. Either I'd become inured to the cold, or my winter suit was working.

Walking was easier too. Despite the added pressure from dragging the sled, my new snowshoes were up to the challenge and kept my feet from plowing through the snow with each step. All in all, trekking across the tundra had become almost... pleasant.

It was a thought that had me chuckling for hours.

Near the day's end, I noticed shapes on the horizon. At first the sighting excited me, but then I realized what they were.

Hyenas.

Perhaps two dozen of the creatures were shadowing me. I suspected they were from the same pack whose members I'd slain a night ago. For myself, I didn't fear the scavengers. But my possessions, on the other hand... they would be vulnerable should the pack pay me another nighttime visit.

Hmm. I'll have to come up with a means of securing the sled tonight.

Breaking for camp early that day, I set about making more rope. When I was done, I wove it together into a loose net which I threw over the sled. The contraption wouldn't stop the hyenas for long, but if it worked as I hoped, it would give me enough warning to catch them in the act.

Running a longer piece of rope between the net and my igloo, I strapped it around my ankle. Then I lay down and went to sleep.

✳   ✳   ✳

Right on cue, at the stroke of midnight, I awoke to a fierce tugging on my leg. Opening my mindsight, I scanned the area. As expected, there were some twenty feral minds gathered around the sled.

The hyenas had arrived.

Closing my eyes, I called on my psi. This time around, I didn't intend on leaving the warmth of my igloo if I could help it.

The moment my casting was ready, I released the spell, leashing the five closest scavengers to my will. *"Attack,"* I ordered the creatures.

They obeyed immediately and a fight broke out.

The skirmish didn't stay confined to my five minions and their victims though. It spread out, embroiling the entire pack. And, to my delight, it continued even after my charm spell lapsed.

Snug in my shelter, a small smile playing on my face as I listened to the pack's snarls, growls, and yelps of consternation. The hyenas' fondness for fighting was remarkable, and they kept at it long past the point I expected, dealing grave injuries to each other but, sadly, few mortal blows. Eventually, though, the fighting drew the pack away.

But that wasn't the end of the matter.

The pack returned three more times, each time as a unified group and with their pecking order reestablished.

That didn't last, of course. Once I charmed a few of the beasts again, the hyenas fell into chaos anew. Finally, the pack got the message and fled into the night, never to return.

Closing my eyes, I went back to sleep.

✳   ✳   ✳

The night's encounter proved to be the most eventful occurrence for some time.

The next day passed without incident. And the one after that. *And* the one after that. And so on. And so on.

Soon, the days blended into one another, passing by in a blur. I tried to stay upbeat, but despite my best attempts, the harshness of the landscape and the sheer monotony of the days chipped away at my resolve.

Day by day, I grew more despondent.

Every morning, I stepped out of my night's refuge, hauled my sled to nowhere, then went to sleep again. Over and over. Rinse and repeat.

A week after my encounter with the hyenas—*or maybe it was longer?*—I was ambushed by a pair of snow tigers. The skirmish was hard-fought, but I prevailed in the end, and while the respite from tedium was welcome, it was all too brief.

Another week passed, and another attack occurred—this time from a half-dead ice sloth. Then it was the turn of a hyena pack. A leopard. Then more hyenas.

And almost without me noticing, my existence fell into a new pattern: days of endless trudging through the icy plains, interspersed with sporadic attacks from its inhabitants.

I was grateful for the encounters—they saw to it that my supplies were replenished, after all—but otherwise, they did little to relieve my spirits. I no longer believed that the region I explored was any more trafficked than anywhere else in the frozen wasteland.

One spot of tundra was much like any other.

Lifeless.

Barren.

With nothing else to do but walk and think, I spent most of my days in fruitless speculation. Would I ever find the exit portal? Was there even a sector boss? Or was the tundra itself the sector's true test? And why, oh why, hadn't I questioned the gnomes more closely about the dungeon?

Round and round my thoughts went. Regret heaped upon impossible questions and maddening what-ifs.

Then one day, I just stopped.

Letting the sled's ropes go slack, I thudded to the ground, head bowed and listless.

Why? I wondered. *Why should I go on?*

I had no answer. I'd been avoiding facing this question for days. But day by day it had loomed larger in my mind, growing more insistent until now, when I could ignore it no longer.

This is it, Michael. Either lay down and die, or…

Or?

Or get up and keep moving.

But why? Why spend another day walking an unknown distance in an unknowable direction? Why should I expect the next day to be any different? Or the next?

Where there's life, there's always hope.

I snorted. Hope couldn't sustain me. Hope couldn't keep madness at bay. Hope was a dish fit for only fools and simpletons. It was empty and absent of true sustenance. No, hope couldn't save me.

Then get off your bloody arse and save yourself!

Chin knocking on my chest, I cackled, the sound devoid of joy. Like I hadn't been trying.

Try harder then.

Impossible. I'd done everything I could think of. I'd come into the sector with nearly nothing yet had managed to both feed and clothe myself. I had survived where countless others would not have.

Oh, stop singing your praises, you damn fool! You may have kept yourself alive, but you've failed at the most important task.

My head creaked up. And what task was that?

Finding a way out of the sector.

How could I do that? There was nothing to navigate by.

There's always a way.

Another worthless truism.

Admit it. You gave up.

I didn't.

You did.

"I didn't!" I yelled, throwing back my head and roaring at the uncaring sky. "There are no bloody landmarks!"

Then make your own.

"Make my own?" I howled with laughter. "*Make* my own? How would I bloody do—"

I stilled.

My inner monologue vanished, and the two dissenting halves of myself reunited. There *was* a way. It would be difficult, tedious, and quite probably pointless.

But it could be done.

Hope resurgent, I rose to my feet.

✳   ✳   ✳

Constructing a landmark would be a huge undertaking.

There was only one material available in anything like the quantity I needed: snow. I had no true conception of the tundra's size, but after traipsing across it for days, I suspected it to be immense—that, or unknowingly I'd been wandering in circles. I refused to believe that though.

To build a landmark visible across the entire tundra would be... difficult— I would've said impossible, but in the spirit of my newfound optimism, I settled for something softer.

For one, I didn't know how well any snow construct would hold up. Would it remain sound after months? And for another, if one of the frequent snowstorms destroyed my landmark, I would be back to square one.

No, I decided. *Better not to build one landmark but many.* Something that was simple to construct but stable too, easily visible, and not too labor intensive. *I know. Cone-shaped spires.*

Snow cones. That's what I'd build.

I could make them fast, and on the flat tundra, each would be obvious from miles off. I would need hundreds. Or perhaps thousands.

One way or the other, I intended on escaping the sector, and if I needed to transform the entire tundra into an array of snow cones to do it, then that's what I'd do.

Chapter 228: An Icy Existence

It took me the rest of the morning to construct the snow cone.

In one sense, it was much like building an igloo, except I filled the inside as well and expanded the structure upward as high it would go while taking pains to keep it stable.

I packed the snow as densely as possible and smoothed down the sides in the hopes that they would eventually ice over. I did one more thing too: scratching deep lines in a large bone, I shoved it into the center of the cone. If I ever ran across my landmark again, the markings on the bone would tell me when I'd built it.

When I was done, I stepped back and tilted my head back to study my creation. The conical-shaped spire rose high over my head and would be visible from a long way off.

Too bad I can't make them in anything other than white.

The color would make the cone harder to spot from a distance, but there was no helping that. The constantly falling snow would hide any coloring I added.

Satisfied I'd done everything I could, I picked up the ropes of my sled and resumed my journey across the tundra.

✳ ✳ ✳

I spent the next few hours navigating by my landmark. I kept it squarely in my rear and paused frequently to recheck its position. When the snow cone had all but disappeared over the horizon, I stopped and constructed the next one.

It wasn't a perfect way of navigating by any means, but it was a darn sight better than what I had been doing.

By nightfall, I'd constructed three cones, and the next morning when I rose, I began anew. While I worked on my first landmark of the day, I reflected on the previous day. By my reckoning, it had marked the start of my second month in the tundra.

And it had been a dark day indeed.

Just recalling it was unpleasant. I shuddered, remembering the grim fatalism that had gripped me. I'd never experienced hopelessness like that before. Such overwhelming despair. I had felt cast adrift, without purpose or means to alter my fate.

I glanced up at the half-built snow cone. In the end, the landmarks might prove worthless. The tundra could simply be too large to map. *No, not worthless. Insufficient, perhaps, but not worthless.*

Today, with my mind unclouded by despair, I grasped something else too. The act of creating the snow cones was as equally important as their navigational value. Building them gave me a vital measure of control.

"Control what you can," I murmured, recalling the words I'd spoken to myself weeks ago.

It was the small things that would keep me going, I realized. The bigger picture might very well be outside my control, but the small things... those were the things I needed to focus on.

If I wasn't careful, despair would creep up unseen and swallow me whole again. It was a deceptive beast. Ruthless. Cunning.

And I couldn't afford to lose hope, not again.

I had to start believing again. Believing I would get out of the sector and prepare for that day. I couldn't go on just surviving.

If I wanted to escape the icy tundra, I had to be methodical, careful, and resolute. If it took months, then so be it; I would still escape.

But I wouldn't if I let despair drown me again.

Focus on the small things, Michael.

Train. Advance. Grow.

I might be stuck on the tundra for now, but that didn't mean I had to waste the passing days. In some ways, this sector could be an even better training ground than the scorching dunes.

And it was high time I took advantage of that.

✳ ✳ ✳

In the coming weeks, I kept myself busy.

I made sure my days were full, be it through building landmarks, crafting, or hunting game. My proficiency at constructing the snow cones increased, and after countless iterations, I was able to produce them sturdier and taller, ensuring they were visible from miles off.

While not trekking across the snow, I worked on my gear, stitching and restitching my winter suit and improving it in whatever manner I could think of. One evening, I hit upon the idea of lining the furs with bone splinters and, when I was done, received a surprising message from the Adjudicator.

You have modified a winter fur suit, transforming it into a set of winter bone-hide armor. This light armor set reduces the physical damage you sustain by 10% but, due to its crude construction, penalizes your Magic and Dexterity by 70%.

A smile twitched at the corner of my mouth—the first in what felt like weeks. I had armor again! In light of the unlooked-for benefit, the equipment's penalties didn't bother me, and I donned it without hesitation.

You have equipped a set of winter bone-hide armor. Your rank 6 light armor skill has reduced the penalties incurred to 40%. Current armor modifiers: -13 Dexterity, -4 Magic, +10% damage reduction, and +5 sneaking.

Last but not least, I changed the way I fought.

My skirmishes against the tundra's denizens became less a rush to kill and more a dance. Even weighed down by the bone armor, with my buffs cast I was nimbler than most of my foes. Drawing out the battles, I took the time to train my skills and forwent one-shot kills. Instead, I dodged, parried, slashed, and riposted.

I closely scrutinized each encounter too. Replaying the battles in my mind, I assessed the results of every exchange and actively sought to better my blade work beyond the Game-gifted rewards I earned in each fight.

The improvements were startling.

My skills in dodging, shortswords, two weapon fighting, and light armor all advanced steadily. I honed my mind skills as much as I did my physical ones too.

During particularly monotonous stretches of hiking, I removed bits of my protective gear and chain-cast chi heal to mend the resulting weather damage. Then I meditated to recover my lost psi and repeated the entire process again.

I even attempted using chi heal in battle. The spell wasn't a combat one and had a long casting time, but with steady practice, I improved my control enough that I was able to hold my concentration between dodges and strikes and successfully cast the spell. Some of the time, anyway.

Employing telekinesis in battle became second nature too. Constantly blinking and two-stepping while fighting, I became adept at repositioning and striking at my foes from above and even when airborne.

I didn't ignore my telepathy either. I fought as many battles with only my astral daggers as I did with my shortswords and learned to strike my targets with pinpoint accuracy from afar.

I even managed to train insight and deception by using ventro and facial disguises repeatedly in battle. Thieving was harder to raise. I lacked the proper materials for it and only managed to fashion the crudest of traps. Nonetheless, I managed to raise the skill by a few points.

My overall player level was the only aspect that didn't advance significantly. The tundra beasts were nearly the same level as me, and the experience I gained from fighting them, even after dozens of battles, was negligible.

More weeks went by, and little about my situation changed.

Day in and day out, I built snow cones, refined my armor, and trained in battle. Small things. But they kept the madness at bay.

Loneliness ate at me constantly. And despair too. They hadn't been vanquished, after all, only beaten back for a time. Still, I soldiered onward, resisting every attempt of the tundra to crush my spirit.

My second month ended, and my third began. Once more, my skill gains slowed. Although, I suspected it was more because I had surpassed what my foes could teach me than due to any lack on my part. I kept up my training though. Some of my skills had reached rank nine, and it was only a matter of time before they crossed over to the next tier.

The many weeks spent wandering had also convinced me of the tundra's immensity. Despite having built hundreds of snow cones, I'd yet to encounter one after I left it behind. The implications of that were frightening, and I shied away from considering them too carefully.

Still, I didn't waver from the commitment I'd made to myself. I remained determined to find a way out of the sector. No matter what.

Then, in my fourth month on the tundra, something extraordinary happened.

✳   ✳   ✳

The day started like any other.

After munching through my usual breakfast, I scored a mark on the bone stick that I used both as a walking staff and as a means to track the passing days. Today was day one hundred and three.

What should we do today, Michael?

Why the same thing we do every day, friend: march across the tundra.

Chuckling, I rose to my feet. After months of being starved of company, I'd taken to talking to myself more. Maybe it was a sign of incipient madness, but I no longer cared. It was better than lying down and letting despair overtake me.

Gathering my belongings, I loaded up the sled. Like all my other possessions, it too had undergone multiple upgrades in the passing weeks. Now, the sled sported handlebars, side rails, spikes, and even a top cage to keep the scavengers away.

Without further ceremony, I oriented myself using my latest landmark and got moving.

Even though the sled had grown heavier in the intervening time, pulling it had become effortless. Since first making the bone sled, I'd gained four more levels—disgustingly few, I know—and each time I'd invested the attribute points in Strength. Now, it sat at rank ten.

It's probably time to stop investing in Strength, I mused. *But what should I invest in next?* Frostbite was no longer an issue, so more Constitution wasn't necessary. *Back to increasing Mind, I think.*

Turning my attention inward, I opened my player profile. Reviewing my improvements was one of the few spots of brightness in my otherwise bleak existence, and it had become the favorite part of my day. Every morning, I scrutinized each Game message, relishing every skill gain, no matter how small.

Alrighty, let's see how I did yesterday.

<u>Player Profile (Partial): Michael</u>

Level: 119. Rank: 11. Current Health: 100%.

<u>Attributes</u>

Strength: 10. Constitution: 14. Dexterity: 22 (33)*. Perception: 25. Mind: 60. Magic: 7 (10)*. Faith: 0.
*** denotes attributes affected by items.**

<u>Skills</u>

Dodging: 96. Sneaking: 89. Shortswords: 98. Two-weapon fighting: 80. Light armor: 81. Thieving: 61.

Chi: 77. Meditation: 101. Telekinesis: 73. Telepathy: 76.

Insight: 98. Deception: 96.

Well, well.

Meditation had reached tier three! Dodging, sneaking, insight, and deception weren't far behind either. *Now, if only there was somewhere to buy abilities here,* I thought wistfully. *Imagine what I could—*

AHH-WOOOOOOOO.

I froze. That sound... I hadn't heard its like on the tundra before.

AhhhooOOOOOooowhoooo

A second howl cut through the tundra, and my head jerked to the left, the direction it had come from. *Am I imagining this?*

A third howl answered the first two.

A fourth followed, then a fifth.

My head whipped around, tracking each sound eagerly. *It can't be. I must be—*

It doesn't matter if you're hallucinating or not! Answer the call!

Craning my head back, I howled.

The sound was long and mournful and went on and on. Once I started, I couldn't seem to stop. I poured everything of myself into the call, giving vent to my desolation, despair, loneliness... and hope.

Desperate hope.

The other howls cut off.

I ran down, my voice hoarse, and waited in dreadful anticipation. If hope had betrayed me... I wasn't sure I could go on.

A shape appeared through the falling snow. Then a second. And then another until, finally, padding soft-footed and silent, the entire pack surrounded me.

My eyes widening in shock, I turned about in a slow circle to study the beasts. My ears hadn't deceived me. There were wolves on the tundra.

And they had answered my call.

CHAPTER 229: RUNNING WITH THE PACK

They weren't dire wolves. That much I could tell immediately from size alone. None of the wolves stood taller than waist-high. They appeared bulkier, though, but that could just be a result of their puffed-out coats, which were all shades of white or gray.

A wolf larger than the rest pushed to the fore. The alpha. His fur was the color of snow, and his eyes were arctic blue. Coming to a stop a few feet from me, he sat down on his haunches and studied me quizzically.

I stood still under the alpha's inspection, waiting.

A drawn-out moment passed. Then another.

"Hello, brother," I whispered finally.

The alpha tilted his head to the side but didn't respond.

I frowned. Did he not hear me?

The wolf raised his snout and sniffed.

An arctic wolf has recognized your Wolf Mark!

A second later, an image was pushed into my mind's eye. It was me. But not me as *I* saw myself. This picture was strangely distorted. My canines were longer and my features were distinctly lupine...

It was how the alpha saw me. He's trying to communicate, I realized. *He can't talk. Not like the dire wolves can.*

Another image appeared in my mind—that of a giant wolf. The new image superimposed itself on the first, and the two merged, transforming the picture of wolflike-me into that of a wolf with human eyes.

The alpha raised his head to stare at me, an expectant look in his eyes.

"That's me," I agreed cautiously.

The alpha lowered his head in satisfaction. While I was uncertain if he understood my words, I sensed he grasped the meaning behind them. A moment later, I felt the image flash across the minds of the rest of the pack as the alpha shared his thoughts with them.

In response, the wolves raised their heads and howled.

No images accompanied the sound, but in the chorus of their voices, I sensed... acceptance. My brows crinkled in confusion. *What are they trying to say? Why would—*

My thoughts broke off.

The wolves were lowering themselves to the ground. My eyes jerked back to the alpha. He, too, was on his belly. It was a surprising display of submissiveness, and for one stunned second, I was speechless with shock.

The arctic wolves of sector 107 have recognized your authority as a scion of House Wolf, and the pack alpha has temporarily surrendered leadership of the pack to you.

*   *   *

My emotions were in turmoil.

Disbelief and unease warred with happiness. I was overjoyed the pack had accepted me but shocked they had raised me above even their alpha. I stared at the white wolf. "Why?" I blurted.

There was no response, nothing but serene acceptance, a sense that this was the right order of things.

I measured the wolf's resolve. There was no hint of doubt or regret in his emotions. I sighed. There would be no changing the alpha's mind, I suspected. Reaching out with my will, I analyzed him.

The target is a level 108 arctic wolf and alpha of the pack.

Arctic wolves are a rare breed of wolves that have evolved to survive in some of the harshest and coldest regions of the Forever Kingdom. Tougher and hardier than most wolfkin, they can go days without eating and run all day and night if necessary.

I studied the encircling wolves again. The rest of the pack were of a similar level to the alpha. Strangely, there were no elders or pups. Every wolf was of fighting age. "Is this the entire pack?" I asked, turning back to the white wolf.

Fleeting sadness touched the wolf's thoughts.

It was answer enough, and I didn't probe further. The tundra was not a forgiving place. One of the things that had puzzled me early on was how the wasteland's denizens survived. Then I'd realized that most probably didn't.

The tundra lacked vegetation, and the only beasts that seemed to inhabit it were predators. To survive, the denizens surely had to feed on each other. Even then, I suspected the beasts' attrition rate was high and left little chance for their weak, old, and young to survive, much less flourish. In fact, it was likely that the only reason there were *any* creatures to find on the tundra was because the Game repopulated the sector daily.

I considered the pack again. It was a large one, numbering thirty wolves in total. *How can I take care of so many?* I wondered worriedly. I wasn't exactly thriving myself.

But the thought of abandoning the wolves didn't cross my mind. They had made me their leader—if for no other reason than I was a scion of House Wolf—and it was my responsibility now to see the pack fed and to give them a chance to prosper.

I sighed, feeling the mantle of leadership settle on me. "Up," I commanded, and the thirty wolves, still on their bellies, rose smoothly to their feet. The day was still young, and it was time to get moving again.

And besides, I had thirty more mouths to feed.

*   *   *

Without needing to be told, the wolves formed a large screen around the sled, the groups on the left and right flanks ranging so far as to be barely visible. Only the alpha stayed at my side.

Every so often, he would glance up at me as if waiting for a command or glance back at the sled and sniff hungrily. Undoubtedly, the pack smelled my frozen store of meat, but quite conspicuously they kept their distance. If, come nightfall, we failed to find game, I would share my supplies with the pack, but as far as possible I wanted to keep my stores intact.

My concerns about the pack's ability to feed itself proved unfounded though.

An hour before nightfall, in response to a howl from the wolves ranging ahead, the alpha stiffened. Drawing to a stop myself, I glanced at the wolf in concern. I couldn't decipher the message in the howl, but I was sure it contained some kind of warning.

After a moment, the alpha turned to me and pushed a single image into my mind: a picture of two saber-tooth cats. A hint of question followed.

I grinned at the white wolf. "Let's go get them."

✳   ✳   ✳

Hunting with the wolves was different.

The pack had their own methods, ones that played to their strengths, and rather than impose my own techniques, I let the alpha take the lead.

Stretched out flat in the snow and with psi held at the ready, I watched the wolves slink toward their prey. The two big cats were aware of the pack's presence. Drawing together, they growled in warning at the circling wolves.

The saber-tooths out-massed the wolves appreciably, and individually the wolves were no match for their prey. But the pack had numbers—and cunning.

Two wolves rushed in—the alpha and another just as large—provoking a response from one of the cats which took a swipe at them. The wolves were too fast, though, and dashed away unharmed.

A second pair darted in, repeating the same maneuver. Again, the cats chased them away.

The pack's tactics were obvious. They were attempting to separate their prey, but it was a dangerous game they played. The cats were too agile to be thwarted for long, and sooner or later, one of the wolves would get struck.

Time to pitch in.

Releasing the psi I held, I cast slaysight.

You have terrified your target for 10 seconds.

Howling in terror, one of the cats took off running. Wolves scattered, letting the senselessly fleeing cat past. The second cat, suddenly abandoned, roared at her mate, but the bespelled creature paid her no mind.

The pack alpha turned around to stare at me. Somehow, he'd sensed what I'd done. Drawing my blades, I rose to my feet and gestured him forward. "Go, finish her."

✳   ✳   ✳

A few minutes later, both saber-tooth cats were dead.

The male cat had returned the moment his fear had dissipated, but by then it had been too late to save his mate. With my help, the pack had dispatched the pair easily, and I could still feel the alpha's surprise at how quickly the deed had been managed.

Sitting down cross-legged, I watched the wolves feast on the remains. The pack had waited for my say-so before digging in, but now they fed with gusto.

Observing the pack, I felt a deep sense of satisfaction. Thanks to my help, *all* the wolves had escaped injury. With a start, I also realized that the despair that had become my constant companion since entering the tundra had lifted. Normally my days passed torturously slow while I counted off my steps and my fears replayed in my mind.

Not so today.

Today, I had been... content.

The hours had passed almost unnoticed. And it wasn't just from the change in routine. It was the wolves. The pack with their presence alone had soothed my unease.

It was good to have company. To not be alone.

Sensing my mood, the alpha broke away from the feast and, sitting beside me, rested his head on his paws, a silent sentry—and companion.

Greatly daring, I ran my hand through his coat. "Snow," I murmured. "I shall call you Snow."

The alpha's only response was indifferent acceptance.

Smiling, I stared off into the tundra. And for the first time, the prospect of being stuck in the sector didn't seem so bad. I had a pack now, and that made all the difference.

Perhaps, I mused, *at long last, my fortunes are changing.*

In the coming days, the wolves and I roamed the icy plains.

The pack was better than me at finding game. For one, they had the numbers for it, and for another, they were more fleet of foot. Every day, without fail, the pack's far-ranging scouts discovered something and reported back their findings.

Sometimes, depending on the prey, I chose to forgo the hunt. Sadly, as skilled as the pack was at finding game, they weren't equally adept at taking it down, not without losses anyway.

The wolves' attitude toward injured or dead packmates was one of stoic indifference. The pack had to eat. And no beast on the tundra made for easy prey.

I, on the other hand, was less accepting.

But even as their leader, I couldn't force the pack to let me tackle the fights alone. Nor could I not protect them all in battle. Still, despite some minor losses, the pack grew steadily.

I don't know if it was just this section of the tundra that was more numerous with wolves, but every day, the pack's calls brought more recruits until, one day, the pack was over one-hundred-strong.

The weeks passed easily after that.

By day we hunted, and by night we huddled together, sheltering for warmth. The wolves loved the igloo, and once they tasted its warmth none willingly slept out in the open again. Needless to say, my nightly shelters grew in size, and constructing them became more time-consuming.

I didn't give up building the snow cones either. Day in and day out, I erected my icy spires—much to the amusement of the watching wolves, who seemed puzzled by my antics stacking and packing snow.

I kept up my training as well, honing my mastery of both mind and sword, even if, as busy as my days were, I had less time to practice. My second shortsword had grown battered and blunt, and outside of training served little practical purpose. Ebonheart, though, remained as sharp as ever.

Of course, I questioned the pack too. Or tried to as much as I could anyway. I wasn't sure how long the wolves had been on the tundra, but I got the impression that some were more familiar with the terrain than I was.

I'd projected the image of a nether portal into the minds of the wolves several times, and though I sensed a spark of recognition in a few, it was quickly swamped by feelings of overwhelming dread.

The wolves *knew* something about the portal, that much I was sure of, but no matter how hard I tried, I couldn't persuade them to talk about it. Even Snow refused to converse on the matter.

A week went by, then another, and another.

Then five weeks after we first met, Snow came to see me.

✳   ✳   ✳

"What is it, brother?" I asked cheerfully as the alpha sat down beside me. We'd just slain a large group of hyenas and the rest of the pack was still eating.

The white wolf licked his reddened muzzle and blood-soaked paws. His coat was no longer as pristine as it had been when we first met. I thought Snow the canniest fighter in the pack, but not even he had escaped the intervening weeks without earning a scar or two.

Done cleaning himself, Snow looked at me with somber eyes. For a moment, he didn't say anything. Then an image flashed in my mind.

I drew in a sharp breath.

It was a nether portal.

But it wasn't the generic image I'd shown the wolves. This one was subtly different and seemed one of Snow's own memories instead of an imagining.

"You've seen it?" I whispered.

Snow exuded a single sharp thought that I'd learned denoted assent.

"Where?" I asked, a thrill coursing through me.

The wolf's head swiveled to the left and almost perpendicular to the direction we were traveling, I noted.

I studied the pack alpha for a moment. "Why tell me now?" I asked finally, my initial excitement fading.

Snow radiated a welter of emotions and thoughts too complex for me to interpret.

I rubbed my jaw, pondering. I needed to frame my question in simpler terms if I wanted to make sense of his response. "Is it close?"

Assent again.

"Dangerous?"

Emphatic assent.

I sighed. I'd been hoping Snow's attitude toward the portal had changed, but it appeared not. "I must still go there, you know."

Quiet acceptance.

"I'll go alone. You will be in charge. Keep the pack here until—"

Instant refusal.

Then another avalanche of images. This time, I grasped their meaning. Neither Snow nor the rest of the wolves were willing to stay behind.

"It'll be too dangerous," I protested. "There's no reason for any of the pack to risk their lives."

Stubborn denial.

I sighed again. There was no way I could keep the pack away if they insisted on accompanying me. My authority as a scion extended only so far, it seemed.

"Very well. We leave tomorrow."

*　*　*

It took three days to reach the nether portal.

I remained on high alert the entire way. Although the wolves were emphatic that the portal was dangerous, they were unable to articulate why that was the case.

At first, I suspected the danger to be hordes of beasts or even savants, but as we drew closer to the portal's location, the tundra grew more barren—not less—and a day from our destination, even the pack's scouts were unable to find any game to hunt.

The region had been completely abandoned.

The implications were clear. It wasn't only the wolves that feared the area. The other beasts were similarly afraid. It was confounding. If the nebulous threat wasn't beasts, savants, or some other powerful dungeon denizen, what could it be?

When we reached the gateway, I still didn't have an answer.

I was lost in thought, pondering the mystery, when Snow, keeping pace beside me, suddenly stopped. Jerking to a halt, I stared at the white wolf in surprise. "What is—"

I broke off.

His hackles raised and fangs bared, Snow's eyes were fixed unerringly on something ahead. Following the direction of his gaze, I spotted a familiar glint through the falling snow.

The glow of a portal.

I turned back to Snow. "Wait here," I ordered unnecessarily. Neither the pack alpha nor any of the other wolves were making any move to get closer.

Dropping the ropes of the sled, I left the pack behind and stomped toward the gateway. As I drew nearer, more details became clear.

The portal shone a luminescent white, indication enough that it was active. Like the other gateways I'd seen, it was bordered by a thick band of silvery metal.

My frown deepened. There was nothing scary about the portal. It looked... ordinary.

Still, I kept my hands on my blades and my senses extended as I came to a halt before the glowing gateway. Craning my head to the left and right, I searched the surroundings for any hint of a threat.

My intuition remained quiescent.

Mindsight turned up nothing.

Trap detect neither.

Glancing behind me, I saw the wolves watching intently. They were afraid. Tense. But their wariness was unfocused. I didn't doubt the wolves' instincts though. I was certain there was danger here.

But what?

I padded a slow circle around the gateway.

Still nothing.

That left only one thing to investigate: the portal itself. Made more nervous by the pack's anxiety than I cared to admit, I reached out and touched the rim of the gateway.

A Game alert unfurled in my mind.

Congratulations, Michael! You have discovered a hidden exit from the Endless Dungeon. This is a two-way portal and leads directly from level 3

of the Guardian Tower to the surface of the Forever Kingdom. This location is a key point and has been added to your Logs.

I gaped at the Adjudicator's message. *A hidden exit?* There had been no suggestion of anything like this in the gnome's notes, and I wasn't sure how I felt about it—about how I *should* feel about it.

Disappointment vied with elation.

The portal didn't lead to the next sector. Which meant I was no closer to finishing the level.

On the other hand, the portal was a way out. A *two-way* exit at that. I could leave *and* return. The Game wasn't forcing me into a choice between abandoning my dungeon run or continuing, which was a relief.

Just as importantly, the wolves could leave too. Nearly anywhere else would be better than here for the pack.

Turning around, I waved the pack forward. "Come on," I yelled. "It's safe!"

None of the wolves budged an inch.

I frowned. *Why won't they—*

I broke off, realizing the problem. The wolves couldn't see the Adjudicator's words, and they likely had no idea what the gateway was. *It must be the portal itself they're afraid of.*

My shoulders sagged. It wasn't an insurmountable problem though. *I'll just nip through and have a look around. Once I've seen the sector on the other side with my own eyes, I'm sure I can convince the pack it's safe.*

But I would take every precaution before doing so. I couldn't discount the pack's fear entirely. After all, it was entirely possible it wasn't the portal—but what lay on the other side—that terrified them.

I didn't want to believe that though.

It would be too cruel a joke for even the Game to play. Why dangle hope, only to wrench it away? But further speculation was pointless. There was only one way I was going to know for sure: and that was by going through.

Closing my eyes, I saw to my preparations.

You have cast reaction buff, increasing your Dexterity by +4 ranks for 20 minutes.

You have cast lighten load, reducing your total armor penalties to 10% for 20 minutes. Net effect: +2 Dexterity and +1 Magic.

You have cast mind shield.

Glancing back, I met Snow's gaze. "I'll be back," I assured him.

Grim foreboding greeted my words.

He didn't believe me then. "I will," I repeated, not sure who I was trying to convince.

Turning back to the gate and eager to escape the tundra—if only for a moment—I crept through the gateway.

Transfer through portal commencing...

...

...

Passage completed!

Leaving sector 107. Entering the Forever Kingdom.

I stepped out of the portal into a world enveloped by heavy banks of smog and was immediately assaulted by a barrage of Game messages.

You have entered sector 18,240 of the Forever Kingdom, a closed and unclaimed sector. You are the first player ever to have visited this sector!

Congratulations, Michael! You have accomplished the feat, Pioneer of New Realms! Requirement: be the first player to enter an unexplored sector. You have been awarded the trait: budding explorer.

This rare trait is normally reserved for rank 4 rangers and grants you knowledge of all key locations in any sector you are the first to discover, automatically adding them to your Log. In addition, when in the sector, the locations always shine bright in your mind, ensuring you are never lost.

Analyzing key locations in sector 18,240...

Nether portal location 1, entrance to the Guardian Tower... added to your Log.

Nether portal location 2, entrance to Draven's Reach... added to your Log.

Safe zone location.... cannot be established.

Sector 18,240 is under assault by the nether and is in danger of being pulled into the Nethersphere!

A young void tree has taken root in the sector, establishing a permanent ley line to the Nethersphere. The region is being polluted with free-floating nether. Until the void tree is destroyed, the safe zone will not form and the nether toxicity in the sector will continue to rise.

Warning: you have entered the nether! The nether toxicity at your current location is at tier 2. You are unprotected. Your health, psi, stamina, and mana are degenerating at a rate of 15% per minute.

Bloody hell.

Of all the places to end up, why did it have to be the nether? The urge to verbally vent my frustration was great, but somehow, I restrained myself and remained tight-lipped.

And you're not in the nether, not really.

That was true enough. If the Game message was to be believed, the sector hadn't fallen yet. It only teetered on the edge of falling.

Biting back my disappointment, I dropped into hiding, cloaking myself in the mists. The portal was still at my back, and I could retreat at any time. In fact, the temptation to do just that was strong, but I fought back the impulse.

I had about six minutes before leaving became necessary. And in the interim, some exploration was warranted.

Turning my attention inward, I scanned the Game alerts again. The message about the feat I'd accomplished was intriguing and explained why the gnomes hadn't mentioned the gateway.

I was the first player—ever—to venture into this sector or, for that matter, to find the portal!

Extraordinary as that sounded, I had no trouble believing it. It had taken me nearly five months of wandering the tundra *and* the help of the wolves to locate the hidden portal.

If only the sector weren't imperiled by the nether.

I closed the Game messages. While the other information they contained—especially with regards to the void tree and safe zone—sounded equally intriguing, I would have to ponder on it later. Right now, I had to focus on what lay before me. Rotating my head slowly from left to right, I surveyed the area.

I couldn't see much.

The air was hazy with smog, and beyond a few yards everything was a wall of white. In fact, my surroundings were frighteningly similar to the rift I'd entered with Simone's party, and if not for the Game messages, I would've believed I was in the Nethersphere again.

I understood the reason for the pack's fear now too.

Recalling what Moonshadow had told me about the effect of the nether's toxins on non-players, I knew any wolf that had entered the portal would've ended up fatally ill.

Just like they had, I thought, my gaze dropping to the ground. Two leopard corpses lay just beyond my line of sight. Both bodies were pockmarked, shrunken, and covered with ugly sores. It looked like they had died painfully, and I didn't blame Snow and the others for not wanting to—

Pebbles crunched.

I froze.

The sound had been soft, barely audible, but I was certain something was moving up ahead. Unfurling my mindsight, I expanded my awareness.

Six dark minds sprang into view.

I swallowed. *Stygians. Has to be.*

Reaching out, I analyzed the closest—a creature about fifteen yards away.

The target is a level 158 stygian shambling horror.

Urgh. The creature was too strong to take on, not alone and without nether protections or a safe zone. *Maybe its fellows aren't as strong.* Reaching out to the next creature, I analyzed it too.

You have failed a Perception check and are unable to analyze your target. Your analyze attempt has been detected!

Damnation!

A failed analyze attempt could mean only one of two things: the creature ahead possessed deception—improbable—or it was over level two hundred—a disturbing but more distinct possibility.

Hard on the heels of my failure, an angry shriek shattered the silence.

A hostile entity has detected you! You are no longer hidden.

I didn't hesitate. It was time to flee. Throwing myself backward, I fell into the gateway again.

Transfer through portal commencing...
...
...
Transfer halted! A second entity has entered the portal. Analyzing entity...
...
...
The entity has been identified as a nether creature and has been denied access. Resuming your transfer...
...
...
Passage completed!
Leaving sector 18,240 of the Forever Kingdom. Entering the Endless Dungeon.

✳   ✳   ✳

You have entered sector 107 of the Endless Dungeon. This sector is level 3 of 5 of the Guardian Tower.

Reeling in shock, I staggered back from the portal. Whatever monster I'd roused had attempted to follow me through.

Bless the Adjudicator for stopping it!

A shape blurred through the air and, hitting me in the chest, bowled me over.

It was Snow. Keeping me pinned down, the white wolf inspected me minutely. Around us, I sensed the rest of the pack gathering. In their minds, I sensed worry and relief. I felt no small measure of both myself.

Reaching up, I tried to gently push Snow away. "Told you I'd be back," I said, laughing as the last vestiges of my fear and adrenaline faded.

The pack alpha stared at me for a second longer. Then, finally satisfied with whatever he saw, he stepped off and let me up.

I rose smoothly back to my feet and turned to face the portal. Even nether-infested, the sector beyond was fascinating. But it wasn't a region I was equipped to explore—yet.

If I ever get out of here, maybe I'll come back one day.

Now, though, it was time to resume my search for the next level. Returning to the sled, I picked up the ropes, and with wolves rushing around me, tugged it into motion.

✳   ✳   ✳

More weeks went by, and slowly any hope I ever had of escaping the sector eroded.

The pack kept me going though, and despite my loss of hope, my mind remained free of darkness. Roaming the icy plains until the end of my days with one hundred and sixteen wolves didn't seem such a bad fate, after all.

One day, that number became one hundred and twenty.

I was putting the finishing touches on my latest snow cone when a bitten-off yelp caught my attention. Pausing, I listened intently for a moment, but when no other sounds of distress followed, I shrugged and returned to work.

Just young wolves playing, I decided.

The spire complete, I scrambled down its side and pulled out a folded piece of cured leather from one of my pockets. Unrolling the parchment on the ground, I wrote down the snow cone's number using a pen cunningly made from bone, sinew, and blood.

Since leaving the portal, I'd been carefully mapping the way back. If I ever needed to return to the gateway, I could do so by following the snow cones whose numbers I'd recorded. That was the theory anyway.

Returning the parchment to my pocket, I rose to my feet.

A muted growl sounded. It was quickly followed by a warning howl. I frowned. *That sounds like a fight in the making.*

In-fighting among the pack was rare. Life in the tundra was harsh enough as it was, but occasionally there was a battle for dominance, or two wolves would rub each other the wrong way, especially after an influx of newcomers.

But the pack hadn't had any new recruits in weeks—which either meant we'd left the region they typically spawned in, or the Adjudicator had stopped replenishing their numbers.

I favored the latter explanation. After all, the Game had to set an upper limit on the number of dungeon denizens, and with so few wolves dying these days, it was no wonder the Adjudicator rarely brought more of them into the sector.

I had spent many hours wondering about the origin of the arctic wolves—and for that matter, all the sector's denizens. Where did they come from? And how had the Game brought them here?

All the wolves had memories of a time before the tundra, but it was beyond any of them to explain where they had lived or how the Game had transported them here. And while knowing wasn't especially important, speculating about it was a good way to pass the time.

Another growl cut through my musings.

Setting down my snow shovel—made from bone, what else?—I moved toward the ruckus. Usually, I tried not to interfere, but this time I'd recognized the growl: it was Snow.

In all the time I'd been with the pack, the white wolf had never been challenged for his position, and the fact that he was being challenged now was cause enough for investigation.

Weaving through the pack—they'd all congregated around Snow and his challenger—I shoved my way to the fore, intent on ending the fight before it began.

But I stopped short when I reached Snow's side. The pack alpha wasn't facing off against another male.

He was in a stare-down with his mate, Star.

The white wolf was trying to edge past the female, but she was having none of it, even going so far as to nip at him when he got too close. I frowned. *Now, what has Snow done to anger her?* I'd never seen the two quarrel before.

Movement behind Star attracted my eye. What I'd first taken for a smear of dirt in the snow was not.

It was a wolf pup. *Four* wolf pups.

"Ah," I murmured, finally realizing what was going on. "Congratulations, both of you."

Sadly, given the pack's numbers and my own busy days, I often lost track of the individual wolves—except Snow, who often sought me out—and I hadn't known Star was pregnant.

I took a step closer. Star's head jerked in my direction and her gaze met mine for a moment before lowering submissively.

I showed Star my empty palms as I inched closer. "I'm not going to hurt them," I assured the worried mother. I could feel the waves of concern rolling off Snow too, and I didn't think it was for me or himself.

Star tolerated my approach—barely.

Reaching the pups, I knelt in the snow before them. The four huddled together for warmth but still shivered uncontrollably. As I suspected, they weren't doing well. The open tundra was too cold for the tiny creatures, what with their thin gray coats providing scant protection.

Snow's head appeared over my shoulder, a whine deep in his throat. "We'll save them," I assured him, not letting him sense my own fear. The four were already in a bad way and urgently needed warmth.

I turned to Star, who appeared on my other side. "I'm going to pick them up."

Reluctantly, she consented.

Opening my fur overcoat, I picked up the smallest of the pups. He mewled in protest and tried to scratch me as I snatched him away from his meager source of warmth.

"Easy there, fighter," I murmured as I brought him to my chest. Sensing my body heat, the pup stopped trying to escape and pressed close to me.

Gathering up the remaining pups, I closed my overcoat and rose to my feet. Then, with the entire pack trailing me, I jogged to the sled and the heaps of skins stored there.

Leaving Star, Snow, and the four pups huddling beneath the piles of furs, I got to building.

It was time to construct a den.

CHAPTER 232: FIGHTING HOPE

I didn't build a den, not really.

What I did was assemble a second sled with a closed top, tightly insulated with layers of furs and fat. The movable den became Star and her pups' new home, one that Snow and the other wolves gladly pulled.

It was a solution that allowed the pack to keep moving while at the same time ensuring the pups were protected from the weather.

I don't know why it hadn't occurred to me before that pups may be born, but after Star's litter, I made sure to check the other females in the pack. At least two others were heavily pregnant.

And so I built more moveable dens.

At first, the pack's response to the newborns was muted. I suspected that this was due in no small part to the fate suffered by other pups before I joined the pack. But once Star's pups left the safety of their den to frolic in the snow, I sensed true joy kindle in even the most hard-bitten members of the pack.

They had finally begun to believe their young would live.

Watching the four pups—and those who followed soon after—play among their more somber elders brought a smile to my own face. It gave me a deep-seated sense of accomplishment too to know that I had had a part to play in youngsters' survival. If not for my coming, Snow and Star would likely be dead already, and their pups would never have been born.

The pups' addition to the pack meant the wolves had a real future in the sector now—even if I didn't. I'd stopped railing against my own fate though. The pack had become family, and I was content to spend my days seeing to their well-being.

But only a few days later, all that changed.

* * *

On my two-hundred-and-fifth day in the tundra, I came across a surprising sight.

A fifteen-foot-high pillar of ice.

I stumbled to a halt, unable to believe what I was seeing. Closing my eyes, I snapped them open again. Then, for good measure, I rubbed them—hard.

The pillar remained. I wasn't hallucinating.

I'd found one of my snow cones.

Dropping the reins of my sled, I rushed forward. The wolves streamed behind me, barking happily. The pack might not understand the reason for my excitement, but they sensed my sudden burst of joy.

Out of breath, I stumbled to a halt before the snow cone. Just from its size alone, I could tell it was one of my earlier attempts. Digging furiously into the spire's base, I found the bone I'd buried within and yanked it out to read the markings.

Thirty-eight.

It was one of my very first snow cones then. I swiveled my head to the left and right and, sure enough, spotted two more ice spires.

Numbers thirty-nine and thirty-seven.

I'd arrived from a heading almost perpendicular to the line formed by the three snow cones. Clearly, my wandering across the tundra hadn't been in a straight a course as I'd imagined.

But what does this mean?

Very little, I thought, my initial giddiness fading. At best, it meant I could retrace my steps through the tundra, but beyond that? Nothing.

It didn't put me any closer to finding the exit portal.

I shrugged off my disappointment. *It does mean something,* I insisted to the doubting inner voice. *It means my plan to chart the tundra is feasible.*

Returning to the sled, I shooed away the inquisitive pups and tugged it onward again, aiming for the snow cone I guessed to be number thirty-seven. I planned on retracing my steps all the way back to snow cone number one.

And then, I would resume my mapping.

✻   ✻   ✻

Days later, the pack and I were back in virgin territory. My first ice spire was behind us, and I'd begun constructing snow cones again.

We moved quicker too. A new urgency filled me, a sense that perhaps escaping the sector was finally in my grasp. As a result, I spent less time building my nightly shelters, forcing most of the pack—excluding only the new wolf mothers and their pups—to spend their nights out in the open again.

None of the wolves complained, but often I felt Snow's eyes resting on me, his thoughts opaque. I wanted to reassure the alpha, but of what, I wasn't quite certain.

As the days passed and we kept up our relentless march, my thoughts returned more frequently to the Game and those I'd left behind.

Were the mantises still hunting me? What did Loken make of my disappearance? Were all the careful plans I'd prepared still valid? And how were those in the valley—Saya and the dire wolves—faring?

But most of all, I wondered if fate—the Adjudicator, the Game, call it what you will—was just toying with me again. After all, this wasn't the first time hope had been dangled before me.

Was it only so it could be snatched back again?

Time will tell, I thought grimly.

✻   ✻   ✻

Day two hundred and thirty. And another breakthrough.

I was trudging through the snow—as always—and doing my best to ignore the twelve pups tugging at my clothing when, suddenly, the entire pack of them scampered off.

I heaved a sigh of relief. The pups were a joy, but sometimes they could be trying.

Glancing to my left, I saw that the younglings had their heads bent over one particular patch of the ground and were sniffing at it furiously. They'd found something.

What is it this time? I wondered. *Another bone?*

Yapping excitedly, all twelve began to dig. Shaking my head in bemusement at the pups' antics, I dragged the sled past. The pack's mothers would herd the little scamps onward soon enough, but in the meantime, I had a few moments of peace.

Looking over my shoulder, I checked my bearings. The last snow cone was still in sight. *A few more hours before I need to build the next one,* I thought, turning around to face forward again.

A flash of dark brown caught my eye.

I paused. Whatever the pups had uncovered, it wasn't a bone.

Shrugging out of my harness, I made my way to their side. All twelve had their teeth into something and, yanking hard, were trying to drag it free of the snow. Ignoring the pups' growls of protest, I shooed them away and inspected their find.

It was a corpse. One frozen solid, and with its face mangled beyond recognition. Still, I knew what I was looking at.

It was a ratman.

Narrowing my gaze, I swiveled about in a slow circle. There was nothing that marked the spot I stood on as different from any other on the plains. Nonetheless, I waved the pack over.

"Dig," I urged. Following my own instructions, I retrieved my shovel from the sled and began digging too.

A little later, just as I suspected, we uncovered another ratman. Like the first, he wore no clothes.

But then again, I stole their garments, didn't I?

I was sure now that this was where I'd slain the ratmen who'd followed me over from the second level what seemed like a lifetime ago.

I had found my origin point in the sector.

✳   ✳   ✳

A few minutes later, the pack and I uncovered the remaining ratmen bodies. They lay in the same position I'd slain them, and based on my memory of the battle, I could almost pinpoint the portal's location.

Of course, the discovery didn't mean much.

Although, technically, I supposed it meant I was no longer lost. I knew where I was now, after all. A wry grin split my face at the thought. *Not that I can do much with the—*

At a sudden yelp of pain, my head whipped about.

Bored with the dead body, the pups had wandered off, and not a few dozen yards away they were chasing each other in circles. One pup, though, was sitting on his haunches with a dazed expression on his face.

Rising back to his feet, the pup shook himself and scampered forward again.

Only to bounce back again.

Huh?

It was almost as if the pup had hit an invisible wall...

Snow sensed something amiss too. Rising from where he lounged at my feet, he quickly covered the distance to the pup. The other wolves followed on his heels, hackles raised.

Drawing my blades, I raced after them.

The pups hadn't missed their elders' sudden concern. Play forgotten, they padded silently back to their waiting mothers. Snow waited for the pup to reach the safety of his mother's side before shoving his nose forward.

He, too, was rebuffed.

My hands tightened around my blades. I was slower than the wolves across the frozen ground and was still only halfway to the alpha. But I was ready to shadow blink into action at a moment's notice.

Yet, like the pup, Snow had suffered no injury. A quizzical expression on his face, the alpha turned around to look at me, his intent to wait for me clear.

Nearing the alpha, I slowed to a halt and approached more cautiously, eyes roving over the ground in front.

There was nothing unusual about it.

The plains ahead were just as bleak as in any other direction, and the wind blew just as strongly. Truly, it looked ordinary. *Remember the last time you thought that?* Readying psi, I reached out with a tentative hand.

Congratulations, Michael! You have discovered the lair of the sector boss. Deactivating the veil of concealment...

I stared at the message in disbelief. *Un-bloody-believable.*

CHAPTER 233: A QUESTIONABLE FUTURE

...
Illusion deactivated.

The air before me shimmered, transforming into a glittering wall of towering ice that marched off in both directions. Yelping in surprise at the wall's sudden appearance, Snow and the other wolves danced backward.

I, though, stood frozen in place, still flabbergasted.

"Un-bloody-believable," I repeated, unable to think of anything else to articulate my...

Anger? No, that was too mild.

Rage? Not that either.

Towering fury? Perhaps.

Another Game message flashed for attention. Ignoring it, I turned slowly around and measured the distance between the newly appeared ice walls and where I thought the exit portal to be.

One hundred yards.

One hundred measly yards were all that separated the two.

I sat down, a stupefied expression on my face. My time in this sector could have been measured in minutes or hours, not months!

But for a hundred yards.

Flinging myself back into the snow, I stared unseeing into the gray snow. *A hundred yards.* A giggle escaped me. Then another. It blossomed into a cackle—a chortle—a guffaw—before transforming into a maniacal howl. With my sides heaving and tears rolling down my face, I curled up on my side. I kept laughing, unable to stop.

A face appeared over me. Snow. His eyes bright with concern, the alpha licked my face.

My black mirth subsided.

Ah, but for the Game's cruel joke, I would never have met Snow, or any of the other wolves. And despite everything that had happened, I realized I wouldn't change anything—even if I could.

I rose to my feet, embarrassed by my lapse. Wiping my eyes dry, I regained my composure. "I'm alright now, brother."

With Snow brushing my side, I moved forward and inspected the ice wall. It curved away in three directions—left, right, and up—and was more properly a dome. It looked inches deep and blisteringly cold. Even in the freezing temperatures of the tundra, the dome gave off its own waves of cold.

Reaching out, I laid a hand on its surface again, prompting the previously ignored Game message to reappear.

Do you wish to retract the barrier formed of ice? Taking down the barrier will release the blizzard trapped within its heart and thaw the inhabitants inside.

Interesting, I thought. The dome's design was another deviation from the previous two levels. It seemed I would have to take down the barrier to get to the boss, not the other way around. *But then again, nearly everything about this sector has been unusual.*

And what did the Game mean by "thaw" and "blizzard"? Both sounded ominous. *I need to better understand what I'm facing before deciding anything.*

Replying in the negative to the Adjudicator's question, I stepped back from the barrier. With the curious wolves sniffing at my heels, I paced a slow circuit around the dome. "How big is that, do you think?" I asked Snow when I was done. "Eighty yards in diameter?"

The alpha just stared back at me, having no conception of human measurement.

I chuckled. *Alright, maybe I haven't entirely recovered from my episode.*

Leaning forward, I placed my palms against the dome and peered inside. The ice wasn't opaque, but nor was it translucent. Everything inside appeared hazy. I frowned. Was that because of the trapped blizzard? Or an effect of the ice walls?

Still, despite the blurriness, I spotted multiple conical shapes within the barrier. They were all of uniform shape. Suspecting what they may be, I opened my mindsight.

"Wow," I breathed.

In just the small section of the dome that my mindsight reached, there were over a dozen consciousnesses. Curiously, though, their mindglows were dull and subdued. It was almost as if they were... dormant. *Hmm.*

Reaching out with my will, I analyzed some of the closest.

The target is a level 143 yeti grunt.
The target is a level 151 yeti berserker.
The target is a level 162 yeti chieftain.
The target is a level 172 savant adept.

Removing my numb hands from the ice, I rubbed life back into them while I considered what I'd discovered. I had no doubt now that I'd found the savant sector boss and his minions. But where was the exit portal?

Walking ten yards along the rim of the dome, I pressed my face against the ice once more. Then I did it again another ten yards farther.

I kept at it, intent on circling the entire dome as many times as necessary. Until I found the gateway and had an accurate count of the waiting enemies, I wasn't going to stop.

✳   ✳   ✳

One savant and one hundred and three yetis.

That was my final tally. I'd found the gateway too. I'd spotted the familiar glint of light at the far end of the dome and, after straining my eyes to squint at it for a while, had managed to analyze it.

The target is a one-way nether portal from sector 107 to sector 108.

So, I've finally found what I've been searching for all this time, I thought as I sat down heavily in the snow. *Boss and exit both.*

What did I do about it though?

Did I do as the Game bade and lower the barrier?

One hundred yetis and a savant were a helluva lot of hostiles—too many for me to defeat alone.

My eyes drifted to the pack. Always quick to grab what rest they could when an opportunity presented itself, the wolves lounged in the snow. The pack would fight if I asked, no doubt. But how many would be lost in the battle?

Half, at least. More, probably.

I swallowed. I couldn't do that to them.

Then there was the question that had been staring me in the face but I'd been steadfastly ignoring: what happened when it came time to leave the sector? Did I take the pack with me?

There was nothing stopping the wolves from following me to the next sector, but would letting them do that be wise? I had no idea what awaited me on the fourth and fifth levels. How many of the pack would die there?

And even assuming any of the wolves survived the dungeon, what then?

Nexus was a closed sector. I wouldn't be able to get the wolves out of the city, and the streets of Nexus were no place for them. Protecting the pack from the hordes of players—who would only see them as an easy opportunity for experience—would be impossible. I bowed my head, finally accepting what I'd known to be true all along, no matter how much I might rail against it.

The pack couldn't go with me.

They would have to stay.

But do I have to leave?

Unequivocal assent.

I glanced at Snow. The pack alpha met my gaze unflinchingly. He'd been following my thoughts, I knew. I'd made no attempt to shield my mind, realizing I had to be honest with both myself and him about the future.

"I could stay…" I began.

No, Snow projected, refuting me forcefully. Images of the dire wolves, Saya, and even Cara and Kesh appeared in my mind. It was Snow's way of reminding me that I had responsibilities beyond the pack.

He was right too. I rose to my feet. "I'll go."

A sense of rightness emanated from the alpha. It was the Wolf's way, he seemed to say. But despite the alpha's desire to appear stoic, sadness colored his thoughts too. And buried even deeper beneath that was also grief.

Snow ruthlessly squashed both emotions, but not before I'd sensed them. The sadness was for our parting. The grief, though… that was for the pups that were and those that *would never be.* Snow feared that once I left, the pack wouldn't be able to nurture any more of their young.

"No, brother," I said, shaking my head. "Don't fear that. I may need to go, but I will not abandon the pack."

Turning my back on the ice dome, I returned to my sled and tugged it into motion. "Come, there's something we must see done first."

＊　＊　＊

I spent another week crossing the tundra, meticulously documenting the way back to the exit as I did. When I judged we were far enough from the entrance portal that no future dungeon parties would stumble upon the pack, I called a halt.

Then, I got building.

On the way here, I'd thought long and hard about what the pack needed to survive the tundra. It wasn't me. The wolves were capable hunters already. No, what they required was shelter—a refuge from the freezing nights and a den to raise their pups.

So, that's what I built.

First, I constructed an oversized igloo, one reinforced with bones—lots of bones—insulated with fat and lined with furs. I used every bit of knowledge I'd accumulated over the two-hundred-odd days I'd spent on the tundra, employed every building trick I'd learned, and utilized every feasible source of building material.

When it was complete, I was sure that nothing, not even the wildest tundra storms, would destroy the igloo. I wasn't done yet though. After the first igloo, I built a whole series of smaller ones. They would serve as birthing dens and as a backup in case anything untoward happened to the central igloo.

Lastly, I packed all the meat I'd accumulated in snow and showed the wolves how to bury the excess food from their own kills to serve as a stockpile for leaner times.

When I was done, I stood back and surveyed the fruits of my labor. Spread out before me were nearly two dozen igloos—a village in the making. *It will suffice*, I thought in satisfaction.

"What do you think?" I asked, turning to Snow. "Will the pack be able to make a home here?"

Emphatic agreement.

"It's no more than you and the others deserve," I murmured. "I only wish I had better materials to work with. Then, I could have—"

I broke off.

Game messages were tumbling heedlessly through my mind.

You have completed the hidden task: <u>Establish a new Pack</u>! You have forged the scattered refugees of sector 107 into a true pack, providing them with shelter, food, and the means to raise their young safely. Thanks to your efforts, the tundra has become a real home to the arctic wolves, and they will henceforth thrive in the sector. Wolf is pleased.

Your Wolf Mark has deepened!

Your Wolf Mark has deepened!

Congratulations, Michael! Your Wolf Mark has advanced to <u>Pack-hunter</u>. Hunters are protectors and providers of a pack and valued members within any pack hierarchy. Most wolfkind will accord you the respect this Mark demands and welcome you with open arms into their ranks.

As a result of your new Wolf Mark, your Class trait, nightwalker, has evolved to <u>wolfwalker</u>!

"Well," I grinned. "That's an unexpected bonus."

A smile tugging on my lips, I scanned the alerts again, studying each avidly, especially the one describing the change to my nightwalker trait.

Your deepening Wolf Mark has brought more of your lupine heritage to the fore, granting you the trait <u>wolfwalker</u>. This trait enhances your senses not just in the dark but in all environments. From this moment on, your senses will be akin to a wolf's and sharper than most players.

My smile deepened. My acute senses had saved me more than once while sneaking in the dark. To have them enhanced all around was a more powerful benefit than was apparent at first glance.

So caught up was I in my musings that I almost missed what the pack was doing. But eventually, I noticed that the wolves were gathering around me.

"What's going on?" I asked, turning my gaze outward and looking at Snow worriedly.

He didn't answer.

"Snow?"

Still no response.

More wolves streamed in to join the burgeoning ranks. Wrenching my gaze away from the alpha, I turned my attention to the rest of the pack.

Standing stiff-legged and three lines deep, they formed a large circle around me. What's more, I realized with a start, *every* wolf in the pack was accounted for, even the pups. *Now, what's gotten into them?*

Before I could question Snow again, the alpha raised his head and howled.

Immediately, the cry was taken up by the rest of the pack.

"Snow..." I began uncertainly.

My words ran down as the pack's actions triggered another flurry of Game messages.

Snow has relinquished the title of alpha!

By unanimous accord, the pack has proclaimed a new alpha!

Congratulations, Michael! You are now the pack alpha of the arctic wolves of sector 107!

I blinked in astonishment. I didn't want this. I hadn't asked for this. "No, no," I protested, raising my palms in denial. "Snow, don't do—"

You have completed the hidden task: <u>Become an Alpha</u>!

Earning the trust and respect of a pack is no easy thing. Wolf packs are notoriously independent, and even House titles and Marks will sway them only so far. Through your actions, you have earned the undying loyalty of the arctic wolves. As a result, the pack has seen fit to declare you their alpha.

Your Wolf Mark has deepened!

Congratulations, Michael! Your Wolf Mark has advanced to <u>Pack-alpha</u>.

The transition from pack hunter and alpha is small but significant and it is one that most scions fail to make, even after a lifetime of trying.

The Alpha Mark cannot be achieved by completing any number of tasks. Nor can it be bequeathed or granted by any player or Power. There is only one way to earn the title of Alpha, and that is by pack proclamation.

Alphas are leaders among wolfkin—sometimes beloved, oftentimes feared. The Mark is a stepping stone, one necessary to climb through the ranks of House Wolf. Without it, a scion will never amount to anything more than a House follower, but with it... With it, he may become one of the House's elite and perhaps one day even aspire to Prime.

But beware. While the Mark will compel instant obedience from most wolfkin, other alphas are likely to see you as a threat. Tread warily among them.

As a result of your new Wolf Mark, you have earned the new Class trait: arctic wolf! This trait increases your Constitution by +5 ranks, your Mind by +2, and your Strength by +3.

CHAPTER 234: BREAK OUT

It's a day for surprises, it seems.

For a long time, I couldn't move. Frozen in place and with my attention turned inward, I replayed the Adjudicator's words over and over in my mind.

The pack's gesture—*no, it was more than that*—the pack's faith in me left me speechless. And if I was interpreting the Game messages right, the implications were far-reaching.

A wolf nuzzled my hand. Looking down, I saw it was one of the pups. The alpha—beta now, I supposed—stood behind him, his blue eyes serious.

I met Snow's gaze. What did it mean that the wolves had made me the alpha, I wanted to ask. Did the pack want me to stay?

No. Snow followed the denial with a series of images.

With difficulty, I worked my way through them, then nodded slowly. The pack didn't *need* me to stay. But they wanted me to know that I had a home here. That I would always be welcome among them.

That I, too, was an arctic wolf.

"I see," I said gravely and inclined my head to Snow. "Thank you." The pack dispersed from around me, and I made my way back to the central igloo.

It was time to prepare for my departure.

$$* \quad * \quad *$$

The next morning, I was ready to leave.

I left the better part of my belongings with the pack for safekeeping. Among the few things I took were the tundra map, my winter gear, and a backpack with enough meat to complete the journey back to the portal.

I'd chosen the spot for the wolves' den with care. It was no accident that the den was only a few days' hike from the hidden portal. Some day—not too far in the future, hopefully—I planned on returning to the tundra, both to revisit the pack and to explore the nether-infested sector. And when that happened, the den would serve as my base of exploration as well.

My farewells were short, perfunctory almost.

All the wolves came to see me off, but to them this wasn't goodbye, only a brief separation, and if everything went as I hoped, I planned to ensure that remained the case.

The trip back to the portal was lonely and contrasted starkly with the many weeks that had passed before. After only one day, I began to miss the pack. Still, it was an easy hike, and with the snow cones to guide me, finding my way was almost laughably simple.

A day before I reached my destination, I pulled up my player profile.

Player Profile (Partial): Michael

Level: 125. Rank: 12. Current Health: 100%.
True Marks (hidden): Pack-alpha.

Attributes

Strength: 13. Constitution: 19. Dexterity: 26 (33)*. Perception: 25. Mind: 69. Magic: 8 (10)*. Faith: 0.
denotes attributes affected by items.

New Traits

Wolfwalker (hidden): improved senses in all conditions.
Budding explorer: all key points in newly discovered sectors logged.
Arctic wolf (hidden): +5 Constitution, +2 Mind, +3 Strength.

Skills

Dodging: 106. Sneaking: 101. Shortswords: 112. Two-weapon fighting: 104. Light armor: 107. Thieving: 78.
Chi: 103. Meditation: 131. Telekinesis: 107. Telepathy: 104.
Insight: 121. Deception: 106.

Equipment

ebonheart (+30% damage).
shortsword, +1 (+15% damage, +10 shortswords), **blunt!**
slim dagger.
amulet of fire (+10% fire resistance).
amulet of earth (+10% earth resistance).
backpack with frozen meat.
winter bone-hide armor (+10% damage reduction, -70% Dexterity and Magic, +5 stealth in snow).
snow-cone map of the tundra.

I was coming up on my two hundred-and-fiftieth day in the sector, and you would think most of my skills would be close to tier four already. But sadly, after reaching level one hundred, my skill progression had slowed dramatically.

I was all but certain it was because the foes I'd been facing simply weren't skilled enough. If I wanted to keep advancing, I would have to find better enemies to fight.

It wouldn't be in this sector though.

I had a plan for getting through to the next level, and it didn't involve me fighting the yetis, or the savant, at least not in the normal sense of the word.

✳   ✳   ✳

Early the next day, I reached the region with the exit portal.

The barrier had turned invisible once more, which I'd expected, given that the dungeon reset every day. I found it without too much trouble, though, prompting the same response from the Game.

Do you wish to retract the barrier formed of ice? Taking down the barrier will release the blizzard trapped within its heart and thaw the inhabitants inside.

Replying in the negative, I readied myself.

You have cast reaction buff, increasing your Dexterity by +4 ranks for 20 minutes.
You have cast lighten load, reducing your total armor penalties to 0% for 20 minutes. Net effect: +7 Dexterity and +2 Magic.

Opening my eyes, I laid a hand on the ice dome. It was a trap for the unwary, of course. As much of one as the tundra itself had been.

After the months I'd spent in the sector, I was certain the tundra's entire purpose on this level was to dissuade players from retreating, to push them into facing the challenge that awaited in the dome head-on. After all, who wanted to risk being lost on the cold, inhospitable plain?

I grinned wryly. Of course, there were those—like me—who ran willy-nilly to that fate, but I doubted many, if any, had survived the experience. I considered the ice dome again.

Two paths lay before me.

One: spring the trap. Open the dome, play hide and seek with one hundred yetis and a savant, kill the boss, and then escape. Crucially, I would have only one day to do all that.

Difficult, but not impossible.

Risky, though, as the yetis were an unknown quantity.

Or two: bypass the first trap entirely. *Don't* open the dome, steal the amulet, and flee. It wouldn't be that easy, of course, and I was sure a second trap awaited those who attempted it. But I fancied that I'd grown familiar enough with this level to know the nature of the second trap.

Time for a calculated risk.

Drawing ebonheart, I exhaled a slow, careful breath. I'd come this far, and I couldn't fail now. Unfurling my mindsight, I located the savant adept.

Then shadow blinked to him.

You have teleported 8 yards.

Immediately, icy winds battered me, whipping snow into my eyes and trying to push me off-balance.

You have entered a blizzard!
Warning: the temperature in this region is unconducive to life. Staying will cause your body to freeze over, locking you in stasis until released.

I was prepared for the weather.

You could even say I'd spent two hundred and fifty days preparing for it. And when a second message followed hard on the heels of the first, it revealed that my preparations hadn't been in vain.

Your body has begun to chill.

My winter armor and the layers of winter fat I'd slathered all over me stymied the weather's icy touch. It didn't stop it from penetrating altogether, of course. But the chill had been slowed enough for me to do what needed doing—I hoped.

Narrowing my eyes to slits, I studied the savant. My supposition was correct.

He was frozen solid.

From head to toe, the creature was encased in a cone of ice. Given the Game's messages, I presumed the icy coffin was holding the savant in stasis. I pressed my face against the surface, trying to see beneath.

But no matter how hard I looked, I couldn't make out the details of the creature within, nor the location of the amulet. I was certain I was looking at the sector boss though. Fairly certain, anyway.

Tapping the hilt of ebonheart against the savant's frozen coffin, I tested the hardness of the ice. I didn't so much as scratch it. I tapped harder. A chip flew free.

Good. The ice could be broken then.

Flipping the black blade over, I took it in a two-handed grip and thrust it straight forward—and directly toward where I thought the savant's neck might be.

A thin crack appeared in the ice.

Drawing the sword back to my chest, I shoved it outward again, causing another crack to form. Then I hit the frozen corpse thrice more, always targeting the same precise spot.

Eventually, a large spiderweb of cracks extended outward from the impact point.

Judging I'd weakened the frozen coffin sufficiently, I raised ebonheart above my head and hacked downward. I kept at it, hitting the ice over and over with great overhanded chops.

A chunk of ice fell free.

I was making better progress than I expected. Unfortunately, the seeping cold was also having an effect, and already my movements had begun to slow.

I have to speed this up. It was time to play my trump cards.

In an instant, stamina flooded my arms, doubling their speed and empowering my attacks. My sword flashed forward again.

Once. Twice. Thrice.

In a frenzy of motion, I battered at the ice, my blade moving blisteringly fast despite the hampering cold.

Three seconds later, my blows slowed down to normal speed. I didn't stop though. I kept going until, finally, I'd carved a fist-sized hole in the coffin.

Time remaining until you are completely immobilized: 1 minute, 30 seconds. Movement speed reduced to 60%.

Peering through the gap, I spotted the savant's right shoulder and, running down it, a thin chain. I grinned, albeit crookedly—the right side of my face was freezing over faster than the left.

Better work faster.

I resumed chopping, speeding up my attacks with whirlwind as soon as the ability was ready. More ice broke off, exposing more of the boss's chest.

Shortly, the amulet itself was revealed.

That's enough, I decided.

Time remaining until you are completely immobilized: 1 minute. Movement speed reduced to 40%.

Yanking back ebonheart, I thrust it forward again—moving in slow motion now—and into the savant.

It was like cutting into ice, if only slightly softer ice.

You have killed a frozen savant adept. The third sector boss has been slain! Sector bosses remaining: 2 of 5.

No experience accompanied the kill. *Huh.* Was that because the savant had been in stasis? *No matter, all I need is the amulet.*

Reaching into the hole, I yanked it free.

You have acquired an amulet of ice, the third piece of the guardian amulet of elements. In its present form, the amulet grants the bearer +10% resistance to water magic.

Ex..ce..ll..ent, I thought.

Even my thoughts were slowing down. Exhaling a frosty breath, I pivoted around and orientated on the portal. It was over thirty yards away. Too far to walk as I was.

Luckily, I didn't intend to.

Time remaining until you are completely immobilized: 30 seconds. Movement speed reduced to 20%.

Drawing on my psi, I shadow blinked.

You have teleported into the shadow of a yeti berserker.

Immediately, I spun psi again and hopped to the next frozen creature.

You have teleported into the shadow of a yeti grunt.

Time remaining until you are completely immobilized: 20 seconds.

Two more jumps to go. *Al...most th...ere.*

You have teleported into the shadow of a yeti grunt.
You have teleported into the shadow of a yeti chieftain.
Time remaining until you are completely immobilized: 10 seconds.

Thankfully, the portal was within touching distance of the pair of yeti chieftains standing beside it. They were its last line of defense, I supposed.

My gaze fixed on the gateway. Wherever it led to, I hoped it was warmer. Stretching out my hands, I deliberately overbalanced.

Falling was faster, after all.

I pitched forward, gaining momentum with each passing heartbeat. I was almost entirely frozen over now, and even if I wanted to, altering my trajectory was beyond me.

But I hadn't messed up. My timing proved impeccable, and I hit the glowing light dead center.

Transfer through portal commencing...
...
...
You are no longer chilled. Movement speed restored.
Passage completed!
Leaving sector 107 of the Endless Dungeon.

CHAPTER 235: LEDGES AND BRIDGES

You have entered sector 108 of the Endless Dungeon. This sector is level 4 of 5 of the Guardian Tower.

I emerged on a cliff face.

In a split second, a flurry of images flashed through my mind. Sheer rockfaces. Jagged peaks. Blue sky. A narrow ledge. And space. An infinite amount of yawning space, ready to swallow me.

Thankfully, the magical chill gripping my body had dissipated, and I was moving at full speed again. Twisting sideways, I avoided the endless tumble that beckoned and instead fell onto the slender ledge.

A heartbeat later, my face smacked up against cold hard rock. *Ooof!* That had hurt.

But it was better than the alternative.

Picking myself up gingerly, I took stock of my new surroundings.

I was somewhere in the middle of a sheer cliff. The rock wall extended vertically both above and below me. The portal had deposited me on a slim outcropping barely wide enough to stand upon, and because of the manner in which I'd entered the gateway, I had almost tumbled right off when I'd come through.

I guess that was another trap set for the unwary, I thought drily. If I'd been only a little slower, I would be dead.

Spreading my arms and bracing them against the cliff, I peered downward and tried to measure the drop. But the ground wasn't visible. Concealing it was thick white banks of clouds. *Down isn't an option then.*

I craned my head upward—carefully. The azure blue sky stared back at me, and for a moment I just drank in the sight. It made for a wonderful change after months of seeing the same dreary cloudbanks day in and day out.

Unfortunately, the sky looked out of reach.

From where I stood, I couldn't see the clifftop. But I *could* see the few hundred feet of rockface separating me from the top. It was smooth and lacked handholds. *Unclimbable.*

I faced forward again. Directly opposite me was another cliff, nearly identical to the one I was on. But it too was out of reach, with nothing bridging the three hundred feet between me and it except empty air.

Finally, I turned my gaze to the ledge itself.

To my right, it ended sharply in a steep drop. But to my left, it continued onward. Never widening more than three feet, the thin rock shelf traced a ragged path along the cliff face.

I sighed. It was the only viable path and, clearly, the one I was meant to take. And while having a defined route made for a welcome change after the trackless tundra, I was wary of what dangers it hid.

The ledge wouldn't be safe. I was certain of it.

I glanced around again. But where were the threats hiding? I could spot none, not even with mindsight. I sighed again. There was no helping it.

I had to follow the ledge and see where it took me.

✳   ✳   ✳

It was slow going.

Shifting carefully sideways—always with my weight pushed back and my hands skimming the rock at my rear—I followed the ledge as it meandered along the cliff.

Sometimes the rock shelf shrank to less than a foot wide and stayed that way for a seeming eternity. That made for tricky footwork. Matters weren't helped by my bulky armor either.

I'd shed my snowshoes before entering the dome but had retained the rest of my gear, including my fur overcoat. Now I had cause to regret it. *Doing this would've been a lot easier in newbie clothes,* I thought crossly.

But despite my grumbling, I didn't discard my armor. Who knew when I would need it again? And thankfully, heat wasn't a problem. The two cliffs—my own and the one opposite—marched parallel to each other, casting the space in between in perpetual shadow.

An hour later, I was still edging along the ledge.

I should find somewhere to rest soon, I thought. One of the wider spots along the ledge should do. Pausing for a moment, I scanned the path ahead.

There, that looks like a—

I stilled.

A deeper pool of black had flitted over the cliff face ahead. In the shadows it was hard to tell one patch of darkness from another, but my sight was keen enough to pick out the differences.

And I was sure something had just overflown the cliff.

Slowly, I turned my face up. A shadow swept over me. It belonged to a familiar shape, one with a wide wingspan, sinuous tail, and snaking head.

Wyvern.

I was sure of it. My fear spiked. There was no way I could fight the flying beast. I was too exposed on the ledge, and without room to maneuver, I would make for easy pickings.

But the creature hadn't seen me. Nor did it appear on the hunt.

It was gliding unconcernedly on the air currents, carving huge circles in the sky and, by all appearance, flying only for the sheer pleasure of it.

I'm safe, I realized, tension easing. Staying where I was, I drew the shadows tighter around me. Then carefully, I extended my will and analyzed the beast circling overhead.

The target is a level 165 brown wyvern.

So, I'd called it right. The creature *was* a wyvern. The beast above wasn't as powerful as Besina had been, but I didn't fool myself; in this environment, the brown wyvern would be nigh impossible to defeat.

What to do? I wondered.

Keep going until I find a secure place to rest and, if need be, fight.
Pressing deeper into the cliff wall behind me, I crept onward.

✳   ✳   ✳

A little later, I came to the end of the ledge.

Unfortunately, there was no safe ground to be found at the end of it. In front of me was a rope bridge. It was bolted to the rock wall and expanded away from my cliff to the opposite one. Worse yet, while I could see the bridge's far end, its middle sagged so deeply it was concealed by the cloud banks below.

"Bloody hell," I mumbled under my breath.

If I wanted to continue, I'd have to step onto the bridge. That idea had little appeal though. If anything, the bridge looked less secure than the ledge. But what choice did I have?

Unhappily, I contemplated the rope bridge again.

Both ends of the bridge appeared to be firmly fastened, and the bridge didn't seem to be in danger of collapsing. But it had no guard rails, making falling a distinct possibility.

The bridge was only two feet across, wide enough not to make the crossing hazardous, but it was far from ideal. Its bottom consisted of slatted wooden pieces, each individually attached, and I could only hope they, too, were properly secured.

I glanced upward again, as I had taken to regularly doing since I'd first spotted the wyvern. The creature hadn't made a reappearance, but I wasn't reassured. It still lurked somewhere in the mountains.

I turned back to the bridge. *Sooner started, sooner done.*

Placing one foot on the bridge, I pressed down lightly. A slight tremor was the only response. Moving with glacial slowness, I stepped fully onto the bridge.

It shook, but only a touch.

Exhaling a careful breath, I took a step forward. Then another. The bridge remained stable. *Alright, it appears sound enough.* Spreading my arms, I advanced down the bridge, placing each foot with exaggerated care.

Thirty feet. Sixty. Ninety.

Then the clouds billowed upward, swallowing me into their depths, and visibility dropped to nearly nothing. Mid-motion, I froze. I was barely able to see my feet, much less where to place them next.

I grimaced. Another complication.

Keep moving. This is exactly the wrong place to stop. Flexing my knees, I slid a foot forward, making sure to keep it in contact with the bridge at all times. Another step completed. Then, I brought the next foot forward. Continuing in this manner, I resumed my crossing.

One twenty feet. One fifty.

I'd reached the bridge's lowest point. From here, it sloped upward. *Halfway there.* I slid my right leg forward.

A shape whizzed past.

A hostile entity has failed to detect you! You are hidden.

The entire bridge swayed with the creature's passing. Throwing myself forward, I clutched at the closest rope.

Another unseen shape rushed through the cloud. Its presence was also very much felt as the bridge was set to rocking again.

A hostile entity has failed to detect you!

Damnation!

Wrapping my arms across the base of the bridge, I hugged it tight and flung open my mindsight. I was just in time to catch three more mindglows flash past.

Multiple hostile entities have failed to detect you!

The bridge lurched violently. Swaying like a pendulum, it cut one-hundred-and-eighty-degree arcs in the air. I held on—barely. But despite my predicament, I retained the presence of mind to interrogate one of the flying creatures before it flew out of range.

The target is a level 161 brown wyvern.

Well, now I know what this level is all about: wyvern and bridges.

Closing my eyes, I prepared to ride out the bridge's bucking. *Gods, I hate this sector already.*

✴ ✴ ✴

I spent another five minutes hugging the bridge. By then, its tremors had subsided.

I'd waited this long in case the wyverns returned, but seeing that they hadn't, I resumed my crossing. Staying prone, I fast-crawled across the bridge—dignity be damned.

I reached the other end safely and dropped lightly onto the waiting ledge. My gaze flew upward. Now that I was out of the clouds, I could see the five wyverns clearly.

They swooped and glided in a carefree fashion.

Clearly, I wouldn't find safety above—my gaze dropped to the clouds from which the wyverns had emerged—nor from below.

I glanced along the ledge. It stretched beyond my line of sight, following the cliff. I sighed, realizing what this meant. *Let's have at it, then.*

Rising to my feet, I began edging along the ledge.

I crossed ten more ledges and just as many bridges, zigzagging between the two cliff faces which I now realized were the two sides of a deep canyon. One whose bottom I couldn't see.

And which housed a nest of wyverns.

Time and again, the flying beasts rushed up the gorge, circled the skies, and dived back down, seemingly for no other reason than because it was... fun.

After my first close encounter, I kept my mindsight continually open. If not for it and my stealth, I would've died many times over.

At some point, the sun peeked over the gorge, and when it did, I hid in a cloud bank until it crossed over to the other side. It was too dangerous to be on the move without cover. The wyverns may not have detected me yet, but that was only because of the concealing clouds and shadows.

From the brief glimpse I'd gotten of the sun, I gathered I was traversing south to north along the canyon. The gap between the cliffs had begun widening too, and with each crossing the bridges grew infinitesimally longer.

But as nerve-wracking as my journey along the canyon proved, I navigated it safely, and a little past noon, I reached its end.

✳   ✳   ✳

The canyon terminated in a valley.

At least, I assumed it was a valley. I still couldn't see the bottom. Over the last mile, the gap between the two cliffs had raced apart before curving around and meeting each other to form the canyon's bowl-shaped end.

I, unfortunately, was still lost somewhere on the cliff face. The series of ledges and bridges had taken me neither up to the clifftops nor down to the ground.

Instead, I was left staring at the sea of puffy white clouds below me. They blanketed the entire valley, completely hiding whatever lay beneath. Only one structure dared to pierce their billowing depths: a thin rock spire in the valley's center.

And atop it was the exit portal.

Nestled on the end of the final ledge, I studied the gateway. It rested on the flat top of the spire, which itself was barely a few feet wide.

Covering both the gateway and the spire tip was a familiar dome. This one was formed of crackling white energy, and when I analyzed it, the Game confirmed its nature to be exactly as I expected.

The target is a protective barrier formed of air. Until it is removed, you cannot pass through, nor can the nether portal be accessed.

Crossing the valley to reach the gateway wasn't the problem. A rope bridge connected the ledge and the spire.

Unfortunately, the bridge was over half a mile long and its entire length was uncovered, with even the lowest point firmly above the clouds. And as wide as the valley was, it was almost entirely bathed in sunlight. It was only to the cliff walls on the rim that the shadows still clung.

Then there were the wyverns.

Two dozen of the flying beasts winged high above the valley, little more than specks in the sky. Periodically, though, they snapped their wings closed and plummeted in a screaming dive through the clouds.

It was then that I noticed that three of the wyverns had riders on their backs. Not unexpectedly, analyze confirmed the trio to be savants.

The target is a level 186 savant master.
The target is a level 151 savant aeromancer.
The target is a level 148 savant aeromancer.

Frowning, I considered the challenge before me.

To get through to the next level, I would have to at least kill the savant master, who was undoubtedly the sector boss. But accomplishing that would be no easy task.

My foes were both numerous and powerful. Worse yet, they were more mobile too and could strike at me from any direction. In fact, the *only* advantage I had over the wyverns and savants was my stealth. It, however, had been negated by the sunlight glaring down.

I have to wait for nightfall, I realized. It was my only hope of getting through the level.

Closing my eyes, I settled down to wait.

✳ ✳ ✳

The hours passed quickly, and before I knew it the sun was dipping below the horizon. Shaking myself out of the light trance I'd fallen into, I studied the valley anew. The shadows had expanded out from the cliff walls to touch the spire and bathe it in darkness.

Time to get going.

Stepping onto the bridge, I cast my buffs. Then, with my eyes peeled on the wyverns still wheeling in the sky above, I crept along the bridge.

Multiple hostile entities have failed to detect you!

A wyvern rushed past, then another. Ignoring them, I kept moving. They had both been riderless. There was only one particular beast I was interested in. Cloaked in shadow, I advanced along the bridge. When I neared its end, I dropped into a crouch and made myself as small as I could.

Readying a spellcasting, I waited.

There was no way I could reach my prey. That left me with only one option: wait for him to come to me.

Ten minutes passed. Then an hour.

I didn't twitch. I didn't fidget. The tundra had taught me patience, and despite the strain in my shoulders and the ache in my haunches, I remained unmoving and perfectly poised to strike.

I would wait all night if necessary. But sooner or later, I was sure my target would come down from his lofty height.

And then I'd have him.

✳ ✳ ✳

Two hours after full dark, the last three wyverns—those ridden by the savants—spiraled downward. All the other wyverns had long since disappeared in the cloud banks below, presumably to rest for the night.

Eyes fixed on my target, I mapped his trajectory and shifted my position closer to where I projected he would pass by.

Six hostile entities have failed to detect you!

In any event, circumstances were almost perfect for what I intended. Buffs recast and psi ready, I waited.

Hurtling down from above, the sector boss and his wyvern closed to within a hundred feet of me. For some reason, the flying beasts seem to enjoy whizzing past the bridge. Perhaps it gave them a thrill of pleasure. In any event, it served my own purposes well.

Fifty feet.

Thirty.

Now.

Releasing psi in a rush, I cast shadow blink.

You have teleported into the shadow of a savant master.

I emerged out of the aether on the wyvern's back and behind my foe. A startled tremor shot through the beast at the sudden addition of my weight.

The savant master, though, was slower on the uptake.

He was still stiffening in surprise when my left hand snaked around his throat and stunned him. In the same motion, my right hand swept forward to plunge ebonheart through his back and up and out of his chest.

You have killed a savant master with a fatal blow!
The fourth sector boss has been slain! Sector bosses remaining: 1 of 5.

There was no time to delay. Releasing ebonheart's hilt, I searched frantically for the amulet. The fingers of my left hand brushed the chain and yanked the amulet free from the corpse's neck.

You have acquired an amulet of air, the fourth piece of the guardian amulet of elements. In its present form, the amulet grants the bearer +10% resistance to air magic.

Smiling in grim satisfaction, I shoved the corpse off with ebonheart still buried in it. The soulbound blade couldn't be lost and would return to me of its own accord.

Meanwhile, I had other problems to attend to.

Namely, the bridge. We were already below it and racing for the clouds. *Damnation!*

My plan had been to kill the savant, grab the amulet, and two-step away. That was no longer possible. I'd misjudged the amount of time I'd have and now I was trapped on the wyvern's back. *What am I going to do now?*

Improvise.

My gaze flitted left and right, searching for inspiration.

My assassination had been so swift that the other two savants hadn't caught onto the fact yet. Not the wyvern, though. Whipping his snakelike head around, the beast stared at me even as we continued our alarming descent.

I tensed, readying myself to dodge while I spun psi.

A plan had coalesced in my mind: charm the wyvern, fly him back to the bridge, and escape. I wasn't very optimistic about it though. The green wyverns in the wolves' valley had been immune to mental assaults, and while I didn't think the brown wyverns had the same immunity—the savants had dominated them, I was nearly certain of it—once the beast alerted the others to my presence, I was sure the two remaining savants would dispel any spell I cast.

Plan B then: in case of plan A failing, stay alive until landing, kill my unwilling mount, flee, then find some way to climb back up the spire.

It was a plan. Not a very achievable one. But a plan nonetheless.

But before I could enact even the first element of my plan, the other two savants—still oblivious—and their wyverns plunged through the clouds.

At almost the exact same moment, the wyvern I rode banked out of his dive. "FREEEEEEEEEEEE!" he screamed as he skimmed over the top of the clouds. "I'M FREE!"

I refrained from releasing the spell I readied. My suppositions were correct. The brown wyverns *had* been mentally dominated, which meant I could still go ahead and try charming my mount, but there was perhaps a less risky way. "You are," I yelled loudly against the wind. "All thanks to me."

A startled hiss escaped the wyvern. "You can under-s-sstand me?" Before I could frame a reply, he went on. "Get off me, little human." The beast curled up his upper lips to reveal rows of gleaming teeth. "Now."

"I will," I replied equably, ignoring his threat. I gestured to the portal atop the spire. "Once you get me there."

The wyvern cut a tight arc through the air, forcing me to clutch tightly onto him for a moment with my legs and hands. "Why s-s-sshould I?" he asked lazily, continuing our conversation as if nothing had happened.

"Because if you don't, we fight," I replied evenly. "I slew your master easily enough. The chances are high I'll be able to kill you too. And even if I don't, can you afford a protracted battle?" I looked down meaningfully. "Sooner or later those other savants are going to realize something is amiss. Do you still want to be here when that happens?"

The wyvern was silent for a moment, then all he said was, "Get ready."

I nodded curtly and hugged the beast tightly as he climbed almost vertically.

We shot past the spire's tip, and the wyvern flipped over, flying upside down for a brief moment. If the beast thought he could get rid of me by dropping me, he was mistaken.

"Are you trying to kill me?" I growled, my voice strained.

There was no response, and for a split-second I was tempted to cast my charm spell, but I held back. Fortunately, it turned out.

Reaching the apex of his flight, the wyvern dropped back into a dive before leveling out and hurtling at the portal at a pace that left me breathless.

He isn't going to stop, I realized at the same moment as the wyvern hissed, "Jump!"

I jumped, throwing myself off the wyvern's back just as he flew past the spire. Landing on the hard-packed ground, I rolled across it and straight through the glowing gate.

Transfer through portal commencing...

...

...

Passage completed!
Leaving sector 108 of the Endless Dungeon.

You have entered sector 109 of the Endless Dungeon. This sector is level 5 of 5 of the Guardian Tower.

I landed in a sprawl, but rose quickly to my feet and spun around, ready to fend off any threats.

But I was alone.

After a tense moment of waiting for something—anything—to jump out at me, I relaxed.

I'd made it.

I'd reached the final level of the dungeon. Sheathing ebonheart—which had reappeared in my hand—I turned around to study my surroundings.

I was in a verdant plain under a bright blue sky. Vegetation—plants, bushes, and shrubbery—of a type I didn't recognize surrounded me on all sides. The ground underfoot was soft and loamy. And wet grass rose to my knees.

Yet, as normal as the landscape appeared, I suspected it was anything but.

For one, it was deadly silent. No birds called; no insects buzzed. For another, there was no wind. No sun either. Just as startling, the dungeon exit stood to my right—undefended and welcoming. *Its* message seemed clear: I could leave if I wanted to.

I wouldn't do that, of course. Not until I'd gotten what I'd come for.

I turned to my left. An expanse of white marble walls lay in that direction. They'd been set in a square forming an enclosed compound, but its walls were too high for me to see within.

Entry into the compound was provided by the glittering door, set in the wall facing me, and while it was sealed, it beckoned in clear invitation. *That's where I'm meant to go.* It bore further investigation, but not just yet.

Turning my attention inward, I considered the waiting Game messages.

You have reached level 127!

My passage through the previous level had been so swift that I'd barely gained experience or skills. Still, killing the boss had netted me two levels, and I didn't hesitate in reinvesting in Mind.

Your Mind has increased to rank 71.

Another, more interesting message was also waiting.

You have acquired all four pieces of the guardian amulet of elements. Do you wish to combine the pieces?

I replied in the affirmative, prompting another response from the Game.

Congratulations, Michael! You have created the artifact: guardian amulet of elements. This item grants the bearer +15% resistance to air, earth, water, and fire magic.

Looking down at my chest, I saw the four amulets I'd collected had disappeared. In their place was another: a medallion with four precious stones.

I smiled in satisfaction. Assembling the artifact had taken a lot of blood, sweat, and tears, more than I'd bargained on. And I could only hope it was worth all the effort in the end.

Swiveling to my right, I approached the nether portal—cautiously—lest it held some undetected threat. The eerie surroundings had me on edge and I feared the worst. But when I closed to within three yards of the gateway, a Game message arrived that soothed my worries.

You have entered a safe zone.

"Ah," I breathed. I'd been afraid the portal might be trapped or that it was a cleverly disguised illusion. But it was truly what it appeared.

After assuring myself that the portal was functional, I glanced behind it and found the rebirth well. *So, both resurrection point and retreat are in easy reach.* I didn't know what to make of that fact though. Was the Game encouraging me to leave or stay?

I shrugged. It didn't matter, I knew my own mind already. Swiveling around, I faced the walled compound.

Time to see what this level is all about.

✳   ✳   ✳

Thirty minutes later, I completed my slow circuit around the outside of the compound. Each wall was roughly fifty yards long and, except for the first one, had no windows or entrances of any kind.

The walls themselves were smooth and polished, and when I ran my fingers along one, it set my hand tingling. I didn't sense any traps or wards in the vicinity, but the tingle was warning enough that the compound's protections were more than just physical in nature.

Beyond the compound, the rampant vegetation extended to the horizon. I declined to delve into their depths though. After my time in the tundra, I'd had just about enough of wandering through endless plains, even if these appeared more pleasant.

Returning to the first wall, I approached the glittering entrance. The door was made entirely from translucent crystal. It caught the ambient light—whose source I'd yet to identify—and reflected it back, giving it its sparkling appearance.

Taking care not to touch the door, I pushed my face right up next to it and peered through. Inside the compound, I could just about make out hundreds of blurry shapes—which was odd, because my mindsight didn't register anything.

Frowning, I leaned back. Were they constructs? It seemed the most reasonable explanation. I turned my attention back to the door. I would find out soon enough.

The door had no handle or keyhole, but in its center was a circular-shaped groove. Knowing what I knew already of the dungeon and seeing that the indentation's size matched the amulet's medallion exactly, I was certain how to unlock the door.

But what awaited me inside once I did that—*that* I didn't know.

I glanced at the brightly lit surroundings. There weren't any shadows around, and it hadn't escaped my attention that the sky had neither brightened nor darkened since I'd arrived. And with no sun in evidence, I was fairly sure it wouldn't.

That made waiting for any sort of nightfall pointless.

Best get this done now then.

Drawing on my psi and stamina, I cast my buffs. Then I drew ebonheart. I left my second blade sheathed; it was too blunt to be effective anymore. Lastly, I fitted the medallion in the groove.

Key detected. Assessing artifact's validity...

...

...

Key has not been used previously. Access granted.
Opening the final chamber of Guardian Tower.
Note, this amulet may not be used to unseal this chamber again.

The door began to slide back, smooth and silent. Removing the amulet, I danced to the side and ducked behind the right wall.

There, I waited.

The door retracted fully, but nothing emerged, not even the least whisper of sound. Mindsight was empty too. *Hmm.* Now what?

Tightening my grip about ebonheart, I peeked around the wall.

Little by little, the compound's interior came into view. The ground was the same spongy soil and knee-high grass. Alas, there was no shrubbery.

There were no buildings or any other structures either. Only... marble statues.

The statues were clumped together in the center of the compound, haphazardly strewn among the grass. Some stood tall, others lay flat, and many looked like they'd fallen over.

But despite their poor care, each sculpture was incredibly lifelike. Not only that, they were familiar too. Fire slugs, ratmen, yeti, and wyvern: there were multiple statues of each—all frozen mid-motion in warlike poses.

On the left wall was another sculpture—notable for the fact that it stood alone.

Just like the others, it too was made from marble. But that was the only similarity it shared with the rest. For one, it was humanlike in appearance. For another, it was tall, stretching almost the full height of the compound's walls. And where the expressions of the other statues were violent and angry, its own face was calm. Serene.

That wasn't the only reason the lonely sculpture had captured my attention, however. I'd seen the statue's like before—outside the entrance to every one of the city's public dungeons.

I bit my lip. The sculpture had to be decorative, but what was it doing here? Unable to come up with an answer, but not considering the giant statue a threat, I swept my gaze across its fellows in the middle of the compound.

They definitely weren't natural. Reaching out, I analyzed the closest statue.

The response was... nothing.

I wasn't reassured. Suspecting a trap, I scanned the compound again using every ability and sense available to me, but once more I didn't pick up anything amiss.

Huh. That just means the trap is well-concealed.

I still had to enter the compound though. But perhaps I could do so with some degree of stealth. The grass was just about high enough to make that feasible.

I glanced down at my white fur armor. *I'll have to do something about all this white though.* Retreating a few steps from the entrance, I picked up a handful of loamy soil.

The fur should soak up the—

Door to the final chamber sealing in 5 seconds...

My head jerked up in shock at the Game message. It couldn't mean what I thought it meant, could it?

4 seconds...
3 seconds...

Not good, I thought. *Not bloody good at all.*

Flinging aside the dirt in my hand, I dashed through the gates a second before they closed.

Chapter 238: The Statue Garden

Door closed. To unseal the chamber, slay the final sector boss.

Panting heavily, I took a moment to recover as the crystal barricade slid shut behind me. I was trapped in the compound now, and there were only two ways out: death or victory.

The good news was that if I died, I had a quick trip out of the dungeon. The bad news? The Game's messages made clear I would get only a single shot at this. *I'll just have to make the most of it.*

Swiveling my head from left to right, I searched for a threat. At first glance, nothing appeared to have changed in the compound.

But then I noticed a fine crack in the nearest sculpture.

Narrowing my eyes, I focused on the statue in question—one of a ratman. A second crack formed. Then a fine haze of white powder fell away from the face, revealing a patch of brown fur beneath.

A mindglow, dull and weak, appeared in my mindsight. But second by second, it strengthened. My gaze jerked away from the statue to the next. It, too, was cracking. As were many others.

Damnation! The statues were coming alive.

Hefting ebonheart, I advanced on the awakening ratman, intent on killing him before he became a threat.

A wisp of movement drew my eye.

Whipping my head around, I fixed my gaze on the half-caught glimpse. At the far end of the compound, something was already moving.

It was a savant.

Reaching out with my will, I analyzed him.

The target is a level 191 savant grandmaster.

Immediately, I altered my course. Lurching away from the ratman, I made for the savant. He was assuredly the sector boss. The grandmaster was already encased in a flickering multi-hued shield and was scanning the compound intently—for me presumably.

He must know I'm here.

This just keeps getting better, I thought morosely. Racing flat-out, I made for the boss.

The other hostiles didn't matter, not as long as I could kill the savant. And with my enemies multiplying by the minute, playing the long game—using stealth—would only make the encounter more difficult.

Nearing a stone wyvern, I cast two-step.

Striding through the air, I landed on the statue's marble head. Not pausing, I leaped off again and onto a yeti's broad shoulders. Another jump and I was on a stone fire slug.

A savant grandmaster has awoken the first of his minions! A level 120 ratman brute is no longer petrified.

At the Game message, my brows crinkled. I'd been mistaken. The boss hadn't been searching the chamber earlier; he'd been awakening the statues.

Raising my head, I surveyed the compound again. While all the statues were cracking, most were still inert stone without mindglows. I had some time before I was mobbed then.

Up ahead, I spotted the newly awoken ratman. He was a few yards away and shaking himself free of the last flakes of his marble prison.

Racing down the fire slug's back, I shadow blinked to the brute and, before he could react, two-stepped onto the next statue.

I was halfway to my target.

But the savant grandmaster wasn't standing idly by either.

Clapping his hands together, the sector boss fired a beam of light in my direction. Somersaulting forward, I let the attack pass beneath me.

You have evaded a savant's magical projectile.

I dropped back to the ground, landing lightly on all fours. Another ray of energy was already flashing toward me. Diving sideways, I threw myself toward the nearest statue.

You have evaded a savant's magical projectile.

The beam blistered the air only a few inches from my nose but, crucially, missed. Huddling behind the statue, I opened my mindsight and spotted a still-weak mindglow up ahead. It was en route to the savant.

Perfect. Spinning psi, I readied shadow blink.

Light flashed three times, and the statue sheltering me detonated, showering me with loose rocks.

A savant has killed a petrified yeti.
You have taken minor damage from falling debris.

Yikes. Flinging my hands up, I covered my head. My ears were ringing, and dust from the expanding cloud clogged my eyes and mouth. But I held onto the spell I was weaving and a second later blinked out.

You have teleported in the shadow of a wyvern.

The half-awakened wyvern tried to swat me with its wings. The blow was slow and easily evaded though.

Another beam flashed.

I tensed, but the attack passed me harmlessly by. The sector boss hadn't realized I'd repositioned and was still targeting the dead yeti's remains.

I couldn't stay where I was though. Hurtling forward, I resumed my charge. At the blur of movement, the savant's cloaked head whipped around to face me. Knowing another attack was inbound, I readied psi.

A savant has cast a frost ray of doom.
You have cast two-step.
You have evaded a savant's magical projectile.

Once again, the savant missed as, running atop a cushion of air, I leaped over his attack.

Frost ray of doom, eh? That doesn't sound very pleasant. Still airborne, I cast again. My target was finally in range.

You have teleported into the shadow of a savant.

I emerged from the aether behind the savant with ebonheart already in motion. Snaking out, the black blade struck the multi-hued bubble dead center.

Your target's shield has blocked your attack, absorbing its damage.

The boss whirled around, hands outflung. Ducking, I rolled away, avoiding the magical flames spewing out of his palms.

Safely out of range, I bounced back to my feet. The torrent of flames had not stopped pouring out of the boss' hands. *A persistent spell then.* Readying psi, I charged forward again.

The savant recentered his hands on my new position, but a second before I could drop back into the inferno's range, I blinked.

You have teleported into the shadow of a savant.

Emerging behind my target, I hammered at his shield again with one combo after the other.

You have cast whirlwind, increasing your attack speed by 100% for 3 seconds.
Your target's shield has blocked your attacks.
You have cast piercing strike.
Your target's shield has blocked your attacks.

It wasn't enough.

Turning around—his own motions much slower than mine—the boss tried to hit me with his deadly flames again. Flipping backward, I sprang off my hands and out of range.

Out of the corner of my eye, I spotted a charging figure on my right. A ratman was attempting to flank me. Pivoting on my heel, I lunged forward, leading with ebonheart's point.

You have killed a ratman brute.

The black blade drilled a neat hole in the ratman's chest. Retracting the sword, I turned back to the savant. He'd changed tactics, I saw. Muttering under his breath, the boss was preparing a longer spell.

I risked another glance at the compound. Four more of the boss' minions had awoken and were closing in on me. The two lumbering yetis would be no threat—they were too slow. The fire slug too. The wyvern, though, would be a problem.

Spreading her wings, the beast glided toward me. Drawing psi, I prepared to meet her.

The savant, meanwhile, had finished his spell, creating a pulse of crackling white charge that radiated outward from his position.

My gaze flickered to the expanding circle of lightning. It was fast approaching, and on the fly, I changed targets.

You have teleported into the shadow of a savant.

I landed *inside* the growing ring and, before the startled savant could react, struck at him again. Once. Twice. Thrice.

Your target's shield has blocked your attacks.

The pulse kept going, not discriminating between its victims.

A savant has killed a fire slug.
A savant has stunned 2 yetis.

Out of the corner, I saw the wyvern flapping her wings furiously. She had avoided the boss' spell by the simple expedient of flying higher. The savant was also turning to face me.

I grimaced. Soon, I would have two dangerous foes to fend off simultaneously. Keeping a wary eye of both, I kept striking at the savant. Speed was my best ally.

The wyvern opened her jaws. The boss raised his hands.

Now.

Selecting the closer of the two stunned yetis, I dived into its shadow—leaving my two foes suddenly bereft of a target.

The startled wyvern tried to swerve. The boss tried to pull his flames back. Both were too slow.

A wyvern has been critically injured by a savant's scorching flames. A savant's shield has absorbed the damage of a wyvern's dive.

The wyvern crashed headlong into the boss, shrieking as his flames burned into her. The savant himself was uninjured, but his flames cut off abruptly as he was tossed clear across the compound.

I chased after him.

The wyvern alighted on the ground not far from me. Crooning to herself, she nursed her smoking face. Ignoring the beast—she appeared out of the fight for the moment—I kept charging toward the boss.

The savant, meanwhile, had come to a grinding halt against one of the marble walls and was back on his feet. Turning around, he contemplated me for a second.

Scared you, have I?

Attempted mental intrusion detected! A savant has failed to dominate you!

Guess not.

The mental assault, coming from nowhere, had caught me off guard, and for a moment I was tempted to raise my mind shield.

But I *had* resisted the attack.

And I couldn't afford to fight without my psi, not now. I needed to end this fast, which meant closing with my target quickly. Going airborne, I rushed across steps of air.

You have passed a mental resistance check! A savant has failed to dominate you!

I smiled grimly at the boss' repeat failure as I sailed through the air. I didn't want to give him a third chance at charming me, but I'd nearly reached him. Shouldering the risk, I left my mind shield down.

A savant has failed to dominate you!

I grinned in relief as I dropped to the ground. *That's it,* I thought. *I'm in range.* Spinning psi, I shadow blinked.

You have teleported 9 yards.

Emerging on the boss' left flank, I launched a frenzied attack on his shield. I threw everything I had at him and used both whirlwind and piercing strike to hasten and empower my strikes.
The boss' shield had already suffered a torrent of abuse, and under my latest assault, it didn't fare well.

A savant grandmaster's shield has been destroyed!

I smiled in savage satisfaction, and before my foe could so much as blink, I rammed ebonheart through his chest.

You have killed a savant grandmaster with a fatal blow!
You have freed 36 hostiles from captivity!
Unsealing door...

Chapter 239: Fate's Key

Barely taking the time to acknowledge the Game messages, I spun around, ready for the worst. There were still multiple hostiles in the chamber after all, and among them were too many wyverns for comfort.

But I needn't have worried.

My foes were stampeding for the exit.

With the sector boss dead—and their minds unfettered—the dungeon's denizens were making a bid for freedom. My gaze slid to the right, where the injured wyvern had huddled. But even she was retreating. Where they were going, I had no idea. Perhaps they hoped to find shelter somewhere on the plains, but it wasn't my problem anymore.

I was done. The dungeon defeated.

I could scarce believe it.

Slumping to the ground, I inhaled a tremulous breath. Game messages were vying for my attention, but for the moment, all I could manage was breathing in and out, gulping in deep lungsful of air.

What plagued me wasn't physical exhaustion. It went deeper than that. I was emotionally and mentally wrung out.

I had spent the better part of a year in the guardian tower. If not for the wolves, I wouldn't have lasted that long, but even with their support, the dungeon had taken a toll on me.

Maintaining my resolve after months of delays, failures, and hardship had been difficult. Keeping my fears at bay—about the mantises, those I'd left behind, and the course I'd chosen—hadn't been easy either.

I'd survived only by narrowing my focus to the dungeon and not looking too hard at matters beyond it.

But, now that I was done... the future stared me in the face.

Had I made the right choice in coming here?

Time to find out.

Rising to my feet, I turned my attention inward to the waiting Game messages.

You have reached level 129!

Your dodging has increased to level 107. Your shortswords has increased to level 113. Your chi has increased to level 105. Your telekinesis has increased to level 109. Your insight has increased to level 124.

The final sector boss has been slain. Congratulations, Michael! You have completed the Guardian Tower.

You have accomplished the feat: <u>Solo your First Dungeon!</u> Requirement: Complete a dungeon while not in a party. As only the 534th tier 3 solo player to finish a tier 4 dungeon, you have been awarded the item: <u>Fate's Key</u>. This artifact is a non-saleable, single-use soulbound item that can only be applied to unopened dungeon loot chests.

When you activate the Fate's Key, it will create three different variants of the loot chest in question, each with items of comparable level that have been tailored for your use.

You must choose which of the three chests to retain as your reward.

I blinked in astonishment.

The level-up and skill-gain messages came as no surprise. The feat I'd earned, though, was unexpected. Slowly, my gaze dropped to the key that had materialized in my hand.

It was ordinary looking, indistinguishable from any other, but going by the Adjudicator's message, it was an item of incalculable value.

And aptly named too.

The key wasn't the only item that had appeared in the wake of the Game messages. Sitting innocuously in the middle of the compound was a loot chest. Not a wooden one. Nor even a silver one.

But a solid gold one.

Excitement bubbled up in me. "Gold," I breathed. In my time in the Game, I'd encountered only one chest that wasn't wooden, and inside it I'd found my psionic Class. *That* chest had been bronze.

The gold chest had to be at least two tiers better—if not more. What would I find in this one? I squatted beside the sealed box, my fingers itching to open it.

But I restrained myself.

My gaze flickered from the artifact clenched in my hand to the chest. It seemed... hasty to use the item so soon after acquiring it. But would I ever get a better chance to use the key?

And it was now that my need was greatest.

There will never be a better opportunity, I thought. Uncurling my fingers, I placed the key on the loot chest.

It's time to decide my fate.

A Game message unfurled in my mind.

Activating Fate's Key...

Before my eyes, both chest and key disappeared. I held my breath in anticipation. A moment later, they were replaced by three other sealed boxes.

All identical. And all gold.

Fate's key activated.

The existing loot has been discarded, and in its place three new sets of items have been generated. The choice is now yours, Michael. Determine your reward for completing the Guardian Tower.

A smile that was as much an expression of nerves as of excitement twitched at the corners of my mouth.

Let's see what's behind door number one, I thought and reached out to flip open the first chest.

✳   ✳   ✳

There were only three items inside.

Stilling my momentary disappointment, I analyzed each.

This is a greater attribute gem. It grants you 3 attribute points.

This is the advanced ability tome moderate chi heal. You have the necessary skill, rank -5 chi, to learn this ability.

This is a master Class stone. It contains the path of a stygian magus and is not aligned to any Force. This Class specializes in wielding magic, not just elemental magic but also magic born of the nether.

Those with the ability to wield the nether are few and far between, and while a stygian magus may learn other types of magic, it is nether wizardry that is his most potent tool. But beware, magic of the nether is not without cost. As a magus' knowledge of the nether advances, so too do the debuffs he suffers when outside the Nethersphere.

This Class stone bestows a player with three skills: elemental sorcery, nether wizardry, and channeling. It also permanently boosts your Magic attribute by +6. Note, both elemental sorcery and nether wizardry are Class-unique skills. And as with all master Class stones, this stone grants you a free Class ability and its skills start at rank 1. This Class stone cannot be sold and is only usable by you.

The air rushed out of me in a whoosh.

A greater attribute gem was unexpected but pleasing. So, too, was the advanced psi ability tome. It would save me two thousand gold—the cost of an ability upgrade gem—and made clear that the loot in the chest had been matched to me specifically.

It was the last item, though, that was the most shocking.

A master Class stone—and one whose likes I hadn't seen before. Not only did the stone contain a Force-unlocked Class, it granted *two* unique skills: elemental sorcery and nether wizardry.

I hadn't heard of either skill, but I could guess what each entailed. Elemental sorcery had to be some combination of air, earth, fire, and water magic, while nether wizardry was probably magic similar to what the stygian creatures themselves wielded.

No matter what the other two chests contained, I knew that the items in the first chest were ones I'd be overjoyed to accept.

But there *were* two other chests.

How about we find out what's behind door number two first, eh?

With a wry smile for my overeagerness, I opened the next chest.

✳   ✳   ✳

It, too, had three items, and without pause for breath, I analyzed each in turn.

This is a greater attribute gem.

This is the advanced ability tome, improved astral blade. You have the necessary skill, rank 5 telepathy, to learn this ability.

This is a master Class stone. It contains the path of a Force adept and is not aligned to any one Force. This Class specializes in mastering the raw might of the cosmos. Where most players can wield only a single Force, the Force adept can wield the Forces of Light, Dark, and Shadow equally well. But while a Force adept may learn all types of Force skills, he is constrained from acquiring any Force Marks himself.

This Class stone bestows a player with three skills: tri-force, aether mastery, and channeling. It also permanently boosts your Faith attribute by +6. Note, both tri-force and aether mastery are Class-unique skills. This Class stone cannot be sold and is only usable by you.

"Wow," I gasped. The loot in the second chest was as good as the first one. A greater attribute gem, a tier two spellbook that advanced another of my scion-acquired abilities, and, of course, a master Class stone.

Once more, I was hard put not to reach down and grab the Class on offer. A force adept sounded like it had all the advantages of a faction Class but *without* any of the strings they came with.

Like the stygian magus, the force adept Class also had two unique class skills: tri-force and aether mastery. I was less certain what these skills encompassed, but it was clear that the Class would let me accomplish what none of the new Powers could: wield all three Forces simultaneously.

I edged over to the last chest. Surely, whatever it contained couldn't outdo the other two, but for the sake of thoroughness, I threw back the lid and peered within.

✻　✻　✻

It came as no surprise to find that the third chest also contained three items: a greater attribute gem, a tier two shadow blink tome, and a master Class stone.

Of course, my attention fixated on the Class stone's offering once more.

This is a master Class stone. It contains the path of a void mage and is not aligned to any Force. This Class specializes in damage absorption and resistance.

Where other players use their mana to weave complex and elaborate spells, the void mage trains his magic with only one objective in mind: nullifying hostile attacks. However, while this allows the void mage to soak up incoming damage and, sometimes even resist unfriendly abilities altogether, it also prevents him from using his mana for anything else.

This Class stone bestows a player with three skills: elemental absorption, null force, and channeling. It also permanently boosts your Magic attribute by +6. Note, both elemental absorption and null force are Class-unique skills. This Class stone cannot be sold and is only usable by you.

I rocked back on my heels.

The void mage seemed almost the polar opposite of the other two Classes. Where the stygian magus and force adept focused on spellcasting, the void mage shunned magic altogether. Indeed, the Class appeared purely defensive in nature.

But that didn't make it worse. Only different.

In fact, the void mage Class looked every bit as good as the first two, which fortunately—or unfortunately—only served to make the task before me harder.

Backing away from the chests, I dropped into a cross-legged stance and cupped my chin in my hands.

Magus. Adept. Void.

Which will it be?

Sighing, I closed my eyes. I had a difficult decision ahead of me.

I didn't rush my decision.

I had at least until the day's end and the sector's reset, and I was determined to think matters through before choosing. It was a monumental decision and likely my biggest one yet in the Game.

"Magus. Adept. Void," I muttered.

All three were fantastic and superior to the master Classes in Erebus' dungeon or, for that matter, the one Loken had proposed. I snorted in disdain. Truly, both the blood siphon and Shadow-operative Classes paled in comparison to the guardian tower's offering.

For what felt like the umpteenth time, my gaze flitted between the chests. Each of them offered a mana-based Class and hence fulfilled the requirements of Wolf, but they did so in dramatically different ways. The stygian magus focused on Magic-based spells, the force adept on Faith-based castings, and the void mage on... defense.

Alright, time to decide.

Letting my gaze linger on the first chest, I reviewed what I had surmised over the last few hours.

The stygian magus would let me wield more powerful magic than even a dozen players combined, I suspected. But its debuffs were concerning.

I'd been to the nether. And I didn't fancy spending the greater part of my life there. If I was reading the Class restrictions correctly, I would be forced to do just that in ever-increasing durations as I advanced my nether wizardry. So, as much as the thought of the Class' magic appealed to me, I wouldn't choose it unless forced to do so.

My eyes drifted to the second chest.

The path of the Force adept was more attractive. With it, I could wield the magic of all three Forces. Theoretically, that meant I could duplicate the magicks of Loken, Arinna, and Erebus—all on my lonesome.

It was a Class built for going toe to toe with my foes, and while it was certainly powerful, I worried it was *too* similar to the powers my enemies wielded. In a very real sense, it would leave me trying to beat them at their own game.

The new Powers had spent centuries perfecting their own magics, and even if I wielded three Forces as opposed to their one, I feared my foes would understand my abilities better than I did. I shook my head slowly. I didn't think I had centuries—or even decades.

I turned toward the last chest.

At first glance, the void mage was the least enticing and seemed to run counter to my own fighting style, which focused on burst attacks. The Class wouldn't provide the plethora of spells the first two did, and going by its description, it focused on one thing only: countering enemy abilities.

Of the three Classes, it was the least aggressive choice.

Safe almost. And hence unsuitable.

From my—albeit limited—experience, the Game was all about high rewards for high risk. And on its own, the void mage Class wouldn't let me take on further risks. It lacked the... firepower for that.

But I don't need more firepower, do I?

Arguably, my existing Classes already provided me with all the offensive tools I needed. And if it wasn't more offense that I needed, then the void mage would make an excellent choice. It should complement my current skills nicely—and admittedly better than the other two Classes on offer—and provide some much-needed defense too.

Just as importantly, the Class didn't seem like it would slow me down. I wouldn't have to lumber around in heavy armor or waste time casting magic shields. I smiled. If anything, becoming a void mage would let me dive more boldly into danger than I already did.

Closing my eyes, I imagined the possibilities. What if I could become...

... a thief no ward could stop?

... a psionic who could shrug off hostile magic?

... a spy who couldn't be detected?

... an assassin who kept going no matter how hard he was hit?

Throwing my head back, I laughed. It made for a nice daydream, but I was a far cry from achieving any of it.

Although...

It wasn't inconceivable that someday it could all become reality. That was the potential inherent in the void mage Class. That was its promise.

Decision made, I rose to my feet.

✳   ✳   ✳

Your choice is acknowledged.
The Fate's Key has been destroyed.

The moment I willed my choice to the Adjudicator, the first two chests faded from sight. I didn't spare them a glance though as I reached into the remaining one and grasped the least important object first—the greater attribute gem.

Closing my eyes, I activated the item.

You have gained 3 attribute points, increasing your total available points to 5.

Next, I picked up the ability tome and read it from end to end.

You have upgraded your shadow blink ability to medium shadow blink. This mind spell allows you to teleport to any living entity within 20 yards, taking your shadows with you. You have 47 of 71 Mind ability slots remaining.

Finally, I retrieved the Class stone and activated it.

A Game window opened in my mind.

You have one remaining Class slot. Do you wish to acquire the void mage Class?

I willed my assent to the Adjudicator, and a moment later the gold marble turned warm in my hand before melting into my skin. More words appeared in my mind.

You have acquired the void mage Class!

This Class focuses on nullifying hostile attacks and increasing your resistance through the use of mana. It permanently and irrevocably transforms your mana pool into a passive protective layer that does not require focus to maintain. As a result, you will be unable to cast any mana-based spells in future.

Note, the specific type of damage absorbed and the added resistances you gain are dependent on the Class skills you acquire.

You have gained the base trait: void touched. This trait increases your Magic by +6 ranks.

You have gained the base trait: spell illiterate. This trait prevents you from casting any Faith and Magic spells.

You have gained the Class ability: basic void armor.

Basic void armor is an ability that infuses your body with mana, strengthening and protecting vital points. It works in conjunction with your Class skills. As they improve, so too does the performance of your void armor.

This ability consumes mana only when absorbing or repelling damage and can be upgraded with Class points. It does not require activation and does not occupy any ability slots.

You have gained one basic skill, channeling, and two master skills: elemental absorption and null force.

Channeling is a discipline that allows a player to replenish his store of mana from the surroundings.

Elemental absorption is the art of using your void armor to ward off hostile air, earth, fire, and water-based attacks. It is more than a simple resistance skill though. Working in tandem with your void armor, it allows you to repel an elemental attack or, failing that, absorb a portion of its damage.

Null force is akin to elemental absorption but instead attunes your void armor to Light magic, Dark magic, and Shadow magic, allowing you to repel—or absorb—their harmful effects.

You have 3 of 6 void mage Class skill slots remaining.

Your skill in channeling has reached rank 1, increasing your mana recovery rate.

Your skill in elemental absorption has reached rank 1, increasing your chance to resist harmful elemental effects by 2.5% and decreasing the damage you suffer from them by 5%. Note, the benefits provided by this skill are only active so long as you have mana remaining.

Your skill in null force has reached rank 1, increasing your chance to resist harmful Force effects by 2.5% and decreasing the damage you suffer from them by 5%.

"Ah," I exhaled, swaying slightly in the wake of the Game's modifications to my body and mind. This time they felt more intricate than the incremental changes I'd undergone previously.

Closing my eyes, I tasted the new knowledge filling my consciousness. The null force and elemental absorption skills were more complex than any other I'd acquired before, and I instinctively knew training them would be harder.

The pool of mana inside me felt different too. No longer did it sit idle at my center, waiting to be used. Now it flowed through my body, filling my organs, running through my veins, feeding my muscles, and sheathing bone.

My scrutiny prompted another Game message.

Void armor operational. Current charge: 100%.

Active buffs: +5% damage reduction and +2.5% resistance to air, earth, fire, water, Shadow, Light, and Dark magic.

I grinned in delight. Before acquiring the void mage Class I could only guess at the benefits it would yield, and I was only too thrilled to discover that it was everything I hoped for—and more.

The nature of the elemental absorption skill came as no surprise—its name had been mostly self-explanatory. But the null force skill... its workings I found particularly pleasing.

In one fell swoop, I'd gained a counter to my foes' most potent weapons: their Force magic. Sure, that would only hold true as long as I had enough mana to keep my void armor charged. And resistance and damage reduction were far from immunity. But both factors were manageable.

Which reminds me...

For my new Class to be effective, it was vital that I increased the size of my mana pool. While I didn't have any spells to cast, every hostile ability I repelled or resisted would drain my mana. Without further ado, I invested my available attribute points.

Your Magic has increased to rank 21.

Immediately, I felt the magic flowing in my veins surge in volume, leaving me feeling stronger, more able. Less vulnerable.

I smiled, certain now that my choice of Class had been the right one.

CHAPTER 241: A RUDE AWAKENING

I didn't leave the walled compound immediately.

There was still the matter of where I went from here. I'd spent months in the dungeon and gained much in the process. A new Class. Upgraded skills. A hidden sector. And not least, a pack.

But now, it was time to contemplate the future.

I'd ventured into the guardian tower primarily to confirm my supposition about the mantises and acquire a Class. I'd done one but not the other.

I wasn't sure what it meant that the assassins hadn't followed into the dungeon. Had I been wrong about why they were hunting me? And did it even matter anymore?

After all, the better part of a year had gone by.

Whatever the case, I didn't fear the mantises anymore. Now that I had my final Class—even if its melding was incomplete—I felt ready to face them and their shadowy employer.

The dungeon, or rather the arctic wolves, had given me something else too. Something priceless.

A sense of purpose.

A goal for the future that went beyond mere survival or the accumulation of power. My plans were still nebulous, but in my mind, I held the makings of a grand strategy.

One that would see House Wolf rise again.

Much would depend on what happened after I re-entered Nexus, the mantises' own actions, and *if* I found Ceruvax.

But I was certain I could see it done.

First, though, I have to get out of here.

Rising to my feet, I swung around in the direction of the savant's corpse, but before I took more than a step, another Game alert intruded.

Congratulations, Michael! You have completed the task, <u>Stay true to Wolf!</u> You have taken another momentous step on your journey to becoming Prime, deepening your Wolf Mark.

I smiled. I'd almost forgotten about the task. Its message was welcome though, especially the news that my Mark had deepened.

Events in the dungeon had made clear just how significant Marks were in the Game. My Wolf Mark, I realized, was as important to my player growth as my levels, skills, and Class—if not more so. It had granted me priceless traits, triggered my Class into evolving—not once, but twice—and if I was right in my suspicions, it would be vital to the founding of House Wolf.

Deepening it further was essential to my plans.

Reaching the sector boss's corpse, I broke off from my musings and rifled through his clothing. Sadly, he had nothing of value.

That's it then, I thought. *All done here.* Turning around, I made for the crystal door.

As I strode through the compound, I let my gaze wander over the deserted interior. In the aftermath of the battle, the compound was tranquil, if eerily silent. Besides the savant's corpse and the mounds of white powder peeking through the long grass, little evidence remained of the fight.

All the statues had awakened or turned to dust.

My gaze slid to the right. Well, that wasn't quite true. The statue of the giant human with the benevolent smile remained.

I stumbled, almost missing a step.

Benevolent smile? When did that happen?

I was certain there had been no smile on the sculpture's face earlier. Granted, I'd had bigger things to worry about at the time, but I had scrutinized the statue, and I *definitely* didn't remember a smile.

Hmm...

For a moment I contemplated ignoring the anomaly, but as slight as the discrepancy was, I thought it warranted a closer look. And it wasn't like I was in a hurry.

Altering my course, I made a beeline for the sculpture. Reaching its base, I craned my neck back and took in its entire length.

I picked out no other anomalies.

The figure stood with his arms folded across his chest and his chin bent, looking down—or in my case, smiling down—at whoever stood directly before him. Walking a half-circle around the statue, I studied it from every possible angle but identified nothing else odd about it.

It was, by all appearance, an ordinary statue—I tapped ebonheart's hilt against the marble—and solid too.

Drawing on my will, I probed it with my abilities. But analyze didn't turn up anything. Trap detect and mindsight didn't provide any insights either.

Sighing, I sat down on the ground. "What are you?" I asked, staring up at the figure.

Not unexpectedly, there was no response.

Tugging free a stalk of grass, I toyed with it in my hands. Unlike the statues outside the public dungeons, this one had no animal familiar. Was that significant?

I had no idea.

Despite the lack of a beast companion though, something told me this statue was related to the others in the plague quarter. Call it suspicion or the paranoia of an overworked mind, but I was certain there was a mystery here, even if it was one I wasn't sure I could solve.

Still, I was reluctant to leave the matter alone.

Given the inclusion of beasts in the statues—in the other ones, if not this one—it seemed self-evident that the statues had something to do with the Primes.

What though? I wondered, chewing on the end of the grass stalk.

Finding remnants of the ancients in Nexus wasn't strange. According to Ceruvax, the city had belonged to the old Powers before the new ones had moved in. What *was* surprising, though, was that the new Powers had allowed the statues to remain.

Maybe, I thought drily, *that's because the statues are simply that—statues. Nothing more than ordinary, inoffensive stone.*

I sighed. Maybe I was deceiving myself. Maybe there was no great mystery here. My gaze dropped to the figure's feet. They rested on a stone plinth, I noted, and over time had become covered by soil and grass.

I frowned. *Maybe the key to unlocking the statues' secrets lies not above but below?* I threw away the bits of grass from my hands. *It's worth a try*, I decided.

Leaning forward, I began to dig.

✳   ✳   ✳

It took longer than I expected to free the statue's base.

I kept at it, though, because not five minutes after starting, I realized the stone plinth was more extensive than I'd initially thought. It extended three yards in a half-circle all around the statue.

And on its flat top was a carving.

"Well, well," I murmured when I was done uncovering the plinth. Standing back, I looked between the statue and the carving at his feet. The image revealed was centered directly beneath the giant figure's gaze.

"So that's what you've been staring at all this time, eh?"

Once more there was no answer, and I chuckled.

My mood had improved considerably. I'd been right; the statue *had* been hiding something. And all it had taken was a few minutes of manual labor to uncover. My eyes drifted to the carving again. I'd seen it before and had recognized it immediately.

It was a blood talisman.

There were slight variations, of course, but otherwise the intricate lines of silver engraved in the marble were identical to those in the artifact I'd encountered in the Wolf Trials.

Dropping to my knees, I crouched before the carving and let my gaze rove over the fantastical beasts depicted. One of the differences between the two talismans was the portrayal of the wolf. Here, he wasn't snarling.

Sitting on his haunches, the wolf stared at me with penetrating eyes. Gently, I brushed my fingers against him.

Nothing happened.

Hmm.

The last time I'd touched a talisman, the reaction had been instantaneous. So what was wrong with this one? Was it broken?

Hells, I hope not.

Leaning forward, I placed both my hands flat down on the marble surface.

Still nothing.

Urgh.

Clenching my hands into fists, I pounded on the inert stone. When that didn't work, I banged harder. *Maybe it just needs a good shaking...*

A deep metal gong sounded in my mind, and I grinned. *There, that's fixed it.* Staying still, I waited expectantly. Words wrote themselves across my mind.

Analyzing offering...

What?
Offering? What offering?
Not me, surely?
Hastily I removed my hands from the talisman and sat back. Another Game message unfurled in my mind.

Analysis completed. The offering has been deemed sufficient. Do you wish to tithe this artifact to the guardian?

Relief was my first response. One, I was being offered a choice, and two, *I* wasn't the offering.
Confusion followed.
What was the mentioned artifact? I hadn't placed any of my items on the plinth. My gaze slipped downward. Or had I?
In all my banging, the medallion around my neck had slipped down and touched the talisman. *I should stop calling it that.* I didn't think it was a talisman anymore. *What* it was, I had no idea.
Removing the amulet from around my neck, I placed it on the marble plinth. The same Game message reappeared, but this time with a warning.

The offering has been deemed sufficient. Do you wish to tithe this artifact to the guardian? Warning: the amulet will be lost in the process.

I pursed my lips. Just who was the guardian mentioned? Involuntarily, my gaze jerked upward toward the statue's face.
Him, I thought. The guardian had to be the statue itself.
My eyes narrowed. One of the many things that had struck me as odd about this dungeon was its name. The titles of the other two public dungeons—the scorching dunes and haunted catacombs—had been self-explanatory.
Not so this dungeon.
Nothing I'd encountered in the guardian tower had alluded as to *why* it was called such. Until now.
The Game message appeared again, prompting me for a response.

Do you wish to tithe this artifact to the guardian?

Did I? The amulet provided a nice buff, but it wasn't irreplaceable. And this mystery was too tantalizing to ignore. *Time to find out what this is all about*, I thought and willed my response to the Adjudicator.

Tithe accepted. Item lost.
Awakening guardian...

✷   ✷   ✷

THE END.

Here ends Book 3 of the Grand Game.

Michael's adventures in Nexus and beyond will continue in **House Wolf**.
Get it here!

I hope you enjoyed the story! If you did, please leave a review and let
other readers know what you think.
Click here to leave a review.
Happy reading!
Tom Elliot.

MICHAEL AT THE END OF BOOK 3

<u>Player Profile: Michael</u>
Level: 129. Rank: 12. Current Health: 100%.
Stamina: 100%. Mana: 100%. Psi: 100%.
Species: Human. Lives Remaining: 3.
True Marks (hidden): Pack-alpha.
False Marks (fabricated): Lesser Shadow, Lesser Light, Lesser Dark.

Attributes

Available: 0 points.
Strength: 13. Constitution: 19. Dexterity: 33. Perception: 25. Mind: 71.
Magic: 21. Faith: 0.

Classes

Available: 1 point.
Primary-Secondary Bi-blend: mindstalker (fabricated), mindslayer VI (hidden).
Tertiary Class: void mage.

Traits

Slayer's heritage (hidden): +2 Dexterity, +2 Strength, +4 Mind, +4 Perception.
Beast tongue: can speak to beastkin.
Marked: can see spirit signatures.
Wolfwalker (hidden): improved senses in all conditions.
Anointed scion (hidden): bound to House Wolf.
Inscrutable mind: +8 Mind.
Secret blood (hidden): conceals bloodline.
Mental focus IV: increases effectiveness of Mind skills by 40%.
Budding explorer: all key points in newly discovered sectors logged.
Arctic wolf (hidden): +5 Constitution, +2 Mind, +3 Strength.
Void touched: +6 Magic.
Spell illiterate: cannot cast mana-based spells.

Skills

Available skill slots: 3.
Dodging (current: 107. max: 330. Dexterity, basic).
Sneaking (current: 103. max: 330. Dexterity, basic).
Shortswords (current: 113. max: 330. Dexterity, basic).
Two-weapon fighting (current: 104. max: 330. Dexterity, advanced).
Light armor (current: 107. max: 190. Constitution, basic).
Thieving (current: 78. max: 330. Dexterity, basic).
Chi (current: 105. max: 710. Mind, advanced).
Meditation (current: 131. max: 710. Mind, basic).
Telekinesis (current: 109. max: 710. Mind, advanced).

Telepathy (current: 104. max: 710. Mind, advanced).
Insight (current: 124. max: 250. Perception, basic).
Deception (current: 106. max: 250. Perception, master).
Channeling (current: 10. max: 210. Magic, basic).
Elemental absorption (current: 10. max: 210. Magic, master).
Null force (current: 10. max: 210. Magic, master).

Abilities

<u>Constitution ability slots used:</u> 5 / 19.
minor lighten load (5 Constitution, advanced, light armor).

<u>Dexterity ability slots used:</u> 27 / 33.
crippling blow (Dexterity, basic, shortswords).
minor piercing strike (5 Dexterity, advanced, shortswords).
lesser backstab (5 Dexterity, advanced, sneaking).
improved trap disarm (5 Dexterity, advanced, thieving).
superior lockpicking (5 Dexterity, advanced, thieving).
set trap (Dexterity, basic, thieving).
whirlwind (5 Dexterity, advanced, two weapon fighting).

<u>Mind ability slots used:</u> 24 / 71.
simple mass charm (5 Mind, advanced, telepathy).
stunning slap (Mind, basic, chi).
two-step (5 Mind, advanced, telekinesis).
simple reaction buff (5 Mind, advanced, chi).
simple astral blade (Mind, basic, telepathy).
medium shadow blink (5 Mind, advanced, telekinesis).
minor chi heal (Mind, basic, chi).
simple mind shield (Mind, basic, meditation).

<u>Perception ability slots used:</u> 22 / 25.
improved analyze (5 Perception, advanced, insight).
improved trap detect (5 Perception, advanced, thieving).
conceal small weapon (Perception, basic, deception).
facial disguise (Perception, basic, deception).
superior ventro (5 Perception, advanced, deception).
lesser imitate (5 Perception, advanced, deception).

<u>Other abilities:</u>
improved slaysight (hidden): (Class, advanced, telepathy).
basic void armor (Class, basic, channeling or elemental absorption).

Known Key Points

Sector 14,913 exit portal and safe zone.
Sector 12,560 nether portal and safe zone.
Sector 1 safe zone.
Sector 101 exit portal and safe zone (scorching dunes).
Sector 102, 103, and 104 exit portals and safe zones (haunted catacombs).

Sector 105, 106, 107, 108, and 109 exit portals (guardian tower).
Sector 18,240 nether portal 1 (guardian tower), and nether portal 2 (Draven's reach).

Equipped

ebonheart (+30% damage), concealed.
winter bone-hide armor (+10% damage reduction, -70% Dexterity and Magic, +5 stealth in snow).
shortsword, +1 (+15% damage, +10 shortswords), blunt!
slim dagger.

Backpack Contents

<u>Money</u>: 0 gold, 5 silver, and 3 copper.
1 x snow-cone map of the tundra.
1 x leopard cloak (-20% movement speed).
1 x tavern bill of ownership.
1 x Tartan token.
1 x Viviane token.
1 x BHG ID.

Miscellaneous Loot

None.

Bank Contents

<u>Money</u>: 0 gold, 0 silver, and 0 copper.
2 x full healing potions.
2 x full mana potions.

Open Tasks

Find the Last Wolf Envoy (hidden) (find Ceruvax).
Heist in the Dark (steal chalice from the Power, Paya).
Probie (complete two tier 4 bounties).
Preying Mantises (stop the assassins hunting you).

Books by the Author

By Tom Elliot

The Grand Game (<u>series page</u>)
Book 1: The Grand Game: <u>ebook</u> | <u>audiobook</u>
Book 2: Way of the Wolf: <u>ebook</u> | <u>audiobook</u>
Book 3: World Nexus: <u>ebook</u> | <u>audiobook</u>
Book 4: House Wolf: <u>ebook</u> | <u>audiobook</u>
Book 5: Wolf in the Void: <u>ebook</u> | <u>audiobook</u>
Book 6: A Scion's Duty: <u>ebook</u> | <u>audiobook</u>
Book 7: Ancient Debts: <u>ebook</u> | <u>audiobook</u>
Book 8: The Lost Reclaimed: <u>ebook</u> (coming soon)

The Grand Game Box Set (<u>series page</u>)
Book 1-3: Birth of a Player: <u>ebook</u>.
Book 4-6: Rise of the Elite: <u>ebook</u> (releasing 31 December 2024)

The Grand Game, Elana (<u>series page</u>)
Book 1: Empyrean's Rise: <u>ebook</u>
Book 2: Empyrean's Flight: <u>ebook</u>

By Rohan M. Vider

The Dragon Mage Saga (<u>series page</u>)
Book 1: Overworld: <u>ebook</u> | <u>audiobook</u>
Book 2: Dungeons: <u>ebook</u> | <u>audiobook</u>

The Gods' Game (<u>series page</u>)
<u>Crota, the Gods' Game Volume I</u>
<u>The Labyrinth, the Gods' Game Volume II</u>
<u>Sovereign Rising, the Gods' Game Volume III</u>
<u>Sovereign, the Gods' Game, Volume IV</u>
<u>Sovereign's Choice, the Gods' Game Volume V</u>

Tales from the Gods' Game
<u>Dungeon Dive (Tales from the Gods' Game, Book 1)</u>

Thank you for reading the Grand Game!

If you enjoyed the book, please consider leaving a review on Amazon [click here]. I'm already working on Michael's next adventure.

If you have any questions, comments, or want to support my writing, please feel free to contact me through my site, TomLitRPG.com or Discord.

Alternatively, if you wish to learn more about the world of the Forever Kingdom, understand the system of the Grand Game better, or are just looking for the latest news on the Grand Game, please visit my site at TomLitRPG.com or signup up here for my: Newsletter.

Regards,
Tom
Support my writing on **PATREON**
Amazon Author page | Goodreads | Facebook | Reddit | Discord |

Definitions

Accord: old agreement between new Powers ceding control of Nexus to the Triumvirate.

Adjudicator: controller and arbitrator of the Grand Game.

alchemy stone: a device used to store alchemical components.

ancient: old Power.

anointed scion: a scion who has bound himself to a bloodline.

ascendant undead: term the Adjudicator used to describe Stayne, meaning unknown.

blended Class: a combined Class.

blood awakening: the process of recalling blood memories.

blood infusion: the absorption of the essences from former scions.

blood memories: gifts from your forebears containing the power of the ancients themselves.

bi-blend: a combination of two melded Classes.

bloodline: reference to the ancient the player descends from.

civilian player: a player without a Class or combat abilities. Civilians do not have a player level.

class-unique skill: a skill that is unique to a Class and can only be acquired through a Class stone.

closed sector: a landmass that does not physically border another, making the area inaccessible except by portal.

controlled sector: a sector owned by a faction. Ownership of a sector gives the faction's players increased privileges in the region.

Class: a defined path or vocation that gives a player access to specific skills.

Class evolution: the advancement of a Class, generally to a better-ranked one, due to particular traits, skills, or Marks acquired by the player.

Dark: one of the three Forces.

Darksworn: a player pledged to the Dark who values the self over the collective.

ebonblade: soulbound weapons found in the Twilight Dungeon.

Elite: a tier five player, i.e. someone above level two hundred.

envoy: a trusted representative of a Power authorized to speak on their behalf.

Endless Dungeon: a section of the Nethersphere where dungeon mechanics are active.

evolution: the advancement of a player's core characteristics.

follower: a player who has pledged themself in a binding vow to a Force or Power.

Force: Light, Dark, Shadow. The building blocks of the cosmos and energy in its rawest form.

Forever Kingdom: the world of the Nethersphere and Kingdom.

Game: refers to the Grand Game.

gatekeepers: holders of ancient lore, guardians of the ancients' trials.

House: House of the Ancient.

House of the Ancient: a grouping of followers pledged to one Prime.
Kingdoms: the collective name given to sectors located in the aether.
ley line: magic threads connecting nether sectors.
Light: one of the three Forces.
Lightsworn: a player who champions the cause of the many, even to his own detriment.
meld: the process of combining multiple Classes into one.
mindglow: the visible signature of a mind as seen with mindsight.
neutral sector: a sector unowned and unclaimed by any faction or Force.
Nethersphere: collective name given to the sectors in the nether.
new Power: one of the Powers who usurped the ancients.
Pact: a binding enacted between a Power and player, overseen by the Adjudicator.
Power: an evolved player.
Prime: head of ancient bloodline. An ancient.
rift: unstable portal from the nether. Ley line created by stygian seed.
scav: short for scavenger. A player who loots the kills of others.
scion: one bearing the blood of an ancient.
scion abilities: the abilities Michael had earned during the Wolf trials: astral blade, chi heal, mind shield, shadow blink.
seeking spell: spell that distinguishes friend from foe.
soulbound: an item that remains with the player after death.
sworn: as in sworn servant. A sworn is a follower of a Power who has sufficiently deepened their binding Mark.
trials of the ancients: tests created by the Primes for their successors.
tri-blend: a combination of three melded Classes.
upgrade gem: a game item used to advance an ability a single tier.
wolf trials: ancient trials created by Wolf Prime.
wolfkind: used interchangeably with wolfkin.

Key Characters & Factions

Factions

Albion Bank: major non-aligned bank in the Forever Kingdom.
Awakened Dead: a Dark faction.
Axis of Evil: an alliance of Dark factions.
blackguards: policing force in the Dark quarter.
Dawn Brigade: policing force in the Light quarter.
Gray Watch: policing force in the Shadow quarter.
mantises: a Dark faction of assassins.
Shadow Coalition: A power bloc of Shadow, made up of like-minded Shadow Powers.
Tartan: the faction of Tartar, the god-emperor.
Tartan legion: the military forces of Tartar.
Triumvirate: a unique faction composed of Light, Dark, and Shadow that controls Nexus.

Guilds and Non-Factions

bounty hunters' guild (BHG): headquartered in the plague quarter, mercenaries.
information brokers: A gnomish organization in the plague quarter.
Kesh Emporium: merchant company owned by Kesh.
Stygian Brotherhood: headquartered in the plague quarter, experts in all things nether.

House Wolf

Atiras: dead Prime Wolf.
Ceruvax: last envoy.

Non-Players

Arden: gnome information broker.
Cyren: gnome senior information broker.

Players

Anriq: werewolf criminal.
Barac: crusader, male centaur.
Bornholm: Michael's companion from Erebus' dungeon, dwarf.
Cara: alias given to Kesh's agent in plague quarter by Michael.
Devlin: Viviane's guard, unknown aquatic species.
Ent: guard outside emporium, armsmaster, giant.
Eyes: The BHG HQ doorkeeper, species unknown.

Jasiah: duelist, human male.
Genmark: ward architect, gnome male.
Gintalush: mantis assassin, insectoid.
Hannah: BHG client liaison officer, human female.
Kartara: huntmistress at Stygian Brotherhood Chapterhouse.
Kesh: master merchant, owner of the emporium, human woman.
Lake: guard outside emporium, berserker, giant.
Michael: protagonist.
Moonshadow: aeromancer, male elf.
Morin: Michael's companion from Erebus' dungeon, the painted woman.
Orlon: Triumvirate knight-captain in the plague quarter, human.
Richter: constable in Triumvirate citadel, human civilian.
Saya: apprentice alchemist, tavernkeeper in wolves' valley, gnome.
Shael: red minstrel, half-elf.
Simone: sharpshooter, half-elf female.
Stayne: Erebus' henchman.
Stonebeard: Triumvirate captain, dwarf.
Talon: the captain, Tartar's envoy.
Tantor: Michael's companion from Erebus' dungeon, high elf male.
Teg: Michael's escort in citadel, human.
Toff: player outside haunted catacombs, ogre
Trion: Triumvirate holy knight, Herat sworn, human.
Trexton: herbalist in Triumvirate citadel, Simone's contact, dark elf.
Wengulax: mantis assassin, blade dancer, human.
Wilsh: Blackguard captain, human.

POWERS

Arinna: Light Power.
Artem: Shadow Power. Goddess of nature.
Erebus: Dark Power, leader of the Awakened Dead faction.
Herat: Light Power, member of the Triumvirate.
Ishita: Spider goddess, Dark Power, member of the Awakened Dead.
Loken: Shadow Power.
Menaq: Dark Power, leader of the mantis faction.
Mydas: Shadow Power, member of the Triumvirate.
Paya: Dark Power, junior member of the Awakened Dead ruling council.
Rampel: Dark Power, member of the Triumvirate.
Tartar: Dark Power, also known as the God-Emperor.
Viviane: Power owning the Albion Bank.

WOLFKIN

Aira: dire wolf dame.
Barak: dire wolf elder.
Duggar: dire wolf alpha.
Oursk: dire wolf sire.

Leta: dire wolf elder.
Monac: dire wolf elder and former alpha.
Snow: arctic wolf pack alpha.
Star: Snow's mate.
Sulan: dire wolf healer.
Suva: dire wolf elder.

LOCATIONS

bounty hunters' guild headquarters: in the plague quarter.
Dark quarter: eastern side of Nexus.
global auction: auction in the safe zone.
guardian tower: public dungeon.
haunted catacombs: public dungeon.
information brokers' office: in the plague quarter.
Kesh Emporium: merchant house in the safe zone.
Light quarter: western side of Nexus.
market square: square housing global auction.
plague quarter: southern side of Nexus.
saltmarsh district: area in the southeast of plague quarter.
scorching dune: public dungeon.
Shadow Keep: central castle in the Shadow quarter.
Shadow quarter: northern side of Nexus.
Sleepy Inn: Michael's tavern.
Southern Outpost: tavern in plague quarter.
Wanderer's Delight: hotel in the safe zone.

www.ingramcontent.com/pod-product-compliance
Lightning Source LLC
Chambersburg PA
CBHW051553100726
47898CB00001B/75